This novel is dedicated to my daughter.

Okay girls... time to pack a bag, head to the beach, and find a secluded spot under a brightly striped umbrella in the sand. You may want to ice down a bottle of something bubbly because you will want to read this last-summer-fling-book from cover to cover in one sitting. Leighton Summers (doesn't the name alone just scream "Texas Oil Princess"?) is a sixth generation, world-travelled Texan who has given us a view into the fishbowl of high society and their take on relationships and lifestyles. More importantly this is a story of the "aha" moments that ultimately brings the realization that to be loved well, one must learn to love smarter.

Never imagining that life would be anything but a reflection of the idyllic Houston home where she grew up, Melanie St. John (the novel's main character) looks back on every romance from their fairy tale beginning to their crushing end. Though she is a trust fund baby, her fortune is still tied up until she is forty, forcing her to examine her limited skill set and find work to support herself and daughter.

Stupid by Choice is an enticing "how the other half lives" novel that takes us on an exotic world tour to the most luxurious places imaginable, and explores the hidden vices of the privileged class, complete with addictions and consequences, while also providing insight into how they handle divorce, infidelity, family problems, motherhood, and career goals with grace and fearlessness. It is a fun but often sad story of finding courage in the face of the unknown, taking risks, and following your heart on a journey to personal happiness.

—Carol McCoggins, *The Islander Magazine*

What grabbed me initially was the title of this book. I think most people can relate to having consciously made stupid decisions, especially when it comes to love, which is a main feature of this novel. What I loved: I loved her sister's antics! And I really loved seeing Melanie's growth, especially towards the end of the novel. I liked that she focused on making herself strong not just for her daughter, but for herself too. I am sick of reading about weak heroines, so this was such a refreshing change of pace! All in all, a really strong first novel for this author. I look forward to seeing what she writes next!

—Whitney, *Barbetti's Books.com*

When I was asked to review this book, I thought it would be a fun read... but it's so much deeper than I was expecting. Melanie St. John lives an enchanted life. Being the daughter of a wealthy oil attorney, she wants for nothing. But in so many ways, Melanie is just like any other girl. She suffers through the issues all girls do... What I enjoyed about this story is that Ms. Summers portrays these characters who have everything, but are also regular people. They navigate early adulthood, etc., trying to figure out where they belong in life, just like everyone else. They just have more means with which to go through it all. The glimpse inside this glittery lifestyle is interesting, to say the least. It was fascinating to watch Melanie grow up. Melanie approaches life, sometimes storming, sometimes stumbling, in her own way. She makes mistakes but, in time, learns from them. And eventually she blossoms.

The supporting cast of *Stupid by Choice* is amazing. Melanie's dad, Oldie, is larger than life...just like a Texan. ;) Her mom... sister Whitney... and even friends like Eva (who I wanted to strangle for the life choices she made) and Victoria added so much to the story. *Stupid by Choice* ended up being so much more than the fun read I was anticipating. It's much more a feelgood story with lots of lessons. And it was very satisfying.

—*Bookworm Brandee.com*

The story is all at once funny, dramatic, sad, and everything in between as we relive Melanie's life from Texas, Monte Carol, Manhattan, Newport, and Palm Beach where she faces destructive love affairs, financial trouble, family issues, unplanned pregnancy, and more of the same with her sister and her friends. Melanie suffers a lot of the same trials and tribulations as women of lesser means, despite having been born with the proverbial silver spoon in her mouth. With a surprising and unprecedented opportunity to have lasting love with the most unlikely person, will Melanie squander it on principle, will she experience the epiphany she needs to free herself from being "stuck on stupid," or will she remain "stupid by choice?" Find out for yourself. Make *Stupid by Choice* one of your summer reads.

—*L. V. Lewis.com*

Stupid By Choice

Stupid By Choice

LEIGHTON SUMMERS

SBC Publishing
Texas

Stupid By Choice
SBC Publishing
Copyright © 2012

Author: Leighton Summers
Editor: M. L. Cutter
Proofreader: Joey Abisso
Book Cover Design: Leighton Summers
Book Cover Layout: Joey Abisso

SBC Publishing, Texas
© 2012 by Leighton Summers

First electronic edition published 2013 in the United States of America and worldwide. First printed edition published 2014 in the United States of America.

ISBN: 0-9889969-1-X
ISBN-13: 978-0-9889969-1-5
Library of Congress Control Number: 2013909564
SBC LLC Houston, TX

The photo for the eyes on the book cover is by William Leatherman and is reproduced by permission.

The poem in chapter 18 was written by J. Berchman Bernard Stewart and reproduced by permission. Another one of his poems is listed at the front of this book and is also reproduced by permission.

www.StupidByChoice.net

For Melanie... Platinum Texas Oil Princess

Lithe limbs of lily willow
Ten tiny tea-rose toes
Her pet's a pearly tortoise
some porpoise chum behind her tows

Venus and Mars for earrings
Shady hat of Saturn's rings
That comet wait's outside?
The gold one? ...it's her ride

By J. Berchman Bernard Stewart

Contents

Chapter 1

◦✄◦

$\mathcal{I}$ realize, of course, how stupid I'd been. There were signs. I can see them now—vibrant, crushing red banners waving like Spanish muletas down a highway straight to Doomsville. We'll get to those, in all their hindsight-is-a-bitch glory. For now, all you need to know is that my marriage was an empty, hollow nothing. Appearances had gone out the window long ago—we did our own thing. It was a good day if we stayed out of each other's way, a bad one if I called the cops.

And yet I stayed. I chose to stay, every day in fact. The absurdity of this concept still surprises me, or at least the version of me who now knows better. I've learned that stupidity is often masked stubbornness, resignation, or fear—and for five straight years of my life, I was stupid.

When I realized the mess I'd gotten myself into… *really* examined the events and decisions that got me to where I am now—the full, shocking brunt of it—I realize that I was propelled into my catastrophe of a marriage as much by momentum as by design. And though I do take full responsibility for it, there were also others at work here, cranking on the propellers of the winds of fate, whether I consciously knew it at the time or not. It was all just too—

"Ding-dong," the doorbell rang out loudly. It was time. I quickly scooped my soapy toddler Blakely out of her bath, wrapped her in a giant fluffy towel, and motioned for her to put on her robe while I located the key to her bedroom door as fast as I could.

"Ding-dong," the doorbell rang again.

My now-awaked but still hung-over husband shouted from the master bedroom, "Somebody answer the DAMN DOOR! I'm trying to SLEEP!"

What else is new? I thought as I picked Blakely up and went to the foyer. *After today, he would have to get the 'damn door' himself.* The thought brought a smile to my face as I swung open the front door.

There stood three hulking men in green jumpsuits standing in the doorway. Blakely's big blue eyes widened at the sight of them; I don't think she'd ever seen such large men before. Their names were written on each breast pocket in cursive script: "Big Al" was a stocky, tank of a man, "Nick" was tall, chiseled, and lean, and "Joey's" balding, oversized head sat atop a pair of massive shoulders.

They're perfect, I thought as I patted Blakely reassuringly.

"Good morning... ah, *Melanie—?*" Big Al asked, glancing at some paperwork.

"Yes," I said with a nod to hurry him along.

He held out the stapled set of papers with their moving company's name written out across the top in big, black, bold letters: Three Men & A Truck. "We got a contract here that says you need us to pack up your whole apartment and move it to Texas."

"Yep, that's right," I said as I glanced at the papers. "I just need one minute though, do you mind waiting here? I'll be right back..."

I shut the door and took my daughter down the hallway and into her bedroom. I sat her on the edge of her bed while I reached for the clothes I had laid out for her the night before.

"Quickly now," I whispered as I helped her pull her favorite lace-trimmed sundress over her head. She looked so beautiful in it since she was still bronzed from our recent trip to Newport for the 4th of July. She looked like a tiny, blond, sun-kissed angel. Blackout shades kept the room mostly dark, but the pink and blue light from her oscillating nightlight still illuminated the walls.

I'd decorated her room with a Palm Beach theme for her first birthday last July—stark white walls, turquoise and lemon accents—because I thought it was cheerful, and because it reminded me of a different time. There was a huge fishbowl sitting on top of Blakely's dresser filled with seashells she'd collected from South Beach, Newport, and Monte Carlo, and a photo wall documenting our family's happier times together at Disney World, Disneyland, and the Parrot Jungle in Miami. As a new mom I'd taken photos of almost everything she did—there she was happily sitting on the beach with her grandmother Helen at the Beach Club in Newport, playing in the sand with her nanny Joy in Monte Carlo, and taking her first swim in her grandfather Foxy's Olympic-sized pool at his fabulous Palm Beach estate. There she was again sitting in her father's lap with a huge bowl of pasta as we all sat at our favorite outdoor cafe in New York City, Le Madeline, back when the possibility of having a normal, happy, family life still felt within reach.

This was the world I revisited in my mind each and every time I entered my daughter's room. But this morning, I fought back tears as I drank in the photos with steely resolve. I would not cry today. There was too much to do.

As I bent down to put her sandals on, Blakely giggled and didn't resist. It wasn't often she awoke this early in such a good mood, and I was overcome with gratitude. Maybe she knew something was up.

Maybe she knew I needed her today, I thought.

"Look Mommy!" Blakely chirped as I looked up—just as she tore off the lid from last night's Sippy cup. Its orange remains sprayed me from head to toe as she squealed with delight from the explosion.

So much for Blakely being on my side, I thought as I breathed deeply, resisting the urge to get upset over this impromptu juice shower from my mischievous two-year-old. I was already dressed for the day, having gotten up hours earlier to pick out just the right outfit, flat iron my hair straight, and put on mascara. I'd chosen a preppy, tight-fitting, bright green and cool pink Lilly Pulitzer dress, "Palm Beach chic," that had always had a way of cheering me up. I'd purposefully reached for this dress knowing this was going to be one ugly day. "Dress for success," I always said, and today I could really use fashion on my side.

Now, as I looked in the mirror, my blond hair sprinkled with orange pulp, I realized my attempt at looking put together today was moot. No time to change, no time to redo my hair.

Great, so this is how one of the biggest days of my life is starting out? I thought.

But I couldn't be mad. Blakely was one of my main reasons for doing what I was doing. Besides saving myself, I also needed to set a good example for her before she got old enough to understand what was really hap—oh, there was no time to remind myself of all of this now, not on the morning I planned to change our lives forever.

I took the cup out of her hand and smiled. "Hey pumpkin, where's Mario?"

"Here," Blakely said as she toddled over to her toy basket and picked him up lovingly. He was a larger, fancier version of a Ken doll and Blakely took him everywhere. She even had a toy closet in the corner of her room filled with only his clothes. I quickly grabbed his mini travel suit.

"Blakely, Mario needs to get dressed now too," I told her. "This is going to be a very special day for him, so he needs to look really nice, okay?"

"Okay," Blakely nodded.

I left her happily playing on the floor while I slipped out and shut her bedroom door, locking it behind me.

I hurried down the hallway, glancing out the grand window overlooking Central Park. I could feel the heat index rising as the subtle moisture on the nape of my neck grew, even with the air conditioning on. It'd be a scorcher by nine for sure. I suddenly felt bad and hoped I didn't leave my three thick gorillas-for-hire waiting outside too long. I opened the front door widely.

"Alright boys, hop to it as quietly as you can, please—oh, and by the way, the faster you go, the higher I tip," I said pointedly towards Big Al.

He winked and said, "Lady, we'll work like the wind if it'll make a pretty woman like you happy."

Joey gave me an appreciative glance as he put on his work gloves and snapped his gum.

Stale orange juice turns you on? I thought as I grabbed for the phone and dialed.

"Ron? Hi, it's me, Melanie," I said into the receiver. "The movers just got here... Yep... same time, same place, right? You've got the flight info? And Mom, too? ...okay, and thanks again for picking us up."

Joey was still giving me the once-over as I hung up, but I quickly glanced away.

Like I have time for this, I thought—though it wasn't like I wasn't used to it. At five seven and thin as a rail (but with just the right curves), I knew what I had to work with. Even after having Blakely my figure stayed intact, so as tastefully as I could I always accentuated my frame with hip-hugging, leg-bearing styles. I was used to the ogling eyes of men, so no meathead like Joey was going to rattle me, not on a day like today. My heels clicked the floor of the hallway briskly as I ignored Joey and motioned for Big Al to follow me into the den.

"You can start here," I said.

The three did, quickly and methodically. As they packed, taped, and transported box after box from the apartment I stood apart from them, as if from above it all, watching the proceedings with detached excitement.

I couldn't believe it was finally happening. Up until this point my whole married life had been foggy, thick and murky like sour milk. But today my nerve endings were firing with crystal clarity. Today was the day I lifted myself and my daughter out of the thick oily muck of our past and led us both into a new life, a new beginning. After five dark, dreadful years I could finally see the brighter path before me. We were driving towards the sun with no rearview mirrors and only the foggiest idea of where the road led, but still, the course was visible, and we'd started down it now. There was no turning back.

In the living room the movers kicked into overdrive, manhandling my belongings like the oversized sausages that they were—and for the first time in years my objects became loosened from their footholds, roots snapping, causing all of my memories of what led me here to crack open along with them as the dust of yesterday got jostled high into the air...

"Listen Squirt, I know you're only thirteen, but if you ever want to talk to me about boys or sex and stuff, you can. I've even got condoms," my seventeen-year-old sister Whitney said matter-of-factly as we sat in her brightly neon-colored, '70s-styled butterfly-themed bedroom. As she started to rip open a small black plastic wrapper, her sapphire eyes twinkled with anticipation.

"No!" I shrieked as I blushed and ran back to my books and stuffed animals in my own room right next to hers. I didn't want to see what she was about to pull out of that strange packaging, but I also knew my sister well enough to know she only took the word "no" as a challenge.

Whitney appeared in my doorframe in no time, but instead of the fight I was expecting she now had a somewhat protective attitude about her, which took me completely off guard.

"Look... I'm only showing you what to do because I can tell you're going to be pretty someday too," she said as she sat down next to me on my bed. Her long, flowing, straight, honey-blond hair grazed her perfectly tanned skin as she continued, "And I want you to be prepared because boys usually *aren't.*"

"I don't want to have sex until I'm in love and married," I said.

My rebellious, usually detached sister immediately reemerged as she laughed in my face. "Why? Because that's what 'Oldie' always says?"

"Yes," I answered defensively, not liking the sarcastic tone she used in reference to our father's nickname. Ever since I was young Oldie was the world, literally, to me. There wasn't anything he couldn't do, anything he didn't know, and any place he didn't go. I followed him everywhere he went, first around the house as a toddler, and then, as I got older, all the way across the globe. He traveled a lot for both work and pleasure and when he did Oldie often brought me along on his trips; mainly because I always begged to go along, but also because he couldn't say no to me, his precious, "Lil' Bit." He was known by our family and his close friends as "Oldie" ever since a Mexican waiter had mistaken him for my mother's father on a Christmas vacation at the hotel Las Brisas in Acapulco several years earlier.

"Would you and your daughters prefer to dine on the patio?" the waiter asked innocently, and my sister, Mother, and I laughed all the way back to our seats until our eyes were wet with tears. At the time he really did look "old," but that was not always the case.

With his thick chest, light blond hair, and bright blue eyes, Courtlin "Oldie" St. John had once been considered a very handsome man. Photos of him commanding an LST boat during World War II showed him muscled and strong; for just like his father had done before him, Oldie had joined the United States Navy right after college when he was only twenty-one. After the war he immediately set off for Yale to secure both a law degree and a future for his family. It was not hard to imagine why my mother Louise—a shy, striking, blue-eyed brunette debutant nine years his junior—was immediately attracted to such a brave, headstrong, and confident fellow (nor him to her beauty, kindness, and intelligence). But as he aged, Courtlin's light blond hair turned into silver fringe circling a shiny, round dome and an even rounder belly—one he cultivated carefully on a steady diet of ribs and scotch despite my mother's protests. Time, stress, and booze then continued to line his face and expand his stomach, and by the time Whitney and I were teenagers the only resemblance he had to his former, strapping self was the bright blue twinkle in his eye and his signature, booming voice.

His nickname fit him well. He'd always been shrewd and wise both in life and in business, and he often seemed more experienced than his years, even when he was young. He enjoyed playing counselor to friends, family, and clients alike, and, like most of his fellow high- powered attorneys, he was exceptionally gifted with words. He was part of the Greatest Generation and he'd let anyone who'd listen know it. For his fiftieth birthday a friend had a special T-shirt made up for him that read, "I'm an Oldie, but a Goodie." He wore it constantly.

He was also your typical Texan—rotund, outspoken, and convinced of his invincibility. As a lawyer to some of the biggest oilmen in Texas his business was lucrative and powerful, but also extremely high-pressured. Though he was most often jolly and amicable, his mood could turn on a dime if provoked and his temper was legendary, most notably for throwing things—usually chairs—out the windows of board rooms, hospital suites, and once from an eighteenth story hotel room at the Plaza Hotel in Manhattan.

That was my favorite place to stay with him when I was little. Oldie and I always stayed in the Eloise suite where my love of Henry the IV era furniture was born. I'd play in the fancy drapes and pretend I was a royal queen in silken robes, my court a couple of carved chair legs and a row of tasseled pillows. If I was good, Oldie would have the butler bring up a tricycle for me to ride on. I still have memories of this man's perfectly starched, white gloves delivering the bright red vehicle to me personally. I'd ride it all over our suite and sometimes later across the street in Central Park with the hotel-provided nanny. I would also get to ride on bumpy carriage rides pulled by strong, white horses through the park and order room service of ice cream floats and peanut-butter-and-jelly, crustless sandwiches whenever I wanted. When I was with Oldie on these trips and he was his typical, doting father-like self, I felt like a real-life princess dancing on the edge of the world, New York sparkling all around us.

But when his temper flared I was always scared. I had vivid memories of my father's ferocious roar echoing through the halls of our large, sprawling Houston mansion unexpectedly, and it soon became a necessary survival skill to be able to decipher who it was directed at—a business associate, Mother, Whitney, or me—before the actual words could even be made out. His rage was mostly inflicted upon anyone who had caused him worry, cost him money, or had in some way disappointed him, and on any given day that could have been any one of us.

"Come with me," a ten-year-old Whitney instructed once as she hastily grabbed my trembling hand when Oldie was on a particularly frightening rampage one afternoon.

We ran into our mother's sewing room.

"Hide behind here," Whitney ordered as she held out the thick, velvety fabric of the long drapes.

"Wh—" I started to ask, but Whitney put her finger to my lips, quieting me. She put her other arm around my shoulder and we both squeezed in close together behind one panel. Even at our young ages we knew his tantrum would pass and it would all be forgotten by dinner. For our father loved nothing more than to sit at the dining room table each night and listen to my sister, Mother, and me prattle on about whatever was going on in our lives, even if it was just meaningless chatter to him. With no sons to focus his attention on, Oldie took a deep interest in his daughters and was a fiercely protective father. He relentlessly doted on Whitney and me by showering us with constant clothes, jewelry, and impromptu trips. We never wanted for anything, for he simply liked being in the presence of happy, pampered women—and my sister and I never once forgot how lucky we were to be "Daddy's little girls"—or so I thought.

"You're not going to be 'Daddy's little girl' forever you know," Whitney said sternly.

"Why not?" I asked, afraid she was already starting to forget how lucky we were *to* be.

"Because other boys are more *fun*." Whitney winked like a wildcat about to pounce on its prey. She took after our father in every way except stature—she was extremely thin—but like Oldie, Whitney had a flair for the dramatic and a tendency towards excess, and just from her tone I could tell she was about to expand on the word 'fun.' "Especially Chad. Can you cover for me tonight while I'm out with him?"

"You're going to try and sneak out already?" I couldn't believe it. It had only been two hours since she was told she was grounded for totaling her *third* Mustang convertible so far this school year—and it was only December. According to her it wasn't—or ever was—her fault. Her last "boyfriend du jour" was at the wheel yet again and the poor Mustang ended up nose-first in a ditch during an impromptu drag race.

The worst of the mustang accidents happened on Halloween night when Trevor, her boyfriend at the time, drove her home from an all night party and smashed into the back of a parked police van in front of a twenty-four-hour I-HOP. Trevor went through the windshield, but luckily he was dressed in a full-body gorilla suit, which the doctors' said saved his life. He was promptly charged with a D.U.I. but later told the judge, "That fire truck came out of nowhere!"

It was a miracle that Whitney was surviving her senior year of high school at all, and Oldie really wasn't any help. Every time she totaled a car he would simply call up the Mustang dealership and order her a new one in a different color, so she knew the next one was already on its way.

Whitney was not exactly my idea of a role model, but she sure was a lot of fun... and since it was pretty clear by now who the "good" child in the family was to our parents, Whitney often looked towards me to help get her out of a bind like this. I have to admit I secretly loved conspiring ways to get her out of trouble too, for since we didn't have much else in common overall, it was our "little secrets" like this that always kept us talking.

"Okay, I'll tell them you were in your room alone the whole night while Emily was here studying with me in mine," I vouched—and she knew I took my loyalty very seriously. I also knew my new friend Emily Brown wouldn't mind coming over on such short notice since she looked for any opportunity to leave her empty, boring house on Saturdays when she knew her mother would be trying to get a double-shift for the extra tips. It embarrassed her to have her mother work as a waitress, but since her dad split on them directly after Emily was born, she also knew her mom was doing the best she could to raise her all alone.

"You're the best, Squirt," Whitney said. "Why don't you change into my blue chiffon sweater before Emily gets here?"

I went directly towards her room—she knew that was my favorite reward. She followed me into her walk-in closet.

"Can I wear these too?" I asked, pulling out her tall, knee-high, dark leather boots.

"No," Whitney said, taking them from me and putting them on. "These are Chad's—and many other boys'—favorite footwear. I want to make sure I stand out just in case I decide Chad isn't as much fun as he appears."

It sounded cold, but I knew she really meant it. For since she became a teenager, Whitney never thought much about anything else other than herself, her looks, and boys—and as a result she was rewarded with a steady stream of male attention, bouncing from one boyfriend to the next as often as she wished. She was considered a very popular girl at her high school, and even though I went to a different school I knew this to be true because nearly every weekend, particularly in the summer, we'd wake up to our trees and lawns covered with white, stringy sails of toilet paper that had turned into a big, pasty sop during a sudden rain fall. It would routinely take our gardener hours to clean up the mess and the whole thing drove Oldie nearly out of his mind with fury, though secretly we teen girls knew it was the ultimate form of flattery. "Wrapping" houses was a favorite weekend pastime for beer-fueled Texan high school jocks, particularly for those on the all-important football and soccer teams, and having your house wrapped meant you were an "it" girl in Houston, for sure.

But among her female classmates this also meant Whitney St. John was a major threat, so nearly every girl in her high school was jealous of her. It was hard for her to get along with most of them, so eventually she gave up trying to make any female friends at all. She instead focused her attention on her guy admirers and did just fine.

That is, until Whitney met Eva Mueller. Eva was anything but the typical American blond—her father was German and her mother was Argentinean, resulting in Eva's sultry, dark, and striking features: olive skin, high cheekbones, and exotic, almond-shaped eyes. She was as voluptuous as she was tall with well-shaped legs and thick, raven-black hair that fell below her shoulders in large, voluminous waves. By most accounts, Eva was drop-dead gorgeous.

But despite her beauty, exotic was not exactly "in" in Houston 1971 high school circles where Miss American Barbie dolls like Whitney reigned supreme. In fact, every race other than Caucasian was generally considered second-class, so by most of the populace's standards Eva was just another low-class immigrant.

And Eva always felt that. Though she was pretty, she knew she didn't quite fit in. She also had a loud, raspy voice that could pierce a room and curves that got all the wrong kind of attention. But when Eva met Whitney at tennis camp before their senior year started, Eva felt she'd hit the jackpot. Then, when she discovered they were both boy-crazy and loved to party, Eva knew Whitney was her ticket out of mediocrity and into the high life—so she never left her side.

Eva was at our house constantly, and even when Whitney wasn't home Eva would stop by and ask if I wanted to play tennis. I could tell she didn't really want to hang out with me, but I guess it was just her way of still spending more time at our house and even less at hers, which was not a place she—or anyone—ever wanted to be because of her dominating, strict, over-protective father.

The story most people knew was that her father, Dr. Helmut Mueller, was just an old, quirky physician who simply left Germany when Hitler came into power. Except for those Eva confided in, no one had any idea that her father had in fact served under the Third Reich for several years before he was actually able to escape. Like most of the best and brightest German physicians at the time, Dr. Helmut Mueller was hand-picked by Hitler's SS to assist Dr. Josef Mengele in the medical labs at Gross Rosen and Auschwitz, and then finally at Mauthausen. He was an assistant to the assistant of the Angel of Death himself, drunk with power, who got to decide the fates of the newly arrived concentration camp victims' with a flick of his wrist; gas to the left, life to the right. Eva never elaborated more than to say that her father had been permanently scarred by this experience—and we could only guess at what she meant by that. (We also pondered over what having a Nazi war criminal for a father could do to person's psyche but that, too, remained an elusive subject.)

Eva's parents arrived in Houston with a few dollars to their name and only the luggage they could carry. But soon her father was able to resume his surgical practice under a new identity and within a few years the couple had established a modest, middle-class lifestyle. Eva was the third in a line of four children, a lost middle child scratching for attention amongst a brood of overachieving, Type-A brothers and sisters. Since her parents both came from affluent backgrounds in their native countries they held onto a fierce pride and never let their children forget who they were or that they came from "Greatness." The children were instilled with a burning ambition to better themselves, unspoken or not, and it was understood that this meant through any means necessary.

Luckily, the Mueller children were given a good head start since their mother was a strict, devout Catholic woman and enrolled all of them in parochial school early on. As a result, Eva and her siblings read grade levels above their peers and were all fluent in at least three languages. Eva in particular, whether through her parents' influence or her own natural born social sense, became acutely aware of 'status' and the fact that other kids had a lot more of it than she did—and at a very early age. She focused on this discrepancy, even obsessed over it, and became determined to change it. Her dream was to one day live in a big mansion in our Houston neighborhood of Highland Park where membership to the country club had a ten-to-fifteen-year waiting list and real estate started in the millions.

Their friendship seemed to work because Eva wasn't a threat to Whitney since Eva came from a relatively 'poor' background compared to ours and was otherwise unknown in Whitney's circle of Houston's "Heirheads," which is what kids like Whitney and me were called because we stood to inherit Oldie's money and people knew it. And though we were considered wealthy, we really weren't overly so by Texan standards. In fact, we were far from the richest Heirheads in town or even the richest ones on our whole block in Highland Park. But Oldie hobnobbed with the biggest and the oldest money in town and even won legal battles for some of them at his prestigious, well-known law practice. In Houston, social rank had a lot to do with whose daddy could charter a private jet and whose couldn't—and even though we only flew first class when we were on our own, we'd been on enough private jets through friends, clients, and otherwise to know that Oldie did just fine for himself and our family's respectable reputation. We showed our faces at all the biggest annual galas and were long-standing members of the most prominent country clubs, therefore full members of the elite Houston social scene.

From where I sat it was obvious Eva only doted on Whitney (and believe me, my sister certainly didn't need any more doting on) and did things for her—like drove her to school every day or picked up her dry cleaning—solely because she was desperate to fit into this otherwise exclusive social scene. Even at thirteen I could sense Eva's needy, troubled loneliness and thought she tried too hard. But she faked it well and Whitney didn't seem to notice. Or maybe she just didn't want to, for Whitney had finally found someone she could shop and share lipstick with—and, above all, someone she could finally gossip with.

The two could be incredibly catty together. They'd chatter non-stop about this person or that person, fueling rumors or just being bitchy, loud, and obnoxious, completely oblivious to the world around them. Though the feeling seemed to be mutual, I could certainly see why all the other girls in their high school couldn't stand them.

I really didn't care much for that kind of behavior either—or Eva in general for that matter, but that was mostly because I was shy and more of a loner overall, so I didn't have many people other than Whitney to hang out with, ever. And whenever Eva came over to our house, which was a lot, I'd always get left out of the fun; though I was able to witness it, for Whitney and Eva did a fair amount of entertaining there.

Our house quickly became known as the official party house their senior year, and it wasn't as if Oldie discouraged it. Though he was a prude about sex and a raging control freak when it came to who Whitney dated, he was very lenient about drinking and partying. He sanctioned alcohol use in the house as long as it was imbibed responsibly. Car keys would be taken at the front door if you were going to drink, no exceptions, and no one was allowed to leave unless they passed a sobriety test. Ron, our personal family driver, was always on hand to take anyone home who needed a ride, and those too drunk to face their parents were sent out to the pool house to "sleep it off." Considering most party-goers were underage, this arrangement made our house a very popular hangout spot, even amongst the very same girls who harbored a secret hatred for Whitney. They tagged along and played fake "nice;" and I got used to the fact that there were a constant stream of Whitney's so-called friends at our house at any given time that year.

When Oldie and I traveled to New York and Europe, my mother always had to stay behind to babysit the house—more to prevent Whitney from destroying it in a week long drug and booze-bender than anything else. Whitney was hard to control, but her friends were worse.

I felt glad I had recently met Emily at a book club for underprivileged teens benefit that my country club had sponsored. She and I were becoming more like sisters than Whitney and I now (or ever) were, especially since Eva arrived on the scene, which is why I was thrilled when Oldie said Emily could come with us on our annual holiday family vacation to Aspen that Christmas. I just hoped with Whitney being grounded it meant Eva wouldn't be able to come too.

"Why can't you get to our luggage? The plane can't be off the ground if we're all still standing here waiting to board!" Oldie's voice boomed across the airport with a big, throaty drawl as his hands accompanied it with some sort of embarrassing gesture towards a very tired-looking stewardess at our gate. As unapologetically friendly as he was ornery, he didn't much care where we were when he acted this way—whether in Greece, Italy, Spain, or the South of France, Oldie offended all equally in his unabashedly brash, outward way. When he asked for his signature J & B Scotch with soda and a city didn't provide it, it was every countryman's fault. If we couldn't find adequate transport to the railway station or airport for what *he* considered to be a reasonable price, a Texas-sized tantrum was sure to follow, like one was happening now.

"Again, I'm sorry for the delay, sir," the stewardess said as calmly as she could, "but until the Aspen airport reopens no planes are boarding for there from anywhere, so even if we *could* give you back your luggage, no other plane would book you and your family now to get you there any faster."

My mother, Emily, and I stood off to the side like we didn't know him at all. Though she was still happy to be there, I had warned Emily about this happening before we left, for Oldie's tiresome tirades at the airport before take-off had now become part of the family tradition. When the Aspen airport would get shut down due to inclement weather, which happened nearly every year, Oldie would act like the TSA was purposefully and personally trying to offend him.

And his attire didn't help to draw less attention to us all either. No matter what the temperature was going to be at our eventual destination when we landed, he insisted on dressing in his usual "travel uniform" consisting of long, baggy shorts, a brightly colored polo shirt, black wool knee socks with Gucci loafers, and a white, crumpled tennis hat to protect his bald head from the sun. Once we were out sight-seeing somewhere he would then accessorize it with at least one camera and usually a pair of binoculars as well, each dangling from his neck with a zigzag strap. He might as well have been wearing a nametag that read, "Tacky American Jackass." Oldie stuck out like a large, cranky, old rooster in a too-packed henhouse everywhere we went in the world for sure.

"This is exactly why this will be my *last* family trip ever," Whitney whispered to our mother in a tone that was dead serious. She was also still upset that Eva wasn't allowed to come along as part of her continued punishment, so her annoyance with Oldie was even more elevated now.

"It might be mine too," our mother whispered back, almost as seriously.

My father just looked back at us all and grinned as if he was doing this for our own benefit. It was not until years later that we all found out Oldie actually would dress and act like this on purpose just to get a reaction from us girls, my mother included. Truth be told, he took great joy in messing with us any chance he could, and heck—the locals, too, mostly for his own amusement. After all, "Mischievous," he'd say, "is my middle name."

"Boarding will now begin for flight one-eight-two for Aspen, Colorado," a loud voice said over the speaker.

The stewardess couldn't have looked more relieved. "Enjoy your flight, sir," she said as she took his boarding ticket and quickly opened the gate's door.

"I will once you give me my scotch!" Oldie said as he gestured for us to come over to join him now. No one else in the entire area dared to move until we had all safely disappeared out of sight down the boarding tunnel.

Once we arrived in Aspen and were settled into our beautiful Swiss-styled chalet, which was perched on the top of Red Mountain and overlooked the whole, quaint village below, Emily was completely awestruck as she looked out at the view from our bedroom window. "It's like a postcard!" she exclaimed.

With the newly fallen, crystal white snow covering the mountain just outside our house, I had to agree. It looked spectacular. "Yes, it will be great skiing tomorrow," I told her.

"Is it hard?" Emily asked. I had forgotten this would be her first time on skis since she never left Houston to go on trips like this.

"Not really. But we'll just stay on the bunny slopes at first, until you get the hang of it."

"What if I don't?"

"Then I'll ask Oldie to sign you up for lessons."

And that's actually what I had to do. Emily wasn't as naturally athletic as me and Whitney were, so when she tried to balance on the long, thin fiberglass skis she immediately slid uncontrollably until a big snow bank finally stopped her.

"Are you all right?" I asked once she pulled herself free.

"I don't think skiing's my thing," she said wearily.

"It was just your first run. Why don't you take a lesson like Oldie said you could at breakfast?"

Emily looked over at a group of three- to six-year-olds nearby, all holding onto each other's poles like they were elephant's trunks lined up in a circus, as an instructor pulled them along sideways across the slope.

"I'd look ridiculous in that group," Emily whined.

"You don't have to take a *group* lesson," I said.

"You mean I could have a private one?"

"Of course," I offered. "I'll just put it on our resort tab."

"Oh, okay, thanks then."

Just then a very fit, attractive, dark-haired man came out of the ski instructor's building wearing an instructor's patch on his neon jacket.

"I want to be taught by *him*," Emily grinned. "My future husband!"

I laughed, knowing she was joking since he had to be at least ten years older than us. After all, what would a thirteen-year-old want such an old man's attention for?

"I'm going back to our room now," Emily said only moments after we arrived at my parents' friends' annual Christmas Eve dinner party.

"What? Why?" I asked with concern. Attending this party was part of our family's Aspen tradition and I knew the hosts spent months personally planning it so each guest would be sure to have a wonderful meal and time. Leaving during hors d'oeuvres would be an insult for sure, let alone what Oldie might do if he thought it would embarrass him as well.

"I don't feel so good suddenly… maybe it was all that skiing and fresh air."

"That's supposed to make you feel great, and you look it." She really did too, which wasn't a surprise since she spent more time in the bathroom that night getting ready than Whitney—which was a real feat.

"I'm sorry Melanie, but I just don't want to be here. I don't even know anyone but you."

"So let me introduce you—"

"No, really, I'm not comfortable being here."

I was completely shocked. Why wouldn't she feel comfortable? She was wearing my new suede pants and cashmere sweater—she fit in more than I did fashion-wise for God's sake. I felt bad, but all I had been trying to do since we landed was make her feel comfortable everywhere we went. What more could I be doing?

"Why not?"

"I just don't."

"Well, let's ask Oldie if it's okay. If he says yes then you can go back to our house, but you have to ask him yourself."

We went over and found him knee-deep in shrimp.

"I don't feel very well," Emily stated. "Is it okay if I go back to your house and go to bed?"

"Aw, sorry about that kiddo," Oldie said. I could tell he was already well into the scotch just from his tone. "Hope you'll feel better for tomorrow night's party we'll be going to."

"Me too," Emily said.

"But *you're* staying, right?" Oldie asked towards me in a manner that was purely rhetorical.

"Oh, yes," Emily answered for me. "I don't want to ruin Melanie's good time."

"Okay," I agreed and was glad, and not just because Oldie wanted me to stay. There were people here I only saw once a year at this particular dinner party and I really was looking forward to catching up with some of them.

"See you later then," Emily said in a rush and was soon out the door.

When we got back home, it was well after midnight and my mom and I helped a very drunken Oldie get straight into bed. He was snoring in our arms before his head even hit the pillow.

I entered my own bedroom quietly and moved around in the dark, hoping not to disturb the large lump I saw in Emily's bed. I changed into my nightgown and got under my own covers. It had been a long day between skiing and the dinner party, and sleep couldn't come fast enough.

Suddenly I heard the front door open. Whitney was the only one still out, so I figured it must be her just now getting in. But then my bedroom door opened and the light was flicked on.

It was Emily, as drunk as Oldie had been.

"Hi roomie!" she said happily as I jumped up and shut the light back off. I quickly shut the door and sat her down on her bed, now realizing the "lump" was all her own, old clothes rolled up into balls to make it look like she was asleep under there.

"Where have you been—and what have you been *drinking?*" I whispered. I was used to seeing Whitney and Eva in this state and had helped them both come out of it more times than I could count, but I was sad to see Emily doing this kind of partying too. I thought she didn't like to drink like I didn't.

"I was with 'Steve,'" she said as her tone changed to one of sadness.

"*Who?*"

"Steven—my ski instructor. He wanted to give me a more 'private' lesson tonight, so I went to meet up with him so he could give it to me."

"You *what?*" I was completely irritated by her tone. It sounded just like when Whitney talked about the condoms to me that day in her bedroom.

"Oh grow up Melanie—we're almost sophomores for Christ sake!"

"You went off with some strange guy you just met without telling me or anyone where you were going?"

"*So?*"

"So I thought you were back here sleeping like you said you were going to do! I told you not to leave—God, what if something had happened to you? We're responsible for you you know—what if he had tried to kill you—"

"No one would care."

"What? Of course they would! Your mother, me, Oldie—"

"'Steve' didn't even care right after he finished. He just brought me back here… he couldn't get rid of me fast enough. But I thought he *really* liked me…" She started to cry, and I knew this regret was bigger to deal with right now than any list I could come up with about whom else on the planet really would still care.

"I'm sorry." I tried to console her as she wept in my arms. She seemed so small, like a baby who really needed its mother. I didn't know what to do to help.

"Oldie really wanted you to be there with him tonight at the party," she stated tearfully. She appeared to be sobering up.

"Yes. And he wanted you there, too."

"I know. But that's only because I'm your friend. I wanted to be the main reason a man wanted me around, and I thought Steven really wanted me, not just what he could 'get' from me… You know, you're really lucky to have what you have."

"I know."

"I don't mean the clothes and money. I mean Oldie. I've never even met my dad. But even if I ever do I know he won't be as good a father as Oldie."

I suddenly felt ashamed for all the times I was embarrassed or even scared by Oldie and realized she was right. No matter what he did occasionally when he was 'acting out,' overall he was a good, loving, and very attentive father. I was lucky.

"You're probably right," I agreed.

"I'm so sorry for all this Melanie," she said earnestly. "I'll never lie or do this to you ever again. You're the best friend I've ever had."

"You're mine too," I said, and truly meant it. Eva could have Whitney. I had my own best friend now.

Chapter 2

❧

"This will look great on you with your brunette hair," I said as I handed Emily a tan wool sweater that still had the tags on it stating it was imported from Ireland.

"No thanks, it's kind of scratchy, which is probably why Whitney left it here," Emily said as she put it back on the shelf. Since she was now used to the 'finer' things in life from getting all my hand-me-downs as well as treated to new clothes and jewelry whenever my allowance allowed it, she was very discerning and instantly knew just what she liked—and didn't.

"You're probably right," I agreed as we continued to go through my sister's closet like it was our own private boutique.

"Have you heard from Whitney since she left?" Emily asked as she tried on a bright yellow, form-fitting T-shirt that left nothing to the imagination once on. She was already quite "blessed" for a sophomore... and she seemed to like the attention it gave her by making it as obvious as possible. I admired her confidence about her new, womanly curves, or at least that's what I thought it was, for I still wasn't sure how to act about my own.

"Yeah," I said as I tried on a pair of four-inch Gucci heels. Since I was only used to wearing kitten heels I felt like a giant, but liked how they made my legs look even longer. Suddenly it made the rest of my 'beginning curves' make more sense too. "She says college is even better than she thought it would be because you can party all night and day and all the other 'Heirheads brats' she's met there seem to agree..."

When Whitney went off to college at the University of Texas in Austin earlier that September, she immediately fell into a group of Heirheads who were some of the wealthiest in all of Texas. Most had known each other since childhood and they had all ended up at UT together. Being the spoiled, incessant partiers that they were, a small group of four immediately formed

19

a bond that was unbreakable. Their clique was soon known on campus as the 'Fearsome Foursome' and consisted of Whitney, Eva, and two male Heirheads named Travis Phillips and Austin Brinkley.

Leading the Foursome was Travis, whose campus nickname was Muy Malo—or "very bad" in Spanish. Travis was a brilliant student at UT on a full, four-year petroleum-engineering scholarship, but all he really cared about were cars and parties.

Travis was more of the strong and silent type, but he was also stubborn, moody, and unpredictable. Witty dialogue (known in Foursome lingo as the "the good bullshit") was about the only thing that could make his slightly upturned aquiline nose crinkle and the ends of his full lips rise in a Cheshire-cat grin. This elusive, mischievous smile melted hearts all over town, along with his electric blue eyes and strong, squared-off jaw. Not even an incident involving a drunken fraternity prank where his fellow frat brothers shaved off one of his eyebrows while he lay passed out on the floor of the Alpha Delta Tau house could change the fact that Travis was a stone cold fox.

But, it took a lot to impress him. He could be brutally indifferent to anyone he didn't care about, which was most people on the planet. Girls weren't a priority for Travis except on the very rare occasion he found one who caught his eye. Then he would pull out all the stops and he'd shock everyone with a grand display of over-the-top affection. He enjoyed sweeping a girl off her feet, but the trouble was, after she was properly swept and bedded, Travis would lose interest and dump her with a casual, "Sorry babe, didn't work out."

Just a week or two into their freshman year Eva caught the attention of Travis and she was the perfect target for his sexual antics. Though she dated a lot of guys in high school (and preferably only those who had money), Eva remained a virgin throughout her high school years and her sheltered innocence was fully intact—which made her even more of a lure for Travis, and him a good candidate for her to want to lose her pent-up "innocence" to.

For it wasn't until her strict German father dropped her off at UT's McCain Hall dormitory that fall that, for the first time ever, Eva was completely on her own. Eva was free from the shackles of her strict Catholic family, and so she instantly began experimenting with the sexual freedom and recreational drug use that was coming into fashion on all college campuses in the early 1970's. It was common knowledge that Eva's father would pack her up and ship her off to a convent if he found out she wasn't a virgin any longer—but like a lot of "good" Texan girls, she figured what her father didn't find out couldn't hurt him.

Eva willingly slept with Travis for several weeks while of course harboring a secret crush on the more affluent Austin Brinkley the whole time.

Whether or not Travis respected her as a friend or even as a person in the beginning is debatable. It was because of Whitney that Eva even got a free pass into getting to know the Fearsome Foursome's two male members in those first few weeks. And despite becoming a full-fledged member of the Foursome afterwards, her inclusion in one of the most important social groups on campus just wasn't enough... Eva wore her insecurities and naiveté like a see-thru slip dress, and her desperate attempts to always fit in were just as transparent, especially after Travis made it clear it was over and he was "moving on" for good.

And despite rumors to the contrary, Whitney and Travis always kept it strictly platonic between them, for Whitney claimed she had "bigger fish to fry" when he once asked her out. When Travis didn't take that personally, they became fast friends. Whitney enjoyed playing the diva of the group—high maintenance and proud of it—and Travis enjoyed indulging her whenever possible.

Travis and Whitney were then always considered the alphas of the group, and Austin Brinkley was the true Adonis—a tall, tanned, well-muscled Texan who, according to the ladies, was six-feet-three-inches of pure animal magnetism. He was also by far the wealthiest of the Foursome, and one of the most eligible bachelors in all of Dallas County, which meant he funded much of the Fearsome Foursome's fun—subsidized the top shelf liquor, paid for table service at the best clubs, and sprung for frequent surprise trips to fun, exotic locations. He stood to inherit an absurd amount of money when he turned twenty-one and only attended UT so he could live on his own.

Austin's grandfather had amassed a great oil fortune and his father was a famous heart surgeon in his own right, but sadly, Austin was only fifteen when his parents' private jet crashed into the side of a mountain while trying to land in an Aspen blizzard. Austin then spent the rest of his teen years living with his half-senile, aging grandfather and a nursemaid-turned-nanny, who, though she meant well, never could get Austin to accept the nurturing she tried to provide. It didn't take a psychologist to figure out that he was deeply wounded by the loss of his parents and he spent most of his time looking for someone, or something, to blame. But he hid his angry, wounded heart well with a calm, Irish charm and a very cool bravado (one that could only come from the knowledge that he'd never have to work a day in his life). At every opportunity he flaunted his wealth openly, as if he was pulling it up from a bottomless well.

Not exactly an official member of the Fearsome Foursome but always around just the same, Jack Hartley was the Foursome's henchman, or court jester. Though he acted arrogant because of his own pending trust fund one day, like many of his circumstance, Jack was really just insecure deep down and required constant petting of his fragile ego. The Foursome kept him around because he was a good instigator: typically, when it was time to wrap up the night, Jack was the one who pushed everybody to keep the party going until the sun came up, sometimes long past. Travis and Austin never needed much coaxing, but Jack did seem to know just how to get them all going again. Jack followed his two heroes around like a Rottweiler puppy and whenever the Foursome needed a fifth, Jack was always first in line.

When Whitney and Eva could finally leave McCain Hall and move off campus their sophomore year, it was only natural that they moved into Austin's place, a condo penthouse in a gated community that he shared with Travis (but which Austin paid for entirely). They all made ideal room-mates and became a true campus institution by the start of their junior year.

Meanwhile, by my own senior year of high school the rest of my curves had grown in to rival Emily's, and I finally understood what Whitney meant the day she told me how much 'fun' other boys could be, especially when one very special one noticed how tall I looked in my heels...

"Happy Valentine's Day," David said as he handed me a small, neatly wrapped box with a pink bow. His dark brown eyes sparkled in anticipation of my reaction.

I had butterflies inside. Though we had only been together for six months I knew this must be what real love was supposed to feel like. I was only ever happy around him, even now, when we were just sitting in his old, beat-up muscle car in my high school's parking lot like it was our own private suite.

David Weinstein and I had met at an open lecture about the Vietnam War that we both attended in August at Rice, a local private university in Houston. He thought I was a student there like him, and I was so smitten by his eyes right away that I didn't actually let him know I wasn't until our third date, and by then he was completely smitten too and didn't mind that I was still a senior in high school.

David was mature, kind, sincere, passionate, and also persistent—per-suasive, even. He had the best G.P.A. of his whole senior class and was one of the smartest boys I'd ever met. Besides being intellectually stimulat-ing, David held radical, extremely liberal political views about the war and other things that I'd never even heard mentioned before. He also had a very impressive way of going about his daily business like he didn't care what anyone else thought. I couldn't imagine living my life that way… but I liked being around it.

But I also felt guilty too. The truth was I'd been keeping my relationship with him secret from my family the whole time. Oldie had some stupid rule that I wasn't allowed to date college-aged guys until I turned eighteen—an antiquated policy, in my opinion, but limiting nonetheless. And, it wasn't the only thing about our relationship Oldie would disapprove of; on the scale of one to conservative, my father was a pure, red-blooded puritan (I wasn't even allowed to wear short skirts to school; most mornings I'd change outfits in my girlfriends' cars and now most recently, in David's), and he would not be happy with David's much more liberal views. So in the tradition of keeping things "like the rest of the family"—meaning of course, Oldie—there was no escaping the fact that David did not belong in ours. But my heart kept telling me I could change that.

I carefully unwrapped the shiny white paper and opened the small gray velvet box inside. It was a pair of tiny pearl earrings. They were charming. I knew he must have skimped and saved just to get them for me, and I thanked him with a kiss. "I love them," I whispered.

"Not as much as I love you," he responded. I knew he meant it too. We had already talked about what it would be like to get married after we both graduated this spring. Though he was my first and only boyfriend ever, it felt right and I knew I could be happy with him for the rest of my life.

"Here," I said, handing him a bright red box.

He opened it and gasped. Inside was a twenty-four-carat-gold Cartier watch that was most likely worth more than his car. He fingered it a moment, then opened the gold band and read the inscription inside:

To D.
My Eternal Love,
M.

"Now who loves who more?" I teased.

He grinned and kissed me so deeply I felt I would melt right into him and we would never be two separate people again. And at that moment, I never wanted to be.

"You're so lucky!" Emily said as we poured over the latest issue of *Vogue* for formal dress ideas. "I've been out with tons of guys and I don't think anyone has ever kissed me like that."

"That's because you don't stay with any of them long enough to really fall in love," I pointed out. She was becoming more like Whitney with her attitude towards men every day—one mishap and it was suddenly time to find another, no second chances ever allowed.

"Most of them are the ones doing the leaving, not me," she corrected, then abruptly changed the subject. "What do you think of this one?"

She pointed to a picture of a stunning, sexy Halston cocktail dress that draped the model's curves tightly in all the right places.

"It's pretty," I said, imagining David's reaction if he were to see me wearing it.

"Yeah, but I'm sure it costs a fortune though."

I could see how much the dress meant to Emily and felt bad I was thinking of David and not concentrating on my time being with her. Since I met David our time together was now much more limited, though my parents thought we were practically inseparable since I always used being with Emily as my 'cover.'

"Tell you what," I said. "I'll treat you to it to wear to the Full Moon dance at the club this weekend if you promise to get ready for it here with me and play along when I tell my parents I'm meeting Beau there for my date instead of David."

"The beautiful, very 'popular' Beau from your school?" She grinned.

"Yes, we've become quite close lately in Spanish class. Probably because I'm the only girl there *not* throwing themselves at him daily."

"Do you think he'll really go and want to be my date?"

"I'll ask him to for you if you want me to."

"Oh yes, please! Oh Mel—this is going to be the best night of our lives! But aren't you afraid of what Oldie would do if he catches you there with David? It's your family's club, people might talk."

"Good point… I'll make sure Beau does go then so we can all sit together and switch dates if needed on the spot—people will think we're all just there together as friends then."

"Great!" Emily beamed. "But we don't have to all *leave* together, do we?" From the look in her eye I knew Beau was going to get as lucky as he wanted to this full moon.

"Here I am, Oldie," I said, entering Oldie's library, which was normally off limits to all of us, especially when he was working on a big case like he had been for the past few weeks. "Mom said you wanted to see me?"

"C'mere, Lil' Bit," Oldie said cheerfully, puffing away at one of his cigars. "I want to show you something." He ruffled my hair as I came around the table. This wasn't like him; since he'd started on this case we hadn't seen him this jovial in weeks. Plus, now that it was only a few months until graduation and freedom, 'family' had become something of an annoyance these days, so I preferred as little contact with them as possible.

Oh God, I thought. *Please don't let this be one of those awkward father-daughter talks where Oldie tries to make sure I'm not smoking or having sex. Gag! As far as he knows, I'm still an angel.*

I cautiously gathered around the table to see what he was getting at as he pointed to a legal-sized document in a cardstock manila folder. "That, baby girl, is your trust fund balance. Have I ever shown you this? I don't believe I have."

He opened the folder and put his finger next to the amount. I just stared at it. It was a big number I supposed, but then again, money didn't really mean much to me, numbers even less.

"You'll still have to find your own career and work for a living of course, but this represents a sizeable cushion should you ever need a little extra padding in life, some 'security' to fall back on. Got it? Did you know this inheritance was coming to you, Lil' Bit?"

"Uh, I guess so." I mean, I knew we had money. After all, my sister, Mother, and I had credit cards that didn't seem to have any limit unless Oldie was having a grouchy day, and we had our own spending money as a weekly allowance in cash too. It was fairly common knowledge at my school that we were what others considered "rich," and I had no reason to doubt it wouldn't always be this way. Actually, I never really thought about it much at all.

"Great. That's good, I'm glad you understand the concept. Now, did you also know that as long as your old man is alive I have control over when and what amount you have access to? At what age, I mean?"

"Uh... I don't know... sort of." This line of questioning seemed highly irrelevant, but I could tell something was up. Why was Oldie messing with my head? I took a step backwards, edging towards the door.

"So, Dad, seriously, is that all? 'Cause I need to go pick up that dress for Emily for the dance before she gets here, and I'm already running late."

Ignoring my question entirely, Oldie slowly turned over an eight-by-ten photo as he said, "This... if I'm not mistaken, is your date tonight, is it *not?*"

I took a short intake of breath. The photo was of David helping me out of his car in front of my high school. The image was taken from far away, but you could clearly make out the closeness of our bodies, the shortness of my skirt, and most revealing of all—the adoring look in my eye. My worst nightmare had come true. Oldie was on to us.

"This young man, 'David' is it? This is the fellow you've been hanging around with lately? Quite a lot of hanging around with... no?"

CRAP, I thought. He knew for sure.

"Yes," I admitted, hoarsely.

"Hmm... is that so..." Oldie took the photo and turned it back over, folding his hands neatly on his desk as he remained calm. "The same David who you swore up and down was 'just a friend' when I found out he drove you to school 'just that one time'? Is this the *same* boy?"

I gulped, but the dryness made my tongue catch on the back of my throat. "Yes."

"Now, I'm just your daddy that begot you, who created you… and if you can find it in your heart to deceive me it sure as hell makes me wonder who else and what else you've been lying about," he said, still infuriatingly calm.

I burned red with shame as my eyes welled with tears. He took a puff of his cigar and tossed me his handkerchief.

"It just so happens that I know a business associate of this young man's father, and you know what he told me? He told me that this boy is a student at SMU. Not a high school student—a <u>college</u> student!"

I didn't bother answering him. I could no longer see through the hot tears blurring in my eyes, and my voice was useless against what was coming next anyway.

"Didn't think I'd figure it out, did you? Well this is *me* darling—I got word of you two 'lovebirds' the same week you started carrying on, but I kept my mouth shut knowing what a 'good' girl you usually are. I figured you had something to prove, you know, schooling all the other girls in the art of attracting an older man, etcetera. I thought it wouldn't last, but it did. And then you lied about it! If you feel you've got something to prove dammit then *prove* it! But not *this* way—"

"YOU SPIED ON ME!" I yelled incredulously. Whatever embarrassment I felt suddenly turned into rage as I realized that he had probably had me followed around for weeks, maybe even months, taking pictures of David and me together. The one photo was proof enough, but I knew that only meant he had to have many more. Worst of all, he was using it to force me into some sort of admission. He knew I couldn't lie to his face, not under this much heat.

"You… spying SPY!" I spat, the only words my mouth could form. I was blinded by fury.

He waved his cigar dismissively. "And lucky I did! I thought this little young pup romance would pass like a harmless sidewinder, but now I hear there's talk of an engagement? No sirree, not on my watch—"

"YES!" I said defiantly. "Yes, there's been talk of marriage because I love him and he loves me! He's good to me and he treats me right. He's driven me to school every day for months and he tells me he wants to marry me all the time!"

"Oh Melanie honey," Oldie sighed, rubbing his temple with his fingers. "*Every* boy in Texas wants to marry my daughters… you could have your pick, but then there you go getting mixed up with this smart-ass, struggling, college pervert... He doesn't have a trust fund coming his way ever, you know." He shook his head. "If you weren't talkin' dim-witted and threatening marriage, involving my own future grandbabies, then I'd just as soon let you run off and do as you please. But what about college, huh? You just want a 'Mrs.' degree like everyone else? Get fat and pregnant? You're only seventeen-years-old for Christ's sake! You think you're really ready for that kind of commitment? Hell no, you aren't!"

"Yes I am! I'm old enough to—"

"*Furthermore,* if I catch wind that you two have had 'relations' there will be a death warrant out for him, and Lord have mercy on your soul too— you'll be grounded for the rest of your LIFE! Do you understand me? You are far too young for any of this and that's FINAL!"

I started to cry uncontrollably and then, like a clean spring breeze pushing off a storm, Oldie calmed down, feeling bad that I felt so bad and he truly tried to console me. "I'm telling you right here and now that you should be playing the field, like Whitney's always done. Give those others boys a chance. Don't let just one ship dock in your harbor, there's an entire fleet out there to be considered. That's all I'm saying."

"I don't want to have a bunch of meaningless flings like Whitney and I don't need to because I already have David and he's a good guy Daddy!" I insisted, still crying freely. "You think he just wants to marry me for my money, but he would never do that!" I wailed. I regretted it before it was even out of my mouth. Oldie darkened ominously.

"Measure your words, child." He flicked the ashes from his cigar. "Because I've said nothing of the sort." He walked over to the window and looked out. "I know he's a good boy, Lil' Bit... but he's not 'good enough' for you and that's *really* the problem here, see? He can't take care of you."

"You don't know him if you think that," I said proudly. I knew that if David were here he'd say just the right thing to make Oldie pause and think, maybe even change his mind. "Dad, please—you don't understand. David's not just any guy or a passing fling... at least meet him and see how happy we are together," I cried.

"Oh, I'm sorry... I forgot—you're in 'love.' Well then, let me re-acquaint your sudden 'rose-colored-glasses-world' with the price you'll pay if you carry on this rebellion and continue to see this boy against my wishes. You see, I created you in more ways than one. I know what you *truly* need and can't live without—"

"You mean *this?*" I scoffed, gesturing around to Oldie's library, the sprawling books and worldly trinkets sitting atop the behemoth mahogany desk. "This is just stuff, Oldie. It doesn't matter. I don't need *any* of this! I'm in love with David and he's in love with me and we both need each other—that's all! Please understand that!"

"Sugar, I'm betting on you understanding what being with this 'dream' boy really means to your future…" He looked at his watch. "Come on now, or else we'll be late."

"*Late?*" I said, unsure of what he meant.

"We have reservations." He winked and I instantly knew my plans for tonight would now not include going to the dance or seeing David.

Moments later we were in a limousine headed for the private jet that would take us to Monte Carlo. I listlessly laid against the soft leather seat looking out the tinted window with my back turned to Oldie. I refused to look at him I was so angry, and he knew it.

He argued into the limo's phone with yet another one of the ten-plus lawyers on this big case; this one was nicknamed "Screw Job." When he hung up he began to talk to me in an overly-jolly manner that only made me angrier. "I have a two-hundred-and-fifty-foot yacht waiting for us in St. Tropez and we can hit all the beautiful ports on our way to Venice. Won't that be great?"

I didn't answer.

"Lil' Bit?"

"I may have to go with you," I said, "but I don't have to talk to you."

He was impervious to my heartache and only determined to win. It was the only thing that mattered to him—and he was brilliant at it. He talked while rubbing his hands together in victorious delight already. "We'll get off and stay at the Lido, 'cause I know how much my 'Lil' Bit' loves that Lido joint!"

"Be sure to eat tons of fettuccini Alfredo there… then maybe you'll drop dead."

He cackled as he rubbed his hands together, greedy-like. "You are a caution, Lil' Bit! You know, you got a lot more of me in you than you think!"

"That's right Daddy, I do." I finally looked at him, smiling sweetly. "Too bad you won't be there to see me rub *my* hands together like that when all your loot hits my bank account."

He nodded, laughing, "That's my girl!" Then he leaned in, whispering, "There's another eighty percent I got hid off shore… you don't even know about all that yet. Yep, believe you me, you'll be a rich'un."

"Oh mercy me… what joy," I sarcastically rejoiced. "I'd still rather be with David. Can I at least call him? He's going to think I stood him up!"

Now he really roared. "I'm saving that boy from you, you know!"

"No, I'm saving him from YOU!" I said, sobbing.

"Child, I'm saving you from a disaster," he said earnestly. "Okay, okay… you wanna sell your daddy south for this boy? You think he loves you, do you? Well, your daddy's love ain't a shallow, changin' kinda love… it ain't no fleeting romantic love that's here awhile and then gone. This is a long haul, 'arm-in-the-fire for my child' kind of love... the cut-out-my-heart-for-you every day until-the-day-I-die Daddy kind of love." He leveled his eyes on mine. "And your daddy, who *really loves you,* is telling you this is OVER and DONE with, you *hear?* Inevitable—like the Titanic... the moment it hit that iceberg it was already over. It wasn't a question of where the ship was going afterwards, it was all about living through it then. And I'll tell you what... life ain't about the card you're dealt, it's all about living through the one you *get*... always remember, when life happens, you happen back! Melanie honey, you will grieve, but you will also accept this all soon enough... believe me, in ten years you won't even recall that boy's name."

"Please... just... please, be quiet!" I sobbed, and then, just for a moment—for a tiny skipped heartbeat—the thought crossed my mind that Oldie could be right and maybe it had already happened... Could my relationship with David really be over? Had Oldie won? How was I going to live through this?

At that moment our limo turned directly onto the tarmac and pulled up to the jet as it was idling. There was the singular smell of jet fuel in the air, piercing to the nose. As I slowly ascended the stairs up to the hatch door a feeling of dread was quickly descending on my heart. I had to speak to David, had to reach him somehow... how could I get around Daddy long en—

"SURPRISE!" A familiar voice shouted as soon as I entered the hatch.

I gasped. Lo and behold, Emily was inside the jet with two packed suitcases tucked neatly beside her. She was as jubilant as I was miserable, but we exchanged air kisses anyway.

"Well, isn't this fun?" Oldie said with a grin.

I shot him a look that said I wanted him dead.

Soon we were in the air out over the Atlantic Ocean. I was reading the latest issue of *LIFE* magazine when Oldie came and sat in the seat across from mine. He was holding a sable throw he always packed for plane rides just in case it got chilly, and he now tried tucking it all around me. "Can't have my Lil' Bit gettin' cold," he said lovingly.

Another wave of rage roared over me as I threw the throw back at him, snarling, "Get away from me!"

He ignored this and continued to talk in soothing tones, "Now you got to at least eat then baby, so I got some food coming...Your favorite... 'Happy Meals' for both you girls!" he said towards Emily, winking.

"I can't eat," I said.

He yelled loudly to the stewardess, "What's the hold up HERE? These girls want their HAPPY MEALS!"

A stewardess came down the aisle with two trays that each contained a crystal glass flute of Dom Perignon, a plate of Beluga caviar, and a small box

of handmade dark chocolates molded into the shapes of cowboy boots—
what we "Texas Oil Princesses" (or "TOP" for short) called our "Happy
Meal."

"Dig in girls… but mind your figures if you wanna catch a rich husband." He chuckled.

Emily squealed in delight. "Yeah! Par-tay, par-tay, par-tay!"

I guzzled the champagne and turned towards the stewardess. "Keep this
glass <u>full</u>."

"Yes miss," she said.

I looked at Oldie and said defiantly, "I'm getting drunk."

"Good," he said. He took the tiny spoon and loaded it high with caviar,
then leaned in, putting it up to my lips. "Here, have some of this… does a
body good."

If looks could kill he would have been dead, but from my mouth came,
"A rich husband, *huh?*"

I opened my mouth and he put the spoon in it. I shut my lips tight and
scooped up the large pile of fish eggs with my tongue, then started to spit
them right back into his face when suddenly he roared, "YOU GO TOO
FAR CHILD!"

Right then I knew I was about to, so I stopped and swallowed, hard.

Oldie sighed, shaking his head as he muttered, "That was *too* far child…"
He stormed off towards the back of the jet as I downed another glass of
bubbly.

Two hours later he was back, and I was tipsy. Maybe he was too, for he
was clearly feeling festive coming to sit on the arm of the seat directly across
from mine again. Emily sat next to me, looking excited.

"Now as you know Lil' Bit, every good girl gets a 'toy' with her Happy
Meal…" Then, like most Texas millionaires who for some reason always
give jewelry with no box as if they just found it lying on the street, he
pulled a diamond bracelet from his shirt pocket and held it out to me.

"*Jesus!*" Emily gasped.

"'Jesus' won't get you one of these, sugar." He grinned.

Slightly off-balance, I grabbed the bracelet from his hand, shook my
head and said, "You're pathetic!" as I threw it back at him.

Unmoved, he held the bracelet out again, staring into my eyes, expres-
sionless. This was a moment of truth, like when Eve first looked at the
apple, but didn't take a bite, yet. I took it and threw it again. This time it
hit him in the face.

Patiently, like the serpent waiting in the tree, he held it out again. I hic-
cupped, and then stuck out my tongue, sneering. I wasn't ready to give up
my 'innocence' to him, now or ever. It belonged to David.

"Daughter of mine," he started, "this is the third time you have refused this blessing."

"So? You think I care about a stupid bracelet? You think you know what I really want and 'must' have? Ha! Well you DON'T! I don't need any of this… all this 'junk' you rich daddies give your daughters just to aggrandize yourselves, to show off your *own* EGOS!"

He laughed. "You think all this grandeur we pour on our little girls is for us? No baby… it's payment rendered in advance to assure your future job is done well… For 'Daddy's little girls' are the instruments of our own incarnation, our future flesh and blood, so all our grand gestures really aren't free at all… which is why I'm now not asking, I'm *telling* you what you will do. You will send David away and you will pick an heir from *our own crowd* and you will marry your two fortunes together and create our future descendants together."

"You can't make me do that!" I cried, not even believing what I was hearing from him. "And I could just elope with David as soon as we get back you know!"

"Oh?" he questioned as if he actually enjoyed the threat. "Well then, okay, if you really are crazy enough to run off and marry this bonehead instead then you know that hefty trust fund we talked about? The one you currently get when you turn twenty-one so you can have a *secure* future? It's *gone* baby girl, <u>GONE</u>! Just like this bracelet can soon be…. so you have to choose now. It's David, or your trust fund and this bracelet." He stamped out his cigar. "I'm not telling you now, I'm *asking* you."

I sobbed and hung my head, shoulders heaving, as I cried, "I pick David!"

Emily looked on like I was nuts. I knew she'd pick the latter.

"Precious, I'd cut off my arms and legs for you, for both of my daughters, in fact," Oldie said, "but I know tellin' you a thing like that ain't enough to get you to understand what I'm *really* asking of you here…" He held up the bracelet as he motioned for the stewardess. "But this will."

The stewardess approached. "Yes sir?" she asked.

He spoke still looking straight at me as he held out the bracelet towards her, "This one-hundred-carats of diamond perfection cost me two million dollars. If my daughter refuses this gift one more time to my face, I'm gonna hand this over to you, and it will be yours to keep…" He paused for dramatic effect, and then continued as his eyes dared me to react. "You know as well as anybody Melanie that I've never made a threat I didn't uphold… It's a matter of strict personal policy of course, for they'd eat me alive out there if I wasn't known as a man of my word… Now, I'm gonna count to three, and if you don't take this bracelet from my hand, a gift from your own flesh and blood father, then I will hand it over to this nice young lady and it will be hers forever and ever… ONE…"

I glared back.

"...TWO..."

I glared harder, willing time to stop, the jet to crash, my life to end, or this airplane cabin to just stop spinning— then it suddenly dawned on me that he *really* meant it...

The stewardess held her breath. Emily put her hand over her mouth as her eyes bulged...

"THRE—" he started to say, and I immediately snatched the bracelet from his palm before he finished.

"You and your damn dramatics!" I spat.

He got up triumphantly. "I *knew* you wouldn't let me down! Now, more of that champagne—for all!"

I lay down and closed my eyes, exhausted from the drama. Emily admired the bracelet as I dozed, then gently took it from my hand and put it on my wrist for me, carefully snapping the clasp.

"For safe-keeping," she whispered, then added, "and don't worry Mel, you did the right thing." She got up and went back to her seat.

Sleep was fretful—I dreamt of snakes, burning crosses, and a glittering bracelet slung from a fiery tree. When I snatched that cold bracelet from Oldie's hands I didn't hear the iron door slamming behind me along with it. I didn't know I was now fallen like Eve, never to get my innocence back. And I did not know I had become Judas, a traitor, snatching the forty pieces, which, by the way, was an insult because back then forty pieces was the cost of a slave... That poor fool Judas tried to give the forty pieces back, tried to buy back his soul and his innocence, but it was too late for him... and now it was too late for me, too. The iron door was locked and I could bang on it all I liked, but it was still sealed shut no matter how hard I willed it to open back up. Judas and I, we had both done something out of pure greed... and could never take it back.

And poor David was the innocent victim who was offered up onto that altar of greed by me when I took the bracelet over his love as we glided over the Atlantic Ocean. Forgive me for my sins... I didn't mean to choose it! But I felt I had no other choice.

Oldie was not innocent in all this, of course. He was in the business to win, and no one ever stopped him by getting in his way. And whether God was on his side that day or not, Daddy certainly got his way this time. And deep down he knew what had just happened; I had just had an abortion, the 'other' kind of abortion, you know, the one that is done on your soul's innocence from your own poor, selfish choosing... But Oldie didn't care about 'that' kind of innocence, only my future security, and over the years when I would curse him for his crime of playing God that day by making me choose between money or love, he would protest that it was all for my own good, that I was too young and naive back then, and then he'd end it with, "Hey! You took the money, so stop crying about it!"

It was then I realized the truth. Yes, like Judas, I <u>did</u> take the money as a form of future security over forever love. So thereafter, I accepted at last what I had done and stopped crying about it. And I never spoke about David again.

Chapter 3

*A*fter that I couldn't leave for college fast enough. I decided to go to the University of Texas in Austin like Whitney, and Oldie was glad to send me since he felt I was on the "right" path again. I was thrilled when he said he'd also help out Emily financially once she was accepted there too; I guess it was partly his way of making sure I still had one person who meant a lot to me around so I couldn't complain that I was "all alone." And with Emily I wasn't, at least at first.

We signed up to be roommates together, and then, just like Whitney and Eva, we were assigned to stay in McCain Hall dormitory. McCain Hall was a chaperoned dormitory where all the 'proper' girls stayed their freshman year, which meant that's exactly where my mom and Oldie insisted I stayed quarantined (little did they know there were tricks for staying out late, hiding beer, and sneaking boys back to our rooms though, which everyone knew about—I'd learned them all from Whitney years ago when she lived there).

"Travis Phillips…" Emily read out loud our first day there as we both stood in front of the student activity bulletin board outside the dormitory's group lounge. "Isn't he one of Whitney's roommates?"

"Yes," I answered. From all the stories I heard Whitney tell over the years about the Fearsome Foursome, I wasn't surprised to see that Travis Phillips's name topped the McCain Hall "Bad Date List" posted before us. The "BDL" was a list developed and maintained by Mrs. Hayden, the robust, matronly figure who ran McCain Hall. She took her job of looking after the freshmen girls—most of whom were fresh off the boat from small, Texas towns—very, very seriously. She came up with the Bad Date List to warn her inexperienced residents about the biggest and most badnews male students on campus—whether that meant they were dangerous, mean, or just plain dumb. She posted the list the first day of school and then updated it on the last Friday of each month as the year went on. Travis considered it an honor to be named the 'best' of the bad dates and took his reputation and all the rumors it stoked very seriously… A dead giveaway that he'd just concocted some new scheme to egg Mrs. Hayden on was a sudden sparkling, sideways glint in his eye—a sure sign that the devilish gears in his mind were cranking overtime. By the time Emily and I arrived at UT in the fall of 1975, Muy Malo's name had topped the BDL for three years running.

In fact, by the time Travis, Austin, Whitney, and Eva got to be seniors they were some of the most notorious kids at the whole school—both for their non-stop partying, legendary pranks, and notorious scandals, and also for the extreme wealth they flaunted everywhere they went. And Travis, though brilliant, was also known for being on academic probation ever since his second semester of freshmen year, solely because he never went to class.

Austin had finally inherited his absurdly huge family trust recently, so finishing college was a moot point to him. But he continued to hang around and never bothered to stop paying his UT tuition just so he could have access to girls, parties, and all the campus hijinks with the rest of the Foursome. Instead of studying, he spent most of his time partying and cruising around in a fleet of fast sport cars ('the penis mobiles' as he lovingly referred to them, a habit that only fueled the rumor that Austin was well-endowed in more ways than one). He also loved to take his girl-of-the-week out to extravagant dinners, yacht parties, and impromptu trips around the world.

Whitney and Eva enjoyed being the divas of the group—and campus— together by now, and it was like high school all over again when other envious girls were around them. I didn't think it was possible, but since they were both now armed with stronger vocabularies, they had learned to take their cattiness to a whole new level.

I disliked their mean girl and constant party behavior even more now that I was feeling grown up and finally on my own as an adult, and I felt sorry for everyone they put down. Deep down, I guess I really was a 'good girl' like Oldie always said, and I soon realized that that meant I had zero in common with most of the freshmen girls I was living with at McCain Hall, including Emily, as she began to turn into Whitney and Eva more and more. For unlike them (and every other girl it seemed at UT), I wasn't out to just party and earn myself a "Mrs." degree— I actually wanted to learn something and graduate. So after a few weeks of feigning interest with most of my hallmates, I gave up.

If I had to put my finger on it, I'd say it was because I was always a bit more interested in what was going on in the world outside of campus and a little less interested in the nearest rodeo or kegger, and it showed. A therapist once told me that traveling the world at such a young age with Oldie had made my "box" a little bigger than most people's. I was proud; I liked being considered worldly. But so far during that first semester at UT my box felt like a big crate set beside a stack of small pencil boxes. While most kids at UT had never once left Texas, by halfway through the semester I already couldn't wait to get out.

Though I was a good student and paid attention in class all week, on weekends I was starting to get bored of just going to movies and reading alone. It seemed everyone—especially Emily, who hardly ever came home most nights and was now referred to as "E.E." for "Easy Emily" by most fraternity houses on campus—was always trying to 'cut loose;' so I finally figured if I was going to have any measure of fun my first year in college I'd better stick close to the experts, so I started hanging around with Whitney and her Fearsome Foursome group.

Even though I was nothing but a lowly, pipsqueak freshman at the time, they tolerated me because I offered to be their constant designated driver and I also played the group's documentarian, holding their cameras up for them and snapping group photos whenever they demanded it. Though I was never a full-fledged member, I was soon around them almost as much as their faithful follower, Jack.

Towards the end of my freshman year, three of the Fearsome Foursome were finally about to graduate. Their easy, worry-free lives seemed paved in gold before them as both Whitney and Travis knew trust funds were within reach, and Eva knew she could count on her friends to "help her out" for at least a little longer. They all felt they were each anointed for greatness and wanted to make sure their time at UT would never be forgotten. That's when Travis and Austin decided to throw the biggest party of the year at their Alpha Delta Tau fraternity house—one they knew would make them legendary—that is, *if* they could pull off their biggest, most ambitious prank yet during it before dawn.

The ADT fraternity house was first home to a brotherhood of young college men that, shortly after the Civil War, sought to reunite North and South by teaching young brothers the value of 'tradition.' The building the fraternity was housed in was once a grand, multi-level, arched mansion. But the building hadn't been remodeled since the 60's and the abused, two-story wooden structure was now home to a brood of over-testosterone-filled, rowdy frat brothers. Every Saturday morning, the poorly manicured lawn was littered with empty top-shelf liquor bottles, and a still-damp, booze-stained, orange shag carpet lay moist and stale in the main sitting room. Decades of hard partying perfumed the air and cigarette-burned couches with countless stains of unknown origin were peppered haphazardly throughout the house. The kindly housemother, Ms. Peyton, tried to keep order, but every semester her rowdy inhabitants kept her outnumbered and fretful.

Travis and Austin carefully formed their plan and decided Bevo's—the UT Longhorn's beloved school mascot's—birthday was the perfect date for the perfect party (and prank) since it would be after semester finals and the last big event right before graduation. Bevo had been gracing the UT football field since an alumnus decided the school needed an imposing, real-life Longhorn stomping around the sidelines during games. He collected donations of a dollar each from students to buy a burnt saffron-colored steer, which was presented to the UT student body on Thanksgiving Day in 1916. But that night a group of Texas A & M "Aggie" pranksters visited the Austin campus and branded him with a red-hot branding iron, searing the new mascot's backside with the numbers 13-0, the score of a recent and unfortunate Civil War game in which UT lost. Legend had it the embarrassed steer's handlers came up with a clever solution to save face: they converted the number 13 into a "B," the hyphen into an e, and inserted a V in front of the zero to spell "Bevo," which was also the name of a popular non-alcoholic beer at the time. Bevo became one of the most popular college mascots in the country and his birthday soon became a revered holiday on UT's campus with students celebrating it with gusto every year. Travis and Austin were determined to make sure this year was his biggest party to date.

And girls, of course, were one of the most important ingredients for making sure they would have a successful evening—for the mission of the Alpha Delta Tau fraternity had changed significantly since its founding. Currently the goal of its male members appeared to be to bed as many co-eds as possible and compare notes later. The more an ADT brother scored, the bigger the campus stud rep. How they all survived their non-stop party marathon college years is a mystery—but even more baffling is that ten years later some of these same big-boozing, dirty-mouthed womanizers would go on to run some of the biggest Top Fortune 500 companies in the country. Go figure...

Still, the night of the big event, everyone who was anyone on campus was excited about attending in the hopes of hobnobbing with these now still-only frat rats—especially every gorgeous, gullible girl on campus who had been aggressively invited. Whitney and Eva were of course on the top of the invite list, and Whitney brought me along too so I could drive them.

"We have to look stunning—it's our last chance to rope them in, girls!" Whitney said jokingly as we dressed for the party... but there was a nugget of truth in that, for most girls attending UT were looking to graduate with a proposal, or at the very least, a rich boyfriend. "That way, once we graduate we won't have to search out a party ever again." She winked.

Eva pulled mascara through her wide-eyed lashes, adding, "Or better yet... *pay* for anything ever again!"

I was starting to get annoyed. They'd been primping for hours. "Well, quit spending so much time on your make-up then! You guys won't be able to catch a man if you don't actually GO to the party," I said, annoyed. "Let's get going already!"

"Shut it, Squirt." Whitney flicked her hair and smoothed her skintight dress. "This is probably the last big party we'll go to in our entire college careers, so lighten up. You can't rush perfection." She pouted her red-lip-sticked mouth into the mirror and patted it with a roll of cotton. I rolled my eyes.

By this point, Eva was like a caged animal. She had already done several lines of cocaine and was so charged, she looked like she was about to go berserk.

"Heeeere we go, kittens!" She giggled manically as we finally left and climbed into my small sports car.

When we arrived at the party, I could feel all eyes were on us as we walked from the car to the front porch. The frat rats practically licked their lips as we entered the threshold of the already rocking, packed house.

"Want any lemon and butter with that?" I said sarcastically towards them all.

Whitney turned around and glared at me. "Shut up, Mel!"

"Well they're looking at us like we're lobsters in a tank," I whispered to Whitney as I saw Travis and Austin approaching us from across the crowded room.

"Look, I don't care if you have fun tonight or not, just quit being such a spoilsport," she scolded.

"If you think I ruin your good time then why even bring me?" I asked, amused.

"Are you kidding?" Whitney raised an eyebrow. "We need you to drive!"

Eva giggled.

Travis and Austin finally pushed their way through the crowd. Travis stretched his arms out in greeting, "Hellooo my favorite ladies! The Fearsome Foursome, together again! So, Muy Malo, at your service, along with my faithful man-servant, Austin."

"Fuck off," Austin said, elbowing Travis out of the way. "You'll have to excuse him. Too many shots to the head—liquid and *otherwise*—"

"Where have you two been? It's late!" Travis complained.

"You can't rush perfection," Whitney cooed.

"Time to play catch up, girls!" Austin said as he handed both Whitney and Eva a shot glass.

Travis poured from the bottle of alcohol he was keeping under his arm. Eva and Whitney brightened.

"Thought you'd never ask!" Whitney said cheerfully.

Eva beamed as she accepted the offering and the four each tossed one back together, with only the slightest grimace as it went down. They all came up smiling.

"Any for you?" Travis winked towards me as he lifted up an empty glass. I shook my head no.

Just then Jack arrived with a tray full of red cups filled to the brim with the infamous ADT punch known simply as Rocket Fuel. "Drinks for all," he said and all eyes went on me as they each reached for a glass. I hesitantly took the last cup. I went to sip it cautiously and, just like I thought, the alcohol burned my nose as I inhaled. I could immediately tell it was spiked with 180% proof Everclear—the strongest booze money could buy, and dangerous when combined with nearly any other alcohol.

Over the course of the next hour I had only sipped about half of the cup when my head started swimming and my legs started to get that warm, tingling, tipsy feeling. I tossed the rest of the cup away, but noticed my sister and her friends gulping theirs down repeatedly.

"Whatever," I muttered as I walked away.

The music was loud and pumping, and there were good-looking guys everywhere, but none were sober enough to talk to. I went outside hoping to find something a little more interesting to do, but nothing could be found. I did, however, see Emily in an upstairs bedroom window making-out with a frat rat before someone finally turned off the light. I knew it would probably be days before I even saw her again now. Then finally, after two hours of feigning interest in random, incoherent conversations and swatting away drunken guys trying to campaign me into drinking with them, I headed back inside to find Whitney and Eva; I was ready to go.

I knew better than to let my guard down around all these drunken cretins, so I walked through the sea of frat rats quickly, searching for my sister. When I finally found her I was amazed to see how the other students looked at her like she was a goddess. She told jokes and yelled across the room like she owned the place—and the true fraternity brothers willingly let her rule. Finally she came over to me with a fresh drink. I could tell she was trying to be nice, but I sullenly folded my arms.

"Come to socialize with the 'common' folk?" I asked sourly.

"Quit being so bitchy, little sis. We'll leave soon, I promise," she said.

"So early? It's only three A-M," I said sarcastically. "Come on, let's go now!"

Whitney leaned in and whispered, "We can't, Eva's.... *busy*."

"What do you mean, 'busy'?"

"I think she's had a few too many cups of Rocket Fuel because Travis and Austin dared her to have sex with them on the Sacred Greek Cross—you know, the one in the forbidden chamber—as a prank, and now I think she's really doing *IT!*" Whitney was drunk too, so her sloppy whispers were more like moist shouts by the end.

Even as a freshman I knew this was incredibly taboo, but it sounded exactly like the sort of thing Travis and Austin would do just to get a rise out of people. It was childish— and incredibly disrespectful.

The Greek Cross—or 'Square Cross' since the four arms were of equal length in the shape of a plus sign—represented honor, tradition, and the passing of the torch from one generation to the next and it was the sacred symbol of the ADT brotherhood. To a Greek fraternity, their sacred symbol might as well have been the American flag, or the sword of knighthood to the Queen of England. Alpha Delta Tau's historically significant and long-standing icon was an impressive, six-foot-tall relic housed in a special room called the "hidden chamber." It was completely off-limits to most, an inner sanctum used only for formal ceremonies such as inducting new members or hosting exclusive planning meetings for important events like Hell Week. The underclassmen were made to believe that the room could only be used for these purposes, but the upperclassmen knew better... important memorabilia like beer-drinking contest trophies were housed there along with old alumni rosters and a TV set available to the upperclassmen only.

The room was always kept under lock and key and only one person—the current ADT president, who was now John Roper, an unattractive but very wealthy rancher's son from Fort Worth—could hold possession of it. The men in his family had been proud members of Alpha Delta Tau since the fraternity's formation, and John's father was a big alumni donor who gave to the fraternity generously—then demanded that his son be made president of the chapter. John was pre-law and took his role of Key Keeper very seriously. He only opened up the room on special, invite-only evenings like the Super Bowl, Movie Nights, and weekly screenings of *Charlie's Angels* reruns. He knew which of his brothers were the obnoxious pranksters and he kept the key as far away from them as possible—Travis and Austin being chief among them. But the mere fact that the Greek Cross was so sacred and the room in which it was housed was so off-limits was what made it an irresistible target for both of them.

"What do you mean—how'd they get in?" I asked incredulously.

"Jack did shots with John until he passed out and then they stole the key from his pocket!" Whitney was trying to hold in her laughter. "I think they're in the chamber right *now... doing IT!*"

"Oh, you have got to be kidding me..." I was aghast. Why did hanging out with Whitney always make me feel like a hall monitor?

"Crap, *shhh*! Here they come..." She tried to straighten up.

Jack, Travis, Austin, and Eva were hastily making their way through the room towards us. Eva was struggling to straighten her dress while Travis cursed up a storm.

"Fucking spoilsport! He woke up! Wouldn't even let us finish," Travis grumbled to Austin. "Or even get started actually—I had barely gotten my pants down—but fuck! So close!"

"Hey Trav, Roper's shitting bricks—we're gonna have to split, man," Austin said as they finally got to us. But I could see Travis' gears still spinning. He looked pissed.

"No fucking way—he's not gonna drop me in the grease like this, not that measly prick," Travis said. "Doesn't matter—we'll say we did it anyway." He climbed up on the closest table and shouted, "CAN I HAVE EVERYONE'S ATTENTION!"

Shocked, the partygoers all stopped what they were doing and the music was lowered.

Wow, they really did own the place, I thought.

"I just wanted to let everyone know that I, Travis Phillips, and he, Austin Brinkley, both of the Fearsome Foursome, have just nailed this lovely chick, Eva Mueller, upon the Sacred Greek Cross of the fraternity!" he said proudly.

The crowd started whooping and hollering their approval. Beers were sloshed up into the air as people cheered, and a drunken Eva beamed cluelessly, lapping up all the attention. I turned away in disgust.

When Travis had had his fill of the crowd's boisterous applause, Whitney and I grabbed a stumbling Eva and made a hasty exit. Travis, Austin, and Jack all shouted their good-byes as we shrank out the back door. As we left, I watched both Travis and Austin accept high-fives and slaps on the back from their fellow envious fraternity brothers and grew furious.

I drove home angrily. Travis was such a jerk! How could he lie like that just for attention? And worse—Eva was now the laughing stock of the entire campus, and I was her get-away ride.

Throughout the night and over the next few days the story roared through the campus like a raging wildfire. The event only stoked the Foursome's notoriety. Those who were at the party let their imaginations run wild and the tale was told with various levels of graphic embellishments and ad-libbed details. The prank elevated Travis and Austin to the frat equivalent of Greek immortality, while Eva suffered an unprecedented level of humiliation.

The Dean of Students found out about the incident and Eva's parents were called. Dr. Helmut Mueller showed up on campus livid and ready to take Eva home for good. Eva couldn't convince them that nothing had actually happened, even when the boys denied everything too. But in order to save herself from expulsion just days before obtaining her degree—and worse—punishment from her father, Eva lied and admitted to engaging in oral sex with one of the boys, but adamantly swore up and down that she was still a virgin. After the tearful confession, her parents and the school bought it. And then after the lecture of the century from her dad, Eva was finally allowed to stay and graduate.

But this new "admission rumor," started by Eva herself, turned out to be an even more horrible mistake. It only fueled her already crumbling reputation, and her phone rang off the hook from endless crank calls from the young, always-horny frat rats who'd heard the rampant rumored confession. They all wanted a taste. Guys stood in droves outside of the Foursome's apartment, trying to get a peek of the now-infamous nymphet. They even climbed the tree outside Eva's window as a joke, or in a bizarre effort to get her attention. Perhaps these young men hoped to get lucky, or maybe they just wanted to see what all the fuss was about. It was ironic that the one event that kicked Eva's already promiscuous reputation into overdrive was the one in which nothing actually happened at all.

Eva was mortified. She was so distraught and overwhelmed by this ugly turn of events that she decided she not only needed to leave Texas, but the entire country—and fast. She immediately started making travel plans to go to France that summer right after graduation, a plan she convinced Whitney to get on board with. Travis and Austin, feeling bad about all the negative attention Eva was getting—for she still was their friend after all—offered to assist with the finances to help her skip town and she gladly took them up on it. My sister, it seemed, had a very different reason for wanting to leave the country after graduation altogether.

"Why in the world do you want to go to the French Riviera for the summer?" I asked Whitney. Traveling abroad was usually more my thing, and she didn't even know any French!

"Eva needs to get out of dodge and why shouldn't I keep her company? It sounds like a lot of fun," she said.

I gave her a look that told her I knew something was up.

"Okay, okay," she relented. "I'm just a little upset that I'm leaving college minus an engagement ring. I mean, what's so wrong with me that I can't find a guy who really appreciates me, you know? Maybe I'll meet someone in France."

"Oh Whitney, that's so tacky. Who cares about that?"

"ME! Besides, those jerks Travis and Austin feel so bad that they're going to help put us both on a plane as soon as graduation is over. They bought our tickets and they're going to pay for our dorm and *everything!* That will help make my own trust fund go even further."

It made some sense, and I could tell my sister was ready to shake off the end of her college experience. I felt bad for Eva, too. Maybe it was a good thing for them to be going to France.

"You ARE going to have to learn French, you know," I said.

"Oh yeah? Well you're going to have to quit being such a smart-ass," she said, but I could see her mulling the idea over in her head. I could tell that she thought it was a good one.

The girls soon presented the idea to Oldie and Dr. Mueller together. Despite Oldie having served in the war and Helmut—according to my father—having the "misfortune" of being born German, the two had actually managed to become quite chummy over the years. Oldie was completely unaware of Dr. Mueller's service under the Third Reich however, and I knew if he had ever caught wind of it that would be the end of it. But today they sat side-by-side enjoying scotch and cigars while they listened to Whitney and Eva's post graduation plan proposal.

Whitney showed them a brightly colored brochure of a three-month summer program at the University of Nice where Whitney could take beginning French and Eva could work towards a master degree's in French. The program promised to be a "highly intensive immersion course" designed for serious students interested in "foreign language applications and international affairs." Eva stressed that she hoped to 'one day' work as an interpreter at the United Nations, or perhaps meet and marry an international diplomat instead. To Oldie and Helmut the thought of learning and mastering French in the heart of the French Riviera sounded like a great idea, so the two men gave the go-ahead for them to enroll, both writing a check out for the school's tuition that very same night. They were each very pleased with their daughters' bold and ambitious next move.

That weekend, three of the Foursome proudly walked across the sun-lit stage, though for one of them it was only by the skin of his teeth. Eva graduated with a B.A. in Humanities, Travis with a B.S. in Engineering, and Whitney received a B.S. in Psychology.

B.S. is right, I thought to myself. My sister knew as much about psychology as I did about string theory.

Our parents joyfully watched it all though, and I could tell they were both silently relieved she had actually made it to this milestone.

When it was time for Whitney and Eva to leave for France the very next day, my mother, Oldie, and I drove Whitney to the airport. She was in hyper overdrive about her trip and couldn't stop talking the entire way. I secretly wished I was going too, but couldn't imagine going anywhere with Whitney and Eva, and I'm sure the feeling was mutual.

We finally arrived at the international terminal and were greeted by Eva, Travis, and Austin. The boys had come along to pay for Eva's incidentals at the airport and to say good-bye to Whitney.

Whitney had loaned Eva some suitcases and between the two of them they collectively packed enough Louis Vuitton luggage to stay at least six months.

Eva started checking in at the Air France ticket counter first when suddenly a petite French woman started clucking from behind the counter. "These bags are well over the limit of fifty pounds," she declared in disgust. "Surely they are not for only *one* person?"

"Yes, the bags are for 'seulement une personne,'" Eva sneered in perfect French, "and what's it to you?" She tossed Austin's credit card over the counter and ordered the woman to charge it, not even bothering to ask what the total in overages were.

It was early, but Austin and Eva had clearly already been drinking, or perhaps they were still drunk from the night before. Austin put his arm around Eva while Travis came over to say good-bye to Whitney. Oldie, Mom, and I hung back to give the Foursome some privacy while they all said their personal good-byes. Even I could tell in the truly heartfelt ways they each looked into each others' eyes that there was a lot more going on than anyone ever knew.

Travis, however, kept looking over at me. I was wearing a tight, white, lycra dress with long, lacey sleeves which looked fantastic against my lightly tanned skin. I went back over to say one last good-bye to Whitney and he leaned over and whispered, "Hey kid, you look *great!*"

He couldn't stop staring at me and smiling. Whitney playfully slapped him in the chest with her carry-on bag. "Stay away from my sister while I'm gone, Muy Malo!" she warned.

Travis grinned and backed away with his hands up in compliance.

Eva wiped away her tears and produced a camera. "Melanie, can you take our picture?" she asked. "This could be the last time we all see each other."

Travis cupped Eva's face in one hand. "I sincerely doubt that, okay?" he told her with a confidence that made everyone feel good, even me.

The four of them lined up and I snapped their picture, their smiles frozen in time. After the flash they embraced each other one last time and Austin slurred, "I guess this is the end of the 'Fearsome Foursome,' huh?"

Whitney then went over to hug Mom and Oldie. I saw Oldie lean over and whisper something to her that made her cry.

"Take care, Squirt," she said, hugging me and kissing me on the forehead. I couldn't figure out why Whitney was being so sentimental—she was just going away for three months! But maybe she really was planning to meet an international billionaire, marry him, and never come home. Or maybe she was just nervous about leaving. It was hard to tell with Whitney.

Eva and Whitney made their way down the terminal and we watched as their plane took off. Travis and Austin invited me to go out with them later that night, but I just blushed and declined. I knew that no matter how handsome and charming the two of them were, or how much they seemed to care about my sister, they really were bad news. I was also still mad about the Sacred Greek Cross incident and knew no good could come out of hanging around with them.

Thus, with a puff of the plane's engine taking Whitney and Eva up into a cloud of early morning Houston fog, the brief reign of the Fearsome Foursome at UT—as well as my first year there—came to an end.

*   *   *

"I heard you're not finding any interesting guys to date at UT," Kathy Hamilton, an old acquaintance from my family's Aspen holiday trips, said over the phone unexpectedly later that week while we were just supposedly 'catching up.'

"You heard right," I said into the receiver as I waited for what she meant by that. I wasn't aware Oldie was discussing my relationship status with his friends, but apparently he was since Kathy was married to Lloyd Hamilton, the son of an oil heir. Lloyd's father had been a friend of Oldie's forever—and he was also a well-known chatterbox throughout all of Texas's social circles.

"Well then, I have someone wonderful I'd like you to meet. His name is Matthew Peyton and he's one of the most sought-after eligible bachelors around right now. Can you come to Newport this weekend?"

"Rhode Island?" I asked, but really already knowing that was where she meant. There were always a lot of preppy, East-coast-type families like hers in Aspen over the holidays who talked about their summers in Newport fondly as they drank from their steaming mugs of hot Irish coffee in front of the lodge's roaring fire. In fact, that is how Kathy and Lloyd met.

"Yes," Kathy replied.

"Sure, why not?" I said. I was up for a challenge and still had the travel bug in me from leaving Whitney off at the airport, and though Newport wasn't in another country, it would still be foreign to me since it would be my first trip there. Besides, since I figured "Oldie" was really the one behind all this anyway and was now playing match-maker, I knew he'd pay for it and must have approved of the guy already, so I was safe on all accounts.

The thought of going on a real date actually sounded nice, too, after not having one for so long... Though I really was enjoying all the interesting things I was learning at school and intended to get my degree eventually in a foreign language (Spanish being the front-runner for now), I still wanted to be in love again eventually. I could have both after all, so why not take a chance and see if one was in Newport?

"Great!" Kathy said excitedly. "I'll set it all up then!"

"Thanks," I said as we hung up. I was suddenly very curious to see what kind of guy Oldie did think was 'good enough' for his Lil' Bit.

I flew to Boston early that Friday morning, then rented a car at the airport. I thought I had left early enough to beat the heavy weekend traffic Kathy had warned me about, but by mid-afternoon it was already close to gridlock on I-95, and when I got to the infamous Newport Bridge it was all bumper-to-bumper and all I could do was pray the weight of all those vehicles didn't send us careening into the ocean. But once I finally entered the picturesque, coastal town, I could immediately see why it was so popular. The grand, impressive, historic mansions along Bellevue Avenue were breathtaking. This city by the sea certainly merited its "Queen of Summer Resorts" nickname.

Kathy and Lloyd were anxiously awaiting my arrival at the hotel. And though all I really wanted to do was relax from traveling all day, they both started in right away about how glad they were I was finally there and that we had to hurry—they had already made reservations for an early dinner at a popular restaurant called The Black Swan, and we had to beat the traffic it seemed to get there now too.

"You're going to love Matthew," Lloyd said as we drove bumper-to-bumper again, though this time thankfully with him behind the wheel since I turned my rental car in. "He's from Greenwich and has his own mergers and acquisitions firm on Wall Street."

"And his family not only belongs to two of the most *exclusive* country clubs here in Newport, but also to the very exclusive Lyford Cay Club in the Bahamas," Kathy added.

"Wow, impressive," I said, knowing that was what they wanted me to say, but really I had no clue at all what any of those clubs were or how much they meant to people waiting to join—which often could be decades, like the ones in Texas. I enjoyed going to my own country clubs in Houston though, so I assumed I would enjoy the ones here just as much too.

When we arrived at the restaurant, Matthew was already there.

"Matthew Peyton," Lloyd said as we all stood in the bar, "this is Melanie St. John."

"Nice to meet you," Matthew said in a polite demeanor, already seeming interested with his eyes.

"You too," I answered. I was immediately stricken by how tall he was, six feet at least, but wasn't as attracted to him as he seemed to be to me immediately. He seemed fit enough, but his hair was a dull, muddy brown color and his eyes were hazel, not blue or brown like I usually liked. Still, he was very attentive as we all sat down at our table—pulling out my chair for me and making sure that I was comfortable. It was nice to finally be around a mature, older man with manners again. No one had done that for me since David.

"We'll have two bottles of Chateau Margaux and four glasses," Matthew said to the waiter.

"No, only three, thanks," I corrected. "I don't drink."

"*Really?*" Matthew said, looking a bit concerned. "Oh, okay then, one bottle then *and...?*"

"I'll have an ice tea," I said.

The waiter returned right away with our requests, a sure sign Matthew was a regular there whom they liked to keep happy. But it turned out he should have brought the two bottles of wine right away anyway, for in less than an hour Matthew was already on his fourth glass alone while we all sipped our drinks and enjoyed some delicious, but very small grilled scallop and truffle appetizers.

I was beginning to get really hungry and could tell Kathy and Lloyd were too, but we each didn't want to rush what now seemed to be Matthew's main course as he ordered yet a third bottle of wine.

"No problem," the waiter nodded, "and are you also ready to order?"

"Yes," I said, looking at the menu I had been staring at for over thirty minutes now. "I'll have the lobster."

Suddenly Matthew's entire demeanor clouded over and his posture changed from upright to completely hunched-over. "Holy COW!" he exclaimed loudly. "I guess you really know how to take advantage of being a guest!" he chided. "You went straight for the most expensive item of the menu!"

Everyone was completely taken off-guard by this seemingly new personality he now displayed, everyone that is except for the waiter, which told me he had seen this all before.

"Matthew," I started, "I have no idea how much the lobster costs... the menu doesn't have prices for women, remember? But if it's a problem I'll be happy to pay for it myself." Oldie had made it perfectly clear when he dropped me off at the airport that I had 'no limits' on my spending this weekend. In fact, he was so happy I had accepted the offer to go that I wondered if Whitney's disappointment in not having a husband by the end of college was partly brought on by pressure.

Matthew immediately dismissed my offer as he waved it off with his one free hand, muttering something under his breath right before he took a drink that sounded a lot like "spoiled bitch."

The waiter took everyone else's orders and made his escape.

When our entrees arrived Matthew made loud, rude comments throughout the entire dinner, making a huge deal out of the "fifty dollar lobster" I was eating; though I knew it was far from the most expensive thing that would be on the bill that night since he recently switched from the costly bottles of wine to top-shelf cocktails for himself, Lloyd, and Kathy.

"Look, could we just drop it?" I responded, shocked at his blatant disrespect.

Kathy looked uncomfortable and tried to change the topic. "What time is your tee time tomorrow?"

"Ten," Lloyd said.

"So I guess that means you'll be having lunch at the club," she said.

"Yeah," Matthew answered. "And maybe dinner too. The tournament usually goes all day. We'll call you when we're done."

Where they were playing, the Newport Country Club, was one of the oldest golf clubs in the country and had a strict members only policy, and Matthew wasn't bothering to offer to put Kathy or me on the tournament's guest list to be able to join them it seemed, though he had no problem talking about all the fun he and Lloyd intended to have there all day without us. And as the evening wore on, things only got worse...

Matthew was a name-dropper, a pompous one at that, and he inexplicably continued to be a jerk about the lobster throughout the entire evening long after our dinner plates were cleared. I couldn't believe I'd flown halfway across the country to meet this guy. What was I thinking, agreeing to spend an entire three-day weekend with a perfect stranger? Am I so desperate that I have to rely on blind dates now? Is this who Oldie really foresees as his future decedent's father figure?

Matthew and Lloyd played golf together the next two days straight from morning 'til dusk, taking the one rental car between us all and leaving Kathy and I stuck at the hotel all day since there were no more cars available to rent due to the tournament. We had to walk into town just to go shopping for something to do, and after two days of this, I was completely bored and was glad the long weekend trip was finally coming to an end soon.

But then, while browsing in a Cole Haan shoe store on my last full day there, I spotted an extremely tall, attractive guy trying on shoes. He spotted me too, and after making eyes at each other from across the room, he finally came over to introduce himself.

"Hi," he said. "I'm Michael Baldwin."

"Melanie St. John," I responded. He had beautiful blue eyes.

"Charmed," he began, "is that a southern accent?"

"Yes. I'm from Houston."

"So what brings you all the way from there to Newport?"

"An adventure," I lied just as Kathy joined us. She must have thought that was a good cover, for she just smiled as she introduced herself to him too.

Michael then told us how he'd just completed construction on a new summer home for himself in Newport, a property he was planning to live in full-time now since his divorce was finalized. At the word 'divorce,' my ears perked up and I then confessed my real reason for coming there. He couldn't believe that Matthew and Lloyd had abandoned us all weekend and was baffled that we'd been in Newport for two days but hadn't yet been on a single sailboat or seen any of the island.

"Newport is famous for sailing!" he said with gusto. "It would be a horrible shame for you two to miss out on sailing while you're here. Listen—it's a gorgeous day. It would be my absolute pleasure to take you ladies out this afternoon on my boat."

"That sounds great," I said, for I thought it sounded like a fantastic idea—and a lot more fun than anything we'd done in Newport so far.

"Oh, no, we shouldn't," Kathy said. "After all, my husband wouldn't approve of such a thing, we just met you..."

Michael looked disappointed, but also that he understood.

"I'll still go," I said, and he beamed.

Kathy looked a little put off by my decision, but I wasn't about to deprive myself for her, Lloyd's, or Matthew's sake. I had to have some fun this weekend before I flew back in the morning. And I'm glad I did, for I had the most wonderful afternoon. Michael had a beautiful sailboat and it was stocked with chilled Dom Perignon. Even though I normally didn't drink, out on the water with the sun's warm rays beaming down on us, it seemed like the perfect thing to do. The afternoon flew by as we sipped bubbly, enjoyed the most magnificent views of the island, and got lost in conversation. I told him about being a student at UT and he told me about his job as an investment banker at Smith Barney. He was polite, interesting, and very amusing. The day soon faded into dusk.

Noticing the color of the sky, I realized I'd totally lost track of time. "Oh my gosh!" I said. "What time is it?"

"Six forty-three," Michael replied as he looked at his watch.

"I'm supposed to meet my friends for dinner and the tournament's closing ceremony at the club, and cocktails start at seven." I was definitely going to be very late!

Luckily, Michael had a phone on the boat, so I immediately called Kathy and Lloyd at the hotel to tell them of my delay, but they had already left.

"Do you really have to go then?" Michael said. I could tell he didn't want our time together to end either.

"Yes," I said sadly. "This is our last night together before I leave in the morning, and I should spend it with them."

About an hour later Michael dropped me off at the country club in his beautiful new black Jaguar. I definitely didn't want to say good-bye to this guy, but I also didn't want to be rude to Kathy and Lloyd (though Matthew was another matter entirely).

"Thank you so much for a truly wonderful day," I said.

"You're most welcome," he said. "I had a great time."

"Yeah, me too," I agreed. "Well, good-bye... it was really nice to meet you."

"You too," he said. "Hey, do you want to meet back at your hotel for some late night dancing after dinner?"

"Yes!" I said, and then gave him a quick peck on the cheek before exiting his car.

I briskly walked through the parking lot and into the building and was immediately greeted very coldly by my already drunken, so-called 'date.' Matthew stood by the front door of the club actually waiting for me, red-faced with anger. He must have seen me get out of Michael's sportscar.

Great, I thought. *How am I going to explain this one?*

"How nice of you to join us," Matthew slurred sarcastically. He put his arm around me, but I recoiled from his horrible alcohol breath. "You're lucky things haven't started yet, or else I'd *really* be upset," he said icily.

My senses must have been dulled by the champagne I had had on the boat earlier, because instead of hearing his actual words I instead actually thought I'd been forgiven, so I committed myself to salvaging the evening with him until dinner was over.

Just then dinner was announced and everyone went to sit at their assigned tables where a lavish New England-style clambake was spread out in the middle of each one: crocks of red-hot lobsters, steamers, boiled new potatoes, hot buttered rolls, and bright yellow, freshly picked corn-on-the-cob. The room was full of all of the golfers from the tournament and their wives, nearly two hundred people total, and enough food to feed at least double that.

"Oh look, we're having lobster, your *favorite*," Matthew said sarcastically as we sat down and he offered me a ruby-pink crustacean. "At least it's free this time, so eat up!"

"I will, thank you," I said, also sarcastically.

But as I went to set the lobster down on my plastic plate, it slid off. Embarrassed, I laughed, but Matthew glared at me and shook his head. "I guess 'Texans' don't know anything about a clambake… all you know is barbeque and beer, right?" He lowered his head and muttered, "Bunch of hicks…" though it was louder and much more audible than he thought.

I looked down at the plastic utensils at my place setting. "Oh my, I'm high class now! Look, I get to eat lobster with a plastic knife and fork! Who are you kidding?"

Matthew completely lost his cool. "How dare you criticize my club's clambake!" He slammed his fist on the table and stood up as if he was going to give a toast.

The whole room fell silent; all eyes were on him, thinking there was going to be an announcement. He looked at me, pointed, and shook a furious finger, screaming, "I've completely HAD IT with YOU, you—*BITCH!* Do you have ANY idea who I *AM?* I'm one of the most sought-after bachelors in America! I could've had not one, not two, but THREE different dates this weekend, and you behave like *THIS?* You show up an hour late, get dropped off by some asshole in a Jag—that's right—I saw you, you tramp! And you *kissed* him? How DARE you!"

Everyone was staring at both of us. I pointed to a telephone on the wall. "Well, excuse me, Mr. 'Most Sought-After-Bachelor.' I suggest you go over to that pay phone there and call one of your other possible dates, cause this one's had enough of your bullshit. I'm not going to sit here and be berated in front of a room full of strangers. I'm out of here!"

Lloyd tossed me the keys to the rental car, whispering, "Matthew's out of control, you should probably go back to the hotel."

I ran out of the Newport Country Club never having been so humiliated in my entire life. The only good news, I thought, was that I was flying back to Texas the next day and would never have to face these people ever again.

Matthew ran after me in the parking lot with Lloyd and Kathy racing behind him, yelling for him to calm down.

"You'll NEVER be allowed in this club AGAIN—or Lyford Cay for that matter!" Matthew screamed at me. "And you'll NEVER be welcomed in Newport *EVER* AGAIN!"

I spun around just as I reached the rental car. "If this is where YOU'LL be then I consider that a *gift!*" I jumped in and sped off.

Later I told Michael I had changed my mind about the late night dancing and then had a nightcap with Kathy and Lloyd in their hotel room.

They apologized profusely for Matthew's behavior during the whole weekend, and especially for earlier that evening at dinner.

"I've never seen him act that way before," Lloyd said.

"Maybe he has a drinking problem," Kathy wondered, "since it was such a quick change from 'Mr. Wonderful' to the terrible 'Mr. Hyde.'"

"Are you sure it isn't *me*?" I asked them, wondering if it really could have been. Since I didn't have a lot of dating experience I thought maybe I really didn't know how I was supposed to behave all weekend, but waiting around for whenever he seemed to be able to 'fit me in' didn't seem right.

They assured me it was not—or that there was anything wrong with me.

The next day I was very glad when I saw the word "HOUSTON" light up on the departure flight list at the airport. I boarded the plane without looking back. The only thing I didn't regret about the too-long weekend was that I had put everything—the hotel room, rental car, and my roundtrip plane ticket—on Oldie's credit card like he had instructed, so I didn't "owe" Matthew Peyton anything ever again. The blind date weekend was not a great choice, but at least I wasn't that dumb—and neither was Oldie.

I found out later from Kathy that Matthew had only been interested in meeting me because he thought I had access to major oil money like Lloyd did. As soon as he found out I didn't he couldn't have cared less, and that's why he acted the way he did. Kathy was very apologetic, but from that point on, we saw very little of each other.

After that, I vowed no more blind dates. My luck with men thus far post-David was unimpressive to say the least, but at least I still had the rest of the summer to hopefully change that.

Chapter 4

꧁ॐ꧂

$\mathscr{N}$ot long after I got back, Oldie decided we should all fly to France to surprise Whitney with a luxury cruise in the Mediterranean on a yacht named the *One Lucky Lady*. Oldie had chartered it to celebrate Whitney's completion of the first half of her Beginning French program at the University of Nice. My parents were so proud of Whitney they could burst, and Oldie thought the cruise would be a much-earned reward for her having shown such initiative in her future—perhaps for the very first time in her life.

When I told Emily, she hinted that she would love to come along too, but I said this was a family-only outing since it was all arranged around Whitney. This was mostly true, but there was also a part of me that wasn't as comfortable hanging around Emily anymore since she was so into partying and boys. But I hoped it was just a college phase, for Whitney seemed to have grown out of it now that she was suddenly so focused on her 'future.'

After twelve hours, with a lay-over in Paris, we finally arrived at the Nice International Airport.

"Oh my God," I said, popping my neck. My carry-on bag weighed a ton and my back was killing me.

"Twelve *hours!*" my mother exclaimed, shaking her head. "Did you enjoy that, Oldie? For Pete's sake—we could have taken the Concorde from New York and only had to be in the air for three and a half."

"I told you—it's too damn expensive! Besides, I enjoyed the long flight. Finished my book, caught up on sleep, the food was good, and the scotch was <u>fantastic</u>!" he said.

"You can't be serious," I said, groaning.

"I don't care what you guys say—that flight was fine! Now, let's go get the rental car... I reserved us something *nice*," he promised.

Mom sighed. "Courtlin, we're exhausted. Let's just go to the hotel... Melanie and I would like to freshen up."

Oldie shook his head. "Ooooh no! We're *not* going to the hotel—we're here and we're surprising Whitney right NOW!"

"What?" I said, appalled. "Dad! We just spent half a day sitting on a plane. Can't we at least take a shower first?"

"No-can-do! The reservation is waiting on us. I'm jetlagged, too, but your sister will be so surprised! You'll get a second wind, you'll see. C'mon, it'll be fun..."

Outside the car rental place, my mother and I couldn't believe our eyes as Oldie ordered us into the obnoxious, bright orange Citroen, which was a fancy French sports car meant for drivers half his age. Mom and I teased him about his belated, mid-life crises for having picked out such a tiny, silly-looking thing. What in the world was he thinking? But as usual Oldie didn't care, and there was no changing his mind.

The University of Nice was just a short, fifteen-minute drive from the airport, so we soaked in the view. We had all only read about Nice and seen pictures of the famous Promenade des Anglais in magazines, but now here it was, a beautiful, palm-tree-lined, sparkling boardwalk hugging the pebbly shore of the Mediterranean; a half-moon highway and beach nestled in a turquoise expansion of water. It made Newport completely disappear from my memory.

Photos from the university brochures where Whitney was taking classes showed an attractive, pristine campus. We were also anxious to see the historic old town it was near, which held picturesque monuments and historic treasures of its own. The hills that currently overlooked us were forest green, and the stunning panoramas were breathtaking. But as we made our way into the city proper towards the university, the stunning panoramas faded into a much more mediocre metropolis. And as the streets wound into the exact section of the city where the actual university was, the streets became a little more rundown, a little more unclean—to say the *least*.

We arrived at the dormitory building where Eva and Whitney's quarters were. It was a small, newly constructed high rise on a rather dull-looking street on the south side of the university. And when we entered the building, there was no one sitting at the reception desk.

"That's odd," my mom noted. "With all these young girls staying here, you'd think there'd be someone around looking after things."

We made our way upstairs to Eva and my sister's dorm room, which we already knew the location of from the student registration packet mailed to all the parents. We were stunned to find the door wide open and the room completely empty. It clearly hadn't been cleaned since the inhabitants moved out, but whether that was Whitney and Eva, we couldn't tell.

My mother and I immediately looked worried.

"Relax, we probably just have the wrong room," Oldie said to us before turning to a young male French student who happened to be walking down the hall. Oldie was clearly panicked, but he attempted a half-polite smile and steady tone. "Excuse me, do you know anything about the two American girls who were staying in this dorm room?"

Luckily, the student spoke a little English. He smiled as he said, "Oh... oui, monsieur—uh, yes, two *American* girls, non? Very wild and 'crazy' girls? Yes, I helped move their things, I remember them very well. Oooo— soo much luggage! *Loius Vuitton,* non? After a week or so, they say they don't like it here so much, in Nice—they tell me they think it is a very loud, unattractive city, and that the school is 'trés *boring.*'"

"Sounds like them alright. So where are they <u>now</u>?" Oldie demanded.

"Two weeks ago I help them carry their luggage out to an auto—a rouge Renault convertible, non? I ask them, 'What are you doing?' And they tell me they are 'going to Monte Carlo to stay at 'Hotel Paariss!'" The French student had attempted to do a Texan accent at the end of his story for effect, but Oldie wasn't amused.

Classic Whitney—she'd never stay anywhere she didn't want to be. It was just like when we were little at sleep away camp one hot, sticky summer. I was having a good time, enjoying the lake and making new friends, but after daily phone calls from a whiny, whimpering Whitney who demanded to be picked up, Oldie eventually gave in and came to drive us both home. I didn't speak to Whitney for a whole month after that.

Oldie paced the hall and started cussing profusely at no one in particular, stunned to hear of their departure. Monte Carlo was not a far distance and The Hotel de Paris was only about a half-hour drive from Nice, depending on traffic, but even I knew it was worlds away from this dumpy university.

It was obvious what had happened... Whitney had taken one look around the cramped, drab university dorm rooms and decided that she and Eva simply couldn't stay there. And rather than hop the first flight home, they probably figured they'd come all this way, so why not have a little fun first? The glamorous hotels, high-end shops, and famous clubs probably beckoned her from the lower Cornice, the winding yellow-brick-road that led pleasure-seekers to what the locals called "The Emerald City." How they were funding such a trip wasn't entirely clear, but I imagined it had something to do with Whitney draining her savings account—or perhaps even dipping into her recently opened trust fund she received on her twenty-first birthday last month before she left. And rather than call to ask permission and risk getting a "Hell NO!" from Oldie, as usual, Whitney knew it would be much easier to just ask for his forgiveness later on.

"I was sad to see them go, they are very funny girls. They are in non trouble, I hope?" the young Frenchmen said, with concern.

"Oh, they're in trouble alright," said Oldie. "Thanks Pierre. Let's go, girls."

"My name is Philippe, monsieur—but you are very welcome," he said, puzzled by my father's pushy, rude tone.

I turned and shrugged to Philippe apologetically. We'd probably just reinforced every stereotype he already had in his mind about Americans, but sadly, this wasn't the first time, and with Oldie, I knew it wouldn't be the last.

We all squeezed back into the ridiculous orange sports car and went after the girls in hot pursuit. Deep down I tingled with excitement—I'd never been to Monte Carlo and already I was succumbing to the same irresistible urges my sister most likely had about this mythical, world-class playground just a few miles away. Suddenly, chasing Whitney all over the French Riviera seemed like a great idea.

Nestled in a cove of rocky and steep coastline between the French Alps and the Mediterranean sits Monte Carlo; a tiny principality in the city-state of Monaco. It's just two miles across and half the size of Central Park, but it's also the most densely populated independent country in the world. Its luxurious casinos and world class hotels have earned Monte Carlo the coveted reputation as the world's most prestigious and elegant place to recreate.

Despite their reputation for having nearly perfect weather year-round, this day was unusually hot at ninety-five degrees, and with no waterside breeze the air in the toy car was stagnant. Oldie, refusing to admit he'd made a poor rental choice, was determined to get the air-conditioning working and kept turning the dials—also refusing to roll down any windows.

"Damn this thing," he sputtered. "It's probably stuck..."

To make matters worse, Oldie was a nervous, agitated driver. Growing up he'd always been driven around by his family's chauffeur, and he now had our own family driver, Ron, to take him everywhere, so Oldie never fully mastered road skills. Just navigating the streets of Houston was hard enough when he was left on his own, so an incredible wave of midsummer traffic on the French Riviera was nothing short of a nightmare for him, and us.

"*HONNNK!*" Aggressive, restless French drivers sounded off loudly as Oldie timidly weaved through tight lanes and vague, blinking stoplights bottlenecked with congestion. Bumper-to-bumper the entire way, the three of us were crammed into the bright orange Citroen like hot, salty sardines.

As our car crept toward Monte Carlo and my mother and I fanned the heat, Oldie waxed nostalgic. It was the first time he'd been back to the South of France since he'd been stationed here during the war, and the sight of the ocean was bringing back memories. During his fourteen months of service as the skipper of a Landing Craft Tank, or LCT—an assault ship that carried tanks and supplies from the merchant vessels to the beaches—he'd seen three invasions. Oldie explained how he had arrived at Anzio in the second group, about two weeks after the initial assault.

"The guys there really caught it from February to April," he said. "The Germans were in the mountains with long-range artillery... they blew the allied forces all the way down the Anzio plain. Day and night they were under fire—three, four air raids a day for months. It was *hell...*"

He told us of his narrow escape when the Nazis landed a 280-millimeter shell in the water only four feet from his small LCT. "Water covered our ship, shrapnel was everywhere. It was a damn miracle we survived, I tell you!"

It was strange to think of Oldie as a young man fighting a war on the beaches of France. I usually thought of him more as a jolly, benign tyrant, but underneath that he was a true man of honor. It was hard for Mom or I to relate though; Oldie had seen a war and the closest we'd each ever been to any real "fighting action" was witnessing a bar fight once at our country club—which my mother quickly took Whitney and me far away from. But out of a deep respect for having seen things we would most likely never see, as well as all the other enduring, honorable things he probably did that we'd never even know about, we both tried to show Oldie that respect by letting him rattle on about War World II all the way to the edge of Monte Carlo. I was proud of him; he'd shown up and did his part—and it felt memorializing.

Just as Oldie had finished his reminiscing, the traffic opened up and we began speeding down the highway to make up for lost time. Oldie was now clearly reminded of his new mission for being here—his delinquent, missing daughter and our quest to find her (and of course to read her the riot act). My mother and I held onto our door handles tightly.

According to the brochure, The Hotel de Paris has hosted some of the most rich, famous, and sophisticated guests including American Presidents old and new, English Prime ministers such as Winston Churchill, elegant actresses like Grace Kelly, and in particular European royalty like Princess Caroline, Princess Stephanie, and Prince Albert. The very first of the Old World hotels, the palace was built in 1864 and to this day it exudes a by-gone era, sitting elegantly in the heart of Monte Carlo and situated in the golden square of the Place du Casino. Of the one-hundred-and-eighty-four suites, most overlook the Mediterranean with sublime views of the water, where sparkling white yachts topped with heliports dot the harbor. One could spend an entire day sipping champagne, the quintessential national beverage, and eating spoonfuls of caviar off of one of those balconies, simply taking in the view.

We arrived at The Hotel de Paris with a screech and a crash—Oldie ran up over the curb and onto the sidewalk as he pulled up to the imposing front entrance. The valet attendant, dressed in a fine, Karl Lagerfeld-designed uniform, shook his head in disapproval as he approached us and opened Oldie's car door with his white-gloved hand.

"Bienvenue," he said, without really seeming to *mean* the welcome.

Oldie climbed out and dashed off into the lobby, not even waiting for me or my mother to extract ourselves from the Citroen. The valet, Mom, and I all watched as he nearly ran straight into the prominent, ten-foot-tall, solid bronze statue of Louis XIV jutting out of the center of the grand foyer.

Oldie ran up to the empty front desk and angrily rang the little bell sitting on the counter. Without even waiting for a response, he yelled, "SERVICE! Excuse-me-ma—someone *HELP* around <u>HERE</u>!"

The concierge appeared from behind a wall and approached my father as if he were some kind of deranged, recently-escaped zoo animal. He didn't even bother with French as he said, "Welcome to ze Hotel de Par—"

"I'm looking for two guests by the name of Whitney St. John and Eva Mueller—I'm *Ms.* St. John's father—they're NOT hard to miss," Oldie said in a rush.

"Of course, monsieur," sniffed the concierge, clearly miffed at the interruption. He searched through his records in a large, leather-bound guest book with raised eyebrows as if to confirm his suspicions, and then nodded primly. "Sir, Miss Mueller and Miss St. John have been staying in the presidential suite for approximately two and a half weeks… and they've reserved this suite for the rest of ze summer."

There was a visible twitch in Oldie's jaw. He shook his head as if he hadn't heard him right. *"Pardon?"*

My mother and I now approached and stood beside Oldie, listening in attentively.

"Indeed, sir," the concierge continued. "Miss Mueller and Miss St. John have been very 'special' guests of ze hotel in a *seasonal* rental for several weeks now, and—"

"Merci—thanks," Oldie said, waving him off and heading straight for the hotel's bar as my mom and I tried to keep up.

He ordered a scotch and soda and silently swallowed it down as if it were a long, cool drink of water. My mother and I knew not to either disturb him or even say a word until he was completely finished. Once he was and his nerves were now 'settled,' we all returned to the front desk.

"Now you're tellin' me," Oldie said to the same concierge in a Texas drawl that only surfaced when he was *truly* angry, "that an American teenage girl has been staying at *this* hotel unsupervised, in some 'penthouse party suite' for two goddamn WEEKS and *NOBODY* called to alert *me?* Just whose goddamn credit card is paying for such a thing?!"

"Monsieur, Miss St. John gave us a credit card and passport and we gave her ze room. A person has to be twenty-one-years old to book a room here, and she showed us proof that she was. She *is* an adult, *non?*" The concierge turned the guest book towards Oldie to confirm his records with him. The pages clearly had Whitney's correct American passport information on them showing her age was indeed twenty-one—which my mom and I both already knew, but apparently Oldie was somehow in denial about.

"It doesn't matter! She's too young to be gallivanting around Monaco spending this kind of money! And just how much does this 'presidential suite' cost per night?" Oldie asked through clenched teeth.

The concierge grimaced as he pulled out a calculator and began punching numbers. "About one thousand and nine hundred per night in American dollars, sir."

Oldie's face began to flush pink.

"Ze girls, they tell me they come to France to learn to speak French and didn't like ze, uh... how do you *say?*—'summer school?' No good. So viola! Here they come, begging for a room in ze hotel. I informed them we are unfortunately at capacity, we only have ze presidential suite available and it needed to be booked for the season only."

"Uh huh, I *bet* you did," said a clenched-jawed Oldie. The concierge pretended not to notice.

"The dark-haired girl—ze one who speaks French *very* well—she tell me the blond girl likes only ze 'very best'—so yes, a suite would be 'magnifique'!" he continued to explain.

Oldie's pinched face was losing patience. It wouldn't be long now.

"Consider your surroundings, monsieur..." the concierge continued calmly. "If you take a moment to enjoy it I think you'll find they made a very *wise* decision, *non?*" He winked at Oldie. "The girls are very sweet and very popular at ze hotel, especially with ze boys!" He grinned and winked again. "I do not believe the girls are in their room at ze moment, but would you like me to leave them a message, sir?"

My dad was about to lose it big-time, and after hearing all that war talk on the ride over, the thought crossed my mind that he just might jump over the reception desk and strangle this tiny man right in front of us. So before he totally lost control I quickly leaned in and whispered, "Dad... don't forget she's spending *her* money—not yours. You just gave her access to her trust fund on her birthday last month, remember? This is the first chance she's had to spend any of it."

Oldie paused and looked at me, somewhat confused, so I continued. "She's going a little overboard I know, but really, she's only hurting herself."

Oldie took a large, powerful breath and sighed. "You're right, Melanie, you're absolutely right."

I, too, sighed in relief—crisis averted, at least for now. He tussled my hair and said, "Thanks, Lil' Bit." Oldie turned his attention back to the concierge. "So, what time did my daughter leave the hotel today?"

"I believe I saw ze girls leave just a few hours past. I would be happy to leave Miss St. John a message."

"No—no, don't do that. We'll wait for her at the bar, and don't say anything when you see her, please." Oldie slipped a crisp, one hundred dollar bill into the concierge's hand. "I want you to come find *me* when she gets here, do you understand? Can I count on you to do that?"

"Certainly, monsieur," the concierge said with real conviction now. "You will be notified as soon as she arrives at valet. Will you require any additional…?"

He continued, but his voice trailed off as Oldie stormed away, not listening. My mother and I tagged along behind him.

We went back into the bar for some more, much-needed cocktails and Oldie sat stewing as he drank his second scotch and soda. My mother and I sipped our cool drinks as we watched uniformed dignitaries and tanned, beautiful women sparkling with diamonds enter and exit the lobby in droves. After listening to Oldie rant and rave the last two hours, it was nice that he finally had nothing more to say.

Four hours passed. We each had had three cocktails each; I was of legal drinking age in Monte Carlo and Oldie didn't pay any mind when I switched from ordering ice tea to champagne because he was so furious with Whitney. I still didn't like to drink, but with the stress of the waiting, I felt it was needed to help take the edge off of the whole situation. But by now, Oldie had finally calmed down. And now it was all about delivering a 'different' sort of surprise to Whitney, not quite the celebration he'd originally had in mind, but an ambush nonetheless. I partially wondered if Oldie had already expected to sneak up on Whitney doing something completely out-of-line before we even got to Nice.

Finally, the concierge came to our table. "Excusez-moi, monsieur St. John?" he said. "Mademoiselle St. John and her friend have now arrived. The valets are attending to her car."

We darted into the lobby just in time to see my sister bouncing through the entrance of the hotel holding-hands with a man who looked well over twice her age. My mother gasped. Whitney was nearly unrecognizable—her long, natural, honey-blond hair had been cut short and dyed platinum blond, which, combined with what looked to be some new, European-styled, sophisticated designer fashions, made her look at least ten years older.

Whitney and the older man giggled and kissed each other as they passed by us unknowingly. They were very tipsy and each carried a crystal flute half-full of rose champagne. It was clear they were still planning to keep the party going…

Oldie marched up to them. As his recognizable shape lumbered nearer and nearer to my sister, her eyes were slowly pulled toward his direction as if by instinct. Then we saw the recognition suddenly register as he reached them directly in front of the hotel elevators. Whitney's tanned face faded to a pale shade of ash, and then flushed into a bright bloom.

"Oh my God…" she said, stopping dead in her tracks.

"Whitney… Michelle… St. John! You have NO idea what *deep* trouble you are in!" Oldie said, fingering the loose change in the pocket of his tacky-tourist cargo pants. I could tell he was going to enjoy this.

"Oldie!" Whitney shrieked. "What are you doing here?" She stood in disbelief, staring at Oldie as if he was a deer and she was about to run him over. Busted.

"What am *I* doing here?" Oldie bellowed. "What in God's name are you doing *here?* Why aren't you in school in Nice?"

"Dad—"

"Don't 'Dad' me! We flew in to take you on a cruise—a surprise trip to congratulate you on a job well done this semester, no less because we were so 'proud' of you! Not to mention I paid a goddamn fortune for that school! But here you are, playing hooky in an entirely different country, spending money like its coming from an endless well… And just who in the world is this man you're with? He's older than I am for Christ sake!"

The old man extended his hand. "Hello Mr. St. John, I'm Dr. Jeremiah Fane, pleased to meet you." Oldie glanced at Dr. Fane's extended hand, but made no move to shake it. "I'm a heart surgeon from New York—friends call me Dr. No Pain Fane… but you'll have to ask my patients about *that* one." He grinned.

When he realized his attempts at levity were failing to amuse our father, the 'doctor' retracted his hand. The telltale, fake-sounding, New York accent gave him away instantly… it appeared my sister was really being escorted around town by an old—and obvious—male gigolo. I could only imagine what kind of equally crazy story Whitney had told Dr. Pain—and everyone else in Monte Carlo—about where she was from and actually did for a 'living.'

Disdainfully, Oldie turned back to Whitney, waiting…

"Oh yes, *that,*" Whitney responded casually. "We went to Nice first Dad, I swear, and we *wanted* to like it… but when we got there it was nothing like the brochures, not at all! It turned out the university was in the *bad* part of town, Daddy. And the dorm rooms were so tiny there wasn't even enough room for our *luggage!*"

Oldie rolled his eyes. "We went there first Whitney, we saw those rooms. They seemed perfectly decent to me."

"But that's not all! There was this kleptomaniac on our floor, Jeddah—people kept getting their *things* stolen. We had to keep our door locked at all times—in fact, we barely felt safe to leave our room at all because who knows how much stuff would have been stolen when we returned, and after awhile we just couldn't take it anymore... The whole experience was just *dreadful*. I mean, I know I didn't finish the program, but it wasn't for school credit anyway, right? So no big *deal?*"

"Whitney, this whole situation is ludicrous. You need to go find Eva, go upstairs to your hotel room—or 'suite,' or whatever it is you're paying a Goddamn fortune for—and pack your bags. We're leaving. This party's *over* and I mean 'over' with a *biggg* FAT O!"

"Uh... darling, I'm going to go for a massage," Dr. Fane said to Whitney, totally unphased by Oldie's tirade as he kissed her on the cheek. "I'll ring you later, ma chérie." He squeezed her buttocks as he left. Oldie looked disgusted.

"So glad you've been keeping such good company while on the lam in Monte Carlo, Whit," Oldie said sarcastically. "Your new companion looks like he could have been alive when Napoleon was on the prowl."

"Dad, I don't care how old Dr. Fane is—he knows everybody in Monte Carlo, and Eva and I have been having the time of our lives with him. Plus, I'm twenty-one now... I'm an *adult*. I can date whoever I want," she said confidently.

Whitney had transformed from a young, bright-eyed, UT co-ed into a sophisticated, worldly socialite seemingly overnight, and there was no budging her now. In fact, I could tell Whitney was highly irritated that we were there at all. We had interfered with her day, interrupted her good time, and she knew we'd probably insist on ruining the rest of her summer now as well.

"Daddy, do you have any idea who I've met? I've been hanging out with super-duper billionaires, heirs to fortune five hundred companies, and kings of countries I can't even pronounce! I'm not going anywhere Dad, except maybe to a party later tonight, and you're just going to have to get over it."

Oldie closed his eyes and put his head down. I don't think I'd ever seen him so speechless. Without a word he walked away towards the hotel bar and, as usual, our mother followed behind him but said nothing. She hated confrontation.

"Nice, Whitney," I whispered through clenched teeth. "Way to ruin everything. Did you for even a millisecond think of anyone but yourself?"

"Can-it, Squirt. You guys are the ones who've screwed-up everything! Why did you even come here? To ambush me?"

"It was supposed to be a 'nice' thing for you! A family vacation!"

"Yeah right, whatever... I don't care what Oldie says. It's *my* money that's paying for this and I'm *not* leaving."

Whitney was being bold, but one look at our father's stern face across the room looking back at us told her she knew she'd have to come up with something far better. I'd seen her Daddy's-little-girl routine played out a million times and was pretty confident I knew what was coming next. She inched her way towards the hotel lobby bar, mentally preparing a plan to placate him.

Inside the bar, Oldie nursed a scotch and soda as our mother tried to soothe him. Whitney approached him from behind and launched herself onto his back as she wrapped her arms around him, giving him a giant, bear-sized squeeze. "Daddy, I know you guys came all the way out here just to make me happy, and I'm *really* sorry I've disappointed you... I know you wanted me to attend that language school this summer, but I'm really doing well here in Monte Carlo, I wish you could see me! You'd be so proud of how I've been representing our family... and I've already learned so much about many different cultures and met many interesting, fascinating people..."

Oldie just sat and sighed hopelessly into his scotch. But Whitney had one more trick up her sleeve.

"Listen Dad, why don't you all go up to my suite and relax for a bit. Tonight we'll go to dinner at the famous Louis the Fifteenth. The food is simply amazing, you won't be sorry. After all, we're in Monte Carlo—let's at least have *some* fun!"

Whitney's silver tongue did its work. My sister, bless her, knew what a little world-class food and wine could do to our father's mood, and so there was nothing left to do but go up to her suite—which was a lavish palace practically—where we napped, showered, and dressed for dinner. Already we all felt a little better about being unexpectedly transported to Monte Carlo.

The opulent Louis XV experience worked wonders on a distraught Oldie. Great food and fine wine always had a calming effect on him, and he was visibly relaxing more and more as the evening progressed. In fact, Oldie seemed to be enjoying the fact that, at least temporarily, our 'happy little family' was back together again. Whitney however, only continued to use his new calm demeanor to her advantage as she still defended her position about staying put.

"...and you *know* how I've *always* been a big reader, Dad? How in school I always read all those things about Monte Carlo and its famous Hotel de Paris? And of course we've *all* seen it showcased in so many films—how could Eva and I be *so* close to it and not check it out? It's just down the road! So, we got in the car—Eva drove—and you know how she already speaks fluent French so we found it right away. It just felt right to stay!"

"First of all, making a move like this without at least telling anyone..." Oldie started. "What were you thinking? What if something happened to you here? Second of all, Eva's parents will need to be told too of course, and then you two 'birdbrains' will have to suffer the consequences of your actions with Helmut *too.*"

For the first time all night Whitney looked irritated and noticeably nervous. "But...but Daddy, please... let's not go there. Eva's off having fun for the first time since that whole Greek Cross incident... let's not bother her with all this quite yet. Let's decide what *we're* going to do first, then get Eva involved, okay? Please don't tell her father anything."

"Fine, cause that's easy. *You're* coming home with US!" he ordered.

"But *Daddy!*" she exaggerated the title like a whiny little child half-jokingly, but still played up her classic stubborn streak. I couldn't believe what I was hearing, yet I knew somehow it would work.

When Oldie realized his orders were going to be pointless, he changed his approach. With a calm and rational tone he said, "Whitney, we flew all the way to France to take you on a surprise cruise through the Greek Isles and damned if you're not going with us. You don't have to go back to Texas right now... but you *do* have to join us on this trip."

Oldie was thinking that once he got Whitney out of Monte Carlo and away from the black-tie parties and presidential room service—and the sleazy Dr. Fane—he could finally talk some sense into her. But I knew it was already too late. She was too caught up in a fairy tale world of hobnobbing with the rich and famous. If schmoozing were a drug, the girl was definitely hooked on it.

"I appreciate the gesture Dad, really I do. But I wish you would've asked me first! I'm having too much fun here to leave. Why don't you and Mother go on the cruise by yourselves? It would do you guys some good to spend some much-needed time alone... You can leave Melanie here in Monte Carlo with me—she'll have a blast! It'll be great for her to experience the city with an insider like me. Dr. Fane and I can chaperone and introduce her to the world of billionaires and princes." She glanced at me and winked. "Maybe I can even introduce her to some of the men I've met here! There are *lots* of eligible bachelors..."

I looked at Whitney as if she'd momentarily lost the use of all her faculties. The last thing in the world I wanted was to be left alone in Monte

Carlo with my party-crazy, relationship-obsessed older sister and her geriatric escort. Especially after my last blind date disaster in Newport! I wanted to scream, "No more fix-ups!" but before I could Oldie spoke again.

"Hmmm," he began, mulling it over. "You know what Whitney? By golly, you might just be right… Melanie really does need a break… she's been far too serious in college. Now don't get me wrong, Lil' Bit, we're *very* proud of you, but all work and no play makes Mel a dull gal on campus, right Whit?"

Whitney agreed as Oldie reached over and ruffled my hair. I couldn't believe it—Oldie was actually falling for this nonsense!

"She could really use some new experiences, Dad, with a much more sophisticated crowd than those beer-guzzling, low-life, frat rats at UT—believe me, I *know*," Whitney chimed. "And I'll make sure she gets the royal treatment she deserves and only meets the very best, most *suitable* contenders."

Oldie, my sister, and my mother then continued to discuss how I needed to 'branch out' and experience 'new things' and learn about the 'different kinds' of men in the world. It was like I didn't even exist in the conversation anymore.

"Um, *hello?!*" I finally interrupted. "I'm sitting right here, people!"

Whitney went in for the kill. "Well, Mom? What do *you* think?"

Our mother looked at me earnestly. "I have always thought you needed to be with someone older and more sophisticated than a boy your own age, Mel…" Then she glanced at Oldie lovingly. "Besides, it would be nice to spend some time alone… just the two of us. Our last vacation together was nearly ten years ago."

"That *long?*" Oldie said, completely unaware of the time passing… but it was indicated clearly by his adoring eyes as he looked back at her that this was not done intentionally. Both Whitney and I knew our parents were still truly in love, and they deserved this much-needed time alone to celebrate that.

"And it's not like Eva and I haven't already been on our own for *weeks* now…" Whitney continued when she really didn't have to, ruining the moment, but also putting the attention now back on her—which was most likely her main objective anyway. "Plus, I *promise* to come home with you guys when your cruise is over, okay? So how about it?"

Oldie slammed his fist onto the table, causing several startled restaurant patrons around us to listen in too. "I'll be damned if I'm going to let my spoiled-rotten daughter ruin my beloved wife's and *my* good time! Whitney, if you *insist* on staying put with your senior citizen boyfriend, then so be it—I've already paid for the Goddamn boat, so your mom and I are going on the cruise alone!" He looked pointedly at me, softening his voice. "Mel, it's only for a week—I'm sure you girls will be fine. Have some fun, for Pete's sake! I know that wasn't the best time you just had in Newport, but put it behind you now. Like I always say, when life happens, you happen *back*."

I looked at Oldie as if he'd lost his mind. He'd been played. And as usual, Whitney had gotten our father to think it was all now somehow *his* idea for me to stay in Monte Carlo and try and find a 'suitable relationship partner' here. I knew firsthand how wild my sister could be from college and I wasn't sure I wanted to see how wild she could be here—especially in a foreign country that was known for being crazy and over-the-top at times. I felt I would be better off being chaperoned by Alice Copper.

"Well—" I started, but Oldie instantly cut me off.

"Great! Then it's all decided then," he said triumphantly.

"Oh, but do be careful, girls," Mom said. "I hate the thought of you alone over here with us so far away out on the open water."

"Don't worry," Whitney assured her. "We'll be fine."

"Of course they will," Oldie agreed as he signed the dinner check. "Say, why don't we all go across the street to the Place du Casino? We can play a little high stakes blackjack, my treat. Mel, I'll even stake you at baccarat— we'll charge everything to my account. Come on girls, it's our last night in town! Let's go have some fun!"

He really was in rare form tonight.

Chapter 5

※

*D*r. 'No Pain Fane' was thrilled to learn that my sister and I were staying at the hotel alone while our parents sailed off to Greece. He became our official chaperone and took us on an endless frenzy of parties, charity balls, art openings, and jewelry exhibitions—two or three events a night the first three days alone.

Monte Carlo was called "a sunny place for shady people" by the writer W. Somerset Maugham, and he was right, for during the high season the city plays host to a hotbed of criminals, con-artists, hangers-on, and opportunists like Dr. Fane who descend upon the city to take advantage of the bejeweled and gowned women coming in for the summer season— particularly the lonely widows, rich divorcees, and now apparently recipients of their recent trust funds.

"What more could a guy ask for?" Dr. Fane would say as he put his two blond bombshells (as he'd always refer to us) under each arm, and then introduce us as 'The Texans' to all the Monte Carlo socialites who would come to his coveted table at 'the bar' each night to either see him or be seen by him.

The table was considered coveted because it was impossible to get a table at The Hotel de Paris' bar during the busy summer months because every one of them was reserved for the entire season quarterly—just like Whitney's upscale hotel suite had to be. Luckily Dr. Fane had been there for the summer many times before (of course), and was now one of the legendary 'regulars' who had a table waiting each night. And at it each bottle of wine or champagne had its own nametag placed around its neck to ensure that there was no mix-up between someone's Chateau Lafitte and someone else's Chateau Margaux.

I soon found out Dr. Fane's real age was close to sixty, but Whitney clearly didn't care, for age had nothing to do with their little 'arrangement.' Upon her arrival in Monte Carlo, Dr. 'No Pain Fane' had immediately picked out my sister as a wealthy Texan heiress looking for a good time while she and Eva were in town. In exchange for entrance into his clique—an exclusive group of socialites and prominent dignitaries—Whitney paid his way as they hopped from exclusive social engagement to even more exclusive social engagement. As long as she kept her credit card handy, Dr. Fane made sure my sister kept good company and had plenty of parties, alcohol, and party-people to play with.

Thus, each evening the three of us would meet at Dr. Fane's always "exclusively reserved table" where Whitney always seemed to be having the time of her life. I was having an okay time—until I found out he'd been telling everyone about Whitney's recent, large inheritance. Once I learned that and realized that was the *real* reason everyone wanted to flock around Whitney and Dr. Fane, I didn't want to be there or go out anymore. But Eva was still off having her own 'good time' Whitney assured me, so the only other option I had was sitting alone in our hotel suite the rest of the week. So, like a piece of driftwood, I let myself be swept up into the current of my sister's 'Monte Carlo summer' and tried to enjoy myself like she was obviously doing.

"Try on this," Whitney barked as she handed me a sapphire blue, rhine-stone-encrusted, sexy cocktail dress at a fabulous designer boutique where they served complimentary rose champagne in the hopes that if you drank enough you'd buy more without paying attention to the outrageous price tags.

"What's wrong with my own dress?" I asked, referring to the simple sundress I already had on. It was similar to all the other ones I had packed and had been wearing the whole time.

"It's the reason no one is paying as much attention to you like they are *me*," Whitney bragged as she pushed me into the dressing room and closed the door. "God, don't you even care about fashion like 'normal' women?"

Apparently not, for all the women we saw in Monte Carlo seemed to wear designer evening gowns and expensive jewelry every night like they were plumed-up peacocks in costumes on display. And besides my lack of European fashion sense, the other main difference between all of them and Whitney and me was that they were all over fifty—at least—and many looked like they had had so much plastic surgery their faces were stretched and stiff to the point of barely being able to smile. I'd never seen anything like it, except for maybe on television occasionally.

I was also discovering, as I 'expanded my world,' that the city was over-run by aristocrats in their fifties, sixties, and seventies—I couldn't find any-one even under forty to talk to—and Whitney didn't seem to be bothered by this in the least. But I was as I zipped up the unforgiving evening wear and tried to make sense of how the various crisscrossed straps should look. I really needed a guide...

"Whitney, it goes without saying that you've totally lost it," I said, "by ditching school, acting crazy, going out with the totally gross 'Dr.' Fane... but actually wanting to hang around with all these old geezers *every* night? I don't get it. You used to be so much more fun!" I finally gave up on the straps and started to wiggle out of the dress completely.

"Mel, you're far too young to appreciate any of this," she fired back, irritated. "Trust me; you'll understand when you get older."

"You're only a couple of years older than I am! 'When I get older...' give me a break!" I declared as I opened the dressing room door and jabbed her in the side with the dress. "Don't you get sick of talking about the same things over and over and going to the same, tired old parties 'hobnobbing' with the same people practically—people all at least twice our age? I've only been doing it for three nights and I'm already sick of it! Where the hell is Eva, anyway? I haven't seen her once since we got here."

Whitney stiffened and swallowed a big gulp of her champagne as we approached the petite clerk to pay for the dress.

"Let's talk about it later," she said dismissively.

"What do you mean, let's 'talk about it later'? Where is she? I'm bored out of my mind! This whole scene depresses me—it's all hangers-on and *non*-count counts all wearing ascots!"

"Shut up!" Whitney said sternly as she signed the credit card receipt and left the shop upset.

I followed her, still on my free champagne-induced rampage, as we briskly walked down the crowded street. "If I meet one more faker from 'Podunk middle America' with a phony British accent I'll scream! Ugh—I can't stand it anymore! Eva is annoying—but I'd hang out with her any day over *these* people," I said. I couldn't understand why Whitney couldn't see things my way. What was wrong with her?

Whitney quickened her pace even more as I tried to keep up. "Well..." she finally admitted, "I guess you could say that I'm not exactly sure *where* Eva is..."

"What do you mean you're not sure where she is?"

My sister's eyes started to look a little glassy. "Okay—she's missing, all right? Last weekend she hit it off with some rich Arab guy—there was some big party on his yacht we both went to—and she decided to stay there with him instead of going home with me that night. I haven't seen her since, and she hasn't called the hotel or anything." She took a deep breath in like it was a relief to finally have said it all out loud.

"Oh my God Whitney!" I freaked out, stopping her. "That was like four or five *days* ago! We have to DO something! We have to tell Oldie... or call the police!"

"Mel..." Whitney whimpered, putting her hand on my shoulder to keep me calm, but I could tell she was choking back tears. "She could just be off partying or something, you know, shacking up with that new guy for awhile like she's done before with other men.... she still might be okay and it's all no big deal."

"Then why'd you wait so long to tell me? Was she gone when Oldie and Mom were here too?"

Whitney exhaled. "She'd only been gone about a day or so at that point, so I really wasn't worried about it. And after that I kept thinking she'd just show up like she always does. I'm sorry I didn't tell you earlier, but Eva and I are adults now... we don't have to get permission or tell people where we are if we don't want to."

I couldn't believe what I was hearing. "Well, does she do this a lot? Just disappear like this?"

"Well, sure... I mean, for a night or two—we usually just do our own thing and have since our freshmen year in college. I trust that Eva knows what she's doing—I mean; she's a grown woman, right? But this is partly why I persuaded Oldie to leave you here with me; I really didn't want to be here alone anymore because for the first time I'm now starting to get a little worried about her... I'm sorry I didn't have the heart to tell you all this before."

"We have to tell Oldie!" I insisted.

"NO! Melanie, please—I don't want to tell Oldie right now because I don't want him to think that this is the sort of thing that could happen to us while we're here—especially when it all could be nothing—and Eva would never forgive me for embarrassing her like that if it is—especially now she's finally forgetting about her last few miserable days at school... and besides, Mom and Dad are far away right now having a good time on the cruise. Let's not ruin that for them, *please?* I'll tell him as soon as they get back *if* she doesn't show up before that—which I'm sure she probably will—okay? I promise."

I reluctantly gave in, "Fine." But how could I not? Everything she said made sense, and I'd known Emily to do the same thing throughout our whole freshmen year, and she always came back okay. It was just usually the very next day or two, tops. "But what about Dr. Fane, can he help? You said he knows 'everybody.' And we should tell the hotel concierge too so he can keep a lookout for her."

Whitney sighed and gave me an unexpected hug. She even kissed me on top of my forehead. "Thank you, Mel. I'm so glad you're here... seriously. I knew you'd help me figure this out! As soon as we get back we'll talk to the concierge about it—and I'll talk to Dr. Fane, too."

"Is there anything else I can do to help make it easier for you? You know, while we look for Eva and stuff?"

Whitney suddenly changed the subject. "You know, I'm going to ask Dr. Fane if there's anyone in this town under fifty he knows that *you* can have a conversation with tonight… someone who doesn't have a walker or a cane." She laughed as she glanced around; hoping no one passing by heard her.

"We're still going out?" I said, astonished.

She laughed even harder now. "Oh Squirt, you're making me feel better already! Don't worry so much, we'll figure all this out, *okay?*"

Whitney did speak to Dr. Fane, and though he didn't know anything about the Arab, that night he did produce a funny and unusual guy from Nepal named Subir who we all met for drinks at Dr. Fane's coveted table. At first the mention of his foreign-sounding name made me pause, for after the upsetting news about Eva I didn't want to take any chances with meeting a foreign stranger, but Dr. Fane pointed out that Nepalese-Indian and Arabian were far from the same thing, and besides that, Subir had been a trusted friend of his for years. Still, there was no way I was going anywhere with anybody alone if I didn't want to—and I was glad Whitney and Dr. Fane were going to be close by the whole time.

Subir was tall and thin with dark skin that contrasted nicely with his solid white Nehru jacket and baggy cotton pants. He was probably in his late thirties, but he still looked great for his age and was clean-cut, pressed, and extraordinarily polite.

"Hello miss, I'm Subir," he said. "You must be the 'bored' Melanie from Texas."

"Guilty as charged," I said, laughing. "I'm probably the only person who comes to Monte Carlo and can't find a thing to do."

"Well, that's going to change starting right now," he said intriguingly. "I've been coming here since I was a child and know every place in town. I don't take any of these silly people too seriously, and I hope you don't either."

I must have glanced unknowingly at Dr. Fane, because he immediately added, "Don't worry… I've known Dr. Fane for over twenty years." He leaned in and whispered, "It's true—he's a gigolo—but a very nice one and he'll take good care of your sister. Also, I can guarantee you won't be bored any longer by only *his* company."

I looked at this gentle, kind, attractive man and wondered how much fun we could really have in this town full of senior citizens, but at the moment I had a more pressing concern. "Subir… did Whitney or Dr. Fane mention that we have a friend who is missing?" I asked him. "She hasn't come back to our hotel in nearly a week."

The last part caught Whitney's attention and she shot me a look that immediately told me to 'shut up,' but then decided it was really too late. "Yes," Whitney took over calmly. "Her name is Eva—she's American and half-Argentinean."

"She's *not* hard to miss," Dr. Fane added with a wink. "She was last seen hanging out with some Arab guys out on their yacht. I didn't recognize their names, but I was hoping you might."

"Oh my goodness, that's terrible," Subir said, truly concerned. "What were their names?"

"The one she was hooking up with was named 'Abdul' or something," Whitney said, trying to remember. "His yacht was parked at the port about a week ago where he hosted a party we attended. *Everyone* was there."

Subir thought this over carefully. "I do know some people who might be able to help us, they'll know more about who you're talking about. I'll go see if I can contact them now so they can at least start asking around."

"Thank you, Subir," I said, truly liking him already. "We really appreciate it."

And with that, Subir and I became friends as I went with him to the hotel lobby where he made several phone calls at the pay phone, leaving word with everyone he could think of who might know something about Eva and the Arab. Though no one had seen her, he assured me his contacts would be following up with him throughout the week. I suddenly felt safe with Subir and that everything would turn out alright now that more people knew about it, just as Whitney said it would. I was grateful for his sincere help with getting some of the locals to help us look for her too.

And even though Eva was now heavy on all our minds, Dr. Fane insisted that we all still try and have some fun that night. "After all," he pointed out, "Eva might be doing just that without worrying about any of us."

Whitney agreed.

So Subir took us to the Sporting Club Casino where we gambled for hours and started to relax. And it was true—like Dr. Fane—Subir seemed to know everyone in town... I was finally having some real fun being in The Emerald City. But it appeared to be short-lived, for suddenly Dr. Fane and Whitney announced they wanted to leave to go to yet another 'exclusive,' boring, late-night social engagement.

"It's back at the bar, so luckily with Dr. Fane we can all get in," Whitney slurred excitedly as she sipped from her already-empty cocktail glass.

"So?" I said. "You promised tonight we'd do fun things, like we're finally doing now."

"If it's alright with your sister and Dr. Fane, they could go on without us," Subir said.

"*Really?* Would you watch her awhile?" Whitney asked like he was a potential babysitter, not a fix-up. I was mortified.

Subir didn't know how to answer the strange request. I was hoping it was 'lost in translation.'

"That's a wonderful idea," Dr. Fane said, turning to me. "Melanie, I assure you, you will be in good hands with Subir. Has he not already shown what a perfect gentleman he is?"

I had to admit, he was treating me like a princess, and I liked it. "Yes."

"Then if it's okay with you, Melanie St. John," Subir said earnestly, "I'd love to continue to have the pleasure of your company on our *own* for the rest of the evening."

"Okay," I said, truly feeling I'd be safe with him.

Whitney and Dr. Fane couldn't have disappeared into the crowd fast enough.

I thought we were going to stay put gambling, but Subir surprised me by offering to take me to Jimmy'z, an exclusive local nightclub where—lo and behold—every young person within a twenty-mile radius had congregated. I don't know where they had all been hiding, but here they were, dancing the night away to extremely loud music. We danced until dawn, breathless, and ended the night around six A.M. at one of Subir's favorite twenty-four-hour local hangouts, Le Tip Top, for breakfast. I was finally not only having fun—but an actual blast—and Subir continued to treat me better than anyone had for a long, long time.

It went on like that for the next two evenings too. We stayed out all night and I slept until three in the afternoon each day. The elevator man in the hotel nicknamed me the "blond night owl." I was also starting to understand my sister's draw to this incredible fantasyland, though I definitely thought Subir's version of Monte Carlo was better than hers. And I also realized I liked drinking—champagne, that is. I didn't have to get drunk off it, just have enough to feel a little tipsy and then stop. I still liked to stay in control, but it was also fun to 'cut loose' like that once in awhile. So though I had a rocky start, I managed to survive my first international vacation week without my parents just fine by the end. Texas seemed like a million miles away, and I never once thought about school. Oldie would have been proud.

"So, are you and Subir hitting it off?" Whitney asked suggestively after I finally pulled myself out of bed our final day there.

"I think so," I shrugged.

"What do you mean you 'think so'? Has he tried to kiss you or make a move by now?"

"No," I said, and then realized I was actually surprised that he never once made a pass at me at all. I was having too much fun to care really, but still, most men did try something at some point.

I knew from Dr. Fane that Subir wasn't married and I had never seen him with a woman besides me for almost three straight days now. With the way he dressed and his slick, polite demeanor, I secretly wondered if he might be gay—and if he wasn't he certainly missed a 'sure thing' considering I thought Subir was quite handsome and probably would respond if he made a move. But in Monte Carlo, distractions abound. And all I really cared about was having someone young enough to spend time with and who had enough energy to take me dancing, gambling, and sight-seeing all around town. Romance was the furthest thing from my mind and in the end we made fantastic friends.

"Did anyone at the hotel mention they saw Eva yet?" I asked Whitney, still concerned of course. Subir and I always showed her picture everywhere we went to everyone he knew, but still, no one had seen her. We both wondered why she wouldn't try to contact Whitney to let her know she was okay, but I had to trust Whitney's constant, repeated answer that it was "just how Eva was sometimes..." and I assured Subir that Whitney had known Eva long enough to really know her well—more than anyone else would, for sure.

"No," Whitney said, annoyed with me for bringing it up yet again, and also trying to hide her own growing concern as she drank her cocktail—alcohol now being her drug of choice for keeping herself in a state of seemingly constant denial mixed with optimism. "But there's always a chance she'll show up any minute now!" she added convincingly.

"I hope so," I agreed. "But if not we have to tell Mom and Oldie as soon as we see them tonight."

"Of course," she said.

Hours later my parents returned from their week-long cruise gushing about their fabulous time, and Whitney and I both filled them in about the good time we had with Subir and Dr. Fane, trying to decide how to also bring up Eva's disappearance.

"What a great idea for us to all take separate vacations," Oldie said to both of us. "But now it's back to the real world... our flight leaves tomorrow at ten, so let's go to a 'bon voyage' dinner at the Louis the Fifteenth again—you girls can even invite your two companions, and tell Eva to come along too."

Whitney shot me a look. "Uh, Eva's a little hung-over from last night, Dad," she outright lied, "so she won't be joining us."

I couldn't believe it. What was she thinking? I gave Whitney a death-glare and started to say something, but she shot me another look that told me I'd better not—or *else*. All I could think about was how much Eva had been through at the end of the school year, and how if this all really wasn't a big deal then it would only make things even worse for her and her family's already rocky relationship. It still didn't seem worth it to risk it.

"Suit herself, but she's missing out," Oldie said.

Later, as we all took our seats at our elegantly set, lavish table, all I could focus on from my seat's direction was the restaurant's immense, famous gold clock filled with heavenly angels floating all around it, practically daring me to do something about my now-growing, guilty conscience—and I finally couldn't take it. I pulled Whitney aside and asked her outright, "When are you going to tell him the *truth* about Eva?"

Whitney whispered back sternly, "I'll tell him later tonight, I promise. I'm just not ready to ruin everyone's good time yet!" But what she really meant was *hers*... she was clearly already tipsy. And apparently so was Dr. Fane as he stared at the linen napkin displayed on his plate in the form of a fan with glazed-over, confused eyes.

I just sighed and went along with it. Truth be told, I was dreading the moment Oldie found out myself. But I knew the angels were right, tonight it was finally time...

I don't know if it was because of the angels watching, the flowing champagne, or the fact that we all had had some time away from each other for awhile, but the evening was magical. Oldie, thank God, was on his best behavior; he didn't over-imbibe with his scotch, cuss, or insult anyone over the course of the entire dinner—Whitney and I were truly amazed, and Subir and Dr. Fane were actually glad they came. Oldie toasted everyone to a great time in Monte Carlo, and as soon as the bill came, he promptly stood up and said his good-nights. He and Mom were beat.

I swiftly kicked Whitney under the table, feeling the angels would understand since this was appropriate action under the circumstances.

"Ouch! Oh—g'night Dad! Thanks for dinner—and thanks for everything!" she said, and then mouthed to me that she'd tell him in the morning. Subir and Dr. Fane were both too drunk to notice what we were referring to as we then all said our good-byes as well and Whitney and I headed back up to our hotel suite.

Fuming, I resolved to bring it up myself at breakfast no matter what, whether Whitney had the guts to or not.

But the next morning I awoke to find neither Whitney nor any of her Loius Vuitton luggage present. The closet was empty and all her stuff was missing.

I immediately called my parents' room. "Oldie? Is Whitney with you?" I asked frantically.

"No," a still-sleepy Oldie answered. "Why?"

"All her stuff is gone!"

"What the—what do you mean?"

"I mean she's GONE! It looks like she snuck off in the middle of the night… all of her bags are gone too. I didn't even hear her packing!"

Oldie slammed the phone down and came over to see for himself in mere moments—he must have flown. There was a long silence as he inspected the empty room and closet, and then slowly turned over the information in his head. I knew I was going to have to tell him everything now.

"Dad… I have some other news, too. Whitney was supposed to tell you, but… but I guess you better know that—that we haven't seen Eva in over a week."

"What do you mean you haven't seen her? Melanie… what are you telling me?" Oldie's stunned voice was quiet and hoarse, as if I'd awoken him from a bad dream.

"I mean we don't know where she is," I continued. "Whitney says she's been gone since last Saturday."

"You mean she *lied* about where Eva was last night?"

"Yep. She played you… and she played *me!* She told me she was going to tell you at dinner, and then when she didn't she said she was going to tell you this morning… and now she bailed entirely!"

I went on to tell him everything I knew about Eva's disappearance.

As suspected, Oldie went ballistic. First he screamed at me for not calling him in the Greek Isles, then at my mother once she joined us for raising *two* such irresponsible children, and then he stormed down to the hotel lobby to scream at the poor hotel staff for a myriad of transgressions, starting with letting Whitney sneak out of the hotel in the middle of the night with all of her luggage.

The concierge who had first helped us locate Whitney attempted to quiet a roaring Oldie down, but there was no placating him. He pounded his fists on the counter and demanded answers.

"Just WHO was on duty last night? <u>Who</u> saw Whitney leave? Was she with that low-life Dr. Fane? WHEN was the last time you people saw *Eva?!* How was this not cause for concern?" Oldie ranted on and on, but no one knew anything.

"Je n'sais pas," they each said, throwing their hands into the air.

When the nightstaff were all finally located, they too seemed to have developed a convenient case of amnesia, which I suspected was caused by a sharp decrease of Whitney's cash reserves, for even I knew her trust fund wouldn't last in a place like this for long. Even more, everyone at the hotel had clearly had enough of us—we were loud, frightening, and causing scenes left and right. In fact, everyone we dealt with seemed secretly relieved Whitney had departed, and probably couldn't wait for her crazy, dysfunctional family members to all leave the hotel too.

The manager of the hotel was, however, very concerned about Eva's disappearance. After speaking in private with Oldie he admitted to knowing the person Eva had taken up with; he was a certain powerful Arabian Sheik named Rasmi Abdul-Malik who was an extremely wealthy oil businessman and a supposed arms dealer who had a terrible reputation for abusing women. His concern was for Eva, but it was clear he didn't want a lawsuit from her, her family, the Sheik, and especially from Oldie. He kept what information he did have close to his sleeve, and Oldie spent several minutes attempting to pump more information out of him. It was difficult to get anyone to cooperate.

Finally, Oldie sent my mom and me back to Houston via the Concorde. This time he didn't care how much it cost.

"Just get the hell out of this crazy place. We don't belong here—everyone is playing some kind of game, and I'm not playing it anymore!" he said as we left.

Oldie, however, stayed behind to try and locate the girls. Eva's family was notified and Dr. Mueller flew to Monte Carlo to help Oldie look for them. They both searched in vain for a couple of weeks. And even after Oldie was forced to return stateside for work, he offered to pay for a private investigator to try and track down the girls. Helmut was very appreciative.

I went back to the University of Texas in Austin that September stunned—and worried that I may never see my sister or Eva again. I still roomed with Emily in an apartment my father paid for, and she stood by me all throughout the crisis. She really was a great friend I now realized, and I was grateful she put aside her partying for awhile to help me cope. After I had experienced some of my own fun partying now too, I realized she wasn't completely out of line for wanting to do it so much, but we both agreed this wasn't the time for partying or dating. All I could do was study and think about Whitney and Eva both being gone, possibly forever.

One day while I was at the library I looked through an upscale travel magazine of Europe, wondering where either of them could be on any of the pages. I flipped through a section on France and stopped on a gorgeous, centerfold spread of the famed Promenade des Anglais road we traveled when heading from the airport towards Whitney's university in Nice. I teared up instantly.

Suddenly a kind, soft voice with a thick Southern accent spoke out, "That's the saddest face I've ever seen for someone looking at one of the most beautiful drives in the world."

I looked up and saw what looked to be a true Southern belle—she had bright, golden- blond hair, deep blue eyes, and was wearing a very con- servative-length pencil skirt and a completely buttoned-up top that each looked like they belonged in magazines themselves, they were so perfectly fitted, starched, and pressed. She was stunning, and not the typical blond, UT co-ed type like me.

"Oh, I didn't mean to interrupt," she apologized. "But you just looked like you could use some cheering up. And if it helps at all, I've been on that drive many times if you want to even ask me anything about it… in fact, I've been to most all of the countries in that magazine over the years. I just *love* to travel… especially internationally."

"Me too," I said, realizing we already had 'big boxes' in common.

She seemed glad about that too. "Have you been there, on the Promenade?"

"Yes, but my father isn't the best driver to have experienced it with unfortunately, so all I remember is clutching the door handle most of the way," I said, not ready to bring up my troubles with someone I just met, especially a fellow world-traveler whom I also hoped would become a friend.

"I understand *that* experience," she said wearily. "My older brother, who thinks he's Mario Andretti, is the same. Oh, land's sakes! Where are my manners?" She extended her hand and I shook it as she continued. "I'm Victoria Lane, from Tuxedo Park in Atlanta. I just transferred in this semes- ter from Georgia State."

"Melanie St. John," I said, "from Houston."

And just like that I made a new friend who was able to help make being away at school during my family crisis a bit easier to take as the days slowly crept by…

Six weeks later, the P.I. finally caught up with Whitney—she was found in Spain at the exclusive Marbella Club, casually sipping sangria by the pool. The investigator had found her by watching her credit card charges. The minute she was located, Oldie instructed American Express to suspend Whitney's card indefinitely. It turns out she had long-ditched Dr. Fane in favor of a much more attractive friend of his who was in his mid-forties, a supposed heir to a champagne company in France, though he immediately walked away when he learned that Whitney had been cut off. Without her credit card and with her trust fund now completely drained, she had no choice but to agree to return to Houston.

"Why'd you leave?" I asked her one weekend in late October when I came home from school just so I could see for myself that she really was okay.

"I wanted to try and find Eva myself," she said. "I remembered that night suddenly that the Sheik had said he would be heading to Turkey next, so I thought I'd give it a go."

Oldie and the P.I. grilled Whitney until they had the names of everyone she had ever associated with in her travels, including the names of the Arabs in Monte Carlo. Oldie and the P.I. followed up on every single one of them until they had enough information to take it up with the international crime investigators of Interpol.

Meanwhile, Whitney started hitting the country club circuit of Houston's elite, dating a string of wealthy men as if there was an endless supply. But without her trust fund 'security cushion' to fall back on ever again, she was now realizing if she didn't land a rich husband she was actually going to have to find something to do to support herself for a living, and work was never something that appealed to her. So she really was going out each night hoping to find love among the trays of fresh, raw oysters and well-aged Brie.

One weekend in mid-November, Oldie got a phone call that left him speechless. He took a fast weekend trip and was very secretive about where he was going. He returned on Monday with a very skinny, very gracious Eva in tow. She was only a shell of her former self. Both Whitney and Eva each picked up some nasty habits during their sojourn in Monte Carlo, but Eva clearly had the worst of them. She had become as thin as a rail, almost anorexic, and went into withdrawals from all the drugs she'd been supplied by the Arabs that summer. The once-bold Eva was now a scared, humbled little girl. She never once spoke about her ordeal escaping and getting home, or spoke about what she actually experienced during her whole disappearance, but I had the feeling she came a little closer to death than any of us realized.

Chapter 6

✦

*T*hat Christmas Oldie rounded up the family for a beach trip to Acapulco for some much-needed relaxation as we all left 1976 behind. Whitney was still completely unapologetic about the craziness she caused the whole family throughout the last few months since she insisted she and Eva were allowed to make "adult-sized mistakes" now that they were "actual" adults. She also continuously whined about not being able to bring anyone 'fun' along to Mexico. I couldn't believe how she was behaving. I mean, I knew she was selfish, but now it seemed she'd taken the concept to a whole new level... or maybe it was all an act to help mask the fact that she was just plain scared. Her only real 'life plan' of marrying young and into a wealthy family wasn't working out, and she didn't seem to have any intentions of coming up with a Plan B. She also dreaded spending—or what she considered wasting—most of her time in this fabulous beach resort for two whole weeks with our parents, who now kept a very watchful eye on her.

I, on the other hand, was allowed to bring two girlfriends this holiday vacation, so I invited Emily and Victoria. It was an interesting mix, for I couldn't have found two more opposite best friends on the planet if I tried. Though we all barely weighed over a hundred pounds each, nothing else about any of us was alike—especially between them.

Emily's mother, an attractive, petite brunette like Emily, did her best to support them with her fluctuating waitressing tips the whole time Emily was growing up, but since she worked most days and nights, Emily became quite used to being on her own most of the time, and therefore she was completely uninhabited and untamed in most situations. Her mother also had quite the reputation when it came to who went home with her during last call, but she didn't seem to care what others thought as she told Emily she was always just looking for her supposed 'prince.' She'd bounce from man to man, hoping "Mr. Right-Now" would turn into "Mr. Always," but they never did. And whether it was by her mother's example or not, by this time of our sophomore year, "Easy Emily" was even more widely known all around campus and seemingly proud of it as well.

While Emily was tough and rough around the edges, Victoria truly was a refined and proud Southern belle the more I got to know her. She was always done up "as pretty as a peach" and her strong southern accent melted like butter. It was also easy to like her—she was genuinely sweet with no agenda except to experience new adventures and have fun. She cared about her body more than anyone I'd ever met too. She kept lithe and toned, and worked-out like a fiend. Her main aspiration was to model in New York City one day, so she didn't care too much about college. She thought most of the frat rats were silly and immature, and she preferred to go shopping and to the movies on weekends instead of their parties.

Victoria had grown up in Atlanta where her father had been a prominent banker, but he died of a heart attack when Victoria was in her early teens. Luckily before he passed away he had made sure that her, her older brother, and her mother were well-provided for—should anything unfortunate like that ever happen to him—so the three relocated to Miami, Florida, where Victoria split her time between her mother's house in Miami and her grand-mother's estate in Palm Beach. She'd clearly experienced a little more than your average Texas-raised girl, and perhaps that's why she and I clicked right away. But with Victoria and Emily, it took a bit more time to finally see eye-to-eye.

Emily, not having grown up with the same privileges as either Victoria or me, always lived on a very meager budget. She had a part-time waitress-ing job at a bar on campus, but it still left her "cash short" and constantly needing to borrow clothes and money from us whenever we went out (but mostly from me). Oldie didn't want to see her turn out like her own mother, so he continued to pay her tuition at UT along with her living expenses as my roommate in our shared townhouse apartment. And whenever my fam-ily could, we also took her along on expensive trips, hoping to introduce her to a world that would be completely unknown to her otherwise. Since she didn't have her own father around or any siblings to bond with, I knew she looked up to both me and Oldie as if we were the missing parts of her own family she desperately wished she had. Victoria didn't quite understand our connection at first, since in her Atlanta country club circles people of differ-ent economic levels normally didn't mix, but Emily soon grew on her, too.

So while I drove the latest model Porsche, Victoria drove the latest model Mustang, and Emily drove a twenty-year-old car bomb, somehow, we all had synergy. Christmas vacation promised to be both fun and interesting...

Acapulco was gorgeous. White sand, blue water, and smoking-hot men as far as the eye could see. The private beach near the Las Brisas Hotel where we were staying was covered with sunbathers sunning themselves on the rocks, glistening like wet seals.

On the very first day, Victoria and I tanned near the hotel's pool while Oldie drank scotch and sodas next to us and told loud, off-color jokes. Emily stopped by on her way out, dressed in a tight micro-mini and high heels.

Victoria looked her up and down as she said, "*Hmm*, just a guess... not tanning with us today?"

"Fraid not, gals! Sun reaks havoc on my skin—I'm hitting the shops," Emily said. "Besides, when will I get to Acapulco again?" She turned to Oldie. "Thank you so much for allowing me to join you, Mr. St. John!"

"No problem-o, ladies... if Melanie's happy, I'm happy! And Emily, please, I've told you before, call me 'Oldie,'" he said warmly.

She seemed glad to. "Sure thing, Oldie! Oh, and 'Mrs. Oldie' told me to tell you her and Whitney would be at the spa most of the day, so they'll see you all just before dinner. Back in a while, girls!" she said towards Victoria and I and then sauntered off.

Oldie whistled. "*Whew!* No offense girls, I'm aware your female friend there is my daughter's age, but hot damn! That is the shortest skirt I've seen in *all* of Mexico... maybe even in Texas!"

Victoria and I rolled our eyes because whenever the subject of short skirts came up we knew Oldie's favorite, new joke about them was soon to follow.

"Reminds me of the time I was at a crowded bus stop in downtown Houston..." he started. "I saw a beautiful woman there wait'n for the bus, all decked out in a tight leather mini-skirt, zipper up to here in the back," he said, motioning halfway up on his meaty, hairy thigh. "The bus rolls up and the woman starts boarding, but then notices her skirt is too tight to allow her to lift her leg up onto the first step of the bus!"

Victoria feigned polite amusement, but I didn't.

"She's quite embarrassed of course," Oldie continued, enjoying the sound of his own voice, "so she flashes a smile to the bus driver, reaches behind her, and unzips her skirt—just a little bit... She figures this'll free up some space to get her leg up, you know. So she tries a second time, but still, her leg doesn't reach the first step! So, she reaches back behind her and unzips her skirt down just a tiny bit more... She then tries to swing her leg up again but still, her leg won't reach! So, smiling apologetic-like, she unzips the offending skirt again—then suddenly a big 'n burly Texas cowboy behind her picks her up and puts her up onto the platform of the bus!

Well, the woman went absolutely ballistic!" Oldie said; gesturing wildly with *his* version of what an absurd and hysterical woman would look like. "She turns to our would-be hero and screams, 'How dare you! I don't even *know* you—and you have the <u>nerve</u>?!'"

Oldie's fake-falsetto now dropped into a deep, southern man's drawl, "'Well ma'am, normally I'd agree with ya, but see'ins how you've unzipped my fly three times, I kinda figured we was friends!'"

Oldie laughed so hard his stomach bounced up and down. Victoria and I groaned and rolled onto our stomachs to tan our backs.

"Excuse me," a strong, Kennedy-sounding Boston accent said from behind, "but are you from Texas?"

I spun around and there stood a tall, tanned, terrific-looking guy—boyish, but strong and dimpled. He reminded me of Ryan O'Neal from *Love Story*—which Victoria and I learned early on was both one of our favorite movies, mainly because of its sexy lead.

"Damn right!" Oldie said proudly in his own deep, Texan drawl.

"I hate to admit this," he said to Oldie, "but I've been eavesdropping on you guys for awhile now, and I just have to say your jokes are hilarious, sir! I love that Texan humor and I just wanted to introduce myself. My name is Morgan Walsh and I'm from New York." He reached out his hand and shook my father's beefy hand like he was a huge fan, which only egged Oldie on even more.

"Is that right?" Oldie said. "Well then... allow me to tell you about the two old Texans putt'n one back in a small-town saloon, right outside of Antonio... Great little watering hole, all the fellas liked to hang out there. One says to the other, 'Ya know, I've had me every woman in this whole dang-gum town, save for my mother 'n sister!' And his buddy replies, 'Well then... sounds like between you and me, we got 'em all then!'"

Our new friend snorted with laughter and Oldie joined in. Victoria giggled, flirting with Morgan openly. I was mortified—how could such a gorgeous man be laughing at my father's tacky jokes? Or was he just humoring him? I wanted to crawl under my beach towel and hide.

"Uh, Dad's a bit eccentric," I said, pretending to laugh it off. Here was this cool stallion that practically arose straight from the sea and I wanted nothing more than for him to join us, sans Oldie, of course. I tried to think of any excuse to get rid of my father as we all continued to converse, but nothing worked. He had an audience now and he was not about to give that up. So I finally did.

"Ah, anyone thirsty? I'm going to get some water at the bar," I said, standing up from my loung chair. I immediately noticed Morgan checking out my figure, but then pretending not to because of Oldie's presence.

"Naw, you go on ahead, Lil' Bit," Oldie said. I wanted to die—how could he have just said that? Morgan was already clearly at least ten years older than me, but I didn't need Oldie pointing that out to him by using my childhood nickname!

Victoria seemed glad I was leaving. I knew she was already interested in him, and I also knew if she pulled out the Georgia Peach charm while I was gone then he would be hers instantly. Most men were when she wanted them to be. Though this was the first time ever that I could think of where we both wanted the same man's attention; besides Ryan O'Neal, we normally had quite different tastes. But Morgan seemed to have all the traits any woman would want all rolled up in one—good looks, a sense of humor, politeness, great style, confidence, and intelligence.

I went to the bar alone across from the pool from them, but I could still hear Morgan and all of them laughing from whatever Oldie was saying as I sat and sipped my water. They were the only loud group of people on the whole patio. I finished my water and decided it would be pointless to go back over. He was either Odlie's best new friend or Victoria's next date by now. I got up and headed down onto the beach towards the hotel.

Then I noticed Morgan standing up. He seemed to say his good-byes to both Oldie and Victoria quickly as he ran towards me.

"Melanie! Hey—!" he yelled as I stopped in the warm sand, waiting for him to catch up. "I was just heading back in too... can I walk with you?"

"Sure," I said, a bit confused, but also happy for his company. I could see Victoria's dagger-eyes staring at us and knew she had wished he had stayed next to her.

We started chatting as we went inside the hotel lobby, and found it difficult to stop once we reached the elevators.

"Hey," he said while blushing, which I found irresistible. "Would you like to have a drink with me?"

"Yes," I answered, and we went inside the hotel lobby bar and continued our conversation there all afternoon while looking out at the gorgeous view of Acapulco Bay.

Morgan was friendly and sophisticated, and seemed quite well off—he knew all the best places in New York and was familiar with many of Texas's elite clubs and restaurants as well in both Houston and Dallas. He had graduated from Princeton several years earlier and came from a large, Irish-Catholic family that lived in New Jersey, but his family spent most of their time in New York which is why he always referred to himself as being from there. He had an apartment in Manhattan, but traveled a lot for work and seemed to always bounce from place to place.

"But maybe one day," he said with melancholy, "one day I can settle down somewhere permanent, you know?"

"That sounds nice," I said, already imagining I could be happy just about anywhere he wanted to land. He was so handsome and polite, and just the kind of man I would want to settle down with.

"I've been down in Texas for a while now though," he continued, "working for the C.E.O. of Seagull Energy. I don't know... so far, Texas hasn't really been my scene," he looked down, a little sheepish. "But maybe that was because I hadn't met any fun, sophisticated Texan girls yet until now, you *know?*" he said half-jokingly, slipping a sly wink my way.

"What kind of girls have you been meeting?" I asked as I took a sip from my crystal champagne flute.

"Only ones with over-bleached, over-teased hair and nails out to here..." He demonstrated some atrociously long talons. "And I've heard some pretty horrific accents—I mean, these girls might as well be from Jersey!"

Though on the exterior he was playing it ultra cool, I could detect a lot of interest going on below... within each of us actually... and once we discovered we both knew a little Spanish we decided to converse in nothing but it for the next hour, laughing and talking until our whole bottle of champagne was gone. By then, I found him irresistibly sexy, but I also knew I had to go meet my family and friends for dinner.

"It's been great hanging out with you," I told him, switching back to English again, "but I have dinner reservations with my family at—"

"Meet me at El Bella Vista for dinner instead," Morgan said rather than asked. I instantly liked his confidence—and obvious hint that we had definitely made a connection he didn't want us to break. "We can sit under the stars and look out at the glittering lights of Acapulco... I know you'll love it."

I was suddenly glad he had laughed at Oldie's tasteless jokes earlier and knew somehow instantly that because of that he would understand... Victoria, however, I wasn't so sure about...

"Where's he from?" my mother asked understandably as I put on my make-up, making sure it helped to make me look as old as possible so he didn't think of me as the young co-ed I really was.

"New York," Oldie answered for me, "and don't worry Louise, I met the boy and checked him out. Seems like a real nice fella."

"*Very* nice," Victoria said. "I wish I were going!" she only half-joked.

Thank God Emily never set eyes on him, I thought, and was silently glad she and Whitney had already gone down to the restaurant before I even arrived back to get ready.

"I'll be fine, Mom," I assured her.

"I know," she said, still trying to convince herself of it. "Just, just—"

"She _knows_!" Oldie said sternly and we all looked at each other understandably, knowing we didn't have to say anything more. "Now come on, I'm starving!"

"Have fun Mel," Victoria said as they left, but with her accent I wasn't quite sure if it was meant to be sarcastic or not.

When I arrived at El Bella Vista the champagne was chilled and the candles were aglow. It was the perfect setting for an enchanting evening under the stars. Morgan and I enjoyed a long, luxurious dinner of fine French wine, crusty bread, and grilled shrimp. But as romantic as the evening was, Morgan seemed to be purposefully keeping his distance from me as the night went on.

I couldn't understand why. He seemed very into me earlier. It was very mixed signals. But, I resolved to just accept his sudden change of heart and let the evening continue on graciously; after all, at least we'd always have the afternoon to look back on fondly.

Like the true gentleman he was, he walked me to the hotel elevators once we were back at our shared hotel. I didn't want this to be the last time I saw him, but I also knew how we said good-night would immediately tell me if it was going to be.

Morgan opened up his muscular arms and gave me a slight, but generous, hug.

Hmmm, I thought, feeling safe and comfortable in his arms, but there was no sudden move at all towards a good-night kiss.

Instead, he just looked into my eyes as he said, "I'm going sailing to Puerto Vallarta tomorrow for a picnic cruise on my uncle's boat...would you like to come along?"

I was happily surprised and would have gone with him anywhere as I stared back into his beautiful brown eyes. We planned to meet on the beach right after breakfast the next morning.

As I rode the elevator back up to my room alone I thought, _What a pleasant change of events... and you certainly have to respect a man willing to take it slow in this day and age..._

The next morning at breakfast with just me and my friends, Victoria insisted on joining me down at the beach, even though I had mentioned I wanted to go alone.

"C'mon Mel," she said, giggling. "This tan isn't going to apply itself! Why don't you really want me to come? Are you meeting Mr. 'sexy-pants' there?" she teased, but I knew she had already figured out that I was.

Emily jumped in, indignant. "Uh? Who's sexy-pants? What did I miss?"

"Sexy-pants is Melanie's new *friend*," Victoria said teasingly—and with a touch of mischief. It appears Morgan's good looks had not been forgotten by her since yesterday. "The one she went to dinner with last night, but..." she continued, poking me in the ribs, *"nothing happened!"*

"Aw, knock it off, Vic," I said. "So we didn't kiss... big deal. Morgan acted like a perfect gentleman all night. Finally, a guy who isn't all hands!"

Just then Emily caught our teenage Mexican busboy staring at her perky breasts spilling out of her top as he refilled her water glass. "Go fuck yourself!" her foul-mouthed tongue spat, jarring him as he quickly walked away, embarrassed.

Victoria was appalled, but I admired Emily's spunk. I could never imagine blurting out a phrase like that—not even under my breath!

The event instantly forgotten, Emily then continued right on with our conversation without skipping a beat. "Yeah right—he didn't even try to *kiss* you? Sounds like he's gay," she said, taking a big bite of jam-covered, homemade toast that was still warm from the oven.

I remembered having that same assumption about Subir in Monte Carlo, but Subir had female tendencies and mannerisms that warranted thinking that. Morgan was nothing but pure masculinity through and through.

"He didn't look gay to *me!*" Victoria said suggestively, affirming my own thoughts. But I was also becoming more than a bit surprised by her behavior. I had never seen her act like this—she was really still into him, even after he'd taken *me* out. Why wouldn't she just give up already?

"Then you just have to jump his bones and find out," Emily said to me matter-of-factly.

"I could never do that!" I said—and both Victoria and Emily knew that.

Emily groaned. "It's the sexual revolution, Mel, get with it!" She checked her make-up in her pocket compact. "Well girls, have fun no matter what you decide to do with 'what's-his-name' today, because you're on your own again... I'm off to the jewelry district to find some deals on turquoise." She left in a rush.

When Victoria and I got to the private beach near the shore, Morgan was sunbathing under a shade umbrella with two empty chaise lounges to the right of him. Victoria squealed and ran over to where he was. He seemed a bit surprised to see her, but polite nonetheless. She greeted him flirtatiously and stripped off her cover-up to reveal the tiniest string bikini I'd ever seen. As soon as I saw both it and her behavior towards him I instantly regretted letting her tag along—especially after the "just jump his bones" comment was mentioned and was still running through both our heads. Victoria had always been more experienced and aggressive when it came to men like Emily was, and I should have known she'd pull out all the Southern belle charm and stops to get his full attention now that I knew she really wanted him.

She twirled between us, batting her eyelashes, and Morgan didn't seem to mind that she was there anymore at all as she placed her beach towel and tote bag on the unoccupied lounge chair right next to him—leaving me to take the one on the *other* side of her. It was as if she'd already decided she had won him away from me, so why put off the inevitable awkwardness of moving our things around later...

"Gosh," she started in a soft, sexy voice, "I was just thinking of going on my morning run down the beach, but now we're all set up here I don't want to leave all the fun! That is, unless either of you care to join me and soak up some of this magnificent sunshine we're having today? *Morgan..?*"

"Sounds 'tempting,'" he said, and I could clearly hear the underlining innuendo in his tone. He threw me a look. "Care to join us, Melanie?"

It was the first time he even seemed to notice I was there. "No, I'm good," I said. "You two have fun." I could accept defeat gracefully.

Morgan raised an eyebrow at me, but then Victoria playfully tagged him on his muscular shoulder. "Come on, she's fine!"

The two took off down the beach, chasing one another like they were playing tag and laughing flirtatiously. Even from afar—and more than a few times—I could see Victoria surreptitiously trying to adjust her string bikini, and then they both disappeared around the bend of the coastline.

After nearly an hour they returned, breathless and giddy, with Morgan glistening in the sun as he ran towards me. Victoria went towards the water to "cool off" while Morgan came up and plopped down beside me on *her* beach towel. "Melanie, I hope you don't mind," he said, "but I've invited Victoria along to Puerto Vallarta today... if it's okay with you."

Considering what I'd been imagining happening around that secluded bend for the past hour, the statement didn't surprise me in the slightest. It did, however, surprise me that he actually thought I'd go along with it and risk the humiliation of watching the two of them get 'cozy' on the cruise. I'd rather stick acid in my eye.

"Of course," I said, as pleasantly as I could. "But listen—I'm starting to feel a little queasy. One too many cocktails last night perhaps, so I'm sorry, but I can't join you guys today."

Morgan looked upset. "Melanie, no—what a shame!" He leaned forward and whispered sincerely, "I was looking forward to some quality time with you..." He cupped my chin with his hand and looked deep into my eyes, adding, "This isn't over, you know."

I had never felt such a strong connection with anyone and couldn't image it only being one-sided, yet it seemed to be. "We'll see," I said coyly.

Just then Victoria returned, dripping wet, and coughed uncomfortably. He instantly pulled away so she could use her towel.

I turned back to my beach tote and packed up my belongings. Surely Morgan was attracted to Victoria—how could he not be? But I also knew from our chemistry that he still at least had a little interest in me, too. But he'd broken an unspoken law of dating by inviting Victoria along on *our* date and to me, that only meant he'd break other rules. The cruise promised to be fun, but only if I was the only one on board with him.

"Mel! You're not going to stand up this fine young gentleman are you?" Victoria said in a mock accusatory tone, her eyes sparkling in victory.

"Surely you'll find a way to entertain him without me, Vic," I said, my voice as cool as silk.

She just smiled and winked at me playfully.

Now that Victoria and Morgan were going to be alone on the cruise together all afternoon there was no doubt in my mind that they would hit it off. I spent the rest of the afternoon sulking, wandering the markets with Emily, and browsing for tired trinkets until I couldn't stand it anymore. I finally left Emily to her jewelry shopping and climbed back down to the beach where I waited for Morgan and Victoria's return. Surprisingly, I didn't have to wait too long—the sun was still high in the sky when Victoria found me on the beach a half hour later.

"Hey Mel... feeling better? And yes... I'm back *already*," she said, rolling her eyes.

"Well? Don't leave me hanging... spill!" I said, trying to sound supportive, though I was secretly jealous deep down. "You practically had him eating out of your hand this morning. I figured you'd be off sailing the globe together by now."

"Yeah, well, once we got out on the boat he wouldn't even <u>look</u> at me!" she huffed. "What a weirdo! We were all alone out on the water, right? And I took off my top to sunbathe like I always do... and he didn't even blink! I walked right by him, like, a bunch of times topless—and he wouldn't even look at me *sideways!* Never tried to touch me, kiss me, NOTHING! I don't even know why he even invited me along..." She folded her arms, truly upset, and I could tell she was about to tear up. "Mel... is there something *wrong* with me? I mean, I'm pretty enough, right?"

Just when I wanted to believe Victoria had only wanted to win the guy from me her true reasons and insecurities bloomed right in front of me— and when it happened, I knew it wasn't Morgan she really wanted. She wanted the same thing I wanted, which was someone to find her beautiful, desirable, and unspeakably wonderful; someone to love her fully.

"Victoria, of course you're pretty enough! Who knows what was wrong with that guy? Obviously we need to find you someone who can appreciate you, clothed *and* not! Forget him," I said, and meant it. "Let's grab Emily and get a margarita."

One good thing that came out of the experience that day was that Victoria and I vowed to never compete over a man again. And even though Emily never actually had with either of us, she agreed to the rule too as we all washed the pact down with our salted drinks. Instead, we decided our friendship was now like a second family, and love 'em or hate 'em at times, we always deserved each other's respect and support because no matter what, we'd always have each other's backs—including giving rides to the airport, whenever needed.

But after we got back to Houston, I kept having these strange dreams where I saw Morgan Walsh always around me, seemingly watching me from a distance with those intense, beautiful eyes. I couldn't help but wonder if this meant Morgan might still one day take me up on his promise that things weren't really over between us. If nothing happened on the boat with Victoria like she claimed, then maybe there was still a chance Morgan hadn't forgotten about me all along. And if it was okay with Victoria, I would still like to know what he had meant that day. I just didn't feel it was truly over, and the dreams seemed to confirm that.

Then, sure enough, one day I got a phone call from him just a few weeks after we were back in school at the start of our second semester of sophomore year. Morgan had been transferred to his company's San Antonio branch, which was only about an hour and a half from the UT campus, closer than he'd been in Dallas. We agreed to meet for dinner in Austin and he said he'd have his limo pick me up.

Victoria had moved on and gave her blessing, so with that Morgan and I began meeting up every other weekend—or whenever Morgan was free. He'd wine and dine me at all of the top restaurants in town with door-to-door car service and with what appeared to be a bottomless expense account. But strangely, just like with Victoria, he never made a move, even after several long evenings together. At this point I'd been out with enough college guys to know that this was highly unusual and I began to wonder if Emily was right—was he really gay? But somehow I just couldn't see it... Morgan was the picture of masculinity, and I'd even caught him looking at me every once in a while in a way that was not just 'admirable' of my fashion sense. But when it came time to "close the deal" each night, his looks were all false advertising and I continued to get nothing more than a hug. Were we on the same page about our feelings for each other?

By the fourth evening we'd spent together I was going out of my mind and by the fifth—as we were enjoying dessert—I unexpectedly found myself leaning in and planting a full assault on his lips. Morgan softened for half a second, enjoying it, but then quickly stiffened and pulled away. I wiped the misplaced-intentions and chocolate mousse from my mouth and turned bright red.

"Congratulations," I said towards the floor. "I do believe that is the first time in my whole life I've ever been so thoroughly rejected by a man. Gotta admit, it's kind of a drag..."

"Mel, listen," he said, truly feeling bad. "I'm so sorry. Please don't be offended, but you should know I'm really only interested in keeping our relationship platonic for now. You're ten years younger than I am—still in college—"

"You do realize I'm nineteen—and that's *over* eighteen—an adult, *right?*" I said with a brattiness I didn't even know I was capable of.

"Of course I know how old you are! But, if something were to develop between us... well, I'd like for you to be absolutely sure you're serious about me—and vice versa, you *know?*"

I felt so ashamed. Here I'd finally met someone with more manners than a caveman, and it was me who couldn't control herself. Morgan continued to be as warm, charming, and friendly as he always had been for the rest of the evening, as if to reassure me that our feelings for each other could be much, much deeper than some superficial, meaningless make-out session. I was beginning to really fall for him now—and not just in a 'lusty' kind of way. It also didn't hurt—as Victoria and Emily both pointed out—that he was playing the ultimate hard-to-get. Fair observation, I conceded, but whatever it was, it was working. I wanted more of Morgan Walsh.

Our friendly, platonic weekend excursions continued all throughout the semester and I began to wonder what else Morgan needed to be sure he wanted to be with me... and what other assurances I could give him that I wanted to be with him. As school was letting out I finally mustered up the courage to bring it up again. "Morgan... I want you to know that as much as I've been enjoying spending time with you, I'm starting to have.... well, real *feelings* for you," I said, staring into his eyes.

He shifted uncomfortably. "Mel, I need to tell you something," he said seriously. "You won't believe the timing, but I'm being transferred back to New York. I was going to tell you tonight after dinner, actually." He looked genuinely apologetic and even a touch sad. I couldn't believe my horrible timing—and luck.

"But, I want you to come visit me," he insisted. "I have a huge apartment on Park Avenue with a guest bedroom; it'll be fun—I want you to come next weekend after your finals are over. Have you been to New York before? And, if so, do you like it there?"

"Yes—and I don't just like it, I *love* it there! I went with my father all the time when I was little and always had a blast."

"Good, it's all settled then."

And so I flew to see Morgan every chance I got that summer, which was practically every weekend. I stayed in the guest bedroom of his spacious bachelor pad and no expense was spared when I came... we traveled the city via limo and dined at five star only restaurants with elegantly set tables and dim lighting (and the occasional, exciting, top-celebrity sightings, of course). It was always a much more serious and sophisticated setting than anywhere we went in Texas, but somehow, Morgan always managed to keep things light and jovial anyway. I felt important and secure with him.

However, in New York, Morgan Walsh also changed and became an extremely evasive person. He was always very vague and mysterious when it came to his background. As we got to know each other better in these new surroundings I began to wonder what his *real* story was... He carried himself with perfect poise, yet I also got the impression he was always looking behind him, watching doorways, and keeping a watchful eye out for some invisible, ambivalent enemy.

"He's probably in the mafia," my mother warned me one night after I got back while my family was all dining together at our country club.

"He's not in the mob!" Oldie said dismissively. "That's just the way people have to be in New York. There's more criminal-types there to rip you off everywhere you go, and it sounds like he's just always looking out for you like I always did, Lil' Bit."

"Sounds like he's always looking around for a better *date*," Whitney slurred as she drank from her cocktail glass. It was already her third and we hadn't even finished appetizers yet.

I wasn't sure if she meant it or if she only said it because she was still upset from hearing the "big news" earlier that Eva had gotten engaged. Actually, it was more of a "big shock" to everyone rather than just news...

We had all been genuinely worried about Eva because of all she had been through over the past year, and I secretly wondered if she would ever even be able to have a normal life again. But now, after nine months of very expensive therapy and drug rehabilitation treatments, Eva had met, dated, and was newly-engaged to a truly caring, bright, and generous young man named Brian Sanderson. Like Eva, he was half-Hispanic and very passionate about life. He was a history teacher at a Houston public high school and enjoyed coaching the boys' winning soccer team each fall. He truly loved his job, his large, close family, and Eva. And Eva truly loved him. We were all thrilled and happy for her when we found out; well, at least three of us were. All Whitney heard when Eva called to tell her the news was that she had now lost her only friend to go out looking for men for *her* to date with—and how was she supposed to get engaged without going out to find available men?

"Well, at least Morgan treats you the way he should," Oldie said; nodding towards me approvingly and snapping me back into the conversation. "And you're still young, there's no rushin' a wedding here, so just continue to enjoy yourself with him, Mel."

So I did, for several more weekends that summer. But with all the talk about Eva being in "true love" whenever I came home—and Whitney seeming to be searching for it herself now endlessly—I finally couldn't take not knowing where I stood with Morgan when it came to being involved in an actual, committed relationship anymore. I only knew I wanted to be in one with him and know for sure that it was truly going somewhere—but before I could bring all that up, I also needed to find out about his secret life in New York...

So one evening, at one of the classiest restaurants I'd ever set foot in, Le Bernardin—where even after being away for several months before his last visit there the Maitre D' called out to Morgan by name as we entered and had steamed Alaskan King Crab at our table before we'd even ordered our first drink—I decided it was time.

"All right, that's it! What is it with you and *New York*?" I asked him outright as I glanced towards the wait staff. "They're acting like you're some kind of celebrity or something!" Morgan rimmed his water glass with his finger as I leaned in closer and continued. "Seriously, what is it? Tell me about your super-secret life here—people are always fawning over us like you're the King of England everywhere we go. What's the deal?"

Morgan sighed, looked up at me, and finally spoke, "Okay, okay... you're right. You've proven I can trust you. I suppose it's time you knew anyway, huh?" He drew in a deep breath. "So, it may not mean much to you, but it just so happens my mother is the daughter of Lorenzo Caliglio... Of course, you've probably never heard of Lorenzo Caliglio, but plenty of people around here have, and some might even have reason to *fear* him. He's got his hands in nearly every important deal in New York right now—not exactly 'on the books' understand, but all of them—the docks, the unions—he pretty much controls it all and keeps a low profile doing it, if you know what I mean." He shrugged his shoulders forward. "And as his only grandson, I guess you could say I'm 'well' taken care of..."

"What are you saying? That your family's in the *mob?*" my voice nearly squeaked.

"Shhh—keep your voice down, okay? It's not polite to talk about it, really... And on top of that, my father is one of the most famous judges in the state and he's notorious for getting members of our 'family' off when they get pinched, so I guess you could say he's not the most popular judge around."

A piece of King Crab dripping with butter cooled on my fork mid-flight to my mouth. I was stunned, but also fascinated. *My mother was right,* I thought. Suddenly I got very self-conscious and slightly nervous. "So what about you, are *you* involved with anything 'interesting?'"

"Of course not!" he said, offended. "Mel, you have to trust me on this, you have nothing to worry about. I'm not proud of my family or my connections, understand? Why do you think I kept it from you this whole time? I've got zero underhanded shit going on and you have to believe me on that—I'm *not* my family!" He pounded the table with his fist, but even that, he somehow did gently, not at all like a mobster would. "Trouble is, I'm being 'watched' all the time here in New York—everywhere I go. I can't go two blocks from my apartment without those two 'goons.'" He discreetly pointed to two large, bulky men dressed in expensive suits sitting at a table across the room from us; two men I recognized as having seen many times before. "They're watching over me," he continued to explain. "But they're also here for *both* our protection, but believe me—except for keeping you safe, which you *are*—this is, in fact, my personal nightmare! And I've lived this way my entire life."

The two sharply-dressed men casually chewed a slow meal of seafood pasta and wine. One of them was wearing a large gold chain, and suddenly he glanced lazily in our direction and nodded.

I gasped as I looked back at Morgan. "Are you serious? I can't believe it! I feel so... 'presidential?' Famous? I don't know.... I suppose this explains why you always eat with your back against the wall!" I giggled, but then stopped. Suddenly the weight of this information—and the meaningfulness of his sharing it with me—dawned on me. "Morgan, I'm so glad you feel like you can trust all this with me... it means a lot." We were definitely on our way towards a true, committed relationship now with *this* much trust involved!

"It means a lot to me too, Mel," he said earnestly. "I'm glad I could tell you, and it feels good to get it off my chest. Now... these crabs are getting cold—let's eat!"

I felt like we'd made a real breakthrough in our relationship. Surely this could change his mind about us being together romantically, right? *Time would tell,* I told myself. I never wanted to stop believing that it was only a matter of time before things "happened" between us.

But weeks went by… Our friendship grew stronger than ever but still, Morgan showed little romantic interest. Instead, he surprised me one visit by saying he wanted me to have a big career like him in New York, so he set up appointments for me with the three top modeling agencies in Manhattan. All three showed interest, but when I approached the topic with Oldie, he was opposed.

"Absolutely not!" he barked. "No daughter of mine is going down the toilet like <u>that</u>!" He was referring to his belief that *everyone* in the modeling industry either had an eating disorder or was on drugs. "You're still in college," he continued to rant, "and there's no way over my dead body you're moving to New York NOW! You want to ruin your life, do it *after* school!"

And with that, Oldie forced me to turn down all three modeling offers. I almost never forgave him for that since it also meant giving up moving to New York to be closer to Morgan, but I was also surprised when Morgan suddenly changed his mind and agreed with Oldie.

"Maybe your dad's right, Mel. School is important," Morgan said, and with that, he crushed my dreams of moving to New York to model and be with him—which was the *main* reason anyway. I would have done anything he wanted me to just so I could stay there with him, modeling was just a convenient option (and one I never planned on sharing with Victoria since I knew that was really her dream anyway, not mine).

I returned to UT to start my junior year of college. I was sad to be leaving Morgan and New York behind, but, deep down, I knew he and my father were right. I had a lot of living still left to do. And that living also included now wanting to have a real boyfriend of my own. I wanted it to be Morgan—but since that was still difficult I decided to try for a UT local instead. But none of them kept my interest like Morgan did… and besides, whenever I did agree to go out on a date it was really only so I could then work it into a conversation with Morgan the next time I talked to him so I could monitor his reaction. He usually played it pretty stoic, and it infuriated me.

Then suddenly Morgan stopped calling and I found out his home telephone number had been disconnected. His secretary told me he had been transferred abruptly again, but wasn't supposed to say to where until things were more 'settled.' I was upset and devastated—had something *else* really happened to him? I had no way of finding out. Victoria and Emily tried to console me, but it was no use. I missed him and moped around for weeks, wondering about his fate.

Then, three months later, I got a call from Morgan out of the blue. He apologized for losing touch, but said things had been 'crazy' and now he was being transferred yet again—this time to Austin. I couldn't believe it! What an amazing stroke of luck! Not only that, he was planning to move into a brand new high-rise just minutes away from my townhouse. I forgot all about the last few months and was just glad he would be arriving next Tuesday.

The night he moved in, I put on a form-fitting dress and shook my hair out long—Morgan had admitted once that he liked it best that way. Finally it seemed like the fates themselves were aligning to bring us together—to deny it any longer seemed fruitless. We could finally admit to one another what we'd been fighting for so long...

I tucked a bottle of the nicest champagne I could find under my arm and knocked on his door. When he didn't answer right away I imagined him inside somewhere, unloading boxes, with earphones on. I knew he wasn't expecting me, so I knocked again, louder, with the bottle of champagne now in one hand.

The door opened.

"Mel! You're here!" Morgan said while looking genuinely shocked to see me. He must have forgotten that he'd told me his exact arrival date.

"Housewarming gift," I said, smiling, as I handed over the champagne. "I thought I'd come over and help you warm—"

"Listen Mel," Morgan interrupted. "I don't know how to say this, but I'm entertaining a guest tonight. This is Juanita," he said, opening the door wider and gesturing behind him towards a sultry, attractive, well-dressed woman closer to his age who was sitting on the couch. "She's my next-door neighbor. It's... not a great time right now. Can I meet you for lunch tomorrow instead?"

Flustered, I said, "Oh, sure, I mean—yes, of course! Just give me a call in the morning." I waved good-bye to both of them like an eager schoolgirl scurrying from his front door, embarrassed and confused.

After what seemed to be the longest night of my life, Morgan called in the morning to make plans to meet me at a cafe near his place. On the way over, I prayed the conversation wouldn't go the way I feared.

"Melanie, I felt just awful about last night," Morgan started, "but I need to be honest with you. Juanita's not my neighbor. She's someone I've been seeing for some time now, ever since I left Dallas, in fact. She's the daughter of an important Venezuelan government official in charge of the country's oil production. We really hit it off when we first met, and to be honest, she makes me feel as great as you make me feel."

My jaw dropped as I said, "What exactly are you *saying*, Morgan?"

"This is just my situation, Mel. I care for you very much, but you should know that my priority is and always has been to get out from under the influence of my family. I've worked hard to make my way in the oil business on my own and my relationship with Juanita is an important one. I knew if things went well with her and me I'd finally have the resources and connections I needed through her to get out from under my family's thumb. And so, last night, just before you arrived, I proposed to her and she said yes."

I was dumbfounded and heart-broken. Did I hear him right? Did he say he's getting *married?*

"We're going to stay here in Austin for a few months, then move to Venezuela to be married—" he continued.

Oh my God... My heart stopped. *He is...*

"Her family already has a palatial home ready in Caracas for us to live and raise a family in, and her father has arranged for me to take control of one of the top oil companies there once I arrive. I know it all probably sounds crude to you to say I've been looking for both financial security and safety over love all this time, but it's the truth. I'll always have enemies, but at least now I'll be able to keep a safe distance away from them by living well in Venezuela. But if you and I were together here, well... you should know that though I'd do my best, I could never fully guarantee your safety, ever, and I just can't do that to you."

I couldn't believe what I was hearing. He was doing just what I had done with the bracelet! I wanted to tell him no, don't—you'll regret it! But I also knew (even more than he realized) how strong a choice based on factors and influences other than your heart *really* was to make. It was even stronger than true love... I tried to summon the words to explain this, but they refused to arrive, so I simply swallowed my tears instead as Morgan continued.

"Melanie," he said with only warmth in his tone. "You and I have the kind of relationship where I feel I can tell you all of this honestly. As my friend I wanted to tell you about Juanita the moment I met her—I felt very lucky to have—but I knew it was all very complicated. I was afraid you might be hurt—plus, I wanted to be sure that this is what I really wanted first. But, I'm sure now, and she is too. Juanita is what I've been looking for, to get out of my whole nightmare 'situation.'"

His crude honesty wasn't so much the problem, it was the fact that I'd been so stupid for so long, so blind to see it, or that, once again, I'd failed so miserably at choosing a man to fall for.

Morgan continued, "Don't get me wrong. I do care for you, Melanie, I have since the beginning. But now that you know what my motivation has been all along you know why I've always been so careful about pursuing a romantic relationship with you. I never wanted to hurt you, Mel, and I'm hoping we can still be friends."

Despite what felt like a swift punch to the stomach, I couldn't muster anger—he was right, we'd never had an 'official' romantic relationship, and even when I was practically forcing myself on him at times, Morgan had never once taken advantage of the situation by allowing the relationship to go beyond platonic friendship. Still, it hurt hearing his confession out loud just the same. I felt like a pawn in a big game of financial-safety chess.

"We'll see," I said sadly, thinking back to when I also said this to him the time he invited Victoria along on our date on the boat in Acapulco. I should have just gone with my first instincts about him back then and stayed away after that—but somehow I thought deep down things would turn out differently from this if I just gave him another chance. I hugged him and quickly left the table. I needed air and to process what had just happened.

I jumped in my Porsche and drove through the streets aimlessly. I didn't smoke, but Emily had left a pack of her Virginia Slims in my car the last time she had borrowed it, and I urgently grabbed for one, lighting it up as I thought things over. How was I going to let Morgan Walsh go now I knew I *really* had to...?

How 'lucky' he felt for having have 'met' her, I thought bitterly. He seemed sincere enough when he said it, but I kept seeing an image of him browsing through a catalogue of oil executives' daughters all around the world until he found exactly what he was "looking for" in one of them just to get out of his own family situation. It then dawned on me that at the end of the day, I might have always only been a list of stats to him like she was. It was now obvious he only dated woman solely for their wealth and connections. But so what if he did? Lots of women I knew did that too with men... By the time I had finished the cigarette I still wasn't sure if I was more upset at him, or at myself for seeing only what I wanted to see about the whole situation the entire time.

At long last, Morgan was finally free of his family's influence. He'd gotten everything he'd ever wanted. And as his true friend, I should only be happy for him. The fact also was I never really even knew the 'real' Morgan Walsh, just the facade he chose to show me at any given moment over the last fifteen months. Maybe it was the not knowing that made him so fascinating to me, but it was all really just an illusion, like the dreams I had of him were.

We tried to keep in touch once he was married and settled in Venezuela, but eventually communication sputtered and then fizzled out altogether. He started traveling the world putting oil deals together while I stayed in school in Austin putting together A's.

Victoria and Emily did their best to try and make the rest of our junior year bearable, but I just wasn't into dating or meeting anyone new. All I wanted to do was study and concentrate on school—not men. And it stayed that way over summer break and even at the start of our senior year too. I wasn't sure if I'd ever meet a man who would mean as much to me as Morgan Walsh, and frankly, I didn't even honestly ever care to.

Chapter 7

⟐

"Another 'ace?'" Victoria asked knowingly as we looked over our midterms from a Spanish class we both shared.

"Sí!" I responded proudly. Since I spent all my time studying instead of dating, I was currently on track to end my first semester of my senior year with a perfect 4.0 G.PA. I was also taking enough extra classes to graduate with a duel major in both Spanish and Portuguese, much to the delight of my parents, who were now encouraging me to keep studying if these were the kind of results. They knew that unlike Whitney, I actually had plans to have a career after graduation, and since I wasn't dating anyone seriously—or at all actually—being in the top of my class in *two* majors by May was just as good for 'bragging rights' at the clubs as an engagement announcement would be.

"Well, I should have sat closer to you then," Victoria said sarcastically as she showed me her grade, which was a C. "But hey, at least I'm set to pass this class now and that was my only true goal. After all, it's not like I'll need to speak Spanish once I'm living in New York!"

"Are you really going to move there right after graduation?"

"Well, not the next day—my mom wants me to spend some time with her this summer in Florida before I 'head out into the world.' She calls it mother-daughter bonding time, but I know what she's *really* up to... she plans on trying to set me up with every eligible bachelor in the Miami area to see if I can land a husband there. I keep telling her I don't want a husband yet, just fun, you know, but she's eager for grandkids it seems."

Just then Emily burst through the front door of our shared townhouse, upset, as she blurted out loudly, "SHIT—I don't *believe* this!" as if we should already understand what she meant it in reference to.

"What?" I asked, truly curious. With Emily you never knew what it was going to be...

"Billy Baker has just asked me out—*finally!*" she said.

"You mean 'Billy with the pending trust fund' he receives immediately after graduation?" Victoria asked, already knowing the answer was yes.

"Of course!" Emily said. "I've been trying to get his attention for *weeks*... which you wouldn't think would be hard to do since no one else on campus seems to want his pimply-faced, fat ass, but still... he was definitely playing hard to get! Not as hard as Morgan *did,*" she said, shooting me a look, "but still, it wasn't easy. Then again, I knew trying to go after an 'M.R.S. degree' this late in the game would leave me with few choices."

"Well, congratulations," Victoria said. Though she and Emily were really friends, it still made her uncomfortable to think of Emily trolling for dates in only the "trust fund section" of men. She found it tasteless, though I tried to tell her it was only because Emily didn't have her own money like we both did to fall back on. But maybe my family had gotten her a little too used to the finer things in life, for she wasn't about to stop having them after graduation if she could help it.

"I have to go, girls," Victoria said as she picked up her purse. "See you later, Mel."

As soon as she left, Emily looked at me strangely. I could immediately tell something more than just getting this date with Billy was up. "*What?*" I asked.

"Okay," she started, "now, you know how much I've wanted to give dating Billy a go..."

"Yeah," I said. She had made a list of all the available men left on campus with trust funds at the start of our senior year, and Billy really was her first pick overall; for besides being rich, he was also known around campus as generally being kind, sweet, and generous. He was a bit of a nerd and not involved in any fraternities or any school sport teams though, so the fact that he was still single really wasn't a surprise. Most women wanted a stud, and Billy was not even close to one. Emily had also seen some of the other women he had dated over the years and knew next to them she was considered a supermodel—so it didn't surprise me that Billy was interested in taking her out. I just hoped he wasn't going to get hurt. Besides knowing firsthand what it felt like to have someone date you for how you looked on 'paper,' Emily had never even had a real boyfriend for longer than a month since high school, and now she was planning on creating her first, long-term one with Billy this year and then making him become her permanent, life-long husband by June. I hoped she understood what that all *really* meant...

"Well, I just found out I'm pregnant and I have to get an abortion before our first date, otherwise I could blow my chance with him," she stated flatly.

"<u>What</u>?!" I said, completely shocked. She was acting like she just asked to borrow my sweater she was so nonchalant about it.

"My doctor said he could do it tomorrow, but he's very reluctant to schedule it because he's worried about how I'll handle it 'emotionally...'" she said sarcastically, then added, "I told him that *wouldn't* be a problem—I don't even know or care who the father is—and I just want this thing *out* of my body *fast!*"

I was horrified—she was talking about a living thing! I knew she slept around a lot, but she had always said being on the pill was full-proof, so she didn't have to worry about something like this happening.

"Emily," I stuttered, "how can you be so irresponsible?"

"I forgot to take my birth control pills for a few days, but I didn't think it was a big deal since I've been on them for years."

"Well, it's a *huge* deal! Getting an abortion is a HUGE deal—how can you be so heartless?"

"I'm not heartless! I just don't want a baby right now!"

"Well maybe this will be a lesson *not* to have so much random sex!"

Emily rolled her eyes. "I don't need a lecture, Mel, I just need to borrow eight hundred dollars to cover the hospital bill... you know it would take me months to save up that kind of money waitressing, and I don't have time to waste here!"

"You want me to *pay* for it?" I said, appalled.

"Look, you know I can't... I basically live hand to mouth... and Mel, I really, *really* need your help with this... I'm desperate here! I need this thing out of my body! It's not at all what I planned—I want to graduate this May, get married to someone nice and respectable like Oldie, and have a *good* life... I don't want to be like my mom!" She broke down, crying hysterically.

Suddenly I understood and felt bad for her. "Okay," I reluctantly agreed. "I'll help you out, but only this *one* time. If this ever happens again you either have to have it or pay for it yourself. Understand? An abortion *isn't* a form of birth control!"

"I know, and I'm sorry I had to ask you to help me with this," she said, still crying. "But thank you for understanding... you're the best friend anyone could *ever* hope for... if things work out with Billy and we do really get married someday, I promise I'll start paying you back for all you and your family have done for me."

"Don't worry about that," I assured her, "just worry about yourself right now."

"Thank you, Mel," she wept. "I love you."

"I love you too," I told her, rubbing her back. This was one time when our "second family" bond was truly being tested, and I prayed silently that it would never be tested like this ever again.

Emily and I decided what happened would only stay between us, so when she came home the next day from the hospital I told Victoria she had the flu and we both let her rest for several days undisturbed. No one suspected anything else, and just over a week later, Emily finally went out with Billy. They hit it off over a lavish, gourmet dinner at one of his family's country clubs, and Emily came home truly surprised by how nice he had treated her the whole evening, including only expecting a peck on the cheek after walking her up to the front door. I don't think she realized there were men who could treat her better than the frat rats she normally settled for (and slept with), and was actually glad she had seen it was possible. Emily told me she planned to take it slow with him, and I was very relieved. She was actually acting like she truly wanted a real, meaningful relationship for the first time in her life. Maybe having such a life-changing experience like getting pregnant actually did teach her a lesson she never would have learned otherwise… She was not the same Emily afterwards, and it was a good change in her to see.

By Christmas vacation Emily and Billy were officially a "campus couple," and Victoria and I were still happily single and concentrating on finishing up finals week successfully. Emily— now sure she was on her way to achieve her "M.R.S." degree by May—skipped most of her classes and did the bare minimum just to stay in school so she could be with Billy. He was completely unaware of this, but so in love by now I'm not even sure it would have mattered. He looked at and treated her like she was his queen, and though Emily showed she really did have feelings for him too; I kept hoping it was real feelings of love. He deserved that, as did she.

Whatever the situation, it was sure to be tested though, as the two campus lovebirds were now about to spend their first few weeks apart as Christmas vacation approached. Billy was going to Europe with his family like they often did this time of year (London for Christmas and then Paris for New Year's Eve), and his strict, religious mother wouldn't dream of letting him invite someone he wasn't married to. (I wondered what she would have thought of Emily's past if she ever found out, for I knew Billy was only telling her what he wanted her to know in very small doses.) So that meant Emily was free to come along with me and Victoria to Aspen instead.

It was going to be a "girl's only trip," for Oldie and my mother were going on a cruise to the Caribbean since it had now been over two-and-a-half years since their last vacation alone together, and Oldie promised my mom he wouldn't let more time slip away since he was more aware of it passing with me graduating so soon. He told me to consider taking the house in Aspen for the week as an "early graduation present," and I was thrilled to do so. I was finally feeling better for the first time since

Morgan and I ended, and I planned on having a blast with my two best friends.

I called Whitney to join us, but she was off having her latest fling and couldn't have cared less.

"Sorry Squirt," she said, "but I have much *better* plans than hanging out with you and your pack on the slopes." I could tell she really liked this new guy she was seeing, but she always did in the beginning of any relationship she started. It just never lasted. "Why don't you call Eva?" she asked.

I hesitated. "Okay, maybe," I finally said. I wasn't really sure how I felt about Eva coming along though—or even about her in general these days. She seemed perfectly fine and better than ever the whole time her and Brian were engaged, but as the wedding date last fall grew closer, she suddenly realized she couldn't abandon her (and her parents') lifelong dream of luxury and her desire to have a big house in Highland Park and a country club membership. Brian, a struggling teacher, couldn't provide this for her, so she gave him back his grandmother's heirloom ring—and though her heart was truly broken—she set off in an earnest pursuit of someone who could. That was over a month ago, and no one had heard from her since.

But, after I hung up with Whitney, I decided to bite the bullet and call her. After all, I knew how hard break-ups were, and maybe getting away would be just what she needed to do right now.

"Hello?" Eva said into the phone.

"Hey, Eva," I said. "It's me, Melanie."

"Oh, hi Squirt," she said, sounding just like Whitney. "What's up?"

"Well, I'm going to Aspen for Christmas and I thought you might like to come... you know, take a break from the break-up and everything for a few days, maybe even get a different perspective on things—"

"I appreciate the invite," she interrupted, "but actually, things are going great now!"

"*Really?*" I said. Wow. It took me *months* to recover from my relationships. It had only been a month since her and Brian's ending.

"Yeah, I found Brian's perfect replacement! Dawson Clarke the Third, the son of a financier—Sanford Clarke of Clarke Management. Needless-to-say, his family is *extremely* wealthy. He's your typical nerd—very smart and not good-looking at all—but hey, he's got what I *really* want!"

She sounded just like Emily, and I found it much more unsettling this second time around. "Seriously Eva, is money all you care about?"

"Yes," she said proudly. "He could have half a face for all I care, but as long as he can give me the kind of lifestyle I want, I'll put up with anything." She then went on to tell me how he was studying to become a doctor and was always known as 'The Doc' at his hundred-year-old Connecticut boarding school, Hotchkiss, growing up. He graduated magna cum laude from Yale for his undergrad and had recently returned to his native Texas to go to the Baylor College of Medicine in Houston to become a heart surgeon.

He sounded like a great catch to me, and I wished Eva well with her pursuit of him as we hung up. I then thought about both David and Morgan—did they both only try to date me for my money and status? I still didn't want to think so, but the evidence of seeing how others did this kept stacking up. Maybe Oldie was right that day on the jet—it's best to only date amongst your own kind, otherwise, you never know what someone's motives are deep down. I mean, I was glad to have money and happy to share it too, but I also didn't want to be used or taken advantage of... after all, no one would.

Victoria, Emily, and I arrived later that week at Oldie's fabulous Swiss-styled chalet home in Aspen. Emily had been there once before with me of course, but for Victoria it was her very first time.

"It's all just lovely!" Victoria exclaimed just like Emily did the first time she looked out at the view of the mountains and quaint town below. "I didn't think 'cold' could be so inviting!"

"It's worth it once you see how much fun skiing is," Emily said.

"Oh, I've been skiing before," Victoria said. "In the Swiss Alps when I was little, with my dad." She teared-up, missing her father, and I felt bad for her. I didn't know what I'd do without Oldie.

"You guys have been *everywhere!*" Emily said, somewhat envious and also to change the subject—fast. She never liked talking about fathers. "But I'm ready to be just like you now."

"Things going *that* well with Billy?" Victoria asked.

"I'd like to think so," Emily said.

"Do you miss him?" I asked.

"Actually, I do," she said, seeming a bit surprised. "But I won't as much once we start the party now!" She took out a small vile of cocaine and set up three lines of it on the table.

"Where'd you get that?" Victoria asked, for she knew how expensive cocaine was and not something Emily could afford—though Victoria could and often bought it strictly to use as a 'diet aid' at least once or twice a week since it suppressed her appetite fully. It did that for a lot of girls actually and that is why it soon became a very popular drug among the wealthy set—especially for any girl who wanted to keep their bodies x-ray thin like Victoria always did. But I knew better than to go there. After all, I had seen what it did to Eva.

"It was a 'gift' from Billy," Emily said with a wink. I was surprised; I didn't even think of Billy as a partier—especially in regards to doing drugs.

"He likes his girls thin, so I told him if he supplied me with the goods I'd use it to stay 'Twiggy-thin' for him."

Emily did a line and then offered the rolled-up bill to Victoria, who happily did her share. Then they both looked at me.

"That's okay," I said. "I'll stick to champagne tonight."

"Come on, Mel!" Emily urged. "You're always such a 'goody-goody!' God—*live* a little tonight… come on, if you do, I promise I won't make you do it ever again! But I just want to see you really cut loose, just *once.*"

"Yeah," Victoria agreed. "This is the best you've looked since you stopped seeing Morgan—I think you're finally over him. And maybe a little 'all night' craziness is just what you need—just to focus on having fun again!"

I looked at my two best friends' eyes as they each started to glaze over with that "high-energy, anything goes" optimism that the drug delivers at first and figured they might be right. I was tired of always following the rules… after all, what had that gotten me? I wanted to have one wild night—and hopefully trip—to remember from college. Why not let this be it?

I looked at the line of coke hesitately, mulling it over, but just couldn't bring myself to actually do it.

"Oh God, forget it!" Emily said, pushing me aside as she did the line. We all left to go hit the bars.

We went to the most popular one we knew of, The Tipper. It was a cozy, wood-paneled bar and restaurant with a large fireplace as its main focal point, and it was packed. Victoria, Emily, and I all got a drink and sat down at a table. Feeling the high energy of the crowded room, I knew I was ready for anything the evening held…

Just then an attractive man in a black parka walked into the bar. I caught my breath—I had never seen such a good-looking guy in my entire life! He was even more attractive than Morgan—tall, lean, muscular, and with thick, dark hair and a perfectly white, charming smile. He reminded me of Clark Gable in *Gone With the Wind.* I couldn't stop starring. Then suddenly, to my delight, he came straight over to our table. I was about to say hello when suddenly he bent down towards Emily and gave her a big, wet kiss on the cheek.

My heart sank.

"Hunter! Get *off* me!" she yelled, pushing him away. "I told you, I have a *boyfriend* now! So cut it out…" She gestured towards me and Victoria. "These are my two 'available' friends, Melanie and Victoria, but I wouldn't be so cruel as to *ever* introduce them to <u>you</u>… trust me girls, he should be wearing a 'beware of Hunter Wells Carrington the Third' sign around his neck! He's *major* bad news…" She laughed and patted him on the arm as she continued berating him, obviously enjoying it. "I'm sure you're up to no good as usual. Where's your ski bunny of the week?"

He smiled, but was visibly miffed at her comment.

"Thanks for all the compliments," Hunter replied dryly. "Believe it or not, I didn't bring anyone this trip. I'm just here with a few guy friends."

"Yeah right!" Emily said, rolling her eyes.

He looked across the room and pointed towards two, attractive men his same age—which was about five years older than all of us—sitting at the other side of the bar. "There they are," he proved. "Look ladies, I've got to go join them, but why don't we all hook up later for drinks at Little Annie's? Say, around nine?"

He looked directly at me and I wanted to faint.

"Thanks for the invitation." Emily crossed her arms. "But we already have plans. For the *whole week.*"

"Oh, well, see you around then..." Hunter looked me in the eye sadly before he turned and sauntered back across the room towards his friends. I could tell he was a little pissed and embarrassed by Emily's comments.

"Oh my God, Emily! Who in the world was *that?*" I blurted out. "Where does he live—how old is he—why haven't I ever seen him before—and why on earth did you tell him we have plans for the whole week? I definitely want to go meet him for a drink!" I could hear myself chattering away nervously from the alcohol, and couldn't stop.

"He's an *ex,*" she said ominously. "And I wouldn't introduce him to my worst enemy, so forget my best friends! Trust me, he's *awful*—like the kiss of death."

"*Why?*" Victoria asked, sizing him up from across the room.

"He thinks it's a sport to break women's hearts. He has a great lifestyle and trust fund to support him, so he doesn't ever work—he just likes to travel and 'work out' all over the world—jogging is his favorite work-out next to sex—and after he gets that, he's on to the next town, country, and conquest."

"But he's *sooo* sexy," I purred. "Surely he can't be *that* bad."

"I'm warning you Mel, stay as far away from him as possible. I saw the way he was looking at you and I'm sure he'll be calling me for your number. But believe me; you don't want to get involved with him. He will break your heart over and over again like he did mine and every other girl I've ever seen him bring to the bar I work at back in Houston over the summer. Trust me."

"So that's how you know him?" Victoria asked.

"Yeah," Emily said. "He came in one night two summers ago and swept me off my feet—literally—for several days straight. It was great, but then, just as fast as he wined, bedded, and dined me—in that order—he dropped me.

You guys know I don't fall for a man that easily because I've got street smarts and watch their every move, but this one *really* fooled me…"

"So he's from Houston then?" I asked, not listening to her warnings.

"He's from *everywhere*," Emily said. "But one of his family homes is in Houston. He also has a family home here."

"So we already have *two* things in common," I said dreamily.

Victoria spotted a handsome man at the bar. "I think I found my 'private ski instructor' for tomorrow," she joked.

Emily quickly shot me a look and I knew just what she was thinking as Victoria's truly harmless comment stirred up a very bad memory—we didn't need words to communicate it was something she still regretted. And between that and seeing Hunter she now seemed to lose her excitement for being out.

"You know what girls? I'm kind of beat suddenly," Emily said. "I think I'll go back to our place and call Billy to say good morning, then turn in."

"Ah, the night's just getting started!" I said, truly revved up.

"I think I'll stay and try to find out more about my 'skiing lesson' for tomorrow," Victoria said suggestively as she strolled towards the man at the bar.

"You coming back with me?" Emily asked me.

"No, I'll stay here with Victoria," I answered. But it turned out to just be the first of two lies, for about an hour after Victoria hit it off with Todd—her new 'ski instructor' for the next day—I told her I was bored and wanted to go do some late-night shopping, but what I really planned to do was take a risk for once and go meet Hunter at Little Annie's. It was only minutes past nine.

He was not hard to find in the crowd. I was immediately and magnetically drawn to him. Hunter was so alluring in a dark blue polo shirt and jeans… his shirt matched his eyes perfectly, and when he saw me he rushed over, happily surprised, and picked me up instantly. "You came! You came!" he exclaimed, spinning me around like we were old, life-long friends.

Then, before I could think, he lowered me towards the floor and stole a quick kiss. "You're beautiful," he whispered, then gently pulled me back up to face him.

I confess I fell in love with him right then and there.

"So Melanie," he said, starring deep into my eyes. "Can I get you a drink?"

"Yes, champagne," I said.

He raised an eyebrow. "'Champagne' is it?" he joked, for most people our age were drinking bottles of beer all around us.

"Yes," I said. "It's all I ever drink."

"'Champagne Mel,'" he said, already turning it into a nickname. "I'll have to remember that."

He went to the bar and returned with a bottle of champagne on ice and two flutes. "I figured 'when in Rome...'" he joked as he poured us each a glass. "So, what's your story?" he asked earnestly.

"I'm just here at my family's house for the week," I started, hoping to let him know we already had that in common, "having fun with my friends."

"And *are* you?" He grinned.

"So far, *yes*," I replied.

"Me too," he said. Our chemistry was unmistakable. He fussed all over me, and though I tried to remain poised, after awhile I totally threw caution to the wind and flirted, danced, and kissed him until the wee hours of the morning and Little Annie's was about to close.

It felt incredible to have this gorgeous man lavishing his full attention on me—as well as his soft lips—after over a year of platonic hell with Morgan. I had even forgotten how much fun kissing was!

We shared a cab ride home and found out, conveniently enough, that his parents' house was just above mine. We stood in front of my front doorway kissing good-night for what seemed like hours without taking a single breath.

"Can I..." he started to say after we finally came up for air.

I was hoping he was going to ask to come in for a nightcap, because I was definitely up for some more making-out. And who knows if I'd even stop there...

"Yes," I said instinctively.

He laughed. "You don't even know what I was going to ask you!"

I giggled, realizing he was right. But really, at that point, it didn't matter. I was ready to say yes to anything he asked—or wanted.

"I promised my friends I'd ski with them in the morning," he seemed to apologize. "But after that can I take you to lunch at Ruthie's on top of the mountain?"

"Sounds great," I said. "I'll be there by eleven."

"Isn't that kind of early for lunch?"

"Okay, ten then."

He laughed and kissed me one more time. "Good night, 'Champagne Mel,'" he said, and then walked up towards his family's home. I had never felt so fully alive and happy ever in my whole life.

I woke up the next morning around ten groggy and hung-over.

Emily pounced on me while I was still in bed. "Let me guess," she said with the energy of a high school cheerleader. "You had the time of your life last night when you snuck off to go meet the infamous 'Hunter—' He focused on you *completely* all the way up until closing time, then he took you home and made mad, passionate love to you like a wild beast!"

She wasn't the least bit jealous or upset, so I knew she was truly over him. This was really good news for Billy actually, for I think she was actually really starting to care only for him. Definitely a first for "E.E."

"Sorry to burst your bubble, but wrong!" I said. "He did treat me like a princess all night, but then he dropped me off here and asked me to meet him for lunch later today… though I have to tell you, I wouldn't have minded a little 'wild beast action,' cause you have no idea how long it's *been!*"

Victoria walked into the room already dressed in her full, cute, form-fitting ski outfit. "Yes we do because we know you more than anyone, well, besides Oldie probably—but this is something he *shouldn't* know about you—*ever*—even after you're married!"

"You're playing a dangerous game starting to see him, Mel," Emily warned again. "But, since it has been awhile since you've seen any action at all, I have to say you couldn't have picked a better one to get back in the saddle with. Though he's a complete ass—he's *fantastic* in bed… and you know I've had *a lot* of experience to compare him too, so that's saying something."

I had to admit though the thought of being with someone Emily had already been with was a bit disconcerting, I was also intrigued by her endorsement of his bedroom skills. Though it was the decade of women's lib and sexual experimentation was encouraged, I didn't have much experience in this department really. I was definitely a 'late bloomer,' but suddenly interested in seeing what all the fuss was about if given the chance to with *him…*

"Come on, let's hit the slopes!" Victoria said. "My guy's waiting."

"You both go on ahead," I told them, then hurriedly jumped in the shower.

I got to Ruthie's just after eleven, and Hunter was already there.

"I thought you were going to be here by *ten?*" he said flirtatiously.

"I thought even eleven was too early for *lunch,*" I flirted back. "Besides, I was giving you extra time to ski with your friends."

"Oh, I blew them off by nine just so I could spend the whole day with *you,*" he said. "They saw you last night, so trust me, they completely understood!"

He kissed me and made me feel so special and beautiful that I melted inside. I thought that happy and alive feeling I had with him last night was partly only alcohol related, but here it was again—all coming back and even stronger now—as we sat, talked, ate, and kissed all through lunch. I was totally smitten.

Since I had taken the ski lift up without my skis, skiing back down the mountain wasn't an option, so Hunter found his skis and we rode the lift back down together, kissing passionately the whole way. I never wanted to reach the bottom.

"Meet me for dinner tonight?" he asked when we finally did.

"Do you even have to ask?" I said, wondering if dinner would lead to 'real' romance afterwards tonight… I felt ready for it to.

With a kiss we parted and I went directly to the best designer shops I knew of in the center of Aspen. I knew I didn't pack anything sexy to wear for the whole week and I wanted Hunter to know I was ready to be treated like a real, desirable woman that night. In fact, I decided if I wanted to pursue Hunter for the rest of the trip too—which I did—I'd better have a whole closet full of sexy options, so I made sure to stock up on several of the sexiest, hottest outfits I could find before heading back home.

After my shopping bonanza I got dressed in the sexiest one consisting of a pair of tight, camel-colored suede pants with an even tighter sweater and a matching, camel-colored suede coat. I felt the prettiest I'd felt in a long time and couldn't wait to see Hunter's reaction to my new outfit.

I walked into the Caribou Club—the best club in Aspen for dancing—where we were to meet, and it was exactly as I had hoped. Hunter's eyes said it all… he liked what he saw, and he truly wanted me. I was in paradise. This man was so intense, and he was now intensely focusing all on me. I had never had this kind of attention from any man before, and it was exhilarating.

We talked about everything, our families, travels, school years growing up, college years (he had graduated from Duke five years before), and our hopes and dreams for the future. The conversation bounced easily back and forth like a well-played tennis match with both of us getting all the time we needed to talk and be heard. I felt like he was truly listening to my every word, and I was also doing that to his. I felt hypnotized by his voice and it appeared he was to mine too. He made me feel like we were the only ones in the whole room all night long, and again, we stayed until closing time.

"Take me home," I wantonly whispered in his ear as we got into the cab. I was shocked at my own aggression. But it just felt so right…

We went back to his family's place and he sprung into action. Candles were lit, music was played, and a bottle of champagne was already chilling on ice. It was as if he had hoped the night would wind up like this too. He took me in his arms and laid me down on a bearskin rug in front of the fire. In the back of my mind I felt the entire scene was all a little cheesy, but I couldn't deny how good it also felt. It had been so long since a man made me feel this good…

He pulled me in close to him and looked deep into my eyes. "I want you, Melanie..."

I melted as he kissed my neck, and then moved down to my breasts... it had been so long since I had felt this way, and I was ready to shed all my inhibitions...

But then his hand reached down to the top of my new suede pants, gently fingering the zipper, and suddenly I remembered Emily's warning of what 'bad news' he was... *she wouldn't just be saying that,* I thought as doubt crept into my mind... and as I looked around at the "perfectly staged setting" we were in, I realized this wasn't the real me at all.

"Hunter... wait," I said, gently pushing him away. "Things are going a little too fast for me... I mean, you're great and *very* tempting, but I don't want to rush into things tonight... and I'm sorry that I asked you to take me home tonight if *this* is what you thought I meant, but I'm not into one-night stands, only relationships."

I almost couldn't believe what I was saying, for Morgan had practically used the same kind of lines on me, but I really wanted to see how Hunter would react to this. I mean, I really wanted to see if he wanted to have a relationship with me, not just a fling.

"Sure, okay," he said, pulling himself up without any fanfare. "Well, this gives me an opportunity to talk to you about my change of plans for the rest of my vacation then... A spot on my friend's private plane to Houston has opened up for tomorrow morning, and I need to take it. I unfortunately have to go back home to take care of some business, so I'm afraid I won't be able to see you again for awhile."

"And were you planning on telling me this *after* we had slept together, if we had?" I asked, wondering if he was really just trying to get rid of me with a lie.

"Of course," he said. "I believe in honesty and I'm telling you the truth, either way. Of course, I would have rather have made love to you *first*." He grinned, but he also didn't seem upset that it didn't happen. He really could have had it occur either way.

I was smitten, but also relieved that I hadn't succumbed to his wiles. He was just after a one-night stand after all, and I felt like I owed Emily a great big thanks. I still had faith in Hunter, however, since he did seem sincere about keeping things honest between us, and I hoped he would call me someday after I returned to Houston myself, or even later back in Austin.

"I still enjoyed being with you these past two days, 'Champagne Mel,'" he said playfully as he kissed me tenderly.

"Me too," I said. "But I'd better go so you can pack."

He laughed and walked me to the front door.

My friends and I enjoyed the next day of our ski trip together, but I couldn't stop thinking about Hunter. Emily was all over me about it.

"I can't believe he's gotten into you this fast," she said, blowing smoke in my face without a thought. She had always smoked, but she only chained-smoked like this when something was really bothering her—like me thinking about Hunter seemed to be doing. "He's only going to hurt you."

"Emily," I started, "I've already told you I'm not ignoring your warnings. You're one of my best friends and I trust you—that's why I took your advice last night and didn't become another one of his 'trophies,' ah, no offense."

"None taken, for I always considered him one of *mine*," Emily said.

Disgusting, I thought. *I would only be with him—or anyone—if it truly meant something more.*

"Anyway," I said, taking both her and Victoria's hands. "I'm sorry I ditched you guys for the past two days. This is supposed to be our big senior break trip! I'm coming back down from my cloud now, so let's go hit the slopes!"

"What are you gonna do with all the new clothes you bought for him?" Emily asked. I could tell she wanted them.

"Return them," I told her. "Well, at least the ones I didn't wear yet."

"Why? They're all really hot and I'd love any of them!" Emily whined.

"Emily, where in the world would we wear winter clothes like these again? It's summer most of the year in Texas," I reminded her.

"Well, if you keep dating Hunter," she said, "which I think you foolishly will cause you're just the type to, I can bet you he'll start taking you to all kinds of exotic places where you just might need clothes like these. That's his style, you know."

"How do you know so much about him?" Victoria asked. "I thought you said you two just had a fleeting, couple of days together?"

"You both are *so* naïve… I do *lots* of things I never tell anyone about…" She smiled proudly.

I had had enough. "Well, thanks for all the info Em, and when and *if* I see him again I'll keep it all in mind, but I'm still returning everything I didn't wear. It was all very expensive and I don't really need it. If Hunter takes me somewhere cold maybe I'll just ask him to buy me some sexy, cold-weather clothes once we're there, like I'm sure *you* did."

She just looked at me and smiled again as she inhaled.

I tried to forget about my time with Hunter, but after we got home to Houston all I could do was think about him and wonder where he was. I couldn't concentrate on anything else it seemed but him—I was like a woman obsessed. I went to our country club trying to either run into him or find out from friends if he was still in town, but it seemed he was always just coming from or going to somewhere within the same timeframe I was asking. Emily was right, he was impossible to pin down.

I went back to Austin to finish my senior year and resolved to give up on Hunter. Emily was still dating Billy and Victoria was content on finishing school and keeping herself focused on her New York modeling goals. I was glad this was my last semester at UT and felt if I could just stay in the top of my class in both majors 'everything' would happen for me after graduation, but fortunately, I didn't have to wait that long...

"Remember me from Aspen?" Hunter asked over the phone. It had been over a month since I'd heard his voice; an eternity. "I just saw your picture in the *Houston Press*... you look great!"

Victoria, Emily, and I had recently attended a high-profile tennis tournament in Houston and a photographer snapped a picture of us sitting in the stands.

"Can I see you tomorrow night?" he asked.

"Is that a trick question?" I replied flirtatiously. I was equally surprised as I was pleased to hear from him.

"Great, cause I really need a date for this wedding tomorrow night at the country club here in Houston... it's going to be *huge*—probably over six hundred people—and very formal, black- tie only. I want you to look *amazing*."

What a narcissist, I thought, but accepted the invite anyway just to see him. "Okay, I'll try to find something suitable in my 'vast' wardrobe."

I chose a beautiful white gown from Yves Saint Laurent. When Hunter picked me up at my house in Houston he said, "Wow, you look like a three-layered wedding cake that I'd *love* to eat later..."

I ignored him and went to his awaiting car, which was a brand new, black Mercedes. Nothing had changed... he still only wanted a one-night stand it seemed.

We arrived at the wedding late because he had gotten the time it started wrong, but we were luckily there just in time for the full course, seated dinner. The main ballroom of the club had been beautifully decorated with white and pink roses. Hunter led me through a sea of tables to one close to the bride and groom's table, and then held out my chair for me to sit down. As I did, I noticed the place card in front of me read: *Wendy Smith.* I was baffled.

"What happened to Wendy Smith? Am I her last-minute replacement?" I asked, thinking either he had obviously just dumped her, or she him.

Hunter just grinned. "Oh, I think she's sick or something... it came up at the last minute yesterday."

I found out later through gossip in the ladies room that Hunter had done the dumping, and it was all done at the last minute just for me. I was mortified, and felt bad for Wendy. She didn't deserve that. No women did. And it was the first lie he had now told me that I could call him on.

I went back to the table to do just that. "Hunter!" I began, and he could tell immediately that I wasn't happy. Still, the attraction between us was so thick you could cut it with a knife, and my anger towards him only seemed to make him even *more* attracted to me.

"*Yes?*" he said, as if daring to edge me on and fight with him publicly. I was afraid to say anything more in front of all these people I didn't know, especially since they all knew of me and my family's reputation among Texas' elite. Oldie never would have forgiven me for causing a scene.

"Let's blow this joint," Hunter whispered in my ear once he could see I had calmed down. I think he felt he had won this one.

I loudly complained of a headache as an excuse, and he stood up and grabbed my purse. Nobody seemed to care if we stayed or left.

Once back in his car, I started to bring up Wendy, but Hunter interrupted, saying, "The night's still young... let's go to my uncle's house. It's only a few blocks away and he and my aunt are gone to their chateau in France, so no one will disturb us."

I guess I was feeling punch drunk from the two glasses of champagne I had already had, because I accepted the offer without giving Wendy another thought.

When we got to the stunning estate Hunter punched in the alarm code at the gate and we entered the property. Then he announced, "Let's go swimming! They have a great pool—"

Before I could answer he immediately started running towards the backyard pool, stripping off his tux and not stopping until he was completely nude... His shirt, pants, socks, and all were strewed around the patio as I followed them like a trail of bread crumbs towards the sound of him already treading water in the deep end. I was amazed at his arrogance, especially after already having told him once I wasn't into one-night stands.

Hunter looked at me as I moved as far away from him as possible and sat on a chaise lounge at the other end of the pool. "Come on," he pleaded. "Just take the damn dress off and join me in here!"

I looked down at my five thousand dollar gown and called out to him, "Are you *crazy?*"

"Come on Mel!" he pleaded again, splashing at the water, but luckily he was much too far away to even get a drop on me.

"No thanks," I answered. He looked alluring and sexy beneath the pool lights, but I wasn't going to be his bait for the night. "I'm tired and just want to go home," I said.

"Alright," he said, swimming towards the ladder. "I'll take you home... but no *peeking,*" he teased as he climbed out of the pool completely unabashed and got redressed in front of me. I was amazed at how well he took rejection, for I knew all this stage setting for what 'appeared' to be just a simple, romantic opportunity by 'chance' really took a lot of planning.

"You know," he said earnestly, "most girls your age fall for this kind of thing."

"Well I'm not like most girls," I said.

He grinned, taking the challenge. Then somehow, once we were back in his car, we wound up back at his huge, *amazing* house—he didn't even have to entertain anywhere else in Houston, ever! It had everything there you could ask for just in the living room: a large, movie-theatre-type-screen with a full stereo sound system along one wall, a pool table and several leather couches throughout the middle, and a fully-stocked bar along the back wall. We drank champagne and blasted Queen's *We Are The Champions* over and over, singing along. We made-out and talked until we both lost all track of time—and because by now I was completely intrigued with him once again. We kissed and danced, but that was all, and he seemed to be fine with it.

He held me in his arms, looked at me tenderly, and said, "I want to take you to Nassau tomorrow."

I kissed him happily, then pulled away to look at my watch. It was 5:30 A.M.

"Oh my God!" I said. "Hunter, it *is* tomorrow—I have to get home, right now!"

"Relax, Mel, I'll drive you home first," he said. "But we're going to have a great time there. I guarantee it."

All I was thinking about was that Oldie was going to kill me—and him. I had told my parents I'd be home by one at the latest.

Hunter took me to my parent's house and walked me through the back gate. I thought I could sneak in unnoticed, but suddenly we both heard Oldie bark, "Where the HELL have *you* been ALL NIGHT?!" from the back kitchen doorway.

"Oh shit," I whispered to Hunter. "We're completely nailed!" I turned towards Oldie. "I've been with Hunter, Dad, I'm sorry…"

"I've been up all night waiting on you!" Oldie said, taking off his glasses.

"Hello Mr. St. John, sir," Hunter said, giving Oldie his best smile and offering him his hand. "My name is Hunter Wells Carrington the Third."

Oldie, unimpressed, refused to shake his hand. "I know you by reputation," he scolded. "You're a no-good, S.O.B. serial womanizer! How *DARE* you keep *MY* daughter out all night! You ought to know better! My God, you're an Exxon heir and should know that this kind of behavior from *your* kind of family name is just unacceptable! Now, get out of my house and leave my daughter ALONE. You *hear?*"

"I'm so sorry to have kept your beautiful daughter out so late, but we were just having such a great time talking and dancing and lost track of the time. Believe me; I've *never* done that before… with any woman," Hunter said.

Oldie put his glasses back on. "Yeah, right!"

Being the smooth operator that he was, Hunter continued to apologize profusely over and over until Oldie, fed up and furious, finally said, "Son, I'm not buying what you're selling. Please leave and *stay away from my daughter,* FOREVER!"

Hunter knew he needed to get out of the house A.S.A.P.

"I'll call you later," he whispered to me as he quickly left.

I went into the kitchen and my mom appeared out of nowhere. "Mel," she started, "you look awful! Your gown is all rumpled and you look tired and horrible."

"I guess staying up all night doesn't really work for me," I said. "But I just had the best date of my life! This guy is so much fun! All we did was go to the wedding, then back to his house to listen to music and talk, for hours… I promise no sex was involved—I told him I wasn't like all those other girls! But now he wants me to go to Nassau with him on a trip—"

Oldie perked up. "Are you out of your *MIND?*" he screamed. "You're not going anywhere except upstairs to bed! That guy has only one thing on his mind, *comprende?* I know his kind!"

"But Dad, not with me he doesn't—"

"Just go upstairs and get some sleep… we'll talk about the birds and the bees later," he quipped. "I've never seen you look so awful and you've never stayed out all night like this—now your sister, she's disappointed us this way *many* times, but you, well… I had just hoped *you* would always have better judgment."

His words stung like a thousand daggers thrown straight into my heart. I didn't mean or want to disappoint Oldie, ever, but I knew I now had, greatly, and the conversation was over.

Needless to say, I didn't go to Nassau, which was only like honey to a bee for Hunter. I went back to UT and he lived up to his name, calling me three times a day with Emily or Victoria always hanging up on him, and then sending me huge, gorgeous bouquets of flowers with a note saying he just needed to get me on the phone.

"Stay away from that *creep,*" Emily would say as I admired the latest arrangement. But as I looked at the notes, always saying something like "can't stop thinking of you… please, just talk to me," or "you're the most beautiful angel on this earth, please give me a chance," I couldn't.

One day when I was alone in my townhouse he called, and I picked up. I agreed to sneak out and meet him at the Elan Club, my favorite campus hang-out. I made up a fake guy I was going to go meet to throw Emily and Victoria off as I was getting ready. I wanted to make sure I looked sexy, and they assured me I did, hoping I would hit it off with this "new, secret admirer" and forget all about Hunter.

I walked into the Elan Club and just like in Aspen at Little Annie's I saw Hunter instantly among the crowd. He looked great in his dark brown shirt and khakis. Hunter looked at me and smiled the biggest smile I'd ever seen.

"Hello, Melanie," he said, giving me a warm, welcoming hug and kiss. "I have your champagne already chilled." He showed me the bottle of champagne in a bucket of ice already on the table with two flutes next to it. He showered me with attention and compliments, and we laughed, talked, danced, and kissed all night. That was it—by the time the club closed, we were an item.

Chapter 8

◦◦◦

$\mathcal{I}$ soon found out that 'instant notoriety' came along with being dubbed as Hunter's girlfriend. He was a constant source of Texas gossip, and incredible rumors of his sexual conquests swirled all around him. There were even sightings, like Elvis sightings, of "little Hunters" that looked remarkably like him seen all over town. No one was ever able to link them directly back to Hunter, however, and he wanted no such responsibility or claim to any of them. But such was the mystique of this 'notorious lothario' I was finding out all about—at least, that was what he was known as up until *now*—for it appeared I was the one who had suddenly 'tamed' him. And it felt fantastic to be the one to finally do so.

As the weeks went by, I felt even more sure of my power over him as his gestures and affection increased daily: bigger bouquets, expensive gifts of jewelry and clothes, constant phone calls, and lavish, fun outings and surprise trips. He said he had never felt so comfortable or had so much in common with anyone so quickly, and I felt the same way. We both enjoyed the same kinds of restaurants, having long, stimulating conversations on various mutual topics of interest, and also experienced the most intense, *incredible* chemistry in bed… We both felt more alive and happy than we've ever been with anyone else.

Hunter also liked the fact that he knew I had my own trust fund and money as well, so I wasn't out to use him like so many of his past girlfriends did, including, he felt, Emily. I shared with him that I had also had the same experiences with men, and it was nice to know that that was not an issue with him and me either. It felt like a perfect match. The only real problem was, we seemed to be the only two who realized that.

Two weeks before graduation, Emily and Victoria came home with me to Houston to have a lazy weekend before we all geared up for finals and graduation-related activities. Hunter was away on "business" (which I had now learned always meant some kind of dysfunctional family-related business he had to straighten-out, since Emily was right, he didn't work), and I promised my two best friends my full attention since I knew I had been neglecting them and my family for the past two months since being with Hunter. What I didn't realize though was that they and my entire family (since Oldie still was not fully on board with the whole 'Hunter situation' since he kept waiting for him to "screw it up") were *really* trying to use this weekend as a last-ditch effort to get me away from Hunter like it was a staged intervention.

Emily, being one of his exes, of course had the most inside information to share the first afternoon as Victoria, her, and I all sunbathed by my family's pool.

"One of his 'conquests' ended up on the sixth floor—you know, the *psych* ward at Memorial Hospital?" she warned while propped up on one elbow and trying to look me straight in the eye.

I just laid back onto my chaise in a state of bliss. Her voice seemed to be coming from far, far away.

"He had made her so dependent on him that she gave up everything just to be with him 'fully' all the time, and it was all in vain!" she continued. "When Hunter dropped the crushing blow on her that he was 'moving on,' she literally lost her reason for living—*and* her mind."

"He told me about that one," I said, defending him like I was always prepared to; Hunter was true to his word and was always honest with me. He told me everything about his soiled past so I'd always be able to explain what others might not know. "And he knew she had some real emotional problems before they even went out. He was just the 'last' straw, not the *only* straw."

Emily looked at Victoria, distraught.

"Mel," Victoria now started in. "Em and I have been talking about this for awhile, but only because we both really care about you and we just don't want to see you become another meal for this guy. Once he sets his sights on a prey, she's his 'trophy' on Monday and out the door by Friday."

"So why is he still with me after over six *weeks* then?" I said defensively. I knew that was what he did with most women, but with me it was different. Why couldn't people see that? "Look, I get that he has a past, but maybe he sees more in me than he did in other girls, no offense, Em."

"Believe me, none taken!" Emily chirped. "It was a blessing when he broke up with me, because now I have a guy who *truly* loves and cares about me…"

"Billy really is sweet to you, Em," Victoria said, seemingly congratulating her on 'catching' him after all. They were still very much a campus couple and everyone—including Emily since she snooped in his wallet and saw the receipt for the ring—knew he was planning on proposing to her the night of graduation at our already-planned dinner celebration at Los Tinos.

"And Hunter is 'sweet' to me," I reminded them. I wasn't ready to give up that easily. I knew I was truly in love with him, and felt he really loved me.

"Okay," Emily said. I could tell she was losing her patience. "Let me at least tell you what he did to me when we first got together... Hunter took me out to dinner at a really expensive place—his favorite kind—and ordered two, *two-hundred-dollar bottles* of wine right away, two tins of Beluga caviar, and then a three-course dinner for both of us."

"There's nothing unusual or bad about that," I said. We often did the same thing several nights a week.

"I know, *but,* when the waiter brought the check Hunter took a long look at it, rifled through his pockets for his money clip, and then said causally, 'Sorry doll, but it seems I forgot my cash tonight... you're gonna have to foot the bill *this* time.' To this day I can still remember the condescending, smug look on his face as he said it..."

I remembered Hunter telling me this was exactly why he knew Emily was one of the many women who was just using him for his money, for he always did this same "test" with a girl he'd been dating for awhile just to see if they were or weren't. And until me, he never once had a women offer to either pay for a whole bill, or even spilt one before the time for this test normally took place. He said it was surprising I was so generous, but it was also very much appreciated.

"I learned later that this was one of his favorite tactics just to 'test' his dates to see how 'devoted' they were to him..." Emily continued like it was a horrible, terrible thing, but I only thought how refreshing it was that he had been so truthful with me—they were both repeating the exact same story; they just each had a very different way of looking at the same situation.

"He *had* the money," Emily stewed. "But it amused him to no end to play games like this with women. And he knew I was no debutante like you—he knew I was only a part-time waitress—that's how we *met* for God's sake! So I told him, 'Are you out of your *mind?* You've got to be kidding me! This bill is more than I make working for *three* whole *weeks!* The waiter came back over to the table, and Hunter just sat there with his arms crossed, not budging. The waiter stared at both of us; then finally asked, 'Sir, shall I call the manager over?' 'That won't be necessary,' I told him. '*I'll* pay the God-damn bill!'" Emily said, changing the tone of her voice to indicate when she or someone else was talking. "So I furiously threw my hard-earned cash—all I had—on the table, I had no choice really, and then Hunter had to cover the rest with his 'American Express' card… I was so mad and thought, 'I'll never speak to *this* asshole again!' I had been around enough to know his type, and I knew I had to stay away. But then he did just what he did with *you*—" Emily raised her eyebrow, gesturing towards me, as her tone got very serious. "He started calling me all the time, pursuing me relentlessly night and day all that summer. I never bothered returning his calls, and suddenly the flowers and notes started… but I just threw them all away."

I didn't know any of this part, for Emily never shared it at the time it was happening, or before now. But still, I felt with us it was different. Hunter and I were not out to use each other. But it still made me question why on earth he continued to pursue someone who he thought would… *if* it was indeed even true…

"And you know what the worst part of it all was?" Emily said, almost like she was just now realizing it. "After I paid for dinner that night—or as much as I could—he took me home and gave me the best sex of my *life!* This almost tricked me into thinking he was worth it—but it's <u>not</u>, Mel!"

I had to admit, though I wasn't nearly as experienced as Emily was, I did feel Hunter was the best lover I'd ever had too. And he told me I was also his, so I guess maybe their chemistry could have been real at the time, but that was two years ago. Things change, and I couldn't see either of them being together now.

"Listen," I told them both sternly, "I appreciate your concern here, but I really think Hunter and I have a connection. And it's *not* just about the gifts he showers me with, which I know he didn't seem to do with you except for the flowers…. you should see the way he *looks* at me! I know he's been known as a 'bad guy' in the past and I'm sorry you were hurt by him like others were, but maybe he just needed somebody to *want* to help out with bills sometimes, someone to believe in him, and really *care* about him… Let me handle this one girls and I promise I'll be the first to admit if I'm wrong about him, but honestly, I don't think I will be."

Emily sighed heavily and lit up a cigarette. "Okay, if you say so, Mel."

I knew she was finally ready to let it go.

"Enough about me anyway," I said, happy to change the subject. "What about you, Vic? Been seeing anyone lately?"

"Well, I've been out on three 'first dates' in the past month," she said with a look that was a bit puzzled, "but I must have the *worst* luck! The first guy was way too into school to even look at me instead of his book, the second 'forgot' the fact that he was *already* married, and the third guy had the attention span of a goldfish and couldn't carry on a decent conversation the whole night! Whatever this guy Hunter seems to have to attract all these women to him he should bottle and sell, otherwise, I'm beginning to wonder if I'm cursed!"

"Oh Victoria," Emily said with a laugh. "Don't be such a weirdo—it's not like you have the plague or something… there are plenty of hot guys around who can't wait to tattoo their names on your ass, I'm sure of it!"

"Really?" Victoria said, impressed. "'Cause that's what I *really* want!"

"Hey you guys!" A happy, familiar voice rang out from the iron-gate door at the far end of the pool. "Is Whitney home?"

I looked over and saw Eva standing there, beaming. She looked fantastic and like she was about to burst from excitement.

"Yeah, but I don't know if she's up yet," I told her as I walked over and let her inside. Whitney had been out extremely late with one of her various, on-again, off-again boyfriends and had told us all not to disturb her until *she* decided to get up. "She's probably still sleeping," I warned.

"And hung over," Emily added.

"Well this can't wait!" Eva said, running over and looking up towards Whitney's balcony. "WHITNEY!" she screamed. "GET DOWN HERE—I DID IT!" She yelled so loud I thought the whole neighborhood would hear.

Moments later a very tired and very hung-over-looking Whitney appeared from above as if she was Rapunzel looking down from her ivory tower. "What is it?" she said, clearly irritated.

Eva lifted her left hand up high for all of us to see. "I DID IT!" she yelled in victory. "Dawson just <u>proposed</u>!"

Whitney and I looked at each other in shock. Her plan had actually worked!

"Isn't it the most incredible ring? It's from Tiffany's and it's *huge*—three-and-a-half-carats—I picked it out <u>myself</u>!" Eva said proudly as Victoria and Emily both got up to admire the big, sparkling rock. I could tell Emily was wishing she could have done that with Billy, but now she only hoped he had gotten her one just as big and impressive.

Eva smiled bigger than I'd ever seen her smile in my whole life; then continued, "I got him, hook, line, and sinker! It's like a dream come true!"

Looking at Eva and Emily together and knowing that they were both now getting their "dreams to come true" by hooking a rich guy, I suddenly got upset that money was all that seemed to matter to either of them. We were talking about *marriage*—a lifetime commitment here!

"Are you in *love* with Dawson, or are you just in love with his *wallet?*" I asked Eva.

Eva laughed so hard she almost doubled over. "*Love?* Hell NO!" she said, almost proudly. "I'm still in love with Brian—and I'm still sleeping with him too… Dawson is a complete bore in bed… he's had very little experience with women cause he's spent most of his life at the library with his head buried in a medical book, and now he spends most of his time at the hospital, so I have plenty of free time for an 'afternoon delight…' You guys have *no* idea how hard these last few months have been for me juggling all this though! And I had to use *every* trick in the book to even get Dawson's attention at first! You would have thought that he could have cared less about sex at all until *I* came along... but it's really hard for me to pretend that I enjoy being with him that way. Sure, I like his company otherwise, but after the wedding I'm going to have to cut off the sex *completely.*"

I could see the wheels in Emily's head spinning as well. She said the same thing about being with Billy in bed—and it didn't help that he was overweight, so she said touching him was like petting a big, hairy walrus too.

"Eva, how could you be so calculating and cold?" I scolded, really upset with all the women who had tried to do this to Hunter too. "How can you marry someone you're not even in love with? Someone you can't even stay faithful to?"

"Oh Squirt," Eva said, waving me off like a child. "Not everyone gets the 'fairy tale' ending."

I couldn't believe what I was hearing as Whitney joined us and she, Emily, and Victoria all congratulated Eva on her pending nuptials. This didn't seem right at all.

The day of graduation came, but it felt like a non-event compared to Whitney's graduation three years earlier. The ceremony seemed so impersonal because there was such a huge class, and even though I was receiving a degree in both Spanish and Portuguese like I planned, I felt no sense of triumph or completion of anything important as I walked across the stage to receive my diploma. I didn't want to admit it, but I was feeling down that my parents hadn't even bothered to attend... After all, they had come to Whitney's graduation, but they said that that was only because it was a true miracle she had graduated at all. With me they always knew I would and they were proud, but it just wasn't a priority for them to make a big deal out of it.

I secretly wondered if that was really it, or if it was more of a form of punishment since Oldie still wasn't happy about me being with Hunter. I had never disobeyed him like this before about anything, but for the first time there was now a man in my life who seemed to mean just as much to me as Oldie did, maybe even a bit more. It surprised and hurt Oldie, and he did just about anything possible to avoid being anywhere near Hunter and me, including suddenly having to "work" the weekend of my college graduation.

"Hi Lil' Bit," Oldie had said just two days ago over the phone. "I just wanted to tell you that your mom and I won't be able to attend your graduation on Saturday. I have to go to Caracas to defend some dumbass who's been violating the Venezuelan laws in a very crooked oil deal."

"Oh my God," I said. "Is it Morgan?"

"They won't tell me until I get there," he said, worried. "But anyway, they're threatening to throw whoever it is in jail, and I was hesitant to take the case because of your big day, but then the thought of any poor American S.O.B. rotting in a foreign jail kept haunting me—especially if it *is* Morgan... he might never get out. Anyway, your mother has to stay home and keep an eye on Whitney—she's getting wilder by the day now. I hope you're not too disappointed."

"Oh, I couldn't care less," I lied. "Most of my friends aren't even going because it's going to take all day and be long and boring. Don't worry about it."

"Well, I'm glad you understand, and just remember—I have a great big surprise waiting for you when you get back to Houston afterwards!" he said.

"I hope it's not another car," I joked. He got me one almost every year, and I told him I really didn't need one that often.

"Hell no," he said. "It's from Tiffany's and I know it will look *great* on you! That guy Steve who I've worked with for years picked it out special, and you know he has really good taste."

"Thanks so much, Dad," I said. "I know I'll love it and can't wait to see it. Have a safe trip, love you, bye."

At least my best friends and Hunter will be there, I thought. Then suddenly the phone rang again.

"*Hello?*" I said, picking back up.

"Hey, doll," Hunter's voice said sweetly on the other end.

"Hi," I said. "I'm glad it's you because I just got some bad news about Saturday..."

"I hope not *too* bad," he said, sounding like there was now even more to come, "'cause that's also what I was calling to talk to you about."

"What?" I asked.

"I have some urgent business to take care of, and I don't know if it will be done by Saturday morning."

"That's okay," I sighed. "I understand."

"But, I promise it will be done by Saturday night, so after your dinner celebration with your friends why don't you plan to come over? I'll have your 'special present' all wrapped and ready for you..."

I smiled, getting his innuendo clearly. "Great, I'll see you then."

So now it will only be Victoria and Emily who I'll be celebrating with, I thought. *My 'second family...'*

But then, on our actual day of graduation, it was suddenly down to only me and Victoria.

"Where's Em?" I asked Billy when Victoria and I got to the ceremony and expected her to already be there with him. We hadn't seen her for the past two days, but whenever that happened it was usually because she was at his place.

"I thought she was with *you*," Billy said, truly shocked. "I haven't seen her since Wednesday."

I became concerned as I immediately thought about Eva, but then realized that a kidnapping on the UT campus was most likely out of the question. There had to be some other rational explanation, like her not being able to graduate and she was just too embarrassed to show up. She had missed so many classes that year I thought it was a miracle she had told me she actually had enough credits to graduate at all when I asked her about it a few weeks earlier; and now, as I walked across the stage with the rest of the class of 1979 to receive my bachelor's degree, all I could think was, *where was she?*

I knew both Victoria and Billy wondered the same thing, and after the ceremony we all spoke to everyone we could think of who might have seen her, but no luck.

"Let's just go to Los Tinos like we all planned," Victoria said, trying to cheer Billy up. "Maybe she's already waiting for us there and she'll give us the scoop."

We were there less than ten minutes when suddenly she walked in the door.

"Emily! Oh my God—where have you *been*—?" I said, and then was stunned into silence when Jack Hartley, the former fringe tag-along member of "The Fearsome Foursome" followed her into the restaurant. They were both extremely—and obviously—very intoxicated.

"Everyone, I have some terrible news!" Emily announced, slurring her words. "I got caught cheating on one of my finals and they kicked me out of school two days ago!"

There was a moment of shocked silence; then we all crowded around her, trying to console her, especially Billy.

"It will be all right," Billy said, rubbing her back. "I'll see if I can talk to someone about you retaking the test. They might let you, if it's a different one."

I couldn't keep my eyes off Jack, who was drunker than she was.

"She doesn't need to retake anything!" Jack said in her defense.

"Who the hell are you and what are you even doing here?" Billy demanded.

"Oh, *him?*" Emily said playfully. "Well, this beautiful hunk of a man just took me to New Orleans to drown my sorrows after I found out... I haven't been able to see or walk straight for the past two *days!*"

Everyone gasped; some in delight and some in horror.

Billy confronted her. "What do you think you're doing? I haven't given you any reason to do this to me! I don't deserve to be treated like this!"

Good for him, I thought as he stood up for himself. He was a nerd, but a truly feisty one in my eyes now.

"Billy, you're a nice guy, but here's the deal," Emily said as she wrapped her arms around Jack. Jack responded by freely roving his hands all over her breasts and buttocks. "You're disgusting. You're fat, and your face looks like a pepperoni pizza. But I love your money—*money, money, MONEY!*—and I love that you take care of me so well. So I'll tell you what, if you go ahead and propose to me right now in front of everybody with that ring I saw the receipt for from Tiffany's, I'll tell Jack to take a hike right now and I'll be yours forever. But, this is also what you're getting.... so what's it going to *be?*"

Billy was stunned and on the verge of tears. He had really thought he had hit the jackpot with Emily. He also clearly thought his whole secret, planned proposal was going to be a surprise. "I thought you loved me, Emily," he said earnestly.

She came out of a long, lingering kiss with Jack. "*Hmm?* Did you say something, *Bill?*"

"You know what? You can take your frat boy and go straight to hell!" Billy said, knocking over a pitcher of margaritas as he made a hasty, embarrassed exit.

Emily laughed uncontrollably.

"Oh my freaking God—can you believe this girl?" Jack said, completely enamored with his new 'prize.' "She the *only* one who's EVER been able to keep up with *me,* this one!"

I grabbed Emily's arm and pulled her away from Jack.

"What in the world is the matter with you?" I asked. "I know things were going south for you with school—"

"'*Going*' south?" She laughed in my face. "Try *gone* 'south'—ha!"

"Yes, but don't worry... we're going to get through this, okay? Just sit down and have some food..." I said, trying to direct her towards our table. "This is supposed to be a party, remember?"

"Woo—a PARTY! Yeah, let's part-*ay!*" she yelled wildly as she tried to stand up on a chair.

"Emily, please, calm down!" Victoria said. "You're making a spectacle of yourself and strangers are starring at us."

"Okay," Emily agreed. "Let's sit."

She seemed to calm down and we all took our seats around the table, glad the entertainment portion of the evening was over. A normal conversation started and then all of a sudden Emily jumped back up and held up a large pitcher of margaritas as if to propose a toast.

"Can I have everyone's attention?" she began; we were all too shocked to interrupt. "Hi—hi, I just want you all to know that Melanie St. John is so 'plastic' that if you put a candle next to her she would literally *melt!*" It was like I was having an outer-body experience watching her, not believing what I was hearing as she continued. "We've been 'so-called' best friends since our freshmen year in high school—over *eight years*—and I have hated and resented her every day of that the <u>whole</u> time! She's nothing but a rich, spoiled brat that's been given everything she's ever wanted her whole life! She has no concept of reality and I am formally announcing to all of *you* what *she's* all about—just in case you haven't figured her out for yourself!"

"Emily—shut *up!*" Victoria said sternly, which was the harshest thing I'd ever heard her say in public.

"I will NOT!" Emily yelled back at her with such anger that it scared her—and the rest of us—silent as she continued her drunken attack on me. "She's such a clueless little bitch! I've used you and your family for *soooo* long! You've given me clothes, paid for my education, and taken me on all your 'fabulous family trips' like I was some kind of poor, third-world exchange student who wouldn't have *ever* gotten the chance to travel otherwise... Oh! And I even got you to pay for my <u>abortion</u> last semester! Whew, was that a close call, or *what?*"

Everyone was shocked at this admission the most. I couldn't believe it. She was crying and seemed so sincere the day I agreed to help her with that, but now, in the restaurant, she laughed about it until I finally couldn't take it anymore.

"Emily!" I said, standing up to confront her. "I hope you're just so drunk you don't even know what you're saying anymore—because this is humiliating!"

"Fuck off 'Champagne Mel...'" she said condescendingly, wrapping her arms back around Jack. "Now I have Jack I don't need *your* pretentious ass anymore. You'll give me anything I want, won't you *baby?*"

"Of course," he snickered back. "As long as *you* give me what *I* want, you can have *anything* you want..."

They began to make out as I began to cry. Suddenly Emily pulled away to look back at me.

"Oh Melanie, don't cry yet! We haven't even gotten to the best part!" she said with glee, and then stood right in my face. "I've been fucking Hunter ever since we got back from Aspen. Oh—you look surprised! Don't you ever catch the smell of me on him when you snuggle up tight with him at night? I tried to warn you about him! He'll *never* change—not for you, or ANYONE! But you're so used to getting whatever you want you just can't accept that!"

"You're pathetic," I said disgustingly, not sure if I even believed what she was saying.

"Well fuck you, Melanie, 'cause I don't need Hunter, you, Billy—or anyone else now besides Jack!" She spun around, tripped, and landed in Jack's arms. "I have him forever now!"

"You two *deserve* each other!" I said as I threw a hundred dollar bill down on the table and left.

Victoria ran out after me as I entered the parking lot. "Oh my God, Melanie—are you okay?" she said, truly concerned.

"No Vic," I said, stammering through my tears.

"Come on," she said, putting her arm around me. "Let me take you home. I'll draw you a hot bath and let you melt this all away—"

"I don't want this all to melt away!" I said. "I want to go to Hunter's to see if what she said is true!"

I jumped into my Porsche and sped out of the parking lot.

I drove to Houston like a mad woman and arrived on Hunter's doorstep way earlier than we had planned. I prayed he was home as I ran the doorbell. Surprisingly, he answered on the first ring.

"Hi, Mel—you're early! What a great surprise!" he said, generally seeming glad to see me. "Come on in... I thought your graduation dinner would go later... can I pour you a glass of bubbly?"

"No you can't 'pour' me anything—unless you want me to throw it right back *at* you!" I said, upset over the fact that he couldn't tell right away how mad I was, and also because from the looks of the baseball game running on the television and the empty take-out boxes thrown about, it appears he had just been hanging out there all day instead of being at *my* graduation.

"What's wrong?" he said, concerned.

"I thought you had 'business' that needed taken care of up until tonight?" I said, deciding to tackle this one first.

"It was done by this afternoon, but I figured I'd already missed most of graduation, and by the time I drove to Austin it would have definitely been all over," he explained causally. "Besides, I knew you were coming here afterwards, and I wanted you to have fun with all your friends for one final, big night out."

"Including *Emily?*" I said, waiting to see his reaction from hearing her name, which was only confusion.

"Yeah, of course," he said. "She's one of your best ones, right?"

"*Was*," I said sarcastically. "Apparently she was just using me all these years..." I started to tear up. I really had no idea, and I didn't want it to be true. I had always thought we were truly there for each other, like family.

Hunter came over and hugged me, rubbing my back. "Oh, honey, I'm so sorry, but she's just that *type*..."

As I stood in his arms all I could think about was what Emily said about smelling her on him at night and I pushed him away. "A type *you* seem to still want around apparently!"

From the look on Hunter's face I immediately knew it was true, but he still tried to cover. "What do you *mean...?*"

I ripped into him with a jealous fury that I wasn't even aware I was capable of. "She told me all about your secret, on-going affair—in fact, she announced it to the *whole* restaurant tonight!"

Hunter looked horrified, and definitely caught. "Calm down Mel, it was no big deal..."

He tried to hug me, but I pushed him away, crying. "You have to be the biggest liar and cheat on the planet! I can't believe you did this to me!"

"You know she's just a tramp... and yes, I was over-served a few times and took her home because she was handy... but you know she's just a bar-fly to me. It was all barely memorable because it was so *totally* meaningless to me... I don't want her... *you're* the one I'm in love with!"

"What?" I said, thinking I must not have heard him right.

"You're the one I *love*," he said, pulling me close to him. It was the first time he had ever said it out loud. "I love you, Melanie St. John," he repeated earnestly and very clearly, "and I've never loved anyone like this before, ever."

I was completely confused. I loved him too and knew it was different from the feelings I've had with anyone else ever before, but now finding out he'd been cheating on me—and even admitting it so casually, not even trying to deny it—that just didn't feel like part of true love, at least, not the kind I wanted.

"That's complete and utter bullshit to say to me right now and you know it!" I said, feeling Oldie would be proud. I was beginning to think Oldie was right all along. This guy couldn't be trusted.

"I was hoping for quite a 'different' response," he said, trying desperately to lighten the mood.

"I..." I started to say, looking deep into his eyes. I truly did love this man, but everything about this night was all too much. I needed to think. "—I love you too," I admitted quickly, "but I can't see you anymore," I added, then ran out of his house and drove home.

Both Whitney and my mom were out, so I entered my big, empty house and went straight up to my bedroom. I tried to sleep, but couldn't. I stayed up all night recounting the events of the day over and over in my head, jumping between what happened with Emily and then Hunter... *Why me? Why me?* I kept asking myself. I had lost the two most important people in my life in the span of only a few hours. How was I going to learn how to trust anyone—male or female—ever again? And the worst part was the man I truly loved more than anyone else I'd ever dated had finally told me he loved me—several times in fact—but this was not how I ever pictured the first time hearing it from him would be... Instead of remembering, I only wanted to forget. I cried for hours until there weren't any more tears left to shed.

The next morning Hunter called a dozen times in a row until my mother finally asked if I would please just talk to him because she was sick of hearing the phone ring.

"Hello?" I said, finally answering it.

"Oh my God Mel—I've been up all night thinking about you!" Hunter said, sounding like he really had been—and possibly even crying, too. "I'm *so* sorry! I didn't mean to hurt you—but please, you have to believe me, Emily means *nothing* to me—she's *nothing* like you—you're <u>magic</u>! No one makes me feel the way you do... you *have* to believe me! And when I told you I loved you I meant it—I'm just crushed thinking it's over between us... please, *please* Melanie, don't break up with me..."

"I'm sorry," I said. "But I don't trust you."

Hunter then went on and on about how much he cared for me and how 'different' I was from all the other women he ever dated. It was killing me to hear when all I kept thinking was he and Emily slept together behind my back.

"I have to go," I finally said, and hung up on him.

A couple hours later the doorbell rang. A delivery man entered the foyer with the biggest bouquet of flowers I had ever seen. I sank down on the floor to read the hand-written note attached:

> Dear Melanie,
>
> I'll try to explain what happened. Well, you know how Emily always flirted wildly with me. She's just that kind of girl. And I won't lie to you—she's hot.

I wished he had left <u>that</u> out, I thought; then continued reading:

> But it was all just a fling, honestly. We'd always been attracted to each other, and

I guess I just needed to get it out of my system still. I ran into her at the bar at the Palm a few months ago when we all got back from Aspen. She was pouring back margaritas like there was no tomorrow, complaining that her new, steady boyfriend was fat and bad in bed... she was getting really down about it because she missed having wild, great sex with someone hot...

I couldn't believe he was telling me all this in such detail—I almost stopped reading, but couldn't stop myself... I needed to know why he did this to me:

I tried to cheer her up by cracking jokes. We started laughing and drinking together. We were having a great time... she was so vulnerable though and said she needed someone to lean on and wanted someone to make her feel sexy again. I admit I was attracted to her, so I took advantage of the situation and took her home. But why didn't we think of you and stop ourselves? I know now that's what we should have done.

We talked about it afterwards and wanted to tell you, but we figured it only happened once and it wouldn't ever happen again, so we promised no one would ever find out. But then she started calling me, and kept calling. She became my secret, late-night date, but that's all. It stayed that way until all hell broke loose this weekend. I just told her it was over though between us, for <u>good</u>. She's history. It was all just sex, and the thrill of it was really in the risk and danger of getting caught. But once I lost you I realized it wasn't even worth it.

Once I lost you Melanie I lost the ability to even pretend to care about her anymore.

You're the real thing. You have to believe me. Sometimes you just have to play the field to realize who you really love. And I love you. I have since the first night I met you and I know I always will. I know I have a bad, playboy reputation and have had a lot of bad relationships in the past, but I only ever kept acting this way because I didn't know there was anything more, or better. Now I do, and I don't want to let you go, ever. Hopefully you can find it in your loving and generous heart to forgive a stud like me. I'll be waiting for you as long as it takes...

Yours,

Hunter

When I finished the letter I felt ill. I ripped it up into shreds and threw it away.

Screw him, I thought. *I can't be with someone who cheats!* I felt so betrayed, both by him and Emily. I wished Oldie was home. I needed to tell him he was right all along.

I felt horrible the whole next day, and by Monday it wasn't getting any better. Hunter continued to call, but I wouldn't talk to him. My mother didn't know what to do, so she just let me mope around the house and told me one day it all wouldn't hurt "so bad." I agreed with her about Hunter, for I had gotten over other men before in time, but it was my seemingly false friendship with Emily that I didn't know what to do about. I also wondered if what she said was all part of a drunken rant that she didn't even remember anymore. And though I now knew the part about the affair with Hunter was true, I still hoped the rest wasn't deep down. I truly thought of Emily as my best, and longest, friend ever. I decided to call her to find out—and give her a second chance.

"Hello?" she said as she answered.

"Hello, Emily, it's me," I said as I played with the phone's cord, trying not to sound as nervous as I was. "How are you feeling?"

"Fine," she said, completely annoyed.

I could tell she didn't want to be on long, so I got right to the point. "Ah, do you remember what you said the other night at dinner?"

"Yes," she said confidently. "Verbatim... would you like me to *repeat* any of it?"

I was completely shocked. "No," I said. "That's all then." I hung up, and instantly knew we would never speak again.

A few weeks went by and I was right; Emily never called back and made sure everyone we both knew—including Victoria—knew our friendship was officially 'over.' She had moved in with Jack and they moved in different circles from me, so luckily I didn't have to run into them either.

Oldie came home, and though he still couldn't disclose who his client was, he told me I had "dodged a real bullet with Morgan" he felt. I never asked if he—or whatever person was on trial—ever got jail time or not. Oldie was sad to see me so upset over breaking up with Hunter, but also secretly delighted as well. He seemed to feel it was his own personal victory just like with the bracelet incident, even though this time it was a decision I had made solely on my own.

Both my parents were shocked and upset when I told them Emily had ditched me completely for a life with Jack. I didn't tell them all the details, wanting to spare them from the hurt I knew they would have felt from being used like I was, but I think they figured it out anyway. Oldie told me when trying to find 'true' friends it was just like dating; it was usually best to try and stick with your own kind, just to be sure—though even *he* always tried to give everyone he met "the benefit of the doubt" at first until they truly did something to prove him wrong.

"Money does strange things to people—whether they have it or don't have it," Oldie would always say when Whitney and I were growing up. "You just never know how anyone's gonna act about it... ever."

I was beginning to realize, for the very first time, what he meant.

A few more weeks went by and each day bigger and better flowers arrived, each with a note that simply said: *Please call me.*

Whitney told me no one had seen Hunter out at any of the hot clubs or country club events either, which was highly unusual. It was as if we had both just stopped living since the split, and no one had ever seen Hunter act this way over a woman. He usually had another one immediately lined up, like when he went from Wendy Smith directly to me. I felt special then, but, if I was so 'special' then why'd he cheat on me behind my back the whole time we were together? It just didn't make sense. This must have been what Wendy felt like when she found out he was seeing me. I felt bad for her—and all the women he'd done this to over the years. I had to take a stand and stay away from that womanizer, for *all* of us.

The next day I received a pair of diamond earrings from Cartier in the mail with another handwritten note:

Dear Melanie,

I haven't heard one word from you and it really hurts. The more days that go by, the more painful it becomes for me. I just can't stand being alone any longer. I'm not even attempting to date anyone else. No one but you can fulfill my needs, help me through the nights. I'm listening to our song right now, "The First Time Ever I Saw Your Face." Remember when we danced to that in Aspen the first time we met? I knew then I was going to love you forever. I'll wait until hell freezes over for you to forgive me. I'm looking at a picture of you right now. Only you fit the bill, beautiful Melanie of my soul...

Yours,

Hunter

Give me a break! It sounds like he's been reading too many Hallmark cards, I thought as I lit it on fire and threw it in the fireplace. I kept the earrings. I figured I'd earned them.

The doorbell rang. I opened the front door hesitantly.

"Hey Squirt, is Whitney around?" Eva asked as she stood in the doorway.

"I hate it when you and Whitney call me that!" I said rudely. "And no, she's *not* here."

"Fine, sorry... man—what's wrong with you?" she said, letting herself in.

"The same thing that gets into all of us—and the reason why Whitney's not here right now."

"Oh, a *man?*" She grinned. "Where's she off to now?"

"I have no idea. There's a new one almost every week she's so boy crazy! It's ludicrous and I've given up even trying to keep track of who she's seeing and where they go."

"That's why I'm glad I'm out of that whole dating scene," Eva said, admiring her engagement ring.

All I could think was *'then why are you still dating Brian?'* but I knew it would be of no use to say out loud, so instead I said, "How *is* Dawson?"

"He's fine, but his parents—well, they're a whole *different* story…" She sat down in the living room, ready to 'visit,' even though I had made no attempt to ask her to stay and do so. But I knew with Eva, she wouldn't leave until *she* was ready, so I sat down next to her as she continued, "You know how they are on the board of many of Houston's biggest charities, right?"

I nodded.

"Well, they expected Dawson to marry someone from, as they say, his 'own backyard.'"

"No surprise there."

"Sure, and that's fine, but then he fell for *me*—and I'm <u>determined</u> to get him to marry me before they talk him out of it! You know they actually take him to dinner every single week at the club just to try and convince him to get rid of me? Even though *I'm* the one wearing his gorgeous ring…" She couldn't stop admiring it. I wondered if she left it on when she was with Brian.

"*Hmm,* imagine that," I said sarcastically.

"Oh shut up! I interrogated him about it all last night—just to see what they were really saying about me—and you know what? He told me his dad told me I was just a gold-digger and that he needed to focus on his schooling right now! And all his mom could talk to him about was my heritage and family and how I would never 'fit in' with any of them or *their* friends… She even said if we ever had any kids they'd have that 'hot, Latin blood' running through their veins—which was 'beneath' them… I am not at all what they expected for him…" she said softly, and I could tell though she was trying to hide it, it really hurt her. "'After all, you're our only son,'" she mimicked mockingly, "'and we only want the <u>best</u> for you!' And when I asked Dawson what *he* said to all of that he just admitted, 'nothing.' He just sat there and took it from them 'cause he would *never* argue with his father—'Daddy' rules because he has *all* the money!"

"So does he usually listen to them?" I asked, wondering if her grand plan might actually not work out after all.

"Yes, but now it's pretty *hard* to…" She laughed as she put a devilish emphasis on the word 'hard.' "Because for Dawson to get rid of me now is next to impossible… especially when I show up at his apartment every night wearing nothing but a Burberry raincoat and stilettos. I'm a seductive breath of fresh air for him. I provide him with a much-needed break from his monotonous, nightly routine of studying."

"Listen to you… you're too much!"

"Hey, I'm hot and I *know* it!" she said proudly. "So I seduce him with all kinds of kinky gadgets I get at this little porn shop on Montrose—plus whipped cream, body oils, you name it! I don't leave *any* fantasy of his unfulfilled and he always folds like a cheap suit instead of ending it with me. And I won't stop until I hit the jackpot—which is walking down that aisle in a pure white, top designer wedding gown. I can picture his parents aghast and disgusted—but I don't give a shit about them."

"Ugh, you're disgusting! I can't believe you'd stoop to those kinds of levels just to keep him!" I said, but then admitted sadly, "Then again, I wish Hunter would have given *me* that kind of attention every night instead of leaving time for his own 'extracurricular activities' with my *ex*-best friend."

"Wow, you're really still torn up about him, aren't you? I don't think I've ever seen you in such a mood…"

"I loved him," I said tearfully, "and still do. I've never felt this way about anyone before, and I don't know if I'll ever again… But he cheated on me just like he did on every other woman he's ever dated, and now I don't trust him."

"Melanie, sex is sex! Everybody loves to do it, so what's the big deal? Why don't you just go with the flow—let him come back to you— then get yourself a little 'boyfriend' on the side too—then you'll forget all about his extracurricular affairs! Women do it all over the world, you know."

"No way, I'm sorry, but that just doesn't work for me. Hunter screwed up and now I'm letting him sweat it out. And if I ever *do* decide to take him back and give him another chance I will make him promise to *never* cheat on me again!"

Eva smiled understandably, but also like I wasn't getting it, and never would. "Oh Mel, I know his type, and it's pretty rare that a leopard like him is *ever* going to change his spots."

I nodded, but didn't want to believe it. I still had faith in Hunter.

Eva knew my mind was made up and didn't want to waste her time trying to convince me I was wrong. "Well, since Whitney's not here, I'm going to get going," she said as she stood up. I walked her back towards the front door. "Maybe I can offer you some more insights when you're ready…" Eva offered. "Will you call me when you take him back and things get bad again in the future?"

"Sure, Eva," I said as I opened the door for her. Then, as I shut it behind her, I thought sarcastically, *so you can reassure me that it can always be worse…*

Chapter 9

$\mathcal{A}$ few more weeks went by and the flowers and expensive gifts continued, each with a note that stated: *Melanie, I'm so sorry, please call me.*

After awhile even Oldie was starting to get impressed. "Well my God, Melanie," he said one particular day after admiring the recent love bracelet gift from Cartier's that was sent along with a huge bundle of roses mixed with wild orchids that all together must have cost a mint. "Maybe the boy's finally growing up and truly trying to change his ways... these kinds of gifts and flowers mean *business...*"

I was starting to think the same.

Then a few more days went by and I received a third note in the mail with a first class ticket to Monte Carlo.

> Dear Melanie,
>
> I can't take it any longer. This has become a hell that I have created for myself. I know no one is to blame but me. Please try to see me as just the dumb, unthinking fool I am. Please give me some hope that I can have another chance to make things right with us. It is all I think about. You are the only thing that matters to me. There is no one else I could spend the rest of my life with. We'd have such beautiful children together. Don't let the beautiful future we could have together slip through your fingers. I can promise you that you would come to regret it as much as I already do now. The time we aren't spending

together is a waste. Don't you see what we are missing by not being together this very minute? Our love gave my life meaning. Now I am lost and astray. Only you can light the way for me.

I've had so much time to think about the pain I've caused you and to know my thoughtless, shallow actions were only the actions of an immature, careless rogue. But this is just the kick in the ass I needed to wake up to just how much I truly do love and need you. Once again, I am so sorry. Just tell me what I must do to earn your forgiveness and respect. If I knew, I would do it this very moment. I am so ashamed of myself. Only you can take this self-loathing away. No one else understands me or loves me more than you do. This I am certain of.

I am enclosing a ticket to Monte Carlo. Please, go there with me this weekend so we can talk about all of this. Please call me Melanie... call me...

Yours,

Hunter

This time I felt he truly meant it. His words were so sincere, and he was talking about a future with me; a future that included children and spending the rest of our lives together. He did want a real, committed relationship like I did after all. He truly did feel the same. And I was ready to forgive him and start over. Besides, it was Monte Carlo, a place I loved, so there was no way I would have turned this trip down...

But then Hunter surprised me! He said we were going to Monte Carlo, but once we landed he changed his mind and took me to what he called the most "romantic Inn" he knew of in the South of France. It was called La Colombe d'Or and was nestled in the tiny French village of Saint Paul de Vence. It was a far cry from the Monte Carlo glitz and glamour. The inn opened in the 1920's and the walls were covered by paintings from some of the world's greatest artists. Some even lived there and exchanged a painting for a room and a meal. It was like a mini museum and you never knew what you would find around any corner… works from Chagall, Miro, Braque, Picasso, Matisse, and a great mobile by Alexander Calder even watched over the pool. It only had twelve, beautifully decorated suites and was like stepping back in time to another era when we were in ours. It had a grand bedroom off the parlor-like living room that was hidden behind a large, old French door. It also had a great balcony that was perfect for champagne breakfasts.

Hunter really put the romance factor to the highest level when he chose this place, and it was perfect—for we hardly ever left our antique, king-sized bed the whole trip… we made love, ate fresh fruit and delicious homemade pastries delivered by room service, and had a never-ending supply of chilled champagne always on hand. But most of all, we talked about our future… what our wedding would one day be like, what our children would look like and be named, and how our lives would be together until 'death do us part.' It was all just what I had hoped for and more. Hunter had learned his lesson and I gave him another chance out of pure love, for I truly believed he could and would change. He swore he would never cheat on me again. He was completely devoted to me now, and I to him.

On our way back to the airport, Hunter couldn't resist the allure of Monte Carlo since we were still so close though, so we spent another week at The Hotel de Paris enjoying fine food and wine, going out dancing and gambling, and growing even closer together as we spent even more time in bed. It was incredible—way better than the first time I was there—and I never wanted to be anywhere without him ever again by the time we boarded our plane home.

We were soon back to being the couple everyone talked about when we got back to Houston, and I was finally back to feeling alive and happy again. So was he. And this time, so was everyone else, even Oldie. It seemed I really had 'tamed' the modern day Houston Casanova—and I couldn't have been more thrilled. I knew it would all work out and I'd have the complete fairy tale beginning, middle, and ending now….

"Someday," Hunter said, "you'll be my wife and walk with me."

I was on cloud nine every time he said it, which was a lot over the next full year. And he continued to take me on trips all over the country and world, sharing all his favorite haunts and hideaways with me. I was now a part of his once secretive world, and he was all of mine. Everywhere we went we were treated like royalty, and I loved it. I now understood what Oldie meant when he said it was just more natural to be with your own kind, for Hunter and I were definitely cut from the same cloth when it came to enjoying the finer things in life, and we both appreciated it in each other as well. Oldie also appreciated how well Hunter took care of me, just as he always had, by treating me like a true princess. He and my mother looked forward to our wedding day as much as I did.

As we approached our one-year anniversary of making up, Hunter took me to his most favorite place of all—Las Vegas. He was a well-known high roller at Caesar's Palace there and every member of the hotel staff, including the manager, was subservient and obsequious to him the moment we arrived. In fact, the only thing I found out they couldn't do for us was redecorate the tasteless palatial suite Hunter always preferred to stay in, and I was a bit surprised at how much he *really* seemed to actually like it the first time I saw it...

I had never gone with Hunter to Las Vegas before because this was where he went with his guy friends to unwind, or to concentrate on his only chosen 'career' when he felt like having one—which was playing high-stakes blackjack. But I had heard so much about this 'fabulous place' over the past year that I wanted to finally see what all the fuss was about, especially since it was so important to him. But when I first entered the marble foyer to our suite I was bowled over by the tawdry brass and crystal fixtures stuck on every inch of available wall space. There were at least ten competing varieties of marble in the place. It was disorienting. *Tacky,* was all I could think of, but this was only the beginning... the entertainment space had a floor so polished you could see your reflection in the black marble titles, and faux Persian rugs so loud a maharajah would choke. It looked like it was decorated in the style of a Bedouin's tent... no, a Bedouin's tent looked better. All the cocktail tables and end tables were mirrored glass with brass legs. The artwork on the walls was nauseating—a perversion of badly done copies of surrealistic nudes. The artist's signature was as big as the images, and I wondered who would want to be so prominently associated with such a series of visual atrocities.

"Isn't this *great?*" Hunter said excitedly as he waited for my approval. I knew it meant a lot to him.

I immediately reached for the nearest magnum of Dom Perignon and was glad to see there were quite a few strategically placed throughout the suite on silver-plated wine stands; I was going to need them to survive *this* trip. "Oh, yes, just great," I said as I sipped away; then noticed a gold, completely nude ceramic nymphet wrapped around the stem of my crystal flute.

"Wait until you see the master bedroom!" Hunter exclaimed as he led me to it like a kid in a candy store and opened its huge, gold, double-doors.

It made any whorehouse décor look tame. I mean, since it was Vegas I was anticipating vulgar, but this was lightyears beyond my expectations... The bed was a huge, round island in the center of the room and it was covered by red and pink velvet drapes. Hunter drew them back and in the overhead mirror I saw the reflection of a jungle of gold, tasseled pillows and bolsters. In the wooden headboard there was a carved-out, gold-colored, bad artist's version of a Roman orgy. Only a few yards from the bed was an oversized, marble Jacuzzi. They clearly expected their guests to step from the bed immediately into the bath, or vice versa. I could only image what kind of sexcapades had preceded our visit to this den of iniquity.

The suite gave me the creeps; I wanted to get out of there as fast as possible. But these salacious surroundings seemed to only aggrandize Hunter's already over-inflated ego right off the charts and send his lothario-like-libido into overdrive as he looked at me.

"I'm so glad you could be here with me, Mel," he said earnestly, "for I've thought about you often whenever I've been here without you this past year."

I was glad to hear that since all I could think about was sex in this room, and lately I was starting to wonder if I could still trust him since we were starting to spend more time apart. Though I had no evidence of any other woman being in his life, at times, when he was away in places like this either alone or with friends, doubts still crept into my mind. After all, I knew what a great catch he was, and so did many other women. But he was always careful to shower me with attention and assurance whenever we were together that I was his *only* love—his future wife 'someday'—and I desperately wanted to believe that, so I decided to make the best of it and keep him happy without ever bringing up my suspicions. After all, they could all just be in my head...

"Thanks for sharing all this with me," I said, pretending to be impressed with the surroundings and suppressing my true mortification at the sheer tastelessness of it all. After all, I was in Las Vegas, and this flashy boudoir epitomized what 'The Strip' was all about. "I know it was the last private place you had, and it means a lot to me that you wanted to bring me here."

"I don't want to have any secrets from you, ever," Hunter said, taking me in his arms and kissing me. "You're the only one who can make me happy, 'Champagne Mel.' Do you realize that now?"

"Yes," I said. The last year did prove a lot and I realized I needed to relax and just trust him completely from now on. After all, he was going to be my husband someday soon... and I was very anxious for that. "And it's the same with me," I assured him.

Hunter seemed glad to hear this as he kissed me again.

"You know, you never cease to surprise me, Hunter," I told him, referring to both his day-to-day behavior and this room I still couldn't believe we were standing in after all the breath-taking, extravert, gorgeous places he'd taken me to around the world.

"Good," he said, "cause wait until you see this..."

He led me outside onto the three-tiered, white marble balcony, and I was immediately impressed with the beautiful, full view of the flashing neon strip below. It was the whole suite's one redeeming factor, and I knew because of it I could stay there awhile.

We drank several bottles of Donnie P that were waiting for us on the terrace as we watched the colorful lights of the strip twinkle on and off like a disco light show, and after awhile I really was beginning to like the place. Besides, I could be anywhere with Hunter and be happy. We kissed and gazed out over the neon jungle as he enthusiastically imparted to me all the illicit secrets he knew about the professional gambler's game—high-stakes blackjack.

I listened intently as he trained me in all the lucrative, veiled subterfuge of blackjack and relished the excitement of becoming a card shark one day myself. Here, I realized, Hunter was truly in his element and I now understood why he came here so often. Gambling unleashed all his ruthless lust for money and let him let go of his insidious distain for the "safe and ordinary" kind of lifestyle most people lived. He felt he had more passion than most people did for life, and taking these bold, arrogant—and often even lawless—high risks at the blackjack table allowed him to prove that, to himself and to others.

"The two times I feel the most alive and unstoppable on this whole planet is when I'm either here gambling," he said earnestly, "or making love to *you*."

The power of his unflinching confidence as he said it transferred into my veins like an electric current, and suddenly the danger of being with a dark, handsome, 'outlaw' gambler here in sin city—or anywhere—felt mesmerizing; and the security that only his expertise could provide for me in this reckless, lasciviousness environment made me sink against his tan, muscular chest like a worshipful kitten, hungry to be in his potent grip forever.

"Show me," I purred in his ear, and he picked me up and carried me back inside to the bed.

I continued to carry on my fairy-tale-like romance with Hunter for the next several months, having romantic adventures with him all over the world, seemingly oblivious to anything else happening around me. We were in our own world, and it was one I never wanted to get out of.

Victoria and I talked occasionally over the phone, and when we did it was always about the same three things: Hunter's and my latest fun, romantic trip, the latest man her mother was trying to fix her up with in Florida, and how she still hoped to one day go to New York to try and model. Her older brother was now living in Manhattan and working in banking like their father once did, so Victoria felt once he got a bit more settled she would ask him if she could stay with him for awhile until she could get a place of her own. Her mother didn't want to lose both her children to the big city though; therefore she kept Victoria's social calendar as full as possible, but no man ever seemed to make Victoria change her mind about wanting to stay.

Whitney didn't seem to be having any better luck, though she dated twice as much as anyone I had ever known—including Emily. But she just didn't see the point of sticking around with one man once she already knew she had found someone else 'better.' I told her if that was her attitude, she would always *be* looking.

Meanwhile, Eva had gotten her wish of finally walking down the aisle in a pure white, designer wedding gown at an extravagant, no-expense-spared wedding at Houston's most exclusive country club. Once the date was set she had come over to our house to show Whitney the guest list, and it looked like she had invited half of Houston.

"How could you possibly know all these people?" Whitney snipped.

"Oh Whitney, don't worry so much!" Eva responded. "Who cares if I know them? I'm sure Dawson's parents know them—or 'of' them all anyway—because they keep telling me they know *everyone...*"

Eva and Dawson tied the knot a few weeks later (Eva didn't want to waste any time), and of course after the lavish wedding she wanted the most elaborate, magical honeymoon possible. After all, money was no object anymore, so she went to a travel agency and told some underpaid, overworked agent there that she wanted a "trip around the world in forty-five days." She insisted she would only stay in five-star hotels and only fly first class the whole time. The travel agent cobbled together an extremely luxurious trip and Eva was thrilled. She told Dawson about it and he was so tired from the wedding and medical school that he just nodded and gave her his credit card... his first *big* marriage mistake... never, ever give Eva a "limitless" credit card!

The "unrefundable" trip was a complete disaster. Eva and Dawson spent most of their time in airports hopping from one country to the next. The travel agent, trying to impress Eva, had put too many destinations on the itinerary, and Dawson was furious at both the cost and how exhausting it all was. The rest of us couldn't stop laughing when they returned; knowing Dawson was in for a lifetime of these kinds of 'adventures' with Eva as his wife.

I wished Eva had called me for advice about her honeymoon plans, for I had become quite the world traveler with Hunter and could have given her many pointers to make their whole trip go a lot smoother. Hunter and I went everywhere together and the next couple of years just seemed to fly by as we continued to travel the globe endlessly: London, San Francisco, Paris, Maui, Rome, Sydney, Montreal, Cozumel, Madrid, the Greek Isles, Nova Scotia, a voyage on *The Queen Elizabeth II*, and many, many more. It was the beginning of the eighties—the decade of indulgence—and we both loved being able to indulge and live a life of pure leisure.

We also naturally settled into a routine of going to places like Las Vegas at least once a month, Aspen every Christmas to celebrate where we met, both France and Monte Carlo every summer to celebrate where we made up, and then we used the rest of the world as a place to explore in between. It was a life of fun, adventure, and romance as we lived off our now-shared trust funds and didn't have to think about making a living; though Hunter did make quite a bit from gambling overall and I always knew he could use that as a way to support us, if needed. I knew I would always be taken care of just the way Oldie expected me to be as long as I stayed by Hunter's side. But I wanted to do so as his wife—not just his girlfriend—and as the years went on this desire grew stronger and stronger. But whenever I'd bring it up, Hunter would always change the subject or simply say he wasn't quite 'ready' to settle down, but would be 'someday,' for sure. I couldn't imagine marrying anyone else, so I stayed, and waited....

"I don't know, Lil' Bit," Oldie said one day when I was waiting for Hunter to pick me up for dinner to celebrate our fourth anniversary of being together. "Seems to me if Hunter was serious about getting married to you, he would have done it by now."

"Oh Daddy," I heard myself saying in a child-like tone just like Whitney did when she was trying to either win him over, or change the subject. "It's the eighties—people don't get married at eighteen anymore! I'm still only twenty-four, and Hunter's not even thirty."

"He's just about," Oldie pointed out, which was true. He'd be thirty soon.

"He'll ask me soon, maybe even tonight!" I said hopefully as I saw Hunter's car pull up to our house. I quickly left before Hunter or Oldie had time to cross paths. I knew Oldie would only bring the whole marriage thing up, and I was already doing that in specific time frames that were more appropriate than the obvious—like an anniversary dinner—though I hoped for *these* events Hunter would choose to bring it up himself any-way... but he never did.

And it wasn't long after Oldie said that to me that I suddenly seemed to have even bigger problems to worry about with Hunter than whether or not he was ever going to give me a ring—for he didn't always call when he said he would and he would occasionally stand me up altogether, something he had never done to me before. My doubts about being able to trust him again resurfaced, frequently. We had an unmistakable chemistry and attraction to each other still, but besides that, some of our initial magic was definitely gone and I didn't know how to bring it back—though I was determined to try, for however long it took...

Then, one day out of the blue it seemed, strange women suddenly started "popping up" everywhere around us, acting surprised to still see me at his side. Hunter always had some reason for somehow knowing them from his 'past,' but some of these women would have had to have met him when they were thirteen to be able to go back before the last *five* years of being with me. And I was also finding evidence of these women around his house in the form of clothing or lipstick stains that I knew weren't mine. But every time I called him on it I was always given either a 'reasonable' excuse, or an all-out apology that he had 'slipped' and it would never, *ever* happen again. But it did, often. And we soon found ourselves in a hellish merry-go-round of "together-today, broken-up tomorrow, then back-together-once-*again.*" I wanted to get off this crazy, dysfunctional ride, but I was too deep into both him and all the time I'd put into the relationship by now to have the strength to jump off. So, I stayed... despite everyone's warnings, especially Oldie's.

Then, one night I was out late with some friends celebrating my twenty-*seventh* birthday, and as I blew out the candles on the cake I couldn't believe that I had reached this point in my life without getting married and starting the family I had always wanted. Hunter had always said we would do it all 'someday.' Well, to me, someday was right now.

I drove straight to Hunter's house even though it was two in the morning to tell him how I felt. We were supposed to leave for Aspen the next day for a two-week Christmas vacation, so I figured he'd be up packing like he normally was before going on a long trip. But to my surprise another woman's car I knew was parked in front of his house. I knew her name was Rosa and she had liked him for awhile now. Whenever she saw us at the country club where she worked as a waitress she always flirted with him just like Emily used to.

I went to the door and rang the bell at least a hundred times, but Hunter never answered. I went home and called him for the next two hours straight, but he never picked up. I finally fell into a fitful sleep.

Hunter called me the next day and acted as if nothing unusual happened. "Are you ready for Aspen?" he asked causally.

"Why was Rosa's car in front of your house last night?" I said, confronting him.

"*Whose?*" He pretended not to recognize her name.

"Rosa—the waitress from the club who always over-serves you and drools all over you!" I reminded him.

"Oh, *her*," he said like she was a complete afterthought. "Yeah, she came by so we could do a séance. She's really into that sort of thing, and it was something I'd always wanted to try."

"A *séance*?" I repeated, dumbfounded. "You must think I'm utterly braindead to believe such an absurd explanation! Well, I hope you enjoyed it, because you can now continue *it* over the next two weeks in Aspen with *her*—'cause I'm not going!"

We argued and screamed over his cheating on me again until I finally hung up on him, telling him *this* time it was *really* over before I did. Then I immediately began to pray that it truly was.

A few days later, Hunter called me from Aspen. "Melanie," he pleaded with me over the phone. "Please, *please* come see me. I can't bear being here without you. We've never been apart for Christmas for the past seven years... we can't start now... I promise it was just a mistake and it won't ever happen again. I promise to be good to you and you know I always am here!"

I missed him so much I convinced myself that he meant it and gave in. "Are you *really* going to change and *never* do it again?" I didn't even want to think of how many times I had asked him that before.

"Yes, I promise," he said, as usual, through his tears. "You're the only one who can stop me from being like this Mel... I don't care about anyone else enough to, but with you, I just know I can finally give up needing any other woman, ever. I only need *you...*"

It hurt so badly to hear this over and over from him because all I really wanted to believe was that Hunter was a good guy deep down inside and that he truly did need and love me. I wanted to be the one to save him. I wanted to be the one who could make him realize what he did was wrong because—like he just said and *always* said—I felt I really *was* the only one who could stop him from being like this. No one ever told him how to behave with women before I came along, and he was grateful to learn how to treat them from me. Every time he 'slipped up' like this I felt like I had somehow failed at getting through to him, but yet, I also truly believed if I just showed him even more unconditional love it would sway him enough to finally stay faithful for good because no one else had ever given him that much love.... I loved him so much, with all my heart and soul, so I was always willing to forgive him and get back on the merry-go-round for another ride. But this time, I *really* thought he had finally learned his lesson for good and was really, *finally* going to change...

So the next day I once again found myself perched on top of Red Mountain, in Hunter's family home, while my own family went on a cruise that year. (Oldie had sold our Aspen house a few years earlier since no one besides me went there anymore, and when I did I always stayed with Hunter anyways.)

Two blissful days went by and everything seemed to be perfect between us amongst the idyllic setting. We skied, visited the shops, and visited with his parents and older sister Catherine (who was recently divorced) over good food and wine. I felt so warm inside at the thought that everything was *finally* going to be okay from here on out. The wild ride was over, or so I thought...

"Hunter," I said on our third night there at the start of our first dinner out together alone. He seemed distracted and kept looking across the room behind me. "Hunter! Did that last run down Spar Gulch wear you out? You're not your usual self tonight."

"What? No, I'm fine," he muttered, starring over my shoulder. "You're so paranoid. Have some more champagne."

Moments later a beautiful woman walked by wearing a full-length mink coat. She seemed to slow down momentarily near our table; then quickened her pace as she continued on towards the back of the restaurant. Hunter reached down towards the floor.

"Did you lose something?" I asked.

Ignoring my question, he abruptly stood up and muttered, "I have to go to the men's room!"

After he left I turned around to see if I could determine what had been commanding his attention. And then I saw her—the woman who had just passed our table, seated with a large group of people at the far end of the room. She was very exotic-looking with long black hair, dark olive skin, and slightly slanted, pretty eyes. As I stared at her I recognized her immediately as a personal shopping salesclerk from the couture department at *Neiman Marcus* back in Houston, only now here she was, dripping in diamonds and fur from head to toe. I had been there with Hunter several times to buy clothes from her department, and I had last heard she had hooked-up with an entourage of Arabs and left her job behind. Her name was Julie something...

"Come on Mel, let's go," Hunter said as he suddenly appeared back at our table. "I'm tired and not very hungry, so I just paid the check for our drinks."

I actually was very hungry, but I didn't want to cause a scene with so many people around, so we left. We drove back to his parents' house in silence, and once inside he was completely unresponsive to anything I said or did. I finally gave up trying and went to bed.

The next morning he flung open the bedroom door very early and shouted, "Get up, Melanie! I'm taking you to the airport... there's an empty seat on my dad's best friend's Lear jet and it leaves for Houston in less than an hour."

"What are you talking about?" I said, confused. "I just got here practically and I'm supposed to stay another week!"

"Get your luggage packed," he ordered, pulling out my suitcases for me. "Something has come up and I have to fly to Vegas on business, so you're going back to Houston, like it or not."

"What could be happening for 'business' in Vegas? Your whole family is all *here!*" I said.

"It's not 'that' kind of business," he said. "And don't ask me about it or even argue with me—just pack!"

I didn't understand why he was being so dismissive and cruel. This was definitely a new side of him, and I didn't like it at all. But I had no choice, so I quickly packed and went downstairs.

I hugged his sister and Mother good-bye sadly. It was clear by the looks of their faces they knew something I didn't.

Later that night, when I was back in Houston, Catherine was quick to contact me. "Melanie?" she whispered into the phone as if she was a secret spy. "Mom doesn't want to get involved, saying that what happens between you and Hunter isn't our business, but screw *that!* My brother's a scumbag and I'm sick of seeing him do this to you!"

"What?" I said, shocked at what I was hearing, for I didn't really know Catherine all that well since she was ten years older than me and lived in California, so we didn't see each other much or have much in common besides Hunter.

"Melanie, you're a really nice girl, the nicest one Hunter's ever dated actually, and you deserve so much more than him."

"What do you know that you're not telling me, Catherine?" I was shocked I even asked the question; for I wasn't sure I really wanted to know.

"You know what his sudden 'business' was in *Vegas?*"

"No. He wouldn't tell me."

"Well, it wasn't even to go! Mom found a matchbook that had the name 'Julie' with a note telling him to meet her at the first lift in Snowmass this morning at eleven. So now you understand what all the urgency to get *you* out of Aspen early was for!"

"Oh my God," I said, realizing she must have dropped the matchbook right in front of both of us at the restaurant. "I know who that is—she dropped that matchbox right in front of my eyes, only at the time, I didn't see it."

"Well Hunter sure did," Catherine said with disgust. "Anyway, you need to stay away from him. He's now treating you like every other girl he's ever dated and back to thinking he's above everyone else. It's disgusting!"

Hearing that cut through my heart like nothing else ever had… I had always thought I truly was 'different' like he said. But apparently, I wasn't.

"I have to go," I told her before I fell apart. "But thank you for telling me this, Cath."

"I'm sorry I had to because believe me—I *know* what it's like from hearing about my own cheating, scumbag-*ex*-husband—but I just don't want to see you keep getting hurt."

"Thanks," I told her, and hung up. I buried my head in my pillow, screaming and crying. I truly had believed Hunter could change, but now I realized I was just stupid for thinking that all this time and Eva was right. He was <u>never</u> going to change his spots!

I started receiving flowers the very next morning (of course), which I repeatedly kept sending straight back to the florist with a "return to sender" message. The day after Hunter arrived back in Houston—which was ten days later—I received flowers *and* a hand written note.

I read the note and felt ill as it said all the same, tired old words of "sorry" and "needing 'only' me still…" I ripped it into shreds and walked towards the garbage can.

Screw him, I thought. *More of his B.S.—and I'm not taking it anymore!*

I started to throw it away, but then had a better idea. I went straight to Hunter's house to confront him. "This is complete and utter *bullshit* and you know it!" I told him, throwing the pieces of his letter right back at him like confetti as soon as he opened the door. "I can't do this anymore Hunter… it's killing me emotionally and physically. We're through!"

"Melanie, please, no—don't say that—" he said, grabbing my arm so I couldn't leave. "I'm really sorry, but I was just being selfish again… I'm sorry I keep screwing up."

"You mean 'screwing' period!" I said, still thinking of him being with Julie this whole time and not me.

"Look, she meant *nothing* to me. She was just a whore like all the rest. You saw how *she* came after *me*—what kind of girl does that? Not the kind like *you,* the kind I want to be with for the rest of my <u>life!</u>" He said it with such sincerity that it made my heart skip a beat.

He could tell I was softening at the sound of spending our lives together. It had been a long time since either one of us had brought it up. "Listen, how 'bout I make it up to you by taking you to Vegas tonight?" He rubbed my arm up and down affectionately.

"*Now?*" I said. His spontaneity always both excited and irritated me.

"Yeah," he said, stroking the side of my face. "Let's just go on one more trip, and I promise, if it doesn't go the way you hope it will, we'll never see each other again…"

He was daring me, which only showed he was already in 'Vegas mold' and truly meant it. Hunter never bluffed when gambling unless he had something 'wild' hidden up his sleeve. I was dying to know what that was.

"Okay," I agreed. "*One* more trip to make this right, Hunter. But that's *it*."

After we arrived in Vegas later that evening it took me awhile to acclimate myself to Hunter's usual, tacky, Caesar's Palace palatial suite after we were led up to it by the bellboy. Hunter was unusually thrilled to be in his "gambler's paradise surroundings" again. It had been at least two months, which for him was like a lifetime.

"Champagne?" Hunter offered as he poured the chilled liquid into two awaiting flutes, knowing I wouldn't refuse one.

"Thank you," I said, taking the glass and sipping it.

"Thank *you* for coming with me and giving me another chance," he said. I could tell he still knew he was in the doghouse, and he was doing his best to get out of it.

"I'm hoping it will be the last time I have to," I said, "because I mean it Hunter... I do love you, but I can't keep doing this. No one deserves to be treated this way."

"I know," he said, and I could tell his head was spinning with the weight of the situation.

No sooner did we finish our one glass of bubbly each when Hunter insisted we go downstairs to gamble. It was already close to midnight, and in the world of high-stakes blackjack that meant the night was just about to really begin.

Hunter sat down at the table with enthusiasm as I sat next to him, wondering how long we were going to be there that night.

"Well, it looks like *somebody* is ready to gamble!" the young, sexy female dealer said in a seductive tone towards Hunter, not even paying attention to me. I looked her over and was not impressed. She was a freckled, blue-eyed redhead who wore the regulation, skintight bunny suit well. Her nametag was prominently displayed above her ample cleavage and read: "Candi," which didn't surprise me a bit.

Hunter gambled without abandon and quickly lost ten grand. Naturally, he was very angry about it, but Candi only encouraged him. "That's the breaks, sir. But hey, you're just getting started, right? Ante *up?*"

I had seen this kind of thing happen before and knew she was paid to keep him playing if he was on a losing streak—which also could have had a lot to do with the fact that she was also trying to keep him 'distracted' from his cards the whole time—so I finally pulled him away from both her and the table. "Hey, you need to take a break from the gambling and the 'double-D's,'" I told him. "…In fact, you're more focused on *them* than on the cards, which is probably why you're losing so much!"

"I am not!" Hunter said, denying it.

"She has you totally mesmerized—though I can't see how cause she's totally tacky!"

"Stop being so paranoid—"

"I'm not paranoid, I'm completely sober and I can tell every little trick she's doing to get your attention and money from you! 'You're just getting started, sir,'" I mimicked flirtatiously. "Give me a break! Listen, I know you'll make that money back in no time later, but why don't *we* now take a 'break…?'" I gave him a look that let him know I wasn't talking about a smoke break. We went back upstairs to our suite.

We ordered some room service and drank more champagne. It didn't take long for Hunter to calm down and completely focus all his attention on me again. It was back to normal, and I was happy.

"Melanie," Hunter started, seeming a bit nervous, which I found sweet. "Thanks for pulling me away from the table down there. You really understand me… I don't walk where others walk, and you're not afraid to walk with me no matter where I go anywhere in the world. And now, I want you to walk with me somewhere we've both *never* been…" He reached into his pocket and pulled out a sapphire and diamond ring that exploded under the Vegas strip lights. It was stunning and beautiful, but clearly not your typical, traditional engagement ring—but with Hunter, nothing ever was. My heart melted when I saw it.

"Will you walk with me, Melanie St. John?" he asked.

"Anywhere," I said as I kissed him. He kissed me back ravenously and then ripped open the top of my blouse as buttons went flying. His powerful hands searched for my breasts as I removed his shirt and did the same with his hard pecs… I surrendered to his strong, muscular arms and he picked me up, carried me into the bedroom, and laid me down onto the soft pillows. He desperately grasped at his belt buckle and ripped off his pants, then my skirt, and he climbed on top of me. The more I sighed with pleasure the more impassioned he became. He rolled over and over me, cradling me in his arms, as he whispered, "I'll love you forever, Melanie."

"And I will love you too, Hunter," I said looking straight into his eyes, "for the rest of our lives."

I pledged to spend the rest of my life with him in bliss, and he agreed to do the same. I felt bound with him in one body, mind, and spirit. I knew nothing could come between two people who loved each other this much, who had fought this hard to stay together. It had all worked out perfectly now, and if such a profound bond could exist between such an irresistibly, desirable man and myself, then I felt I must be the most alluring and beautiful woman on earth—or even the whole universe. He made me feel like a goddess, and making love to him so passionately made me feel invincible. I loved him more in this moment than I had ever loved him before. In an instant it seemed our love had grown even deeper, and it continued to do so with each thrust.

Afterwards, as I laid there cooing and snuggling contently against his broad, muscular torso, I dreamed of our loving, magnificent future together. After an appropriate, but also calculated smidgen of time, Hunter stood up in a regal manner and got dressed.

"I just got my 'power' back," he said jokingly while I gazed at his Adonis-like body, still wrapped in my cocoon of security. I smiled at him seductively as I rose up from the bed, completely nude, and stepped into the Jacuzzi for a sensual bath.

Hunter kissed me good-bye passionately. "If my luck doesn't change downstairs I'll be back up sooner than later."

I only smiled back as I let the soapy suds wash over my wet, bare breasts and run down towards my torso, and then sank down beneath the water. Hunter sighed with anticipation and left in a rush.

He was gone quite a while, so I felt tonight must really be his "lucky" night.

We flew back to Houston the next morning and I immediately called Oldie to tell him the good news.

"So you're really engaged?" Oldie said as if he needed to hear it twice before he'd believe it.

"Yes," I repeated. "We are!"

"Well," Oldie said, still a bit apprehensive, "then I guess now it's time to call that S.O.B.'s bluff."

"What do you mean, Oldie?" I said. "Hunter really proposed this time! I even got a ring!"

"That's great, Mel," Oldie said, but I could tell he still wasn't convinced. "Then let's all have dinner tomorrow night together to celebrate... we'll call it a 'celebration showdown.'"

I just sighed and agreed. I knew it was going to take a lot of convincing for a lot of people to understand that we were finally getting it all right.

We went to dinner at the Confederate House the following night. After several scotch and sodas, Oldie confronted Hunter at the table in front of my mother and me. "Hunter," he started in full lawyer mode, "you've been dating my daughter for *how* long now?"

He knew the answer, but wanted to hear Hunter say it out loud as evidence.

"Seven years," Hunter replied.

"Seven years..." Oldie repeated slowly. As I heard him say it out loud like that it suddenly dawned on me that it seemed like a very, *very* long time, but throughout most of the last seven years I was just so focused on this particular moment of engagement as my main goal that it didn't seem too long, well *most* of the time. "Well, since you made us all wait so *long* for this happy moment to finally get here, I think we ought to waste no time announcing the engagement properly to everyone. Melanie's mother and I would like to give you an engagement party at the club, and I'll put the announcement in the newspaper myself. I've already talked to the club's event planner and she's just ecstatic about it."

"Yes," my mother added happily. "She thinks she can have a fabulous party arranged in just a few weeks even."

As my parents spoke I could see Hunter getting visibly uncomfortable. He shifted in his seat and kept adjusting himself.

"We'll have one hell of a good time and serve only the *best* champagne," Oldie continued gleefully. "Melanie can choose the menu, the guest list, and whatever else she wants—flowers can be flown in from wherever—Holland even!"

Hunter's usually suntanned face went ashen. "Well... um, sir—I mean, Mr. St. John," he stammered. "Are you saying you want to announce our engagement to like... *everyone?* Because I don't think I'm quite ready for a public announcement."

"What do you mean?" Oldie said, seeming stunned.

"Well, I'm really fine with the way things are... Mel and I are together, well, 'engaged,' and you know it, and my parents know it, and it should just be left at that for now."

Oldie stared at Hunter for what seemed like an eternity. Suddenly, he pounded his fist on the table, getting the whole restaurant's attention, as he yelled, "That's BULLSHIT Hunter and YOU *KNOW* IT! This whole engagement thing to my daughter is bullshit to you! Either you agree to this engagement party *and* newspaper announcement in <u>print</u> right now, or else—"

"You know what?" I interrupted, stopping my father in mid-sentence, which wasn't easy to do. "I agree with Oldie, Hunter..." I turned towards Hunter and looked him straight in the eye. "If you're really serious about being with me, then what in the world is wrong with announcing it and having a party? If you don't want to do that then it must mean you have no plans to actually *get* married, and you're only using this ring as a way to get me to keep hanging around waiting for another seven, eight, or even *nine years!*"

"'Engagement' ring," Oldie muttered. "That supposed 'engagement' ring you gave my daughter is a <u>joke</u>! It looks like a Goddamn cocktail ring! No one would ever even *know* it meant marriage unless you told 'um!"

"Yeah," I agreed, now studying it. "You've taken me to *Tiffany's* to look at *real* engagement rings so many times I've lost count, so you had to have known which one I liked. Or is engagement ring shopping yet another one of your favorite sports to do with women that I'm just not aware of yet?" My anger grew by the second as I thought about the reality of what I'd just said. "Hunter," I continued, "if you don't agree to this engagement party right now then we're finished and I mean it—finished, over, <u>period</u>!"

"And I'll make sure she keeps her word on that *this* time," Oldie added sternly.

Hunter looked at both of us with stone cold eyes and released his pent-up anger. "I'm not going to be forced into having an engagement party— and if you dare question my intentions then this engagement is <u>off</u>!" He threw his napkin on the table, got up, and stormed out of the restaurant.

I got up from the table and chased after him like a complete lovesick fool. I caught up with him in the restaurant's parking lot just as the valet was bringing his car around.

"Hunter, what are you doing?" I cried hysterically. "Is this really over after all these years? Is this how it ends, in the parking lot, just like that?"

Hunter glared at me with eyes completely void of any emotion at all as he fired back, "Yes Mel, it's *over!* And don't bother calling me to try and change my mind—*ever!* We're 'finished, *over,* <u>PERIOD!</u>'" He mocked my same exact words, though I knew he really meant it as he said each one.

I was completely stunned as I watched his black Mercedes drive off into the cold and rainy Texas night. He said those last three words to me with such clarity and conviction that I could never have failed to get his real message. Oldie and I had really rattled his cage and shaken him to the core, and he had made up his mind and told me it was over between us, finally, for good.

As I stood in the parking lot a light went off in my confused brain. I realized that I had done nothing wrong by wanting to have a formal engagement party. It's every girl's right, especially after dating for so many years. But when called out to go through with it, Hunter bent like a cheap piece of tin. This time I had to summon the courage to stay away from him and let it really be over. *Oh my God, it's <u>really</u> over,* I thought... the realization of that hit me like a lightning bolt and I suddenly felt very, very tired.

I then felt Oldie's strong arm around my shoulder, and I was grateful to rest my head on his chest as I sobbed into his arms. "Oldie, Hunter just left me... he told me our engagement is really over and to not call him again, ever! Can you believe anyone could be so heartless and cold?"

"He's an S.O.B. and I never liked him from day one," Oldie said. "He was never going to be good enough for you, Lil' Bit. He tried at times, but I could always still see right through him. He was a complete ass and I want you to remember this isn't your fault. You're a very beautiful girl and you're very smart… there are plenty of more fish in the sea that will be lining up just waiting to take you out. I hate to see you this upset and your mother and I will do anything we can to help you get through this nightmare, but I know you will because you are strong… Remember, when life happens, you happen b—"

"*Back…*" I repeated with him in unison, trying to smile through my tears.

The next few days were awful. Though I knew I shouldn't, all I did was lay around the house in my pajamas and stare at the phone, hoping Hunter would call me, but he didn't. I'd put all my energy, hopes, and expectations into this one man who'd I'd grown from a teenager practically into full adulthood with. And now sadly, we'd never grow old together like we always talked about, and as I always anticipated. I wouldn't have his beautiful children. I would never wake up to his beautiful, sleepy smile ever again. I would never feel his hot, muscular body against mine ever again. I was going crazy missing him, but I was also realizing I was also scared because I didn't know who I really was without him. To love Hunter fully meant I had to suppress who I was in order to please him most of the time we were together. And I had done it for so long now—from age twenty to twenty-seven—that there was now very little left of me except for an empty shell filled with unbearable pain. Recovering from Hunter and finding out who I was again would be a long road back to full emotional wellness. My life, stripped of illusions, didn't look very pretty or rosy at the moment. I was dead inside, stung, and scorched. I felt no one would ever want to marry me and I would become a bitter old maid. All I could do was sob… and my parents were truly great, for they just left me alone and let me.

No flowers came, or gifts, or notes…. I couldn't actually believe it. Hunter had never stopped everything like this cold turkey before, so I knew he really meant it. It was over, and I was just going to have to accept it… somehow… someway. And just when I thought I'd never hear from Hunter Wells Carrington the Third ever again—exactly thirteen-and-a-half days after our break-up—he finally called, 'just to see how I was doing.'

Hmmm… let's see, I thought. *Well, I can't eat, so I look like a walking skeleton, I can't sleep, so I stay up all night watching bad movies, I've been in the same jogging suit every day because I never have the energy or desire to put on anything else, or clean…. I've talked to two therapists who both said I'm suffering from 'deep depression' and they each want me to go on a different medication… oh—and I can't stop crying, but aside from all that, I'm—*

"Doing friggin' great!" I told him sarcastically. "Never been better!"

"Good, because after the last time I saw you, I thought you'd be an emotional wreck by now," Hunter said.

He sounded surprised that I was doing so well, so apparently he didn't get the sarcasm, but I was too afraid to start a fight. It was good just to hear his voice again at this point. "I'll be fine, Hunter," I said, trying hard to sound sincere. "How are *you?*"

"Well actually, that's why I called," he said, and I only hoped he was about to say he was going through everything I was, and worse. "I wanted to tell you first before you heard it from someone else..."

My heart sank, for just from his change of tone I knew it wasn't anything about him wanting to get back together with me. He was happy and excited, almost giddy even.

"I've moved to Las Vegas and I'm living with Candi, the girl I met the last time we were there—"

"The *blackjack* *d*ealer? The one who wears a *bunny* suit?" I almost dropped the phone.

"Yes!" He gloated over his new possession. "And I could care less if she's a blackjack dealer... having an Ivy League education and a major background doesn't matter to me anymore. She's struggling and hard-working and I admire that in her. And I'm not in lust like usual either—I think this time it's actually <u>love</u>!"

I couldn't believe what I was hearing. "So you didn't love *me* then?"

"Not like this—it's hard to explain, but it's just so 'different'... she's a single mom too, and I'm really enjoying being a step-dad to her three-year-old son. It's like we're already a family!"

"Wait—" I said, now letting it all fully register. "So you're *really* living there, in Las Vegas, with *her?*"

"Yes, for over a week now."

"A WEEK!" I screamed, thinking of what I had been through for the past almost two full weeks trying to let go of him—of us—and now he's telling me he only took a few *days* to move on...? "So you've gone from debutantes to casino dealers now?" I asked in disbelief.

"Yes, and I've never been happier."

"If this is your choice Hunter then I think you're out of your fucking *mind!*" I was so sickened by this conversation and the fact that he could think so little of me and our relationship that I suddenly felt he wasn't worth crying over anymore. I gathered strength I didn't even know I had left and added, "Don't *ever* call me again." I hung up and threw the phone across the bedroom as hard as I could. It smashed an heirloom mirror, but I was too numb to care.

The next day I got a surprise visitor.

"How are you doing?" Catherine asked as she entered my room. My mom must have let her in, because I didn't even hear the doorbell. Luckily

Oldie was away on business, because I don't think if he were home he'd let her up due to her association with the 'enemy.'

I tried to straighten myself up, but it was no use. I looked awful, but Catherine looked like she completely understood.

"Don't worry," she smiled. "I didn't expect to see you at your best."

"Oh Cath," I cried, glad for someone who really knew Hunter to finally be able to talk to. It was the first time she had ever been to my house without him, and I felt grateful she bothered to come to check up on me at all. "I can't believe any of this!"

"I know," she said, hugging and consoling me. "I'm so sorry my brother has done all this to you... but now that he's moved to Las Vegas for 'good' as he says, I went over some of the boxes he left behind, and you won't believe what I found!"

She pulled out a large box from a tote bag hanging from her side. She opened it and put her hands over the large stack of pictures inside. "Now, I'm only showing you these as evidence so you can remember them as you're trying to forget my scumbag, cheating brother and move on... They're to ensure that he will *never, ever* hurt you again, because after you see the proof of his indiscretions—which he apparently proudly documented *himself* over the years—I don't think you'd ever even *consider* taking him back... do you want to see them?"

Still reeling from the shock of everything over the past few weeks—and feeling completely stupid for putting up with Hunter for so long now overall—and believe me, it is really, really hard to take back stupid—I only signed and said, "Yes."

She handed me the first one. I couldn't believe it—it was of Hunter and Candi, together, with her wearing only *half* of her bunny suit (the tail half)—and him admiring her double-D's up close and personal... and, oh my God—could it be? .... Yes, Hunter was wearing the *exact same shirt and pants from the night he proposed*... to <u>me</u>.

"Oh my God," I stammered.

"I know," Catherine said with disgust. "Can you believe how fake those are?"

"No... that's the last time he was there with *me*... the night we got engaged... He went back down to gamble after we—" I didn't have to explain the sex, for Catherine could tell from my ashen face what I was leaving out. "He was gone until morning, but I didn't think anything of it... I mean, I didn't think he'd actually *cheat* on me the same night he <u>proposed</u>!"

"Oh my God, I'm so sorry!" Catherine said, truly shocked. "That has to be the biggest asshole move for a guy, <u>ever</u>! Oh Melanie, I thought this one was more recent than that, I didn't know— I'm sorry, maybe you shouldn't even see the rest—"

"No, please... these are very educational..."

She showed me another one of a completely nude woman lying on a float in the middle of the pool at his parents' million-dollar ranch in the Hill Country of Texas. Her body was incredible, very toned with enormous, fake breasts, and I recognized her immediately as Julie, the exotic woman from Aspen. They must have gone back and forth from Aspen to Texas over that holiday week they spent together. They looked like a couple of lovebirds in the next photo together, and then Catherine handed me one of Julie's body only—much more close up—and I saw something so shocking I wanted to throw up. She had a tattoo of "R.A.M." displayed prominently on her private area, and no pubic hair what-so-ever.

"Why are there so many pictures of this tattoo?" I asked, seeing several more from various angles.

Catherine sighed. "Julie had been the concubine of a powerful Sheik named Rasmi Abdul- Malik, and this man tattoos his initials on all the women he's with... down there... as if to 'brand' them as his property, just like she was a cow! It's disgusting."

My heart was thumping. This was the same Arab Sheik oilman who had abducted Eva all those years ago—and the thought that he had done this to her possibly too was so gross I couldn't believe my eyes. I put those pictures away and then saw a picture of Hunter at what looked like a huge party shaking hands with Rasmi Abdul-Malik himself. I was appalled that Hunter would even be associated with such a piece of trash, let alone be so happy and proud to be with one of his 'branded' concubines.

My eyes welled up with tears and my throat tightened as I took this all in. I flipped through the rest of the pictures only to continue to find myriads of women I didn't know or somehow recognized throughout our travels, and all of them were in various, hypersexual positions. There were even a few of Hunter in the act of having sex with them. Once I reached the count of at least twenty different women over the past year alone, I stopped looking and put the box down. I ran into my bathroom and threw up.

"I'm so sorry, I guess these were just too much," Catherine said, coming in after me and wetting a facecloth so I could wipe my mouth.

"Yeah," I said. "But thank you for bringing them over. I needed to see the truth... what I wasn't willing to allow myself to know before. I can't deny anything to myself now about him and what really happened when we were 'supposedly' together."

"No," Catherine agreed. "Fraid not."

We came out of the bathroom and I took one more, very brave look at the pictures... I knew these images would keep me from ever being tempted by Hunter again, for sure. They were truly enraging. "Thank you for showing me these. I will never have anything to do with your brother ever again now."

"Good," Catherine said. "Because you really need to move on this time, like he always seems to do."

"I know, but I was just so in love with him that I'd listen to whatever lame excuse he gave me and take him back. I resented anyone who told me he wasn't good for me, but now I know everyone—including you—was only trying to wake me up and tell me the *truth*."

"Well if I had known about these photos years ago I would have shown them to you right away!"

"That would have saved me years of my life, but it's not your fault I stayed with him, it's mine, and I need to accept that. I just need to sever all ties with him now." I looked at her sadly, but she seemed to understand why.

"I understand completely," Catherine said. "And don't worry, I won't take it personally. I had to do the same thing with many people when I got divorced. It just happens. But right now you need to take care of yourself and do what's best for you only. Don't worry about me or anyone else. We're all *fine*."

"Thank you," I said, with feeling. We hugged for a long, sincere moment, and then she gathered up the box with the photos, put it back into her tote bag, and left.

I looked into the mirror and thought, *I'm a smart women... how could I have let this happen to myself?* My state of mind was horrible, but I knew I had to examine this all while it was still fresh in my mind. The good times with Hunter had been so much fun I had chosen to ignore the bad things, like the fact that he cheated on me repeatedly with all these women—some of whom I knew, but most of whom I didn't. He did not really love me if he was able to act like that. It then dawned on me that I had been repeating a pattern throughout my life of picking men who were not capable of giving me the love I was seeking, and then trying to stay and make things work out anyway. I realized that I had been stupid by choice! Why had I willfully chosen a man like him, or Morgan? It wasn't for reasons like Emily or Eva, for I didn't need a man to pay my way since I had my own money. So what then, was *my* excuse? I guess I kept hoping to find true love, and maybe I felt I had to earn it by saving someone from himself. Whatever the reasons, I was not only stupid, but also stubborn. I really had to get hit hard by the truth to let go of someone. And this time, I felt I was hit harder than anyone else ever had been before. But I was determined to get over it, starting hopefully, tomorrow…

The next day it took all my strength, but I finally managed to get out of bed and take a bath. The water felt warm and comforting. I was proud of myself for accomplishing what used to just be an afterthought of my day. And then, to make it even more of an accomplishment, I put on something new, clean, and different to wear. I felt like I had taken a big step, but it was the most I wanted to take at the moment. I crawled back into bed and cried, praying for the strength to finally get over Hunter completely, another day…

Another week went by, or maybe two even. I was so depressed I barely got out of bed again. It seemed my one day of two small victories was a false alarm. I was not getting better. In fact, I felt like I'd never leave my bed ever again.

"Okay Squirt!" Whitney said; entering my room one night and putting all the lights on, which jarred me awake instantly since I was so used to it being dark. She immediately took charge. "Out of that bed and into the shower…" she ordered.

"What? Why—"

"We have reservations at eight."

"Reservations?" I said, confused.

Whitney gathered the few clothes I had been wearing for the past two weeks and winced. "Oh my God—these are going downstairs into the fire-place! Come on now, hop to it!" She put the shower on in my bathroom and dragged me from the bed towards it. "I'll pick out what you're going to wear tonight," she continued to bark as she stepped into my walk-in closet to consider the choices.

Whitney is coming to my rescue? Impossible, I thought as I stepped into the shower and got clean. But it was also intriguing, so I didn't argue. I mean, I must really be a mess if even *she* thought so.

Once we got to the restaurant, just the two of us, Whitney continued to be in charge as she ordered the drinks and food. I hadn't eaten much of anything for several days, so anything on the menu sounded good.

"Wow, I think I really needed this Whitney," I said, coming out of my major funk as I took a big bite of delicious, homemade, pumpernickel bread. "Thanks for taking me out."

"Hey, with Oldie away that leaves *me* in charge," she said playfully, "and besides, even though we don't hang out a lot, you're still my little sister, and I hate to see you like this."

"I'm surprised it's just you and me tonight though… Eva seems to always want to tag along whenever you go out lately."

"Yes, she sure did—*when* she was here to..."

"What do you mean?"

She laughed. "Well, let's just say the dog got her bone, but things aren't turning out the way she planned they would in 'married-life-land.'"

"I could have told her that was going to be the case. What happened now?"

"Dawson got offered a residency position at a hospital in New York City to train with some of the best heart surgeons in the country last month, and he accepted the position without even discussing it with Eva."

"You're kidding!"

"No, and I don't think I'd ever seen her so distraught! Picture them sitting in a nice restaurant, like this, and Dawson just told her the 'good news'..."

I nodded eagerly, for I knew she was getting ready to do an impression of Eva's response—and Whitney could do Eva even better than Eva could at times. Whitney got into character and suddenly spit water halfway across the table, "'Excuse me? What did you say? We're moving to fucking New *where?*' She then went completely ballistic on him right in the middle of the restaurant. 'What are you telling me Dawson—that we're moving where it fucking *snows?* You know I hate cold weather, crowds, and I don't even know a single soul in New York! How dare you accept a position there without even discussing it with me! Have you forgotten I'm your WIFE— you fucking son-of-a-*bitch!*'"

I laughed so hard I forgot all about Hunter. Whitney was glad, and she let me catch my breath before she continued. "But here's the 'big' surprise..." she whispered.

"I can't believe there's more!"

"Well, the puppy finally became a dog, because Dawson shut her up pretty good. 'We're moving to New York and that's *final!*'" she said in a mocking, burly-man tone.

"Wow, he's not Eva's pet anymore, huh?"

"No, but I mean, think about it. He's just so focused on his career, and New York would be a great opportunity for him. Eva continued to protest it, but Dawson just got up and left her in the restaurant to sulk."

"No way!"

Whitney nodded as she took a sip of her cocktail. "She came over that night and she was *so* pissed! He really tore into her in the car on their way home for embarrassing him with a drunken tirade like that in the restaurant. He went off on her and told her that his parents must have been right about her all along—and that he thinks he's made the biggest mistake of his life for marrying her."

"He woke up to that a little too late though, didn't he?" Saying that out loud suddenly made me realize I was glad I found out everything I did about Hunter now too.

"Looks like it. Eva was shocked at his response. She said she had never seen such a cold-hearted attitude from Dawson before."

"So when are they moving?"

"They already did, last week... she calls me five times a day telling me how much she hates it already—they live in a tiny, cramped apartment next door to the hospital, and Dawson has spent every night there instead of coming home to see her. She told him yesterday, 'This isn't what I had in mind when I married you!' And he put his hand in her face to shut her up, then said coldly, 'You and I *both* know why you were in such a hurry to marry a *Clarke,* so quit your bitching. It's both boring and low-class. You should be grateful for what you've got!'"

Whitney nodded her head for emphasis.

Good old Eva, I thought. *I could always count on her to let me know things really could always be worse.*

"Wow," I reflected out loud. "So I guess the fairy tale life she dreamed of won't be coming true for her any time soon."

"At least not for another six years... that's how long this residency program lasts! We'll see how long she can hold out."

"If she doesn't meet another, even richer guy first," I added.

"Naw, my guess is she'll probably stick it out with Dawson and hope it gets better, for now she knows that it will probably just be the same with *any* rich guy she chases after—none of them <u>ever</u> change."

"Is it just me, or are you trying to give me advice through what's going on with Eva?"

"I don't know *what* you're talking about!" Whitney said sarcastically as she signaled towards our cute waiter. "Excuse me, but we need another round."

Hearing about Eva's situation did seem to snap me back to reality. Hunter wasn't going to ruin my life. He wasn't worth it. I had to toughen up and move on.

Chapter 10

※

Now I knew I wasn't going to marry Hunter and live happily ever after, I needed to figure out what I wanted to do with my future, which at the moment seemed very, very depressing. For even though I was only twenty-seven-years-old and still attractive, any female over twenty-five was considered an 'old maid' by Texan standards, so I felt very old, tired, and unattractive overall. So the question was if I wasn't going to be planning a wedding and fulfilling my life-long dream of having Hunter's children, then what do I do *now?* How do I start over?

I had honestly never thought about my future without Hunter. And a life with him only ever included attending lavish parties, shopping for the best, most stylish clothes, traveling to every corner of the world, and maintaining my size-four figure. I never had to work—and never had to before him either. But now I knew I was going to have to enter into that world; for though I was much better at managing my trust fund money than Whitney was, it still wasn't going to last forever, and I needed money coming in if I was ever going to move out of my parents' house and start supporting myself.

I didn't want a run-of-the-mill, mundane, nine-to-five routine existence either. My globetrotting ways and decadent lifestyle may have come to an end, but I still didn't have to let my daily life be boring. I could find something to do that would be challenging, stimulating, and fulfilling as a career. Something I knew I'd enjoy. That way I knew I could make a great living doing it and still be happy. The question that plagued me for days though was, *What could that be...?*

"The world is your oyster!" Oldie said encouragingly as he held up a spoonful of his Oyster's Rockefeller appetizer on his fork and savored the bite that followed, chewing it slowly. "And you're smart, so you can do whatever you put your mind to doing," he added once he had finished his tasty morsel, and then reached down with his fork for another big, gooey bite.

"I know," I said. "But it's overwhelming just thinking of all the choices there are for careers."

"You like to cook," my mother said. "Why don't you become a chef?"

I looked around the posh restaurant we were in and observed the dozen or so wait staff bustling about as they served delicious, art-like cuisine. I did like to cook and people have always said I was great at it whenever I threw a dinner party, but that was when it was just me alone in a kitchen. The thought of spending my days and nights in a hot, crowded kitchen with a whole crew of cooks and wait staff somewhere like this didn't appeal to me, so I said, "I think cooking's more of my hobby."

"Well, don't worry, Lil' Bit," Oldie said. "It will come to you. I know you're anxious to get out and start a new life for yourself, but there's no rush. You can stay at home as long as you need to while you're getting started. After all, Whitney's still living there, and it looks like she'll *never* be leaving now."

He was referring to Whitney's last birthday celebration—her thirty-first, which she celebrated still very wild and very, very single—which also meant it was doubtful she was ever going to change and settle down. Oldie used to fight with her about never taking responsibility for herself, but Whitney only pointed out that he had raised his 'Daddy's little girls' to not think about things like money, ever, so why be so surprised that she didn't? I had to agree with her to a point, but I also didn't want to be her age and still living at home, single or not, so I was determined to find a career as soon as I could. After all, it was the '80s and most women were career-minded, or at least the ones with ambition like me were.

I tried to get in touch with Victoria to find out if she had any suggestions, but her and her mom were off on a grand, once-in-a-lifetime world cruise that her grandmother had bought and paid for and then left as a surprise for them in her will. She had died right after the holidays and knew Victoria was still considering going to New York to live with her brother. Since her grandmother knew she was ill and wouldn't be around much longer to help constantly fix her up with men from Palm Beach, she figured booking a six-month cruise that started in February would at least keep Victoria close to her mother (and the idea of staying in Florida with her) for a bit longer. Victoria had sent me postcards when they docked in South America and Europe already. I was looking forward to seeing where their next stop on the globe would be.

"What do you like to do with your time?" my old high school friend Beau asked me one day when we were out for a walk at his fabulous new estate. He had invested his trust fund money well over the years and was now living in one of Houston's most prominent neighborhoods. He showed me his beautiful, peaceful Koi Pond in the backyard just off the pool's deck, and I was enjoying both his company and the wonderful surroundings.

"Being in places like this!" I only half-joked, for it was mostly true. I had imagined living in a home just like this with Hunter and my own family. I had also spent a lot of time in these kinds of lavish abodes with our mutual wealthy friends over the years and knew a lot about high-end real estate by observing different architectural styles and top interior designer creations. "Oh my God, what a wonderful cresting," I said as I pointed up towards the top of the mansion's roof. "Simple, but very classy... was this home designed by John Staub?"

"Yes. How'd you know that?"

"He was known for his 'understated elegance' of grand homes like this, and that particular cresting he designed is a nice feature to have, for it's attractive to look at and it will *also* help to keep debris from going into your pool by where he strategically placed it."

"You know, you would be great at selling homes, especially ones like these," Beau said with confidence.

"You mean as a realtor?" I said, actually liking the sound of it immediately.

"Why not?" Beau said. "You look the part in your designer labels already, and people would see you in one of these houses and think 'wow, she looks beautiful, smart, and comfortable here, so it must be a great place to live!'"

The thought of both showing and selling beautiful homes like this sounded attractive to me, so the next day I enrolled in a real estate course and promptly got my license several months later. Thanks to Oldie's connections and support, I was immediately hired as a real estate agent by one of the oldest and most prestigious firms in Houston. I took my parents and Beau out to dinner to thank them all for their help and support, and also to celebrate the start of my new, promising, exciting career.

I started the next day and was eager to work hard and have a good attitude about my new job, but within a few weeks I realized real estate wasn't really my thing... I was trying to enjoy it, but after having lived such a glamorous, adventure-filled lifestyle since the age of nineteen with men like Morgan and Hunter, this career thing was not measuring up. And it didn't help that it was also starting out as one of the hottest summers in Houston on record, so no one who could even afford the kind of million-dollar homes I was listing would be around to show them to by July. They were all off jet-setting to Monte Carlo or somewhere fun for the summer like I had always done, so the idea of working at a hot, stuffy office and trying to survive the blistering heat for the next two months was hard for me to deal with.

"I can't stand it anymore!" Whitney complained as she came inside from the pool before dinner. "Look, the water already evaporated from my skin *and* bikini!"

"Well what do you want me to do about it?" Oldie said. He was tired of both Whitney's and my mother's constant complaints about the heat. I tried not to join in, but it was getting hard not to as the Texas heat index continued to rise daily. We were all in for a terrible scorcher by August for sure, and it was only days away from the fourth of July still.

The phone rang.

"I'll get it!" Oldie barked; glad for the excuse to escape and go into his library. He shut the door so we couldn't eavesdrop.

"Hello?" Oldie said into the receiver as he sat down behind his desk.

"Courtlin—good, I'm glad you're home," Chase Martin said on the other end of the line.

"Oh my God—*Chase?* Well, I'll be damned! How are you?"

"Been better Court, that's for sure," Chase said wearily, and Oldie immediately knew this wouldn't be a 'fun' social call. Chase Martin was Oldie's roommate from his days at Yale law school, and after graduation he had become a successful lawyer in New York City. He was from a wealthy East Coast family and married a very prim and proper woman named Anne who was also from a prestigious East Coast family herself. They had two twin sons a few years after I was born. They led a comfortable life in Greenwich, Connecticut and we all exchanged Christmas cards every few years with updates of how 'well' everyone was doing. No one ever mentioned the bad times, so the last Oldie knew things were fine at the Martins. But that was several years ago...

Chase went on to tell Oldie that after thirty years of marriage he was bored and left his 'prim and proper' wife Anne for his very sexy, very exciting, thirty-year-old Puerto Rican paralegal named Carmen the year before. They eloped, but the marriage fell apart last month when Chase came home and caught Carmen in bed with their new, sexy, twenty-three-year-old pool cleaner in his family's Southampton home. They had just opened it up the weekend before and had hired him together.

"There's no fool like an old fool," Chase said. "I really thought Carmen was in love with me, but when I look in the mirror and see my bald head and wrinkles it becomes painfully obvious that she was only in love with my wallet the whole time."

"Hell," Oldie said, "that's the oldest trick on record and you're a smart, shrewd man, so she must have really done a number on you to convince you it was love."

"She did."

"Hey, aren't your two twins about twenty-three now too?"

"Yes, which is why this whole situation just keeps getting more and more embarrassing... *The New York Post* won't let up on making it all front page news... I need to get out of dodge until fall and the whole divorce is final, but I can't go to my house in Southampton because it's part of the property settlement and the judge ordered that it was 'off limits indefinitely' to both of us due to the situation, which is why I'm *really* calling... Do you want to borrow it for the rest of the summer to get out of that awful Texas heat I keep hearing about?"

"Do *I?*" Oldie said happily. It didn't take him long to get both the address and security code.

Oldie, my mother, Whitney, and I all eagerly arrived at the grand estate on Gin Lane and Oldie drove our rental car up the long, winding driveway to the massive front entrance. We saw portions of the beautiful, white, wooden Colonial mansion hidden behind immaculately groomed private hedges as we rode along the pavement. Oldie had already explained that it had a tennis court, a great pool cabana (without a pool boy now, of course), a croquet area, a screening room, and a putting green. There was also a sixty-foot Hatteras fishing boat docked in Sag Harbor, just in case any of us ever felt like fishing. There was a full-time chef, two housekeepers, and a car and driver always on hand throughout the summer as well. Hearing all this was like a dream come true—I was back to living lavishly again and could forget all about needing a career, at least for the time being. Before we left, Oldie had set me up with a meeting with two of his top stockbrokers and they had told me I could tell them my "future financial plan" upon our return from Southampton, so I had the whole summer to think about it. That was plenty of time.

As we parked in the circular driveway, a pretty Hispanic housekeeper named Carina came out to greet us and help us with our bags. "Welcome, St. John family," she said warmly.

"Thank you," my mother said back graciously. We were all grateful to be there after having been rescued from the horrific Texan heat and were all looking forward to spending the rest of the summer in Southampton, enjoying our heaven-sent "home away from home."

I went inside the living room and plopped down on the plush down sofa covered in light blue chintz and breathed in the ocean air coming from the opened French doors. Life slowly re-entered my body and a smile formed across my lips. After a few lingering moments I got up and then amused myself by looking at all the comfortable, stylish antiques. The walls were filled with clever illustrations by Saul Steinberg, and I recognized his witty drawings from the covers of the *New Yorker* instantly.

"Isn't this great?!" Whitney said as she looked around in awe.

"Yes," I agreed, and knew instantly that I was going to like it here. Best of all, nothing here reminded me of Hunter.

Life in the Hamptons was a bit like Monte Carlo with its endless party circuits, beautiful, lavish estate homes, and fabulous yachts. Seeing millionaires and heirs was routine, though not too many princes or kings, and many young, beautiful, and fun people were everywhere. The parties were incredible and lasted until dawn. Chase had arranged guest passes for us at the local country clubs, so we were right in the middle of all the action all the time. We loved it. My mom enjoyed peaceful days reading by the pool and walking along the beach. Oldie spent most afternoons at the local watering hole called The Driver's Seat relaxing with his signature scotch and soda, which the bartender always made right. Whitney had a different date every night and couldn't believe her luck in meeting all these new, very eligible suitors. Since she had gone through all the available men in Houston, this was like a whole new playing field. I normally just tagged along with each of them on a revolving schedule, taking it all in with whomever I was with at the moment. Though I was feeling a lot better, I was still too much of an emotional wreck when it came to men to even attempt dating at this point, so I was just happy to observe.

The summer seemed to fly by and our wonderful family vacation was going to end in a couple of days. As soon as the thought of going back to Houston crept back into my mind I started to get depressed. I didn't want to go back to my job; though they had said when I left I was welcome to at any time. I think they knew with my family's connections to all the wealthy country club members I would bring in a lot of prime, upscale, repeat business, but I still didn't think selling real estate was my passion.

"So, have you decided what you're going to do back in Houston, Lil' Bit?" Oldie asked me as we each sipped our cocktails on the patio of The Driver's Seat. We were going back to Houston in two days, and I was dreading every second that ticked by towards our plane's departure, for Oldie told me he had spoken with the two stockbrokers I met with before we left, and they were both eager to know my "future financial plan" as soon as we returned. I had none. And my biggest fear, even worse than not having one to tell them, was that I would find out Hunter and Candi had split up while I was gone, and I would then end up back in the same old dysfunctional, "going nowhere" relationship with that complete jackass for lack of anything else better to do. I swirled my flute in my hand, thinking of that doomed fate...

"Excuse me, but are you Melanie St. John, from Texas?" a polite man with very dark skin asked me. He was dressed in purple polka-dots from head to toe, complete with a matching tie, and looked like an over-tanned clown.

"Yes," I said, completely perplexed at how in the world this odd-looking man would know my name. Oldie just stared at him too, waiting to see as well.

In a very thick accent he said, "'Bored Melanie!' Don't you remember me? I was your Monte Carlo escort during that infamous summer with your sister and Dr. Fane!"

I gasped. "Subir?" I jumped up and hugged him, not believing it was the funny person I had met there from Nepal. I hadn't recognized him because his hair was much longer and he also had a whole different style of dress. He must have thought it was more "American" or something to be wearing such bright colors. "Oldie, remember Subir from that crazy summer?"

"Of course I remember him and that whole Goddamn summer—I'd have to be braindead not to remember *that* ridiculous summer—sit down Subir, have a drink with us," Oldie said in a loud, Texan drawl.

"Oh, is it okay if my fiancée, Cindy joins us too?" Subir asked, and suddenly a petite, pretty woman with black hair appeared at his side. I don't even know where she had been hiding, but at least this told me my assumption back in Monte Carlo was wrong—he definitely wasn't gay.

"Of course," Oldie said, and both Cindy and Subir joined our table and we went into a lengthy reunion lunch as we all caught up on all the things we had each been doing over the last decade.

It turned out the year after our summer in Monte Carlo Subir had become the Nepalese Ambassador to the United Nations and moved to New York City where he had now been living for the past ten years. He had met Cindy there and they lived in a quaint, one bedroom apartment on the Upper East Side of Manhattan. He said the funny outfits he always wears are designed by him and typical of his country. He hoped to market his clothing in the U.S. someday.

Good luck with that, I thought as I stared at him in the most ridiculous outfit I had ever seen. He looked like he was going to a costume party.

"I suggest you keep your day job at the United Nations, just in case this 'fashion thing' doesn't work out for you," Oldie said tactfully, then burst out laughing. Everyone else soon joined in.

We drank bottles of Dom Perignon as if it were going out of style. I told Subir and Cindy about my dilemma and how I was supposed to figure out my future.

After politely listening to my whole saga Subir thought for a long moment, and then finally said, "Melanie, it sounds to me like you need a change. You should move to New York and start over. You've wasted all of these great years of your life in a bad relationship, wandering aimlessly around the world following Hunter everywhere, and you have now ended up back in Houston with absolutely zero to show for it. You're still only twenty-seven, which is not considered old at all in New York."

"Even thirty isn't considered old there," Cindy added encouragingly. She looked to be just over that age herself, so I took her comment seriously. "Everyone your age is still single there—it's not like the south where everyone gets married and starts having children right after high school or college."

"Yeah," Subir agreed. "So you shouldn't go back to Houston and waste away your—"

"Are you out of your MIND?" Oldie yelled. "That's the most ridiculous idea I've ever heard! Melanie has no skills and hardly any job experience except for a few weeks in a real estate office—what on earth would she *do* all day in New York? Everyone there has either a career or a hefty trust fund to live off of. Thanks to spending over half of hers with Hunter, Melanie now doesn't have enough money left to live off of, and she has no career either—"

"Thanks for all your encouragement and moral support 'Dad!'" I said angrily. I only called Oldie "Dad" when I was upset with him, and he knew it.

"Wait! I have the perfect solution," Subir said once he could see an argument between Oldie and me was brewing. "Cindy and I are on our way to Nepal to visit my family for the next six weeks. Melanie, why don't you stay in our apartment while we're gone? This will give you some time to explore the city and look for a job... or even see if you like living in Manhattan."

I could barely contain my excitement. "Perfect! I think that sounds like the best—"

"Melanie, I don't think you could even *last* six weeks on your own in New York," Oldie said, shaking his head. "The only time you've ever been there was with me or with Morgan, and you always stayed in the best hotel suites or his upscale, *huge* Upper East Side apartment—no offense to yours, though, Subir."

"None taken," Subir nodded. "For it's nice, but not something that comes with amenities like door men or room service."

"Exactly," Oldie said, knowing Subir understood how I was used to being treated. Then Oldie turned to me. "You're used to being in New York with unlimited shopping allowances and a car and driver to your avail. You'll go into complete culture shock if you stay in Subir's place and have to live there like a local—the crowds, the noise, schlepping groceries on the street, being yelled at by nasty cab drivers with foreign accents—'gain, no offense," he said towards Subir.

Subir nodded as if he understood yet again.

"Plus," Oldie continued, "you'll never be able to deal with the harsh, cold winters or learn how to navigate the subway system to get around—"

"Well why not at least give me a *chance?*" I asked.

Oldie rolled his eyes, which made me upset.

"You're wrong, and I'll prove it!" I said, meaning it.

Oldie looked at his glass for a long moment; then looked back up at me seriously. "Okay Lil' Bit," he said reluctantly. "If this is what you *really* want to do then we'll just wait and see if you can make it there. But if you try to do this you'll have to do it *completely* on your own without *any* help from me. And I can't let you use the rest of your trust fund money either... not after watching Whitney waste all of hers in one summer like that. You have it invested in some good places, and I'll tell my boys to just keep investing it for you for now until you're older and more 'settled.' So if you think you can do this with whatever you have left in your savings account from this summer only, then go ahead. But you're not getting a penny more."

It was just like the moment when he held up the bracelet on the private jet and dared me to take the 'security of money' over love. Only now, it was money over freedom... freedom from Hunter, and freedom from my family's—or really *his*—money. Both Subir and Cindy held their breath just like Emily had done as they looked at me, and I knew I would only get one chance to answer.

"I'm going to New York," I told Oldie firmly. Subir and Cindy both exhaled happily. "I have to do something for myself Oldie, and this is the perfect time and chance. After being here all summer I am finally really moving on from Hunter and my old life back in Texas that was going nowhere. I'm going to show you that this will be a good move for me—I'm going to give it my all and I'm going to make it work no matter what!" I hugged Oldie, then Subir and Cindy. "Thank you so much for this opportunity," I told them both gratefully.

"It's our pleasure to help," Subir said as Oldie glared at him. I knew he took this as a personal defeat and it would take awhile for him to let it really sink in.

I felt invigorated by the path I had laid out for myself as we all left The Driver's Seat.

I flew back to Houston two days later with my family and packed three very large suitcases to take to New York. I put the rest of my clothing and things in boxes and left everything in my room, then gave all the shipping information for Subir's apartment to my mother just in case I liked New York and decided to stay longer after my six weeks was up.

"I'm so proud of you, Melanie," my mother said as she hugged me and kissed me on the forehead. Oldie still couldn't believe I was going, so he said nothing, hoping it was all a bad dream. And then, when the cab came to take me to the airport early the next morning, he held true to his word and didn't offer a dime to help me start off on my new path. But luckily I hadn't shopped a lot or spent much of the summer allowance money he had provided in my Southampton savings account, and I knew I could make it last six weeks if I budgeted it well for food and the basics while being able to stay in Subir's apartment rent free.

"Good-bye Oldie," I said as I hugged him. "I'll call once I'm there."

"Take care of yourself there in the city," he said softly, and I knew he was choking back tears.

"I will," I told him. "And don't worry so much about me. I'm tougher than you think, you know!" I joked, silently praying that I truly was...

I arrived in Manhattan later that day. It was the end of August, and both the atmosphere and the heat of the city overwhelmed me. Subir and Cindy's apartment was in a nice, tree-lined area of the Upper East Side, but it was far from the kind of place Morgan lived in. It was only a very small one bedroom with a tiny bathroom, efficiency kitchen, and a basic living room that also doubled as the dining area, but it was all very clean, neat, and cozy. It was filled with exotic antiques from Nepal, Tabriz carpets, and paintings from India. It was beautiful, tasteful, and stimulating to my imagination.

What would it be like to travel to the Orient? I thought. I'd never been there. And suddenly I realized there was half a world I'd never explored with Hunter, so that meant there was still plenty of adventures left for me to have. Through Subir's reality my imagination was carried away to a place where I never had to think about Texas or Hunter Carrington the Third ever again. Just what the doctor ordered.

A tall, silver hookah adorned with beautiful animals sat on the floor. A carved wooden statue of a smiling Buddha was placed atop a marble pedestal. The full-sized bedframe taking up most of the bedroom was hand-carved from teak wood, and one wall was all completely exposed, rugged-looking, red brick. The entire environment was new to me and delightfully simple and inspiring. My mood was immediately uplifted, and I was ready to have a good time being a big "city girl."

Subir and Cindy were right, a twenty-something woman from Texas could have a lot of fun in New York. It seemed I fit right in being single and available here, and I felt like a kid in a candy store there was so much to do all the time, and so many eligible, available men everywhere. Even though I had no interest in having a relationship again at this point, it was still fun to receive the attention. I was amazed at how little I was missing Hunter as the days went by.

Out of sight, out of mind, I thought as I went out each day and night and met all different sorts and types of people from all over the world. Then eventually I even started going out on real dates again, not to form a relationship with anyone particular, but just to have a good time receiving the attention of a man.

To make sure I broke my bad pattern of being attracted to men who couldn't give me the kind of love I wanted—and also to make sure I never got attached to any of them too soon—I decided my idea of a "great date night" would be to have three dates in one night—one date for cocktails, one for dinner, and then one for late-night dancing. It worked great and I was soon doing it quite often, but it was a ridiculous schedule and I would routinely fall asleep in the cab on the way home from the last dancing date.

"Please, wakey up and pay now—we are now home, miss!" A heavily-accented cab driver said to me one particular time after I had fallen asleep on the way home, again. I guess it says a lot about the kind of honest, trustworthy men New York City cabdrivers really are, for it was amazing I was never kidnapped, raped, or murdered in the wee hours of the morning by any of them and always got home safely.

I had been in New York for a month when I finally decided to go visit Eva. Whitney had told her I was living there now and she kept complaining to Whitney that it wasn't fair that I didn't go to see her since we were 'old friends.' I never thought Eva actually considered me a friend, but I also wondered if anything had changed in her life since she moved. After all, I was having a blast, so I couldn't see how anyone didn't like New York.

"Oh, I'm so glad you're here and could come see me Mel!" Eva said as she hugged me with desperate abandon in the doorway of her apartment. "I've been so bored and lonely up here. I'm so glad you're living here now too."

"Yeah, but I can't see how you can be bored, Eva," I said. "I'm having the time of my life—New York is great! I've dated the most men I've ever dated in my life and I've been partying the nights away with friends I met over the summer in the Hamptons as well as new ones I make here at all the great parties."

"Oh man, I'm so jealous of you!" Eva said, not smiling any longer. "You're still young and have nothing to worry about... you remind me of *me* in college—and after."

"Eva, I'm only three years younger than you, and that time you're talking about was only a few years ago! I was there, in Monte Carlo with Whitney—rememb—" I caught myself just as I finished that last sentence. There's no way Eva would have remembered that I was even in Monte Carlo since she was missing the whole time I was there.

Eva was visibly affected by my comment and I felt bad, but she shook it off. "Oh, I made us some coffee..." she said and I followed her into the kitchen, which admittedly was not that far from the living room we had just been standing in. "So you finally got away from that guy what's-his-name, *Hunter?*"

"Yes, and it feels *sooo* good," I said as I sat down at the kitchen table.

"Well that's great. I'm glad you finally realized I was right about him," she said with almost glee as she placed a full cup of black java in front of me.

"I appreciate the coffee, but it's really not my thing."

"Oh, okay." There was a long, awkward silence, broken only by random sips as Eva drank from her cup, but didn't offer to get me anything different.

We talked small talk about people back home, which I hated to do, and I could tell she was trying to find out any of the latest gossip she thought I might know, but I didn't know any. After awhile it was clear we had nothing in common and nothing to say to each other. She was Whitney's friend, after all, not really mine, and this visit made that painfully clear. I finally rose to leave, but it looked like a bomb went off in Eva's eyes.

"Leaving so soon?" she shrieked. "I was just about to watch a movie. Do you want to join me?"

"I really have to get going, Eva."

"Oh man..." she groaned. "It's just that I'm so lonely here! I haven't been able to make any new friends since I'm cooped up here all day doing everything for Dawson. I just miss the chatter and company, you know?"

I sat back down. "Okay Eva, what's the deal here? I thought this guy was well off. Isn't that why you married him? You should be able to do anything you want to do all day long."

Eva sighed heavily. "Yes, he is... but he's cheap and stingy with 'his' money. I mean, look at where we live! My place in Houston before we got married was *way* bigger! He only gives me enough money to cover the basics."

"Well why don't you go out and find a job? I have to look for one while I'm here living at my friend's place, but that's only for a couple more weeks, because then he's coming back home. I'm on a tight budget here too and not getting any help from Oldie, and if I don't find a job so I can get my own place soon then I'll have to go back home to Texas."

"Melanie, please. I haven't worked a day in my entire life and I'm not about to start now. Especially while I'm married to this asshole who *should* be supporting me *better.*"

"If you're so unhappy then why don't you leave him?"

"I worked hard to get where I'm at! It took a long time to get that ring on my finger and fight off his parent's attacks and I'm not going to give that up now! He's still rich and his family's even richer. I'm <u>not</u> going to throw all that away."

"Okay then, I don't know what to tell you," I said as I got up to leave again.

"Mel wait!" Eva grabbed my arm and pulled me back down next to her. "I know this guy who works with Dawson. His name is Charles Evans and he is so cute! He's a brilliant doctor and he always talks to me while he helps me ferret out Dawson at the hospital—we've become good friends and he's *very* single. Do you want me to set you up with him?"

I could tell that Eva was going to do whatever she could to keep me close, but I wasn't interested in being close with her and I really wasn't interested in dating a man from her world, even if he was a successful doctor. "No offense Eva, but wouldn't someone who works with Dawson be just as unavailable as he is?"

She gave me a look that told me he was.

"I respectfully decline," I said.

"What about Whitney? Is she seeing anyone right now?"

"That changes hourly," I laughed. "Haven't you spoken to her lately?"

"C'mon… she's so wrapped up in her own life currently she says she doesn't have time for me whenever I call her…" She handed me the phone. "Can you call her for me?"

"Sure, but the chances of her being home are pretty slim." I dialed the number and to both our surprise Whitney picked up.

"Hello?" Whitney said, sounding either still hung-over or half asleep. It was always hard to tell.

"Hey Whitney!" I said happily.

"Oh, hi Squirt, how's New York?" she said.

"Still great! And you won't believe it, but I finally managed to get up and visit Eva… in fact, I'm here right now and she wants to talk with you about something—"

"Is it the clap?" Whitney said sarcastically.

I shot Eva a look, hoping she didn't hear her. "No, it's not that… okay, here she is…" I handed the phone to Eva.

"Hey Whits! Hold on, I'm going to put you on speaker… okay, there we go! So, what's up with you? We haven't talked for *days!*"

"I've just been busy working on my tan… and last night I went to a cocktail party with Brad Johnson. Remember him? I ran into him while I was out jogging the other day and he invited me to an engagement party for Maggie and Robert. Their wedding is next Saturday. Everyone in Houston is getting married now—it feels like I'm the only single girl left!"

"Well I'm glad you feel that way because I want to set you up with someone up here. His name is Charles and he's a doctor who works with Dawson at the hospital."

"It's been a while since I've been to New York…" Whitney thought out loud.

"You can even stay with me while you're here!" Eva said excitedly. "We can hang out and go to some parties too—Dawson is never around and I'm so lonely!"

"Sounds good to me… I don't have anything planned for this weekend, and no offense, but I'm going to talk Oldie into letting me stay at the Plaza. If I hit it off with this guy I can't bring him home to your couch!"

Eva laughed. "Well I'm sure he has his *own* place."

"I want to impress him, especially if he's a 'doctor!'" Whitney's mind was made up, and Eva knew not to argue.

"Okay, great," Eva said. "Call me later after you talk to Oldie and we'll make final plans."

"Great—see you all soon!"

Eva hung up the line and I gave her a congratulatory look. "It's nice when a plan comes together, eh?"

Not surprisingly, Eva's mood towards me suddenly changed as she shuffled me towards the door. "Mel, thanks for stopping by, and maybe I'll see you when Whitney's in town."

"Yeah, sure," I said. I couldn't help but laugh as the door closed fast behind me.

That weekend Whitney flew in early the day of her big blind date. We didn't tell Eva her arrival time so we could spend the whole day alone without her, shopping up and down 5th Avenue for the perfect cocktail dress to accentuate Whitney's near-perfect figure.

"Okay Melanie," she instructed. "You have to help me find something that's really going to grab this guy's attention as soon as I walk into the room. Oldie is getting sick of funding these kinds of blind date trips, and I'm sick of hearing him complain to me about them."

It didn't take us long; for I already had something in mind I had seen early that week in the window of Bergdorf Goodman's. Whitney loved it and after we bought the deep pink, sexy number along with some killer matching stilettos, we went back to the Plaza where we went to work making her look as fabulous as possible—which was easy to do since she still looked great overall. It was nice to hang out with Whitney again and be "girly" with her just for the sake of being girly. As she put the finishing touches on her make-up the phone rang. It was seven o'clock. Right on time.

"Hold that thought," Whitney said into the receiver. "I'm on my way."

She hung up and turned to me, almost giddy. "He's in the bar and was told he should be watching the door for a 'five-foot-four, beautiful, tanned blond to appear.'"

"Oh wow! Well then, we mustn't keep him waiting! Come here and let me touch up your eyes for at least another fifteen minutes." We both laughed.

We went downstairs exactly twenty minutes later. As we entered the bar, a tall and extremely good-looking man in his late-thirties came up to us and kissed us both on our cheeks. He was dressed fantastically, well-groomed, and smelled great. I silently wondered if I had made a mistake passing him off to Whitney. He stepped back and said with a grin, "I wasn't expecting two such gorgeous blonds, but I'm certainly not complaining. I'm Charles Evans, which one of you is Whitney?"

Whitney stepped forward, fast. "That would be me, handsome."

He smiled happily. "I'm charmed, for sure."

"This is my sister, Melanie," Whitney said.

He beamed at me. "A pleasure to meet you too, Melanie." He took Whitney by the arm. "I have a great table for us by the window with a view of Central Park. We'll have to weave our way through the crowd though. Will your sister be joining us?"

"No, she has her own plans, and don't wait up, sis!" Whitney said, ditching me as fast as she could now she knew she was in such good, *handsome* hands.

"Have a wonderful evening," I said as I watched them disappear into the packed bar. I knew they would be out late, so I went back up to the room and relaxed with a romantic movie, a hot bath, and a couple of glasses of champagne as I thought about my "future plan." Subir was coming home a week from Monday, and I still wasn't sure what I was going to do...

Whitney really hit it off with Charles and stayed all weekend to be able to get to know him better. To Eva's dismay she then left on Monday, promising to be back soon to see Charles, but not necessarily Eva. It seems Eva's scheme of getting Whitney to New York mainly so they could hang out didn't go as planned, but I was glad my sister was finally interested in a man for more than two seconds.

As the week went by I spent most of my days looking at various types of want ads in the newspaper instead of partying, but I either didn't have the right degree to apply for the job or enough experience. I didn't even have a resume to send anywhere. It was getting quite depressing.

I woke up the following Sunday morning feeling ill as I opened the Sunday edition of the *New York Times.* I was overwhelmed by the amount of job ads even listed. *Where on Earth do I even begin?* I thought.

Thankfully, the phone rang.

"Hello," I said, answering on the first ring, happy for the distraction.

"Hello Mel, it's me," Hunter said sheepishly on the other end of the line.

"*Hunter?* How did you get this number?" I asked, completely shocked and not sure if I even wanted to know or to keep talking to him. I had finally gone days—maybe even a full week even—not thinking about him or us, and I didn't want to go backwards from here.

"It took some doing," was all he offered. "Anyway, I miss you, Melanie…"

I wanted to scream, *Good—but it's too late you asshole!* and slam the phone down, but my curiosity got the best of me. "What happened to 'Candi' and your sudden family?" I asked sarcastically.

"Ah, she turned out to be just like all the rest…" Hunter said, hoping to get some pity from me, but he didn't. He then went on to say how they had been in a crazy kind of 'on-again, off-again,' intense relationship for the past nine months and he was having a hard time dealing with it all. "I'm not ever sure if she's interested only in my money or actually *me,* she keeps playing so many games… and then I keep thinking of her compared to you and what *we* had. I don't know, love is just so *confusing…*"

I had had enough. He didn't even seem to care that I had been feeling just as bad about him once—actually, only weeks ago still. He was completely selfish.

"Well, I hope you figure it out," I said. "But I'm kind of busy with a whole new life here in New York, so please don't call me again."

"What?" Hunter said, realizing I was trying to end us from even ever being friends. "But Mel, I *need* you right now—"

"Bye Hunter," I said and hung up. The pain of our break-up hit me like it had just happened all over again and I realized I missed him much more than I was admitting to myself. Going back to Houston *definitely* wasn't an option anymore.

The phone continued to ring the rest of the day and night, but I always let the answering machine pick up, afraid it would be Hunter. Most of the time the caller hung up, so I assumed it was indeed him.

No, please, just leave me alone, I thought as I laid in bed, too upset to even look at the want ads or even sleep. The calls started first thing in the morning again as I waited for Subir and Cindy to come home.

"You can't talk to him or go back to Houston," Subir warned, and Cindy nodded. "You've come too far now."

I agreed, and they let me stay living on their couch for a few more days while I tried to figure things out. I found out from Whitney that Hunter was hanging around all our old haunts in Houston, moping about our cancelled engagement to everyone and not even talking about Candi. I found it pathetic after all this time, but also strangely alluring as well. The thought that his woes may have led him to now be a better man crossed my mind frequently, but after what he told me about being "on-again and off-again" with Candi this whole time I knew I couldn't take that chance and get back together with him. He could just be trying to play both of us now.

By the end of the first week of all three of us living together in such a small space, I knew I had to make a decision soon. I didn't want to overstay my welcome, but I also didn't know what I was going to do. I was almost out of money, and my job prospects were non-existent.

I took a walk down the street with Subir, trying to come up with a plan. But all I could really think of was going back to Houston and admitting to Oldie he was right.

"Is that *really* what you want to do, give up?" Subir asked.

"No," I said, almost in tears. "But I have no other choice."

"Yes you do," he said with confidence just like when my friend Beau told me I could be a realtor. That made me think of my only job experience ever.

"What if I tried to work in a real estate office?" I asked.

"I think that's a splendid idea! I know of one close by even. Come on!" I followed Subir quickly down the street, intrigued, as he led us to Sotheby's auction house.

"*Sotheby's?*" I asked, confused. "Isn't this an auction place?"

"And real estate… *international* real estate, which you would be great at! Come on, I know some people here," he said, stepping towards the front door.

"But I'm not dressed for a job interview and I don't even have a resume ready!" I said, stalling.

Subir stopped and stood directly in front of me, looking me straight in the eye. "You look great, as always Melanie, and you have to stop worrying so much! You have to stay positive, *always*. Negativity will get you exactly where you do not want to be, nowhere—and then this city will eat you alive. The sooner you realize that the best things in life are the things that you earn and are not just 'handed' to you, the sooner you can take control of your destiny. Now, shall we enter and see if someone inside needs any *help?*"

I couldn't believe it, but in less than two hours later I had a job at Sotheby's International Realty. It turned out someone had just given their notice the week before, and since I had a valid real estate license I fit the requirements for the vacant part-time position. Due to my lack of experience I couldn't actually show any condominiums or buildings, but I was perfect to be an "administrative assistant," updating the real estate listings on the company's computer database. I also loved the part-time aspect of it. My hours would be all day Tuesday through Thursday with both Fridays and Mondays off. That would give me a four-day weekend every week, and that suited me just fine. The only downside of the job was the pay—only $6.50 per hour—but with a schedule like that I didn't care. The people were all really nice and friendly, and there seemed to be an endless supply of girls just like me on hand from all over the world working there, each willing to work for peanuts just to hobnob with the wealthy clients and British gentry.

My new boss, Alexandra Wynn, was right out of college, and she was the head of the whole Sotheby's listing department. She was a fellow Texan from Dallas and a major T.O.P. heiress as well. She could care less about the pitiful salary we were all making. Her focus was squarely on enjoying the experience of the city at the ripe old age of twenty-two. We became fast friends and party-buddies my very first week there.

Subir's words stuck with me the whole time, and I stuck to them. He was right. I just had to stay positive and see what else good could happen to me there. I persevered, and ended up finding a room for rent in a large but very old one bedroom apartment in a pre-World War II building on 97th Street between Madison and Fifth Avenue. The neighborhood was very scary and only a few blocks from Harlem, so it was not at all what I was used to; but I realized that I was going to have to sacrifice some things if I was going to get anywhere at all in this city.

"So, can you pay month-to-month, or week-to-week?" Wallace, the woman who owned the apartment asked me during my interview. She had stringy brown hair to her waist and called herself a dress designer, but I didn't see any evidence of sewing anywhere in the living room or kitchen which were both fully in view. The sofa we were sitting on was an old, scratched up, leather thing that looked like it came from the Salvation Army, and the rest of the place was sparsely furnished with only the basics. "I only ask 'cause it seems I'm always having to look for new roommates, and I just want to know how long you plan on sticking around."

"Why doesn't anyone stay?" I asked, wondering if it was because of the poor state the Murphy bed was in. It was currently pulled out from the wall and taking up half of the living room right next to us. It looked very old and uncomfortable, and it would be my—or *any* roommate's—sleeping quarters.

"Oh, you'll see! I'm a bit 'nutty' to live with," Wallace laughed, taking my down-payment for the next month, which was mostly all the money I had left. I knew I had a challenge in front of me, but I also couldn't afford anything better.

Subir and Cindy were proud of me when they helped me bring over my things to move into my new place, though they tried to hide their look of horror when they actually saw it.

"It's called 'Harlem renaissance décor' darlings," Wallace joked with them as they stood speechless in the living room. "And hey, great suit!" she added towards Subir, who was thrilled that she noticed his brand new green and orange striped number.

I soon learned that "Wacky Wallace's" (as I started to refer to her) fashion designs could easily rival Subir's collection, for her favorite saying was, "When the going gets tough, the tough go shopping—to the *thrift* store!" Her bedroom, which was off-limits to me, was filled with beads, baubles, and little scraps of fur which she'd sew together into the most ridiculous party outfits I'd ever seen (next to Subir's normal daywear, of course). When she didn't have enough money to buy more scraps of fur she would resort to wearing her white cat around her neck like a live mink collar. She fed the poor creature an antihistamine to keep it placid as she headed out each night to the latest dance spot. All she ever did besides make her own outrageous outfits was party all night and sleep all day.

In an effort to make the apartment more chic before anyone else I knew saw it, I went to a thrift store Wacky Wallace recommended and purchased two large Chagall posters framed in wood for the large, bare, living room wall. Little did I know, however, that the wooden frames housed termites, which I soon found out the hard way one morning when the wicked-winged creatures "buzzed" around the room, waking me up. I had to scrape together pennies to afford a bug bomb, but fortunately, it did the trick.

The building didn't have a doorman, of course, but it had a double-locking mechanism on the entrance's front door, which was New York's best recipe for a quick rape or robbery while someone was fumbling for their keys. So I made sure I always had my key out and ready to get inside as fast as I could every time I came home, night or day. The apartment was truly disgusting and I even nicknamed it the "rat hole" because I could routinely watch mice scampering about the kitchen floor from my Murphy bed at night. It was a pretty grim place for a completely spoiled, twenty-seven-year-old woman from Texas who had spent her summers in Monte Carlo and her Christmases in Aspen annually, but it was all I could afford on my meager salary from Sotheby's. But I was also really learning how to survive on my own in the big city, and I was proud of myself. I hoped my family would be too, especially Oldie.

I soon settled into a busy, enjoyable routine of working three days straight, then going out with Alexandra (or "Alex" as I now called her), and my other New York friends both day and night the other four. It was fun and I was making it all work financially—though just barely. I soon began dating again, and Alex joked that I got more calls than her real estate listing agents did most days, for the rat hole didn't have a phone, so I could only give out my work number. I was happy to be so sought after and the only person I wished *wouldn't* keep calling was Hunter, for he still did, though now more randomly. But Alex and my other co-workers all knew never to forward his calls on to my desk whenever he did. Everyone was helping to look out for me as I continued to get over him, and I appreciated it. I had a lot of truly great friends and support.

"Are you kidding me? This has to be a *joke!*" Whitney said on her first visit to the rat hole two months later. She had been a frequent New York visitor in recent weeks for she was continuing to hit it off with Charles. In fact, she wouldn't shut up about him whenever I called home and always wanted to spend every moment with him in New York when he wasn't at the hospital, which was a lot, just like Dawson. But, she finally had a few moments while he was called away on an emergency this particular morning, so she came to see what my new 'home' was like.

I unfolded my Murphy bed to show her where I had been sleeping. Whitney stared at it, and for the first time I could ever remember, she was speechless. She looked at me like I was from Mars.

"Isn't it cozy?" I said, trying to remember Subir's words and sound positive as I outstretched my arms to put the full place on display. "And it's no joke. I'm going to make this work, even if it kills me."

"Ugh... that shouldn't take long," she groaned, then lost her patience quickly. "This is bullcrap Melanie! You can't live here. Let's go back to my hotel room."

"Well, fine, for tonight, but this is where I live now Whitney, like it or not."

"You just better hope Mom never sees this place. She'd have a coronary and then Charles would have to save her!"

"You're just trying to bring up 'Charles' again into the conversation," I joked, but as we left the rat hole and rode in a taxi back towards midtown towards the Plaza, I thought about Whitney's reaction and knew she was right. I couldn't believe I was living such a pitiful existence. But I did my best to hide those feelings in front of her.

"So my job's going *great*," I told Oldie on the phone as Whitney kept giving me a look of annoyance as she eavesdropped.

"That's great, Lil' Bit," Oldie said, but not like he really meant it. I knew he still wanted to be proven right that I wouldn't be able to handle a New York life. "And how's your new place? As good as the *Plaza?*"

"Close," I lied.

"It's *nothing* like—" Whitney stared to say loudly, but I quickly interrupted.

"Ah, I have to go. Say hi to Mom for me!" I hung up and turned to Whitney. "Please, don't say anything to Oldie or Mom, okay? I know they want me to move back to Texas, but I can't. Especially with Hunter now being there. He calls me all the time now at work, but luckily I don't have a phone at the rat hole, so I can at least avoid him there."

She looked at me understandably now. "You're really trying to stay away from him, aren't you?"

"Yes, but it's still hard."

"Well, okay then. You know, I never understood how much a guy could really affect you, or anyone, but I'm beginning to now, so I get it."

"Does that mean it's getting serious between you and Charles?"

"Oh, I don't know," she said, blushing. "But we're sure having a lot of fun! He's well traveled and talks a lot about his European escapades. Of course I have a few of my own to add to the mix, and he never judges me for any of them. It's just nice to be with someone who's really got it together."

"Wow, who are you and what have you done with my sister? The real Whitney would be bored with him by now..."

"What can I say? He's not boring!"

"So do you think it's really going somewhere then?"

"Let's not get *too* carried away. It's only been two months, and the only place I'm concerned about going with him is to wherever he's taking me tonight!"

We laughed as she began to get dressed, and I helped her get ready.

Sure enough, Whitney couldn't keep her mouth shut once she was back in Houston and a few days later my mother showed up at the Plaza Hotel and then came to visit me in my new "place." I thought I might turn a negative into a positive and tried to tidy the place up as best I could, but she only lasted thirty seconds in the rat hole before she covered her mouth and gasped. "Melanie, you can't possibly be living like this! This is worse than a ghetto!" She used her heavy Texan accent and had tears of disbelief in her eyes.

"I know it's awful," I retorted, "but I'm never home. I'm only here to sleep and change clothes really."

Her tears began to fall as she pleaded with me. "Mel, you *really* need to come back home to Texas. Why would you ever even want to live up here like this?"

I hugged her. "Mom, it's okay. I've been having a great time and I've made a lot of great friends. One is even from Texas. I've been putting away some money too, and with a little help from Oldie I've been thinking of getting a summer share in the Hamptons this summer, so I won't be here all year. Don't worry, it will work out. After all, Oldie thought I was unemployable, and I've got a job I'm good at now, so I proved him wrong about that, right? I'll show him I can do well here again if I can just get a great place for the whole summer too."

"Okay, I'll talk to him. For now though I'm getting you out of here! As long as I'm here you're staying with me at the Plaza!"

"No argument there. I'm determined, but not 'crazy!'" I told her.

My mom begged Oldie to send me more rent money, but he thought New York was just too damn expensive so he said no. But we both knew it was really because he secretly wanted me back in Texas and thought I would soon get sick of living so badly and come crawling back. But I didn't. He did, however, tell me he was happy I was actually employed and surviving 'on my own.'

Then, after four consecutive months at both my job and living with Wacky Wallace in the rat hole over the holidays and throughout the coldest, harshest, New York winter months, Oldie was so impressed that he finally agreed to supplement my pathetic income. However, it was still not enough for a better apartment, so I continued to stay on my Murphy bed and used the welcomed, extra money for better food, shopping, partying, and saving up for a summer share in the Hamptons. I was still living way beyond my means though, and as I trudged through the slushy, now sparsely, snow-crusted streets, I often wondered what exactly I was doing in New York and why was I working for this ridiculous amount of money.

I had a college degree from the University of Texas and was fluent in two languages, but, except for my brief stint as a real estate agent back in Houston that now seemed like a hundred years ago, this was my only real, long-term job. I finally rationalized that my whole stay in New York was a good escape from Hunter, and it was all much cheaper than the four or five days a week of therapy sessions that had been highly recommended to me by several of my physicians back in Houston if I had stayed there to try and get over him. They all agreed I needed extensive therapy to recover from my marathon relationship with such a serial cheater. He had beaten me down emotionally for so long they were all a little doubtful that I would or even could ever recover, or be able to trust a man ever again. All I knew was that as long as I was in New York, Hunter wouldn't be around as a distraction because New York was never his 'thing.' The temptation to call him and get back together with him was still great, but focusing on my own survival took my focus off of him and I wanted to continue to get better on my own. And with spring just around the corner, I knew things would only get brighter if I stayed living here, so I did.

Chapter 11

$\mathcal{B}$y the end of April, I had reached my first six months of making it on my own in the big city and I wanted to celebrate, so I arranged an intimate party in a suite at the Plaza Hotel. I invited Alex from Sotheby's; Subir and Cindy, in appreciation for all they had done for me at the beginning of my journey; Whitney and Charles, who were still happily together, and Victoria, who was flying in for the first time since I had moved to New York just to see me. I also reluctantly invited Eva and Dawson, but Dawson 'no-showed' the night of the event, to the surprise of no one.

"Oh my God Mel, it's so good to see you!" Victoria said as she flung her arms around me in the entrance to the suite. Most everyone else was already there and I had been anxiously awaiting her arrival for the past half hour.

"And you too!" I said, kissing her on the cheek. "It's been way too long!"

"I know and we have so much to catch up on, but first, let me tell you my *biggest* news..." She grinned as she motioned to someone in the hallway. In seconds an elegantly dressed, handsome man who looked just like John F. Kennedy Jr. appeared next to her. "Melanie St. John," Victoria began, "this is Christopher Curry, an investment banker from Canada I met while he was working on a business deal in Florida shortly after I returned from my trip. He and I have been dating for the past few weeks, so I asked him to come along as my 'plus one.'"

"Nice to meet you," Christopher said as he shook my hand firmly. "I've looked forward to this trip to the city all week. Victoria and I have tickets to the Met for tomorrow evening."

"Handsome *and* smart, I approve Vic!" I joked.

"Don't embarrass him too much or you might chase him away," Victoria said.

"Ah, he looks tough enough to handle it," I said towards Christopher. "Please, both of you, come inside and make yourself comfortable. I have the bar fully stocked."

"Thank you," Christopher said as he walked ahead of us towards the bar.

"Great catch!" I whispered to Victoria.

She gave me an 'I know' look with her eyes as we both glanced at his firm, muscular frame from behind. He was the total package.

The party was fun and laid back. Everyone got along well and the catered food, drinks, and champagne flowed all night. I was worried about Eva being mopey or acting weird the whole evening like usual, but she was relishing the first social outing she had attended in months and behaved herself. I couldn't have been more surprised.

As the night wore on, the room divided into small groups with people conversing in stimulating, interesting conversations. Whitney, Eva, Victoria, and I soon found ourselves in our own.

"I'm so glad to finally spend time with you," Eva said to Whitney in earnest. "This has to be the first time we've done this since you've been coming to New York all these months."

"Well when I'm here, I'm *busy,*" Whitney said, and we all clearly got her underlying meaning.

"Okay Whitney," I said. "Spill it! You've been all secretive and mysterious the past few times you've come to visit. What's up between you and Charles?"

Whitney grinned from ear to ear as she looked at Charles lovingly from across the room. He was in a deep conversation with Christopher, Subir, Cindy, and Alex, and it looked like whatever they were talking about took all their attention.

"Yeah girl," Eva egged her on. "*Tell*—before I say something that will make you blus—"

"All right, all right!" Whitney said. "We're living together!"

"*Really?* Wow!" Eva squealed. "That's fantastic!"

"Congratulations," Victoria said.

"For how long?" I asked, not believing I didn't already know this. I wondered if Oldie and our mother even knew.

"For a few weeks now," Whitney said. "I've been flying up on all the weekends he hasn't been on call… which he's managed to make sure is most of them for *me!*"

Eva instantly looked jealous. Whitney didn't even blink as she continued, "One time he just offered me a key to his place as I was saying goodbye and told me I could stay with him 'whenever I wanted to now.' It's not that big of a deal y'all, it's just so we can see more of each other."

"Sure," I said sarcastically.

"Whitney, that's so exciting and I'm *so* happy for you!" Eva said, now suddenly thrilled, though it was more because of the thought of having her old best friend around more often rather than Whitney's new romantic endeavor.

"Well, since we're on the topic of revealing 'big' news," Victoria said with a tone of nerviness and anticipation, "Christopher and I will be moving to New York next month!"

"What?" I said, both surprised and thrilled. "Why didn't you tell me before?"

"We just decided really," she said. "My brother has some contacts for him to talk with on Wall Street this week, and on top of that Christopher has some contacts for *me* to meet with here in the modeling world too!"

"Ooohh," Whitney said. "Nice work—*if* you can get it."

"I hope I can," Victoria said. "I've already done several successful shoots in Miami, and now Christopher's used the pictures from them to get me an interview with the *Wilhelmina* agency!"

"They'll love you, I just know it," I told her as I thought back to when I had the chance to go meet with the same modeling agency through Morgan, but never did. I was glad Victoria was following through with the opportunity. "And I'm really looking forward to having you around!" I added, but as soon as I said it I shuddered at the odd parallel between Eva and I now having our two best friends move here at the very same time.

"Anyway," I said, changing the subject in my mind. "I guess it's *my* turn! Attention please—everyone!" I said, turning so everyone at the party could hear me. "Summer is rapidly approaching, and as you all probably know everyone who is anyone is talking about 'summering in the Hamptons,' so of course I want to go to the Hamptons and take a summer share like everyone else! But not because I think I'm 'anyone,' it's mostly because I desperately need a break from that rat hole I'm living in!"

Everyone laughed, for by now most of them had seen it and met my wacky roommate, too.

"So last week I took the Hampton Jitney out to Southampton where Whitney and I stayed last year and had such a fabulous time, and I checked out some great available rental properties there. I've decided to move forward and wanted to let you know that you are all invited to stay with me to have fun—and to help share the cost of course, too!"

The announcement set the whole room abuzz with excitement, with the exception of Whitney, who quickly pulled me aside. "No offense Mel," she started with a protective, worried tone, "but how in the world will you be able to afford this from working at *Sotheby's?*"

"I'm glad you asked," I told her. "I knew between that and the extra money Oldie sends me I still wouldn't be able to afford it, so I searched out the possibility of borrowing against my stocks. I succeeded and managed to get a substantial loan. All I need to do now is select the house and find enough people to live with me and help share the rent so I can pay it back."

"Count us in!" Victoria said after discussing it with Christopher.

"Yeah, sounds like fun and the perfect place to make a lot of great contacts over the summer after we get settled into our new place here," Christopher said with excitement.

"And it's been so long since we've been able to hang out Mel, this will be a way to really catch up!" Victoria added.

"I'd absolutely love to sign up!" Alex exclaimed. "This is exactly why I moved to New York, to do things like this! Oh my God, this is so exciting!"

"Well, with all due respect Squirt, sharing a house with a bunch of people doesn't sound like my cup of tea," Whitney said as she gave Charles a seductive look. "We require *a lot* of privacy, right babe?"

"What can I say? When she's right, she's *right*," Charles said, taking Whitney in his arms and kissing her passionately. All the women in the room seemed to be a little jealous of her instantly.

"I'm not going to be able to go either," Eva said. Again, it only looked like an effort to be closer to Whitney, but to be honest, I was relieved.

"Cindy and I would be happy to take part," Subir said. "And I happen to know a few people who I can ask to move in as well, to help take the burden off of you, Melanie."

"Thank you Subir," I said excitedly. "I knew I could count on you!"

"You've come so far in so little time," Cindy added like a proud mother hen.

"Yeah," Subir agreed. "How can we not continue to watch you grow?"

I was so proud of myself and happy to have such good, supportive friends. The party went on until the wee hours of the morning, but instead of really enjoying it any longer, I stayed busy in my mind making plans for the summer share.

I couldn't wait to sign the papers for my Southampton house and immediately started asking around at Sotheby's that Tuesday for advice.

"It's all about location, location, location!" Alex chattered as we stood in the hallway, not even thinking about work. "Melanie, you simply *have* to be east of the highway and you MUST have a pool, otherwise forget about getting invited to the parties. And once you're out of the party loop, you can just kiss your summer good-bye."

"Can't you help keep us in the party loop?" I asked, knowing it was Alex's thing to be 'in the know' about all things party-related in New York.

"Absolutely!" she squealed. "Now, we have you, me, Victoria and Christopher, Subir and Cindy, and that leaves...?

"At least four more," I said, doing the math for the full rent money needed in my head. We could make it work if we just had ten people total, which was the common number of residence I'd heard in each summer share done like this. It will be a lot different than having one big house all to ourselves like our family did last summer with a full house staff to our avail, but it still had to be better than living in the rat hole. "Subir is checking around for people who want in too."

"Who else do you think we should ask?"

Just then "The Squid"—one of our tall and languid co-workers—lumbered by. Her real name was Grace Kidd and though on the surface she was a gorgeous twenty-six-year-old, adorned with a pretty face and large, fake breasts, constant misery darkened her complexion and soured the air around her almost always. Everyone called her The Squid because whenever she got upset she'd blanket the room with her demeanor until everyone else was also covered with a thick, inky, black cloud of gloom. Grace could turn a whole room's mood from good to bad in an instant.

One sweltering hot, humid night a couple of weeks before, I had invited a group of girls from work over for cocktails before we went out dancing. The Squid had overheard us talking about it, which she assumed was an invitation, so I had no choice but to give her the directions to my place. She arrived at the poorly air-conditioned, boiling hot rat hole later that night wearing a skin-tight, fire-engine-red North Beach leather dress that looked like it had been painted over her exquisite body. As soon as she walked into my cramped, sticky apartment she started sweating, squirming, and complaining about the heat instantly. Then, just to make her feel extra special, a couple of mice scurried by her feet, as if to check her out. I almost burst out laughing at her scampering from the mice in that ridiculous, too-tight outfit. An hour later, after her non-stop whining had annoyed everyone there, we all had to concoct an intricate plan just to ditch her before we went on to the club.

Grace was the kind of social reject who didn't know she was one—case in point, we'd been calling her The Squid for so long at work now that she thought it was some sort of hip approximation of her last name "Kidd" and had even embraced it, telling us to call her "Squid" right to her face. Eager for friends, she often came off as desperate but yet, just as quickly, she'd turn off any potential comrades with her utter negativity. The one appealing mystery about her was that she had had the same boyfriend since college for eight years… no one could see how any man could put up with her for that long unless he himself was a downer too.

The Squid stopped right next to us and asked, "What are you guys talking about?"

We paused awkwardly, unsure if we should continue.

"Well," I hesitated, but then realized she would be good for the rent. She was also from Texas and had a hefty trust fund she bragged about often. "I was just telling Alexandra about my summer share in the Hamptons this year. But I'm sure you won't want to—"

"Right on! Are you still looking for roommates? Because I don't have anything going on this summer and I'd really love to get out of the city," she said eagerly.

I doubted The Squid had any clue what a summer 'share' in the Hamptons meant, but I did some quick mental arithmetic and realized time was short—I needed people to commit. Money was money, right? "Sure Squid, I'll get you the info... stop by my desk later, okay?"

That meant we had seven people for sure, which was enough to make me feel confident, so the next day I took the Hampton Jitney back out to Southampton and went searching for houses. I found a large, two-story house with a pool on Pond Lane. I signed a lease for a three-month summer rental and held my breath—it was incredibly expensive at nearly $50,000—and even at that price, the place was a bit run-down. Thankfully it had eight bedrooms, a great patio area, a clean pool, and it was in a phenomenal location, just five minutes from town.

I knew I'd have to get busy finding more people to share the monthly rent though, for split seven ways that would still be a lot to come up with for any of us. I called Subir to see how he was progressing; so far he'd found four other people willing to move in. I was elated—that meant we'd have eleven people in all to fill the rooms—including couples—and that number divided the rent into tolerable levels for everyone. We were now at capacity with a mixed bag of very diverse and interesting strangers.

On our first day there I soon realized Subir had assembled a truly colorful bunch:

There was Subir and Cindy of course, who both acted different in these surroundings than they had in their own apartment for some reason. I knew they were staying engaged while Subir waited for his family's inheritance so he could pay for a lavish wedding, but it still seemed to always be 'months' from now. *Polite and patient girl,* I thought about Cindy when I met her last summer and first heard this, but now I learned in these surroundings she was a non-stop party animal and motormouth with all the house guests. I started to wonder how a man as quiet and cultured as Subir could put up with that and silently wondered if that was the real reason for the constant delay in their wedding plans. Cindy talked constantly in an endless stream of drunken, verbal diarrhea that we all just tuned out.

Lizzy Jolmson was an acquaintance of Subir's. She was a wealthy intellectual in her early thirties from Toronto who worked for the Canadian

Consulate. She and I were complete opposites. She was the mature single role model of the household, while I was the young single hopeful going out every chance I could to the latest nightclubs and hitting every single's party in town looking for dates. She preferred "mature functions" at the embassies or was even satisfied staying in, reading non-fiction, and listening to Miles Davis. Unlike me, she had a "real" job that paid her "real" money, and she used her brain on a daily basis, which she never tired of reminding us all about.

Reza Imiri was a thirty-five-year-old, ultra-successful Persian realtor from Tehran who drank rosé champagne all day and amused everyone with stories from the old country. He was fond of telling tales from when the Ayatollah took over Iran, forcing his family—who were supporters of the Shah—to flee the country. Unlike most refugees, they managed to escape with their wealth intact and he wowed us with descriptions of parties from the Shah's "townhouse palace" on East 64th Street in Manhattan. Then, when the Shah's assets were frozen by the city of New York, Reza described how his sister rented the Shah an elaborately furnished townhouse, filled to the brim with antiques and original works of art, costing a mere $10,000 a month.

Reza was a colorful character who kept us all laughing and entertained, but a misstep could cost us too, for Reza's temper tantrums were flamboyant and legendary (and often involved dirty acts of revenge). Everyone soon learned not to cross Reza, ever.

Sylvia Riker was the craziest, most confused and mixed-up of the bunch hands-down. I thought it was hard to top Wacky Wallace, but if too much money corrupts then Sylvia and her dysfunctional family were the living examples of corruption. She was a young, 'twenty-something free spirit' from Los Angeles and the rich people from L.A. are "a special kind of crazy," as Oldie used to say. Sylvia's mother was eighteen when she had Sylvia, so she was more or less raised by her wealthy grandparents. According to several of Sylvia's therapists, the fact that her mother was more like an older sister and friend than a mother became the root of all her problems, which were a lot: drugs, drinking, sleeping around, paranoia, and most notably, being a compulsive liar. The outrageous fabrications from her mouth coupled with her discombobulated mind that didn't seem to know what was real or wasn't made us all guess that whatever she said to any one of us at any given time was probably a little bit truthful and a whole lot of crap.

A favorite past time of everyone quickly became to compare Sylvia's stories with one another to decipher how many versions there were. Depending on the day, her biological father—whom she had 'supposedly' never met—was a poor hitchhiker from Mississippi that her hippie mom had picked up on the Ventura Freeway, or sometimes he was a super-rich business mogul living in Beverly Hills, and other times he was a pervert who she did know and tried to molest her once, so her mom tossed him out on his ass. The only part of the story she knew for sure—and that she ever said more than once—was that he was living on the North Shore of Long Island now. One of these days she planned to drive by his house for a glimpse, or even go up to the door for a confrontation. We didn't know how much her garish tales were true, but we did know that after her third arrest for marijuana possession last year, Sylvia's family had cut off her finances. She was still a major pothead, but, like me, Sylvia had moved to New York City with hopes to start a whole new life and forget her past. For that reason alone, I liked her.

Perhaps the most intriguing housemate of all was a woman named Carol Coleman who was from one of Dallas's toniest of neighborhoods. She was beautiful, brilliant, in her mid-thirties, and the toast of the Dallas social scene. She'd modeled in college, had been head cheerleader *and* homecoming queen, and seemed to have it all. But, she had a dark, shameful habit. Not drugs, alcohol, or sex—but to make herself 'feel' better, Carol shoplifted. She started out stealing small items like *Baccarat* animal figurines for her friends, but she soon graduated to stealing designer clothes from *Saks* and *Neiman Marcus*. She said it relieved her of her anxiety—like taking a drag off a cigarette might satisfy a smoker—but when she got home she'd panic, asking herself, "Did anyone see me? Am I on a surveillance camera somewhere?"

Carol soon became completely out of control and was nearly arrested at a *Betsy Johnson* store when she put a dress on under the one she was wearing and tried to walk out. When the alarm went off and security busted her, she whipped out her credit card and played dumb, which got her off the hook, but scared her straight. There was no concrete reason why she'd do it; her family had plenty of money and an arrest would totally ruin her family's carefully polished, public image. She said she continuously risked everything for some dumb piece of wardrobe she could have easily afforded, just for the thrill really.

"One day, when I was out walking my dog through my neighborhood, which was pretty posh," Carol told Alex and me on our first night there as we all bonded over being from Texas. "I spotted a house under construction. Out of curiosity, I went inside and saw some amazing English and French antiques that hadn't been packed away yet. There were several pieces I just loved and had to have, so I returned later with my suburban, loaded it up, and took the pieces back to my own townhouse. No one ever made a fuss about it or mentioned it, so I thought the people forgot all about the items. But then, just a few months later I decided to put my townhouse on the market and I held an open house. Someone from the neighborhood recognized the antiques as 'stolen.' They confronted me about it and there was a big fight—I just couldn't convince them that they were mine because they were so rare, and I had no real explanation of how I came to acquire them. Well, the open house ended and I became violently ill afterwards from the sheer embarrassment of it all... Gossip spread like wildfire, and the event shoved me out of the whole Dallas social scene and forced me to make a move to New York." She smiled at us. "I now look back on that day as the best day of my life because being publicly humiliated like that *finally* got me to accept the fact that I needed help, and I now get to be here for the whole summer with y'all making a fresh start."

I was glad she was there too since she paid up front for the whole summer already, but still, I was going to make sure to lock up my valuables! I looked over at Alex and could tell she was thinking the same thing as me. We were the only ones there so far, and despite the range of ages and personalities, we were all looking forward to our wild summer in the Hamptons.

For that first night there, the start of our very first fun weekend in the share, I had organized an elaborate party with champagne and fresh barbecued lobster tail. The lobsters were a little beyond my means, but it was important to me that everyone be happy in our new home, so I marinated the lobsters for grilling, prepared side dishes, and piped soothing R & B music throughout the house and by the pool.

But as I drank my champagne with only Alex and Carol there still, I fretted over the rest of the food getting cold, and then the reality of the weekend commute started settling in: most of the housemates had full-time jobs, which meant they couldn't leave the city until after work on Fridays, so that meant they would be stuck in "parking lot-like" traffic on the Long Island Expressway for hours most likely, and they were.

Everyone arrived very late and exhausted from the drive. Immediately, there were disputes over sleeping arrangements.

"Why should you guys get bigger rooms, just because you're a 'couple?'" The Squid said to Cindy.

"Yes, because we're two people... it just makes sense," Subir answered in Cindy's and his defense.

"Well I don't see how that's fair! We should have to draw for rooms!" The Squid stomped around loudly, wearing a short, tight, stone-washed jean skirt with black lace leggings underneath, a metallic blue bikini top with a white mesh covering, and silver heels, trying to get people to see things her way. I was beginning to think I was a magnet for people competing in a most outlandish outfit competition.

I looked down at Squid's psychedelic luggage and wondered what other concoctions she'd brought. Her fashion sense would definitely land her on Mr. Blackwell's worst dressed list. You'd think she'd fit in quite well with

Subir, who was wearing a bright yellow and red number, but they were going at it more than anyone.

"And well, I don't mean to be difficult, but there's no way I'm fitting all my clothes into *this* tiny closet. I'm definitely going to need a room with more space," Carol said matter-of-factly to me, eyeing the tiny closet in her assigned room skeptically.

Sylvia barked, "But we already claimed our spots!" She had gotten there shortly after Alex, Carol, and I finished our bonding earlier and taken one of the largest rooms.

"Well some people have to work, you know! It shouldn't be 'first come first serve'—we all pay the same rent here!" The Squid whined.

"Which means some people—single people—just have to have the smaller rooms. There's no way around it," said Christopher calmly.

I was starting to get nervous and whispered to Victoria, "If this keeps up it's gonna be a rough summer!" We giggled quietly.

"I know," Victoria whispered back. "I can't believe the arguments and one-upsmanships *already*. I assumed everyone would be more civil with each other, but at least we're here together, and I also have Christopher with me!"

"Oh—just look at that smile," I grinned. "Are things going *that* good with him?"

"Oh my God Mel, it's so great! He's so sweet to me and we never, ever fight. It's the best relationship I've ever had!"

I wished the relationships of everyone else in the share were as peaceful as Victoria and Christopher's, but there was constant conflict from that moment on and the evening was a complete disaster. I tried my best to ignore the bickering, but I went to bed that night with a raging headache and a queasy stomach.

Determined to make it all work, I tried again the very next day. No one in the house knew how to cook besides me, so I then learned they were all expecting me—as the one holding the lease—to cater all their dinners each night.

I worked all day shopping and cooking up a storm and arranged a dinner cocktail party that night with all the neighbors, thinking an infusion of blood and fresh conversation might lighten the mood and diffuse the growing tension (and get people to behave). No such luck. The quibbles continued, with The Squid as the catalyst.

"My bedroom absolutely sucks!" The Squid complained loudly. "My bed is *way* too small, and my back is killing me! Someone has to switch with me."

Subir stood up. "'Squiddie,' *enough!* I've told you a million times that all the beds in the house are the same! We've settled on this already, and no one is going to move just to accommodate you."

"Even if we did she'd just complain about something else," Sylvia piped in, with a mouthful of prosciutto-wrapped cantaloupe showing as she spoke. "I don't think I've seen her smile once since we've gotten here."

The Squid was outraged. "Oh—can you think of one reason why I *should* be smiling? I'm stuck out here in the middle of nowhere with all of you ridiculous misfits in this sweltering heat, and yes, it absolutely *stinks!*"

"Um, excuse me, but did you just call me a 'ridiculous misfit?'" Christopher asked, glaring at her and leaning in her direction as if expecting an explanation.

"Well, you are *Canadian,*" Carol joked, trying to lighten the mood.

"Look who's talking 'southie,'" Lizzy said sarcastically as she playfully tossed her napkin at her.

Carol took offense. "What's that supposed to mean?"

"Why do you always have to go out of your way to insult everyone?" Lizzy asked.

"I don't," Carol insisted, which we all knew was a lie, for she really did this every chance she got. Then she muttered under her breath, "Whatever, snob. You think you're 'so' much better than *everyone...*"

"I do not," Lizzy said; making it obvious she had heard her. And the bickering continued to escalate from there as invited neighbors quickly and politely made their way towards the exits. I didn't blame them.

My only shelter in the storm that night was Victoria. I pulled her aside a few hours later, "God, can you believe these people *still?!*"

"I know!" Victoria said. "Thank goodness for you and Christopher, otherwise I don't think I could last another minute here."

"Are things still going great with lover boy?"

"Better than great... I think I may be falling in love."

"Oh Vic, I'm so happy for you!"

Aside from Christopher and Victoria, the rest of the house was in a constant state of conflict the whole rest of the weekend, and it only got worse our second weekend together. As the owner of the lease I did my best to try and keep the peace, but keeping a bunch of rich, spoiled brats in line was getting old, fast.

The Squid was totally lost in translation. She became the pariah of the household, complaining about virtually everything and making sure every single person knew just how miserable she was. To make things even worse her long-term boyfriend dumped her, and she asked me daily where all the available men were and accused me of filling my house with complete losers. I didn't know how much more I could take.

Then on Saturday afternoon, as I was preparing a big barbeque dinner and party for everyone that very night, I heard a knock on the front door. I answered to find a distraught and teary-eyed Eva standing on the front porch of my already drama-filled beach house.

What now? I thought. I wasn't sure I could handle Eva's problems on top of my own, but I let her in anyway. "Eva, what's going on? What's wrong?"

"Mel," Eva whimpered. "I stayed in New York because I thought I'd be able to see more of Whitney... but she's always off with Charles. She *never* has *any* time for me!" She dropped an overnight bag on the floor, and I silently rolled my eyes. "I barely see her and when I do, I'm just a third wheel. She might as well still live in Houston!"

"C'mon, Eva...why can't you just be happy for her?"

"Seeing her happy doesn't help. Charles is the perfect, doting boyfriend who makes sure Whitney doesn't want for anything. That's the life *I've* always wanted—that's the life *I'm* supposed to have! Seeing Whitney so happy just makes me resent Dawson even more!"

I tried steering her back to reality. "Whitney's your friend, right? Don't you want her to *be* happy?"

"Well, yeah... but she gets more attention in one day than I get from Dawson in a whole *month!*"

I couldn't stand her self-pity party anymore. "Eva, if you're unhappy you need to *do* something about it. I waited and waited for Hunter to come around, and it almost destroyed me. Just waiting around to see what happens isn't going to help you."

Eva paused and sniffled a little. "You're right, Mel... you really are..." I could see the gears turning in her head. "I'm at square one, and I'm going to have to win Dawson all over again somehow—"

She wasn't getting the point! Frustrated, I said, "You know Eva, you might try a little *sincerity* for a change, it might do your relationship some good."

But Eva was clearly not listening anymore as she mulled over something else she was already considering out loud, though more to herself than me, "...only this time, it'll be different. This time, I'll really win his heart. When I'm finished he'll be just like Charles is with Whitney. He'll *have* to be, if I'm pregnant with his <u>baby</u>!" She looked up at me with happy, swollen, glazed-over eyes.

I was taken aback. I thought I'd been convincing her to leave her unhappy marriage, not create an unhappy family. "Eva no! Come on—"

"Seriously! We talked about having a kid one day, mostly because I've been so down lately with nothing to do, and we agreed to wait until Dawson's schedule was less hectic, but if it just 'happens—'"

"Now you're just talking crazy! Getting pregnant isn't going to make your husband love you!"

"Oh yeah? We'll see about that."

"Look, Eva—do what you want, but I can't support this. Maybe some time away from him would do you some good." I looked down at her bag. "Are you staying over, because I'm throwing a big barbeque tonight and you should stay and think about things… it'll be fun." At least I hoped it would be.

"Could I? Oh thanks, Mel. I'll stay on a couch or something. I could really use a good old-fashioned house party—I'll even help you plan it!"

The evening arrived and I kicked off the barbeque with some loud southern rock. With Eva's help I built a huge spread of standard B.B.Q. fare with chicken, ribs, hamburgers, and sausage and I even hired a bartender for the night. The alcohol and the music were flowing, and this time I was sure everyone would have a great time.

But a few hours later I started to wonder if perhaps the alcohol was flowing a little too freely. Most of the guests were drunk before the food was even served. People were getting quite loud and boisterous. To calm my own nerves I'd even had a few too many cocktails with Eva getting everything ready, and I could feel that I was quite tipsy.

As usual The Squid was being a pill. I happened to overhear her conversation with one of our handsome and very available neighbors just as I was walking by them on the front patio.

"My boyfriend just left me after eight years, can you believe that? What a prick! I'm so miserable. And to top it off, this heat is atrocious. It's really horrible here—I have no idea what all the fuss is about with this whole place. I mean, like, the mosquitoes? No one said anything about how bad the mosquitoes are!" The Squid complained continuously in an ongoing, steady stream of inky gloom.

Just who the hell does she think she is? I thought. My usual calm self had had just about enough of her. She was a guest at *my* summer house, at MY barbeque—and here she was scaring off the guests! I knew if I heard her complain about the heat index one more time I was going to scream. Yes, it was over a hundred degrees in the shade, but the heat combined with her mouth was what was *wholly* intolerable.

I stormed up and confronted her. "Squiddie, our new neighbor is not interested in hearing the petty complaints of a spoiled brat from Texas! If you're so miserable here call the Hampton Jitney tomorrow and you can go home. I'll find someone else to take your room. At this point, I think it's crystal clear that the Hamptons *aren't* your scene!" I gave her the dirtiest look I could muster.

The Squid glared at me, but thankfully, turned on her heels and silently went back inside. I smiled apologetically to our new neighbor. "Sorry if she was bothering you, won't you join me inside for a cocktail?" He seemed relieved to be rescued and happily went inside to take me up on my offer at the crowded bar. We chatted for awhile and he soon found himself in a great, flirtatious conversation with Sylvia, so I left them to get to know each other better as I wandered off to mingle and play hostess.

As I made my way around the crowded room I was met by a hiccupping and sobbing Victoria, who quickly pulled me into a corner. "Oh, Melanie! Thank God I found you!" Tears streamed down her face and I could barely understand her.

"Sweetie, what's wrong?" I asked, concerned.

"Christopher... he... he... just broke up with me!" she sobbed.

"Why? What happened?" I was completely shocked.

"I caught him kissing Lizzy on the beach! That bitch!" Victoria cried. "What's wrong with me, Melanie? Why doesn't anyone want to be with me?"

I gave her a long hug. "Shhh, Victoria... calm down. Nothing's wrong with you! It's just the guys you go out with sometimes... They're the ones who have something wrong with them... You're gorgeous, you're intelligent, and you're a model in New York for goodness sake! What more could a guy want?"

"Lizzy, apparently."

"Screw Christopher. He's obviously thinking with the wrong head."

"I can't stay here—"

"Vic, no! Listen, you don't need him anymore and I'll kick them both out for the rest of the summer! Just totally forget him, we'll find you a new guy. We can hit the clubs tonight, just you and me—just like in college! We'll have a great time, I promise."

"I can't, Mel. I don't want to be anywhere near those two. I'm gonna have to get out of here."

"Oh no, please Vic, don't go! I'm having an awful time here too, and it'll be hell without you this summer! I don't know if I can keep it together much longer..."

"I'm sorry, but I really fell for Christopher, and if I stay I'll be humiliated and also be worried about seeing that son-of-a-bitch kissing Lizzy again anywhere we went all summer—I just can't do it. I'm leaving tomorrow and moving in with my brother!" She ran upstairs to pack, sobbing.

It was awful after Victoria left, and after three dreadful weeks in the Hamptons to the tune of some ridiculous amount of borrowed money, I wasn't sure I could endure a fourth. And on top of my dysfunctional housemates, I was beginning to see that there was very little to do in

Southhampton besides party in our sectioned-off, rented summer houses. It was nothing like the fun summer I had had the year before with my family.

None of us belonged to any of the country clubs nor did any of the clubs there reciprocate with my clubs in Texas, so they were all 'off limits.' There wasn't anywhere to play golf or tennis, and the only beach available to us was a public one and it was a complete pain to go to—there was never any parking, scads of screaming children ran around like wild animals everywhere, and as Reza liked to say in a fake French accent, "It is trés *boring!*"

But it's not like I had much time to play tennis or go to the beach anyway. Since my housemates all expected me to continue to cook *all* our dinners, I'd have to make huge spreads that would take me a half-day to produce, and then I'd be too exhausted to even go to the beach, or even go out later that night. It was all getting to be too much. But when I stopped making food for everyone our dining bills from going out around town quickly got sky-high, and then they all complained about *that*. I worked really hard to keep everyone happy, but my efforts went completely unappreciated.

Soon it was abundantly clear that I'd made a huge mistake. So as the end of our third weekend came to a very welcoming close, I assembled everyone in the living room.

"I'm really sorry to have to do this, but I think it's clear that from day one, this experiment has been a complete disaster," I said. "I've spoken to the realtor and he's agreed to allow me to sublet for the summer. He said there's a long list of people waiting to take this property, but if any of you want to take over the place you'll have first dibs."

Everyone in the room groaned.

The Squid went absolutely berserk. "What the hell? Is this a joke? Do you think screwing around with my life is funny? What the hell do you expect me to do *now* for the rest of the friggin' summer?" She stormed out of the room before I could even answer.

Subir stood up. "Everyone, relax. I will take over the property, and anyone who wishes to stay will be more than welcome. Anyone, that is, except Squiddie."

We all laughed.

"Thank you so much, Subir!" I jumped up and hugged him. "Coming to my rescue, as usual!"

"It's not a problem, my friend," Subir grinned. "You gave it your best shot."

"I'm glad you think so. It means a lot coming from you," I said, realizing I now looked up to Subir like a big brother, and his opinion really did mean a lot to me.

Our meeting adjourned and everyone who wanted to stay huddled around Subir with their list of changes and requirements. I was glad to be through playing landlord.

Alex walked up to me. "You know Melanie, this couldn't have happened at a better time, really. My mother just called and invited me and a few friends out to Newport next weekend for my birthday! I've already invited Reza to be my date. Would you like to join us?"

I remembered my first Newport experience—also a disaster—but that was a long time ago and I desperately needed to get away from Southampton. I wasn't ready to return to the rat hole full-time either, so I took a leap of faith. "I'd love to!" I said, and prayed that it would be better than this.

Alexandra, Reza, and I celebrated Alex's twenty-third birthday that following weekend in Newport in style. On the first two nights we attended a smattering of swanky black tie parties, and on Sunday afternoon everyone had a farewell lunch together at The Beach Club on Seal Rock Beach. It was a wonderful weekend and nothing like my first visit to Newport at all. This time everywhere I went I was treated well by friendly, welcoming people and experienced none of the rudeness I had with Matthew Peyton almost a decade before. (I had found out at the club that he was already on his second marriage, and even that one, though still new, was rumored not to be going very well... I couldn't image *why*.)

As the weekend slowly came to an end, I wasn't looking forward to the very long, four-hour-plus drive back to Manhattan, nor returning to the dingy rat hole after staying in such a posh, wonderful guest room at Alex's family's beautiful seaside mansion (which they humbly referred to as a 'cottage' like all the grand estates in Newport were called). But, such was my fate, so I walked with Alex and Reza towards our rental car after we'd all finished a wonderful, delicious, last lunch there.

"Oh my Gosh! Melanie—is that *you?*" I heard a southern female accent say.

I turned around and there in the parking lot of the club getting out of their own rental car were two old high school friends of mine from Houston, Chrissie and Brady Pennington. I hadn't seen them in years and it was very refreshing to see some "Old Texans" here on the East Coast.

"Chrissie! Brady!" I said as I hugged them and then introduced them both to Alex and Reza. "I'm so glad we ran into each other—I was just on my way back to New York."

"Is that where you live now?" Chrissie asked.

"Yes," I said, "for most of the last year. I just love it, but not in the summertime. The heat in the city is *terrible!*"

"Well," Brady started, "we just arrived from Houston and are going to be spending the next month in Newport visiting my grandmother. She has an enormous house and her passion is hosting as many houseguests in it as possible. You should come and stay with us," he insisted.

"Or at least stay for one more night and have dinner so we can catch up," Chrissie said. "Then you can meet his grandmother, she's a real hoot!"

I was dreading going back to the city heat and didn't have to be back at work until Tuesday, so I jumped at the opportunity. "I'd love to!"

"Have fun," Reza said as he removed my bags from our car and handed them to me.

"Yeah," Alex added happily. "You're in God's country now, so enjoy every moment of it!" She kissed me good-bye and they drove off.

Brady, Chrissie, and I had dinner with his eighty-something-year-old grandmother, Mrs. Nielsen, in a private dining room later that night at the New York Yacht Club. The dinner was incredible and lasted for hours. It included bottle after bottle of three hundred dollar wine, caviar, and seven courses of perfectly plated French cuisine.

These people really know how to entertain! I thought as I sipped my champagne. *I could get used to this kind of lifestyle again.*

Mrs. Nielsen was a major Exxon oil heir, and though now in her golden years, she definitely still had both her looks and her wits about her. Her Newport summer 'cottage' was called Lark's Landing, and of all the town's impressive dwellings, hers was one of the last great mansions to be built by the renowned architect, Charles Platt. He designed the house in 1928 and did so in the style of Louis XVI. It was a stately, elegant, and classical French manor nestled on twelve acres and had two guest cottages, two heated greenhouses, three staff cottages (housing no less than thirty-seven, full-time staff workers) and a potting shed. The property and mansion had been properly maintained over the years and now stood as one of the only privately owned homes in a neighborhood otherwise maintained by the Newport Preservation Society. Lark's Landing was a large house, but it felt more like a grand hotel and its perfect arrangement of rooms created a sense of light and air to the free-flowing entertainment areas speckled throughout the grounds.

There were at least twenty people staying on the property my first night there, "hanger- ons" and "wannabes," as Brady called them, and we were all seated in the private dining room together that evening.

Brady turned to me and whispered discreetly when we first arrived, "My grandmother never leaves home without an entourage. She has to have at least three walkers per night."

"What's a walker?" I asked.

"You'll see," he grinned.

A walker, I soon learned through observing, is a man—often gay—who escorts wealthy, elderly women around town to various society functions. Mrs. Nielsen had three doting on her every move all night. But one of them suddenly began to get a little 'too' doting and started eating off her plate— with his fingers—so she motioned for the waiter quickly.

"The walkers have a tendency to drink too much," Brady informed me as we both watched the drunken man get escorted out of the room discreetly by a busboy. "But when one gets over-served like that, she simply has her driver take him home. She's figured out over the years that 'three' is the perfect number she needs to get through the night. By the time the last walker gets too tipsy, she's finally ready to leave as well!"

I laughed. It seemed that Mrs. Nielsen was still a major party animal, even at her age. I admired her and was having a ball. I didn't want the evening to ever end, and luckily it didn't have to, for Mrs. Nielsen seemed to read my mind.

"Melanie, dear," she said, gaining my full attention. "Are you enjoying your visit to Lark's Landing so far?"

"Oh yes, thank you so much for letting me stay with you," I told her earnestly.

"Brady tells me you have to go back to the city soon," she said sadly.

"Yes. I work at Sotheby's part-time during the week."

"Well, if you'd like to come back next weekend we'd all be happy to have you here again."

It didn't take me long to consider the invitation. "Yes, thank you, Mrs. Nielsen. I'd like that very much!"

Chrissie and Brady looked at me and smiled. My summer was now saved.

Chapter 12

❦

My short, three-day work week couldn't go by fast enough. The city was incredibly hot for July and the rat hole was even hotter. I couldn't get out of both fast enough as Friday morning finally came and I went back to the refuge of Newport.

Mrs. Nielsen had the "Green Room" ready for me, and I then learned that every guest bedroom of Lark's Landing had a distinctive nickname assigned to it based on its décor so she could visualize where everyone was staying at all times quickly in her head. I wondered if it was also a way to refer to people in case she forgot their names, for there were lots of house guests coming and going daily throughout the whole weekend nonstop.

"I'm so glad you could come back for a longer stay," Chrissie told me as we walked towards the main house after a game of tennis on my last day there. The weekend had gone by way too quickly and was filled with delightful time relaxing by the pool, sailing in the Atlantic Ocean, and enjoying wonderful, fabulous food served with only the finest champagne.

"Me too," I said as I relished the beautiful surroundings and took in the fresh air. It was warm, but tolerable compared to where I would soon be going back to in the morning.

"Hey guys," Brady said as he met us near the back patio entrance. His face and forearms were slightly sunburned from playing golf all afternoon. "Hope you two are hungry, we're going to the Yacht Club for dinner."

"Oh good!" Chrissie said excitedly. "Come on Melanie, let's go get ready. That's the same club we ate in last week, so we definitely want to look our best!"

Chrissie was right, for the New York Yacht Club was very upscale, and I was hoping to be able to revisit it. When we got there later that night the place was already packed with eloquently dressed patrons. I was dressed to the nines in couture and felt I fit right in.

"Melanie, dear," Mrs. Nielsen said as she greeted me. "So good to see you again…" She said this to everyone every time she saw them, even if it was only two hours before. I wasn't sure if it was an old-age thing, or just her way of greeting people instead of 'hello.' "And I hope you don't mind, but I took the liberty of already assigning everyone's seats tonight… I felt it would be more 'fun' to split everyone up so they could spend time getting to know some of the other guests."

Chrissie and Brady both looked at me, and I could tell they knew something was up, but said nothing.

A waiter came to let us all know our private dining room was ready, and a large crowd of people from the open courtyard filed into the stunningly set-up room.

"See you later," Chrissie smiled as she and Brady took their seats at the far end of the long table from me.

A tall and strikingly handsome man with thick, sandy blond hair and sparkling blue eyes sidled up next to me. "Well hello, Melanie St. John… it is Melanie, isn't it?" He feigned uncertainty, seeming a little nervous, which I found instantly appealing. "I believe we've been seated next to one another for dinner."

"Oh, well then, it's nice to meet you," I said as I held out my hand in greeting. Mrs. Nielsen winked at me from across the room and I knew she had deliberately sat him next to me as an attempted fix-up.

"I'm Barclay Cunnigham, but my friends call me Barc… I have to say, you are the most striking girl in this entire club, so I insist I buy you a drink. What are you drinking? Scotch? Tequila shots? Wine?"

Normally I'd just roll my eyes at the audacity, but tonight I was feeling a little audacious myself. Maybe it was the welcomed, cool breeze blowing through the opened windows, or perhaps that his name sounded ever-so-familiar … could he be Foxy Cunningham's son from Dallas, possibly? I silently prayed not.

"Shots? I don't 'do' shots," I told him teasingly.

"Well, what do you drink?"

"Champagne."

"Well then—waiter!" He raised his hand to get the waiter's attention. "A glass of your finest champagne for the lady, no, make it two glasses, please."

"I didn't ask you to buy me a glass of champagne," I said flippantly, tossing my blond hair back in the direction of Chrissie and Brady, who were watching me with interest.

"Well I didn't ask you to turn me down, either. You aren't turning me down, are you Melanie?" Barc seemed unsure, and I found his insecurity charming.

It's just a drink, I thought, and he looked into my eyes as if trying to read my mind. "Well... no, I don't suppose I am," I finally answered.

"Good," he grinned, now feeling more confident. "So, you're from Texas too I hear?"

Oh no, he must be the son of Foxy, I thought, wondering if that should be enough for me to know to run away right then and there. Foxy Cunningham was a flashy, well-known son of a Texas oil tycoon and he had quite a legendary reputation thoroughout all of Texas. According to Oldie, a couple of active wells were still very, very lucrative for the Cunninghams, and rumor had it that Foxy had amassed hundreds of millions of dollars over the years sitting on his father's pumps—and he wasn't shy about spending it around town. Oldie had long admired Foxy's enormous success in the oil business and I was aware that the two men shared similar political interests. Oldie often remarked, "Of all the good ol' boys, that Cunningham is a fox AND a hound!" he'd joke, referring not only to Foxy's gift in hunting down lucrative business deals—which he did with endless passion and enthusiasm— but also to the fact that he was a real 'dog' when it came to women, too. Long divorced from his first wife who bore him his first two sons, he was now working on his at least fourth—or maybe even fifth—wife, and they seemed to always stay the same pert, youthful age while he continued to age at least a decade in-between each ceremony.

But this attractive man I was now seated next to didn't seem harmful, and what I'd heard of his father could have all just been idle gossip. After all, Oldie was known to stretch the truth from time to time...

"Yes, Houston," I told him.

"Dallas."

"I know who you are. They call your father Foxy, is that right?"

"Yup, the one and only son-of-a-bitch," Barc said, rolling his eyes as the waiter arrived with our flutes of champagne. He took a long sip like he needed it after hearing his father's name and I wondered if I shouldn't have brought him up.

"I'm sorry, I was only trying to make conversation, for I think our fathers know each other," I said, sipping from my glass as well.

"I'm sure they do," Barc said. "Everyone in Texas seems to be connected by oil. That's why I was glad to get out of Dallas for the rest of the summer... I can't stand all the cliques and gossip back there."

"I know just what you mean. It was one of the reasons I left and moved to New York last year myself."

"That's what I heard."

"Really?" I said, flattered that he had been finding out about me before the evening even began. I wondered if he had been in on the fix-up. "What else did you hear?" I asked him curiously.

"That you left Houston to make it on your own in Manhattan, then left New York to get a summer timeshare in Southampton, but that was a bust so now you're here in Newport to escape from the Hamptons, is that right?" Barc said, amused.

"Yep, that about explains it," I said, equally as amused.

We smiled at each other and settled into a nice conversation that never stopped throughout the whole, five-course dinner.

I found out he was thirty-five and went to the University of Texas in Austin just like me, but he had already graduated by the time both Whitney and I went there. He obviously ran with the 'fast crowd' in college too as he described endless wild, all-night parties and lavish outings. It reminded me of the Fearsome Foursome escapades and I wondered which of the bad parts about that kind of party lifestyle he was leaving out. He said studying was never a priority for him since he knew he had a future working for his father's oil company, but he managed to graduate cum laude with a degree in business anyway, which meant either Foxy had some pull with the Dean, or Barc really was smart enough to get away with cheating often.

I noticed that as the night went on, Barc relaxed into an unassuming manner throughout the whole elegant dinner while other guests at the table fidgeted and seemed uncomfortable at times. I could tell he was used to enjoying long, leisurely dinners of truly fine cuisine without rushing through the meal, just like me.

Later, when dinner ended and we all moved into the courtyard for after-dinner drinks, Barc and I politely split up and joined the friends we came there with.

"So, what did you think of Barc?" Chrissie asked, and I could tell everyone seemed to have been in on the fix-up along with Mrs. Nielsen.

"He's cute," I said; then noticed Barc admiring me from across the patio as he sat with his own group. It felt nice to have someone's eyes on me again. It seemed no one had looked at me like that since Hunter, and I was afraid no one ever would again... But here was this confident, interesting, good-looking man right in front of me, now giving me his full attention, even from across a crowded room. I was smitten.

"His mother, Helen, comes from old ranch money in Texas," Brady said. "Her grandfather left her plenty when he died and she was smart with her investments... made a lot of big purchases in the art world, and now she's a well-respected player in it and runs her own gallery in Manhattan. She maintains one of the most important collections of contemporary art in the entire country there, but I hear her personal collection *rivals* it."

"Really?" I said, impressed. It was hard not to be impressed with Barc's pedigree the more I found out about him. "So they have a place in New York then?"

"Yes, Helen has several apartments in fact at the Carlyle, and she also has a chalice in Aspen, a place at the George Cinq in Paris, a beautiful estate in Dallas, and of course a huge mansion here in Newport."

"She's a real Newport legend, amongst the sort of people who 'know' about this sort of thing, I mean," Chrissie added. "Her estate here is one of the oldest and biggest ones on the whole coast."

I was trying to listen to find out more, but Barc's intense stare kept pulling me towards him more and more.

"Excuse me," I finally said when I couldn't take it anymore, "but I need to go freshen my drink."

I went up to the bar, and in seconds Barc was right beside me.

"Barkeep!" he said towards the bartender. "Please give the lady a glass of your finest champagne, and whatever else she wants."

I smiled and we talked for the rest of the evening. Mrs. Nielsen seemed pleased as she and her last walker finally left, leaning against each other for support as they exited. Barc and I stayed until closing. Neither of us wanted the night to end. Chrissie and Brady were being very patient as they stayed in their own corner of the room, waiting for us to say good-night so they could take me home.

"Well, it was really nice to meet you," I finally said, "but I think my friends are ready to go."

"Yeah, mine too," Barc said as he looked over at the one who was still left. His friend seemed bored and *really* ready to get out of there. "But it was really great talking with you tonight."

"Yeah," I agreed, and meant it.

"Are you going back to New York tomorrow?"

"Yup. Have the 'job' in the morning, which is why my flight's so early. I wanted to stay here as long as possible, and now I'm *really* glad I did."

Barc blushed. "Hey—do you have a ride to the airport?"

What a nice thing to offer, I thought. I hadn't yet made transportation arrangements and I was enjoying his company immensely, so why not? "No."

"Could I take you?" he asked.

"Yes," I graciously accepted, glad that meant his handsome face would be the last thing I would see before heading back to the hot, sticky city I was dreading to return to again.

At dawn, Barclay arrived in his sports car and picked me up from Lark's Landing near its golf green. We slipped right back into a comfortable conversation like we had never stopped talking from the night before.

"So, you fly into the city from paradise just to work at a job you find boring and live in a crappy apartment for a few days, then travel to lavish estates again each weekend, is that it?" Barc joked.

"Pretty much," I said.

"Is the rest of your family as eccentric as you?"

"Me—*eccentric?*" I laughed. "I mean, I'm not normal by any stretch, but I'm normal compared to the rest of my family—you should meet my crazy dad!"

"I'm afraid I have you beat on *that* one. Foxy really takes the cake," he said, once again looking upset.

"I'm sorry, I didn't mean to bring him up." I felt bad and didn't want our last few minutes together to be unpleasant for him.

"No, it's okay," Barc said with some reflection. "I didn't want to talk about him last night because there were so many people around, but now that it's just us I don't mind."

My heart skipped a beat when he said the word 'us' and I was surprised by my reaction. I had only just met him, but it did seem like we were already becoming an "us" somehow.

"He hasn't had to work since he struck it rich in the sixties," Barc began, "and even though he's got real estate all over the country and plays the stock market like a fiend; he's still always sitting there on a giant pile of oil money from his own father's business—but the stingy bastard won't share a penny of *any* of it!"

"Really?" I said. This I had never heard in the Texas oil rumor-mills.

"Nope, I'm completely on my own," Barc said with distain. "Plus, the stocks aren't the *only* thing he 'plays...'"

"I'm guessing you don't mean tennis?"

"Nope... try cocktail waitresses. I think he's got his eye on a couple of girls over at his golf club right now."

"Oh—cheaters... I hate 'em...your poor mother!"

"No sir, not *my* mother! They divorced *lonnng* ago... Foxy's on his, let's see..." Barclay paused to count on his fingers. "...*Fifth* marriage now. A gussied-up little tart named, get this— 'Buffy.'"

"No... her name's not really *Buffy?*"

"Hard to say what's on that marriage license since I didn't bother going to this one, but that's what people call her at the clubs at least. Yes-sir-ee... the younger, the better for good ol' Pops, and this one is just *barely* legal." Barc shook his head. "Though she's no bubblehead, she's got him good— made him sign a prenup and everything. And of course he was so horny for her he signed whatever the attorneys shoved at him. Congratulations old man—Foxy and his 'child bride'! Really, it's quite disgusting when you think about it." Barc gripped the wheel tightly. "It's probably some kind of fetish, maybe he makes her dress up like a cheerleader in bed or something, I dunno."

"So in other words... not your idea of a cute couple?"

Barc laughed. "Definitely not. Try freak show—and he seems to find lots of freaks… quite *often*."

"Doesn't she care that he fools around on her?" I couldn't help but think of Hunter and how his cheating affected me.

"Naah, no way. Buffy wouldn't do anything to compromise her 'security.' He's forty-five years her senior—and I do mean *senior*—so you do the math. The fact that he's not banging down her door every night is probably a relief, for I'm sure she doesn't want to sleep with him now they're hitched! As long as she has her fill of jewels and handbags until he kicks the bucket she doesn't care *what* the old fox is up to… she practically gives him pick-up lines!"

"Surely not?"

"They'd probably have an 'open' marriage if it wasn't so taboo… pretty screwed-up, huh?" He glanced in the rear-view mirror, then at me. "There. Now you know all my deep, dark secrets," he said, winking at me with a sideways glance.

Already, I could feel a kinship towards Barc; like he was a big, awkward kid that deep down really just needed a hug. And what luck! A fun-loving, sweet guy who—straight out of the gate—*didn't* want to take after his cheating father. I smiled, not believing my good fortune.

"Well, your secrets are safe with me," I said. "I suppose that's one thing I can feel lucky about—that my parents are still together. Oldie would never screw around on my mom."

"You're lucky—or maybe you just never knew about it."

I didn't even want to think that that could be true. "No," I told him firmly. "He really loves her. You should see the way they still look at each other… you can tell. It's been that way ever since I was little too."

"You ARE lucky then, because I was little when my parents split up and I *still* remember it like it was yesterday… our mom sat us down at the dinner table—I was seven and my brother Stewart was nine. Out of the thin blue air she told Foxy she couldn't deal with the cheating anymore because it was a humiliation to her and an embarrassment to the whole family. She said that in front of us, can you believe it? We had no idea it was even going on…. Stewart and I were stunned."

"You poor things!"

"Yeah, it caught my dad off guard too… some very expensive Herend china went flying out the window that night—that was a favorite stunt of his, tossing things out windows whenever he was upset. Still is, actually," Barc added, chuckling to himself.

"So what happened afterwards?"

"He moved out of the house the next day and thought Mom was a complete disaster, so— in classic Foxy style—he bribed the next-door neighbor with 'an offer he couldn't refuse' and bought his house, claiming he wanted to keep an eye on his boys. This little 'arrangement' didn't sit well with Mom, of course, so to get back at him she shipped me and my brother off to boarding schools—Stewart was sent to Millbrook Academy in upstate New York, and I was sent to this awful Military School in Missouri—all so *he* couldn't see us. If that's not evil, I don't know *what* is." His eyes darkened.

"Oh, I'm so sorry," I said, rubbing his arm.

Barc seemed to appreciate it as he continued, "After that I only ever really got to see both my parents and brother on holidays, and during the summer me and Stewart stayed in Newport with our dad only, for my mom couldn't stand to be in the same zip code as him anymore and kept away from here back then."

I continued to rub his arm, allowing him to gather his thoughts before he went on. "Stewart and I were young and unruly and Foxy couldn't control us, so he put an ad in the Boston Globe for a nanny. He finally hired one named Sarah who was a nineteen-year-old sophomore at Boston University who needed to make extra money for the summer. She was really cute... a petite blond and a lot of fun to hang out with, like you." Barc glanced towards me. I blushed and wanted to listen to him even more intently now as he continued, "All he did was play golf all day and go to parties every night. We hardly ever saw him after Sarah was hired, and when we did he was *always* in a bad mood. He still couldn't believe Mom had left him even though it had been a full year at that point. He was an egomaniac and control freak and NEVER thought she would dump him I guess... Anyway, as summer went by we started noticing that he spent more time at home lounging by the pool and having cocktails with Sarah. We were too young to understand what was happening, but when summer ended he convinced her to drop out of college and move in with him once we went back to our boarding schools."

"Oh my God!" I said. "And she was only nineteen?"

"Yeah, we couldn't believe it either—nor could our mom. They were together for about a year but then started to get tired of each other—the twenty year age difference was just too much. She was planning on going back to school, but then found out she was pregnant. He married her and they had a baby girl. The baby put more stress on them and he divorced her the next year, basically leaving her penniless because he had made her sign a pretty tight prenup."

"But what about the baby? Didn't he at least want to provide for *her?*"

"Nope. He felt he already had enough to take care of with Stewart and me, and never let us forget what an awful burden we both were."

"That's awful!" I said, truly sympathizing with him. Oldie always took great pride and joy in providing well for Whitney and me. I guess we really were lucky to have been his 'Daddy's little girls.'

"Yeah, so all things considered, I had a pretty shitty, lonely, screwed-up childhood," Barc said, now pulling up to the airport terminal. I was surprised that the normally long drive had passed by so quickly.

"Oh Barc, I'm so sorry to hear this," I told him earnestly.

He parked the car next to the curb. "Yeah, well, now you *really* know all my secrets."

"You seem perfectly adjusted now though," I said, comforting him still.

Barc stared straight ahead towards the row of cars in front of us, lost in thought. "I try... but I guess I always thought—and don't laugh cause this might sound corny to you—but I always thought I'd find the happy home I never had growing up by finding the right woman and getting married." He glanced at me, briefly meeting my eyes. My heart melted.

"Barc, that's not a corny idea at all! I think it's sweet."

"Well, thanks... but don't get any ideas," he joked, and we both laughed. "Right now I'm just traveling the world and having a lot of fun, you know? I truly believe it's never too late to have a happy childhood, so I work at it every day, making up for lost time."

It was touching to hear him say that. I was enjoying getting to know this guy—Barclay seemed so different from anyone else I'd ever met. I was beginning to hope this new friendship would last, and maybe, just maybe... grow into something more...

"Well," I started, knowing I had to catch my plane soon. "I think that's great, and thank you so much for the ride, but I have to—"

I opened the car door, but Barc grabbed my hand and held onto it. "Would you like to come back next weekend? There's a big ridiculous wedding that my mom wants me to go to, but I don't have a date."

I hesitated for a moment, as if I was thinking it over, when all I really wanted to do was scream "YES!" immediately. "Sure, that sounds like fun," I said calmly.

"Fantastic. You can stay with Mrs. Nielsen again and I'll make sure the 'Green Room' will be waiting for you... Oh, and by the way, it's at Rosecliff, so it's black-tie only. I'll send you a roundtrip plane ticket and call you tomorrow with more details."

"Great!" I hugged him and with only a slight hesitation, kissed him on the cheek. It was smooth with only a hint of last night's stubble. "Well then, I guess I'll talk to you tomorrow... and thanks again for a really fun time, Barclay."

"Same to you, Melanie. I already can't wait for next weekend."

I went straight to work after my plane touched down in New York and told Alex all about Mrs. Nielsen's fabulous dinner party 'fix-up.' It turned out that Alex had run in similar Dallas social circles as Barclay's family as a teenager, and both their families were very old friends. A couple of hours after hearing my story, Alex called me at my desk in a tizzy.

"I called my mom and got the scoop!" she said over the receiver. "She told me all about Barclay's family. They're a *major* big deal, one originally from Boston before Texas, and Barclay is very much 'in demand' as a bachelor all over—Dallas, Boston, Palm Beach, *and* Newport!" She squealed so loud I thought all my co-workers would hear her and wonder who I could be talking to that would do such a silly thing.

Well this is getting better by the minute, I thought as I listened to Alex go on, confirming that Barclay was indeed *very* single, was definitely looking to settle down, and was an heir to a vast oil fortune in the *billions*. The only obvious problem I could think of so far was the fact that he lived in Dallas; for though I never admitted this to Alex, I personally never liked Dallas all that much. But maybe I could start to...

"Oh my God!" Alex continued to squeal. "You could be the next 'Mrs. Cunningham' someday soon!"

"Whoa," I said, feigning nonchalance. "It's *way* too premature to start thinking about that. I've never even been on a proper date with the man. I'm going to just have fun with him for now and see where it goes."

Alex agreed that this was best to do, but as we hung up I had butterflies in my stomach. If I had to sum it up I think that for the first time since Hunter, Barclay Cunningham really made me feel alive again, and it was wonderful.

I spent the rest of the week searching Manhattan for the perfect party dress to wear to the formal, black-tie wedding at Rosecliff and I finally found it—a criminally short, strapless, aqua blue Ungaro from Bergdorf Goodman's. It was perfectly flattering to my figure and brought out the sharp blue of my eyes. Ready, aim, fire...

"It's all just perfect," Victoria said as she admired the shoes I found to go with my new killer dress. I was leaving in the morning and she had come over to the rat hole to help me pack.

"Thanks. It feels like forever since I've wanted to really look good for a man," I told her as I neatly packed my suitcase with several more sexy outfits to have on hand for the rest of the weekend.

"I wonder if I'll ever want to again," Victoria said sadly, and I felt bad for her. Break-ups were so hard.

"You will. Just give it some time." I gave her a reassuring hug. She welcomed it. "And at least you'll be far away from New York soon."

"I can't wait," she said, sitting down on my Murphy bed and arranging some jewelry in my travel case. "This will be my first shot at really making the rounds in Europe for the agency too, so I hope I do a good job."

"You will. Which cities are they sending you to?"

"Paris, of course, to start, but then Milan and London too... it really couldn't have come at a better time. I hope I book enough shoots to keep me busy for *years!*"

"I hope you do too!"

"But of course I'll come back if you need a bridesmaid or anything," Victoria joked, trying to stay positive.

"Please, I'm just going on my first date with Barc! I have no idea how it will go."

"I think this one sounds different than every other guy you—or I—have ever dated. I don't know, I just have a good feeling about him."

"Really?"

"Yeah, but then, I could be wrong— I mean, just look at my own track record!"

We both laughed.

"No, really Mel," she said in all sincerity. "I hope he's the one... you deserve to be happy."

"We *both* do," I told her earnestly.

She looked up at me teary-eyed and smiled in agreement, but I could tell it was still too soon for her to believe that for herself. I silently prayed I was truly ready to even try again at attempting another relationship myself...

I flew back to Providence early the next morning and Barc picked me up at the airport and then drove me to Mrs. Nielsen's. I wondered why he insisted I stay at Lark's Landing again when I knew his own mother had an even bigger estate, but all I could assume was it had something to do with his love-hate relationship with her and also that he was staying there, so maybe he was keeping some distance between us just in case we didn't hit it off.

I changed for the wedding in my now-familiar Green Room and Barc came back to pick me up right on time. He looked so handsome in his Armani black tux I couldn't keep my eyes off him. He seemed to be doing the same when he saw me in my carefully selected attire as well.

"Wow!" Barc grinned. "You look stunning."

"Thank you... so do you," I told him.

The weekend was off to a great start already. We drove to the famous Rosecliff estate and arrived a few minutes before the wedding ceremony began. I couldn't help but think back to how different this all was from the first real date I had with Hunter, which was also to a black-tie wedding event, but he had gotten us there late and didn't even care in the least that that was a major social faux pas. Barclay was very mindful of proper social protocol, which I appreciated.

Rosecliff was known as the most romantic cottage in all of Newport, and as I looked around at its heart-shaped staircase and exquisite grand ball-room, I could see why. It created a wonderful atmosphere for romance over-all, and the wedding was the most beautiful one I'd ever attended. There were hundreds of bright red roses everywhere which had been flown in from all over the globe. Gold cages filled with white doves hung from the tall ceilings and several birds were released every hour into the main ballroom while the full Lester Lanin Orchestra from New York played classical music in the background—but they were only one of the many musical choices to choose from throughout the lavish estate. Willie Nelson played in the main dining room, L.A.'s best rock 'n roll band played out by the pool, and a steel band from Jamaica played in a lawn tent set up in the huge, perfectly manicured backyard. It was a truly harmonious, spectacular event.

Glorious Cuisine had been brought in from New York and we were served a sumptuous, five-course dinner by perfectly trained, white-gloved wait staff.

It was a magical evening and I was truly enjoying it all, but Barc seemed to think this kind of entertaining was 'de rigueur.' He'd seen this sort of thing quite often and knew that now dinner was over and the bride and groom had cut their stunning, fifteen-layered, rose-petal-covered cake, social protocol allowed us to thankfully leave.

"Want to go to the Candy Store?" Barc asked me.

"What's that?" I asked.

He grinned. "Oh, that's right… you're not from 'the beach.' Come on, you'll love it…"

Barclay and I made our way towards the outside of the house. Near the front entrance we approached a fashionably dressed, attractive older woman who was eyeing me very obviously up and down—from the top of my head down to my shoes—like she was judging for Miss America or something. It made me highly uncomfortable and I was about to tell Barc when suddenly he stepped ahead of me and straight towards her.

"Hello Mother!" Barc said like he was caught completely off-guard from seeing her. "This is Melanie St. John… Melanie, this is my mother, Helen Cunningham."

Helen gave me the once over again coldly, then spoke in a heavy, Kennedy-like accent, "Oh, so *you're* the 'Texan.'" She didn't even attempt to conceal her disgust.

I replied politely, "Yes, I'm from Texas, but I live in New York now."

"Oh, I see dear... there looking for a *husband?*" she asked rudely.

I decided that she was an offensive snob and that her discourteous question didn't deserve an answer, so I just smiled graciously.

Barc came to my rescue. "Sorry Mother, but we have to go."

To my surprise and his credit, Barc apologized profusely for her conduct as we made our way out to the valet. "I'm so sorry about that... Mom gets like that sometimes. Her dislike of 'Texans' goes back to her long hatred of my father, so please don't take it personally. Anyway, I'm sure you've had your fill of stories about my parents. Let's go have some fun—the Candy Store—also known as the Clarke House—is *the* place to be seen after any private function and it's a favorite watering hole for the local beach crowd. There's a huge tuxedoed-bouncer guarding the entrance named Mickey who knows everyone by name, and if he doesn't know you, you don't get in, period. Townies and tourists have to stay in the rooms below, so it's just a place for us regulars." He seemed to really like being considered a 'regular,' so I was intrigued to check the place out with him as one too.

We drove to the Candy Store and Mickey smiled at Barclay immediately when he saw him. "Hey, Barc," he said, letting us through. *"Enjoy..."* He added, winking towards me.

"Thank you," I said, feeling special from the preferred treatment while other tourist-types stood waiting to get into the other rooms below.

Once inside the bar I didn't understand the appeal, but I soon realized I was in the minority—it wasn't even eleven and the place was already packed. I later learned it was like this every night of the week too.

Barc seemed to know every person we walked by as we made our way up to the bar. And watching him interact with his friends made it clear that he took after his father socially—he was cocky and always had a joke or sharp insult for each one in the crowd we passed.

"Hey Barc...'bout time you showed your face here tonight," his friend who had brought him home the other night from the Yacht Club said.

"I just needed to get drunk enough to be able to look at *you* before I did," Barc replied with a sly grin.

I noticed many, many women watching us as we stopped at the bar. Barc motioned to the bartender, who was a pretty, tanned woman who quickly headed over to us. "Your usual, handsome?" she said, then looked me up and down almost as much as Helen did.

"Yeah, and why don't you make two of them... is that okay, Melanie? I know you're used to champagne, but I'd like you to try one of my favorite cocktails now."

"Sure," I said, wondering what it would be.

In less than a minute the very attentive bartender returned with our two very large daiquiris. "Two New Frontiers," she said as she placed one down in front of me, then handed the other one to Barc.

"It was Teddy Roosevelt's favorite cocktail," Barc explained to me. "It's basically a daiquiri topped with Meyer's dark rum *and* Bacardi one-fifty-one."

I took a sip and was delighted. It was a sweet and very potent concoction, but nice. *"Mmmm,"* I said towards Barc. "It's really good."

"I told you you'd like this place," he said proudly. *New Sensation* by INXS started playing. "Come on, let's dance!"

We joined the crowded dance floor and had fun dancing, drinking our New Frontiers, and talking until closing time, which was only 1:00 AM like all the bars in town—and far too early for all the local Newport party animals who were now wired up—so we then went to a private after-party hosted at Tim O'Quinn's house. Tim was nicknamed "T.Q.," and was a middle-aged D.C. lobbyist with three wild teenage sons. Since he was very fond of young women, T.Q. was currently getting divorced from wife number three. We arrived at his splendid home about 1:30 AM and the party was already in full swing. At least sixty guests, all in haute couture, wandered through the rooms of his palatial Victorian cottage. We milled around for about an hour, and though it was fun, I was really ready to go.

"It's supposed to be a beautiful day tomorrow and it would be a shame to waste it by sleeping all day," I said to Barc. "So could we please go now?"

"Already? We just got here."

"I know, but you live in this beautiful place. I'm only here for two more days, and I really want to make the most of them."

Barclay was very accommodating. "How would you like to spend the day with me at the beach tomorrow then?"

"I would love it!"

"Then let's get out of here. We'll have a great day tomorrow."

Barc drove me back to Lark's Landing. I was a little anxious because though we slow-danced on and off all night, he never made a move yet to kiss me. I could tell we had chemistry, but for some reason, he was holding back. I thought of Morgan and how embarrassing it was to get rejected whenever I made the first move, so I decided to just be patient and let nature take its course. And as Barc's car rolled up the long driveway to the front entrance, I prayed that would be right now.

"Thank you for a lovely night," I said, giving him the most seductive look I could muster. "It was all wonderful."

"I'm glad you had a good time," he said, but made no effort to move towards me. "Shall I pick you up in the morning, say, ten?"

"Sounds good," I said, and then realized he wasn't going to try anything at all tonight. I leaned over and hugged him, then got out of the car fast.

Okay, well… I'll just have to see how the rest of the weekend goes, I thought as I went inside. I wasn't going to wait around for months like I did with Morgan, but it was only our first real date. I decided to give him the rest of the weekend to at least kiss me, and I had sweet dreams of him doing that to me and more all night long.

Barc picked me back up the next morning at exactly ten. I liked his promptness. We drove down to the "Beach Club" (which really was named the "Seal Rock Beach Association," but no one ever called it that). It was supposedly the oldest private beach club on the whole East Coast and impossible to join. Surprisingly, it was a small, unassuming, nondescript gray house with yellow shutters and no sign, casually furnished with white wicker furniture. But the property and beach was unspeakable, occupying the most breathtaking spot overlooking the Atlantic. Lifeguards patrolled the private beach area, preventing tourists and townies from the public beach next door from wandering onto the club's pristine land.

Barc and I walked towards his family's private cabana. "There's a mile-long waiting list for these," he told me. "Most costing well into the six figures."

"Really?" I said, trying to sound impressed, but I couldn't help but note that they were actually very *un*noteworthy; they were just plain, white, small cubicles with a few lounge chairs and a table in each one. I was definitely not impressed—and especially not when I saw Helen already sitting in the particular cubicle we were fast approaching.

Great, I wondered. *How rude will she be to me today?*

"Oh, hello Melanie, dear. This is my step-daughter, Irene," Helen said. I was shocked she remembered my name as she introduced me to Barclay's step-sister, who turned from her lounge chair and smiled as she shook my hand.

"Nice to meet you," Irene said. "Please, call me Bella." Her nickname fit; she was a real beauty.

"Thanks," I replied. "It's nice to meet you too."

"Melanie's from Texas and is working at Sotheby's in New York," Helen went on to explain like we were old friends. Her acidic tone from the previous evening had completely evaporated, and judging by the information she was imparting to Irene, it seemed that she had been checking up on me, just as I had asked around about their family. Obviously, she liked what she found out, so now here we all were 'chumming it up' at the beach together for the day.

While the three of us chatted, Barc headed to the bar and brought back two New Frontiers.

"*Really* Barclay," Helen said, chastising him. "It's a little *early* in the day, don't you think?"

"It's five o'clock somewhere!" he grinned. "Besides, Mel and I have to celebrate. It's our one-week anniversary."

I was flattered that he was making a big deal out of it in front of everyone. But Helen just sighed heavily, making it clear to me that she didn't like alcohol all that much. I suspected Foxy's fondness for the bottle, along with a few of her other exes, might be the reason why.

Barc winked at me and raised his glass. "Cheers!"

Helen responded to his swaggering gesture. "You better warn Melanie how strong those drinks are, especially if you begin in the middle of the morning."

Barc countered, "Don't worry, Mel's a big girl. She'll survive."

I have to give the New Frontier credit for escalating our already-blossoming relationship. After a few sips, I began to relax—even in the company of Helen—who proved to have her own funny way of charming her admirers, most notably with colorful stories about her numerous exes. She first explained that after her divorce from Foxy, she married her second husband, Sam Goodson, who already had one-year-old Bella from his first marriage. Sam died of a sudden heart attack a year later when Bella was only two and left his entire family fortune to her; thus, Bella was a very rich woman. Bella grew up, married a Madison Avenue marketing exec, and had four children. They all currently lived in a four-story townhouse off Park Avenue in New York.

A couple of years after Sam died, Helen explained how she then married Sam's best friend, Jacques, on a whim when the two of them got bored one weekend in Bar Harbor, Maine because they were "socked in" by the fog and couldn't fly out in his private plane. Jacques soon rivaled Foxy in the cheating department and left Helen after less than a year of marriage for Natasha, a beautiful coat-check girl from the Russian Tea Room in New York. The beginnings and endings of Helen's next several relationships continued much in this same manner, and it turned out to be a pretty lively morning listening to all the colorful stories. They continued all through lunch too. By the end I felt Helen and I had bonded and she now approved of me getting to know her son.

"Well, I think Melanie and I are ready to hit the beach," Barc said once our lunch plates were cleared and the conversation had started to wind down.

"Have fun, kids," Helen said approvingly as we both walked down to the sand.

"Why has your mom suddenly changed her attitude towards me?" I asked Barc once we were out of her earshot. "She was a little insulting last night if you ask me, and today she's a completely different person."

Barc sighed. "Let's just say she's incredibly unpredictable. She can be nice one day and awful the next. But don't worry about her... it's *me* you have to hang out with."

He took my hand and held it tightly as we walked down the beautiful, rocky shoreline. I tingled all over from his touch and knew we were slowly but surely becoming an "us" still. I decided it didn't matter if he was going to take his time kissing me; I liked being treated with such respect. After all, Hunter had kissed me right away and then had created well-planned-out staged scenarios to try to get me to sleep with him every date early on, just like he apparently did with *all* women... It was nice to be with a man who wanted to spend some quality time getting to know me first without a pre-planned agenda.

At the end of the day Helen invited us sailing the next evening on her best friend's incredible yacht. Barc took me to a wonderful, romantic restaurant in town, then dropped me off early so we could both get a good night's sleep since we were tired from the sun all day and staying out late the night before.

Barc picked me back up right on time in the morning and we spent the day sight-seeing all over Newport; then we drove down to the pier to meet Helen and her friends in the late afternoon on their truly fabulous yacht. We sailed around the island on a sunset cruise drinking Cristal champagne and dining on smoked salmon crepes and lots and lots of caviar. I was falling in love with Newport and maybe, just maybe, Barclay as well.

The weekend ended way too quickly. As Barc drove me to the airport, I tried not to think about saying good-bye.

"I wish you didn't have to go back," Barc said sadly.

"I know," I agreed. "You know, I've earned a two-week vacation from work that I haven't taken yet."

He lit up. "Well in that case I'd like to rent you one of the small cottages at Lark's Landing. Why don't you spend your whole vacation there? I think you'll be much more comfortable in your own place than staying in the Green Room."

I was amazed. I hardly knew Barc, yet he was willing to do something so wonderful like that for me.

"I'd love to," I graciously told him. "I just have to let them know this week at work, but I could come back on Friday and stay after that."

"Great. And bring a bunch of cocktail dresses because we're about to go into the height of the social season. I'll take you to parties and black-tie events every night! We're going to have a blast!"

We hugged longer than usual as he dropped me off at the curb at the airport, and I didn't care that I was still waiting for my kiss. I knew it was coming soon and would definitely be worth the wait...

I went back to my boring job and rundown apartment, but I was so excited for my two weeks in Newport I could hardly sleep that whole first night back. I put in for my vacation time and of course Alex arranged it so that it was no problem at all to get. Each night I shopped all along 5th Avenue for a few new frocks and dresses and finally went back to the rat hole on Thursday night to pack, for I was happily leaving the very next day.

Wallace came out of her bedroom and stood in the doorway, looking both annoyed and hung-over. "You need to check your messages—that Eva chick's been calling nonstop all day!"

"Sorry Wallace," I said as I walked over to the phone. (I had finally splurged and gotten a phone only a month before—mostly on the insistence of my mother who was still worried about me living in such dire dwellings; having access to the outside world from inside the rat hole seemed to make her feel much better.) "Seventeen messages?" I said in disbelief as I looked down at the number on my answering machine. "You've got to be kidding me!" I hit the playback button.

Message one beeped. "Hey Melanie, this is Eva! Guess what? I'm pregnant! Can you believe it? Call me back girl A-S-A-P!"

I deleted it.

Oh boy, here we go, I thought.

Message two beeped. "Oh my God Melanie! It's *twins!* I haven't told Dawson yet! Call me!"

Delete.

Message three commenced. "I want to tell him so bad! I just don't want to start a fight. It seems like that's all we do. We fight about money, our ridiculously tiny apartment, how I hate the weather here, and other crap like that. Anyway, call me!"

Delete. "Okay, I'm sick of hiding it—I'm about to burst! I wish you were there to talk to me! Whitney's not home either! Please, please call me Mel!"

Delete. "Okay, I've decided to tell him over dinner tonight. I'm going to cook him his favorite meal of rack of lamb, au gratin potatoes, English peas, and a Grand Marnier soufflé. That'll put him in a good mood to then receive my *bombshell*..."

Delete. "Mel... you woan belieheheheve what just happened..." I couldn't even understand what she was saying for that or the next five messages. I could tell she had started drinking by noon, and was getting drunker as the day went on. I was definitely preoccupied with Barc and packing at this point and didn't want to have to deal with any of this drama. But I knew if I didn't call her she would just continue to call and pester Wallace, so I picked up the phone and dialed.

Eva answered right away, sobbing and muttering something completely incoherent.

"Eva! I can barely understand a word you're saying," I told her. "Please, try to stop crying and tell me what's wrong."

"I told Dawson about the twins and he told me I totally disgusted him for trapping him like this and left in a rage. I thought for sure he would be happy, but now I'm *so* upset..." She cried and cried into the phone.

"Eva, everyone knows that a new baby, especially an unexpected one—or *two* in your case—never 'helps' a bad marriage. Tricking Dawson was not very smart and now your situation is even worse than before. I don't know what else to tell you because I told you before I wasn't going to support this plan. But it looks like you're now stuck being a mom *and* staying in this marriage, like it or not."

A wail of heavy sobs was her only reaction.

"Look Eva, I have to go, but I'll call you later, okay?"

She muttered something unintelligible and we hung up. Though her judgment was bad and her motives for marrying Dawson were really warped, I felt sorry for her and wanted to find a way to help her. I hated to admit it, but I saw a lot of myself in her. If things would've been a little different a year ago this is exactly how I could have ended up with Hunter by now. After all, he could have been just as cruel to me about finding out I was pregnant just like Dawson was to Eva. And no one deserves that level of brutal callousness, even if they were trying to 'save' a hopeless marriage.

I finished packing and went to bed, trying to focus on my vacation ahead but also worried about Eva. I woke up earlier than planned so I could keep my promise and call her back.

She answered on the first ring and still sounded drunk. *"Heello?"*

"Eva? Have you been drinking today already?" I asked, truly stunned. "You sound terrible!"

"Oh Mel, I'm *sooo* depressed," she said, slurring her words. "Dawson never came home last night, and never answered his bee-beeper, so yes, I've been drinking... I'm just *sooo, sooo* depressed!"

"It's not even ten... you've got to get a grip! You're pregnant now, remember?"

"I know, I know," she said, choking back tears. "I think I'm gonna go to Houston to try and sort things out..."

"Okay, but be careful," I said, and then suddenly remembered what Emily did when she didn't want her unborn child. "And please think of the well-being of your unborn babies before you do *anything*," I added, hoping she'd get my underlying message, even in her intoxicated state.

"I'll call you when I get there," Eva said, clearly not understanding anything anymore. I knew it was no use to continue talking and hung up.

I didn't want any child to have to go through a bad childhood after what Barc had told me about his, but I also knew Eva would do whatever she thought was best for her, regardless of what Dawson, me, or anyone else said. She always only looked out for herself first, which was the main reason her life was always in such a constant, complete mess.

I unplugged my answering machine before I left for the airport, giving Wacky Wallace some peace until I returned two weeks later. I knew I could still squeeze a lot more summer out of this season.

Chapter 13

❦

Barc was waiting at the airport for me with a gorgeous bouquet of pink tulips. I gave him a big hug and he put all my luggage into his car. I was impressed by how delicately he treated it, making sure not to squish my garment bags in the slightest.

"I have everything all arranged," Barc said confidently as we drove towards the island of Newport. I felt safe in his complete care. "Your private cottage is all set up at Lark's Landing and I've R-S-V-P-'d to events for the next two weeks straight. I'm so glad you could get out of work for so long."

"Me too," I said and couldn't believe how happy I was already. It was as if being in his presence put me under a spell and I couldn't help but smile constantly.

Barc took my hand and held it all the way to Lark's Landing. I never wanted to let it go, but did so we could bring my luggage into my new gatehouse for the next couple of weeks.

The cottage was quaint and romantic. Outside there was a splendid veranda with white wicker furniture that overlooked the wooden area near the golf putting green, so I knew we would have lots of privacy. Inside there was a living room made up of a white wicker sofa in front of a stone fireplace and a small table near the window with two causal chairs; a large bedroom with a carved mahogany canopy bed and a big beautiful wooden armoire; and a full bathroom with a claw-styled, antique bathtub big enough for two. It was going to be delightful staying here.

Barc put my suitcases neatly beside the armoire in the bedroom and hung my garment bag in the closet as I placed the flowers he had bought me in the tall crystal vase on the bedside's nightstand that was already filled with tap water, waiting. The burst of nature and marvelous, warm pink color the tulips gave off was the perfect finishing touch to the room.

"Well," Barc said very gentlemanly, "I'd better let you get freshened up. I'll be back to pick you up for dinner. Say, six?"

"That would be fine," I said.

We both looked at each other longingly and I could tell the bed was giving him ideas. It was for me too, but the moment wasn't right yet.

"Well then, see you soon," he said as he quickly left. I laughed as I set out to decide which of my sexiest lingerie I should wear under tonight's equally-seductive cocktail dress...

Dinner was fabulous of course at a wonderfully romantic restaurant with a spectacular view of the Atlantic and a cool breeze blowing the whole time. Barc said he wanted me all to himself that first night, so there were no parties to attend and nowhere else to go after we finished our crème brulee and second bottle of fine champagne.

When Barc brought me back to the cottage we could both feel the chemistry between us growing with each step we took as we walked up onto the veranda. The moon was out and the night air was crisp, but not hot. It was perfect.

He held onto my hand and pulled me close to him. I didn't want to break the mood with words, so I only looked up into his beautiful blue eyes as he stared back at mine. Then, it finally happened. Barc leaned in and kissed me so passionately I thought I was going to melt all over the wicker chair beside us. I'd been seduced by the champagne, the attention, the fairy-tale-like lifestyle of Newport, and Barclay's considerable attractiveness, humor, and charm. There was also a comfortable closeness I felt with this fellow Texan, and so I continued to kiss him back passionately for several minutes. It felt natural and safe when his arms went around me tightly; it was clear he didn't want to let me go, and I didn't want him to. Soon I felt I couldn't stand up much longer... my knees were giving out...

Barc whispered to me, "Melanie, you're the most beautiful woman I've ever known, inside and out... I could really see spending the rest of my life with you. No one has ever made me feel this strongly."

The kissing then intensified into more than just a "good-night kiss" as he took off his bow tie and led me inside the cottage. Barc laid me down on the white wicker sofa and took off his shirt. His body was tanned, toned, and muscular and his hair was tousled, falling in his face rakishly debonair, but still somehow exuding an animal sexuality. I'd been B.S.'d enough to know the difference between a man who'd had experience pleasing women and those who hadn't, and I knew Barclay wasn't kidding around when he spoke the words, *"I want you, Melanie..."*

He unzipped my Chanel cocktail dress with such panache I could tell it was not his first time. It excited me to think of all the heiresses and debutantes in Dallas, New York, Palm Beach, and Newport he'd been with and yet, he now wanted *me.* It was like a soothing balm to my wounded ego after feeling so dejected by Hunter. And I wanted Barc back badly. I needed him to stop the cutting pain that had left me emotionally frozen for the past two years. Here, in the dark with Barclay Cunningham, it was all now slowing and deliciously melting away...

I let him lead me into the bedroom and we made love intensely like two wild, sex-starved animals in the accommodating, large canopy bed. Afterwards, as I lay in his strong arms, gratified and exhausted from the hours of passion, I knew I wanted this feeling to continue forever. I was too fulfilled to worry about where this might lead, or if it might ever end... all I wanted at that moment was to let him have his way with me as soon as possible again... and my wish was eagerly granted.

Barc was good on his word not only in the bedroom too, for the August social scene in Newport was a nonstop party. We had champagne at breakfast, wine at lunch, and our new "couple's drink," New Frontiers, at dinner. We hit every party on the circuit and had a blast.

First we attended the Preservation Ball at The Marble House, the most sumptuous of Newport's cottages. It was a Beaux-Arts French-styled palace designed in 1888 by Richard Morris Hunt for Mrs. William K. Vanderbilt. The house featured many varieties of marble, gold, and bronze and the front gates, entrance, and central halls were modeled after Versailles.

Next we attended the Newport Art Museum Gala held at The Breakers, a home built for railroad magnate Cornelius Vanderbilt and his wife. A seventy-room Italian palazzo, it was the largest and most magnificent of the Newport cottages, if you could even call it that. Also designed by Richard Morris Hunt in 1890, it took 2,500 workers and two years to complete. It boasted a golden ceiling in the music room, a blue marble fireplace, several rose-alabaster pillars in the main dining room, and a porch constructed by Italian artisans that had them all laying mosaic tiles on their backs for six months straight.

Yet another prestigious Newport Art Museum event was held at the Chateau-sur-Mer, built in a Victorian Gothic style between 1851 and 1852 for William S. Wetmore, a tycoon in the China trade. The Renaissance-styled dining room and library by Florentine sculptor Luigi Frullini—as well as the Gold Room by Leon Marcotte—were all sterling examples of top nineteenth century design.

We again visited the famous Rosecliff, this time filled with flowers, for the Newport Flower Show. Rosecliff was built for Mrs. Hermann Oelirchs between the years 1898 and 1902. Her father owned silver mines in Nevada. The architect, Stanford White, modeled the place after the Grand Trianon at Versailles. The grand ballroom, where the wedding was held before, now had a magnificent sea of flowers taking center stage, to the delight of all.

Our last party of my vacation was a benefit for the Boys and Girls Club of Newport held at Belcourt Castle, which was another Hunt-designed mansion. It was built between 1891 and 1894 for banking mogul Oliver H.P. Belmont and was replicated after Louis XIII's hunting lodge at Versailles. The house was nicknamed "The Metropolitan Museum of Newport" because of the plethora of European and Asian treasures housed within its walls.

Barc and I followed an exciting routine of attending fabulous party circuits by day, and then had rounds and rounds of intense, passionate lovemaking every evening for the duration of my whole two week stay. I felt like a princess and he was my prince, and I never wanted our story to end.

I found out Barc was a man of leisure and though he 'said' that he worked at his father's oil company in Dallas, he in fact had never actually worked a full day there—or anywhere for that matter—in his whole life. He felt working wasn't necessary since he didn't need to make any more money, for he had tons of money from a large trust fund. He paid for everything the entire time and never let me help—even when I tried to, which was often. Barc said he admired me for making it on my own and wanted me to keep my money for my own needs. He enjoyed taking care of me he said, and I could feel Oldie's approval immediately.

At the age of thirty-five, Barc still lived in his mother's guest house in Dallas for most of the year (she kept her estate there to maintain a residency and also give Barc a place to live, but she herself never set foot in Texas because of Foxy). He also stayed at his father's guest house in Palm Beach whenever he wanted to and spent his summers at his mother's estate in Newport (which his father now never set foot in because of Helen). He traveled all over the world whenever he wanted to throughout the year as well in between.

"Why don't you get your own place somewhere?" I asked as we laid in the afterglow of our passion one evening. We both really opened up afterwards and I felt he was always telling me the truth and not just what I wanted to hear in these intimate surroundings.

"I'm looking with a few realtors in a couple of cities," Barc explained. "But I have to admit I haven't been looking too hard because I've been more interested in finding the right woman to share my life with... after all, don't you think two people should look for a home they'd both enjoy living in *together?*"

"Yes," I agreed and kissed him passionately. It was a truly logical explanation. And why would anyone suspect otherwise? Barclay was one of the most eligible bachelors in the country, and heir to one of the largest oil fortunes in Texas. I didn't doubt for a minute that he was just 'in between places' because this was also very enthusiastically stressed by a very spirited Helen whenever I spoke to her about her son's living arrangements. In fact, she was now more than happy to "fill in the gaps" when it came to rumors or questions about Barc's illustrious past or if anything inconsistent about the present ever came up. And there were always plenty of reasonable explanations as to why Barc did not—on the surface—appear to be leading the life of a "responsible adult," the biggest of course being his sad, dysfunctional childhood. But all that was beside the point Helen told me reassuringly, because she knew for sure Barc was quite ready to settle down.

"Men…" she'd say with a sigh. "Can't live with'em, can't live without'em. But I can tell you one thing Melanie—I know my son, and he doesn't seem to be able to now live without *you*."

I was beginning to think she was right…

I watched Barc one night at the Candy Store as I sipped my New Frontier, amused by this rather oafish, hot-shot heir hanging onto my every word in a 'puppish' sort of way. There he was, shouting loudly to his drunken friends across the bar and being all bullish and bravo—ordering rounds of top-shelf liquor for everyone in a brazen, cocky kind of way, and I could feel myself becoming more and more attracted to him, getting tipsy on his testosterone. It's possible that I was also comparing him to Hunter, and that alone should have been enough to give me an inkling that I might also have trouble with this one, but though there were definite similarities, Barc also seemed very different in many ways. Especially with how he talked about our budding relationship to anyone who cared to listen whenever they'd ask him about our 'status.'

He'd first repeat his favorite motto, "It's never too late to have a happy childhood," and then the monologue that followed always went like this: "I never had a happy childhood because I was shipped off to military school when I was only seven and had to grow up there fast. My parents were going through a divorce—my mother was looking for her next husband and was very selfish and self-absorbed and didn't have the time, interest, or patience to take care of me or my brother. So I guess I may seem a bit immature now, but that's only because I've been trying to make up for never having a real childhood all these years and no one ever made me want to change or grow up again—until now… I think I've finally found a true soulmate with Melanie. She's stable and comes from a very normal family. I've never been happier with anyone."

Hearing it always made me feel truly special and adored.

As my last few days approached, Barc and I started to spend more and more time by ourselves and away from the crowds and parties. We couldn't stay out of bed or be in a room without touching each other, and I didn't know what I was going to do the morning I would have to leave. Just thinking about it was unbearable.

"Mel…" Barc whispered as I laid naked in his arms. I could feel his sweet breath against my face and loved how close we were. "I'm falling in love with you."

I didn't doubt that he was, because I was starting to feel the same way. He was gentle, kind, and the passion between us had been slowly intensifying every day—first with words, and then through a physicality I wasn't prepared for. He was able to get close to me and reached a place in my heart and body that no one had touched since that awful night when Hunter tossed me aside so callously.

I hadn't thought I could ever love anyone ever again, yet here I found with Barclay Cunningham, I could.

"I'm falling in love with you too," I told him. He smiled so big I thought he was going to explode; then kissed me like he had never kissed me before…

I went back to New York and it was torture being apart from each other. Luckily it only had to be for three days, and then I flew back to Newport and straight into Barc's arms Thursday night. I soon got into a routine of leaving early Tuesday mornings, working for three days in the hot city heat, and then jet-setting back to Newport on Thursday nights.

On my last night in Newport after two weeks of this, we were sipping Donnie P from our canopy bed when Barc said, "Mel, I'm really sad you're leaving for New York again tomorrow."

"I'm sad too… I don't want to go back—ever!" I said as I buried my head in his chest.

Suddenly he said in a strong, serious voice, "Why don't we just get married? We haven't wanted to be apart since we met six weeks ago."

"Have you lost your ever-loving mind?" I laughed.

He continued, "No, seriously. The summer's about to end, so I can move to New York and live in my mother's apartment since she spends the fall in Paris."

I was having a hard time believing what I was hearing and thought surely, he must be joking around.

"Mel, just think about it… I could get a job on Wall Street with my parents' connections… maybe this is just the thing I need to get me started at a real career. I've been giving this some thought for some time now, ever since we first met, actually."

As it dawned on me that he was really being serious I tried to listen earnestly, even though I was in a state of semi-shock.

"Look, I know this might be weird... we haven't known each other for very long, but I feel like we're in similar places in our lives and it just makes sense. Don't answer now—I want you to think about it."

He held me tightly from behind and settled into his spot on our shared, king-sized pillow. I don't remember anything between his last words to me and when I finally fell asleep... my mind raced with thoughts of him moving to New York, wedding planning, and dress shopping. It was a little overwhelming.

The next day Barc woke me up early. "Let's go back to my house and tell my mom the big news before I take you to the airport!" he said excitedly.

I was still in a bewildered state, but agreed.

As we drove to his mom's estate I said, "You do remember that I haven't accepted yet, right?"

Barc laughed. "Of course, Mel!"

When we walked into Helen's grand 'cottage,' she was climbing down the stairway already dressed and ready for her first "champagne brunch party" of the day.

Barc yelled, "Hey Mom! I have some great news! I've asked Melanie to marry me!"

Helen replied without even stopping or looking at us as she went towards the front door, mumbling, "I'm late and good for you, dahling." Not one to be deterred from her activities, the news didn't faze her for a second—it was as if she was expecting it—as she went out the door without another word.

Helen's unusual reaction stirred up some uneasy feelings about this funny family in me immediately. I summoned my courage. "Barclay, I need some time to think all this over. I need to get back to New York and go back to work now."

"Take all the time you need. Like I said, I want you to think it over carefully."

I just couldn't get over how fast this was happening. I felt a little flattered and dazzled by it all, but I knew that this was going to be the most important decision that I would ever make, and I had to make it wisely. It was scary, but thrilling too!

I left my answer hanging in the air and returned to New York to discover some shocking news on my now-plugged-back-in answering machine: Whitney was a married woman!

I called her back immediately and found out Charles had proposed to her over a romantic dinner at the Astor Court Restaurant in the St. Regis Hotel three weeks ago. He presented her with a four-carat diamond engagement ring from Tiffany's and told her she was the only woman he'd ever loved and wanted to spend the rest of his life with her.

Whitney was thrilled and bubbling over with enthusiasm. Unlike me, she seemed to be a strong, determined bride-to-be with no doubts and no nervous hesitations whatsoever about her decision.

"Marrying him just felt so totally right," Whitney said. She was ecstatic. "He's so good to me and such an altruistic and brilliant young surgeon... I just know we're going to have a wonderful future together!"

In a testament to how much she had changed and how private she had become since she met Charles, they agreed not to have a big wedding. A trip downtown to the justice of the peace on a Saturday morning was all it took, and suddenly, they were legally married.

Their honeymoon was not so conservative however: they vacationed in Rome, Florence, and Portofino for ten days. And now the happy couple had recently returned to New York and was settling into their 'dream home.' Charles had found an estate in Pocantico Hills in Tarrytown, New York right next door to the Rockefeller Estate and overlooking the Hudson River. He "surprised" Whitney with it upon their return.

Whitney adored it immediately and they were now starting to work on redecorating the lavish, six-bedroom, turn-of-the-century Hudson River estate and restoring it to its original grandeur. It was a big project, but the two of them would be doing it together, loving every minute of it. Their lives seemed to just fall into place perfectly over the summer. It was a complete personality shift for Whitney, but she had something good with Charles and she knew not to screw it up. It appeared that Whitney was able to achieve what all of us wanted: a fairy- tale life.

"This old Hudson River estate looked like crap when we first got here, but it's taking shape nicely already," Whitney told me the next evening when I went out to visit her after work. "Charles says it's the perfect place to come home to after a long and tiring day at the hospital."

"You know, it's just like you to go and get married without anyone knowing," I said. I still hadn't told her—or anyone—my news about Barc's proposal. I was still mulling it over, and he was still patiently awaiting my reply.

Whitney rolled her eyes. "Here we go again! Like I haven't already heard it from Mom and Oldie! Please, don't you start too!"

"It can't surprise you... you know how they like to be involved in everything."

"I know, I know. Charles and I just decided to do it one day and we didn't want to make a big deal out of it. That'll be *your* job now whenever you get married!" she said sarcastically.

I laughed nervously and decided to change the subject. "Pocantico Hills is magnificent!" I marveled to Whitney as we strolled through the grand old house.

"Isn't it? I just adore it here. When the maple trees turn pink, orange, and yellow it really inspires me. I feel like I'm living inside a Van Gogh painting."

Their master bedroom had one of the five fireplaces in total and also a large terrace overlooking the Palisades of the Hudson River. It was gorgeous.

"Over here I just planted Japanese maples with star-shaped leaves," Whitney said as she pointed at the trees near us. "When the sun hits them at just the right angle it makes star-shaped patterns across our bedroom walls and ceiling."

"Whitney the gardener—now I've heard it all!" I laughed.

"Charles's favorite room is the library, just like Oldie's is," she pointed out. We went to go see it and it was indeed impressive. The windows were all stained glass and the built-in bookshelves were carved chestnut. They were filled from top to bottom with stacks of Charles's medical books just like Oldie's shelves were filled with law books back home. The walls here were covered with art and paintings as well. There was also a large brass telescope.

"Charles just loves looking at stars and constellations. And we love to go to antique stores and auctions in the Hudson Valley together—as you can see, we've built up quite a nice art collection so far! Charles loves cooking and sailing, too. Isn't he multi-faceted?" Whitney's voice trailed off dreamily.

"I don't think I've seen you so happy. *Ever*," I said, and meant it. It was nice to see her in this state too.

"He's the first man I've ever loved." she admitted bravely. I knew it took a lot for her to be vulnerable, so she really must have meant it too.

"Guess you just needed someone to tame you."

"Well, he can give it his best shot anyway—*rawr!*" Whitney clawed the air at me playfully as we laughed. "You know, we're going to start to throw some parties soon, after we do a little more work on the place of course. You're going to have to bring this new guy of yours over so I can meet him."

"I don't know… I wouldn't want you to steal him or anything."

Whitney mocked that she was appalled by that thought. "Well, for once I don't care how great your guy is… there's no way he can come close to *my* man!"

We burst out laughing.

"But seriously," I said, feeling I needed to talk about it finally. "I just spent the most *amazing* six weeks with Barclay in Newport over the summer. He's really great in bed."

"Wow, six whole weeks…" Whitney said devilishly.

"Good for you! That's the one thing that's…" Whitney hesitated, but just for a moment, "a little 'different' about Charles. I mean, when we do have sex it's *fantastic*… but these days it's only happening about once a week."

"Well he's a busy guy, and once a week is still better than some couples. It's funny though, of everyone I never thought you'd have trouble in *that* department!"

"So in other words you're calling me a slut?"

"If the shoe fits," I said with raised eyebrows; then we collapsed into a fit of giggles. When we'd caught our breath, I decided it was time to spill. "So… I have some *news…*"

"Well go on!"

"Barc proposed to me."

"No way!"

"He did—and after only six weeks since we first met! Isn't that *crazy?*"

"*Wowww!* What did you say?"

"I haven't answered yet. To be honest, I wasn't going to say anything either because I'm having some serious misgivings… He brought me to his mother's house to tell her about it and she wasn't even fazed! It was like she already knew, or maybe he'd done this sort of thing before a lot…"

Whitney looked at me slyly. "So… do you love him?"

"See, that's what I don't know… we've only been together for such a short time—"

"The amount of time doesn't matter. I never would have admitted it, but I was ready to marry Charles less than two weeks into our relationship. You just have to get over 'society' telling you that you haven't known him long enough and go with your heart."

"I guess I have a lot of thinking to do."

"What's to think about? Does he make you happy?"

"Yes, very, very much."

"Well all I can tell you is Charles makes me *so* very, *very* happy too, and all that partying I used to do? All the world traveling? I don't miss it a bit! When you have a man that's devoted to you and *only* you, you never want to leave his arms."

"Thanks Whit… you'll be the first to know what my answer is when I figure it out…"

I went to work the next day and told Alexandra and some of the other girls in the office the big news so I could gauge their first reactions. But before I gathered everyone together I was careful to make sure we were far away from The Squid's desk and that she was busy on a long, important business call—just so she wouldn't jinx the whole thing by being present or even overhearing.

Alex grabbed my arm excitedly as she exclaimed, "Mel! Do you know how rare it is for a girl to get engaged so soon after moving to New York City? It almost never happens! Most guys here just want to sleep around and string you along. Am I right, girls?"

"You'd be crazy not to accept!" all of the other unmarried and slightly jealous co-workers agreed, though they were also very excited for me.

Finally, I called my one true advisor: Oldie.

"Well, what are you waiting for then?" he said at the news.

"Oldie! I'm surprised at you!" I was shocked by his reaction. "I've only known Barclay for six weeks!"

"*And?*" Oldie laughed. "You dated Hunter for how many years? Hell, it was so long I quit trying to keep track. What difference does it make? You've already dated every other available bachelor in the state of Texas besides Barc!"

"Quit exaggerating."

"All I'm saying is it's time to try something new. As you know, when life happens—"

"I know, I know—'you happen back,'" I finished.

"Well, this is surly life *happening!* And besides, judging by his parents' track record, marriage and divorce in *that* family is a pretty routine thing, so if it doesn't work out, no big deal."

"Oldie! Divorce is a *huge* deal!"

"I know, I know, but I still hear great things about his old man Foxy—not about him being a real 'ladies' man' and always having a young wife, of course—but that he's still known as a great guy and an even better golfer—so the divorces haven't tarnished his rep a bit! And most importantly, he's made a *fortune* as an independent oilman... Mel, he's made <u>billions</u>... I seriously think if you even think you love this guy then you should consider marrying *up!* Nothing would make me happier for you, Lil' Bit."

I thought about this. Hunter had money, but it was nothing compared to the world of old- money circles Barclay traveled in. He had introduced me to a completely new world of luxury and affluence, and I thoroughly enjoyed it. And for the first time I also understood what it felt like to have someone I loved also be totally in love with *just* me back. After never being sure of Hunter's true intentions during all those years, I really didn't think I could ever trust a man again, or ever have such strong feelings for anyone else ever again. But now I did. Sure, I'd only known Barclay for a short time, but the chemistry and connection were definitely there. My dating life, as busy and diverse as it had been in New York, felt empty to me—full of quantity—but very little quality. No one I had dated seemed remotely interested in any sort of commitment. So with a gulp, I decided to take Oldie's advice.

I hung up and immediately called Barc. "Yes!"

"Is that a 'yes' to what I think it is?" Barc asked.

"Yes, I'll marry you, you crazy man! After Hunter I really didn't think I'd *ever* be able to trust anyone else, or love again. But I do. I love and trust *you* Barclay, so yes, I'll marry you!" I told him happily.

"That's great, Melanie! We're going to have such a wonderful life together! Listen, I have a few things to take care of in Dallas and then I'll be all set to move to New York. I'm going to call my mother. She's at her apartment in New York right now actually—I'm sure she'll be calling you soon!"

Helen immediately called moments later to congratulate me on a "very wise" decision and invited me to have lunch with her at the Carlyle Hotel the following afternoon. I had to admit, the woman was unpredictable.

The next day I arrived at Bemelman's Bar and was greeted by an exuberant and smiling Helen. "Hello dahling, I'm so glad to see you," she said. "You look marvelous."

I thanked her, and we sat down and ordered lunch. My nerves were shot so I ordered a salad and a much-needed glass of chardonnay. Helen ordered steak tartar and a sparkling water.

When the waiter left, she immediately got down to business. "So, what are your plans for the wedding, dear?"

I nearly choked on my drink. "Wedding plans? Well, there aren't any yet."

Irritated, Helen exclaimed, "Dahling, you should *really* set a date and not let this engagement drag on. Trust me—I know from experience—when a man wants to get married—and most men *don't*—you need to act on it <u>immediately</u>. And don't even think about moving in together before the wedding. That *never* works. Trust me on that, too."

She went on to tell me how she'd never seen her son so happy. "Barclay has been dating forever. He's dated all the major heiresses in Dallas, New York, Newport, and Palm Beach—you name it—but he's refused to settle down until now. You're different from all the other girls Melanie—you're very mature, stable, and no airhead or gold-digger either. You'll make the perfect wife for him dear, and I should say, I think he's been around enough to know what he's *really* getting with you... I think he'll make a great husband for you, too..."

She went on like that for the next several minutes. *Why was she trying so hard to sell me on Barc?* my common sense screamed at me, but I was too caught up in the whirlwind excitement of this new romance to notice or even care.

"I'll send my car and driver over this afternoon to pick up all of your belongings... you're living in a 'rat hole,' is that right?" Helen said with disgust. "Well, I insist you stay here until the wedding. My friend just passed away from lung cancer and her apartment is just sitting there empty until the estate can be settled. It could take months and months..."

Before I could say anything she said, "So everything's settled then, dear. You simply must be comfortable for the next few months—remember, 'we' have a wedding to plan! Besides, Barc tells me your apartment is way up on 96th Street near Harlem... Dreadful! I won't tolerate it."

I couldn't argue. After living in such beautiful places all summer in Newport, I was ready to leave the rat hole, for good.

Helen's black, stretch limousine arrived later that afternoon as promised, and her valet, Joe, loaded all my worldly possessions into it as I said good-bye to Wacky Wallace.

"I'd say keep in touch, but by the looks of where you're heading in *those* wheels I know you'll probably be too busy going to high teas now to converse with the 'common' folk," Wallace joked to me as she looked at the perfectly polished limo parked outside our rundown building.

"Thanks for your hospitality," I told her.

"Ah, it wasn't much... *honestly,*" she grinned. "Now you'd better get going before someone steals the hubcaps on that thing—it would be like ripping off two cars all at once!"

Joe drove me to my new life at the Carlyle Hotel. I felt a little like a character in a fairy tale for real now, for I'd finally been rescued from a struggling, single-girl life in Manhattan by a truly handsome, rich prince, never to look back. I was about to embark on a whole new adventure and it felt exhilarating and wonderful.

My private apartment at the Carlyle couldn't have been more plush or glamorous. It was previously owned by the recently deceased Mrs. Gilbert Wellington Vancouver III, though her nickname was "Bunny" due to the fact that she gave birth to seven children back-to-back. Seven *greedy* children who were now feuding over her vast estate... and it was thanks to the numerous Vancouver offspring's avarice that I was comfortably ensconced in their mummy's luxury digs for the time being. The longer their equally-greedy attorneys fought, the longer I would be allowed to live there. I took some pleasure in the fact that I, not any of Bunny's squabbling brood, was the only person legally allowed to set foot in the family quarters.

The apartment was furnished in nothing but museum-quality antiques, which just happened to be Bunny's major passion. And Bunny's perfectly-pressed, size-four, Chanel suits all hung, still as death, in the overstuffed closet. I could almost feel her presence emanating from her garments as they gathered dust, and every time I opened it I couldn't help but be reminded of her death. A faint hint of Chanel No. 5, obviously Bunny's signature scent, hung in the stale air of the apartment and it was also a constant reminder to me that I was living in somewhat of a morgue. Nevertheless, it was still preferable to the rat hole.

Two days after I moved in, Barclay moved into his mother's place as well. I didn't see why we couldn't just stay together at Bunny's apartment, but Helen *insisted* we live separately until we got married. I had to admit it was refreshing to see evidence of some traditional values from Barc's side of the family for once. I took this as reassurance that I was marrying into a good family after all.

Barc was particularly attentive during this time as we both settled into our new places in New York. He was focused entirely on me. I remembered what Whitney said, that I would never want to leave his arms once I had found this kind of attention, and she was right. Maybe this was my shot at a fairy-tale romance like she had too.

Even though Barc continued to pay for all our meals and I didn't have any rent, I kept my rather menial job at Sotheby's so I could still have my 'own' money since I was so used to it now. Surprisingly, neither Barc nor Helen objected, so I dove into our busy fall season, telling Alex and the others I wasn't going to leave them "high and dry" when I knew they really needed the help. They were all very glad.

Every evening after work I'd join Barc for cocktails at his apartment in the Carlyle. Sometimes Helen would join us, and after much pressure on her part, our wedding date was quickly set for December 18, 1989—a winter wedding. Barc didn't object at all. I couldn't believe we were only going to be engaged for three months with all there was to do to get ready for it, but after Hunter didn't even want to do a formal announcement or have a party it was nice to see a groom-to-be actually be excited for his own pending nup-tials—and even help out with planning it. Barc insisted we have the wedding in Texas since it was 'traditional' to have the bride's family give her away, and Helen countered by saying she would throw us a lavish, elegant reception in Newport. That way we could mingle with 'all' family members from both places—and she, of course, could also get out of not going back to Texas.

There was no way I'd be able to take any time off to fly to Houston to plan anything during our busiest season at work, so I asked my mother to help plan the wedding for me at our family's country club.

"Melanie, don't you worry about a thing. I'll book the club and do the invitations and everything! Oh, it's going to be so fantastic!" she said excitedly.

I asked Alex for the time off for the wedding week itself and the next two weeks after that during the holidays for our honeymoon, which we still had yet to plan.

"Of course you can have *that* time off! It's your big day!" Alex said. "And I'll even help you and Barc find a great apartment here in New York for when you get back from your honeymoon. I know you're busy, so don't worry—I'll do all the looking and you can then just go view what I find around your wedding-planning schedule."

"Thanks so much Alex," I told her. "That would really be a big help."

I couldn't stop wondering, *Is there really going to be a wedding? Is this really happening? Is this all too crazy?* But everyone around me kept assuring me it wasn't and that it would all work out just fine.

Barclay and I were supposed to fly to Houston so he could meet my parents the following weekend, but when Hurricane Josephine came barreling up the Gulf of Mexico I got a call from Oldie who bellowed into the phone, "Melanie, it's just too damn dangerous in the Gulf for you to fly down here during this Goddamn hurricane! I don't think meeting with this Barc character will change anything—just tell him I'll meet him at the rehearsal dinner."

In lieu of a trip to Houston, Barc and I went to visit Whitney and Charles in Tarrytown, N.Y. at their historic estate.

"So this is the famous Barclay," Whitney said when we arrived, offering her cheek.

Barc kissed her cheek and said, "Yes, here I am! It's so good to finally meet a member of the family. I hear you're quite the partier, Whitney."

"Well sure, I know how to have a good time, but I'm not as crazy as I used to be. This man has *really* settled me down." Whitney put her arms around Charles's waist.

"Barclay, right? I'm Charles. Nice to meet you," Charles said as they shook hands.

"Whitney, are you expecting more guests tonight?" I asked, noticing the dining room table was set up for six.

"Yes—and actually, they just pulled in behind you. You're not going to believe this, but Charles has a famous patient!"

"Oh really? Who?" Barc asked.

Whitney said giddily, "Dr. Jillian from the soap opera *City Heart Hospital!*"

Charles laughed. "Well, his 'real' name is Billie Blaine. One day I walked into Billie's hospital room to attend to his bicycling injury—and there was my patient not only in bed, but on the television as well! He said he was doing 'research' for the part. We hit it off so I invited him and his wife over to dinner tonight to join us. Annie's a successful actress as well, do you remember the sitcom *Sheila On the Hunt?* It's not on anymore, but she was on it. Oh, and here they are now…"

Whitney nudged me. "Watch this. It's *so* cute."

As Billie entered the room he rushed toward Charles and they started an intricate handshake with lots of silly hand motions. Billie said jovially, slapping his hand, "Tom-cat, tough-titty, I'm a mofo from the motor city!"

We all laughed.

"So… you're from Detroit, I take it?" Barc asked Billie after a full round of formal introductions were made. Billie was a handsome, clean-cut, dark haired man, and his wife Annie was very attractive as well.

"Oh, I brought this for dessert," Annie said, presenting Whitney with a homemade pumpkin pie that smelled delicious. Whitney brought us into the library where her maid, Tina, took the pie and then served us cocktails and hors d'oeuvres.

Billie was a fun entertainer and suggested a game of charades. We played until dinnertime, laughing and performing for each other. We marveled at how good both Billie and Annie were at pantomiming the clues to the game—and marveled at how different charades is when professional actors are playing!

Dinner was a lively parade of stories by Charles about the E.R., and Billie told us all about being a "minor soap opera star," as he called himself. Annie was a comedian in her own right, and her one-liners had us doubled-over in laughter all night. It was a rip-roaring evening and the six of us partied together until well after midnight.

When Billie and Annie had gone home, I cornered Whitney in the kitchen. "I don't want to spoil our evening, but I was just wondering, have you heard from Eva? The last time I talked to her she wasn't doing so well."

"Yeah, I talked to her a while back, but…." Whitney shifted uncomfortably and I could tell she didn't want to talk about it. "She calls me nonstop these days. She even calls the hospital to talk to Charles. It drives him crazy. She always says she's looking for Dawson and thinks she can just call him anytime there. Anyway, Dawson wasn't at the hospital one time when he said he would be and Eva freaked out. She thinks Dawson's cheating on her now."

"Yeah, she mentioned that to me too the other day," I said. "She thinks it's because she's pregnant."

"I know, and I tried calming her down, but there's no talking to her. I know she's one of my oldest friends and I hate to just avoid her, but she's my past, Mel. I want to focus on my *future.* I know she's gotten herself into a miserable situation, but that's just it—*she* got herself into this. There's nothing I can do to help her anymore."

"I feel the same way… but I just fear for her unborn kids. She was drinking pretty heavily the last time I spoke to her—and every time before that since she told me she was pregnant too."

"She's doing *a lot* more than drinking, Mel… but like I said, I can't focus on any of that, and neither can you. You're getting married soon… starting a new life! And soon, I want to focus on having my *own* children."

Whitney was right about Eva. She'd made her own bed, but still, I couldn't help but feel sympathetic towards her. I tried to push the thoughts about her situation out of my head by changing the subject. "Having children… or just practicing the act of *making* one?"

Whitney gave me the evil eye and shoved me back into the dining room. It was great fun hanging out at Whitney's beautiful home with her artistic, witty friends and her truly charming new husband. I was glad to see her life was turning out so well, and looked forward to the fact that mine now seemed to be heading in that same direction finally too.

Chapter 14

fter a few more weeks getting to know Barc 'better' in New York City, I was beginning to have second thoughts about this whole marriage idea. Red flags were popping up everywhere. I saw a different side to him that I never saw in Newport. For example, he drank an excessive amount of vodka daily and had a very short temper by his fifth drink—which was usually by mid-afternoon. He seemed to only be half-heartedly looking for a job and would find any excuse to cancel the interviews Foxy worked so hard to set up for him at prestigious firms all over Wall Street. Whenever I questioned him about this he said it was because he wasn't in a 'rush' to work since he had his trust fund; and besides, he was only *really* looking for a job so he could set a good example as a responsible adult for our future children someday. But since it would be awhile since a child would even enter our lives, he routinely slept until noon and often smoked pot—acting like an indulgent adolescent himself in the meantime.

I arrived at the Carlyle one evening after work and stepped off the elevator just in time to see a shabbily-dressed young man with dreadlocks leave Barclay's apartment. I immediately went over and confronted Barc. He was still dressed in his clothes from the night before and was opening a bottle of Stoli Vodka when I entered. Another empty bottle was tipped over on the coffee table.

"Who was *that* who just left?" I asked him angrily.

Already drunk, Barc just slurred something unintelligible and waved his hand at me dismissively.

"Barclay," I said sternly. "I want to know who that man <u>was</u>—"

"None of your friggin' business!" he blurted back.

I could see a baggie filled with marijuana stashed in a partially-opened drawer in the end table near the sofa. I put the dreadlocks and the ganja together. "Is he your drug dealer?" I asked, though it was more of a rhetorical statement than an actual question I needed an answer for.

"Okay, okay—if you *must* know that's my mom's gardener's son Maurice," Barc lied. "He was doing some work on the apartment."

Instead of fighting him about this ridiculous explanation and the pot, I instead decided to ask him how his job interview with Goldman Sachs had gone earlier that day.

Again, he angrily dismissed me with a gesture of his hand. "I was too fucking busy to go today."

Busy smoking pot, drinking vodka, and never even bothering to get dressed, I thought. He hadn't even shaved, which was insulting since he knew it bothered me when he didn't.

"I had to wait for Maurice to come over and do the work I just told you about. Mom doesn't like people in her place without someone here to watch them," he continued to lie.

"Well I'm sure you could have asked him to come back tomorrow since you knew how hard it was to line up this particular interview… surly your mother would have understood."

"You know *her*," Barc glared with hatred. "Nothing is more important than what *she* wants done first, so I had to wait."

I realized it was no use continuing this battle, and I was hungry. I was at least able to convince him to go shave and get dressed for dinner.

Once he showered, we dined downstairs on his mother's account. I was still annoyed with his upstairs behavior, and he felt bad.

"Mel," Barc started, "I'm sorry I've disappointed you lately. I'm really trying to get things together, but it's just hard since I've acted this way for so long… I really want to be a good husband and father though. I just don't know how to. Will you please be patient with me while I figure it all out?"

I looked at the earnest expression on his face and melted. I guess he really didn't have any positive role models to follow with his background, which explained a lot about his current behavior. I decided to give him more time to adjust, especially since he was changing his ways just for me. "Of course," I said and squeezed his hand.

I spent the rest of the evening enjoying the live jazz music coming from the piano bar long after our plates were cleared, but Barc only used this time as an opportunity to drink more and more vodka as he went on and on complaining about his sad, lonely, dysfunctional childhood.

When the restaurant closed I had to get the hotel staff to help carry him up to his apartment. After a couple of incidents similar to this I was becoming concerned. This was not who I pictured being my future husband, no matter how hard he claimed to be 'trying' to get it together.

Finally, I summoned the courage to call Helen and asked her to join me at the Carlyle for lunch. She met me the following day.

As soon as we sat down, I braced myself and began, "Mrs. Cunningham—Helen—I believe I may have made a big mistake rushing these wedding plans..." I went on to explain my concerns over Barc's temper, his drinking and pot-smoking every day, and his total disregard for finding a job.

Helen interrupted me in mid-rant, speaking in a soft, persuasive tone. "Oh, my poor dahling, don't *worry!* All these things will settle down after awhile... Look, Barclay has just moved to a new city, he's looking for a job for the first time in his entire life and it's very unsettling for him... In addition to that, he's getting married in a <u>month</u>! What man wouldn't be acting out of sorts dealing with all *that?* This is a lot of stress for anyone to have to handle—for you too, dear!"

"I know, but—"

Helen took my hand and patted it firmly. "I *assure* you everything is going to be just fine. I'll speak to him about it. And I'll have my driver pick you up tonight after work. I want him to take you on a little 'shopping spree' to Tiffany's and Bergdorf's." She smiled and added, "I'd like you to charge whatever you'd like to my account, as an apology for Barc's unacceptable behavior as of late. Now, now that *this* is all settled, can we please order lunch? I'm famished!"

"Of course," I stammered. The conversation was clearly over. Helen ordered her usual—steak tartar and sparkling water—and I ordered two chardonnays.

I soon learned that this was Helen's standard response to any of my concerns about Barc. He'd settle down for a few days after she spoke to him—which was often—but it never lasted. And once his behavior became "intolerable" again, she bought me clothes and jewelry as a trade-off for his bad conduct, saying it was still only his way of dealing with all the stress. I knew I shouldn't accept these gifts of pure bribery to stay with him, but it was hard not to since I couldn't afford these types of extravagant luxuries on my meager salary from Sotheby's, and since I'd gotten engaged Oldie had taken away my allowance from him, saying I didn't need it anymore now Barc and his family were taking care of me. Besides that, every few days Barc did sober up and acted like the attentive, respectful, loving man I first met and fell in love with in Newport; and I kept hoping he would stay like that. It was all very confusing.

Since Helen had offered no true comfort over Barc's latest recent 'relapse' just two weeks before the big day, I called my parents with all the same concerns. Oldie was away on business, so my mother spoke for both of them. "Melanie, *now* you tell me all of this? I've already sent out the wedding

invitations a month ago! And the country club has been booked for *months!*"
she exclaimed.

"Well, can't we cancel it and send out another letter explaining the wedding has been called off?" I asked. "What if I'm about to make the biggest mistake of my life going through with this? I'm not sure who Barc is anymore..."

My mom sighed and said, "Oh Melanie, stop being so melodramatic... Everyone feels this way before they get married. And Barclay is in love with you, he's clearly shown that by wanting to marry you so fast. Don't worry—I've got everything planned for your perfect day... It's all coming together just fine and it will all work itself out." She spoke in the same, soothing tone as Helen always did—a tone that said underneath, *Silly girl, don't you know you're too old at twenty-nine for cold feet?* It was a tone I was becoming a little too used to hearing and it made me feel like I was really being told I was a spoiled child expecting everything to be 'perfect' and only go my way.

Still, I wondered why everyone was in such a rush for me to get married. Nothing about this marriage felt right to me and yet, I really felt I was being pushed from all sides to go forward with it regardless. I felt like I was losing control of my life and I wondered, *Had I ever been in control of it at all?*

I wanted to talk to Victoria, but she was still in Europe and extremely hard to track down. I then wanted to get advice from Subir, but he and Cindy were away in Nepal until after the holidays. I didn't want to bother him with more of my troubles while he was enjoying time with his family, so instead I decided to go visit Eva. If anyone could make me feel better about my own situation it would be her, and just maybe I could help her out in some way too.

I arrived at Eva's apartment late in the afternoon and she answered the door in her bathrobe. I'd never seen her look so horrible; she didn't have any make-up on and her uncombed hair was a disheveled, snarled mess.

Eva mumbled, "Oh, hi Mel... come on in to my 'mini-mansion,'" she said sarcastically, motioning wide with her arms. This was only the second time I'd been to her apartment and I'd forgotten how shockingly small and cramped it was, especially considering the fact that her husband made great money as a heart surgeon like Charles did.

"Coming from someone who's lived in a rat hole Eva, I still can't believe how small your place is! How can you stand it?" I asked her.

Eva motioned for me to follow her into the kitchen where she opened up a cupboard that was full of prescription bottles. "*This* is how I deal with it," she said, quickly opening a random bottle and swallowing three pills.

"What is that, Eva?" I asked, alarmed.

"Does it matter? They all make me feel better." She busied herself making a pot of coffee, obviously forgetting the fact that I didn't drink it. "I'm just so miserable all the time..." she said. "I can't stand it anymore really, Mel."

"Eva, you have to be realistic. You're pregnant, and you have to think of your babies first. Don't you have a place you could go?"

Gigantic tears streamed down her face. She ignored my question and said, "On top of everything else, I'm *convinced* Dawson is having an affair! Probably with some hot intern or slutty nurse—I found out he's been lying about being married at the hospital, you know! And we haven't had sex in *months!* All he says is that he's too tired, but I know that's *complete* bull-shit!"

"Have you checked his desk or looked through any of his credit card statements?" I asked, unfortunately knowing exactly how to find out for sure since I had so much experience with Hunter's cheating record.

"No... I never thought to look at any of that before. He uses a Gold Amex card a lot."

I sighed. "Where does he keep his bills?"

The unknown meds were kicking in, and Eva slurred "over there" as she pointed at an antique desk in the living room; then slumped down on the couch while I immediately started looking through carefully organized folders. Dawson was meticulous about his statements and bills, and it wasn't hard to locate the credit card he was using to entertain his 'on-the-side' girlfriend.

Within fifteen minutes and a little Colombo-like sleuthing, I'd figured out Dawson's complete M.O.: he had carefully itemized credit card statements showing purchases from tickets to the latest Broadway musicals, some of the best restaurants in the city, trendy spas and hair salons, clothing boutiques, and other extravagances. Dawson had been entertaining some other woman on a very grand scale, and here was solid proof.

My dilemma now was how to break the news carefully to an already drugged-up and half-numb Eva. I didn't want to shatter what was left of her world, but I had to tell her. I'd been cheated on by Hunter dozens of times and my wounds of that were still raw. But I didn't want anyone else to ever go through what I'd been through with him. Eva had to know now.

Eva laid on the couch in a glazed stupor. I wasn't sure if she'd passed out or not.

"*Eva?*"

She groggily sat up when I spoke. "Soooo... did you find anything or what?"

"Eva," I said, sitting down next to her on the couch. "Dawson does have a girlfriend... a very *expensive* one," I added as I showed her the Amex bills.

She immediately recognized charges to Dawson's favorite couture stores, out-of-town restaurants, and spa visits that did not match up to any schedule *she* was keeping with him. She now had a complete picture of what kinds of activities her husband had been up to lately—all while she withered away with their two babies growing inside her in their small, cramped, stuffy apartment.

For a moment Eva seemed to snap out of it. The knowledge that her husband was having a full-fledged affair made her hot Latina blood boil. I'd never seen her so angry. Her fury flared-up instantly like a scorching, blue-yellow flame and she screamed, "I'm going to MURDER that SORRY SON-OF-A-BITCH!"

"Whoa girl, just don't shoot the messenger!" I said, getting out of her way as I stood up. "Don't forget, you cheated on him too with Brian back when you were engaged."

Eva ignored the comment as if it never happened as she stood up and hugged me tightly. "Thank you Mel for *finally* helping me get to the bottom of all this!"

"I'm sorry that it wasn't a good discovery. But Eva..." I said, looking deep into her eyes—eyes that shifted in and out of focus the whole time—"maybe it'll help you decide what your next move will be. Call me later if you feel like talking,'kay?"

I left her apartment quickly, feeling my work there was done. Empowered with this new information, I hoped things would definitely now change for Eva, but I also wondered how she was ever going to cope with this new crisis in her current, drug-addicted state. I somehow doubted she could stand up long enough to even pack.

Despite this it did feel good to help out a friend, particularly one that was being so heartlessly trampled on. I bitterly recalled Hunter's serial cheating and was comforted by the knowledge that Barc was not like that. Sure, he was a partier—and a bit immature overall—but at least he wasn't a *cheater,* and I was truly thankful for that.

I still had misgivings about the pending wedding, but like Eva, I felt I had also made my own bed now. And after seeing what was happening to her, I felt secure knowing that at least *my* bed would be a much more comfortable place with a non-cheater like Barclay in it.

The big day finally came. I spent the week in Houston making final preparations, and I calmly told myself that I was ready. I was going to do this, and everything was going to be fine.

Whitney went with me in the limo on December 18th as we headed in a rush to St. Mary's Episcopal Church, a little behind schedule. We drove through the parking lot on our way to the bridal room when suddenly something out the window caught my eye. "Oh my God—Whitney, LOOK!" I said, pointing towards a small crowd.

Barc and his best man, who I'd never met before, plus a dozen or so other men all in black tails and ties, were standing around in the parking lot drinking beer and smoking cigarettes out of the back of someone's Suburban.

Whitney laughed out loud. "Oh man... they look like a bunch of Billy-Bobs at a tailgate party!"

"I can't believe it! He's getting *wasted* before our ceremony! Oh my God, I'm going to vomit!" I clutched my stomach. It felt like I had swallowed nails. I frantically looked for the limo's buzzer but couldn't find it. "Driver! Pull OVER!" I yelled toward the closed partition.

Whitney stopped me. "Mel—stop! You know it's bad luck for a groom to see his bride before the wedding, so listen to your maid-of-honor... we're already late! And besides that, you know your guy is a party animal, so lighten up. Lots of women have boring lives and boring marriages... at least you can say yours *won't* be, huh?"

I couldn't believe what I was hearing. "No, no, no—this is *wrong*—Whitney, this is ALL WRONG! What am I doing here?" The air felt nothing but hot on my face. It was hard to breathe and I started to hyperventilate.

"Jesus Mel, get a hold of yourself! Maybe you should have a drink yourself." Whitney shoved a glass of champagne in my hand, but I brushed it off and fumed the rest of the way to the bridal room.

We entered to a hurricane of activity. All eight of my bridesmaids, half of whom were old friends from high school, were furiously dressing and being primped by a floating crew of hair and make-up artists. Everyone was rushing about, getting ready for the "big show."

I hurried down the line to greet them each individually, and then came to the three in the back of the room I was most glad to see. "Victoria! Alexandra! Chrissie—I'm so glad you guys could all make it down here!" We all hugged and air-kissed so as not to disturb the make-up work already done on each of us.

Victoria gasped. "Oh Melanie... you look absolutely *gorgeous!*" She leaned in and whispered devilishly, "Wouldn't it be nice if Hunter could see you right now? He'd just *die!*"

"Oh hush..." I said, doing my best to smile broadly at the sound of his name. I didn't even want to think of him on my wedding day to Barclay, but it had actually been hard not to all morning. In fact, I hated to admit it, but I had thought of Hunter a lot since the moment I landed back in Houston. I was glad I didn't have too much longer to stay here now.

"Eva! How are you doing, girl?" I said happily, truly glad to see her as she approached us. She was all cleaned-up and looked glamorous, much improved from the last time I'd seen her—though behind her made-up eyes she still looked a little like a deer in headlights, close up.

"I'm doing a lot better Mel, thanks to you. I'll talk to you about it later," Eva said, winking at me. I wondered what she meant by that, but there was no time to ponder it. I was being shoved into a seat and poked at and fretted on by David, my Saks Fifth Avenue hairdresser.

Suddenly I saw Catherine approaching in the mirror's reflection. "Catherine!" I exclaimed. "Oh my God—thank you so much for coming!" I reached over and grabbed her hand. I hadn't seen her since the day she left my bedroom with the box of photos and was happily surprised to see her now.

"It's my pleasure, sweetie," Catherine said. "I'm just so glad that you finally got away from my asshole brother and found someone who *truly* loves you, and I wanted to come tell you that in person on your big day!"

"Thank you," I told her, trying not to cry. "I really appreciate it." The clock on the wall read 4:30 PM, the time the ceremony was supposed to start. I used it as a way to quickly change the subject before tears ruined my carefully applied make-up. "I can't believe how late I am to my own wedding—I'll probably be late to my own funeral!"

Everyone laughed while David twirled tendrils of my hair as fast as he could while someone else applied lip-gloss. I felt a bit like Dorothy in *The Wizard of Oz* when she was in the Emerald Palace.

"Don't worry about it!" Alex exclaimed. "This is your pony-show honey—ride it!"

I couldn't stop smiling. Misgivings or not, it finally hit me—I was getting married! This was supposed to be one of the best days of my life. Suddenly my smile began to feel real.

Ever the artist, David was still primping when Oldie showed up and hammered at the door. "Melanie! Everything's ready, but we kinda need a friggin' bride here! What's the Goddamn hold-up?" he roared.

"I'm still getting my hair done, Dad!" I yelled toward the hall, but since we were all dressed Whitney let him in before I could stop her.

"Well, can't you step it up? All our guests are waiting. And it's not like I'm paying you people by the hour!" Oldie said to the flitting entourage.

David said nervously, "Well Mr. St. John, sir, you DO want Melanie to look fabulous, don't you? It's her big day!"

I gulped and saw Oldie's face turn red. He roared, "How long does it take to fix HAIR? It looks perfectly done to me! I'm giving you all FIVE minutes and then Melanie better be walking down that Goddamn isle, got it?"

Five minutes later on the dot, I was nervously delivered to Oldie's arm and we walked down the aisle past rows and rows of onlookers. I was still in a frazzled daze, but as Oldie lifted my veil to kiss me on the cheek, I realized the weight of what I was doing. In my whole life I had never seen my father cry, and this was as close as I ever got—his eyes were welled-up and sparkling as he smiled proudly at me, his youngest daughter. As long as I live I'll never forget the look on his face.

As I carefully made my way up the steps towards the church's altar, I looked at Barc who stood stiff in his tuxedo next to it. His eyes were tearing up. My eyes were tearing up now too—partially because I was so happy I was finally getting married—but also because in the pit of my stomach the thought still festered inside me that I was making a *big* mistake...

When it was time to exchange rings, there was a small commotion as the best man whispered something into Barc's ear. After a quick pow-wow, the best man dashed down the aisle and out the church doors. I swallowed my mortification as the wedding party stood chatting uncomfortably and the crowd waited. I overheard Barc whisper to a groomsmen that he'd absent-mindedly left the ring where they'd been tailgating in the parking lot. I closed my eyes in disbelief, embarrassment, and silent dread for the moments that were still to come as we all waited for the best man to return.

He finally did and dashed back to the altar where Barclay and I finished our vows. The ceremony was completed with a sweet kiss, a round of applause, and little tufts of white rice thrown into our hair.

Since my mother had decided that I was too old at twenty-nine to have a huge wedding with a thousand guests like you would for a twenty-one-year-old, our small, traditional ceremony was followed by a reception for about two hundred people—a modest crowd by Texas standards—back at our country club. Yet even still, I spent the entire evening in a receiving line—every time I'd walk to another part of the ballroom, a large group of well-wishers would follow. I barely had time to eat or drink, let alone keep track of my new husband.

Barc had disappeared shortly before the main course and was now needed for the first dance. But of course, he was nowhere to be found. A few groomsmen and even Whitney had looked everywhere in the building and parking lot, but couldn't find him. Finally, Chrissie tracked him down out around the side of the building smoking pot with a few of the guys from the tailgate group earlier. Barc arrived back into the ballroom bleary-eyed and stoned, though he pulled himself together long enough to swing me around to our chosen song, *Thank Heaven for Little Girls*. I was so angry as we danced that I had to fight off tears.

As Barc turned me around on the dance floor suddenly—out of the corner of my eye—I saw something that made me forget all about being upset at him and I froze in place. Barc stopped dancing and looked in the direction I was starring in.

Casually, as if he were there only to 'browse,' Hunter strolled leisurely through the crowd with a barely-dressed Candi—the woman he had dumped me for—on his arm, gloating. He didn't even seem to notice that Barc and I were in the middle of our first dance—Hunter just brazenly walked out onto the dance floor in front of everyone and straight up to me.

"Hunter, what the hell are you doing here?" I whispered, astonished.

"What am I doing here? What, did you *forget?*" Hunter asked, amused.

"Get out of here! I don't want you here!" I told him sternly.

"Surely you remember Candi, from Vegas?" he said casually.

"You weren't invited! You need to get OUT!" My voice and tone had decidedly risen above a whisper by now.

"Then why did you send me an invitation? Wait, let me guess, you just wanted to show me you were over me, is that it? Wanted me to sit and watch you get married to someone *else?*" he asked sarcastically.

"I didn't invite you—my mother did the invitations, and why the hell she would invite *you* is beyond me!" I said, but knew deep down she really wouldn't have done such a thing and he was just crashing.

"You didn't think I'd come, did you? Didn't think I'd have the nerve to show up and bring the hottest, classiest babe in the room? You should know me better by *now.*" Hunter laughed scornfully.

I'd had enough so I spat, "Right, she's so 'classy' she slept with you for the first time on the same night you got engaged to *me!* Or did he not tell you that *that* was the <u>real</u> reason he was back downstairs feeling extra 'lucky' that night?" I said towards Candi.

She gasped, so I knew he hadn't. Hunter looked clearly surprised that I knew this even happened as well.

Barc laughed out loud, leaning into the middle of our fight. "You've got *some* cast-iron balls coming here, guy!"

"Nothing against you, man," Hunter told Barc like they were old frat brothers. "I just had to see it for myself. I don't want to give you any problems though, because you're gonna have *plenty* after today!"

Barc leaned his head back towards me and chortled. "Ha—*tell* me about it!"

I couldn't believe it: my new husband was joking around with a man who'd torn out my heart and stomped on it. Looking at them both together made me suddenly realize I had *really* bad taste in men... I should have never stepped foot near either one of them. And that festering feeling of doubt inside me now became crystal clear: it was my suppressed feelings of love for Hunter bubbling back up towards the surface of my heart, even though I didn't want them to. I suddenly knew right then and there that this whole marriage to Barclay was done on the rebound, for it was Hunter I still loved deep down. It was a love I couldn't stop, but one that could definitely still shatter me again at any moment as I stared into his intense eyes, wishing it was *him* who I had just said "I do" to, but it was too late. Luckily, Oldie stormed over—rescuing me at the precise moment I was about to have another complete, utter breakdown...

"You have SOME NERVE, Hunter!" Oldie yelled. "Get the hell out of here—and I *mean* it! Haven't you put this woman through enough? She's trying to move on with her life—without YOU! You've made your statement, now *go.*"

"Fine, fine... sorry, sir." Hunter put his arms up in the air as if to call 'uncle.' He and Candi turned on their heels as Hunter said sarcastically towards Barc and me, "Best wishes to the 'happy' couple." Then they sauntered out of the main ballroom.

The music was still going, so Barc swung me around as if to shake off the encounter, but by this point, I was crying. Most of the crowd had no idea what had just happened and were whispering among themselves to try and be filled in. Catherine looked at me sadly, mouthing the word "sorry" over and over again. I noticed everyone else was beaming at us as we danced, seemingly urging us to just "carry on." And we did.

Later, a jubilant Victoria caught my bridal bouquet. Afterwards I hugged her tightly as I told her, "I hope this brings you luck."

"Maybe now I'll find a man to take care of me, too," Victoria said back happily. "Just like you did."

"Yeah," I replied, but secretly thought, *At least, I sure hope I did...*

The party wound down around 10:00 PM and all I wanted to do was go back to our hotel suite and crash after such a long and exhausting day. We had thankfully convinced Helen to host her party for us in Newport the following evening to allow us privacy on our actual honeymoon night, but suddenly Barc roared, "Let's keep this party going!" to a group of about fifty revelers, and they all headed back to our hotel suite after they had been ransacking the open bar all evening.

So instead of a romantic wedding night with my new husband, I played spontaneous hostess to a rowdy group of drunkards who moved way past champagne and onto bottles and bottles of booze. Most of them were Barc's friends from high school and college, all sloppy and obnoxious, and I felt like I was baby-sitting a group of high school jocks after prom. I pushed the last guest out the door at around 3 AM and vowed to sleep as late as I could before the post-wedding brunch the next morning. But at 7 AM the phone in our hotel room started ringing shrilly.

It turned out two of our married groomsmen couldn't find their wives, and they called to ask if they'd passed out on any of our suite's sofas. Barc looked concerned and got dressed. He left our room and returned a few minutes later with the two missing women—both of whom glowed with the same look of 'fulfilled satisfaction' that Barclay and I should have been illuminating by now. They had spent the night together in one of the extra hotel rooms reserved for out-of-town guests. Barc made up some big story to tell his buddies, but a tense and awkward brunch shared with the husbands and their two very sheepish, now-lesbian-lovers/wives revealed the writing on the wall (divorce, we found out later, happened for both couples just a few short months later).

That afternoon Barc and I caught a flight north to Newport for the huge party Helen was throwing for us at her beachside cottage. I was glad to have left both Houston and Hunter behind, and hoped to now try to make things work better between Barc and I in the same place where our relationship had started out so magically when we first met just months before.

We drove down Bellevue Avenue where all of the major mansions were and continued along Ocean Drive towards Helen's place. As we passed each estate I thought of all the great parties we attended in Newport over the summer and hoped Barc remembered them all too. I silently prayed being here again would turn him back into the way he was then—the way I could truly love him—and also allow me to try to forget about Hunter, for good.

Barc steered the car smoothly through the curve in the road when we passed by Seal Rock Beach, and I knew Newport well enough by now to know if you didn't belong to this famous 'beach club' then you weren't included in any of the town's main social events—including tonight's party—all year. By now I also knew that Helen Cunningham was considered Newport's 'grand dame' and her whole cottage estate, nicknamed Indian Wells, was one of the largest pieces of property in Newport. The cottage sat right on the ocean and had its own private beach as well as a private golf course. But it's most notable feature was "Tommy," a replica of the little English train with the smiling face, Thomas the Tanker. Helen had had it commissioned to be made by a deranged ex-window dresser who charged millions for his artwork. It seated forty persons nicely and ran all over the grounds of the fifty-five acre estate all summer.

The cottage's exterior looked like something out of the English countryside, but inside it contained one of the top contemporary art collections in the country. There were enormous, abstract paintings everywhere and the rest of the décor had a distinctly vintage, 1960's feel. It had twelve bedrooms and every door was painted a color straight out of a box of crayons, making the rooms unique, memorable, and perky. There was the Red Room, Jade-Green Room, Sky-Blue Room, Orange Room, Avocado Room, Golden-Yellow Room, Pink Room, Auburn Room, Magenta Room, Aqua Room, Violet Room, and Alabaster Room—and Helen always had a room assignment ready for her constantly rotating roster of houseguests, just like

Mrs. Nielsen did at Lark's Landing. I wondered which room Barclay and I would get for our first stay there.

Helen told me weeks ago that she was specifically throwing this party so I could meet everyone important from 'the beach.' She had informed me there would be a group of about four hundred or so attending, so the event would be an even bigger spectacle than our actual wedding.

"Oh Melanie dahling!" Helen cooed as Barc and I arrived. "I hope you don't mind, but I took the liberty of commissioning Vera Wang to make you something *extra* special to wear tonight... How you're presented to our friends needs to be perfect in *every* detail."

"Thank you, Helen," I told her. "I'm sure I'll love it." I thought it was odd that she didn't ask about our wedding or even say congratulations to either of us—it was as if the whole ceremony we went through was just a formality and we could now get on with the rest of our 'real life' together, starting with her party.

Helen had booked the Lester Lanin Orchestra from New York to play under a giant white tent on her back lawn. New York's Glorious Cuisine catered the whole evening's menu including delicious hors d'oeuvres, entrees, and desserts. She really went out of her way to top the affair in Houston it seemed.

I realized this was to be my "grand unveiling" to the whole of Newport society, and I felt a little like a debutante all over again. The Vera Wang dress fit perfectly and Barc told me I looked spectacular in it. I then felt more like a real-life princess the rest of the night as I was served a steady supply of fine champagne and formal introductions, so much so that my head started to spin like a top.

I watched the hands on the clock fly by as I put on my best face for the army of strangers. But on what was an unusually mild night, and after hours of being paraded around on my feet for what felt like thirty-six-hours straight starting the day before, I couldn't keep my eyes open any longer. At 4 AM I slunk away from the lingering and exuberant crowd and snuck upstairs, craving nothing but a soft surface to lay my head on. I settled for a Victorian fainting couch in an empty hallway upstairs, where all I had to do was lean into it and I was asleep before my foggy head even landed.

"Melanie! Mel—wake *up!*" I was jolted awake to find myself surrounded by Barc, Helen, and a group of assorted family members. I thought I was still dreaming. I looked at the clock on the wall and could see it was 6:30 AM, but everyone was still dressed for the party; they'd obviously been up all night. They were staring at me—some amused, some angry.

Helen seemed to be continuing a lecture that had already been going on, "This is just *not* the way we do things! You do not leave your own party for any reason until the last guest has left! You should know better than that!"

she said not to me, but to the air around me, and then stalked off. The others stayed behind to taunt Barc.

"Oh you *really* picked a good one this time," Barc's brother Stewart said sarcastically.

"What a lightweight!" Barc's cousin Damien said as he nodded and pointed. "Look at her! Can't even hang! No stamina at all..." He jokingly shook his head and patted Barc on the back. "Good luck, bro."

Barc sat down next to me. "Mel, you need to know that this was *really* not acceptable. We couldn't find you for hours! You have to stay up through the party no matter what—this party was in *your* honor. Anyway, it's over now." He rubbed my shoulder. "So go on and get some sleep... we leave for our honeymoon in Palm Beach in a few hours! Aren't you excited?"

He kissed me on the forehead and they all left, but I was too humiliated and frazzled to fall back asleep. In more ways than one, I wondered what in the world I had done—and what in the world was I going to do now I *legally* belonged in this crazy family...

Foxy had insisted we spend our whole honeymoon at his home in Palm Beach, Florida as his wedding gift to us, so we left Newport a few hours later and arrived at the lavish estate that would be our private retreat. The location was beautiful; it overlooked the ocean and had an underground tunnel to get across the street to the secluded beach. Black iron gates surrounded the whole estate which included amenities such as an Olympic-sized heated swimming pool, putting greens, a tennis court, and of course the four bedroom guest house which was Barc's 'second' home. The elaborate main mansion itself was designed by the acclaimed architect Addison Mizner and was done in a Spanish style with a terracotta roof. It had thirty-five bedrooms and a private movie theatre that could fit fifty people in plush, stadium-styled seats.

The weather was a wonderful seventy-four degrees with a balmy breeze. I felt it was as if we were transported to a sunny paradise just like when we were back in Newport over the summer, and it suddenly gave me a renewed hope that we could really make this marriage thing work.

"I'm sorry I couldn't stay awake all night for the party. I know how much your mom wanted it to all be perfect," I told Barclay as we unpacked our things in the grand master suite that had a marble balcony overlooking the enormous, sparkling pool below.

"Are you still thinking about all *that?*" Barc said jokingly as he looked at me like he had other things on his mind than the past twenty-four hours up north. "Cause to be honest, now that we're finally 'alone,' I can't think of anything else but the fact that we still have one final, *very* important thing left to do to make this marriage 'official'..."

I grinned, knowing exactly what he had on his mind. And as soon as Barc took off his shirt and came over to unzip my dress, it was suddenly on mine too. This was the attentive, caring man I had fallen in love with... the one who knew exactly what I liked in bed in every way too as he slowly removed my lace bra and cupped his strong, firm hand gently around my right breast, moving his fingers in circular motions as he kissed me passionately... though we had our problems elsewhere, when it came to the bedroom, I definitely had no complaints.

"I want to make love to you, *Mrs.* Cunningham," Barclay whispered in my ear. Then he picked me up and carried me across the room to the king-sized bed where we made love for hours on end over the next two days straight, basking in each other's newness and soaking in only the 'good' memories of our wedding that we both wanted to recall and let go of the bad.

On the third day of our blissful honeymoon I felt everything awful that happened in New York and Houston was just a terrible dream and I finally had the 'mature' Newport Barclay back. We went out onto the beach and watched the cool ocean waves lap the shore as we sunbathed while drinking fruity frozen drinks.

"Want to go out tonight?" Barc asked me.

"Sure," I said, thinking it was time to reemerge into the world around us again.

But I had forgotten Palm Beach was one of Barc's old stomping grounds and many of his childhood friends still lived there. His social group consisted mainly of loud, delinquent trust fund brats at least a half-decade younger than him, and a gaggle of major heiresses he used to date there. And from the moment we set foot in the Palm Beach's Liquid Room later that night to meet his friends, it was obvious the men were all players, and the women already despised me. I was from Texas after all, which was salt in their wounds—an 'outsider' who had nabbed one of their most infamous, sought-after playboys—and now here I was in the flesh, sitting at their table, drinking their champagne, and infiltrating their little tightknit world. And worst of all, I wasn't impressed with any of them one bit.

"So... *Melanie? Is it?*" one woman about twenty-five with striped blond hair started with a hint of mockery. "How do you like living in New York? I mean, it must be quite the change from...'Texas.'"

"Well actually, I grew up traveling all over the world and I lived in New York over several summers as a child with my dad," I told her. "So it was pretty easy to get used to living there full time as an adult."

"You must get that a lot though… I mean, with your accent—you really sound *sooo* Southern!" giggled another young woman in a green, skin-tight dress.

I looked over at Barc, but he was at the bar with his male friends and didn't seem to be coming back over to the table to rescue me from his rude female friends, so I decided to just do my best to keep the peace with them all. "Well, my parents are both from Texas and I grew up there all the way through college, so I guess it's understandable that I talk like this still," I said, trying to act friendly.

"Is it true what they say, I mean—about Texas guys?" asked the one in the green dress. "That they all have big *dicks?*" She squealed at her own joke, but no one else did.

"Is it true that most women there are married by twenty-one, with kids?" asked a third woman who looked to be in her late twenties and the closest to my age. She then added sweetly, "Didn't you get started a little late, for a 'Texas' girl?"

"Uh… I really wouldn't know… now if you'll excuse me, I need to go powder my nose," I said, getting up from the table. Barc's girlfriends were annoying and I was already bored out of my mind.

After I'd made my way back through the crowd, I approached Barc from behind as he and his male friends all sat down at the table, now joining the overly made-up harpies. Before anyone had noticed me, I could hear Barc telling them all, "Yeah, she's a little different, but as soon as we get back to New York I'll get her to change her clothes or at least her hair or something—she sticks out like a sore thumb everywhere we go. So 'not' Manhattan at *all.*" He rolled his eyes.

"Well, least she's hot!" said one of his polo-shirted preppy male friends. The other guys all laughed loudly.

Barc doesn't like my hair or the way I dress? Since when? I thought as I waited a beat; then emerged from the crowd, pretending I hadn't overheard anything. A stab of embarrassment tugged at my heart as I sat down at the table.

The women mostly ignored me after that while they incessantly flirted with Barc all night. They told childhood stories, adolescent jokes, and cracked each other up with snide insults masked as humor. It was clear I didn't fit in—and I didn't want to. Luckily the club's music blared all around us so I could mostly just tune them all out.

Later, after waiting for Barc to reappear after what had been by now at least an hour-long trip to the men's room with two of his buddies, I decided to go back to Foxy's place. The girls sniffed a good-bye as I bid them and the rest of the group good-night. I couldn't believe how insensitive Barc was being. I searched the crowd to tell him I was going home, but he was nowhere to be found, so I got in a cab and left.

The bars in Palm Beach stay open until 4 AM each night, and from that night on Barc and his friends "closed down the town." I spent my nights staying at Foxy's grand estate all alone watching movies and my days by the pool or sunbathing on the beach, waiting for Barc to sleep off his hangovers. Before my eyes he'd morphed back into an obnoxious, nonstop party animal all over again. I couldn't believe we were spending our honeymoon this way.

One afternoon as I people-watched from a popular hotel bar's private veranda, I realized Palm Beach was beginning to feel a lot like Newport to me: a place where millionaires played all day and partied all night, and though it was beautiful and enticing, everyone here seemed void of any real substance to me. I could see how empty and dysfunctional all of Barc's friends really were here in Florida—and Barc, it seemed, was quite at home.

The end of the trip finally drew near, and I couldn't wait to get back on the plane and back to New York. I started to pack, even though it was still only the day before we were leaving. Barc woke up and looked at me sleepily from the bed.

"You're packing already? We still have another whole day here!" he said.

"Please, don't remind me," I said as I wondered what on earth I was going to do all day alone yet again.

But instead of starting an argument like I thought he was going to do, Barc sat up and looked concerned. "Don't you like Palm Beach?" he asked, clearly getting for the first time I wasn't having as great a time there as him.

"Not especially," I said as I laid out all my shoes to decide which to pack first.

Barc got out of bed and put his arms around me from behind. "Mel, I'm sorry I've been a little neglectful this trip. I just grew up with these guys and haven't seen them in a long time... I know you understand," he said, turning me around to face him and lifting my chin. I was surprised. For once, he sounded like he cared.

"Barc... a 'little' neglectful? You've disappeared every night for hours for the past three nights and you even did it once at our *own* wedding!"

He looked deep into my eyes. "Okay, Mel, you're right. I've been a jerk. I'm sorry. Let me make it up to you. I want to take you out on an extravagant cruise today, just you and me. Drinks, caviar... it'll be fantastic. "

I hesitated. "I don't know... let's skip the boat and just stay in bed all day like we did at the beginning of our trip. It's supposed to be our honeymoon Barc, just you and me... no one else..."

"Naaaw—let's go wild then! No crew, nothing—we'll rent a speedboat, go down the inter-coastal waterway, and then fuck our brains out on the open ocean!" he said glibly, picking me up by the waist and twirling me around.

"Barc, stop! Listen.... you've ignored me—and frankly, embarrassed me—this whole trip! You've flirted with every skirt in town and you've made me look like a small-town hick from Texas to *everyone*—"

"Lighten up Mel, Jesus—these are my buddies! They're just joking around and it's no big deal."

"Yes it is because I *heard* you!"

"What?"

He clearly didn't remember.

"I overheard you talking about the way I look, the way I dress... that I'm *so* 'not' Manhattan—like I'm *nobody!* You and your stuck-up, bitchy, East Coast friends think you're so great... but you *know* where I come from— you know I have connections too! How do you think it makes me feel to know that you think so *little* of me? Like I'm *nobody!*"

"Melanie, seriously—it's okay..." Barc said, now seeming to get it as he became serious for the first time during the whole conversation. "Listen, I love you, and I'm *really* sorry about everything... I know who you are and you're not 'nobody.' And you're also right—it's our honeymoon. I won't hang out with my friends at all for the rest of our trip and I want to make it up to you, so please, let's have some fun today, just you and me."

I admit his smile and the offer were both appealing now I knew it would only be the two of us.

The sunshine danced off the water near the dock when we arrived at the marina; it was a gorgeous day and our last chance to do something really romantic on our honeymoon. And besides, Barc sounded completely sincere as he kept telling me over and over how sorry he was and that he was going to give me a day I'd never forget now.

"Which of these babies is the *fastest?*" Barc asked the rental agent, a seedy-looking man with a faded captain's hat. He pointed to a sleek white speedboat with *The Gemini* painted along the side in blue script.

"Perfect," Barc said to the man. "It's our honeymoon—and matter of fact, I'm a Gemini too." He gave me a warm smile. The rental agent flipped him the keys.

We got in and sped away. Barc immediately reached into the boat's stocked cooler and pulled out a bottle of iced vodka, then yanked the cork out with his mouth. Not even waiting until we hit open water, he accelerated into the highest gear the boat would go.

"WOOO HOOOO!" he yelled between swigs.

"Barc, jeez—where's the fire, huh? Slow down!" I yelled over the crashing waves. "I don't think you're supposed to be going this fast here... those signs back at the dock said—" but my words were cut off, drowned out by the gushing wind.

Barc kept driving the boat and getting drunk—both with fiendish speed—as he held the bottle of vodka in one hand and the boat's wheel in the other. I clung to my seat in fear. It was worse than driving on the French Riviera with Oldie behind the wheel.

I tried again to yell over the wind, waves, and the sound of the engine, but Barc just smiled and squinted into the sun, offering me a swig of the now half-empty bottle.

"No Barc, I don't want a drink! Please, slow down!" I begged him as I finally made my way over next to him. "I'm getting scared—the water's choppy and this boat is bumpy... I think I might get seasick—"

I had barely finished my sentence when we heard a squawky stern voice over a megaphone: "Attention Gemini... Pull over! Repeat, slow your boat to a full stop. Repeat, pull over!"

A U.S. Coast Guard speedboat was on our tail, now directly behind us.

I thought fast. "Fantastic, Barc—look at you. I suggest you ditch the vodka you nimrod and suck on these." I handed him a handful of breath mints fished out of my purse.

Barc glared at me as he slipped the bottle overboard and away from the approaching Coast Guard. Their boat pulled up beside ours and a uniformed officer in sunglasses shouted to Barc, though politely, "Sir, are you aware you've been going twenty miles per hour over the speed limit in a no-wake zone? This area is a protected manatee habitat."

Barc mustered his most sheepish, innocent face. I rolled my eyes.

"I'm sorry officer, I didn't know. It's our honeymoon, you see. I guess I was just trying to impress my new wife. I'll slow down from here on out."

"Great," the officer said, not at all impressed with his excuse. "Please also pay *this* upon the return of your boat rental later." He issued him a five hundred dollar speeding ticket.

After the Coast Guard boat left, I was trembling with adrenaline and anger. It was too much.

"Barc, what are you trying to prove? You'd have to be blind not to see all the signs posted everywhere! Manatees are an endangered species for Christsakes! Imagine if you ran over one of them." My mind immediately went to the poor animals Barc could have hurt, or maybe already did...

"Fuck you, Mel! I don't need any shit from you—not right now! Besides, those signs are inconsistently marked!" he roared.

"Inconsistently marked?" I snorted. "They were *everywhere* on the dock! And look—one- two- three- four- *five!*" I counted out loud as I pointed to the five signs within eyesight of our immediate vicinity. "You're *really* lucky you didn't hurt a manatee or that that speeding ticket *isn't* for a D-U-I for driving a boat *drunk!*"

"What? I'm not drunk!" Barc said, insulted. "But you're <u>wet</u>!" He suddenly grabbed my waist, picked me up, and threw me overboard in one full swoop. The water's cold, wet splash was a shock to my whole system.

"Now you can play with your 'manatees!'" Barc said, laughing hysterically as he looked down at me. "And you look like a drowned rat!"

"Cut it out and help me!" I yelled as I treaded water. I was beyond furious and humiliated. My new Pucci dress, compliments of Helen, was totally ruined and both my Ferragamo sandals and Hermes sunglasses were now sinking towards the bottom of the ocean.

A life preserver plopped down beside me, splashing my face. I grabbed onto it and Barc pulled me to the boat's side; then lowered the ladder so I could climb back up, cold and wet.

Right then and there I knew I'd made a terrible mistake by marrying this rich, pompous, arrogant asshole. And suddenly Hunter popped into my head. *Hunter would have never, in a million years, thrown me overboard on our honeymoon and thought it was funny*, I thought to myself. In spite of all of Hunter's limitations and how badly he'd treated me, I don't think even he could have behaved *this* badly, ever.

Dripping and furious, I shivered and hugged a towel all the way back to the rental office. As we disembarked, I shirked Barc's help in getting off the boat and back onto the dock.

"I'm going to the Breakers Hotel for some cocktails. See you later," Barc said, leaving me there, hurt and alone. I walked back to Foxy's beach house, soaked, barefoot, and crying. But I wasn't really even angry anymore... I was just sad. I was already shifting my thinking, making plans in my head.

I can't wait to get back to New York so I can get an annulment, I thought. This marriage was bad news, and I wanted out. I decided to call Oldie as soon as I made it back to Foxy's place.

I finally reached Oldie by phone later that night while Barc slept off his cocktails in the other room. I stifled tears while I told him all about the details of our disastrous honeymoon: that we had barely spent any time together; that Barc got drunk with his old high school buddies every night and partied till dawn; that he had gotten pulled-over by the Coast Guard for speeding through a protected manatee zone...

Oldie had been quietly listening to my saga up until this point, but then, just as I told him about getting thrown overboard, 'just for kicks,' I thought I heard a stifled laugh.

"Do you think that's *funny,* Dad?" I said, not believing he could really think that.

"Melanie," Oldie said with a sigh. "Barclay is a rich, spoiled brat—but he's your *husband* now. Those vows mean 'for better or for worse,' and you know that. Just you mind—Barc will settle down once he finds a job, gets himself a routine, and then everything will fall into place."

"Oldie, you don't understand—I've made a *huge* mistake. I can't stay married to Barc! He's lazy and a complete party animal!"

"Melanie, don't you think it's a little late to be wondering if you went and married the wrong man?" There were tears running down my face by this point, but Oldie didn't know that. He just said, "That boy hasn't worked an honest day in his whole life Lil' Bit, and you knew that about him going in, so you're just going to have to be patient with him now. Give him another chance. Your mother and I would be devastated if you tried to annul your marriage so soon—I'm sure you can understand how that would be a huge embarrassment to *all* of us, especially with no divorces on our side of the family. Now toughen up kiddo and go work things out with your *husband.*"

I hung up, crushed. These were the nuggets of truth I did not want to hear from my father, but Oldie was right—I had gotten myself into this predicament, even when I had serious doubts way before. Who marries someone after only a few *months* of meeting them?

Oldie's words rang in my ears and occupied my thoughts all night, and even into the next day as me and a still hung-over and very grouchy Barc made our way to the airport. Oldie was right. I would have to live with this decision, and all of its ramifications, at least for a while. And there was still time for things to calm down—after all, we had only just ended our honeymoon, and we weren't fully established in New York yet.

Now Barc was getting away from his old friends and life in Palm Beach, maybe he'd go back to being the Barclay I knew and fell in love with over the summer, as brief as our wonderful love affair had been. He had a lot of growing up to do, that much was clear—but a part of me believed that deep down he cared for me enough to finally come around. Besides, how long could a grown man continue to party and behave like a teenager?

I resolved myself that it was time to start looking ahead, and not back. Sure, Barc had messed up our honeymoon—but maybe we'd laugh about it later, when we were old.

Things can't be bad all the time, I thought. So with a gulp and a swallow, I told myself to wait and see as we boarded the plane back to New York together, as husband and wife.

Chapter 15

❦

The day we got back from our honeymoon it was early January, and there was a blizzard in New York City. Barc and I took a cab from the airport to the two bedroom apartment Alexandra had luckily found for us to rent just before we left for our wedding two weeks before. It was a brand new building—less than a year old—on 86th Street between Fifth Avenue and Park Avenue. It was so new in fact that it was still having some work done on it while we were gone: we'd asked to upgrade all the kitchen appliances and for the walls to be painted before we fully moved in. The manager had assured us the work would be done in time for when we arrived back from our honeymoon, so we even had most of our belongings moved up from Texas as a wedding gift from Barc's brother Stewart who owned a moving and storage company in Dallas. This included all of Barc's furniture from his mother's guest house as well as my huge wardrobe full of designer clothes and shoes.

When the yellow cab pulled up to our building, however, something was terribly amiss. Yellow and black tape cordoned off the entrance to the building itself. The sidewalk was all torn up, and there were police barricades everywhere, purposefully blocking the path up to the door. It was frigid and snowing like crazy outside. All of our winter clothes were inside that apartment, which meant we were both exhausted, freezing cold in our Palm Beach attire, and apparently staying that way.

I shivered.

"Wait here," Barc instructed. "I'm going to go see what the hell is going on in there."

He stormed out of the cab and tried the entrance to our building, but it was locked, so he climbed over a pile of construction materials and disappeared into the building next door. He finally reemerged and got back into the cab, completely silent.

The cab driver shifted impatiently. "You stay or you go? I don't have all night," he snapped from the front seat.

"Just a minute! We need a friggin' minute, okay?" Barc shouted at the cabbie. He turned to me and explained, "The doorman next door said all of the construction on the building has been halted indefinitely... rumor has it the 'mob builders' violated several major New York City ordinances and the city shut down the building completely. No one's allowed in or out. In fact, all the other tenants were forced to vacate their apartments too—all this happened while we were gone."

"What? This place was ninety-eight percent occupied! How could this happen?" I was in disbelief.

"I don't know. The guy said since it's now condemned it probably won't be resolved anytime soon either—the tenants have all been living in hotels for the past six days on the city's dime, so the union doesn't seem to be doing much of anything about it."

I began to cry. All I wanted to do was go up inside our new apartment, get warm, and start to unpack and feel like I belonged somewhere. Outside the window of the cab I could see the snow piling up on the sidewalk. I knew we had to make a decision fast.

"What's it going to be?" the cab driver said, more annoyed.

"Would you tell him to shut the fuck up already?" Barc barked toward me, making sure the cabbie heard. "I don't need to take any crap from a cab driver wearing a turban at this particular moment. I'm trying to make a *plan!*"

"*You're* going to make the 'plan?'" I snorted. "Yeah right..." I looked around at our condemned building, the empty block, and the snow piling up around us.

"Take us to Hotel Wales," I told the cabbie, sniffling. "It's only a few blocks away, and it's the only place I can think of right now."

"Where? That's extra for two stops—"

"The Hotel Wales God-dammit—just turn left up there!" Barc shouted as he pointed, and we pulled away from the curb of our 'supposed' new home.

We checked into the small, shabby hotel around the corner, which had long seen better days. There was no bell service and the lobby had a noticeably musty odor. Not exactly the kind of place Barc and I were used to staying in, but since the place was practically empty, the manager gave us a two bedroom suite. Barc automatically pulled out Helen's credit card as usual, but this time he hesitated and slipped the card back into his wallet. I pretended not to notice. He turned to me.

"Hey Mel, can I borrow your Amex card for this?" he whispered. "I maxed out mine in Palm Beach. Weird though, I didn't even know it had a limit... anyway, I'll pay you back, I promise."

Why would he lie about that being his card? I thought. I knew the whole time since we had been dating it was usually Helen's credit cards he used. In fact, I only knew him to have one card in his own name at all. But given the circumstances and the fact that the hotel manager was standing there, waiting for us to finish the transaction, I pulled my Amex card out. I mentally added up what a week in this dumpy, overpriced hotel would be, and I could feel my irritation rising.

Once we were settled into our dark, outdated suite, Barc started unpacking his bags, pulling out a few navy blue blazers, khakis, swim trunks, and flip-flops.

"You won't be needing any of that, it's about zero degrees outside," I said.

"God Mel, quit being so negative. This is all I have to wear, and I'm not going outside—I'm going downstairs. They have a nice restaurant and bar here. You can join me if you want, but I really don't care."

"Before you leave and start charging a bunch of cocktails to *my* credit card Barc, where are all yours? I noticed you using Helen's the whole time in Palm Beach. Where's *your* credit card? Where's *your* cash?"

"Oh, that. I got into an argument with American Express and they suspended my charging privileges. Don't worry about it—it's not even worth talking about."

"Well when are you going to get your charging privileges back?" I asked, trying not to sound concerned.

"Probably next week. It's no big deal," he said, clicking on the TV and channel surfing as he sat down on the bed.

"So in the meantime I'm just supposed to pay for everything?"

"Fraid so," he said, staring blankly at the TV. "But I don't see what the big deal is… after all, we're married now, so your money is technically 'ours jointly' anyway."

My stomach dropped. I began to see a pattern taking shape—and I didn't like it. This was not part of the deal. I could barely cover my own expenses, let alone Barc's expensive taste and unpredictable spending habits. Unlike Barc's trust fund, mine was meant to provide me with a little 'extra cushion,' not living funds, and Oldie was still holding onto it all at his two best stockbroker's offices anyway. I still had no access to any of it, and Barc knew that.

If I had the energy I would have unloaded everything I'd endured since our wedding, not the least of which was the fact that Barc was supposed to be taking on *all* the expenses in this relationship, not me. He had assured me that over the summer. But what was the point? For now I only had one main concern: "Barc, how am I supposed to pay for everything on my small salary at Sotheby's when you're the one with the big trust? What about your day-to-day money? Why are you putting everything on credit cards anyway? It's not like I can support us until you turn forty and get your next trust fund either, you know. You *do* know that, right? Cause that's five *years* away..."

Barc continued to watch TV, ignoring me.

"*Barc!*" I was about to explode.

He still ignored me like a spoiled child.

"RIGHT BARCLAY?" I yelled. "Your trust funds are all spread out five years apart... isn't that what you told me when you <u>promised</u> I'd *never* to have worry about money as long as I was with *you?*"

Barc got up from the bed and walked out of the hotel room, leaving the TV on.

That night, I slept in the second bedroom alone. Without Barc hogging up all the space beside me there was finally enough bed to contain my tossing and turning. For the first time since our marriage had become official, I had the room to contemplate what all this meant. Barclay Cunningham had no money left from his last trust fund... and wouldn't for a very, very long time. This fact was hard enough to deal with, but on top of that, being married to Barclay Cunningham was turning out to be a nightmare in every other way too.

Because of the snow and lack of warm clothing, we were stuck inside the entire weekend and we barely spoke to each other. He spent most of his time at the bar downstairs. I spent time watching movies, reading, and worrying excessively about our future.

I was one very unhappy newlywed.

But by Monday morning at 9 AM the snowstorm had passed. I tried Alexandra on the hotel's phone again. I'd been calling her all weekend in vain, but she wasn't home. I knew she had a hot new boyfriend, which probably meant they were off skiing in Vermont or holed up in some romantic inn in Connecticut somewhere. But I knew she was due back at work this morning, and sure enough she picked up on the first ring.

"Oh hi Mel! So how was the honeymoon? 'Fab,' I presume!" Alex shrieked before I could answer. "You're so lucky—you missed three terrible snowstorms while you were off screwing your brains out in beautiful, sunny Florida. It's been so miserable here—"

"Listen, Alex, I'll have to tell you all about it later," I interrupted, not in the mood for idle chit-chat. "We have a major problem. What the hell happened to our apartment? And why didn't you call to warn me about it? We can't get in and they say it's been condemned or something—and all our winter clothes are in there! It's ten degrees outside and I have nothing to wear but a pair of old baggy sweatpants from the Gap and—"

"Shit Mel, calm down—I was about to tell you, but it sounds like you've been there already. I'm so sorry, but I didn't want to ruin your honeymoon—there's nothing anybody could have done about it anyway. We all thought they'd come to some sort of agreement by now, but you know how 'egos' get with these kinds of things… So, you don't even have a coat, huh?"

"I was in Palm Beach—all I packed was a few cashmere shawls. And we were planning on moving right in as you know! What are we supposed to do? I can't even go back to work until I get my regular clothes—and we're staying in this hell-hole of a hotel—The Wales on Park, know it?"

"Eesh, yeah…. okay, honey, I'm on it. The Arcadian is full—that's where most of the tenants are, but I'll try to get you in somewhere nicer, don't you worry—and I'll make sure it's on the city's dime too just like the others who were put out of that place. Oh, and since it doesn't look like there'll be any resolution on the building, I'll just start finding you guys a new apartment too, how 'bout it? I should still be able to get you guys out of the lease… Anyway, I'll call the office manager about getting your clothes out as soon as possible. And Mel," she said, "don't worry, okay?"

"Thanks Alex, I really appreciate it."

We hung up and she called back a few minutes later. "Great news!" she chirped. "The building manager will meet you there at five so you can get your stuff. I'd suggest hiring a car service—just wrap whatever you can in a couple of hotel sheets or something, you won't have long. He said you can keep the rest of your furniture there until we can find you a new place too."

"I'll be there alright—if I have to wear these sweatpants for a minute longer I'll scream. Thanks, Alexandra. Let's definitely get lunch later this week. Oh—and Alex, can I ask you a kinda more 'personal' question?"

"Sure, anything, what's up?"

"Did you know that Barc doesn't have any money?"

There was a long pause on the other end of the phone. "What do you mean Mel? Like cash?"

"Like he doesn't even have his own credit card anymore… and if all the money is gone from his current 'family trust' then it means he won't be allowed to touch any real money again until he turns forty and gets his next trust fund. We stayed at his father's place in Palm Beach and he paid for practically everything else with his mother's credit card."

"Wow… well, that's what I've always heard…. that Foxy and Helen have always covered his whole 'lifestyle' whenever he'd burn through another trust."

"What do you mean *another* trust?"

"Well," she stammered. "I've heard that he went through three by the time he was thirty."

"Fuck Alex! THREE!? And you *knew* this? Do other people know this—or am I just the dumbest girl in New York? This marriage is <u>not</u> what it's cracked up to be!" My voice was starting to tremble.

"Oh Melanie—it was none of my business, hon. All I know is what everyone else knows really... which is that his parents have *tons* of money. Nobody knew anything about a trust—but why would we? That's obviously a very private matter."

"What else do you know about him that you never told me?"

"Nothing you didn't hear already... just stuff about his problem bachelor days after college and his run-ins with the law growing up in Dallas—"

"What? I never heard about that! What did he *do?*"

"I'm not sure exactly 'cause he always got off because Foxy knew the police commissioner."

"Oh Alex, what am I going to do? I didn't know he was *this* much of a problem—and I definitely wasn't planning on supporting him—there's not enough in my paycheck to support MY husband!"

"Oh God Mel, I'm so sorry... but can't you call Helen and straighten things out? I hear she's, you know... 'generous' about these things?"

"I knew it! You guys all knew about all of this and didn't warn me!"

"No Melanie, no—we honestly didn't. I mean c'mon, we've all known Barc's bad rep since he was in college, and everyone knows he's a spoiled fuck-up. I mean, you *had* to have known yourself after only this short time. He's just a big kid who never grew up!"

"I have to go, Alex," I said, feeling ill.

"Seriously... call his mother... she was always very 'kind' to anyone Barc screwed around back in Dallas. Just tell her how you feel and I'm sure she'll help you sort this whole thing out."

I hung up in disbelief. *What was I going to do?*

Barc walked into the room, startling me out of my head.

"We can get our stuff," I said as if everything was fine. "Be ready to go over there in a car at quarter of five."

Barc look pleased. "What'd, you finally do something *right,* blondie?" He grabbed my waist and tried to kiss me. He was obviously already tipsy.

"Get off me, Barc."

"I'm taking a shower—then maybe we can grab a late breakfast next door at the French bistro, huh?"

"Fine, whatever. It's not like I have to change clothes or anything," I said sarcastically, motioning to my sweats.

Barc laughed at my joke. He was obviously in a rare good mood.

With Barc in the shower, I decided to call Helen. I managed to tell her the entire story of our ill-fated honeymoon, the saga of the condemned apartment, staying at the rundown Hotel Wales, and then, I finally asked the *big* question, "Helen... why doesn't Barc have his own money?"

There was a noticeable pause, and I thought I heard amusement in her voice. "Whatever do you mean, dear?"

"I mean, why is Barc paying for things with your credit cards and now asking for mine—as if he's not a grown man and doesn't have his *own* money?

There was dead silence on the other end of the phone, which was very unusual. Then finally, Helen spoke, "Melanie dahling, it's none of my business where Barc gets his spending money anymore, but he certainly doesn't get it from me, or his father. That ship has *long* sailed—didn't you know? Barc gets all the money when we die and not a minute before. I'm not sure what he's told you, but I know he's still in denial about that little fact. No... it's no secret that Barc will need to work for his living dear, but you *knew* that because I've heard you both discuss his job interviews routinely. His father and I have both done our best to help him start a career too—years ago I had him take over a property I owned in Palm Beach for awhile to get started in real estate, but in less than nine months he defaulted on the mortgage and sold the property without telling me to pay off all the gambling debts he'd accumulated. Foxy repeatedly tried to get him to work for him at his oil company in Dallas, but he became a bit of a public relations problem he screwed up so badly there—*when* he even bothered to show up to the office *at all*... So now we have both just let Barclay know that he has to find a career on his own without our help, and luckily he now has *you,* so it's really none of my business anymore. Now, I'd rather not discuss these unpleasant things, if you don't mind."

"So, in other words—"

"—so in other words Melanie *Cunningham,* you should feel free to continue to let me know about any little thing *you* might need dear and I'll try to help *you* out. Otherwise, that boy is now your responsibility, and I will pray for you both that my careless, senseless son shapes up... and hopefully before he becomes a father, too, for that's what Foxy and I are *really* now anticipating..."

Oh my God—there it was; the truth. Helen and Foxy had planned this all from the beginning! They pushed me into this rushed marriage by misrepresenting Barc and tricked me into thinking he was going to change, that he was a different person underneath his 'bad boy' ways... but they were really just looking for someone to take care of him! How could I have been so blind? It suddenly became crystal clear to me as I pieced it all together from the very beginning...

For all their differences, Foxy and Helen could agree on one thing and that was after they were gone they *knew* Barc wasn't capable of taking care

of himself, nor what was to be his vast inheritance. It was only a matter of time before Barc would blow through all the money. So in order
to protect their vast fortunes, Foxy and Helen knew Barc had to be cut
off. And then, to really rid themselves of their biggest financial liability,
they needed an unsuspecting and wealthy family to absorb Barc's bad
habits, a family with a daughter traditional enough—maybe even stupid
enough—to sign up to take care of him on the dotted line of a marriage
certificate.

I knew they had done their homework—they dug around my family's
background and found no divorces on either side of the family. I was well
educated and stable, relatively quiet and drama-free compared to Whitney,
and they knew I had my own trust fund coming someday.

Even more than that, they luckily discovered that Oldie—who had
enjoyed a fair amount of success on his own—was also the heir to my grandfather's holdings in an old telephone company he started in the 1930's.
Back then it was called "Texas Telephone and Telegraph," but today it was
a well-known telecommunications company worth millions.

Armed with all this knowledge, Helen and Foxy made an assumption
that I was their 'Perfect Patsy' for Barclay. They knew Oldie would never
contest the marriage like he did in the past with other men I'd dated because
he felt the Cunninghams were the 'perfect,' most suitable 'Texan' family for
me to marry into. They also seemed to intuit I'd never go against Oldie's
wishes either, and they wanted Barc married off fast once we started dating
and Oldie approved. Their only real challenge was getting Barc to behave
long enough to fool me, which was why it all happened in a whirlwind of
only five months. I felt ill.

"But Helen—"

"Don't worry yourself too much, dear," Helen clucked. "I'll send some
warmer clothes over in the car... and I've been meaning to mention this,
but why don't you start going to the Christian Science Reading Room with
me? They have a location right there on seventy-second and Madison—
maybe it's time to turn to God for guidance in your marriage."

I thought I misheard her. "I'm sorry... did you say 'guidance'? I'm not
really the 'Christian Science' type Helen, but thank you."

"Melanie, there is no typical Christian Scientist. They come from all
walks of life, of different social and economic statuses too. The common
belief that binds us is that we can all be cured through faith and Godly
energy, dispelling negative thoughts in favor of God-like thoughts which
will then follow through with *His* God-like actions."

I really thought she must be joking, but she sounded as serious as I
had ever heard her. I'd seen her play some pretty petty mind games and
hand out some backhanded compliments, but this was perhaps her most

infuriating move yet. Of all people, Helen Cunningham should *not* be playing the 'God' card.

She paused for dramatic effect. "Now, how about this Sunday? You can join me at the Reading Room and then we can go shopping afterwards. What do you say, dear? My treat."

I was stunned as we hung up.

Barc came out of the shower, whistling a tune.

Later, after we'd gotten our clothes back and warmed ourselves with food and sweaters, I thought about what Helen had said in regards to God and how we all needed to think positively so 'He' can then 'take action.' I realized that even in times like these I should just be grateful for the small things in life I now had—like warmth, food, and shelter—but the man lying beside me in bed was someone I didn't even know, and I didn't understand why God would let this scam of a marriage happen to either one of us.

For the next few weeks I spent every free moment trudging around in snow up to my knees in the endless pursuit of an apartment. It was the worst winter I'd experienced in New York, and luckily Helen took pity on me and loaned me one of her mink coats and a pair of knee-high snow boots. I huddled into the winter cold, determined to get us out of what we now referred to as 'Hotel Hell.' All the major dignitaries were in town, so Alex hadn't been able to get us into any other suitable hotels within a hundred blocks of where we were now, and so we stayed—and still on my dime since we weren't evicted by the city along with everyone else when the building was initially shut down.

While I looked for a roof to put over our heads and continued my part-time job at Sotheby's to bring in some money, Barc continued to play cards and drink vodka with the French waiters at the bistro next door to the hotel. It was impossible to get him to do anything else. His rationalizations were always flying: "Look Mel, I can't start interviewing for a job until we have an apartment with an address and phone number," he'd explain to me while dealing out a hand for the table and puffing on a vintage cigar. Or, "You have much better taste than I do in apartments. I trust you to find a good one, Mel," he'd say, dressing to go meet some friends from Newport or Palm Beach for dinner. Then he'd kiss my forehead as he walked out, not even inviting me to join them.

Mindful of Oldie's words that were still only a month old in my head, I motivated myself by saying we first needed a place of our own to call home before we'd ever even have a prayer of saving our new marriage. So I kept my mouth shut and kept looking.

After two more weeks of pounding the pavement in bone-chilling temperatures, I finally found a two bedroom apartment that was completely out of the budget: the building was in a brand new high rise on the corner of

81st Street and Park Avenue, with a circular drive and a huge fountain in the center. Ours would be on the twenty-eighth floor, facing west with a wrap-around terrace. The view of the New York City skyline over the backdrop of the Park was breathtaking from both the balcony and the many large windows throughout each of the grand rooms inside.

I immediately called Helen.

"Oh dahling! I'm so proud and excited that you *finally* found somewhere else to live besides that God-awful hotel! After all you newlyweds have been through, I'd like to offer to pay for the first year's rent plus the security deposit," she announced.

I was stunned. I hadn't done so yet, but I was going to ask Oldie for help. Now I was glad I called her first. "Wow, Helen—"

"No, no—I insist, dear. It's the *least* I can do since you poor kids have been through so much lately." Whether she was bribing me to stay with Barc for at least the first year of our marriage, or truly felt guilty about what her son had put me through so far in this brief amount of matrimony, I didn't care either way. I only wanted to move forward.

Barclay and I moved out of the hotel the following week, and I called my favorite limousine service to take us to the new apartment as a way to celebrate and start anew.

As we pulled up Barc smiled at me, "Mel, this place looks great! There aren't many buildings in the city with fountains. I can't believe my mom is going to pay this enormous rent for a year either... she must have panicked and thought you might be leaving me or something," he joked.

How right he was, but thinking back to Oldie's words, I held my tongue. Instead I said, "You're right, Barc. It's extremely generous of your mother and I know she really likes the apartment too. She told me she stopped by the other day to take a look at it before signing the lease."

"Believe me; if you can impress her, you've done a great job."

We took the elevator up to the twenty-eighth floor. When we entered the foyer, Barc was awestruck. "These views are amazing!" he exclaimed as he came over and gave me a big hug. "Great job, Mel. This place is incredible! All of your hard work really paid off. I love this place!"

I was warmed by his genuine, enthusiastic reaction. It wasn't often that I got to see Barc so happy lately, especially with me.

"I'm so glad you like it, Barc! I'm just shocked I didn't get pneumonia," I joked.

He cupped my nose playfully. "Well, I know things have been a little rough for us so far... but I think we should look at this apartment as a new beginning, what do you think?" He wrapped his arms around my waist. I breathed in deeply.

"I think that sounds wonderful," I said, hugging him back. It felt good to have him there, truly present for once. I stared at our reflection in the balcony's sliding glass door, unsure of the future or what would come next. But right now, we looked like we were a young, happy couple just starting out and all seemed possible.

After we were settled into our new apartment, to my delight, Barc immediately hit the street looking for a job. After a round of interviews with most of the major Wall Street firms (thanks to Foxy's help, of course), Barc was hired by Oppenheimer. Since Barc had no job experience, as a "wedding gift" Foxy and Helen each gave him a check for one million dollars to open up two separate retail accounts to help him start building his portfolio at any firm he decided to work with. I was sure it was the only reason he was hired—starting with two such strong client portfolios for any stock broker was very impressive—and he'd told the firm's president about the new accounts right away along with promising that he could use his wealthy family's connections to bring in many more. It closed the deal and by the end of the interview Barc had the job.

It was a productive change, and the first few weeks were exhilarating. Barc would get up early and go to work excited to finally have a purpose. And I had gotten a promotion at Sotheby's as well, so now I had full-time hours and much better pay. We settled into a routine, and it was comfortable and nice.

Barc settled in fast at Oppenheimer and it seemed predestined that not long after starting work there he met another good-looking trust fund wastrel named Tanner who was newly hired himself. Barc and Tanner took the subway together after work to Lexington and 59th Street, and would then barhop all the way home. His newfound friend kept him in a steady supply of blow and showed him where and who to buy pot from in Central Park. By the time they arrived at our apartment near midnight most nights, they were walking on air.

Tanner often had a 'nightcap' in our apartment, which meant I usually found him crashed out on our couch in the morning, a habit that was getting to be particularly annoying. This disgusting, destructive behavior continued unabated for months while I busied myself at work—and with our mounting debt.

Though we both now had good, full-time jobs, Barc's spending was out of control and what we made wasn't covering it. I knew we needed more money coming in, so I decided to ask Oldie if I could use some of my trust fund money; the extra cushion it was meant to be would really come in handy right now.

"Sorry, Lil' Bit," Oldie said. "It's in a ten year C.D. that has too high of a penalty to touch it now—I thought since you were marrying 'up' you wouldn't really ever even need it."

"I thought that too," I told him. "But it seems his parents are determined to teach Barc some serious 'life lessons' right now."

"That should do the boy some good!"

"Yeah," I said, trying to sound positive and not wanting to burden him with the fact that I hadn't even seen Barc sober for weeks.

"I'm really proud of how you're keeping this marriage together, Mel," Oldie said. "I knew if you just gave it some time, it would work itself out, and see, it did!"

"Yeah," I said again, feeling bad I was lying now, but I wanted to continue to make him proud. "You know what," I started, changing the subject. "Remember that time when Mom said I should be a cook?"

"Yeah," Oldie said. "What's this all about?"

"Well, I think she's right. I really do love to cook, but I don't want to give up my new job at Sotheby's to go work in a restaurant all day. Do you think you could help me out to get some supplies so I could start a catering company on weekends?"

"Sure, Mel, I'd be happy to if that's what you really want to do."

"Yeah," I said, now feeling very optimistic about my decision. "I do."

My new, "Southwestern, Tex-Mex themed" catering company took off and I quickly had events and parties scheduled for all my weekends over the next few months. I used all my mother's fabulous recipes and served delicious spreads of cheese quesadillas, miniature tacos, spicy chili, and special hors d'oeuvres and dips including guacamole—which was a huge hit to all the East Coast attendees who were very excited to indulge in this new kind of "comfort cuisine." And thank God most of them couldn't cook; for my "private cooking classes" at people's upscale apartments soon became a big hit as well. I was booked most every evening after work.

We now had lots of decent money coming in, but I was working like crazy to keep both my jobs going, and Barc and I rarely saw each other unless one of us was coming or going. But I really didn't mind, and he didn't seem to either. We were settling into our new life, which was pretty separate from each other's, but at least with mine I didn't have to deal with his constant partying, which was getting completely out of hand.

One night after Barc's foul-mouthed temper had awoken our next door penthouse neighbors, I was finally forced to call the cops to get him to calm down.

"I'm FRIGGIN' SICK OF YOU and every OTHER ASSHOLE in this CITY giving me SHIT all the FRIGGIN' time—" Barc yelled angrily as he threw a ceramic vase out the window. I remembered him telling me this was one of Foxy's favorite pastimes, but it seemed the apple didn't fall far from the tree.

The officer was on his way up in the elevator and couldn't have arrived fast enough. Barc immediately set the next item he was about to hurl out the window down and straightened up as soon as he saw me let the muscular, stocky cop into the foyer—putting on a complete act of hospitality for him. "Hello, officer," Barc said politely. "Can I help you?"

"Mr. Barclay Cunningham?" the officer said sternly as I stood behind him for protection.

"Yes... is there a *problem?*" Barc asked him like he was truly concerned.

"Yes," I began, but the officer quickly motioned for me to be quiet as he continued to direct his attention at Barc.

"Mr. Cunningham," the officer said. "There's been several calls about some disturbance from this building... the last one was from your wife."

"Is that *so?*" Barc said, then glared at me as he still remained as calm as possible in front of the cop, but I knew I would pay for this admission later.

"Mr. Cunningham, are you under the influence of any substance right now?" the officer asked.

"No sir... I mean, I might have had a few brews earlier after work, you know how some days at the office can be, and it was one of *those* days today, but I'm fine as you can see now..." Barc did his best to stand up straight, but he still leaned over to one side. The cop knew he was lying, but he had to follow procedure.

"Is it okay if I ask you a few questions, Mr. Cunningham?" the officer asked, taking out his notepad with some notes about the disturbance calls already on it.

"Shoot," Barc challenged him. Since he had been in trouble with the law many times before he knew his rights, and knew if he could get the answer right to three silly questions by law they couldn't take him to jail, the hospital, or anywhere—no matter what I or the neighbors said.

"Will you confirm if these answers are correct, ma'am?" the officer asked me. I nodded.

"What's your mother's maiden name?" the cop asked Barc.

"Belmont," Barc said like he was ready for that one.

I rolled my eyes as I nodded to the officer that he was right. What the officer *didn't* know was that Barc ONLY knew his mother's maiden name besides her first married one of 'Cunningham' since she never bothered changing it again after she got divorced from his dad. She figured since she didn't know how many husbands she'd end up having overall, why bother changing it ever again?

"Where was your wife born?" the cop asked.

"Houston," Barc said proudly.

Why are these questions so easy? I wondered.

"When's your birthday?" the cop asked.

His birthday was now the only rote fact that stood between freedom or being put in a jail cell for the rest of the night, and luckily for Barc, it didn't take much more motivation than that to sober up even more.

"June second," Barc said, knowing that his 'test' was now over and he had passed.

But I knew the truth: that it was rare that Barc even knew what day of the week it was nowadays, and I was hoping tonight would be a wake-up call for him if he really was taken away. At least a couple times a month I took secret pleasure watching him rise early for work, shave and get dressed— only to break the news that his office would be closed since it was Sunday. I really wanted him to get it together, no matter what it took, including jail time, if necessary.

The officer quietly pulled me aside and said as kindly as he could muster, "Look lady, I know he's lit, but it's not against the law to get dead-ass drunk in your own apartment. Unfortunately, there's nothing I can do about it unless he does harm to himself or to you—until then, we're not supposed to intervene. Now, there are a lot of folks out there who genuinely need my help and I can't keep coming by your place every time your husband gets too drunk again, ma'am, understand? I'm really very sorry, but this is something you're just going to have to handle *yourself*."

It was mortifying and heartbreaking to hear this. I had never felt more hopeless and alone than I did right then. Calling the cops had always been my worst-case scenario, but now that Barc was surpassing what even my wildest imaginings could have predicted by eluding them, there was nothing left, and nothing more I could do. The officer seemed to confirm that there was nothing *anyone* could do anymore. I couldn't see how it could get any worse...

But then, a few months later, we started receiving brokerage statements in our mail. There must have been three or four different ones a day and they were stacking up on our desk and on our kitchen counters, dozens of them, all unopened. After a few weeks I couldn't stand it anymore. I filled one of those medium-sized brown bags from Bloomingdales with them and presented the bag to Barc.

"Barc, why are all of these statements being sent to our apartment and why don't you open them?" I demanded to know.

Barc mumbled something about me not understanding the stock market. "They're addressed to me," he said, "and they're none of your business!"

I kept pressing the issue. "But look at this pile. This is insane. Go on, look at it!"

"I'm watching a World War Two movie and going to bed. I don't have the time or the interest in explaining this to you right now," he said angrily. "Leave me alone and quit your bitching!"

His reaction was angry enough that I knew he was hiding something... but what?

The next morning after Barc left for work I opened several of the statements. There were so many of them I knew he wouldn't notice. I didn't know much about the stock market, but even I could tell something was up. I could see on the statements that he was buying "puts-and-calls" instead of investing the way his parents had intended him to invest their money. I had overheard some of my private, stockbroker cooking clients talking about this sort of thing while we were sautéing vegetables the other evening and I knew what he was doing... Barc was day trading.

More like gambling than investing, a day trader gets into the stock market in the morning and gets back out of it by the closing bell—it was just Barc's style to try and make a buck quick and fast. It was legal for those who could stomach it, but I knew neither Helen nor Foxy were those kinds of investors. Besides meddling in other people's lives by playing 'matchmakers,' his parents weren't terribly big risk takers. Both Helen and Foxy had given him strict instructions only to invest in safe, blue chip stocks, no exceptions.

"No problem, Mom and Dad," Barc had assured them.

The total disregard Barc showed toward his parents' money and investments made me very uncomfortable. If they found out what he was doing they could pull their money out and Barc could lose his job.

Looking at the amount he was losing on a daily basis, I was sure his boss wouldn't be happy; plus I knew Barc had told the firm he'd bring in additional investors through his parents' wealthy contacts. I hadn't heard him speak about any new clients since he'd started, and a quick flip through the rolodex on Barc's desk confirmed he was doing little else but playing the table with his parents' money each day.

I wanted to say something to someone... but to whom? If I confronted Barc, he'd just start screaming that I didn't know what I was talking about and never let it go that I had 'spied' into his personal, private business. If I called Oldie, I knew what he'd say—that this was a business matter between Barc and his parents and I should stay out of it. If I told Helen, the only one of the two in-laws I actually had a relationship with, genuine or not—it could put our lifestyle in jeopardy because to punish *him* she might reconsider covering our shared housing expenses. I knew Barc and I couldn't afford our new apartment on our own—even with me working two full-time jobs. And besides that, I'd grown rather accustomed to letting Helen shower me with gifts, shopping trips, and jewelry. Just that week, in fact, Helen had invited me to spend the whole summer with her in Newport to get away from the hot city and 'other things,' meaning of course, her son Barc. I now needed to say yes and get away from here more than ever, for there was nothing keeping me here anymore besides work, and I really needed a break from that for a while too. In fact, I needed a break from everything...

Eva had had her twin boys the month before and was calling all the time because they were driving her 'crazy'—and her words were always slurred whenever she spoke, whether it was on my answering machine or over the phone when I called her back. Whitney was blissfully happy still with Charles and their new "best friends" Billie and Annie, so she couldn't be bothered with Eva anymore—or any of my 'silly marriage problems' as she referred to them, because they only brought her own 'always happy' mood down. Victoria was still off traveling the world as a top Ford model now, so I hardly ever heard from her anymore. Subir and Cindy were spending more and more of their time in Nepal and traveling the world, so our lives were slowly drifting far apart. I felt completely alone and on my own, even married, and Newport seemed like just the escape I needed for awhile.

Two weeks later, Barc's daytrading habits became a three-and-a-half-hour away problem, a 'city problem'... one of those nagging irritants I could let go of as I crossed the long bridge leading into the small, affluent harbor town. I felt the oppression of my life in New York immediately melt away as soon as I entered into Barclay's and my old stomping grounds from the summer before. The air was pure and the sea was so calm that contentment engulfed me.

"Dahling, you're here!" Helen said happily upon my arrival. "I insist you take the Sky Blue Room. It has the best views of the ocean besides the master bedroom, of course."

"Thank you, Helen," I said, truly grateful. "I'll start unloading my car."

"Nonsense. My handyman will take care of that. You, come with me." She led me out onto the great veranda. We looked out onto the ocean.

"Thanks for letting me stay the whole summer. I really couldn't wait to get out of the city. It's already sweltering there," I said, deciding to leave the rest unsaid.

"Yes dear, you're very lucky to have such a flexible job, and an understanding husband!"

I let the husband comment slide. "You're right, I am lucky. Here's to a great summer!" I welcomed her warm greeting and was relieved. I'd been anxious about staying under the same roof with Helen for three months, but we were off to a good start, and it continued as we relaxed into a nice, comfortable routine of summer galas and wonderful meals together. I was really enjoying myself for the first time in what felt like forever.

However, as fate would have it, after only two weeks, the weather in Newport took a dramatic turn for the worse. An ominous cold front blew in, dark and unabating, and the weather report called for more chilly temperatures all week. Once again, I found myself totally unprepared for the wind, rain, and cold. I was always a light packer and because Newport was so consistently gorgeous the summer before, I didn't even bother packing a sweater. I remembered how miserable that chilly weekend in the Hotel Wales was when I had nothing warm to wear. Even though I knew I could shop for warmer clothes in town, the beach was dreary and depressing and the house was very drafty, so I decided I could just as easily wait the weather out in the city. After all, I could always return to Newport the following weekend. I told Helen of my plans.

"Oh dear, I wish we were the same size, then I could at least lend you some of my sweaters and pants—all I have is this raincoat. I don't know why you won't just let me take you shopping. I hate to see you make that drive. You'll have to leave dreadfully early if you want to avoid traffic. Won't you reconsider?"

"Thank you Helen, but I'd rather just head back. I'll probably leave around seven."

"Well, if I don't see you in the morning, dear, have a safe trip. Give Barclay a call to let him know to expect you—he'll be so pleased to have you back home, I'm sure."

The thought was amusing to me that Barc would even care if I came home or not. "I'm sure he will. Thanks again, Helen."

The next morning I drove back to city. I had some CDs in the car to listen to, and luckily the traffic was a breeze. I was in a great mood and for once I was actually looking forward to seeing Barc. We had never been apart this long during the whole past year, and though we didn't see each other much while we lived under the same roof, it was amazing how much you get used to someone's presence just knowing they live in the same space as you. I took it as a good sign that I missed him too, for I didn't think I would and was actually surprised I did. I had thought about calling him like Helen suggested the night before, but decided it would be more fun to surprise him instead.

I arrived back at the apartment by eleven. Since I had been gone for a couple of weeks I wasn't sure what to expect—Barc had never been on his own for so long before. I had left him a number for a cleaning service and hoped he had used it.

I opened the front door and my nose was immediately assaulted by the odor of rotting garbage and stale food. I went into the kitchen. The place was a mess. There were dirty dishes everywhere, dozens of empty take-out containers, pizza boxes, and empty bottles of booze.

So much for Barc being capable of taking care of the apartment while I'm gone, I sighed.

I noticed the red light blinking on the answering machine and hit the play button.

"Hii Mell," Eva's drunken voice slurred. "Whhere are youuu? The twins won't shut up—please call me!"

I sighed again and hit delete. *Why'd I even come home?*

Message two: "Hi babe, it's Amy." This voice was unfamiliar to me. "Where are you? I've missed my 'rock'—I mean, I still look at the sparkly one you gave me for Christmas," she giggled, "but sometimes a girl just needs the *real* thing, yeah know? I heard your frigid bitch of a wife moved to Newport for the summer, so why haven't I heard from you, Boo? I'm lonely. Call me as soon as you can." Click.

I was in shock. Who in the hell was Amy? She used 'frigid bitch,' one of Barc's favorite insults towards me, so I knew she was calling the right number. He had a stepsister named Amy, but this was x-rated stuff and not the kind of message she ever left him. I replayed the message again. Hearing her voice, whoever she was, totally repulsed me. I went into our bedroom, got out two suitcases, and started packing everything I could fit into them.

The next thing I knew, Barc was coming into the bedroom.

"Fuck! You scared the dog shit out of me!" he yelped, shocked to see me. "What the hell are *you* doing here?"

"Nice 'welcome home', asshole," I said, my tone flat. Apparently he *didn't* miss me.

"Whoa, what's your problem? I had no idea you'd be here. You were supposed to be gone all summer, remember? What happened?"

"The weather got nasty so I came back to get some warmer clothes. But don't worry, 'Boo' —I've almost finished packing and I'll be leaving shortly. I wouldn't want to interfere with any of your 'summer plans' of course." The sarcasm dripped from my voice.

Barc looked at me strangely, but tried to act casual. "I told you June was a very unpredictable month up there. It can be gorgeous or totally awful like it is right now, but of course you never listen."

"Well it's funny you say that because I *did* just listen—not to you—but to something you've left on the answering machine... Sounds like you've had 'fun' while I've been away!" I attempted to sound like I didn't care, but my anger was bubbling up.

"What are you talking about?" Barc asked. I could hear him straining to sound normal, but I could hear the panic rising in his voice. "I've been working my ass off all week and don't need any of your bullshit, Mel. Just what are you trying to insinuate?" As he said this he went straight over to the bar and poured himself a slug of vodka, which he downed quickly, pulling out a Marlboro chaser to light it.

"I'm talking about someone named 'Amy.'"

"Who?" he asked, unconvincingly.

"*A-me!*" I enunciated, biting off each syllable with rancor. It was comical, his attempt at playing this off.

"Amy... you mean my step-sister?"

"No Barc—I mean the fucking WHORE who's missing her 'rock!' Apparently she's lonely and wants it *bad*—wait—does *this* ring a bell?" I calmly walked over to the answering machine and hit play, turning up the volume to the highest level to make sure he could hear her message loud and clear.

Amy's seductive, raspy vocals filled the room again, and Barc went ballistic. "Amy Lee? Jesus, why is that bitch calling me *now*? She's a psycho! I dumped her over a year ago! She's way too tacky for me."

"You expect me to believe she left you *that* message after a year? She says right there on the message she got a gift from you at Christmas, you asshole—that was the same week as our <u>honeymoon</u>! You must think I'm so stupid," I said, shaking my head. I hit 'play' on the recorder again, just in case he missed something.

"Well what did you EXPECT?" he screamed at me. "You left me alone in the city for the whole summer!"

"Barc, it's only been two friggen' weeks—and even when I'm here I hardly ever see you. This marriage is a joke."

"That's not true!"

"And if you are here, you're either drunk or passed out. Our relationship died long ago, and you know it. In some ways, it never even had a chance..." I said wistfully, and then wondered, *Did we ever have a chance?* Our six-week courtship was fast and furious... even passionate... and during it I truly thought I loved him. But the months that followed leading up to the wedding and this whole six months after it was just not working, ever...

"We still have fun together," he said, trying to sound convincing.

"Who are you kidding, Barc? You know as well as I do that we don't have anything in common. We're rarely seen out in public as a couple anymore, and who cares? I don't. I honestly don't expect anything but tears and heartache from you. So do whatever suits you, seriously—I don't care anymore. I'm packing my bag and then I'm out of here, for *good*."

"Please, don't leave me. I really need you!"

"For *what?*"

I could see him scrambling, trying to think as I packed; meaning it. I was really going to leave him. I was ready to. I had tried and gave it my all, but I was ready to except defeat and head back home to Texas now. Oldie would understand. I knew he would let me stay there at home while I figured out my next move. But I just couldn't stay in this hopeless, loveless sham of a marriage one more second.

Barc gained his composure and switched on the charm as he came over and tried to get between me and my packing, but I kept stepping around him to continue. "Melanie... Mel... just stop... Listen. I admit I haven't been the best husband. I know that. But this is my first rodeo," he said, trying a little playfulness.

"Yeah, well, you know what, Barc? Your first rodeo seriously sucks!" I said, getting out my third suitcase and stuffing it with everything I could from my wardrobe. "If you were riding a bull he would have bucked you off and stomped on you by now. Bulls don't like wimps; they can sense them as soon as they get in the saddle. And that's what you've become. Look at yourself. *Really* look at yourself, cowboy."

Barc was standing there holding an empty rock glass with a cigarette dangling from his mouth and his shirt all rumpled and stained. He looked like shit. "I don't even know what you're talking about right now," he said, truly clueless. "Look, I promise, I can change—I'll be whatever you want me to be, Mel. I love you."

"As far as I'm concerned you're a liar, a cheat... and a drunk, Barc. So it's not even worth discussing this with you because you won't remember it all anyway. Have fun with 'Amy Lee' and the rest of your *pathetic* life."

At that I grabbed my bags and purse and ran out of the apartment, frantically pressing the down button on the elevator, willing it to arrive faster.

"Fucking BITCH!" I heard Barc yell, followed by the sound of his rock glass smashing against the window.

Amy Lee was the first time I actually knew about another woman, even though I had no idea who she was or where she came from. But I vowed she would be the last. I wouldn't put up with a cheater again I told myself as I thought about Hunter. And as I stepped into the elevator and descended toward the ground floor below I could only think of one thing: *I have to get out of this marriage... I have to get out of this marriage...*

Suddenly the elevator stopped and the doors opened. I politely nodded towards Mrs. Milligan and her little yippy Bichon Frise, Sophie, as they got onto the elevator.

I have to get out of this marriage, the voice in my head continued to chant as I watched the numbers plummet all the way to the bottom floor, hoping Mrs. Milligan wouldn't ask where I was headed with so much baggage. Luckily she didn't and I quickly exited through the lobby and was hit by the chilly, late spring air as I went out the front door.

My car was still parked out in front of the building. I loaded it up with my suitcases and got in the driver's seat. I knew this was it. I had a major choice to make. I could go back to Texas and start my life over again, or I could drive back to Newport, let Barclay fret for awhile that I was really leaving him, and see if he changed his ways. Would he love me enough to really change this time? Did I have the strength to really start a whole new life all over again in Texas? And what if Hunter was still in Houston? Would it only be worse going back home and taking the chance of running into *him*...?

I drove back to Newport as fast and furiously as I could. Barc could have his Amy Lee. I wasn't going to let her—or him—ruin the rest of my summer or life—and I certainly wasn't going to stay in *any* city for the next three months now. It was going to be far too hot in both New York and Houston for my tastes. Besides, by the fall I felt I would finally have it all figured out.

Chapter 16

$\mathcal{B}$y the time I got back to Newport Helen was already 'in the know,' for Barc had called to say I was leaving him, but wouldn't say why.

"Your son is cheating on me," I told her frankly. "And there was x-rated proof on our answering machine."

"Oh, is that *all?*" Helen said like she expected me to have—or even need—more, like saying it wasn't really cheating until I caught him in bed with someone, at least.

"There doesn't *need* to be more than that, and besides, he didn't deny it."

"Dahling," she started in the same soft tone she used the months before I got married while she was trying to fool me about matrimony being able to 'change' him. "Men sometimes 'stray'… that's just a fact of marriage… but it doesn't mean he doesn't still love *you*."

"That's a strange way to show it," I said, thinking of all the times I took Hunter back whenever he said something just as similar to me. How could anyone think it's okay to cheat on someone?

"I know you don't want to leave him really," Helen said with a Cheshire-cat grin. "Because if you did you wouldn't be here now, would you?"

"I didn't know where else to go," I lied. I should have gone back to Houston, but I still couldn't imagine going back there, so close to Hunter, but I couldn't tell her that. I felt lost, alone, and stuck—and immediately started to cry.

Not one for nurturing, Helen used this as a reason to end the whole conversation. "Now, now…" she said, not bothering to hug or comfort me in any way. "Why don't you just go upstairs and take a nice long bath? Think things through… then let me take you to the Yacht Club for a fabulous dinner! Oh, and there's a gala at Rosecliff we could attend afterwards, to take your mind off things. In times like these it's best to just stay busy yourself, dear."

The summer flew by as I pretended to ignore what I knew was happening between Barc and Amy Lee back in New York whenever I spoke to him, and Helen did her best to indulge me with all the 'perks' of living in Newport among her family's wealth and reputation. She told me as long as I stayed married and with her all would "work itself out in time," and I decided to see if she was right. Soon I was enjoying myself as much as I had the previous summer, only this time solo, and realized my unfulfilling marriage was only a bad side effect to the whole "arrangement" I was now truly in. I decided it was my choice to stay or to go, but since I really didn't have anywhere else to go, I decided I would just stay put. For as long as Barclay and I stayed married on paper and living separate—but happy—lives, Helen was right; it really was all working itself out just fine.

I went back to New York in the fall and Barc seemed grateful I didn't leave him. For some unknown reason to me, he seemed to want to make this marriage last, even with all its problems.

"I've never had anyone take care of me the way you do, Melanie," he told me my first night back while I was picking up his grease-stained pizza boxes and empty bottles of booze from around the living room. I had called the cleaning service and scheduled regular weekly visits throughout the summer, so luckily it wasn't as bad as the first time I had come home. "And though I've messed up, I promise I'll try to do better," Barc continued.

"Sure Barc, whatever," I said, not believing him and also fully resolved to keep myself happy and content like I had all summer, no matter what he did.

We both settled back into our busy routines of our full-time jobs (both of mine, for me), and living mainly separate lives, and I was surprised how once I had removed myself emotionally from him it was easy to just co-exist under the same roof. We felt like roommates more than husband and wife, but to the outside social circles we were still very much a couple who was beating the odds and staying married.

"Heyy," Barclay slurred to me one night in late October as he climbed into bed, drunk, as usual. It was almost midnight and this was pretty much still part of his 'usual' routine.

"Barc! I'm sleeping!" I told him sternly. I had to get up much earlier than he did for work, and it annoyed me when he woke me up.

"There's a party on Halloween... some ball one of the guys at work is putting on for charity... and I told him we'd go."

"What?" I said, not believing it. We never went anywhere as a couple anymore.

"Do you want to go with me?" Barc asked, seemingly like it was our first date all over again. I was touched.

"Okay, sure, if you want." I told him. After all, it was for charity, and it might even be fun.

"Okay, monkey girl!" he said playfully, nudging my side.

I groaned. This was one of Barc's new favorite nicknames for me, one he reserved for 'special occasions,' like when he wanted sex. He now often drew inspiration from the animal kingdom when addressing or describing females; for instance, all women were chipmunks who did nothing but chatter non-stop and 'squirrel away' his money and shop around for nuts. His two half-sisters? He was frequently quoted as saying they had the collective I.Q. of a squid. He had started these new word choices over the summer for some reason while I was away, and it was really insulting and didn't put me 'in the mood' at all. In fact, since he wasn't very good at creating romance anymore I was *never* in the mood. Besides, I was not about to let him use me for sex since I now knew he was getting it other places.

"I'm not in the mood, Barc," I told him sternly.

"You're *never* in the mood!" he stewed.

"That's because I'm the kind of girl who needs some 'romance' to get in the mood, not just a bad pet name and a nudge."

"I can be romantic!" he said like I had challenged him.

"Yes Barclay, I know you can be because you once swept me off my feet. Why don't you try doing that again sometime and then we'll see what happens?"

Barc seemed to think this through as he settled into his side of the spacious, king-sized bed, far from me.

I didn't think my comment about being romantic would stick because Barc was usually so drunk at night he hardly ever remembered anything that was said or done, even when he got rowdy and broke things. Whenever that would happen, which was often, he would just blame it on the 'wind' swaying the building too much since we were so high up, or a draft coming in from a window that was left open. No mess was ever *his* fault.

But on the night of the charity Halloween Ball, Barc was truly in rare form. He sent me flowers at work with a note simply saying:

Looking forward to tonight. Love, Barclay

Alex and the others didn't know all the details of our relationship, so they just took it as a sign that our marriage was going strong. I didn't want to let them know otherwise since most of them were still unmarried and had grand illusions of what finally getting married would be like. I didn't want to spoil their fairy-tale, for maybe they'd achieve it. After all, Whitney seemed to.

I came home early and Barc was already there, getting dressed up as the dashing Jay Gatsby from F. Scott Fitzgerald's classic novel. He looked great and even more than that, he was actually sober. He had a bottle of Donnie P chilled and waiting with caviar too.

"Wow!" I told him. "You really went all out!"

"I know what you like," Barc said confidently, handing me a flute of champagne.

I couldn't believe it. Was this the old Barclay I first dated again? I couldn't help myself, but deep down, I silently prayed it was…

We went to the ball and had a blast. It was the first time we had had fun in months. I was dressed as Daisy Buchanan in a sexy flapper-styled outfit to portray the era from the same novel, and I could feel Barclay looking at me all night. He said I looked more beautiful than he had ever seen me, and he was jealous of all the other men who stared at me too. It felt good to be getting his full attention again.

I had hoped he would stay sober all night, just to really show me he was changing, but unfortunately the party was open bar and filled with opportunities for smoking pot or doing blow secretly too. Barc did his share of all of them, and by eleven he was flying high. I was getting tired, so I told him I wanted to go home.

To my astonishment, he agreed without a fight.

"I thought you'd want to stay and party with your friends all night," I told him in the cab ride home.

"And let you go out onto the streets alone looking *that* good?" Barc said, putting on the charm. "I couldn't take that chance. I might lose you."

I couldn't figure it out. He was the old Barclay one moment, and party Barc the next. It was making my head spin, along with all the champagne I had been drinking earlier.

We got back home and he offered to help me get out of my costume. I knew what he was really trying to do—seduce me—but since it had been so long since I felt his body on mine and since he had started our 'date' with a beautiful bouquet of flowers earlier that day, I let myself be seduced. We fell into bed and made love for hours. It was nice to be so wanted again.

But it didn't last. Within days of our wonderful Halloween evening, "party Barc" suddenly came out full-force, and he was more out-of-control than ever. I was starting to think I was living with a monster. I didn't know who I was going to wake up with in the morning, somewhat-grouchy Barc or complete-asshole Barc who was still drunk. And even though the first cop had told me not to, I had to resort to calling either them or sometimes the paramedics when I simply couldn't control him or the situation anymore myself.

But each time Barc did his best to answer the three always-silly questions quite easily, and he was never taken away.

Our one-year anniversary came around and it was a complete non-event. Helen "gifted" us another year at the apartment; another bribe to stay married to her son I suspected, but at this point I was too busy to even think about leaving him. My job at Sotheby's Auction House was busier than ever and my catering company had gained so much business over the fall I was now booked well into the next year. I was proud and glad to be making it all work, for the most part. So I continued to ignore whatever Barc's latest bad behavior was and just continued to get through each day in a daze, exhausted when I finally fell into bed.

I wanted to go to Houston to see my parents for the holidays, but Oldie and my mother were already booked for a two-week cruise to the Caribbean. Whitney and Charles were going to Aspen with Billie and Annie and some of their Hollywood friends and told me we could come along too, but the last thing I wanted to do was go to where Hunter and I had spent so many years ringing in the New Year together. I spent most of the eighties with him there, now I was married and it was a new decade, I intended to celebrate 1991 and beyond far from the slopes of Colorado.

"We're going to Newport, it's all already been arranged," Barc said like I had forgotten we agreed, but actually I didn't ever remember talking about it.

"Since when?" I asked. "No one ever asked me about—"

"My mother told me she told you we were all R-S-V-P'd to all the big galas from Christmas to New Year's, and I told her fine since I *doubted* you'd want to go back to Palm Beach again this year."

"Not if all your 'friends' are going to be there."

"They're not, 'cause most of them will be in *Newport* instead," he said, with glee.

We went, and he was right. Barc stayed out partying each and every night with all of the same spoiled, trust fund brats from our honeymoon, and I never saw him once until the day we left.

I have to get out of this marriage, I thought as I sat next to him on the plane ride home, watching him 'nurse' his hangover with several vodka tonics. *But how…?*

I went back to working my two full-time jobs and became so busy I forget all about how miserable I was in my marriage. I realized working was my way of avoiding the whole situation, but since the money I brought in was so desperately needed, it was like I was on a treadmill I couldn't stop or get off of, so I just kept running in place.

In the middle of January a terrible snowstorm paralyzed the city on a day I was to manage an auction of 18th and 19th century English furniture. The weather had shut down many parts of the subways and rail systems in New York, and the TV reports were asking everyone to stay indoors. A combination of dumb luck, poor attendance, and quick thinking on my part allowed me to purchase many of the furnishings at an incredible price. They were all museum- quality pieces with a very high resale value, and I'd scored each one at a very deep discount. Even if I strictly viewed it as an investment, I knew I stood to make a killing if I put the items back up for re-auction someday. I was thrilled, and proud that I'd had the business savvy to recognize the opportunity when it presented itself.

I called Oldie to tell him about it, but he was away on business.

I called Barc at work, and he insisted we meet at our favorite neighborhood French Bistro to celebrate over a candlelit dinner later that night. "To hell with the weather," he said. "Let's celebrate!"

I was glad he was so happy with my purchases and touched that he wanted to celebrate with me. We hadn't been out since Halloween, so it would be nice to share a meal out together again.

But Barc arrived an hour late to the restaurant, and he hadn't even made it half-way across the room before he ordered a bottle of champagne from a random, passing waiter. He was completely drunk, and I was embarrassed as he clumsily made his way towards me at the table.

"Barc! Please, sit down!" I whispered sternly as he took a long time to try to take off his London Fog overcoat. It seemed the wet, snow-covered sleeves were giving him trouble.

Luckily the waiter arrived with our champagne and helped Barc remove his final sleeve, then offered to take his coat for him until the meal was over. Barc didn't understand a word as he just waved him away and then poured the champagne into the two flutes himself.

Barc raised a glass high in the air and toasted loudly, "Cheers to the dumb blond for actually doing something right for a change!"

I was used to his ribbing and insults normally over small things, but in this case, with so much money at stake, his words stung like an icy dagger falling from the bistro's limp, frozen overhang outside. I had finally had enough. "You can't do it," I told him flatly. "You can't even toast me without putting me down, can you?" I asked, stunned.

"Jesus Mel, I'm just kidding!" Barc replied as he sat down. "You can't even take a joke anymore. What the hell is it with you lately? What's wrong?"

Everything is wrong, I thought as I looked outside and studied the storm. "Barc, I can't do this anymore," I said frankly.

"What?" He was so drunk he didn't have a clue what I meant.

"This marriage Barclay! It's not working—"

Now he understood and immediately straightened up. "Jesus Mel, I told you I was just joking with the toast! Come on, please, you know insults are just my way of expressing myself... you've seen me with all my friends."

"Yeah, 'cause you're *always* with them more than me!"

"Listen, you know you married a socialite... it comes with the territory... but there's enough of me to go around, always."

"Well I don't want any of *you* OR this life anymore! It's not worth it."

"Oh yes it is... come on. Why don't I make it up to you?"

"How?"

"Okay. I was going to tell you about this later, as a surprise, but I guess it shouldn't wait... I've booked us two plane tickets and a hotel to Paris for next week... a 'second honeymoon' to make up for last year's."

"You did? Really?" I couldn't tell if he was lying or if he really had done this, but either way I was touched. He knew how much I loved to travel and we hadn't done so abroad yet together.

"So, what do you say, can we just enjoy our meal and then look forward to a romantic trip?" he asked with a winning grin.

I agreed, and thought if he was willing to plan all of this on his own just for me; then maybe this marriage can be saved after all.

Just like for our last real "date" on Halloween, Barclay was attentive and charming for several days leading up to our trip to Paris, and I was hoping to have this be a real second chance at turning everything around between us.

The trip started out normally enough too. We arrived at De Gaulle late from New York and decided to get a nightcap in the hotel lobby bar before bed. It was 2 AM and I had a headache and was exhausted with jetlag. Barc, as usual, was seemingly wide-awake, insisting someone tell him where all the 'action' was. The French bar staff was mostly ignoring him.

Then a very cute, foxy young waitress in a black miniskirt and pouty lips came by our table. She leaned in, refreshing our table water. "I know a place that is very good near my apartment—and I'm finished with my shift very soon," she said coyly to Barc and with only a sideways glance in my direction. "I can bring you, if you want me to—I meet my friends there almost every night. It is, how do you say, really wild and fun, especially for the Americans—if you know what I mean," she winked at him, and Barc grinned widely—it was all the invitation he needed.

As I took the hotel elevator up to our hotel room alone, I could feel a slow, sickening, wrench in my gut.

Barc stumbled in near dawn, disheveled and reeking of vodka and cheap, drugstore perfume. I was already awake when he got into bed, but pretended I wasn't. I waited until he passed out before I dressed and snuck out for the day. I didn't want to know or imagine what he might have been doing last night until all hours, and I didn't have the energy to confront him here in Paris.

So while he slept off his hangover and whatever else, I watched the rain from the hotel's breakfast salon where the menu was partially in English. I picked at the delicious, hot meal I couldn't enjoy. I then read a book in a chilly study I found off the grand hotel's lobby.

I went out for a walk in the rain, but after a few blocks it was a lot wetter than I had first thought. I wandered into a boutique to escape from it.

A willowy French woman greeted me kindly as I shook my coat off by the door. "Salut! Comment allez-vous?" she asked.

"Oh, uh—ca va… parle Anglais? I don't speak very much French," I said apologetically.

"Oh-alo then. Please, please come in, it's best to get dry. It's terrible, no? The rain?" She took my umbrella and helped shut the door against the wind.

"Yes, so much rain!" I said. "I've been going bonkers in my hotel all day—I thought it might be safe to go out in it, but I guess I was wrong."

"Oh, no…" she tsked. "You are here in Paris for business? Or 'pleasure' perhaps?" she said with a knowing, lingering smile.

Not one part of my trip had been 'pleasurable' so far—in fact, it was getting hard to detect a difference between miserable, and desperately unbearable. So instead of answering her, I wandered among the crystal figurines. It was warm in there, and the light made them all sparkle beautifully.

"Neither, I suppose," I finally said wistfully, fingering the delicate trinkets on mirrored trays, then held onto one in particular.

"The elephant... do you like it?" the woman inquired as her eyes searched for mine, her smile warm and inviting. She nodded at the crystalline figurine I was clutching, and I felt it, smooth and cold on my skin.

"Yes, it's beautiful," I told her.

"Elephants... they mean you should never forget... is this a trip you want to always remember?"

I smiled as I thought of the irony of this. I knew she meant as a good, 'pleasurable' memory, but this was far from that. Still, I knew once I got back to New York and back to my hectic, crazy work schedule I would once again 'forget' all about moments like this and days, weeks, months, then possibly even years would pass... and I suddenly knew I couldn't keep doing this to myself—or to my life.

I have to get out of this marriage, I told myself as I purchased the elephant. *As soon as we get back to New York, I have to start looking for a way out of this mess...*

Barc had already left the suite when I arrived back to our room hours later, desperate for sleep. I put the elephant on my nightstand where I could see it as I drifted off, wondering what I would do if I did finally leave Barclay Cunningham. I could make a new life separate from him in New York, my job and catering company could more than support me alone. And since we traveled in completely separate social circles I knew I'd never have to even run into him again there...

I could make this work, I told myself as I looked at the elephant—and swore it was smiling back at me as if to urge me on with these new thoughts of freedom.

Miniskirt was at breakfast the next day when Barclay and I sat down. She was cold as she took our breakfast order, while Barc sat, looking uncomfortable. I just stared at the icy water glasses. I didn't even care anymore. Avoiding Barc since yesterday had been easy and I'd spent the whole day alone, wandering the narrow, bricked streets, soaked from rain and occasional tears, exhausted and lonely, but I knew this whole nightmare of a prison was about to end. I now had a plan...

We got back to New York and I worked on my "plan" of leaving Barclay, starting with finding an affordable place to live on my own, though discreetly of course. But as the days became weeks I was forced to admit that my marriage to him and the stress of trying to get out of it was making me physically ill. My stomach was constantly upset and I was tired all the time.

Each day it became harder and harder to drag myself out of bed; by three in the afternoon I was exhausted, and for the first time in my life, I was constantly hungry. I started going down to the coffee bar for a cookie each afternoon. I never used to eat cookies. Barc was literally draining me of all my energy and willpower. I even noticed I'd put on a few extra pounds, something I never would have let happen before I was married.

Desperate for a distraction, I called Alex to meet me for lunch. She had always been my personal 'relationship confidant' since she'd known Barc's family much longer than I did, and she often seemed to have a perspective on my marriage that I didn't when it came to how the Cunninghams 'typically' handled things. I wanted to get her thoughts about Barc and me truthfully before I decided to do anything more.

"Every time I talk to you Mel, it sounds like you're in a fog," Alex confided as we sat down at our usual table at La Goloue. "Are you okay? I can practically hear it in your voice."

"It's that obvious?" I said; thinking, *Oh great, now I've become like Eva—a walking billboard for being unhappily married.*

"Fraid so. I miss the old Melanie! Barc's dragging you down, girl. I mean, I've known him a long time, but Lord knows that man has problems! You have way too much going for you to give it all up for that spoiled bum."

"I know, I know... but I guess I feel trapped."

"Trapped by who? Barc? He's a mess! No one in this relationship is going to look out for you but *you*. Have you ever thought about leaving him?"

The words sent a chill down my spine. *Was it obvious?* I was trying to do everything discreetly, but it was hard to in a city with so many eyes and ears everywhere.

Alexandra played with her fork as she continued. "I mean... of course *I've* never been married, so I couldn't possibly know what it would be like to leave, how hard it would be..."

Oh good, I thought, relaxing now, *she doesn't really know.* I looked at the ground. "He'd go crazy... both our families would too. It's not that easy to just pick up and go."

I saw Alex start to protest; then hesitate as she sipped from her drink.

"Let's just change the subject, okay?" I offered. "Tell me about you and Tad. Almost three months now? Practically a record for you!"

Alex broke into a wide smile. "I know, right? We're doing really well! He has a great job as an investment banker and a fabulous apartment on Fifth Avenue. He's European, so of course he's way more mature than those American Wall Street types," she said, rolling her eyes. "And he's *so* good to me..."

"I'm glad for you—just don't be like me and rush into anything, okay?" I warned. "You never really know who you're getting involved with until you've spent a long time with them... I mean, look at my situation."

She nodded understandably, and we went on to discuss office happenings and other current topics.

After lunch Alex had to go meet Tad, so we hugged good-bye, but for the rest of the day her words echoed in my mind: *Have you ever thought about leaving him?*

It's all I'd *ever* thought about since that cold hard 'swim' he forced me to take on our hellacious honeymoon... I'd been thinking about it since I found out Barc was destined to be a financial liability on me, my parents, and our own future family—if we ever even had one. And I'd been thinking about it since I realized that Barc's capacity for unabashed self-destruction seemed to have no foreseeable bottom. And even though Oldie and Helen had both persuaded me against it at first—and then settling into our new life here in New York had even stalled it—I could see its inevitability coming toward me like a freight train... Barc was *never* going to change, and I had to move forward with my plan of finally leaving him.

I started auditioning several possible scenarios in my mind. Would I confront him? Just pack up and disappear? Leave a note? Serve him divorce papers at work? Each had their own exhilarating possibilities. But the logistics of it all were, above all else, nauseating. And besides, before I even told him I had to have a place to go, so I couldn't do anything without finding an apartment first, and that was a feat in itself in New York. I decided to sleep on it some more.

The next day though I felt worse than before, so I decided to sleep on it again. Then, a whole week passed of me feeling constantly sick to my stomach. Even the smell of food was now starting to make me feel queasy. Something was unsettlingly wrong—was my body reacting to the thought of leaving and the stress of being on my own again? It couldn't be any worse than being married to Barclay. I called my doctor.

The next day I found myself in Dr. Carlton's outdated, spearmint-colored waiting room. I flipped through a dog-eared *Redbook* magazine from the fall before, trying to concentrate on the "45 Best Autumn Recipes" instead of my dancing, roller coaster of a stomach. I wondered what heading home to make a homemade stew for a grateful husband would feel like.

"Mrs. Cunningham!" an irked voice said sternly.

I suddenly realized the nurse was now calling my name a *third* time. My married name was used so infrequently, I hardly recognized it. 'Mrs. Cunningham' was simply a ghost of my failing marriage to me. I quickly stood up and followed her down the hallway.

Dr. Carlton's assessment was very quick and perfunctory. "I have a perfectly good explanation for why you're feeling the way you are, Melanie, and that's because you're three months pregnant," she said. "You're in the throes of first trimester morning sickness."

My stomach, already floating, dropped to the floor. I went cold.

"You can't be serious," I said, in shock. "Are you *sure?*"

"Your blood test from this morning proves it. It was positive."

The word 'positive,' with all its connotations, hung in the air. There was silence in the office for several moments.

"Oh my God!" I started to cry, burying my head in my arms on her desk. Dr. Carlton came over and gave my shoulder a reassuring squeeze, misinterpreting my reaction as overwhelmed joy.

"Takes some getting used to, doesn't it?"

"Oh my God... I don't know what to do..."

"Well, first we'll get you started on some prenatal vitamins, and then—"

"No, no—not about that. About my husband. I... I was planning on leaving him."

The weight of my words sank in, and Dr. Carlton sat back down in her chair. She looked very serious, so I tried to avoid eye contact as she spoke, "Sounds like you have some very serious choices and obstacles ahead of you. But most importantly Melanie, you need to take care of *yourself.* I'd advise staying away from your husband as much as you can right now until you decide to stay or go, for I assume he's an upsetting influence if you were thinking of leaving him."

I nodded, not able to speak yet.

"I'd also recommend not doing a lot of traveling. Do you understand?"

"Yes..." I finally managed to say. "Thank you, Dr. Carlton." I stood up in a daze. "I have a lot to think about." But as I gathered my coat and handbag to leave, something that felt like new, tingly knowledge tickled my insides. I looked up and smiled.

"I'm going to be a mother!" I cried, this time my tears slipping into joy. Barclay had ruined many things during our time together, but I was not about to let him spoil this particular, truly wonderful moment. I had *always* wanted to be a mother! I hugged Dr. Carlton spontaneously and could feel her ever-so-slightly hug me back, somewhat shocked.

That night I sat in bed with butterflies in my stomach along with my new little one growing inside. I was dying to talk to someone, anyone, but who first? I sure as hell couldn't talk to Barc—not until I knew what I was going to do—plus I needed to tell him in person, preferably sober, which I knew he wouldn't be once he finally stumbled home. I wasn't sure how he'd take the news, but at least sober I'd have a way of knowing best. Calling Helen was completely out of the question. When it came to Barc she was never unbiased, and with a grandbaby involved she'd have jewels, minks, and Lamaze classes dangling over me in no time.

I picked up the phone and dialed Oldie. I knew my parents would be thrilled, but I wanted to tell Oldie first before my mom. More than anything, I needed his reassuring voice and sure-footed guidance out of this unholy mess of uncertainty. The only trouble with Oldie was… you could only tell him *so* much. I was already reluctant to tell him details of my marriage anyway, since I was still 'Daddy's little girl' and wanted him to stay proud of me, thinking everything was always alright.

"Hi Oldie!" I said happily when I heard his voice answer.

"Melanie! I've missed you!" His voice sounded so far away. I imagined him in his library back in Texas, the polished gun cabinet to the right of his mahogany desk. He used to like to threaten bodily harm on any boy who did either one of his 'little girls' wrong when Whitney and I were growing up. I wondered if he would still do that now. "How the hell are you?" Oldie asked.

"Great—I have something to tell you."

"Well, I don't guess there could be a better time than right now then… shoot!"

"Daddy… I'm… pregnant!"

"Oh, Melanie! Finally, I'll be a grandfather! It's about damn time! We've been waiting on this kind of news for a long time now. Have you told your mother yet?"

"Nope, you're the first."

"Well she'll be ecstatic," he said, his excitement jumping through the phone. "We've been wanting a grandbaby since both you girls got married… and you know Whitney won't be headed that way any time soon— she's too worried about her figure still!"

I laughed. "Or at least not until they start making Gucci baby-bags and clothes," I quipped, and Oldie roared with laughter.

"Hell, we might just fly up there to celebrate!" he said.

"Sounds great! But Oldie, before you do… I need to talk to you about something else."

"Well, sure. Everything okay?"

"Not exactly… Things haven't been so good between Barc and me. I was actually thinking about leaving him right before I found out about being pregnant."

Oldie's voice dropped. "Why? What did he *do?*"

Suddenly the thought of answering truthfully felt like I was letting him—and everyone—down. I wanted to tell Oldie the truth—the whole truth—and this was my chance, but I balked. "He's just… being really 'distant,'" I stumbled on my words. "We live very separate lives. I think it's possible that he's even cheating on me."

"But you don't know for *sure?* Well then honey," he continued on before I could even answer. "Nothing brings a family together like a baby. Your mother and I were so happy when we were blessed by both you and Whitney—take comfort, Lil' Bit. That child will change everything!"

"I don't know, Oldie. I may be needing some help from you, off and on—I'm not getting a lot of financial support from Barc these days, and haven't since we were first married. I pretty much support us right now. Apparently he no longer has access to his trust—"

"Baa! Don't you worry about that, I'll take care of whatever you need," Oldie said with that reassuring tone I'd counted on my whole life. "And just remember, you always have a place here. Come south if things *go* south with you and Barc. But right now, you need to focus on getting your family together if you can, and doing everything in your power to take care of that baby! Nothing else matters, you hear me?"

I swallowed my tears, and we said our good-byes. Oldie always had a way of making me rethink my priorities. As I hung up I felt a renewed determination to fight through my problems with Barc. I was keeping this baby with or without him, that much was clear—and so now the only two choices were to try and save my family, or to deny my fetus a fighting shot at a normal life. Did Barc deserve a kid? I wasn't sure. But did my baby deserve a chance to know his or her father and have a *real* family? That I did know. I'd stayed for this long, so I knew I had to give Barclay the opportunity to step up and be the husband—and now father—that I once thought he could be, and he once said he wanted to be. Now, there was just the small matter of telling him...

I waited until we were dining at one of our favorite outdoor cafes just a few days later.

"Wow," Barc said as he watched me devour a large salad with skinless chicken strips. "Take it easy, we can order more, you know, piggy."

"Barclay...," I said, ignoring his sarcastic dig and trying to sound as positive as I could. "I have some news. I finally got my test results from the doctor."

"And?" He took a big sip of a very expensive cabernet.

"I'm three months pregnant!"

Barc's goblet slipped from his fingers and it crashed to the table, instantly soaking the pristine white tablecloth. "Fuck! What the?!" He jumped up, avoiding the crest of red spilling down the edge of the table.

A waiter appeared out of nowhere to assist in cleaning it up, but Barc ordered another glass, pushing him away to go retrieve it, fast. Once the waiter disappeared he said, "No—there's no *way!* I don't believe you! We NEVER have sex! You must be cheating on me! Don't try and trick me—you're lying, I know it!"

"You were drunk Barc, but it was the night after the Halloween ball. You were in a very fun and 'feisty' mood for a change, remember?"

"No, I don't remember, and don't try to play mind games with me!" he sneered.

"Like it or not Barc, you're going to be a father."

"Well we're getting a paternity test—and that's final. There's no way I'm fathering some illegitimate child of yours!"

"This baby is *yours*, Barclay. Who would I be cheating on you with, and when would I have the time? If you've forgotten, I pretty much fund this marriage right now—oh right, except for your little joke of a job 'day-trading' your parents' money away—"

Barc's eyes flashed in anger as he snatched his blazer and stormed out of the restaurant. By the time the door had swung shut behind him, I had dissolved into tears.

Barc never fully came around to accepting the news of becoming a father, but I didn't let it stop my joy of pending motherhood. And it didn't stop Helen's either as she dressed me from head to toe in chic-looking maternity outfits and soon turned our second bedroom into a stunning nursery fit for a child of royalty. I loved it, and wanted to keep giving both myself and my unborn child even more.

I hated to admit it because I didn't consider myself to be materialistic, but I was now getting completely 'hooked' on Helen's money. It was becoming an addiction of sorts. The frivolous buying seemed to fill some kind of void in me from my loveless marriage, and even though I knew it was only a temporary fulfillment, it seemed I now needed to shop just to get through the day. I wondered deep down if this was all part of her 'plan' when she tricked me into marrying her son, knowing once I got used to the money I wouldn't be able to really ever walk away from her family's clutches. I prayed not, but deep down, I knew this was becoming a major problem and even went to a psychologist secretly to try and get some help. The psychologist said it could just be my overactive hormones making me crave shopping instead of food, and I prayed he was right as I kept this particular 'daily craving' to myself.

Alex and the other girls at work threw me a wonderful baby shower, and everything went smoothly with my pregnancy up until I gave birth to a beautiful, healthy, six pound baby girl in July. Barc came to the hospital and bravely watched the C-section birth, almost passing out twice, but I was just glad he was present—and sober—for the arrival of our precious child. I named her Blakely.

Barc pretended to enjoy all the acclaim that came with new fatherhood as the days went by, but he was really secretly jealous since the baby took so much attention away from him. His drinking got worse only weeks after we came home from the hospital, and he stayed out night after night—sometimes not even bothering to come home at all.

"She's so beautiful, really Mel," 'Aunt' Whitney said as she held Blakely for the first time. Our parents had wanted to come visit too, but Oldie's work schedule was so hectic he said it would have to wait. For now just hearing Blakely's "coos" over the telephone to he and 'Granny' would have to do.

"Thank you," I told her. "I think so too, but I'm prejudiced."

"Motherhood agrees with you," Whitney told me. "I haven't seen you this happy since before you got married."

"That's because I haven't been," I told her, looking over at the crystal elephant I kept on a high shelf in the living room as a constant reminder of what my life was *really* like, even when I chose to temporarily forget. "But I'm going to try to be happy from now on, for both Blakely and me."

"I think that's great, Mel," Whitney said. "I think every child deserves two good parents, if they can *be* that."

We looked at each other knowingly, not wanting to bring it up, but I knew we were both thinking of Eva and Dawson and how neither of them wanted to be raising the two boys they now had. As I looked down at my precious Blakely, I couldn't imagine not wanting your own child. I felt like she had given me a whole new reason for making my life work now and I was determined to make it happen.

A few weeks later I hired a six-foot, wonderfully nurturing, middle-aged Jamaican nanny named Joy, who soon had to double as my bodyguard whenever Barc got into one of his drunken rants. Joy wore her waist-length dreadlocks bound in a tall, colorful wrap, which gave her an extra foot of height and somehow an extra sixty pounds on her already rotund frame—though believe it or not, her larger-than-life personality trumped even her size. Joy worked for me and me alone. I paid her well, and she was fiercely loyal. I was very grateful to have her in my life. And though Blakely was giving me a lot of delight overall also, I still felt very stuck in this marriage as I tried to balance motherhood with my two very demanding work schedules. Joy did her best to always make it easiest for me; often even staying late to make sure both Blakely and I were okay when Barc came home drunk.

Joy soon become like part of the family and began to despise Barc more than I did. On a daily basis she encouraged me to leave him, citing two of her three ex-husbands as examples why. But since I was so busy I didn't see how I could get out of the whole situation now, and even though I wasn't pregnant anymore, I still continued to shop daily to ease the stress in my life. Luckily Helen told me I could charge whatever I needed for myself or little Blakely whenever I wanted, so the money for this habit wasn't part of my troubles.

"Oh Mel! She's just *precious!*" Victoria said on a rare, quick visit while she was passing through town a few months later between photo shoots.

"Thanks," I told her. It was nice to see her. It felt like it had been ages since we last spoke.

"You look good holding her too."

"You think so?" she beamed. "Maybe someday I'll get to be a mom too… but I wouldn't hold your breath of it happening anytime *soon.*"

"Then I take it asking about who you're dating is probably moot?"

"Agg!" she groaned. "Yes! I don't get it Mel—I get asked out by a lot of great guys it seems, but I swear after one or two dates something just happens to turn them off, or make them suddenly realize they're actually gay! It's like I jinx them or something."

"You're not a jinx," I told her. "You just haven't found the one for you yet, and don't try to rush it. It's not the worst thing to still have your freedom, you know. After all, being married isn't all it's cracked up to be… just look at *me.*"

"I am," Victoria said, through tears. "But I have to tell you Mel, from where I sit you and *all* this—" she gestured toward Blakely and my impressive, affluent apartment filled with antiques and collectables, "—only looks *great.*"

I didn't have the heart to disillusion her with all my marriage troubles, and besides that, I didn't want to be reminded of them while I was having such a nice, rare visit with my oldest friend. So we just chatted about her exciting modeling career and compared traveling notes until she had to jet-set off again.

Several months later I awoke to a damp fog of Barc's breath, soured with vodka and a mood to match. I didn't even have to open my eyes to know what was coming.

"Let's *chhatt,*" he slurred.

Through cracked lids I could see him peering at me, staggering side-to-side ever so slightly. I shut my eyelids again and willed our ornately carved, four-poster, king-sized bed to swallow me back into sleep. I concentrated on the warm, quilted silk cocooned around me, and listened for signs that Barc would give up and go away, even though I knew better.

"Melanie….wake UP!" His tone meant he wasn't going to shut up or pass out until I gave him what he wanted—or at least yelled at him enough to make him go away.

"Barc, are you crazy?" I said; my voice still hoarse from sleep. "You literally haven't spoken to me in *days*—what could you possibly want to talk to me about right now?"

"Move over, damn it! I want to lie down next to my own wife in my own Goddamn bed! Do you have a problem with that, 'monkey girl?'"

"Why of course 'husband'—I've never been 'hotter' for you," I said sarcastically as I pulled the comforter back so he could crawl in—on his side only.

"I said MOVE!" he growled.

"The sheets are cold Barc, I'm not moving over. Go around to your side."

I could see him struggling with this concept, contemplating completing the task of making his way around to the other side of the room where the two French windows were already casting a shadowy light. Instead, he stumbled around in the semi-darkness stripping off a disheveled, rumpled tux. He looked every inch the idle waster he'd become, aged beyond his years from the late nights, drugs, and booze. Barc was normally a very handsome man, but now, in his boxers with his shirt wide open and hair askew, he looked like a bum from a homeless shelter, not a multi-millionaire from the Upper East Side. I suppose I took some fleeting satisfaction knowing that if Barc continued on this reckless course, he'd eventually end up looking like an emaciated drag queen—he'd lost so much weight in recent months he was already well on his way. I harbored fantasies where I'd run into him one day walking the streets of the Lower East Side turning tricks for dope or vodka, a toothless junkie filthy with his own feces, me haughty with indifference. For a person as pampered and vain as Barclay Cunningham, this picture was an extremely satisfying version of what I thought "justice" looked like.

Tonight he was so drunk he was relatively quiet for a change, a welcomed respite from the usual stream of obscenities. If I got lucky, I could distract him to the point he'd pass out before any real arguments began. If I could get him to his side of the bed, he'd nod off as soon as his head hit the pillow.

"Seriously Barc, walk around," I said as he tried to push his way back onto my side again. "No, not that way.... the other way. And watch out for the—!"

Too late. He crashed into the needlepoint vanity chair where I had my clothes neatly ironed and laid out for work the next day.

Mornings had become so rushed and unpredictable around my house that I'd long ago learned to stick to a morning routine, which meant selecting an outfit the night before. If I didn't arrive fresh, pressed, and polished to my job at Sotheby's Auction House in time to set up the computers and 'ready' the office for the first clients of the day I could be reprimanded, or, even worse, fired—and with our expenses we couldn't do without a paycheck, ever. They always expected us to look our best at Sotheby's too, and

I was looking forward to wearing my favorite Chanel suit in black tomorrow with a brand new accessory: the latest black and red Chanel scarf, a gift from Helen only the week before. I'd set it out along with the perfect pair of Gucci boots to complete the look. It was a killer outfit.

"Ow! Shit! I've told you a hundred times to move this fucking chair!" Barc cursed, rubbing his knee. He grabbed my clothes and threw them on the floor, stomping on them and spiking them with his heel in fury.

"BARC, STOP!" I shouted. "You're insane!" I snapped, getting up from underneath the warm comforter to rescue my clothing from the floor. I attempted to smooth the dusty wrinkles and re-hang them properly on the padded hanger, but it was an ill attempt.

"Well, KEEP YOUR SHIT OUT OF MY WAY!" Barc shouted at the top of his lungs. With my side of the bed now vacant, he was able to crawl into the pocket of warmth I'd left behind.

"Great, Barc. You wanna wake Blakely? Please, just keep your voice down." Our two bedrooms anchored different wings separated by a second bathroom and a study, but still, I worried Blakely would hear us arguing. She often did, and it scared her.

"What, I can't speak in MY OWN FUCKING HOUSE? I came up here to TALK Goddamn it! Stop being such a controlling BITCH all the time!"

"For protecting our daughter *I'm* the bitch?" I spat. "Well you're a pathetic, fall-down drunk!"

He sat up, indignant. "What? What are you trying to fucking say to me?"

It's no use, I thought. *He'll never even remember this conversation anyway.*

"Whatever—I have to be up in less than two hours. I'm going to sleep in Blakely's room."

I snatched a pillow from the bed and tried slipping past him, but he caught the edge of my nightgown and screamed, "YOU FRIGID BITCH— act like a *WIFE!*" He yanked my gown until I lost my balance and we both flew back onto the bed. I knew better than to fight back, so I laid there like cold jelly while Barc, of course, suddenly turned 'affectionate.'

"Melanie... Mel..." he said, kissing my neck. He'd already forgotten the last five minutes, and I wouldn't be surprised if he'd forgotten we'd ever even *had* an argument between us before tonight either.

"Mel... I love you!" He tried to put his arm around my middle while petting my head, but I continued to lay in icy silence, not budging at all to help him.

"How about a 'me too, Barclay'?" he prodded.

He tried to kiss me. His stale breath laced with cigarettes and alcohol was too much. I shoved him off, stood up, and yanked my gown from his grip.

"STOP, Barc! I need *sleep!* I have work tomorrow and then Blakely and I are going to Whit's for the weekend. I can't just—"

"What do you mean you're going to Whitney's? No you're not!"

"It's been planned for weeks, Barc. You just don't ever remember what I tell you."

Whitney and I tried to keep up with each other as best we could, but it wasn't often either one of us made the effort anymore since our lives were so different now. But she adored Blakely and hadn't seen her in over ten months since she was born, so it was important we made it up to Tarrytown for the weekend like I'd promised.

"To hell you are!" he replied. "I'm taking Blakely with ME today!"

His arrogance never ceased to astound me. He wouldn't know how to begin to take care of our daughter for more than an hour at a time; I doubted that he even knew where the stroller or the car seat was stored. "You're not going anywhere *near* her in your condition, and you know that."

"Damn it, she's my DAUGHTER!" he howled. Whatever shred of affection there'd been moments before now turned to fury. "BITCH!"

Barc grabbed for the bedside clock and threw it at me. It missed and shattered against the wall as I turned to run. He leaped out of bed and across the room, managing to catch the door as I tried to slam it shut. He chased me down the hall and we both entered the formal living room on my way to Blakely's room. Barc was only steps behind me when I saw a flash in his eye—a crooked, wild-eyed rage I'd never seen before—and it scared me so much I threw the only thing I had within reach, a heavy sofa pillow. The solid stuffed tapestry was enough to push him off balance, and he lunged forward as he fell, hitting his head on the edge of the coffee table. After a groan or two he laid still, snoring.

I never bothered calling 9-1-1 anymore. Authorities had been to our apartment almost a dozen times in the past year, and most of them had kept telling me what the first cop did: that if I was able to 'handle' him myself; then I should and not bother them. So since I didn't see any blood and knew he was breathing, I felt he was fine to just "sleep it off" on the living room rug. It wasn't the first time he'd passed out there anyway, and he had told me once that it was actually quite comfortable.

I crept into my daughter's room and silently climbed into the daybed I had set-up in there, careful not to wake Blakely in her crib nearby. She usually slept late, or at least until Joy arrived around seven o'clock, so I still had a couple of hours before I had to be up for work.

But at 6:30 AM I awoke to the familiar sounds of Barc vomiting. Even in my half-asleep state the absence of a toilet flush or a running sink struck me as odd, and I couldn't nod off again, worrying over it. I listened for the tell-tale 'thump' of Barc climbing into our big bed, waited the three minutes I knew it would take for him to pass out again, then got up and scurried down the hall.

As soon as I entered the bedroom I could smell it—he'd thrown up on my Chanel suit. The runny mess was everywhere—all over the new scarf, the silk blouse, even the leather boots. He lay in bed snoring, spittle already drying on his face.

It was already starting to get light out as I stood in front of Mr. Lee's dry cleaners less than an hour later, just when Mr. Lee himself was arriving to open the shop. It was not the first time I'd visited him an hour before work hoping for a miracle, nor the first designer label he'd salvaged from complete ruin—but today I had a feeling my outfit *and* my morning were already shot.

I showed Mr. Lee the soiled clothing and he took one look and shook his head. "Ohh, no good, no good!" he said, tsk-tsking with his fingers. "We try to fix but no promises, okay? What happened here?"

"My husband has the flu," I lied. *More like the cocktail flu*, I thought to myself, but that wasn't any of Mr. Lee's business.

I snatched the ticket from Mr. Lee's hand and hurriedly left the cleaners.

Eight hours later, after I'd returned home from work and—with Joy's help—packed the car for Blakely's and my departure, Barc finally woke up. Blakely and I were on our way out the door when he emerged from the bedroom carrying a wedding photo of ours in his hands.

"God, you're so fucking ugly now... why didn't someone tell me this would happen?" he complained. "That you'd keep looking so fat and even older long *after* giving birth?" He threw the photo in the trash as we walked out the door.

I sat in Whitney's pristine suburban mansion later that evening feeling numb, like I was watching a bad movie of my own life. Whitney was sympathetic but her advice, if you could call it that, was of little use to me.

"Maybe he'll hit rock bottom, you know? I mean, look at my life—you know how I was and I totally changed it around... it's possible, Mel," Whitney said while she marveled at little Blakely crawling all by herself now.

I couldn't help but cringe—my spoiled, gorgeous sister, my sister who had everything now—was trying to compare her life to mine. If I could've felt anything at all anymore, it would have only been annoyance.

"Whitney, please. It's not the same," I said.

"Sure it's the same. I mean, I had problems—Barc has problems. But look at my marriage—we were stronger than that and Charles helped me through it all. Maybe you guys are that strong too."

I hoped she was right, for Blakely's sake mainly, not my own anymore.

The following morning a sharp knock startled us while we made small talk and sipped coffee—I had finally started drinking it now that I needed the caffeine to keep me awake most days. A deliveryman bearing three-dozen, long-stemmed red roses peeking out of a large rectangular box greeted Whitney at the side kitchen door when she opened it. There was a glittered envelope on the top that was addressed to me.

I opened it and read the letter inside:

> *For my wife Melanie, who I truly love,*
> *When something needs doing, I don't always do it.*
> *When something needs fixing, I don't hop right to it.*
> *When the checkbook's a mess, I may throw a fit.*
> *When the going gets tough, I've been known to quit.*
> *When I shampoo and shave, I may splash up the floor.*
> *And the junk I collect, may spoil our decor.*
> *When I start off each day, I don't always smile.*
> *When we step out to dine, it may not be in style.*
> *I may have my faults, but one thing is true...*
> *I did something right when I married you.*
>
> *Mel, I can never apologize enough to you and I'm so sorry. I love you so much. Please come home, Barclay*

I cried. It was such a rare moment of atonement from Barc, I couldn't help it. I wondered where in the world he could have found such a poem. It read like he had written it himself and I considered the fact that he did somehow—*had he?* I really didn't know what he was capable of anymore, but it was times like these when I suddenly remembered what it felt like to be the targeted affection of a man who truly cared.

A flood of memories came rushing back like a Tsunami, entering the cracks of my hardened shell, the spaces where my old life tugged at my heart, pulling it further and further away from the life I was currently living. I tried breathing in the roses Barc sent and recalling some of the good times while we were first dating—the spontaneous laughing, the bad jokes he'd make.... the yacht parties in Newport when it was fun to hang on his arm, when I was proud to.

I thought back to when Barclay Cunningham was a true gentleman, with perfect manners and charming charisma. When he was funny, handsome, debonair—and listened to me like no one else had, not even Hunter. We'd talk for hours and hours about our parents, siblings, and affluent upbringings and it felt like we had a lot in common.

It was a bit like when I first moved to New York and had been seduced by the loud, glamorous, glittering lifestyle of the bustling, throbbing city. The fast pace was thrilling for me and I loved being on my own. But it was the warm shores of Newport, where Barclay and I first met in the fantasyland of yachts and millionaires that really won my heart over the city. I was tired of struggling to make it on my own amongst the crowd there, and secretly praying someone unique and different from Hunter would show up and rescue me. Barc seemed to be just what I hoped for… a man of leisure who'd been Dallas society's—and Newport's, New York's, and Palm Beach's—most eligible bachelor. He was exciting and seemed attentive and reliable, at least at first. And who wouldn't have fallen for someone like him—or anyone—after dating a creep like Hunter for so long?

What happened to the man in Newport I first fell in love with? The man who said he'd never been so in love in his entire life? Who begged me to marry him six weeks after we met? Who wined and dined me, bought me beautiful jewelry, and whispered the sweetest nothings into my ear?

I used to love to catch Barclay looking at me back then. He'd usually work his way up and I'd let him, playfully, meeting his eyes at the top, busting him, where he'd then have to grin sheepishly, or sometimes raise an eyebrow that said, "Yeah? So *what?*—" which meant he was in the mood, and we'd then dash off to make mad, passionate love for hours. Now, every once in a while, when we bothered to look at each other at all, I'd search for his eyes after they'd absently wandered over my body, the effort of arousal too draining for much more than an appreciated glance. If he was sober he'd occasionally meet my eyes and give a sad, half-smile. But if more than a couple of drinks had set in his eyes would then become blank, dark holes that didn't say anything at all. It was the latter I had only been seeing for well over the past year, it seemed.

Was it possible he'd hit his head harder on the coffee table than I thought? Maybe this latest drunken tirade had actually been the final straw for Barc and he was ready to *finally* give it all up, get clean, and be the kind of father Blakely needed and the kind of husband I thought I had married. Maybe he really *did* regret his behavior, and maybe my sheer 'willing it' this whole time was enough to save our dying marriage.

I prayed for strength and returned a few days later—but before I tested my newfound thoughts of hope and happiness for my stronger, better, future marriage—I stopped first at the dry cleaners.

"So sorry, we tried everything," Mr. Lee said.

The stains never did come out.

Chapter 17

❦

*B*arclay behaved himself up until Blakely's first birthday, which my mother was able to attend, but Oldie was away on business. My mom was so happy to see her little grandbaby, and it made me proud to have produced one for her. I was also proud I was keeping my family—however fragile—together still.

"Oldie was right," I told my mom over a slice of pink birthday cake from one of New York's finest bakeries. "A baby does seem to solve a lot of things."

"Yes," my mother agreed as she wiped off some frosting from Blakely's nose. "They sure do, like little erasers sent down from above."

At least, for awhile it seemed like that… but after my mom returned to Houston, Blakely, Joy, and I went to Newport for the rest of the summer to stay with Helen. Barc said he'd come see us on weekends, but he never did. And whenever I called home I only heard the sound of my own voice on our answering machine, so I decided to let it be until fall.

But by fall Barc was nowhere to be found. We came home to a messy, booze-stained apartment, and I learned from the cleaning service lady that Barc had told her to stop coming by weeks before because she 'disturbed' his busy day. I didn't want to let Blakely think there was anything wrong, so I told her and Joy to go unpack in her bedroom while I called his work.

"He's not here," Tanner told me. "I think he's in Palm Beach, or possibly Dallas. I don't know… he said he needed to get away for awhile."

I called Foxy's house.

"Hello, Cunningham's residence," a polite maid with a Spanish accent said over the phone.

"Hello, is Barclay there?" I asked. Since I hardly ever saw or spoke to Foxy since the wedding, I didn't want to get into explaining who I was, and hoped they would just say yes.

"No, miss," the maid said. "They are out right now. Would you like me to take a message?"

"No thanks," I said, glad I now at least knew where he was, but also well aware that the "they" didn't refer to Barc and Foxy since they never did anything together... Barc had not gone there alone.

Barc, you are making me so sad I want to cry, I thought as I hung up the phone. *But I have too many tears for other things...*

Barc returned three days later, looking completely disheveled and still obviously drunk. He reeked of booze, cigarettes, and several kinds of perfume, so I didn't even want to think about who he'd been partying with, or for how long.

"Mel! Wow, you're back!" he said, seeming surprised.

"Yes," I told him, wondering if I was going to get an explanation of where he'd been and who with without asking.

He headed straight for the bar and poured himself a scotch.

"O, so *you're* bac," Joy said with disgust in her heavy, thick accent as she entered the kitchen and saw what she knew to be "party Barc" back in full force.

"Joy, could you please take Blakely to the 'pen?'" I whispered, knowing she knew exactly what I meant. The 'pen' was our secret nickname for the building's private playroom and children's garden located on the ground floor, and it was one of the best features of the whole property. It was a sanctuary for Blakely, Joy, and me whenever Barc was drinking or would fly into one of his rages. Joy always knew to pack up Blakely and bring her there, safe from Barc's violent words or drunken rages. Not much of a hands-on dad, Barc had never once taken Blakely there—or anywhere else, really. In fact, it was our suspicion that Barc didn't even know this playroom and garden existed, hence the safe-house 'pen' nickname we created for it. The entrance leading to it was all the way on the other side of the building, nowhere near the main entrance or parking garage, the only two places Barc ever went... in our whole time living there he had never even bothered to get the mail.

"O'course, Miss Melanie," Joy said, her dark eyes glaring at Barc as she went towards Blakely's room where she was playing.

I quickly put as many of the sharp kitchen items that I was using to prepare my latest catering dish into the dishwasher and tried to stay calm until I heard the elevator doors shut and I knew Blakely and Joy were safely gone. "So, are you back for good, or just passing through?" I asked Barc sarcastically.

"STOP GIVING ME SO MUCH SHIT!" Barc barked at me in a rage. "I just got home for Christ's sake and I'm tired!"

"Oh? You're 'tired?'" I said, amazed. It was just after seven o'clock in the evening, and I had already been up since 6:30 AM, worked a full day at Sotheby's, and was now going to be cooking for hours to prepare the food for tomorrow night's catering event for seventy-five people. I knew I wouldn't be done until at least midnight, and I really didn't want to waste any time fighting with him. "Well then, why don't you just go on to bed then? I seem to have everything handled here—as always anyways—so it's not like you need to stick around—"

"DON'T TELL ME WHAT TO DO BITCH!" he yelled.

"Fine, do whatever you want then, like always." I began whisking the sauce on the stove.

"Don't you even want to know where I went for the summer?" Barc asked.

"Palm Beach," I said flatly.

"How'd you know that?"

"I called Foxy's place looking for you."

"No one told me that!"

"I didn't leave a message because I didn't want to interrupt your 'fun.'"

"Well I only went there because you're never any fun anymore! All you ever do is work!"

"Well how do you think you can afford to party and have all your 'fun' if *someone* doesn't make a decent living for us?!"

"A decent living? You're nothing but a short-order cook! It's embarrassing—going to people's houses we even *know* to bring them dinner!" He got so mad he grabbed the pan I was using and threw it against the wall, splattering the hot liquid contents in it everywhere—including on me—then stormed out of the room in a huff.

I was glad I had thought to put all the sharp objects away.

Barc continued to come and go every few weeks over the next few months while I continued to work constantly day and night, clearly realizing he thought very little of my successful catering company. Typical snob. Other people were amazed at my stamina, being an auction manager all day and then catering events or giving private cooking classes at night and on weekends.

I need to get out of this marriage, I started telling myself again, but since I was so busy keeping everything going all on my own all the time I didn't see how I could. And besides, my secret "daily spending sprees" were also starting to get out of control. I was worried Helen might even say something, but she never did. All she ever did was compliment me on my recent new clothes or whatever new toy or outfit Blakely was wearing. She felt I had developed "exquisite" taste, and she was right.

For if there was one thing I learned a lot about since moving to New York, it was designer clothes—and especially shoes. I had over two hundred pairs in my closet by now, half of which had never even been taken out of the box. There were shoes made by Monolo, Ferragamo, Jimmy Choo, Chanel, Prada, and a variety of top-name exercise sneakers in all different colors—to match all of my work-out clothes. It made me feel good to recklessly spend Barc's 'family' money in an attempt to get back at him for all the things he put me through. And I continued doing it well into the whole next year, while we drifted further and further apart. I was stuck on the treadmill of life again it seemed, and I didn't even realize how much time was actually passing...

"Melanie, you need to come home," my mother's weak voice said over the phone. "Oldie's in the hospital."

I got on a plane to Houston with twenty-three-month-old Blakely as fast as I could. On the ride there all I could think of was this would be the first time Oldie would finally see his granddaughter, and I couldn't believe the time had passed by so fast without us trying harder to get together. We both always said we were too busy with work whenever one of us tried to make the trip, but that was no excuse at all really now that I was considering the fact that she was about to turn two-years-old soon without ever meeting him. It was inexcusable, and I planned to take her with me straight to the hospital after we'd dropped off our luggage at home.

But when we arrived my mother was out of sorts in our large home without her husband of forty-plus years, and she thought it wasn't a good idea. "A hospital isn't a safe place for a toddler," she said, worried. "There's so much sickness in the air."

"But Mom, Blakely needs to see her grandfather," I protested.

"Let's just bring her to the waiting room," Whitney said, taking charge as usual in Oldie's absence. She had arrived early that morning and had already been to the hospital twice. "Maybe he'll feel well enough to be wheeled down to see her."

Since I was the only one who hadn't see him yet, Whitney and Mom stayed with Blakely in the large, impersonal hospital waiting room while I went up to Oldie's private room.

Before I even entered, I could hear Oldie complaining to someone about his 'accommodations' as if he expected it to be more like staying at the Plaza. I smiled, feeling he was going to be just fine soon if he was already this ornery.

Oldie was sitting upright in bed when I entered, and he brightened as soon as he saw me. The young, tired nurse looked relieved someone was there to rescue her as she made a hasty exit.

"Well, look who's here—my New York girl!" Oldie said happily. "Melanie, you look great! Have a seat… I can't wait to get out of this Goddamn place… the food is inedible and the nurses aren't even pretty! Every time I turn around one of them is sticking me with another needle, and it's been two straight days of it! I feel like pulling this I-V out of my arm. I'm tired of waiting on the doctor to release me and he sure as hell better hurry up!"

The phone rang and he grabbed it on the first ring. It was his stock broker, I gathered, for Oldie started bellowing orders into the phone about trades and transactions, shouting expletives every other phrase. After a few minutes he slammed down the phone. "I'm going to fire that dumbass as soon as I get out of here… he's a no-good S.O.B.!"

"Dad, you just had a heart-attack… I don't think you're supposed to be getting yourself so worked up in here."

"I know," he winked. "But I was just still testing the old ticker out!" He quickly switched topics, "I want to meet my one and only granddaughter. Go and get her," he demanded.

"Sure, 'Grandpa Oldie,'" I said, and then got up to go and get Blakely. I planned on telling my mother it was fine to bring her in here since he was the same old Oldie. But as soon as I reached the doorway, all of a sudden the color drained out of his face. He looked ashen, and then I heard the foreboding sound of the heart monitor indicating a flat line. I ran over and hit the panic button, yelling out, "HELP! *Please! HELP!*"

Several nurses and two doctors swarmed into Oldie's room like a stampede of buffalos. Everyone was shouting at once.

"Put the paddles on him!" an older doctor shouted.

The second, younger doctor was about to shock Oldie back to life when suddenly my mother rushed in.

"STOP! You can't resuscitate him because he has 'do not resuscitate orders' in his living will!" she yelled.

"Mom? What are you talking about? He's dying, come on!" I pleaded.

"I'm sorry Mel, but he says he doesn't want to be kept alive by a machine."

"Who gives a shit about that Mom! HE'S DYING!" I turned towards the young doctor, who was standing by, speechless. "Use the paddles or DO something—don't just stand there!"

"I'm so very sorry, Melanie," my mother continued, upset now, "but he has *very* specific instructions in his will to make sure no attempt is made to keep him alive if this sort of thing happens… he prefers to go peacefully."

I tried to grab the paddles out of the doctor's hands, but one of the nurses dragged me out of the room. My mother followed, wringing her hands.

"PLEASE, *PLEASE* DO SOMETHING FOR MY FATHER!" I screamed at anyone in scrubs who was within earshot.

My mother just looked at me helplessly.

"HELP!" I howled, running down the hall. "Somebody, please help me! They won't save my dad! I need somebody to help me *save* him!"

I was completely out of control with grief, and people poked their heads out of various rooms and shook them as if to say, "Poor, crazy girl."

My mother finally rushed over and grabbed me. "Melanie! Calm down!"

I was crying hysterically and couldn't stop. "Mom," I said between sobs. "I can't believe what you're telling me. He loved life!"

"Yes, he did... but unfortunately he loved the 'good life' a bit *too* much, which is why this happened. The doctors and I have been telling him for *years* that he needed to lose weight and give up his beloved scotch and sodas, but he refused."

I tried to control myself. "How come I didn't know any of this?"

"Mel, you've been gone a long time now living in New York. It would be too hard to describe, but I've seen him practically self-destruct firsthand over the last few years, and there wasn't anything I could do about it, even though I tried... I tried the very best I could to get him to listen and take better care of himself, but it was *his* choice to be overweight and drink excessively. He wouldn't listen to his doctors or me, *ever.*"

Suddenly I realized my mom had been dealing with some of the same problems I had in my own marriage, and I knew firsthand how pointless it could be to talk to someone who doesn't even think they have a problem.

"I know you're devastated and angry," my mom continued, not really knowing what I was *really* thinking, "but everyone knows I've tried everything I could do to help him, he just didn't want to listen. Please Mel, take some deep breaths. We'll get through this somehow."

I did as she asked, and started to feel only slightly better.

The young doctor, along with several of his colleagues, nervously approached us. "I'm so sorry," he said, "but his organs started to shut down, and once they do it's like an old car... little by little things start breaking down until eventually the whole car just stops going."

My mother turned white and I was stunned. Oldie was gone.

Whitney had taken Blakely for a stroll around the hospital and ended up in our corridor, missing all of this.

"Hey, why is Oldie's bed empty?" she said as she looked into the room. "Where's Oldie?"

Sadly, Blakely never did get to meet her grandpa.

I'd never attended a family member's funeral before. The Saturday of my father's funeral was pleasantly breezy for Houston weather in June. I was grateful God had given us a break from the usual unbearable humidity. Mom looked dignified in a black suit and veil. She was so gracious and strong as she received all the family members and hundreds of friends, business associates, and acquaintances who poured through the carved wooden doors of St. Mary's Episcopal Church, the same church Barc and I had been married in four years before.

The death of my beloved Oldie left a raw, gaping hole in me emotionally. It had happened so suddenly, just when it looked like he was getting better. The worst part of the wound wasn't my guilt about not coming home more often over the last several years; it was his last stated wish to meet his one and only granddaughter before it was too late. Had he had known he was about to die? I felt like I had failed him miserably and for no good reason. All my pathetic attempts to keep my marriage intact by staying in New York or going to Newport over the summer had proved fruitless, like plugging a hole in a large dam with chewing gum and expecting it to hold— and that is what had kept me away all those years. I just couldn't forgive myself for my flawed judgment. I guess I really didn't believe Oldie would ever die on me. He had always been there for me and I foolishly thought he always would be.

I sat beside my mother through the grueling service, emotionally disassociated. Barc sat on the other side of me, but emotionally he was elsewhere. He showed no nostalgia or even respect that we had been married here. His head turned with every attractive blond who entered the church, but I was beyond feeling humiliated by him anymore. I had too much grief, complicated by guilt, and was completely overwhelmed.

Whitney, I must admit, was Mom's rock. She sat on the other side of her and made sure she got through the whole public ceremony in one piece. She seemed to know instinctively that, as the oldest daughter, the task of taking care of Mom would fall on her, and she was a real friend to her. And though she would never admit it, I knew she was there to be supportive of me as well. I was proud to say she was my sister.

However, in the midst of that feeling and my grief, I also couldn't help but feel a twinge of envy towards Whitney and Charles's "happy" marriage. He sat on the other side of her, keeping his adoring eyes always focused on his beloved, beautiful wife. I suddenly wished Blakely was there. I had left her at home with my own childhood babysitter who had offered to look after her since she was too young to understand what a funeral was. We didn't want to upset her, but now I wished she was there if only to distract me from having too much time to think of everything else that was going on around me.

The graveside ceremony was so painful I blocked most of it out of my memory as soon as it ended. There's nothing lonelier than the sound of hard clods of Texas clay echoing against a solid brass coffin. All I wanted to remember were the sprays of red, white, and yellow roses adoring Oldie's casket and grave, and the beautifully carved raw marble monument dedicated to a life "well-lived." My stomach sank as I glanced at the blank grave plot next to his, knowing someday my mom would join him.

The reception was held at home for friends and family only. The house was filled with pictures of happy family vacations in the South of France, Greece, London, Aspen, and Acapulco... pictures of Oldie in the United States Navy commanding his LST boat... collegiate photos from Rice... a proud graduation picture from Yale Law School as he posed with a young Chase Martin... our family growing up over the years in our big, Houston home and at events at the country club... Yes, Oldie's life was laid out with love in these photographs, and I was happy to say he lived a truly wonderful, fulfilling one by the look of his genuine smile in every photo. For that I could be proud, but the gnawing guilt that there were no happy photos of Oldie as a grandfather clutched at me. For that, I was to blame. It was hard for me to mingle and uphold my role as hostess feeling this way. Especially since one time Barc, Blakely, and I took a quick weekend trip down to Palm Beach to visit Foxy when he *insisted* we did, so even Foxy had a few "Grandpa photos" to display now. I couldn't believe I didn't ever do this with Oldie too. Fortunately, Mom and Whitney were there to fill in when I finally excused myself so I could go up to my room and lie down.

Mom never shed a tear in public or during the whole reception. She waited until she was completely alone later that night, then the dam broke. I could hear her down the hall, but I knew she wanted to be alone since that was always her way of dealing with things, and so I left her to her own, private grief.

I couldn't sleep and went downstairs to wander around. I found myself in Oldie's study. I poured myself a glass of brandy that he always kept in his Waterford crystal decanter and sank into his favorite big, comfortable, office chair. The smell of him lingered—the smell of oiled leather, brandy, and Old Spice. Now I could really feel his presence.

The mahogany shelves filled with books lined two entire walls. I ran my fingers over ancient first editions... Had he really read all of these books?

Centered in front of the bay window was his antique English partner's desk that now stood unattended, like an abandoned ship. I stared at the desk and was transported back to all the times I had sat across from him, soaking up his advice. Oldie said he did most of his profound thinking sitting at that desk because it had belonged to a renowned attorney from London, a 'Sir...' well, the name escapes me, but a 'Sir-somebody-important.' My father often said that only people with equally sound minds should occupy this room, to honor the history of that desk; or, as he sometimes put it more bluntly in true 'Oldie' style, "No dumb-asses allowed!"

Looking back, I was grateful my father had been so firm with me growing up. Otherwise who knows how I would have turned out? I could have become a reckless party girl, like Whitney, and had lots of regrets throughout high school and college. But I didn't. Those only came after, when I was on my own, but still always trying to be his "Daddy's little girl" and do just what *he* wanted me to do to make him proud. But now, without Oldie's towering presence, his optimistic assurance, and his larger-than-life charm—I felt utterly alone and helpless, and I knew trying to live for him was a mistake. I couldn't live for Oldie, Helen, or anyone else anymore—I had to start living only for myself and my daughter, like he had done for himself and our family—for I knew he loved us all fiercely. But to do that I had to get out of this dysfunctional marriage now, before it was too late— like it was for Oldie meeting his only granddaughter...

At the very least I knew Oldie would have been a great sounding board for my mounting marriage problems. Though his law practice had dealt with oil and gas issues, not family law, I still knew he'd have keen insights and a smooth hand when it came to getting me the right kind of legal support to get out of my current situation. His life motto was to "live life to the fullest and never back down from a challenge"—which meant I'd feel safe in his care.

Oldie always had the tenderness and patience to sit back and listen attentively to my sister, my mother, and me, and offer his opinion about all our mundane little problems, no matter how big or how small. I realized now that that was how a *real* man should be.

Nostalgia was immediately tempered with the realization that for the first time in my life, I wouldn't have my father's advice and support when I needed it most. With his pragmatic, logical approach to things, he'd always been a wizard at solving my problems—personal, financial, or otherwise. If I got any sense at all, it was from Oldie. Thinking about what he might say, I could almost hear his twang, "I'm not around to help you, Melanie, but you must fight this self-absorbed S.O.B. loser in the legal battle of your life with all of the zeal you inherited from *me*...

"Now, calm down Lil' Bit and dry those tears... Let's examine the facts one at a time... Like dominoes, they'll all fall into place, they always do. Remember, you fall off your bike, you get back on. Your house falls down, you build it up again. When life happens, you happen <u>back</u>."

I fell asleep curled up in Oldie's office chair, soaking it all in.

"POP—POP—POP!"

The sound of the movers bubble-wrapping my formal Chippendale-style, cream-colored, camel back sofa snapped me back to the reality of the present moment only eight weeks later. The rest of my antique furniture from the front room was also there—now all padded, taped, and packed—and patiently waiting for the moving truck too. I could recognize the shapes of the secretary shelf circa the mid-1800s, the two Old English wing-backed tapestry chairs, the mahogany armoire, and the antique Kerman area rug. Once they each stood stately on the Sotheby's auction house floor, holding secrets to their historical past, but now they held memories of my own wrapped in their knotted, plastic-bubble skins. Like ancient relics to my past, bearing witness to the ugliness of the last five years, the furnishings were all, like me, ready to go.

"So... uh.... what about all this glass stuff, lady?" Nick asked as he gestured into the dining room past the long buffet, an antique dining table complete with eight chairs atop a beautifully hand-woven Persian rug. A huge Baccarat crystal chandelier completed the room, and it's light sparkled and danced off a stately corner cabinet displaying all of my crystal collectibles, many of them figurines I'd bought all over the world.

Big Al sauntered up and consulted his list. "Uh, that's right, Mrs. Cunningham ma'am," he said. "It seems the crystal zoo here wasn't included in your price quote—all that stuff needs to be individually bubble-wrapped, each little one—and I ain't got nuthin' here on my list that says anything about no crystal stuff. This is gonna take one of my guys an hour just to do this alone, and we haven't even gotten upstairs yet. You're lookin' at some overtime for sure," he clucked, shaking his head.

I shot him a frustrated look. "Forget it then, I'll pack the cabinet myself," I told him. "Just get to work—we don't have much time."

Big Al gave an annoyed look to the other two men and gestured for them to head back into the sitting room to finish packing.

I walked over to the glass hutch, opened it, and took out the crystal elephant I'd bought in Paris that miserable afternoon years ago and stared at it. The glass edges now held a thin layer of dust. Heavy in my hands, I felt like smashing it against the wall. Instead, I sat it down on the table.

"M'am...? Leave just the two items, right?" Nick asked.

I snapped to. "Yes, just the TV and the painting," I agreed, then took a deep breath, scanning the rest of the sitting room. Barc's only belonging, besides the seventy-two-inch flat screen TV he had insisted on buying, was an original Jasper Johns, a huge abstract painting in dull, muddy colors that I had always despised. It had come to us compliments of Helen. Soon after we had moved in, I came home one day to find the painting prominently displayed above the fireplace. I was furious—but mostly just hurt—that Barc had hung it without so much as even checking with me when the Jasper was ridiculously large, ugly, and clashed with the décor I had so painstakingly picked out the week before. But it was when Helen arrived unannounced, chirping "happy housewarming!" that I knew it was a lost cause. She marveled at how great the painting looked where it was displayed, and mentioned how thrilled I must be to own it, considering it was such a valuable piece of art. I held my tongue, and the painting never budged. Instead I decorated around it and was always slightly at odds with my sitting room.

As I wrapped the rest of the crystal menagerie from the hutch, I realized that Barc and I had never spoken about it—the painting, the slutty hotel waitress in Paris, Amy Lee, his constant disappearances every few months, none of it. I thought about leaving the crystal elephant behind as a remembrance for *him* now...

The front room now stripped, the men then moved into the kitchen. I could hear mumbles of protest coming from behind the closed doors, so I went to see what all the fuss was about. As I prepared to enter the swinging kitchen doors, I overheard them as they muttered something about how "rich people don't ever seem to know or appreciate what they have when they have it." I pushed the doors open wide.

"Oh hello, Mrs. Cunningham… we were just commenting that you have quite a lot of kitchen stuff here," stammered Joey, the one who'd been eyeing me earlier.

"I see you also didn't mention nuthin' about a bunch of restaurant supplies—is *all* of this going, too?" Big Al inquired as he stood assessing the state of my kitchen cabinetry. It was a large, craftsman-style kitchen that contained all kinds of state-of-the-art gadgets, all key assets in my catering company. He was right—I hadn't mentioned my catering business at the time of booking and it was more than your average kitchen's worth of cooking equipment. But it didn't seem relevant at the time. However, it did seem relevant now—it was getting on 7:00 AM. We'd have to hurry—Barc would be up soon.

Nick stood, scratching his unusually large head. "Jeez lady, I've never seen so much stuff. It looks like a Williams Sonoma in here. My wife would go ape-shit, excuse my French. She gets these catalogues right? And she loves to read them, seriously pours over them and gets real upset if I throw them out. I mean, that stuff is ridiculously expensive—they want a hundred bucks for a salad bowl. I've seen it, seriously," he said to Joey, who stared at him, blankly. "But she likes looking at the pictures I guess. Beats me." Nick went back to taping up a box.

I just glared at them and said, "Enough editorials for one day. You're getting paid by the hour, am I right?"

"That's right, no problem, ma'am. Just gonna take some time is all," said Big Al.

Suddenly I heard a thump from down the hall. It was Barc's feet hitting the floor from the master suite. The monster was up.

I jumped into the hall to listen for any sign that Blakely was not exactly where I'd left her, playing quietly in her room. She was humming softly to Mario from behind closed doors and safe, so I rushed back into the kitchen. Where was Joy? She should be here by now. She promised.

Barc stumbled into the kitchen, obviously hung-over, wearing nothing but his rumpled Brooks Brothers boxer shorts. Joey, Nick, and Big Al all stopped what they were doing and stood up.

On a good day Barc was still a decent-looking man; today, however, he looked like a junkie with greasy hair matted to his head and bloodshot, barely-opened eyes, possibly still stoned. He emitted an open-mouthed growl as he limped into the room, a mere shell of his former self.

My stomach tightened and I prepared for battle. I was sure he'd go ballistic. *The bastard will have to come after me,* I thought. But I knew he wouldn't, not with Big Al and his gang to my right and my left.

Barc just stared at everything. He stared into the living room, then the kitchen, then at the three oversized men. When he finally spoke, it was in the low, murderous tone that had always preceded our worst fights. His words were measured, tight. "It is seven o'clock in the fucking morning, Melanie!" he said. "What the FUCK are these people doing in my Goddamn kitchen?"

Frozen with fear, the words would not come and I gave Big Al a look that pleaded, *Can you take this?* I silently prayed for Oldie's help too…

Big Al paused; then pulled out the folded-up contract from his back pocket.

Barc snatched it from his hands. *"Movers?* Fucking MOVERS? What the… what is this, Melanie?" He took a step towards me, but Big Al instinctively took a step in my direction too, and I forced myself to meet Barc's eyes as I stood my ground.

"Please continue packing the apartment," I said firmly to the movers as my eyes never left Barc's.

The men resumed their work, cautiously.

"What the HELL do you think you're DOING?" Barc yelled as he stepped closer towards me, leaning in, expecting an explanation—but I didn't give him one. "Just, just STOP! STOP, GODDAMN IT!" he yelled at the movers, but they didn't.

Barc looked at me and pleaded, "Mel, tell them to stop." He was whimpering now. "Just tell me what the fuck is going on!" His lip was trembling.

I cringed; this wasn't what I was expecting. Barc was acting even more pathetic than I'd imagined. Yelling, sure—throwing things, most likely. But *crying?* I had never imagined this. I could tell he wasn't going to give up until I said it out loud, so I closed my eyes and let myself grow angry, really angry as I remembered the hellish relationship this had been for almost five years of my life. It was the jolt of energy and courage I needed to just come out with it: "Barc, I'm getting out of this nightmare of a marriage and taking Blakely with me. You didn't believe that I'd ever leave, did you? Well believe it now, asshole! Because I can't take it anymore!"

I could feel Oldie's presence, and he was proud as I continued, "I have put up with your abuse, your temper, your drinking and drug use, and all the cheating for too many years—I'm done and we're moving out today! Our marriage is finally over—just like it *really* has been for the last four long, *miserable* years!" I yelled. The words hung in the air like icicles, cold and dangerous.

I braced myself for Barc to smash the wall, or maybe throw the lamp beside him. He didn't. Instead, he just paced the room. "Now? You're leaving me NOW? After *all* we've been through—are you serious?"

"I'm dead serious, Barc. Blakely and I are moving back to Houston and that's final. We have a plane to catch in just a few hours, so until then, I suggest you stay out of our way."

Barc finally seemed to be getting it. The rage was starting to bubble up. "You're not going anywhere with Blakely, you giant fucking BITCH! Are you out of your mind? You're NOT TAKING MY DAUGHTER!"

Go ahead, let it sink in. Might as well get the rest of it over with, too, I thought. I marched across the room and pulled out a stack of legal papers from my overstuffed Chanel tote bag. On top was a thickly stapled document which, having rushed up behind me, Barc grabbed furiously from my hands.

He started to read it out loud: "In the district court of Harris County, Texas, District Court agreed order of divorce for—*divorce?* ... BULLSHIT!" Barc shouted, throwing the papers so they scattered all over the floor. I didn't care; I was almost free. Since we were married in Texas I'd filed there instead of New York, which meant that I could legally take my daughter away without penalty. In New York, state law would have forbidden me from moving more than ninety miles away until Blakely turned eighteen and to me, that was no longer an option.

Big Al watched the whole scene closely. He caught my eye, silently asking if I needed any help. I shook my head slightly, grateful that he and the others were there.

"Fuck you, you bitch!" Barc ranted. "If you leave me nobody will *ever* want to be with you! You're fat, ugly, old, and disgusting!" He lunged across the room and grabbed my arm.

Big Al, Nick, and Joey all moved collectively across the room to intervene—each with a balled fist—while I grabbed the crystal elephant from the table near us and brandished it above my head.

Just then Joy arrived. She strolled in casually, looked at the papers scattered all over the floor, and leveled her dark eyes in a death-glare at Barc, who immediately dropped my arm. I smiled. Barc was terrified of Joy.

"Oh—I do NOT think so, not today," Joy tsked. Joy could have easily picked up Barc with one scoop of her vast arms, particularly now that he was a mere wisp of a man, thinned by age, drink, and self-neglect.

Joy took the crystal elephant from me and handed it to Big Al. She rolled her eyes disdainfully as she bent down to pick up the scattered papers. "I see yo throwin' noth'er one of yo daily fits in here," she said to Barc in her heavy accent. "And so early in da morning too! Usually it at two, three in da aftanoon befo' yo to go out yo mind," she said as she ambled down the hall.

Joy knew the drill; we'd discussed it the day before. She went directly into Blakely's bedroom and loaded her and Mario into the stroller.

"We're goin' to da pen," she said to me as she wheeled Blakely out the door, flashing a sympathetic look in my direction as she slammed the heavy door behind her. My eyes welled up with gratitude. Joy was so good at getting things back on track, for taking control of a situation.

The three movers resumed packing. Barc simply kept circling around the room, muttering to himself in the now-empty living room.

I slipped back into the kitchen, whispering to Big Al that I'd be right back and to keep an eye on Barc. I slipped out and pattered downstairs to the private pen.

Joy and Blakely were playing with Mario on the garden grass near the swing set. Joy greeted me with a hug. I laid my head on her large shoulders, tears already running down my face.

"There now..." Joy said, comforting me. "Every day he be yellin' about somethin', ain't no different today. What kind of life is that fo yoself? Why do yo listen to this bum? No good, I tell yo. That man ain't no good," she said firmly.

"I know, Joy, I know," I agreed. "He's not even as bad today as I expected. But it's still so hard."

"He gets home smellin' of ganja and whisky every night, and then starts in on yo—always criticizn' yo. It ain't no life, I say."

She was right. "I know—and I'm so glad this is finally happening! It felt good to finally stand up to him, but I don't know if I could have gotten to this point without you. You're my personal hero Joy, did you know that?" my voice trembled.

Joy shook her head. "Bah. I just know he no good, that's all! And he got no power over yo no more. It's time. You doin' the right ting, movin' back wit yo momma, and sort da tings out. Yo dada would be proud."

I knew she was right as I watched Blakely play. She was so blissful today, so innocent to the new life I was about to make for us. She looked up at me and her big blue eyes were enormous compared to her tiny round face. I went and sat down beside her, brushing a wisp of sun-streaked hair from her forehead.

"Hey Blakely, guess what?" I said happily.

"What?" she giggled.

"We're going to go see Granny!"

"Gama Ellen!" she said as she raised Mario to the sky.

Of course, I thought. She meant Grandma Helen, Barc's mother. She'd only met my mother a couple of times, and the last time—because of the funeral—she hardly spent any time with her because Mom didn't want Blakely to see her so upset.

"Nope. We're going to Texas, buckaroo!" I said in a ridiculous, exaggerated Texan accent. I made guns with my hands and made 'ka-pow' noises before tickling her.

Blakely squealed, then stood up and imitated me as only a toddler could do with such excitement. She ran to go play on the large, colorful jungle gym.

As I watched her I couldn't believe how lucky I was. Blakely was the only positive thing Barc had ever done in his entire life—and I knew he couldn't possibly ever understand or appreciate how wonderful and precious she was.

Blakely stopped playing for a moment, then looked up at me and smiled. I couldn't resist blowing her a big kiss. "Everything's gonna be okay, baby," I whispered.

Joy tapped her watch. "Betta go move those movers asses now. It's goanna be late soon. Now git, we'll be fine."

I knew Joy was right, so I left Blakely to play as I padded back up the stairs and slipped into the apartment. Barc was still pacing.

As soon as he saw me enter, the yelling began anew. "You want a divorce? FINE WITH ME, YOU TWISTED BITCH! I'm going to hire the TOUGHEST FUCKING HOT-SHOT LAWYER I can find in Texas and I'LL FIGHT YOU TOOTH AND NAIL! My mom will pay for it and I KNOW YOU CAN'T FIGHT BACK without your FATHER NOW— YOU SPOILED, SELFISH, FAT *BRAT*—so you won't get a DIME!"

I tried to steady my breathing as I saw the movers still watching us. "Please stop screaming, Barc. There's nothing you can do—it's done." I knew I should stop talking. It wouldn't help to egg him on. But my newly minted freedom was so close I could taste it, and the words just tumbled out: "Why don't you call up one of your girlfriends and ask them to come over and make you feel better?"

Barc looked taken aback. I hadn't seen him look genuinely surprised in a long, long time.

"Oh… you think I don't know? Seriously?" I asked him. "You think I'm that oblivious? Honestly, Barc. Take a look at yourself when you come home most nights. You don't put *on* boxers with 'lipstick marks' on them in the morning."

"Yeah right. You don't know jack!"

"Jesus Barc, just believe it! I'm finally doing something about our joke of a marriage. I'm leaving you, and you *can't* stop me."

He had nothing to say to this. He knew it was true. I stormed down the hallway and into the master bedroom and started assembling my carry-on bag.

"S'cuze me, uh, Ms. Melanie, is it?" Joey asked from the doorway. He had taken off his cap. He motioned if it was okay if he stepped inside the room. I nodded that it was. He glanced at the bed's mattress that was stripped and already leaning against the dresser, ready to pack up. "So uh… I noticed you're not exactly on good terms with the 'mister' of the house… So I'm just wondering, if you wanted to, you know, how's about you's and me? Later, before your flight? You look like you could use a little something to 'relax' you… I'd be happy to take you out for a nice cocktail, maybe at a hotel bar, if you know what I'm sayin?" His eyes sparkled, and he winked.

"You've got to be kidding me!" I said, shaking my head. Normally I might have let it go, but today was an entirely different matter.

"They call you 'Joey,' right? 'Joey the Jokester…' I'm so fed up with men like you I could throw up! Can't you see what's going on here? You think just because I'm leaving my husband that I'm going to fuck *you*? You think I'm some vulnerable little chickie you can just take advantage of?"

"Hey, whoa lady, I was just talking about a drink… c'mon!" he said, now changing his tune.

"Come on nothing! I'm not going *anywhere* with you, you ogre! Now get back to work—all these clothes *aren't* going to pack themselves!"

"Alright, fine. Just please don't tell my boss," Joey pleaded.

I rolled my eyes, wondering what would even be the point after all I've been through this morning already.

Later, as Barc watched the men carry box after box out of the apartment, reality really started to sink in. "You better not take that Goddamn TV!" he said, defeated.

"Barc, I can assure you I won't remove one thing from this apartment *you* purchased," I said mockingly as I scanned the room. "Aaaand it looks like that leaves you with the chair you're sitting in, the TV, your mother's disgusting painting, a New York Post, and that piece of trash coffee cup. That's about all you've contributed to this marriage, too," I said, newly confident now.

The three men finished loading the furniture and boxes onto the moving truck and I went downstairs to see them off. As they rolled the hatch down and closed it, Big Al asked if I was going to be okay.

"I'll be fine, and thank you for being here... the worst of it is over now," I told him. By that time Joy was heading back upstairs and I motioned towards her as I assured him 'we' could take it from here. The three men drove off in the truck with a roar.

I went back upstairs and surveyed the nearly empty apartment one last time to make sure we had gotten everything, and then looked at Barc. He was sitting in an empty living room on a solitary chair, watching TV. He looked so beaten down. He noticed me looking at him and said, "No man will EVER want you, do you know that? Do you really think anybody would be stupid enough to deal with an old, fat, worthless bitch like you, 'monkey girl?'"

Joy walked towards Barc with destructive intent, but I grabbed her shoulder and stopped her. "You're a weak and pitiful excuse for a man," I said to him firmly. "I hope you enjoyed that last little stab at me, because it's the last one you'll *ever* get. Good-bye, Barclay."

With that, Joy grabbed Blakely, I grabbed our travel bags, and the three of us walked out the door. We were all the way down the elevator before I dared to even look at Joy because I knew what was coming next. Once we caught each other's glances we both started crying immediately.

She gave me a huge hug and handed me a small voodoo doll full of pins.

"Miss Melanie, this doll equals Barc. Stick as many pins in da doll whenever yo feel down or yo doubt yo'r decision for one moment. It will protect yo," she said. I looked at the handmade doll and cried even harder.

Joy picked up Blakely, who immediately started playing with her dreadlocks. "Yo take good care of yo'r mama now, little one! I'm gowna miss yo so much!" she said, hugging her tightly. "I hope I be seein' yo again one day, Miss Melanie and Miss Baby Blakely. Bye-bye!"

She waved her hand at Blakely.

"Byeee!" Blakely said as she waved back happily. She'd been practicing this waving thing a lot with Joy and knew it usually made everyone smile when she did it, but this time no one was smiling back at her. She looked at me, confused as to why Joy and I were so sad. I smiled at her comfortingly through my tears.

"Here," I said to Joy as I handed her a big bonus check. "For putting up with *so* much, for *so* long," I added gratefully.

"Psshaw, yo always so good to me," she tisked.

Joy helped us fill the stretch limo with all of our bags and Blakely's various stuffed animals and toys that we had brought down the night before and stored in our storage unit, ready for this moment, until the whole back seat of the limo was stuffed to the hilt.

We hugged each other one final time, and then it was time to go. I would have brought Joy with us to Houston in a hot second if she wasn't tied to New York by her extended family and children, but she was. I wished her and all of them well.

After Blakely and I were finally on the road, she looked around, asking for Barc, "Where dah? Where dah?" Hearing her say this was like a kick in the stomach. My heart broke.

"We're going bye-bye, to Texas, remember baby? We're gonna go see Granny," I said, stifling the tears that were already on their way. How in the world could I ever explain what was happening to her?

The driver dropped us off at LaGuardia Airport. After checking in the enormous amount of luggage and paying an absurd overweight charge, we went to the gate and waited to board the plane. Blakely was agitated and overwhelmed by the airport's hustle and bustle and became fussy.

I picked her up. "It's okay baby, we're gonna get on an airplane! You remember what that is, don't you?" I used my hand to simulate a plane, complete with soaring noises. At that same moment a plane flew over our heads, fresh from take-off, and I pointed towards it. "Look!"

"Wow!" Blakely said as she got an excited look in her eyes as if to say, 'We're getting on that again?' She liked traveling as much as I did it seemed.

We finally boarded the plane and settled into our first class seats, preparing for the same four hour plane trip to Houston that we had taken to go see Oldie only two short months before. I still couldn't believe I had arranged this all so fast, but I guess once you finally make up your mind to do something, you really can just "get it done" like Oldie always said.

"Look Mommy! Clouds!" Blakely said, smiling at me and then went back to cloud gazing, leaving me to deal with my own disorientation. She stayed glued to the window from take-off all the way up to 10,000 feet before she finally fell asleep, and I was grateful that she was neither restless nor uncomfortable.

But I was a different story. I didn't have a single plan or any idea of what I'd do when I arrived in Houston—not where I'd live, where Blakely would go to school, nor where I'd find work. I figured leaving Barc was the hard part, and thankfully, now that was over, I just had to get back home and reexamine my future and my entire life plan. I figured the four hours

I currently had on the flight down to Texas was probably a good time to start too.

All at once I felt scared, desperate, sad, and lonely. I felt like a failure as a mother, a wife, and as a woman. Not only that, I was about to get reacquainted with my old hometown, a place I'd left over six years ago to escape the biggest love of my life. I hoped I didn't run into Hunter again. I couldn't take that chance feeling this vulnerable. I wanted to get myself together, have a place of my own, and a great job first. Then I'd feel better about myself and be ready to face him.

While Blakely napped, I reexamined my complete bad taste in men, and how none of them actually appreciated or respected all the love I tried to give them. And as much as I tried to pull water from a stone and conjure up any pangs of fondness for my soon-to-be ex-husband since he was always going to be the father of my child, the truth was, I should have run screaming as soon as I met Barclay most of all. The regret overwhelmed me and I knew I was about to lose it big time, so I quickly made my way into the bathroom where I hoped no one could hear me cry.

After a few muffled tears in the restroom, I came back to find Blakely still asleep, sweetly clutching Mario. I stroked the hair of my beautiful daughter napping in the sky somewhere above Missouri and suddenly changed my mind.

No, my angel was worth it all...

Chapter 18

The plane finally landed in Houston. Four long hours of intense reflection had my head pounding, only made worse by the wall of August's heat and humidity that blasted us as we exited the plane.

"Hot, hot!" Blakely announced.

"That's right, baby," I said. "Houston is HOT!" I was so proud of her. She'd been a little saint on the plane.

Ron, our family driver of over twenty years now, greeted us at baggage claim. "Miss Melanie... welcome back to Texas!" he said as he grinned widely, giving Blakely and I both a big bear-hug. He was a sinewy black man with graying hair, and I thought I saw pity behind his kind, brown eyes.

While Ron motioned for a skycap to come help him load our mountain of luggage into his limo parked outside at the curb, Blakely and I piled into the back seat of it. My head was pounding by the time we finally left the airport and drove towards Highland Park.

I didn't know which was worse yet; the fact that I was facing life as a single mother, or that I was being forced to go back home to live with my mother. But I didn't have any other choice really. Being married to Barc had drained my sizeable savings, and I couldn't afford to go anywhere else for the time being.

Stop feeling sorry for yourself, I told the inner me. I knew self-pity and despair were a waste of time—especially since Barc was the prime example of that since he spent so much time pitying himself over his 'unhappy childhood' (and had consequently spent his whole adulthood in a twisted, downward fall to nowhere). But that was beside the point. I'd already been there over Hunter, and now, with my marriage ending, I felt some of those same depression-like feelings starting to bubble-up inside again, but I tried to shake them off. There was nowhere to go from here but up.

Suddenly, out of nowhere, the words to *Don't Stop,* one of my favorite Fleetwood Mac songs, echoed through my mind, and I instantly started to hum the upbeat melody as I looked at Blakely.

She laughed and, inspired by my enthusiasm, clapped along with me.

"That's right Miss Melanie, yesterday's gone," Ron smiled. "Ain't nothing to worry about now," he said as he pulled the limo into a large circular driveway lined with hedges, leading up to the front door of my childhood home.

"We're home!" I announced to Blakely as I gave her a hug. "This is where Mummy lived when she was a little girl, just like you!"

Though I had grown up here and been back many times since my childhood to visit, I was still in awe of its size and beauty as we approached. The house was a large, antebellum-style mansion with six stately columns guarding a large veranda. The front yard was meticulously landscaped in flowering bushes, rose gardens, azaleas, and rhododendrons of varying colors. The oversized lot the house sat on, almost an acre, was wooded in old-growth oak trees with moss draping off them, and the backyard contained both a clay tennis court and a marble swimming pool. A waterfall flowed along one wall and across from it was the pool house, complete with a pool table, ping-pong table, and an original soda fountain for making homemade fountain drinks. Whitney and I loved that feature when we were little.

"Yah!" Blakely shouted as we got out, though I think she was more likely just relieved to be getting out of the car as she ran around to the other side of it and up onto the grass. It was nice to stretch our legs, and I noticed it was turning into a pleasantly breezy afternoon—rare and welcoming for Houston. I'd gotten used to the unpredictable climate in New York where the seasons were brief but wholly distinctive. As they say in Houston, "It blazes from December to March, and then *hotter* blazes from April 'til November."

Ron and I started to unload the car as my mother appeared at the door, elegant as ever.

"Come on in, you two! Let's get everything organized by room, please," she said as she came over and kissed my cheek, warmly.

"Hi Mom," I said back, just as warmly.

"Goodness, I've never seen so much stuff! I'm glad I cleared three bedrooms out for you."

Just then Blakely reappeared from behind the limo and looked up at my mother shyly.

"Hello sweetheart Blakely!" my mother said happily. "You've gotten so big in only the last couple of months!"

Blakely only smiled back as she ran up to me and hugged my legs.

"Mom," I said as my voice trembled. "Today's been the *worst* day. I've been up since dawn, I had it out with Barc, plus all the traveling—"

"Melanie, we're going to get you through this, okay?" She touched my shoulder reassuringly and gave it a light squeeze. Not known for her affection, for Louise St. John, this was like wrapping me in a giant bear-hug in her arms and smothering me in a warm blanket of kisses. I smiled at her, sad and exhausted, as I picked up Blakely and headed towards the front door.

My mother always said a home's front door was an introduction to the people who lived there, and that's why she put an expensive, but welcoming, solid bronze pineapple-shaped doorknocker in the center of the large, mahogany-carved door as a token of greeting to our visitors. And visitors there were plenty; our home was often filled with neighbors and guests of my parents' at dinner parties, social causes, and gatherings for Oldie's business associates. I became used to the sight of grown-ups greeting each other and saying good-bye in the front foyer, placing their umbrellas into the antique Chinese-urn umbrella stand, which also held my mother's colorful collection of Laura Ashley floral print umbrellas.

Today Blakely was a 'visitor' of sorts, and so I let her play with the knocker as we entered the foyer. Immediately the prisms from the large Waterford chandelier created streams of rainbow patterns as it broke up the bright Texas sunlight, which poured through the leaded glass windows on either side of the front door. A set of botanical prints in inlaid wooden frames hung symmetrically across from one another on each side of the walls. But my favorite—the objects that added mystery and excitement to the hallway and always intrigued me as a child—were the matching set of antique, stone-carved gargoyles that graced either side of the doorway into the grand living room. The expression on their faces seemed to change when you studied them from different angles. Mom had gotten them in France and said they protected the house.

Blakely looked around the entrances of the big rooms the foyer flanked with wide-eyes, absorbing her new space. She had only been there once before, and it was still strange to see my daughter in the home I'd grown up in, discovering my old things, my memories, and tracing them with her new eyes. Stranger still, seeing my mother interact with my now two-year-old daughter, attempting grandmother-likeness. She knelt down and put her hands on Blakely's shoulders.

"I'm baking homemade chocolate chip cookies just for you, Blakely— but I need to get back into the kitchen before they burn. Tell Mummy you want to go see her old bedroom, where she lived when she was just a little girl, like you!"

Blakely had seen my room when we were here for Oldie's funeral, but since my mom was so out of sorts she didn't remember. I guess I didn't really pay too much attention to what Blakely was seeing either, for it felt like today was her first real visit there.

We started up the grand staircase, but suddenly a figure appeared in the doorway of the living room that I nearly didn't recognize.

"Aunt Winnie!" Blakely shouted with glee as she ran towards Whitney, now entering the hallway with her long, blond hair flowing behind her.

"Hi pumpkin!" Whitney said as she scooped up my daughter and they both giggled.

"Whitney! What are you doing here?" I called out in disbelief. I hadn't seen her since the funeral and thought she'd be back in New York by now.

"Well that's a nice way to greet your older sister!" Whitney said, walking over to me with a big grin. She was as tan and beautiful as ever, dressed in skintight Gloria Vanderbilt designer jeans and cute Chanel flats. I hugged her.

"Mel, you have perfect timing. I came down here for one of my old high school friends's wedding this past weekend, can you believe it?"

"Not really, that sort of thing normally isn't your bag. I'm surprised you even wanted to go."

"I know, it's not like me, *right?* But then I thought, what the hell—I missed everyone else's over the years *and* my twentieth high school reunion, so maybe it'll be an ego boost or something to just finally show up and see everyone, plus when I heard *you* were coming back, I decided to come and stay the whole week."

"Did you even have anything to talk to anyone about?" I asked, thinking back to my own unattended high school reunions and wondering if as much had changed for Whitney as it had for me over the years since high school.

"Not really… but it was fun to see some of the old gang and hear about who had become more successful than the football jocks everyone used to have a crush on. A lot of the nerdy guys have become high-powered attorneys, plastic surgeons, doctors—oh, and of course, *none* of my ex-boyfriends who were there seem to be aging well! They all had big stomachs and fat wives and most of them were either bald, gray or *both.*"

I laughed.

"But you know I don't care about any of them!" Whitney said. "I mean, you have to admit, I look pretty good for my age, so the looks on the faces of all those 'loser-jock-has-beens' when I walked over and introduced myself to their wives was pretty priceless. Especially when I then got to show them all pictures of *my* beautiful, fit 'Charles' and let them all know how successful he is as a heart surgeon back in New York—he's working this week and couldn't make it down this time with me."

I could only laugh. Whitney had changed over the years—but some things never change. I couldn't help but wonder though that if instead of the wedding, she had actually come home to support me, just like she did the week of Oldie's funeral. If this was true, she would never let me know it—just like she pretended the week of the funeral she wasn't all that concerned about me, but she really was. My heart warmed to my sister, who I knew at times could be very selfish—even superficial—but at her core, she was really growing up and was now there for me.

"That really sucks about Barc, Mel," she said, getting more serious. "He seemed decent the few times I met him... I guess marrying someone after only a couple of months of knowing him wasn't such a great idea after all, huh?" And there it was—the old Whitney I knew who would always get in a 'dig' whenever she could.

Raw and tired from my hellacious day, it was all the opening I needed. "*Must* I remind you that it was *you,* Dad, and Mom who *all* advised me to 'go for it' with Barc when I said I was having second thoughts? Mom was too concerned about the invitations already having been sent out, Dad said he was *just* the kind of man he 'expected' me to marry, and least you forget about the pressure *you* put me under with the wonderful advice of 'just follow your heart and not listen to society's influence of taking a long time to get to know *him*—'"

She brushed me off. "All in the past, aye?" Whitney changed the subject happily. "Now we're all here—and my adorable little niece and I are going to have some fun! Right, baby?"

"Right!" Blakely shouted.

"Actually, if you could take Blakely for the next hour or so that would be amazing. It'll give me some time to get all of this stuff in order," I said, pointing to the piles of boxes and suitcases in the foyer. "I'll have to get a storage unit, but not today." I pulled our carry-on bags out and started up the stairs.

Whitney stopped me. "I'm really sorry that things didn't work out, Mel," she said sincerely. "I mean, I don't even want to *think* about what I'd do without Charles, and I want you to know I'm here if you need me."

"Thanks Whit," I said, hugging her. My relationship with my sister was complicated—and as usual, I felt conflicted. I was grateful that she was trying to be supportive. But I also couldn't help but feel a touch of resentment that she was still happily married and I was not—it was as simple as that. I needed to cut her some slack though; being married was good for her since she now had someone else to focus on besides herself and was becoming a better person overall, but it was still hard to.

I continued on up the stairs and set the carry-on items down outside my door, then went back down the stairs for another load. When I got back to the foyer, Whitney and Blakely were gone and I finally had a moment alone to let what I was doing really sink in. Being back at home was bringing up so many memories it was starting to influence my mood, and I could feel tears filling my eyes. Had I made the right decision? Should I have sought marriage counseling? I walked through the house, trying to calm down. It was strange not to hear Oldie's bellowing voice echoing through the rooms. Everything just felt empty...

But there were happy images emerging too, floating through my mind as I made my way through the house, and I paused at the entrance to the dining room where a sudden flood of memories of Christmas dinners reassured me. I'd always loved the way the Waterford chandelier, with its cascading prisms, cast a twinkling glow over everyone in the room as we ate in here. It was magical.

Our last Christmas together as a family was years ago, before I was married... Mom and Oldie were in top form that day. They had fawned all over each other, still acting like two newlyweds. He was always so impressed with Mom's cooking, and for holidays at home Mom went all out.

Dinner at these engagements always started out with a small amount of Beluga caviar and champagne to set the mood and whet our appetites. The buffet table was carefully prepared with steaming plates of delectable dishes, all hand-cooked by Mom—beef tenderloin with portabella ragout, creamed spinach, perfect, buttery mashed potatoes, a glistening dish of ambrosia, and of course, a shining, golden-brown turkey displayed on a raised pedestal above the other dishes, which my father was in charge of carving with an electric knife. In the adjacent room just off the dining room there was always an extravagant display of miniature desserts and pastries, varieties of seasonal fruit cobblers, and my favorite, rice pudding. My mother loved every minute of those gatherings, for they were an opportunity to display her incredible culinary talents. Talents my father enjoyed to their fullest extent—and it showed in his large, round, always-full belly he proudly displayed.

There was no secret I'd gotten my love of cooking from my mother, and I was always put in charge of making the hors d'oeuvres for all the various events my parents threw at the house. I remember wrapping large trays of dumplings or rice paper as a child, just exactly as my mother had shown me, making perfect folds in a delicate fabric of dough. Oldie would often come in, ruffle-up my hair, and say, "Silly food for silly people, Lil' Bit!" but he'd always swipe a nibble just the same.

But now my dad was gone and things would never be the same.

"Mummy!" Blakely said happily, toddling up behind me and giving me a new perspective. No, things would never be the same ever again without Oldie here, but now, with my own daughter to create new memories with, they could still be great.

I got my bearings as I picked Blakely up and went into the living room with her, starting to feel better as soon as I entered. The Imari porcelain lamps that had flanked the Williamsburg sofa as far back as I could remember still comforted me, and the deep blue shade of the couch's color was still a favorite of mine. A portrait of my mother when she was much younger stood smiling down at us from the tiled fireplace. She was tall, slim, and had her wavy brown hair pinned back so that it just lightly touched her shoulders. Her cornflower-blue eyes were large and sparkling and were set into her slightly round, angelic face. Her ruby-red lipstick highlighted a perfect, perpetual smile that she wore always—even when she was upset.

I'd always thought of my mother as a 1950's archetypical housewife. She reminded me of June Cleaver, the mom on the sitcom *Leave it to Beaver,* because she always enjoyed spending time with her children, cooking, doing charity work, playing bridge, and attending club luncheons. I admired her and had thought I would have a life just like that one day, too.

Whitney reappeared beside me dressed in a bright blue tennis outfit.

"I'm going to the club!" she announced. "Come with?"

"Nah… I just want to roam around the house some more." I looked back up at our mother's portrait. "It's amazing they were married over forty years. They were so different from each other."

"I know," Whitney laughed.

I got quiet thinking of how I assumed I'd find the same happiness.

Whitney seemed to read my thoughts. "Try and cheer up, Mel. I'll be back in a few hours if you want to talk some more."

"Wait—I thought you were going to take Blakely for awhile?"

"Oh, right—sorry Mel. Can it be after tennis? I'll take her when I get back, I promise."

I was not surprised, so I just said, "Of course—go play tennis. Thanks, sis."

Suddenly Blakely tugged at my arm. "Mummy, I want to see your room!" Her demand shook me out of my somber mood and we went upstairs.

Our first stop was Whitney's old bedroom. It hadn't changed since she left for college—still bright pink with the shag carpeting that had been so popular in the '70s, only now it had been layered over with colorful throw rugs. A floral and paisley print covered the chairs, bedspread, and canopy. I tried to show Blakely Whitney's cheerleading pictures, swim team trophies, and her graduation photograph with a boyfriend whose name I'd long forgotten, but Blakely wasn't interested in any of it.

Instead she pointed to a large photo hanging on the opposite wall: a framed print of Whitney in all her glowing glory surrounded by her 'Fearsome Foursome' group of best friends from college: Eva, Travis, and Austin, with a caption reading THE FEARSOME FOURSOME.

Blakely liked what she saw, a younger and more beautiful 'Aunt Winnie.' "Aunt Winnie!" she said, in awe.

"Yes."

"Where's Mummy?"

"Mummy took the picture," I said, rubbing my eyes to keep tears at bay as I remembered that day at the airport saying good-bye to Whitney and Eva, and not wanting to remember the hellish summer that followed. I'd always been the eager younger sister—desperate to be included in the fun—but sometimes there wasn't any to be included in.

We moved on and into my old bedroom, which hadn't changed either. My blue-and-white floral bedroom was still decorated in English chintz with complementary flowery patterns on two matching chairs, the Laura Ashley curtains and dust ruffle, as well as atop my four-poster canopy bed. The rug was a beautiful Oriental in pastel colors which covered most of the deep mahogany hardwood floors. It was ultra-feminine and, like Whitney's room, had a Juliet-styled balcony that overlooked the pool.

My dressing table contained my jewelry box, a large variety of perfume bottles, and numerous photos in silver frames. I looked in my vanity minor, trying to figure out what happened to the girl who used to live here. Disappointment filled me as I looked at the older woman who reflected back, and tears welled up.

"What's wrong, Mummy?" Blakely asked.

"Your momma is very, very sad."

"Why?"

"You're too little to understand, but please don't worry, I'll be okay soon... look—I can show you things from when I was younger to cheer us up," I said, wiping silent tears but determined to keep a happy face for my daughter.

I looked around the room and spotted a megaphone and some gold and purple pompoms from my cheerleading years. I picked up the megaphone and yelled, "Gooooo Falcons! The mighty mighty *Falcons!*"

Blakely stared at me blankly.

"What's a Fal-kon?" she asked.

"A bird—it was our football team's mascot when we cheered for them." She looked at me like I'd lost my head. *"Cheered?"*

"You cheer when you want your team to win."

I handed her the pompoms and she immediately jumped up and down waving them, mimicking something she must have seen on TV while her dad was watching a game, for she looked like a miniature cheerleader. She was so cute that I racked my brain trying to remember the words to a cheer to tell her to chant, but high school was a million miles away.

"Try this," I began to hum, and all of a sudden I remembered one. I perfected out the routine to her, singing as I moved, "We are the Falcons, the mighty, mighty Falcons and everywhere we go-o people want to know-o who we are-rr, so we tell them!"

Blakely joined in and we jumped around, singing.

Our thumping feet got my mother's attention downstairs. She soon poked her head into the room. "Melanie, this is the first time I've seen you smile since you walked through the front door!"

"Well I haven't had a lot to smile about lately."

"Try to keep having fun with Blakely. It's good, for *both* of you." A hugging-sort of mom would have embraced me at this point, but she just left the room. I picked up Blakely and squeezed her tight.

"Don't worry about Mummy so much, baby. Mummy is going to be just fine," I said, determined to mean it.

The week after Whitney left, and I'd attempted to adjust back to life in Houston, I realized how much harder it was to actually be 'fine' now I was starting a whole new life again at thirty-five—and as a single mother too, to boot. Luckily there had been my mom, Whitney, and our longtime maid, Consuela, to help look after Blakely, so whenever I needed to escape for some 'private, reflective' time, I knew Blakely was always in good hands. However, it was getting so I felt like I needed 'alone' time more and more as the days went by, until one day, just like when I was in that no-hope, depressive state over Hunter, I didn't want to get out of bed at all. And so I just stayed in it, and luckily my mom let me, but only for awhile…

The pillow was wrapped around my head on the third morning of my self-wallowing party when suddenly there was a knock on my bedroom door. I ignored it, knowing the door was locked, so I could stay in my safe, warm cocoon. But the knock continued, relentlessly.

"Who is it?" I finally asked.

"It's the Pope… who do you think it is?" my mother said sarcastically.

"Later please, Mom… I don't feel so well."

"Rise and shine! It's a beautiful day today… now, open up!" she insisted.

"Mom, *please*… just leave me here…"

The banging grew louder and relentless until I finally got up and unlocked the door. I got right back in bed and sat up with my arms wrapped around my legs.

"What—is Blakely okay?" I asked, slightly aggravated. I didn't want my daughter to see me like this, but I knew if she really needed me I'd have to pull myself together.

"Blakely's fine, but the Driller's Club is having their annual 'Tux and Boots" ball this weekend."

"So what?"

"You're going... that's *what*. Here's the invitation."

"Are you crazy?—I can't go to a ball, look at me!"

"You'd look *fine* if you just made yourself up a bit," she coached. "Look, you're getting a divorce, so you'll soon need a new man, and the Driller's Club is where you might be able to see who's out there and available to you."

I sighed. "If I never see another man again I'll be—"

My mother cut me off sharply, "As my mother once told me, 'If you want fish, fish where the fish are. If you want a man—fish where the *men* are,' so you're going *fishing* this Saturday night, at least just to 'test' the waters. I don't expect you to actually start dating until the divorce is final, but really, it won't hurt to at least socialize."

"I can't... I can't face it.... the humiliation."

She ignored me. "Yes, it's going to be harder now... you're older and you have a child, but the sooner you get back out there the better."

"I hate men... I just want to be alone."

"The women of my generation didn't have the luxury of 'alone,'" she said. "And now, it appears, neither do *you*."

I groaned. "I'm not in the mood to go to one of those glittering soirees you are always reminiscing about."

"Yes, they are glittered," my mom said fondly. "And your life really still is too... You should count your blessings child; think about poor Beau and his lot in life now."

I suddenly did and felt bad. My old high school friend Beau had been in a terrible car accident two years ago and was now a quadriplegic living at his deceased father's 25,000 acre ranch at the edge of Houston called "El Sueno." Both his parents were dead and he had quietly and seamlessly inherited one of the largest fortunes in America between the two of them, and for some reason he kept all eight of their combined homes around the world and also the ranch he had bought on his own. Rumor had it people were worried Beau was 'losing it' because oddly, he ordered fresh flowers to be put in every house each week in case he were ever to go to any one of them, but he never went anywhere anymore other than the ranch.

"Go and see him," my mother said. "That will douse all this self-pity going on here. One look at him and you'll know how lucky you are. I ran into his cousin yesterday and he said Beau heard about what happened to you and is very concerned. You should go and see him today."

I laid back down in bed. "I'm not sure I'd be good company."

She pointed at me sternly. "Get out of that bed and go see your friend! Besides, it will be good for your daughter to see you up and about too."

She was right. I got up, took a shower, then went downstairs and played with Blakely. She was being such an angel still about this whole thing. She hadn't asked for 'dah' again once since we got here, but, since Barc often went 'missing' from her life for weeks at a time I guess she was just used to him being gone most of the time.

I called Beau's home and Joseph, his valet, said Beau was in his hydro-therapy for his muscles, but that I should come by at two that afternoon. He added that Beau would be delighted to see me.

I drove to Beau's ranch and as I got out I heard Rachmaninoff's second symphony floating out into the sunlight. Joseph greeted me with a kind smile and led me into the dark, cool hacienda with its Spanish Mission antiques.

Beau sat in the middle of the room in a state-of-the-art hospital chair. Though I tried to hide it, I was completely taken back by his appearance. His once superb, muscular frame was clumsily placed into the chair and now, devoid of any real tone or limb animation, he appeared to have faded to the point of looking like a lifeless ventriloquist's dummy dressed in rich Paul Stuart clothes.

Beau smiled and said, "Melli! Oh, bright angel! How I have longed to see you!"

I went to speak, but instead became overwhelmed with emotion. I wasn't expecting to see him looking this way. I went into sobs, followed by a tor-rent of tears.

Finally Beau called out, "Joseph... best bring our Melanie a towel!"

Joseph brought me a hand towel and as I cried into it Beau said, "Notice I don't tell you *not* to cry, Melanie... for I gave up asking people not to. I've learned there's no point in asking them to do something they can't possibly do, so go on and let your tears fly girl, like all the others... but as for me, I'm counting my blessings... if that truck had hit me just two vertebrae higher I would be hooked to a breathing machine for *life*."

I kept trying to speak and either nothing came out or I went into more sobs and tears. I saw some paper and a pen on a writing table nearby and I quickly picked it up and wrote: I'm sorry.

"You should be," Beau said sarcastically, trying to lighten the mood. It worked.

"Oh Beau!" I finally said, finding my words again. "I just can't believe it—what's happened to you..."

"Well, be it ever so humble and simple, 'that's life,' and there's really nothing like life—no matter *what* state you're living it in—and I just try to remember that every day."

I couldn't believe how sad I'd been just hours before over what I now considered my silly, 'little' problems compared to his situation. At least I had my health, my daughter, my family—and that was really everything. My mother was right. I had to count my blessings and get back out there. I picked the paper and pen back up and quickly wrote: Would you like to go to the Driller's Club ball with me this weekend?

Beau seemed pleasantly surprised. "Wow, you need a date *that* badly?" he joked as he mulled it over. "Well, it's been awhile since I went out dancing, but, knowing you, that question is really an 'order' and not a question at all, so I don't *really* have a choice to say no, do I?"

I shook my head playfully as I wrote: Black Tie ... Saturday, 8:00... and don't be late!

I kissed his forehead tenderly; it was so cold. My tears spilled onto Beau's face and he recited a part of a poem I remembered he had written back in high school:

"Is not the first kiss of sweet rain,
rain enough to say 'sweet, it rained?'
More kisses are just 'more rain than this,'
but never sweeter than that first kiss."

I went to wipe away my tears, but Beau shied away his head and said, "No, leave this sweet kiss there... let me retain some part of you with me until Saturday."

I went out to my car and drove away. Once I had left the grounds of his sprawling estate the tears got so bad I could not see and I pulled over to the side of the road. I sat there and sobbed for an hour, but I knew I was crying not just for Beau, but for myself again as well. I had to find the strength to pick myself up and really live again. If Beau could do it after all he'd been through, I had no excuse.

The night of the Tux and Boot ball there was a Texas full moon, a comfortable, rare breeze in the air, and the main ballroom was decorated fabulously for the event. An ocean of Dom Perignon was being served and Beluga caviar was available everywhere you looked on shiny, silver trays. All the men were in tuxedos and every pretty maiden there wore a couture gown and at least a million dollars in jewelry... the night was set to be both grand and magical.

I met Beau outside the front entrance so I could be the one to push him through the main ballroom doors, not Joseph.

"I've got him," I told Joseph, who looked at Beau, unsure.

"Are you sure?" Beau asked. "Because I don't mind if Joseph chaperones."

"What? You don't think I can handle pushing you in *this* for a few hours on polished marble? Do you not remember I have a toddler who I've pushed around in a stroller over uneven, concrete payment all *over* New York?"

Beau laughed and knew I could handle it. "Okay Joseph, looks like you have the night off now," Beau said to him.

Joseph nodded respectfully and went back towards the handicap-accessible van that had brought them both there along with Beau's driver. Meanwhile, I pushed Beau into the same place where Barclay and I had had our wedding reception four miserable years before, determined to have a *better* time tonight at this ball than I did back then.

But I wasn't expecting the immediate looks of shock we got—or even rude, outright stares. It was ghastly; the hundreds of dressed-up partygoers, many of whom had been in Beau's and my social circles our whole lives, now looked horrified that I had even brought him to this event as I wheeled Beau past the dance floor, and then went on to try and find a vacant table for us to settle in at. But it seemed every one we passed was either already filled—or the people already at a partly-filled one gave us a look to say they definitely *didn't* want us joining them—so I kept going.

A few people gasped and some even looked away, pretending we didn't exist, but I didn't care that I was ruining their 'good time' by bringing Beau as my date. Let all these selfish souls hide in their limos and private clubs and pretend there is no misery and disaster in the world... let them face the cold, hard facts as they looked at both me and our once beautiful, healthy Beau now...

"Mel, I think I'd like some air," Beau said once he could sense we were not welcome anywhere either. I felt bad and knew he was right. These were not the kind of people who would even try to understand anything troubling. They never wanted anything to ever affect their perfect, 'carefree' lifestyles.

"Sounds good," I said as I pushed Beau out onto the balcony and into the warm night air. The moon was glowing beautifully above us, and the few people out there soon found reasons to go back inside.

I thought Beau would get embarrassed or upset, but instead, he only laughed. "Well, *that* was a cheery bit of business! One would normally have to go to a funeral to see so many stricken faces saying, 'wow, he *doesn't* look *good!'*"

"I'm so sorry, Beau—"

"Don't be. I know you didn't know how they'd treat me, and actually, this was a real treat, to see all my old friends again," he said, with true gratitude.

"Don't any of them ever come to see you?"

"No. I mean, they did, at first. But not anymore, and it's okay. They are not selfish," he said. "They are afraid. They fear becoming a wretched scrap like me, and who could blame them? The night this happened to me I was coming home from an event just like this one after having the time of my life… but like my father always said, 'life is just a big casino—the cards come at you and you turn 'em up, and—good or bad—you must play 'em as best you can.'"

"You were so good to everyone Beau, especially me, all through school. I hate that this has happened to you."

Beau suddenly looked up at the moon as he reflected back, "I had wanted to die at first you know, I even felt like I had for awhile… I had fresh flowers put in all of my homes every week just like you would on a grave, for the homes were all my 'tombs,' just waiting for me to finally die in one of them. But then, in time, I was suddenly just glad one day that I even had *this much* fragment of life… Oh Mellie, what a thing it is to be ALIVE—to have even the *least* wanted seat at the long table of LIFE! I mean, just look at those stars turning up there—burning with fiery, icy envy at this—*our meager bits* of *glorious LIFE!* And those two, biggest stars are really lifeless, cold, iron giants Jupiter and Saturn out there weeping down with jealousy at all this life *we* possess… what they wouldn't give just to have *my* diminished portion even."

"Oh Beau, I can't believe how positive you are!" I said, truly astonished.

"It's enough that I am still here, and I'm glad that I have lived long enough to have been able to look at you again tonight too. You look beautiful Melanie, did I tell you that yet?"

"No, but thank you," I blushed, actually wondering how long it had been since I received a true compliment from a man. I couldn't recall Barc saying anything nice to me in years.

"Remember that Fourth of July at the fireworks we were all at together—your family and mine?" Beau said, reminiscing now. "A blind man was there looking up and everyone was saying, 'What is *he* doing here?'" And your dad said, 'Well, he showed up, that counts for something!' I never forgot that, and especially not now that I *am* that blind man… I showed up tonight and am still going through the motions of life, and this Melanie, counts for *everything*… thank you for bringing me. But I am tired now, so please, let's go to the van… it's time to go."

"Yes sir!" I said, and proudly pushed him all the way back out to the front of the club.

Joseph and his driver were waiting right where we had left them like they expected this to be a short outing. They worked together to secure the chair in the medical van and Beau was facing me as he was lifted into it.

"Goodnight, sweet Melanie," Beau said.

"No, I'm leaving with you," I told him, trying to get into the van to sit next to him.

"No," Beau said.

"Yes!"

"No... please, stay... stay and *live* Mellie. You belong here, where there is 'possibility' for you."

"*Possibility?*" I asked, not getting his intended innuendo.

Beau smiled before he continued, "Mel, I want you to *really* find love this time."

"What?" I said, thinking, *Where did this come from?* We hadn't even talked about me or my relationship problems, and he didn't seem to keep up with friends enough to know any of the rumored gossip, so I could only imagine it was something he heard from his cousin when my mother ran into him and talked about me being home, and *why*.

"You know what I'm trying to say... most women say they need 'security,' and hence, they don't marry the one they love... count your blessings and know that you now have another chance, a *real* chance at finding true love, so take it, and don't settle again."

I let this sink in as I smiled at my longtime childhood friend fondly. "I will," I promised, and meant it. "Oh Beau, I'm going to come visit you every day now I'm back! You make me feel so happy just being around you!"

"Of course you are," he said; then added, "but Mel, just so you know, sometimes people *mean* to come, yet can't for whatever reason, so if perchance you *don't* make it by tomorrow, the next day, or say, even 'never again,' know that I forgive the well-meaning gesture in advance, and let me leave you with just this; remember how much I love you and always will, especially for tonight."

It took all my strength to control myself, waving, as the van pulled away and I thought good old, wise Beau was letting me know he wanted me to spend my time getting my own shattered, wreck-of-a-life together instead of trying to ignore it by taking on his problems too. I thanked him silently for that, and then, when the van was completely out of sight, I collapsed as I sat down on the ground, sobbing, just as some party guests went by.

I heard one of them mutter, "*Disgraceful drunk!*"

The following Monday morning I awoke with a whole new attitude about things as I forced myself to begin the arduous task of finding a good, honest, and decent divorce attorney, if there was such a thing. I had been trying to contact Barc in order to expedite our divorce ever since I arrived in Houston, but he was not answering the phone or returning any of my messages. I finally stopped calling. An ex-partner in my father's law firm had drawn up the divorce papers I served, but he'd retired and only done it as a favor really. I would now have to find a new attorney in Houston.

I exhausted myself running around town, interviewing a few of the city's finest. But all the lawyers I interviewed were all extremely expensive and demanded huge retainers that I didn't have.

The first was a crotchety old man named James Wooly. He was so rude and clearly bored with my case that in the end, I walked out without even finishing our consultation. Then I met with Beth Newcomb, who, in just the short time I spoke with her, I could tell was highly intelligent and knew her stuff... but she was also a beautiful, petite blond, and it was a "man's world" in Texas. I didn't want to risk losing everything strictly due to a biased or even sexist judge, which was highly possible to get.

Next was a sleazy-looking lawyer with slicked-back hair named Theodore Walters. I saw dollar signs in his eyes when he heard the family names that were involved, and he made me feel like cornered prey surrounded by a very hungry pack of hyenas. "You really shouldn't settle yet, Mrs. Cunningham," he said. "I'd be happy to see what *else* we can squeeze out of this guy."

"Out of the question," I said sternly. "I want to move forward with my life. I just want out, with a fair and equitable settlement."

When he pressed the issue, I left.

The one lawyer I really wanted to hire, E.J. Gilbertson, was, by reputation, the meanest guy in town. "I'm not going to try to sweet talk you, Mrs. Cunningham," Mr. Gilbertson said confidently. "I'll let the figures do my talking for me."

He laid out a series of case summaries in front of me that dated as far back as five years. He had a nearly one hundred percent winning track record.

"This is very impressive Mr. Gilbertson," I said. "But I'm afraid your rates are a bit out of my league."

"It's my thirty-five years of experience, Mrs. Cunningham, and you get what you pay for. Be very careful if you're going to try to 'bargain shop' with a matter like this."

I connected with his personally and he gave me good advice—but he was just too expensive. I didn't want to burden my mother with a $50,000 retainer. Not after everything she was already doing for me by providing a home for myself and my daughter.

Because of the names involved, any lawyer I'd called was naturally very anxious to take my case; however, the only one who wasn't so anxious—or as expensive—was named Ray Morris. But his low rates bothered me after what Mr. Gilbertson said.

"I have to admit, your rates are within my range, Mr. Morris," I told him. "But you must understand my anxiety. I've been advised that it may be to my disadvantage to bargain shop in this field."

I could tell that he felt a little insulted by my comment, but he wanted me to hire him all the same. "I understand your concern, but you have to understand that most of the top lawyers you've talked to are fat cats who run their practices like mini-corporations. I like to think I run things a little more 'personally' here. I'm very plugged into the family court system. I'm friends with most of the family judges in this county—one of whom who will most likely preside over this case—and I'd like to be your friend as well. The reason I got into this practice was so I could help women like you get out of bad marriages. I may be a little cheaper than the others, but unlike them, you will have my full, undivided attention."

He was very convincing and I ended up having a four hour consultation with him at $400 per hour. I explained everything about my marriage to Barc. Mr. Morris seemed genuinely sympathetic and had warmth about my situation. I felt like I could trust him, so I gave him a $10,000 non-refundable retainer and left him two boxes of files containing bank statements, credit card statements, tax returns, brokerage account information, and other important legal documents.

Mr. Morris assured me he could handle everything and that it would be fast and simple. I went home thinking positively for the first time in a very, very long time.

Then, on a dreary, rainy afternoon just over a week later, as I was driving back home from the grocery store, Mr. Morris called me on my car phone. "Melanie, are you sitting down?" he asked. "I have some *really* bad news for you. I've read all the documents you left me and I'm so sorry to tell you this... but you won't be getting *any* kind of settlement from Barc. Zero... zip... nada."

I was stunned as he went on to explain to me that everything Barc possessed during our marriage was in a family trust, so it remained his separate property.

"You and Barc never had any community property together. His mother rented your apartment, and all of the summer and winter homes you enjoyed together also belonged to one of his parents. The bottom line is even after being married to him you have ended up with a big, fat zero. Furthermore, since Barc conveniently quit his job a few months ago and doesn't seem to be planning on getting a new one, he only has to pay the minimum child support in Texas, which is four hundred dollars a month."

I almost dropped my mobile phone and swerved off the road when I heard this absurd and depressing news. "Surely there must be some huge mistake!" I said, trying to steer the car straight. "I'm supposed to live in Houston on four hundred dollars a month with my daughter? That's impossible! How can *anyone* support a child on four hundred dollars a MONTH? Even people on food stamps must get more money than *that!*"

"I'm sorry Melanie, but that is the state minimum, no matter *who* the dad is."

"So," I stammered, trying to contemplate what this all really meant. "You're telling me I'm back in Houston with nothing to show for my failed marriage to this loser except a daughter and no real money at *all* to support her?"

"I'm afraid those are the facts and I can't do anything about it," Mr. Morris coldly consoled.

I hung up and cried the whole way home. It appeared the facts wouldn't have changed no matter which lawyer I had hired, but I couldn't help but feel that hiring Mr. Morris was a very costly mistake.

How could Barc do this to me, I thought, *and to his very own daughter?* It now became obvious to me that Barclay had never cared about anyone other than himself, and that his family had never really been looking out for anyone else but themselves either when they tricked me into marrying him. I felt completely alone and like I couldn't trust anyone.

I needed help and had no one to turn to. My father was dead and I knew I couldn't burden my mother to fight my battles for me with one of the higher-paid attorneys, especially since she was letting Blakely and me live with her rent free indefinitely. I wished I could use some of my trust fund money, but since it was still locked into the long term C.D. for several more years, it was out of the question. I thought of pawning some of my jewelry, but the only really expensive items were all gifts from Oldie, and I couldn't bear to part with any of those, ever.

When I finally arrived home, I sat down with Blakely and held her. I was trying not to cry, but it was hard not to. My daughter looked up at me with pleading eyes.

"Mummy, it's okay," she said, patting my arm. She had always been intuitive and in-tune with my feelings. I hugged her tightly.

Chapter 19

$\mathcal{I}$ tried relentlessly to get in touch with Barc to start the paperwork to collect my "state minimum child support" of four hundred dollars—and hopefully convince him to pay a bit more since she was his daughter, too—but he was nowhere to be found. It seemed no one had seen him anywhere—in New York, Newport, Palm Beach, Dallas, or Aspen—and if they had they weren't about to let me know that. He just 'disappeared' completely; meaning I now couldn't collect any child support at all or get the divorce finalized. It was infuriating.

Blakely was bouncing off the walls more and more each day, and I knew I had to find a way to keep her entertained and playing with other kids. September was fast approaching, so I felt it was the perfect time to get her signed up for preschool. I started researching all of the local ones around.

The school I found with the best program was called "One Step at a Time." It was a very upscale, private preschool and daycare center at an Episcopal church, which met my high standards perfectly. The only problem was the price.

I didn't want to ask my mother to help pay for it, for I still felt bad that she was doing so much already, and since asking Barc to help was now completely out of the question I knew that only left two other options—his parents.

Things with Helen and I had become a bit rocky since I left Barclay, so I decided to call Foxy first. I didn't know him well—he was only present a few times at some holiday gatherings and during that one visit Barc, Blakely, and I all made to Palm Beach—but I of course knew him by reputation and from his occasional drunken, late-night calls to Barc. And besides, he had once told me to let him know if his granddaughter ever 'needed anything,' and she now did.

I had always secretly regarded Foxy as the perfect father-in-law. He was a scratch golfer and was constantly invited to many exclusive golf clubs for member guest tournaments all over the U.S., which meant that he was never at any of his beautiful estate homes located all around the country for very long, and he often encouraged family members to use any of them whenever they wanted to. The last two winters he let me, Blakely, and Joy use his home in Palm Beach to escape his loser son whenever we needed to, and it was a real blessing.

I called to ask if I could meet with him, and Foxy told me the timing was perfect and to just come by his office on Thursday, about 'two-ish.'

I arrived at his upscale office on time the very next week, but strangely, there were no staff members anywhere to greet me.

"Well hello there, Melanie," Foxy said, appearing out of a doorway and warmly greeting me himself with a peck on the cheek. He was about the size of a jockey and all wrinkled-up from too many golf games in the sun as well as now entering his true 'golden' years.

"Where is everyone?" I asked, scanning the huge office suites around us that were all eerily vacant.

"Oh, I told them all to take the rest of the day off after lunch," he said.

I didn't say anything.

"Please, won't you join me in my study?" Foxy asked.

I dutifully followed him. His office was very tastefully decorated in the finest English antiques, and he had signed pictures of celebrities from all over the world on the walls. I took a seat in one of the two leather-padded chairs directly in front of his rather large, imposing desk.

"Mel, you look fantastic!" Foxy gushed, sitting down across from me and behind his huge desk. "Getting a divorce seems to agree with you."

"Really?" I said, and then told him all the facts I'd just gotten from my attorney.

"I'm not in the least bit surprised," Foxy said, shaking his head understandably. "I've been through this shit so much I know *exactly* what you're going through. Say no more—I want to buy you a car, first of all, and then I want you to know that *all* of Blakely's educational needs are going to be met."

I felt relieved and was glad I came.

"So, where have you two been staying?" he continued causally.

"Well, your S.O.B son has basically dumped us out on the street," I said. "So we have nowhere else to live except at my old house with my mother. Can you imagine how depressing it is? A single mom living at home at *my* age?"

"Mel, let me tell you something…" He got up and moved around to the front of the desk, perching on the edge of it right in front of me. "I made sure when I set up the trust for Barc that he wouldn't have access to any *serious* money until he turned at least forty… he's *way too* immature to handle it, I mean, he's already blown through three rather sizeable trusts and still has nothing meaningful to show for it."

He leaned over and rested his hand on my shoulder momentarily, but it lingered there for a breath too long. "I'm *so sorry* that you're just now finding all this out about your husband after years of marriage and a child. But, I may be able to help you, Melanie." He looked at me fondly. "I have more money than I can *possibly* spend in a lifetime dear, and I'd love nothing more than to spend it on *you!* Would you like an apartment? How about the penthouse at The Harrington? It's an exclusive, brand new, high rise condo just around the corner from my office here."

He took my face in his hands and made sure I was looking straight into his eyes to emphasize what he was saying. "I'll pay *all* of your bills and give you a twenty-five *thousand* dollar a month allowance. Believe me, I'm an old pro at juggling wives and mistresses. Hell, I've been doing it my whole life!" He winked; his eyes ablaze with excitement.

"You can of course use my houses in Beverly Hills—did you know I just got one there?" He grinned enticingly, and then continued on, "Palm Beach, Dallas, New York, and Aspen anytime you want—you'll get keys. Fly first-class to any one of them anytime you want, whenever you want to…"

He reached out, and, ever so gently, touched the strap of my bra peeking through my blouse. "I could order you the entire Victoria's Secret spring collection, just for shits and grins. What do you say?" he said teasingly.

I wanted to slap the old sucker, but instead, I politely removed his hand and readjusted myself in my seat, the furthest away from him as I could. He remained uncomfortably close, and I struggled to maintain my composure.

"I'm so bored with Buffy—you remember, my fifth wife?" Foxy whined, seemingly oblivious to the fact that I was rejecting him. "All she does is drag me to every conceivable charity ball filled with the same old bags with their gay 'walkers.'" He chuckled at this, elderly widows arm-in-arm with their gay hairdressers. He moved his leathery hand to the top of my thigh and rubbed it up and down. "I'm tired of buying these expensive tables week after week. She drives to Neiman Marcus every morning to see how much she can charge to my account. She's so addicted to shopping that I've finally had to hire a shopping chaperone! The rule is she can only stay in the store for two hours and then she's done—she has to leave the store. Isn't that *absurd?*"

He waved his hand in the air with disgust, and I was glad it was now off me. He continued whining, "And even wearing thousands of dollars in designer clothing doesn't make her look *any* better either. She's not aging very well, and all she does is gossip incessantly. She's an empty-headed *bimbo!*"

None of this information was news to me, but I was appalled and disgusted by how Foxy was talking about her. After all, she was still his wife.

"But I can tell that you're different, Mel. You and I, we could have 'fun' together. I may be eighty, but I've still got it if you know what I'm *saying...*"

"Loud and clear, Foxy," I said, trying to keep things light-hearted, but I started looking for the door.

Foxy shifted uncomfortably while still leaning back against his desk. "In fact, seeing those bare legs right now has got my soldier standing at attention! I can't even stand up!" Amused by his own comment, he chuckled as he looked at me with a disgusting, vile, wide-eyed grin.

I couldn't believe this dried-up old man was actually propositioning me—and he was my own father-in-law! I wanted to scream, "Stop, you disgusting old fool! I'm not some bubble-headed bimbo you found 'fishing' for rich men at the club!" But I knew because of Blakely I had to keep my cool. He was still, after all, her grandfather too.

Foxy leaned towards me and tried to kiss me with his wrinkled, puckered-up, old and tired lips, which completely catapulted me over my threshold of shock, disgust, and anger—and I knew I needed to flee this salacious scene immediately. I avoided his lean-in by jumping up to grab my coat and muttered, "I need to get home and let the babysitter go. I'll be in touch."

"I think you should go home and think about my offer, long and *hard,*" Foxy said, emphasizing the word 'hard' in case I hadn't gotten his other blatantly obvious comments from before. "Because I really think I'm your *only* way out of this nightmare that my misbegotten son has now handed to you."

I nodded and made my way out. As I left his office I considered the alternative: a few moments of discomfort in exchange for a free ride for myself and my daughter. I instantly started to shake all over—not believing I had actually let myself even *imagine* it!

Oh my God, I thought. I was more desperate than I thought!

I was upset the entire drive home to Houston as I recalled all the times Foxy invited me to his homes around the country and had given me gifts of money, jewelry, and clothes. Now I realized they were all just attempts at luring me into his perverted web one day.

Once I was home I called Helen immediately and told her about the degrading and horrific encounter with Foxy.

"Dahling, Foxy's been a cheat his entire life—that's why I divorced him!" she said. "You know he married his teenaged nanny once, didn't you?"

"Yes," I answered.

Helen then went on to tell me the story of what happened with her *other* ex-daughter-in-law, Lena, who was Stewart's first wife. "Stewart had left Lena for his young, hot secretary—like father, like son, I guess—and also left Lena penniless. She had no family to turn to for help and three young boys to support, so Foxy made her an offer she *couldn't* refuse. She lived rent free on his ranch outside of Dallas for six *years* until she remarried, but even now they still stay 'connected,' if you know what I mean..."

My stomach turned. I had no idea this had gone on, for by the time I had met Lena once at a holiday gathering in Palm Beach she was remarried and all seemed fine between her and Foxy. They each mainly focused on the three boys the whole weekend, who all seemed pleasantly 'normal' too. Though now that I thought about it, it *was* strange that her new husband wasn't able to 'make the trip...' The similarity of the situation sickened me.

"Buffy doesn't like the country," Helen continued. "She says it makes her 'sneeze,' so Foxy must be wanting some 'fresh hot flesh' to go traveling there with him in and out of the city."

I got light-headed with the realization that I, in fact, was just more 'fresh hot flesh' to him. *Who are these people?* I thought. *What's wrong with them? Don't they have any scruples or morals?*

I thanked Helen for this new information, though it didn't make me feel any better. But at least it confirmed my first reaction even more about *not* wanting to go down a path similar to poor Lena. I was desperate, but not dim-witted. There had to be another way.

"Helen, I know we've had our differences, but you've always been kind to me," I said, knowing I now needed to get some distance from the whole crazy Cunningham family. "I just wanted to say good-bye and thank you for all of your help and support all these years."

There was complete silence for a few seconds, and then Helen spoke. "I've seen a total change in you since the baby was born, Melanie. I'm very proud of you. I know how hard it is to work all day and come home to a vivacious preschooler. And men *never* help out either. But not to worry... God will take care of everything." Her Christian Science philosophies still occasionally came out, and this seemed to be an instance where she felt one was necessary.

"Yeah," I said. "Maybe he'll buy me a really nice house in Houston and pay for everything... if I sleep with him!" I added jokingly.

For once, Helen laughed.

We hung up and I called Foxy back immediately.

"Mel! So good to hear from you so soon!" he said, truly sounding excited. "Can I expect you for cocktails tonight?"

"Actually Foxy, no," I told him firmly. "I want you to know that while I appreciate your generous offer, I've thought a lot about it and though I am a bit overwhelmed, I won't be needing your help after all."

"Well Mel, I don't see what other options you could possibly have, but fine. And if you change your mind, the offer still stands. You know where to reach me, dear."

"Thank you Foxy. But really, 'no thanks,'" I said again, even more firmly, for I knew this was a man who was used to getting his way. But there was no way I'd accept his obscene offer—ever—though I still knew I needed to make him think that I thought he was a 'saint' for making it. I didn't want to risk him kicking Blakely out of his life—or will—so I quickly added, "But it was *very generous* of you to offer it all, and I do want you to know I *really* appreciate it."

His ego was kept intact as we hung up.

Foxy was a disgusting human being, but I hadn't made it through everything I had gone through so far in my life just to become some old geezer's glorified prostitute. I knew I could make it another way. After all, I had *other* skills.

The encounter with Foxy had left me only two other options, and since Helen didn't offer to help out financially anymore when we spoke, I now knew I was down to one. It was all up to me. I had to go back to work, and the fastest way I could think of to do that was to start up my catering company again.

My business in New York had been very lucrative for four years, and I now had a lot of experience cooking for both small cocktail events and large dinner parties. My limit was seventy-five people—I'd never catered anything larger before—but I knew this was a great, standard size limit for many kinds of business and private-party type of events. It could be perfect to get it started again here, and I knew just who I wanted to have as my partner for it, too.

"Mom, how would you like to help me start up a catering business here? We could rent a space for a kitchen and use your contacts to get started," I said. My mother's culinary skills were legendary and she often hosted luncheons for her bridge club. I knew they would all want her to cook with me for their other private events too.

"I don't know Melanie," she said. "I've always only cooked for fun. I don't think anyone would actually hire me."

"Don't sell yourself short!" I told her. "I think we can do this! I'll handle the business aspects and we'll hire a few chefs to help us out, so you don't have to do all the cooking—just use your fabulous recipes and guide them. And I'll cook too, of course. It really helped out when I was doing this kind of business in New York when I needed more money, and I know I can make a good living at it here if I did it full time now."

"Okay Melanie...," she said, coming around to the idea. "Let's look into this a little further. I have to admit I've been feeling a bit down since your father died with too much time on my hands. I think this might help to get me out of the house more."

Luckily, my mother had many friends who knew what a great cook she was, so word spread fast about out new business and we were able to get it established quickly. We called it "Caviar Dreams."

With Mom's help I rented a small commercial kitchen near our home and hired three cooks to assist us. We'd make everything from appetizers to large-scale buffets, and then deliver the food to some of Houston's top law firms, corporate businesses, and private family functions. The money I made was significantly lower per gig than what I made in New York, but at this point it really helped just to have something coming in to pay the bills. I was soon working eight to ten hours a day, seven days a week, at the catering business to keep Blakely and I afloat, but I still wasn't making enough to cover the cost of the private preschool I had found that I still wanted to enroll her in.

"Mom," I said, a little uncomfortably. "I really need to get Blakely enrolled somewhere for preschool, but it's really steep."

"Melanie, if you find a good place I'll take care of everything. You know that," she said warmly.

"I know." I hugged her. "I just feel like I'm relying on you so much with everything now."

"Sometimes we *have* to rely on each other. Besides, this is my only grand-daughter! I want her to have only the best!"

"Thank you. But you know once the catering business takes off even more I'm going to pitch in."

"I know Melanie... but please, don't worry about it. We're doing fine. In fact, since you're working so hard at trying to get this business off the ground and being a single mom, I also want to help you out by hiring a nanny for Blakely... a good friend of mine just told me her maid's sister just moved here from Mexico and needs work. It would solve *two* problems at once if we hired her, don't you think?"

"Oh yes—thank you, Mom!" I said, truly grateful. I was really glad I had come home.

I called my mom's friend immediately and arranged to meet her maid Carina along with her sister, Sondra, at a local Mexican restaurant to inter-view her the following day. She was in her early twenties and was pretty with long black hair and very dark skin. Her girlish jeans and T-shirt made her look even younger.

"Hi, I'm Melanie St. John," I said, shaking her hand. It felt good to be using my maiden name again. "You must be Sondra."

"Si, senora," Sondra responded shyly.

"Habla Ingles?" I asked her, using the Spanish I'd learned while earning my bachelor's degree in Spanish.

"No senora," she shook her head sadly.

I then learned through her sister that Sondra spoke a regional Spanish that was much different from what I'd studied. As we ate chips and salsa, Carina translated her sister's long, sad tale of making it to the United States...

It had taken her three months and all the family savings to pay a 'coyote'—a person who smuggles illegal immigrants across the Texas/Mexico border—to get her here. Sondra had walked for miles and miles in the desert at night once she left her tiny village, and then snuck onto three different buses and hitchhiked rides with strangers for several days before she finally made it to the border where her coyote met her. He was extremely paranoid of the border patrol and literally grabbed her and threw her into the back of his beaten-down, dirty, rusted-up truck—then covered her with a huge bag of fertilizer. It was scorching out and smelled horrific, but after all she'd been through just to get to that point, she didn't complain and endured it for the whole four hour drive to San Antonio. Once there, he put her on a Greyhound bus to Houston where her sister Carina met her at the bus terminal.

I couldn't believe Sondra had endured all that and felt that just like Beau, here was someone else who was now giving me inspiration and putting my own situation in true prospective. My problems didn't seem so insurmountable after I listened to *her* story.

A busy but friendly waitress finally came over to our table. "What would y'all like to drink?" she asked, somewhat rushed.

As I ordered a margarita, Sondra leaned over to ask her sister something privately by whispering in her ear.

"She wants to know if she can get a Coke," Carina translated. "She's never had one before. Our village was so tiny and poor they couldn't ever get things like that there."

"Of course!" I said, nodding to the waitress, who also seemed to share my look of surprise and pity.

When the Coke arrived moments later, Sondra started to cry. "Thank you, thank you so much, senora," she repeated twice in halting standard Spanish through her tears. "This is such a treat!"

I had never seen anyone cry over a Coke before. I hired her on the spot.

Having a new nanny made me miss Joy, but I could hear her voice, thick with her Jamaican accent, asking, "Everythin' betta today now, mon?" I knew she would be happy for us.

Sondra helped me quite a bit, too. She worked five days a week and I couldn't have managed without her. Blakely loved her and she was a natural with children. While Blakely was in school she also helped out with the housework and laundry, tirelessly keeping everything organized and handled. This gave me more time to focus on the catering business and make even more money. I felt things were finally falling into place as the next couple of months went by.

Sondra always helped me sort out and organize my closet while she put the laundry away, and I truly appreciated it since now more money was coming in and I immediately picked up my "shopping habit" once again to spend it. I was always under a lot of stress and still feeling somewhat depressed—and a trip to buy new clothes, make-up, or another pair of designer shoes from Saks Fifth Avenue or Neiman Marcus became my standard activity to deal with it, though I knew I shouldn't be spending money this recklessly.

In time, my walk-in closet contained shoes and clothing I'd never even worn—or sometimes had simply forgotten I'd even bought. I felt bad and guilty over it, so to cover my feelings and to thank Sondra, after I paid her on Fridays I'd often send her home laden with a bag of sling backs and dresses too. It felt good to help a fellow woman in need, and it also made me feel less guilty for shopping again the very next day.

But it was on one of Sondra's days off that I found myself rummaging through my over-stuffed closet trying to find my favorite pair of Monolo sandals when I was unsuccessful, simply because there was so much stuff. I looked around at boxes I hadn't opened since I left New York and sighed, then began to reorganize it all. I knew I needed to get my shopping under control. I had too many other bills that needed addressing. So, I decided to take what clothes and shoes I knew Sondra wouldn't want to a local charity as the first step in getting rid of the 'addiction evidence.'

I reached up to try and grab some aged shoeboxes on the top shelf, but the boxes were piled up so high I couldn't reach them. I finally lassoed a box with a coat-hanger. As it fell, four other boxes crashed down along with it, spilling their contents at my feet. When they hit the floor, hundreds of pictures scattered everywhere like multicolored raindrops. It was like opening Pandora's Box. I knelt down and looked at the photos, reminiscing.

They were mostly of my blond and blue-eyed Blakely when she was an infant and throughout her whole first year-and-a-half of life. One was of her being held by a proud Aunt Winnie when she was first born... another was of her happily playing with Joy on the slide in the pen... the next was Blakely's first ride on the train with Helen in Newport... then one of her standing with Foxy on the veranda of his home in Palm Beach. They looked happy together, but I shuddered at the thought of my innocent daughter being around him ever again. In the next photo Blakely was trying hard to climb up onto Barc's lap in our New York apartment—but Barc's eyes were not in focus as he seemed to be pushing her away, not helping her up like she—and I at the time—thought he was doing...

I stared at the photo and tried to understand how I had ever gotten desperate enough to marry such a loser. I used to be smart and confident. When had I become such a victim? Was it after Hunter? Or even before him? I began to sort through the photos and put them back into their separate boxes—soon uncovering even more insights as I found many pictures of Barc and me, but with his eyes either always bloodshot or seemingly looking towards someone else who had caught his interest outside of the frame. I then found several old, long forgotten photos of Hunter, seeming to do the same. Each picture provided a clue to the mystery and brought back memories, both good and bad. I cried, knowing I had to get to the bottom of this or my problems—with men, shopping, and otherwise—would never get solved.

I made an appointment later that week with a psychiatrist named Dr. Ray Julia, a sleekly overweight man who reminded me of a seal. I entered his office and sat down on the leather couch facing him and counted the diplomas that covered the walls. There were seven. I had consulted with dozens of professionals back in New York—psychiatrists, psychologists, and family counselors—but none of them had this many credentials. I prayed he would finally be the one to help me remedy my situation.

Dr. Julia leaned back in his plush chair and opened his notebook, saying, "Melanie, how do you *feel?*"

Great, I instantly thought, they had each always started with this. *So he's going to be just like all the rest... asking the same, meaningless questions...* It made me so angry I almost got up and left, but instead, I simply stated it, firmly, "Angry."

"With *whom?*"

I sighed. "Look, I'm a recent divorcee and single mother who's gone from a very privileged life to struggling to get by. I'm so stressed out all the time I feel like I'm going to pop!"

Dr. Julia nodded and jotted something down in his notebook as he said, "I'd like you to start on an anti-depressant. It'll help stabilize your moods. Is that something you might be interested in?"

I sighed again and sat silently for a moment, then finally said, "Well, no."

All the doctors I'd ever consulted with wanted me to immediately start taking anti-depressants or anti-anxiety drugs, as if they were experimenting on something alien rather than dealing with a fellow human being. But I didn't want to end up a drugged-up zombie. I then realized it was my responsibility to take control of my own life, and sitting on some shrink's couch once a week and popping a few pills a day wasn't going to change a thing. Half the time it didn't even feel like they were listening to me anyway, but they all had told me the same thing, like a broken record: "As long as Barc was in my life, I was 'stuck,' so I had to get out of that situation." Well, I did, but I *still* didn't feel any better. But it didn't seem like this guy was going to be able to help me out now either, even with all those credentials.

So, I decided right then and there to quit wasting my time and money on shrinks. I was the one who was living this life. I was the one who had to learn how to deal with the situation, not them.

I had a long, uphill road to climb.

As the holidays approached I was still having a hard time getting my shopping under control, but I felt if I could just get my divorce finalized with Barc it would help ease a lot of the overall stress. I wanted nothing more for Christmas than to finalize the paperwork and move on with my life as the New Year began, but Barc was still nowhere to be found. So once again I had his family and friends try to contact him on my behalf, but it was still no use. He had 'disappeared' into thin air and no one seemed to ever know where he was. I couldn't believe he wasn't even going to wish his own daughter Merry Christmas, but it only showed me even more of his selfish, petty side really.

Whitney and Charles came to Houston for Christmas, and Mom and I cooked a fabulous holiday meal for us with all the trimmings.

While we were seated around the dining room table it was strange not to have Oldie there, but with both Charles and Blakely now also filling the room with smiles and voices it seemed to make the day special and memorable, if only in other kinds of ways.

"So, have you told them yet?" Charles asked Whitney with a grin.

Whitney smiled as she said, "No, but I guess Christmas would be the best day to…"

"What?" my mother asked excitedly.

"Well," Whitney started, "you know how Charles and I have been trying to start a family for awhile now…"

"*Yes?*" my mother said, clearly anticipating good news.

"Well, the fertility treatments haven't been working," Whitney said matter-of-factly, not noticing the instant look of disappointment in my mother's eyes. "So, we've decided to—"

"Adopt!" Charles said, finishing her sentence.

Whitney kissed him lightly. They often finished each other's thoughts this way. I tried not to seem jealous, but I secretly was.

"Oh, that's wonderful!" my mother said, truly happy just the same.

"Yeah," I agreed. "You two will make great parents together." I felt that for sure, but Whitney on her own as a single parent would be a whole different story. She still couldn't handle watching Blakely for more than twenty minutes at a time it seemed.

"Thanks," Whitney said, and then admitted sheepishly, "I was nervous to even bring adoption up because I felt I'd let us both down by not being able to conceive."

Charles immediately stepped in. "Whitney please—I've told you a million times the body is very complicated and it's not your fault! And besides, we won't miss out on any good genes from *my* side anyway since I come from a whole line of no-good Irish drunks!"

We all laughed, knowing he was joking, of course.

"Well, a child is a true gift from above, no matter if it's biological *or* adopted," my mother said, kissing Blakely on the head as she got up to pass around some warm rolls to everyone.

"That's right," Charles said. "We'll raise him up as 'ours' no matter what!"

"*Him?*" my mother picked up on immediately.

"Uh-oh!" Charles joked, looking 'caught' now—though only playfully.

"Oh, a son!" My mother's face brightened. I knew she wanted more grandchildren and was glad it was now happening for her.

"Yes," Whitney said proudly. "We've already met with a private adoption attorney and started the whole process... we were approved by a social worker immediately, and the attorney came through with several prospective mothers right away. We decided on an attractive couple who had six children, but then 'accidentally' got pregnant with their seventh, a boy... "

"Who will soon be our son," Charles said, taking Whitney's hand.

"He arrives in April," Whitney beamed.

I could feel the happiness everywhere, even filling up Oldie's empty chair at the head of the table. I was glad for Whitney and Charles and decided to let my feelings of jealousy fade away. I was blessed with a child too and knew just how wonderful it truly was, even if I was raising her 'up' on my own without a prince charming like Charles around to help.

We settled back into our busy work and school routines right after the holidays. Then, one Sunday afternoon in early March, while my mother and Blakely were playing outside in the backyard by the pool and I was at my office planning a large dinner party for later that week, a vintage Mercedes pulled into the circle drive, screeching its tires as it came to a full stop. Barc emerged from the vehicle with rage on his face. He rang the doorbell impatiently and my mother came in from the backyard to answer it, with Blakely in tow.

"Yes, hello?" my mother said as she opened the front door, keeping a frightened two-and-a-half-year-old Blakely safely hidden behind it.

Barc immediately tore into her with his vicious words. "I demand to see my daughter right this second or I'm going to fucking call the police!"

"Okay, Barc," my mother said. "Please, calm down, she's right here… Just let me call Melanie at her office and get her to come home first."

"That's right, call that giant BITCH! Get her OVER HERE!" Barc yelled as he walked into the foyer without being invited and slammed the door behind him. He went straight towards the bar in the dining room, not even seeing little Blakely hiding behind the large umbrella stand.

My mother knelt down to her. Blakely was visibly shaken by what had just happened. "Baby, I want you to go upstairs to your mommy's room and play, okay?" my mother whispered.

Blakely nodded her head "yes" and then quickly went upstairs, whimpering.

My mother phoned me. "Melanie, Barc just showed up at the house and he's in a rage. You need to come home right now. I have no idea how to handle him."

My stomach dropped as I first asked, "Is he drunk? Never mind, it doesn't matter—tell him I'll be there in less than ten minutes."

I dropped everything and sped home. My stomach knotted up in anticipation of the impending conflict. I could hear the raised voices of my mother and Barclay arguing as soon as I opened the front door. Barc had a wild look in his eyes and was flushed with anger as he met me in the foyer and got right in my face, unleashing a verbal salvo as he punctuated each word with stabbing motions at the air all around me. "FUCK YOU! How DARE YOU? You fucking BICTH! You FORBID ME from seeing my daughter? You monster bitch! That's NOT gonna HAPPEN HERE!"

I wanted to throw up, but I stood my ground. I didn't even know what he meant. "Barc, we haven't seen or heard from you in over six months. You have no business here. You've neglected our daughter and me! You're totally out of control and I don't even know what you're talking about!"

"I want to see my fucking daughter—RIGHT NOW!" He now made stabbing motions with his forefinger straight at my chest as he emphasized each word again.

"Why now? It's been months! Why do you all of a sudden care? What's up with that? Have all your tramps left you? Did you run out of drugs? Are you lonely and bored? Why the sudden interest?"

Barc snickered and replied, "I got myself an apartment here in Houston. This divorce is NOT going to be on YOUR terms and you're NOT going to take MY daughter away from me, got it?"

"If you're just doing this to piss me off then it's working, Barc," I told him firmly. "YOU are a sociopath. You're so sick that your whole life is about causing everyone else around you pain. You don't care about her, me, or anybody else. You only care about your damn SELF!"

"You know what? Fuck THIS!" He shoved me hard and I almost fell into an antique grandfather clock leaning against the wall.

Barc stormed up the stairs looking for Blakely. "Blakely! Where are you?"

I was right behind him, terrified at what he might do to her. "Blakely no—stay in your room!" I yelled, but it was too late. When we got to the top of the stairs she was already standing in the hall, clutching one of her favorite stuffed teddy bears—the one she only turned to when she wanted comfort.

"Hi baby," Barc cooed at her, but when he tried to pick her up, she started to cry hysterically.

"Put her down now!" I screamed.

Barc looked at Blakely with a confused and disgusted look; then handed her to me. "I'M CALLING THE POLICE!" he yelled. "And GETTING my parental rights! I want her every other weekend and every Wednesday night, you fucking BITCH!"

He went over to the phone sitting on a table next to a wingback chair in front of a large bay window in the hallway, picked it up, and dialed.

I hugged Blakely tightly, attempting to calm her down. I was so angry and hurt I wanted to lose control and scream at him on her behalf, but I didn't because I didn't want to expose Blakely to that side of me.

I overheard him telling the police, "She's refusing to let me see my child... Yes, it is my scheduled visitation time."

"*Liar,*" I muttered under my breath as I continued to rock Blakely, who was still sobbing.

Barc went downstairs to wait for the police. I heard my mother confront him in the foyer. "I won't accept this any longer, not in my home Barclay! You've abused my daughter and granddaughter for way too long and I want you out of my house right now!"

I couldn't believe my shy mother was actually kicking Barc out of her house! I was so proud of her, and thankful.

"Bitch, I'll leave when I'm damn well ready!" he said, then stepped outside and lit a cigarette on the front porch.

The police finally arrived. I came outside and tried to defend myself against Barc's accusations to the officers. There were two, Officer Young, who was callow and fat, and Officer Evans, who was older and more grizzled with wise eyes. They both saw what was going on and the older one said, "I'm sorry ma'am, but by law, we aren't allowed to get involved in domestic disputes over custody. I suggest you both call your attorneys."

Barc waved off the officers, went back inside, and immediately called his attorney. He arranged a meeting for the next day. I thanked the policemen for coming, even though it didn't do anyone any good.

Officer Evans pulled me aside. "Ma'am, I can see the state of mind your husband is in. If this custody battle gets physical, I want you to call this number." He handed me his card. "This is my direct line. If anything happens, I want you to call me. Because if he crosses the line, I can and *will* get involved."

I thanked him again as Barc—thankfully—sped off in a huff.

I went back inside and proceeded to call my lawyer, Mr. Morris, and arranged to meet with him the very next day.

When I met with Mr. Morris the following morning he agreed with Barc's lawyer that we needed to go through mediation and not the family court system. Both the lawyers and the mediator actually all thought they could 'reason' with Barc—what a joke. I knew Barc was going to do whatever he could to drag it out, and I was right. It took us over two weeks to finally even find a time when we could get the mediator, both lawyers, and both of us present.

Then the lawyers wasted over eight hours of both our time at $500 per hour, per attorney—plus the mediator's fee of $2,500—and nothing got resolved. My only focus was to protect Blakely and prevent Barc from having unsupervised visitation rights. But no one could agree on anything.

It became obvious that my attorney wasn't even interested in really helping me either because there was no big money in it for him. I felt that Mr. Morris regarded us as two silly and rich spoiled brats arguing over a cookie. I pulled him aside at the end of the exhausting day.

"What exactly am I paying you for, Ray?" I asked him angrily. "You sat there and barely said one word in my defense all day, and the one time you did speak you couldn't even remember my daughter's name! You're useless and *fired!*"

I knew this move would make the divorce settlement take even longer, but I didn't care. I needed to keep seeking supervised visitations no matter what. It was the only way I could think of to protect Blakely from Barc's incessant partying and drug use, which seemed to have increased tenfold since I left. He had no skills or knowledge of how to take care of a young child, plus I also knew he had Hepatitis. I was afraid Blakely would contract it by sharing food or water with Barc and, unless I could control the visit, I couldn't protect her from that.

I continued to interview more family law attorneys all over Houston. They all told me it was almost impossible to get supervised visitation in Texas. I discovered that in Texas a father had to be nothing short of a monster (meaning conducting extensive physical, verbal, or sexual abuse) in order to warrant reasons supervised visitation needed to be awarded—and there were very few other circumstances. Bad parenting skills, having a communicable disease, partying obsessively, and having overall poor judgment just wasn't enough to win a custody case with supervised visitation rights. And even worse—I couldn't prove Barc's recreational drug use—so no one really believed me.

In desperation, I went to Child Protective Services and pleaded my case. They told me the same thing, but I refused to give up.

Two weeks later I finally found a female attorney who'd been through a similar situation with a deadbeat dad. Lisa Williams was the niece of one of my mom's best friends. She was in her late thirties, tall and preppy-looking, and had short black hair with piercing green eyes. She'd gone to Columbia Law School, which interested me because, for a while anyway, she'd gotten out of Texas, and she seemed more sophisticated than the other lawyers I interviewed. And though I was a bit worried about the fact that Texas was still a 'man's world,' even in the mid-nineties, at this point in Ms. Williams's life she had already been screwed over twice in bad marriages by cheating spouses and now basically hated all men. She told me that was precisely why she had decided to devote her time and energy trying to help women like me in cases just like this, and would be glad to help me fight for supervised visitations.

It was definitely an upward battle in a state where men ruled, but Ms. Williams told me most of her clients were females who were getting screwed around just like me. She'd seen it happen so many times and was sick of it. She seemed tough enough to do the job, and I thought back to when I'd turned down the previous female lawyer because I was worried it would hurt my chances in court. I didn't want to make the same mistake twice. Ms. Williams was willing to take my case and at least she was honest—she told me our chances of winning were very, very slim. But she also insisted we take it up in the family court system this time, and I agreed.

We would have to get on a list to be called in front of a judge, but I was willing to wait for that day. We had waited this long since I had first left Barc, so a few more months wouldn't hurt now.

I was relaxing at home in the living room with Blakely the following weekend when suddenly there were strange sounds coming from the outside of the front door, like someone was trying to break in. My anxiety shot through the roof and I was afraid Barc had come back to cause another scene, or worse, try to take Blakely away this time.

"Go upstairs to your room," I told Blakely as I quickly got Officer Evans's card out of my purse and was ready to call him, but when I looked out the window I saw it was only Whitney, stumbling to try and open the door while also trying to balance several suitcases. Surprised, I opened it for her.

"Whitney!" I said, stunned. "What's wrong?"

She was crying uncontrollably. I brought her inside to settle her down and placed all her suitcases in the foyer for her.

"Mom!" I yelled towards the kitchen.

My mother rushed in and was just as surprised to see Whitney as I was. "Whitney!" she said, concerned. "What on earth's the matter?"

"Oh, Mom! It's just awful, *really!* Everything's a mess..." Whitney said as we all went into the living room and she began to tell us the surprising turn of events that had happened to her 'perfect' life back in New York.

"You know how we've been waiting on the baby to arrive all this time," Whitney said, doing her best to keep her composure.

"Yes," my mother said.

"Well, our friends Annie and Billie had been helping us get ready for him all winter, then suddenly in February they announced they were moving to Los Angeles—Annie had landed a role on a primetime sitcom with a very lucrative contract. She assumed Billie would want to go with her and try his luck in the movies instead of on soaps—but late one night I overheard Charles and Billie 'venting' behind closed doors.

"Billie said he'd auditioned in L.A. before and the only job offer he ever got was for a children's show—and he didn't want to give up his three-hundred-thousand-dollar a year salary for *that!* He also said he didn't want to sit around the pool and be supported by his 'wife,' and that's when Charles chimed in and said, 'Well, at least you don't have to deal with adopting a kid! Talk about babies being expensive... this one's already starting off expensive! And this urchin isn't even *mine*—I don't even want him either! I'm only doing this for Whitney, and what do I have to look forward to now but slaving away—all for the bastard son of a white-trash whore!'"

Both my mom and I gasped. What a terrible thing to say—or even think.

Whitney continued, "I know, I was horrified by Charles's attitude too—which he was obviously only expressing in 'Billie's' company. I mean, you both saw him at Christmas, he seemed completely on board with the whole adoption thing then!"

"Yes," I agreed, for he certainly did.

"I then realized there's a whole side to Charles I didn't even know," Whitney said sadly. "And it frightened me. He sounded so callous and brutal—nothing like I'd *ever* heard him talk like before!"

"But you've heard 'other' men talk like that," Mom said, obviously referring to Oldie when he was on one of his legendary rants. "Not about a child of course, but I mean just over whatever else was under his gaw."

"True," Whitney agreed. "And I mean sure... Charles *has* hardened a bit over the years, I've noticed—only to protect himself from all the medical horrors and deaths he's witnessed being a surgeon, I'm sure—but this seemed to be something much more than that even... But anyway, then Billie announced that he *wasn't* going to Los Angeles with Annie and the two of them decided to get a divorce. It made me so sad to see such good friends fall apart that way... Annie had been helping me prepare the nursery and I tried to convince her to work out their problems, but neither of them would budge on their career choices.

"Finally, Annie moved and Billie spent most of his non-working hours sad, alone, and at *our* house. Charles tried to take his mind off his problems with plenty of bicycling sojourns and sailing trips and he even canceled plans with me to spend more time helping Billie get over Annie leaving. I felt abandoned, but I figured competing with sports was not very unusual for a wife, right? And besides, I was busy looking forward to the new baby that was coming—for we had made a commitment to him, no matter what Charles had said to Billie." Whitney got quieter as she then confessed, "I figured Charles didn't know I had overheard him and he never said anything like that to *me*, so I just busied myself with preparing the nursery—I bought little blue clothes, a crib, and filled the whole room with toys and diapers—I knew Charles would feel different about him once he was living with us and was *real*. After all, how could you *not* love a baby?"

I bit my tongue thinking of everything I had and was still going through with Barc over Blakely after he said *he* wasn't happy about becoming a father, but I knew this was Whitney's time to vent, not mine. So I let her continue uninterrupted.

"Then Charles started spending *all* his weeknights working late at the hospital and *all* his weekends sailing and bicycling with Billie. It was getting on my nerves," Whitney said. "So last week I pleaded with him to tell

Billie that we needed some 'alone' time too, especially since the baby would be coming soon—that day it was exactly two weeks from its due date—but Charles just said it would be cruel to leave Billie alone in his 'fragile' emotional state. I wanted to fix him up on a date, but Billie told me he wasn't ready to 'date' yet, when *really,* the two of th—" All of a sudden Whitney began to sob, and my mother and I both looked at each other knowingly.

"Oh, Whitney, I'm so sorry," my mother said, placing her hand on Whitney's shoulder gently just like she had done the day I returned home from my failed marriage.

Whitney knew we both got it now as she continued, "I'll never forget what he said, 'Whitney, I'm attracted to men. I've finally realized it and I can't deny it any longer. But what kind of life will I have as a gay man? I'll lose everything!"

"Oh no, you mean he wanted you to *stay?*" I said, my jaw dropping at the thought of my sister living her life as his 'beard.'

Whitney couldn't help but now laugh through her tears as she looked at our shocked faces. "I know, I couldn't believe he was serious about that myself," Whitney said. "But he fell to his knees and wept, begging me to. I finally told him that maybe he was just under too much stress and needed to get psychiatric help, but he blurted out, 'The truth is I'm in love with Billie and *not* you! I might as well just kill myself right now!'"

"Oh dear," my mother said, still trying to take the whole situation in.

"He said it with so much pain I actually felt bad for him," Whitney said, reflecting back sadly. "But I was also stunned and felt betrayed. Everything seemed so perfect before, but now we're both these tortured creatures... How did all this happen?"

Whitney cried into Mom's arms. I tried to absorb what I was hearing, but I could scarcely believe it myself.

"So what's going to happen now?" I asked, with some trepidation.

"He told me he wanted a divorce and would be moving in with Billie. He said he doesn't blame me for being mad but says he has no other choice. He told me he wouldn't leave me high and dry—that there'd be a 'generous' financial settlement—but all the things he said seemed rehearsed... like he'd been planning what to say for days, maybe even *months.*"

"What about the baby?" Mom asked.

"Exactly—I asked him about that too, for I still wanted him, and the birth is only next *week!* But all he said was, 'What baby?' He was so cold about it. He said he'd taken care of everyone else his entire life and was now ready to *only* take care of himself. He then said to call the lawyer and call the whole thing off, telling me to tell him he couldn't try to be a father to a child he didn't even want... so, I did, yesterday..." She put her head down on the table and sobbed.

My mother put her hand over Whitney's. "Oh, Whitney, honey... I know how hard this must be," she said. "On top of everything else, I know how much it must kill you to have to come back home, running to me."

My mother then looked at me as she put her other hand on mine. "You too, Melanie. You both had lives outside of Houston, but things went sour and now you're both back where you started. I get that this must be difficult, but I'm telling you both right now not to feel that way. I'm going to be here for both of you no matter what, just like Oldie would have been."

All of us tensed at the mention of his name. Our mother started it, but we all finished it in unison: "Remember... when life happens, you happen _back_!" We all smiled at Oldie's old trademark saying and instantly felt better.

Mom was right. We had a good family, and we needed to stick together and help each other out now. We spent the rest of that evening having dinner, talking about our lives, reminiscing about Oldie, and hoping for better futures.

That night I slept in a state of contentment that I'd not felt for longer than I could remember.

Chapter 20

𝒲ᵂ𝒽itney settled back into Houston life over the next couple of months as she finalized her divorce through e-mails and telephone calls easily and amicably. Since she was getting a sizable alimony check, as well as half of the sale of her and Charles's historic New York mansion, she knew she was at least set financially. Her broken heart though, was a different story.

I wished my ex-husband would have been so mature and giving to me and Blakely financially, but it seemed Whitney and I had complete opposite experiences when it came to both marriage and divorce. But at least I wasn't as heart-broken over my spilt. For me it was more like a relief, and I just wanted it to be over.

Two months later my lawyer finally called.

"Good news, Melanie," Ms. Williams said excitedly. "We have a closed-hearing court case arranged for next week."

Finally, I thought. It was almost a year since I had left Barc.

We both hoped for the best and hung up, but on the day of the case we found out it was all to happen in front of an old, jaded, hick judge who was so bored with our hearing that he actually nodded off a few times during the long, nine hour day.

I took the stand and Barc's attorney, a tall, young, super-aggressive man in a cheap suit, attacked me like a piranha. His name was Rod Dillion.

"First of all, *Mrs.* Cunningham," Mr. Dillion said, emphasizing the 'Mrs.' part. "Your sorry attempts to look like a schoolmarm are neither convincing *nor* amusing. What needs to be known is that you are a selfish woman who only cares about *herself.*"

I had dressed very conservatively for court and pulled at my shirt's collar, which was hugging my neckline.

Mr. Dillion paced the floor as he continued, "You abandoned my client, Barclay Cunningham—your *husband*—and took everything except the sparsest of belongings from *his* New York apartment. But that's not all you took. You also took a young daughter away from her father and out of a stable home. Do you *really* think you are someone who should be demanding supervised visitation?"

"I left because I was being verbally and physically intimidated and abused," I said. "And I'm seeking supervised visitation because of Barclay's hard partying, drug use, and the fact that he has a communicable disease I do not want my daughter to catch."

"Can you prove *any* of that, Mrs. Cunningham?" Mr. Dillion asked scornfully.

I could not and felt stuck. I didn't even have access to Barc's medical records to show the Hepatitis claim, and Mr. Dillion commented that bringing it up was just a vicious lie, insinuating that I was a liar. Then the onslaught of ridiculous accusations and assaults against my character continued. But I wasn't trying to be the controlling, vengeful, histrionic, or hateful person that Barc's attorney made me out to be, I just wanted to protect Blakely.

All the while Barc leaned back in his chair with a satisfied smile, while I gave him the nonstop, evil-eye look back. I tried my hardest to explain my concerns to the judge about the welfare of our child, but my pleas fell on deaf ears.

The judge eventually grew tired of the whole proceedings as they dragged on and he finally stopped them.

Ms. Williams and I both held our breath and hoped for the best, but he ruled against me and said we would have "joint, unsupervised custody, period." And it was just what Barc originally told his lawyer he had wanted too—every other weekend—but luckily he had gotten drunk that day and left out the 'and Wednesday nights too' part that he had originally told me.

The judge's words echoed through my mind as I repeated them over and over in my head: "We'd have joint, unsupervised custody of Blakely this way from now until she turned eighteen. Period."

I couldn't believe that this monster would have unsupervised access to my darling daughter for the next fifteen years, and there wasn't anything I could do about it now. In order for me to cope with this reality, it was necessary for me to start putting many of my negative thoughts, emotions, and feelings aside. Even though Barc had been a complete jerk and messed around on me throughout our whole marriage, he'd always be her father. And despite it all, I knew it was important for Blakely to have a strong and loving relationship with him, if that was even possible.

All I could hope and pray for now was that I could raise Blakely in a way that would not allow her to make the same horrific mistakes with men that I had. Stupid mistakes that somehow or another, I'd chosen for myself all on my own. I was determined to raise Blakely on those mishaps so she'd do things differently. I vowed she would one day have a happy, healthy relationship, home, and life. I just had to make sure Barc didn't do anything during his visitations to mess that possibility up.

Six weeks later, Whitney received her check for the sale of her and Charles' estate, and it was more than enough for her to buy herself a wonderful house right in Houston, not far from where we grew up.

"Congratulations," I told her as I helped her move her things into the warm, comfortable, two-story, Spanish mission-styled abode. "It's really nice."

"Thanks," Whitney said. "It's completely different than what I thought I'd be spending the rest of my life living in, but at least it's all mine and I never have to worry about losing it."

I left and went straight to Saks Fifth Avenue, telling myself I was there to find something as a nice housewarming present for Whitney, but I was only kidding myself. I wanted to buy myself a whole new wardrobe to make myself feel better. My daughter was with her deadbeat dad for her *third* weekend of unsupervised visitations, and I was going Crayola-eating crazy trying not to think of him hurting or neglecting her. And it didn't help that Whitney was now moving out and on with her life while I still couldn't afford to leave our childhood home.

I scanned the rows of designer stilettos, wanting to buy one of each in every color, but I kept telling myself Blakely and I would never get our own place if I kept spending what little money I was finally able to put aside so recklessly.

"Can I help you with a pair of those?" a polite salesman asked, happily sensing I was eager to buy.

I clutched my purse, knowing I had both cash and plenty of credit cards on hand.

"Ah, no thanks, I was just looking today," I quickly blurted out, then used all my strength and resolve to turn around and leave the store—fast. It was the first time in years that I'd ever left a store empty-handed, and it felt like a major accomplishment. In fact, it felt like I had just climbed Mount Everest.

I kept my "victorious" feeling going for days, then weeks, as I continued to stay away from the stores, saving towards a down-payment for a home. Then, several months later during breakfast one morning, my mother presented me with some exciting news. "Mel, you remember the townhouse down the street that Oldie bought as a rental property? The one Tony Rogers lives in?" she said.

I nodded as I ate my breakfast.

"Well, Tony informed me last night that he's taking a job in Atlanta. Do you want the house?"

I dropped my dry toast and ran over to hug her. I had no words.

"I've loved having you and Blakely here, dear," she explained. "But I know how hard you've been trying to get your own place and understand that you need to be on your own. Babysitting won't be a problem—you know I'm always available. After all, you'll only be five minutes away. And we'll still be working together, of course."

"Oh, thank you so much, Mom!" I said joyfully. "I love you!"

Once again, I packed for another change in my life. My goal was to be moved in by the end of the week. Oldie's townhouse was a good place to make a genuine attempt at a home for Blakely and myself, but on the day we moved in I couldn't help but feel a little down. I felt at my age I shouldn't be moving into new places and starting over, let alone moving into a place that resembled the townhouses I had lived in during college. But still, it was a generous offer to be gifted a place to live, so I put on a brave face for my daughter, Mom, and Whitney, who were all there to help.

Still, after Mom and Whitney left, I privately thought of the faux-Colonial, three-story building as the equivalent of a battered women's shelter as I drifted off to sleep.

But after the boxes were all unpacked and Blakely and I spent our first few days in our new home, I realized that this was a place where we could really start over. It had a backyard for Blakely... all my beautiful antique furniture from New York fit in it nicely, and I had also saved up enough money to buy all new appliances and have it professionally painted. Once everything was finished I loved it... and it was my very own.

Soon I had finally developed a steady and fulfilling daily routine. I'd wake up, get Blakely ready for school, have breakfast, and after that I spent my mornings managing my business, preparing whatever events we were catering that week. This went on for just over a year and a half, and even though both Sondra and my mom—and occasionally Whitney—were a lot of help, overall I was still adjusting to being a struggling, single mom inside. I had to admit, it totally sucked. I appreciated having the support of my family, but it was still a very lonely and simple life. I didn't go out much at all. I'd either bury myself in my work or Blakely, or lose myself in television and movies on my 'free' weekends when Blakely was with Barc—too depressed and worried about her to leave the house at all. I never dated anymore either, mainly because every man I met was married.

Then, out of the blue, Victoria called one day from New York. "Hi Mel!" she said happily.

"Oh Vic, it's so good to hear your voice!" I said, and meant it. We had completely lost touch with each other while our lives went separate ways.

I hadn't spoken with her for so long—since I had left Barc actually, almost two years ago.

"Melanie! Alexandra and I are going to Bermuda for the weekend and I can get you a ticket with my frequent flyer miles!" she said. "If you're not too 'busy,' I thought you could use a break and join us." She said 'busy' in the way a kid in elementary school would say it, like she was taunting me.

"I'm sorry I haven' t called you, Vic," I apologized. "It's just been tough juggling my business and Blakely—it's all been nearly impossible some-times even—"

"No need for excuses hon, just come! It sounds like you need to get away!"

"I sure could use a break..."

"Sooo...is that a *yes?*"

I sighed. "Yes, of course!" I laughed. "I've missed you Vic, and it would be nice to see Alex too. Listen, I need to arrange for my mother to babysit this weekend—but I'm sure she will, so count me in."

"Wonderful! I'll set up everything and call you back with details."

We hung up and before I knew it, I was on a plane to Bermuda three days later.

I'd never found the Caribbean to be particularly exciting—just as good a time could be found as close as Galveston, I thought, and even Palm Beach would have been preferable. But these days I didn't want to be near any ele-ment of my former life with Barc, plus, it was nice to have the camaraderie of Victoria and Alexandra again no matter where we were going to be.

We all had a happy, tearful reunion at the hotel, and then they both pursued two full, busy days shopping in the duty-free shops, playing sets of tennis, and snorkeling, but I preferred to soak in the rays on the beach with chilled glasses of white wine the whole time. It was hugely relaxing to sit and watch the turquoise waves lap the shore of Elbow Beach, and swoop-ing gulls lulled me into blissful complacency. This was the sort of thing I hadn't done in far too long.

In the back of my mind, however, I knew I'd soon have to peel myself up off this beach chair and return to my hotel room to pack for the flight back to Houston. Though I missed Blakely, the rest of my life back there wasn't as appealing to return to.

"Melanie!" Victoria said with wide eyes as she ran up to me, still in her tennis outfit. "You won't believe who I just saw at the cafe by the pool! Hunter's here—with his 'flavor of the month,' of course."

I felt a familiar stab in my heart at the mere mention of his name. I hadn't seen him since I had moved back to Houston and thought I no longer had any feelings left for him. Still, I couldn't help but react a bit shocked to this news. "So?" was all I could think to mutter.

"Well... don't you want to go up and 'surprise' him?" Victoria urged.

"Ha!" I scoffed. "That's the *last* thing in the world I want! We were over a long time ago Vic and I really don't want to talk to him." I thought to myself for a moment. "But still, I can't help but be curious... how does he *look?*"

Victoria grimaced and said, "Actually, Mel, I can't lie. He looks great. I didn't see *any* lines, but then, why should he have wrinkles? The man never showed any emotion, right?"

I chuckled as she helped me pick up my beach bag and towel.

"I've got an idea," Victoria said. "Why don't we pass by the café bar on the way back to the hotel? That way we'll come at them from the back so you can see him without being seen—you'll kick yourself later if you don't, Mel! I just know you—"

"Oh, all right. But just a quick *glance,*" I agreed. She was right. I would regret this later if I didn't take the opportunity to see him now.

We sprinted up the path and I stopped to peer around the corner of the bar. There Hunter sat—regal, bronzed, and emotionless—as his trashy-looking, barely-legal girlfriend babbled away, staring at him in admiration. I immediately noticed she was wearing rings on both her middle fingers—definitely a give-away that this was no debutante. The usual bemused expression on Hunter's face was a mask for whatever perverted thoughts he was thinking about while the poor girl continued to ramble on. I knew he didn't care in the least about what she was actually saying.

Even after everything Hunter had put me through, and what Barc had put me through, I still felt the urge to go up and talk to him. I had my cutest bikini on and felt good about myself. It was almost as if he had a hypnotic influence over me... but I snapped out of it.

"Nothing ever changes," I said to Victoria with a sigh. "Let's go."

We went back upstairs to our hotel room and said our good-byes to Alex, who was staying a bit longer than Victoria and me now since she had met a new guy there the night before and they had really hit it off. Over the weekend I had discovered that Alex had turned into quite the party-girl since I had last seen her in New York, and I could tell our lives would be drifting apart from this point on. We really didn't have anything besides Texas now in common.

"Thank you so much for including me in this much-needed Bermuda break," I told them both as Victoria and I packed our bags. "I really, *really* needed this," I added, and meant it, but little did I know before I had even come how much I really needed to see that with Hunter—and even with Barclay—I had now *truly* moved on... and it felt liberating.

Victoria and I shared a cab to the airport. During the drive we reminisced about the paths our lives had taken. She was both concerned and empathetic as I then burdened her with tales of the chaotic life that Barc had created for me—I hadn't wanted to spoil our weekend by saying too much beforehand, but now, in the close comfort of the cab's backseat, it felt like the right time to confess it all to her.

After my long saga Victoria turned to me and said, "Melanie you need to leave both Hunter and Barc in the Bermuda Triangle. You first got out of a long, bad relationship, then an even worse marriage—and you need to be careful not to get into a *third!* Don't carry those painful memories around with you. Leave them somewhere else—this is the only thing that gets me through the ghastly things I've been through with men."

"Thank you, Victoria," I said. "You're my best friend, and I'm not going to lose touch with you again—ever!" I made a vow to call her every Saturday, just as I had done with Oldie. She was thrilled.

We hugged each other tightly as the cab pulled up to our terminal outside of the airport; then went our separate ways once inside.

I had a lot of time to think on my flight back to Houston. I'd completely lost touch with my sympathetic confidant Victoria, and now, thank goodness, I had her back just when I needed her the most to help keep my hopes up about finding true love again. Now I was finally over my past, I was ready to.

Upon my return from Bermuda the following Friday afternoon, I took my car to get washed. It was a hot and humid day, and I was completely bored since my workday was done and Barc had just picked up Blakely for the weekend. I had no idea what I was going to do for the next forty-eight hours until I got her back and could then return to my normal, busy routine of juggling her and work. Normally I had catering events planned all weekend to fill my time, but every so often there was a free weekend like this ahead with no events scheduled—and it was only during these rare, unoccupied hours that I actually had the time to realize that I was indeed, alone. Otherwise, I was so busy it didn't even occur to me.

I took out my cell phone and thought about which restaurant to call for take-out for that night, when suddenly Travis Phillips, the former leader of the Fearsome Foursome, burst through the doors of the car wash with a masculine sort of swagger. I hadn't seen him in years—since that time at the airport when we dropped Whitney and Eva off—and he looked good. He still had all of his sandy blond hair and was in excellent shape. He was wearing navy blue Nike running shorts and a T-shirt that showed off his muscular frame underneath. He wasn't potbellied and bald like most of the old acquaintances I'd run into since being back in Houston, but I figured he was probably married like everyone else.

"Travis Phillips!" I said, going straight up to him. "How are you?"

It only took him a second to register who I was in his memory. Then he genuinely looked surprised and pleased to see me. "Well hey, Mel!" he said, shocked. "What brings you to Houston? Aren't you living in New York these days?"

He hugged me and I gave him a kiss on the cheek. It was then that I couldn't help but notice the absence of a wedding band.

"Not anymore," I said, and decided to skip all the depressing details. I simply said, "A divorce. What's new, right?"

"Sorry to hear it, Mel. What happened?"

"I finally got rid of a guy I shouldn't have ever married in the first place. Turns out he was a real jerk."

"See? That's exactly why I've decided not to ever *get* married," Travis said. "No commitments, no strings, no divorces. My life is very simple and I like it that way. I do what I damn well please."

I was shocked that there was actually a hot, single guy left in Houston, so I couldn't help but turn up the flirt. "I bet you do… I mean, c'mon, I remember you, 'Muy Malo!'" I said, smiling mischievously.

"That's right," Travis said proudly. "I pick'em up and bring 'em home any old time I want to." He winked playfully, but I knew he was serious. He then leaned in and interrupted what was turning into dirty thoughts in my head as he whispered, "So, how long are *you* in town?"

I laughed. "Until my daughter turns eighteen, and she's only almost five. Some hayseed judge downtown awarded my incapable, disaster of an ex-husband joint custody—which means I can't leave the state. Truth-be-told, I'm still reeling from it."

"Well, how about I do my best to get your mind off it?" Travis said as he jangled the keys in his short's pocket just like Oldie always used to do. "… *If* you let me take you to dinner first, of course."

I was caught a bit off guard—even as more dirty thoughts of he and I crept back into my head—but it didn't take me long to answer. "Well sure Travis! I'd love that…. give me a call anytime. Here's my cell number."

I smiled at him as we parted ways. As I watched him drive away in his newly detailed sports car, I felt a little something stir inside me, something feathery and warm. I wasn't sure, but it felt like hope.

I drove back home in my spotless car and thought about how funny it was to have run into two men from my past in the very same week. Fate really was strange.

My cell phone rang as soon as I walked through the door, and I thought surely Travis couldn't be calling me this fast! Still, I secretly hoped he was.

"Hello?" I answered warmly.

"Melanie?" Lisa Williams said back, and I could immediately tell something was wrong just from her tone. I hadn't talked to her since Barc and I finalized all the paperwork after our court date—and was surprised she was even calling since she had said back then things were all set.

"Yes, what is it, Lisa?" I asked.

"Are you sitting down?" she said. "Because Mel, I'm just going to cut to the chase—that son-of-a-bitch ex-husband of yours has filed a lawsuit against you! He's seeking *full* custody!"

"What? *Why?*" I said, now sitting down.

"The lawsuit accuses you of abandoning your daughter and leaving her with your nanny or your mother all the time. It claims you're never home, that you go out every night and leave town on weekends, and that you're so lazy your mother has to drive little Blakely to and from school every day because you're napping or getting ready for your next all-nighter... Not in so many words, but surely you get the picture."

The wind was knocked out of me. It was as if Barc had stuck a dagger straight into my heart. The tigress inside me stirred and shrieked and suddenly I was ready to rip out Barclay's innards with my bare teeth if I had to. But at the same time, the allegations were so absurd I couldn't help but laugh. "That's not true at all! I mean, yeah, just last weekend I went to Bermuda with some friends and left Blakely with my mom, but that was the first time I'd *ever* done that!"

"Were there any 'male' friends?"

"No, why?"

"Barc probably thought that, which now explains this whole ridiculous suit."

"Wait a minute," I stammered. "Barc has grounds to sue me just because he thinks I'm dating someone? We're *divorced* now!"

"Unfortunately, Melanie," Ms. Williams explained blandly. "One does not *have* to have any grounds to sue. One does, however, have to respond to lawsuits that are served, and it sounds to me like he's mounting a full-on custody battle now."

I wasn't planning on needing the services of a lawyer after our divorce and the joint custody agreement had already been settled, and I knew Ms. Williams's rates were high, but since I had looked for so long before to even find someone to take my case I knew I was running out of other options. Now, more than ever, I needed help if Barc was asking for full custody. I sighed and asked, "And how much is this ridiculous lawsuit going to cost me?"

"It won't be cheap. I'll need another thirty thousand dollar, nonrefundable retainer like I started with before, since you know I only take on a few cases at a time, and my rate is six hundred dollars an hour after that."

I can't afford this, I thought, but all I said was, "Why in the world would Barc do this to me? We're divorced and I thought we could just go on with our lives now! Why does he want to do this?"

"You want the truth?" Ms. Williams said. "It sounds like he's doing it to fuck with you, Melanie... bleed you dry, get revenge for leaving him, who knows?"

"Fine, then. What are my options?"

"You have none. You can fight him or risk losing your daughter."

The words hung in the air like caustic mustard gas.

Defeated, I hung up the phone. Blakely was all I cared about, and Barc knew that. The trouble was—on the surface at least—some of what he was claiming was true. I *was* working late at night often with the business and my catering gigs kept me tied-up nearly every weekend. I'd been relying on Sondra and my mother to take up the slack with Blakely, and we all juggled her around whenever necessary. But that was just what every single parent I knew did to survive. So the allegation that I was 'abandoning' my daughter out of laziness, or to go out and party, was what really hurt—but then again, it was Barc—so what did I expect?

He thought I was now 'dating,' I thought, with a laugh. Besides taking Beau to the Tux and Boots ball, I hadn't been out on a single other date since I'd returned to Houston—and even going to the ball didn't really count since Beau and I were just friends. Everything I did here, I did for Blakely. I'd even given up on love entirely until recently. But now this all put me in an extremely awkward position, considering the fact that I'd just met someone I did want to go out on a real date with... but Barc was now screwing that all up, or at least trying to. How completely typical, I stormed. But I knew I couldn't let him win. Not this time. I was intrigued by Travis, and it wasn't breaking the law to at least become friends with him again if I wanted to. After all, he was someone I knew from my past I could always say. Still, I thought about the reality of even being seen with him now very seriously...

People gossiped incessantly in Texas. Oldie liked to say gossip grew like tadpoles in water, and I knew that among 'wealthy Texans' it was from a lack of anything better—or decent—to do, and Travis was a man who I knew people would definitely gossip about.

It was clear if I decided to spend time with Travis I needed to keep him at a distance from my home and business, for the less Barc knew, the better. It was now clear someone—probably a neighbor of mine—was 'spying' on me for my ex-husband and he (or she) had now already gotten Barc to 'assume' I was dating, and the last thing I wanted to do was give them more ammunition. I sighed heavily, wondering if this would all even be worth it, as I looked at the whole picture clearly.

Travis was a long-time bachelor, could he even put up with a child being in his life if we really were to start 'hanging out' anyway? My life was already difficult between balancing Blakely and running the business. I wanted to find more time to spend with her, not less, so why even bring someone else into the situation to compete with that? Also, bringing a new man around would only be upsetting and confusing to Blakely, and we'd already had way too much chaos and drama that her *own* father brought into her life. No, it would be pointless to try and date anyone now, no matter how much Travis made me want to start dating again.

I should just forget about it all completely and stay single, I told myself sternly. But as I settled into the feelings of that reality I got upset as I thought of how unfair this all was… I knew Barc dated—a lot—so why couldn't I date too? I was a legally single, grown woman, and this was all ridiculous. I couldn't let Barclay continue to control my life anymore—he already wasted five whole years of my 'dating' lifetime. It was my right to find love if I really wanted to—and I did!

So, I made a decision. I would start to date again, carefully and thoughtfully this time. And I would never, as long as she lived under my roof, involve my daughter in any relationships I had with men, Travis or otherwise, until I knew for sure it was going to become something permanent. Blakely would always come first, and I'd keep my dating life completely separate from her. I felt good and confident about my resolution.

An hour later my cell phone rang. It was Travis. Somewhere in my mind I had expected it to be Oldie, but I knew that could never be the case.

As I picked up, a deep excitement bubbled up from my gut. "Hello?"

"So, you still up for dinner tonight, Mel?" Travis said in a deep, sexy voice.

My heart skipped a beat while I tried to reconcile what I'd decided about Blakely and my new, fluttering feelings of excitement and confidence for wanting to find love again. "Yes," I said, "but I just received some disturbing news from my ex—so can I ask you a favor? Can you pull up a few houses down and then give me a call to come to you?"

He asked no questions. "Sure. Say, seven? And put a smile on that beautiful face of yours, kid."

I took a long time deciding what to wear. We were going to the Grill Room at Travis's country club, which meant I needed to pull off conservative-but-sexy. I finally decided on a black Chanel dress. I threw on a floral-cashmere Pashmina over my bare shoulders, a pearl necklace, and dainty earrings to complete the ensemble. I looked in the mirror and decided I looked proper, but feminine. It had been a long time since I had gotten ready for a first date—or any date for that matter—but I was excited to finally do it again. Especially since it was with Travis Phillips. My sister always thought he was too 'Texan' for her—yet among the other ladies, particularly the underclassmen girls at UT—he was in high demand. I had to admit, if Travis had paid more attention to me back then, I probably would have gone for it.

My cell phone rang. I answered it. "Hello?"

"I'm here, four doors down, in the same ride as earlier today," Travis whispered like James Bond would on a secret mission.

I was glad he wasn't offended and even seemed to be having 'fun' with my request.

I walked over to meet Travis down the block with butterflies in my stomach. I couldn't tell if I was anxious about being spotted by Barc's spy, about spending time with Travis... or bothered by the fact that I hadn't been out on a proper date for so long.

I only lived a stone's throw from the country club and it was good too, because aside from a little small talk, we both played it cool and didn't speak much for the whole ride over. But with restrained, stolen glances I could see he was dressed very classically in a gray suit with a pale blue Hermes tie—attractive and conservative. In fact, he looked incredible.

We walked into the 'library,' the pre-dinner cocktail area where every blue-haired woman and balding man turned to stare at us. It was a decidedly senior crowd and I was soon disoriented enough to wonder if news had somehow already reached them about Barc's custody suit against me. Why else would they all be staring at me as if I was from Pluto?

Travis noticed my discomfort and whispered in my ear, "I'll be right back."

Irritated that he'd leave me alone in this fish tank, I watched him get up and work the room. The stares from the blue-hairs were like X-ray vision but slowly, surely, Travis table-hopped and shook hands with almost every group, charming them and making them laugh. You would've thought he was running for mayor.

Travis finally returned and gave me a kiss on the cheek. "Sorry kid, but most everyone in this room has known my family since forever. They were all just curious about my new, gorgeous 'mystery' date."

"Oh really?" I smiled and leaned into him. "So, what did you tell them? That I was from New York City?"

"Fuck no because first of all girl, you're from *Texas*—and don't you forget it! Second of all, I just told them I was with the younger sister of an old friend from college. No details."

I was glad about that, but most of the blue-hairs still kept staring—and mostly at me. "Why do they keep staring at me?" I finally asked Travis.

"I suppose it's because I haven't dated much quality lately. In fact, just a few weeks ago," he laughed to himself. "Well, let's just say I *really* made an impression!"

"What'd you do?" I urged. "Come on, you know I already know your name topped Mrs. Hayden's B-D-L list at McCain Hall for four straight *years.*"

Travis grinned like he had forgotten about that, but he was now clearly proud to have been reminded. "Okay, I took an underaged stripper from the Gold Coast Club to a very social wedding at the Oaks Club. People are *still* talking about it." He shook his head in disbelief.

I was dumbfounded. "Surely, you're joking!"

"Not joking. But... it's a funny story really. Wanna hear it *all?*"

"Certainly not!" I said indignantly, but Travis seemed intent on telling me anyway.

"My original date, who I'm sure you'd agree was quite normal, cancelled at the last minute because she was sick," he explained. "And I'd met this stripper the night before at the bachelor party and hell, Mel—it was so dark in the place I had no idea how old she was! Anyway, I called her up and she agreed to go, but when I picked her up she was wearing this incredibly slutty dress—it looked like she'd been poured into the thing, I swear—but nobody said 'when...'" He demonstrated just how much she was spilling out of her dress.

I rolled my eyes, thinking, *Typical...*

"Worse," Travis continued. "I then realized how *young* she looked, like she might still be in high school even—so I said, 'Listen sweetheart, this dress is a little sexy for a church wedding, do you have anything more conservative?' She changed into a pantsuit with a nice jacket, and it was much better—and, thank God—it made her look older, too! I despise weddings and plus, I was sweating balls even bringing this girl there, so to make sure we missed the ceremony I pulled off at El Tiempo to have a few margaritas before we hit the reception."

In near perfect synchronicity, our waiter brought us our round of drinks. Though he'd aged well, Travis still carried over a few other bad habits from his younger years besides dating young strippers—he still drank what he called the "bracers," his concoction of vodka, rum, and fruit juice, because even back in college Travis was never a beer drinker. The waiter set one down in front of each of us.

Once the waiter left, Travis continued, "Anyway, we pull up to the Oaks Club and my 'date' hops out of the car and throws her jacket into the backseat since it's hot as hell out—and the valet takes off with my car. *That's* when I notice this huge, giant tattoo on her left breast, fully exposed. I'd completely forgotten about it from the night before. It was of the little rabbit from *Bambi,* you know the one?"

"Thumper?" I laughed.

"Yes! Thumper!" he said. "And let me tell you... she sure could make that bunny 'hop!' Anyway, I was shocked to see this massive bunny on her boob, but her jacket was gone, so there was no choice but to just go on inside. But of course, the very last person I wanted to see was the very first person we ran into... my Aunt Jeanie. She takes one look at Thumper, pulls me aside, and goes berserk. 'Travis, your date is *totally* unacceptable! Jesus, is she underage? She has a cartoon on her breast!' You know, stuff like that. So, I apologized..."

I feigned shock. "You *apologized?* Wow, let me write this down!" I joked.

"Yeah yeah," Travis smiled slyly at me. "I'm not a Neanderthal—I do apologize from time to time... But Aunt Jeannie got in my face, 'Do NOT bring this indecent girl into *this* wedding reception or you will NEVER hear the end of it!'—and the poor girl was only standing five feet away! I felt bad—I don't know, maybe it was the margaritas—but I couldn't help it... I got really heated and told her, 'You know what Aunt Jeanie? I don't give a rat's ass what you or any of these other people think, everyone can go piss up a rope for all I care! Thanks for your concern, but we're *going* to <u>this</u> party!' And we just walked right past her and into the ballroom. I thought my poor old aunt was gonna fall down dead right then and there!"

"Oh God," I laughed, imagining him dancing with 'Thumper' at the reception. "You really *still* don't care what people think about you, do you?"

"Not in the slightest. These same people have been making shit up about me since college, and who cares? I'm a self-made millionaire and even if I wasn't, I'm not gonna change what I do just to please people I don't care about." He leaned over and kissed me on the cheek, then nodded towards everyone else in the room. "So fuck 'em if they can't take a joke!"

Our waiter, Dennis, showed up to take us into the main dining room. He seated us at Travis's favorite table in the corner. "Mr. P., you want the usual?" he asked.

"Is that a trick question, Dennis? I always want my usual, but I have no idea what my blond beauty here would like for dinner. I'm not even sure she eats she's so skinny," Travis teased.

"I eat! I'll have a petite filet, medium rare, with grilled asparagus," I protested. I found out later when our entrees arrived that Travis' 'usual' consisted of a large New York Strip steak, cooked medium, with creamed spinach.

"So, tell me about your family," I asked boldly. I knew very little about Travis's background since Whitney hadn't told me much back in college.

"You really want to hear about that? Why?" he asked.

"It's my job to dig skeletons out of your closet... especially on date number one," I teased.

Travis grinned. "Alright then, since you asked. In a nutshell, it was no '*Little House on the Prairie*,' that's for sure." He took a swill of his beverage.

"That's not enough, I want *details,*" I urged. "And please, don't hold back. Believe me, I can handle it."

"Okay," Travis said, feeling like he could spill it all now. "My mom was a complete recluse who sat in her bedroom all day drinking scotch, which she hid inside a pile of blankets in the closet. She was lonely and depressed, couldn't really cope with four young children always running around underfoot, so she finally handed us over to 'Cordona,' our nanny, and hung a needlepoint sign on her door that read, 'Do Not Disturb the Artist.' I'll never forget that sign... My three younger sisters were no help and always tormented me. Cordona carried a belt and used it constantly on all of us, but I always got the brunt of it because I was the 'boy,' plus my sisters would gang up on me and blame for everything. There was never anyone around to protect my poor ass."

"Oh Travis, that's so sad," I said, truly feeling bad for him. All that time in school I had thought he had it made. I had no idea he had this kind of upbringing. "What about your dad, where was he?"

"'Big John' as they called him, worked for an international oil equipment company so he was never home. He grew up during the Great Depression and didn't have much, so the first chance he got he climbed the corporate ladder as the company 'yes man' so he could fly all over the world on the company jet. He was well-paid, drove around in a new Mercedes every year, and had company perks too—including big-game hunting and fishing trips all over the globe." Travis looked distant as he reflected back. "Yep, 'Big John' was living the 'good' life—but he left us four kids back home with Mom *constantly*. He desperately wanted another son, so when she produced three baby girls in a row, he was basically done with her."

Travis went on to tell me that Big John served as the president of some of the top country clubs in Houston, and even though he was well-liked and well-respected in the community, all hell would break loose whenever he'd come home. He was a very tall, intimidating man at six feet three inches and frankly, Travis said, he scared the shit out of everyone. No one, including his mother, ever dared to contradict him.

Wow, I thought, he sounded a lot like Oldie.

Big John and Travis fought over just about everything—which meant that really, they were an awful lot alike. The only interest they shared was hunting, and this represented the only quality time "father and son" ever spent together. Otherwise, they fought bitterly. Big John was an avid Texas A&M fan and he fit the mold perfectly: according to Travis, he had the Aggie mentality (hick) and the Aggie personality (none). When Travis accepted a full scholarship to UT, father and son became bitter rivals. It will never cease to baffle me how ridiculous and inexplicable the competitiveness between grown adults can be over these two colleges.

"Big John was also a bully and a tyrant," Travis said. "The old man used to wake me up at seven o'clock every Saturday and Sunday morning when I was in high school—knowing I'd been out late partying the night before. He could easily afford pool cleaners and gardeners, but when he was home he took great pleasure in booting *my* ass out of bed. I used to argue that there were plenty of folks out there happy for the work, but he always insisted I do it. Because of him, I suppose I did learn a bit about responsibility though... a good work ethic and how to do things for myself, you know, things like that... I guess I *at least* owe him for that much."

Travis then went on to explain that despite his reputation as a party animal at UT, he had gone on to become a brilliant engineer after college. He moved to Alaska for two years to work for one of the largest oil companies in the country, and then started his own business back here in Houston, becoming a self-made millionaire before he was thirty. Travis was rich, but not 'super rich' as they say in Texas—but as an in-demand oil engineer his career was never going to end unless he ever wanted it to, so he was very secure.

I thought of how different this all was from both Hunter and Barc, who each were proud of the fact that they had no claims at all to any real responsibility or any sense of a work ethic. I reached over and touched Travis's hand fondly, admiring him.

He looked at me mischievously. "You see, my father and I also didn't get along because even from a young age, I think he was jealous over my prowess with girls."

Amused, I teased, "I see... interesting... So, does that mean you were a 'playa,' even back then, *Mr.* Phillips?" I flirted.

"I suppose it's accurate to say that I was. But that was a *loooong* time ago."

"But didn't you tell me earlier that you always do 'exactly as you please?'"

"That's right... I do. And I guess you could say I still get around... I can't complain much."

I knew Travis had been—and still apparently was from the 'Thumper' story—a wild ladies man, and it explained a lot—like why, for instance, he was near forty and had never been married. "Really?" I urged him on daringly. "Then tell me more about how 'fun' it all is..."

"Alright, you got me," he grinned sheepishly. "So it's a little lonely, too."

We glanced into each other's eyes and then looked away, realizing we were starting a true connection.

Over dessert we caught up about everything I'd been up to for the past ten-plus years, from leaving school, to my bad relationships and marriage, to starting up my own successful business in both New York and now here, and about my troubles over the custody battles with Barc over Blakely. He felt bad for that and told me not to worry, he understood these things happen and would keep our date a 'secret' for sure. We then reminisced about college and the Fearsome Foursome days, talked a little about the Sacred Greek Cross fiasco, and then about the last time we had seen each other at the airport, the day Whitney and Eva left for France.

"I still remember you from that day," Travis admitted sheepishly. "You looked *amazing*."

Inside, I melted. "What? You remember?"

"Of course! You were wearing this tight white dress and your long blond hair was blowing in the wind outside the airport... if Whitney hadn't forbidden it, I would have pursued you back then."

Damn it Whitney! I thought, but instead I said, "I guess things happen for a reason, huh?"

As our coffee got cold we failed to notice that we were the last patrons in the room and Dennis was hovering over our table, cleaning up. I looked at my watch—it was midnight. We'd been talking for four hours straight.

"Oh Travis, I'm sorry about this, but I think we should go."

"Okay kid, I'll take you home. But, just so you know, I don't want this evening to end. I've had a *really* great time."

I felt the same way.

Travis drove me a few houses away from my townhouse and we kissed good-night in his car like two hormone-filled teenagers. When we finally resurfaced, Travis laughed and said, "You know, I haven't mugged with a chick like this since high school!"

"Neither have I!" I laughed. It was so corny, but it felt good.

"Wanna go out for dinner again tomorrow night?" he asked. "I've got nothing planned."

I didn't even wait a beat to answer. "After such a great night? You got it!"

Caught off guard, Travis laughed out loud. He had the most infectious laugh. He watched me walk back to my townhouse and held his hand out through the window as he blinked his good-bye to me with his car's headlights, then drove off.

I couldn't wait to see him again.

I spent the next few weeks trying to spend as much time with Blakely as I could while also running the catering business and surreptitiously continuing to see Travis whenever I could fit him in. He took me to his country club several more times where we always had interesting, stimulating conversations about our common interests over a wonderful meal. Here I was—finally dating a fun and decent guy who gave me hope that it wasn't out of the realm of possibility that I might find love and happiness in this lifetime after all—but Barc was always there, an annoying pin in our sides, a dark plague on both our houses as we kept our rendezvouses a secret. Luckily neither Barc's nor my family was well-known at Travis's country club, so it was a safe place for us to go. Still, just the thought of someone gossiping about us was enough to keep me stressed over it, though I tried not to show I was to Travis.

And there was always the stress of Barc's bi-monthly visitations with Blakely to deal with too. By order of the court we were not allowed in each other's homes, so we met in neutral, public places. But instead of one regular meet-up time and location for the exchange such as at a local coffee bar, Barc purposefully changed the venue or time at the last second to mess with my head. It was always at his convenience too, of course—whatever suited the self-absorbed piece-of-shit best. I did what I could to keep up. There was nothing else I could do, and by law I couldn't stand in the way of, or interfere with, their visits. In fact, I could be sent to jail if I tried to—a fact Barc took great pleasure in reminding me of constantly.

But worse than the mind games was the fact that Barc had recently invited his newest girlfriend—a woman named Mimi who was in her early thirties—to move in with him. Mimi was known around town as a drunk with a gambling problem and had been married four times already. Everyone referred to her as "Crazy Mimi." I'd seen her temper firsthand at some club functions and knew that she hated children, which was the reason two of her last four marriages had ended because she simply refused to get pregnant. Blakely told me she once accidently spilled some juice on Mimi's shirt and Mimi became enraged. Plates, wine glasses, practically anything that wasn't nailed down became a casualty of her violent shouting tirade that followed. I realized then that she was actually perfect for Barc and the whole Cunningham family, who were legendary for throwing things during fights, but I didn't want that kind of person anywhere near my own daughter. Barc was bad enough when he did these types of things on his own.

Mimi also became insanely jealous of anything or anyone competing with Barc's affections—even his own kid. I worried that with Mimi around, Barc's house wasn't a good environment for Blakely even more now, so I instructed Ms. Williams to file a petition with the court restricting Mimi from spending the night during Barc's weekend visits.

This did not sit well with either of them, but, like I did with all of their requests, they had to oblige.

It was soon springtime in Houston, which meant that to the 'Daniel Boones' in the area, it was turkey-time. Travis invited me to his ranch for the weekend so I could accompany him on a "turkey hunt." Travis, being a passionate pursuer of gobblers, thought this was an experience we needed to share.

"Melanie, you'll just love it!" he declared. "I look forward to this trip all year long."

"I don't know Travis... you want to take me *hunting?*" I said, thinking he must know me better than that by now. I'd never been hunting for anything other than designer clothes, and the only turkeys I'd ever seen were oven-roasted, golden brown, and beautifully displayed on a buffet at the country club or on a sterling silver platter on my family's holiday dining table. I had no idea what going on a real turkey hunt even meant.

"Well, it's a lot more than just hunting," Travis persuaded. "We'll spend time on the ranch, have dinner and drinks, and then go hunting in the morning. I'll have you back by Sunday night before Blakely comes home, I promise! You'll have a great time, kid!"

I didn't have any idea what one wears on such a thing as a 'turkey hunt,' so I drove to the local sporting goods store and asked around. It seemed camouflage was the answer, so I bought a big bag of khaki and camouflage clothing for my adventure.

The next day, after I dropped Blakely off with Barc for the weekend, Travis picked me up in his Cadillac Seville for our six hour drive to the southern part of Texas where his ranch was.

"Ooh, you're driving the Cadillac to your ranch! Reminds me of something J.R. Ewing would do," I teased. "I'm surprised you don't have an SUV like everyone else in this city."

"Of course I'm driving my Cadillac. I hate SUVs—all the soccer moms drive them now, makes me crazy. What in the world do they need all that horsepower for, for goodness sake! And those Hummers? Give me a break! I don't have a bunch of screaming brats to haul around town so yes, my Cadillac will do just *fine*, thank you very much!"

I was somewhat surprised at his comment. He meant no offense, but it was now very clear that children were not on Travis's future agenda. *Too bad*, I thought, for I had really been having a good time with him so far, but if this was indeed how he truly felt, it looked like our time together would soon be coming to an end. After all, Blakely came first.

Oh well, I thought. *I could still just allow myself to enjoy the weekend and bring this all up with him later for discussion...*

Off we went to his ranch, which turned out to be literally in the middle of nowhere near the South Texas and Mexican border. I got a little nervous when the foreman of the ranch greeted us at an enormous, black-iron gate wearing what looked like a 57 magnum on his belt.

"Why are you carrying a gun? Is this place *really* dangerous?" I asked the foreman.

"Oh yes ma'am," he answered sternly. "We're so close to the Mexican border you should be armed at all times. Illegal aliens are coming across the border from Mexico constantly."

What in the world am I doing here? I thought to myself, and then quickly thought of Sondra and how much she risked just to make it into the U.S. My mom and I had helped her begin to file the paperwork to become a legal U.S. citizen, but it was a very long and slow process. I silently prayed it would go smoothly as we continued to drive over the bumpy, dusty, desert terrain and went towards the ranch. I looked out the window, studying the vast landscape and how threatening it all suddenly appeared.

South Texas along the Mexican border was known geographically as the Chihuahua Desert. It would be hard to find a more foreboding place anywhere on the planet. Rattlesnakes, pit vipers, and Gila monsters—the most poisonous lizards in the world—were common neighbors, as well as tarantulas and rat-sized scorpions. The landscape had every kind of cactus, thorn, and prickly pear you could think of, and brutal, punishing, 110 degree heat. This was a far cry from the Plaza in New York.

However, once we reached the ranch and I saw the actual house, I was shocked. It was truly beautiful, and Travis had created an oasis within its walls. The Mediterranean-style hacienda had a courtyard patio constructed of colorful Mexican tiles. There was a fountain in the center and a rock garden surrounding it all, which was typical of homes in Mexico. Off to the left was a swimming pool which was decorated with even more Mexican tiles. Marble tables with bright blue sun umbrellas provided shade from the South Texas desert-like atmosphere. The only vegetation was a cactus garden filled with red and yellow blooms. I was amazed at how appealing these thorny plants could actually be when landscaped into a layered desert garden.

Fleets of Mexican workers were briskly moving in every direction making sure Travis was comfortable and happy. They had no idea I was fluent in Spanish and could understand what they were saying. They seemed to be ranting about how impossible "the senor" was to please whenever he was expecting guests, and how he demanded perfection down to the very last detail. I was flattered that Travis would go out of his way to make sure my stay there was perfect, but I didn't want it to be at the dismay of all his workers.

Travis wondered out loud what all the commotion was about, and I found the whole scene quite amusing.

One member of the staff, Maria, showed me to my room, which was a small suite decorated in a rustic and sophisticated Santa Fe theme. She spoke a little English and told me sternly, "Senor Travis likes all guests downstairs and dressed for dinner at seven, sharp. You start with cocktails on terrace."

I had no idea what one wears on a ranch in southern Texas and probably changed five times before I could decide on anything—I was so nervous it was ridiculous. In fact, I was lost in thought when there was a loud knock on the door. "Senora! It's Maria! The senor is waiting for you on terrace. I told you he don't like waiting!"

Well what else does he have to do? I thought. *We're in the middle of friggin' nowhere!* "Okay okay," I told her. "Please tell him I'll be there in a few minutes."

I finished putting on a large turquoise squash-blossom necklace, sprayed some Chanel perfume in the air and walked through its mist, then went to join him on the terrace.

There was a slight chill in the air and the sun was just beginning to set as I walked onto the veranda's terracotta-tiled floor. Looking at the beautiful view was so tranquil... so peaceful. Travis watched me closely as I walked straight towards him. I could tell he was pleased with my final—and very sexy—leather dress selection.

"Mel," Travis grinned. "Please join me for a homemade margarita and let's enjoy this great sunset together. You look... fantastic!"

"Oh, it's just a little something I got recently, but thanks," I told him.

He kissed me lightly on the cheek. "And you smell great, too. All dressed up, huh?"

"Yes, it's Chanel—my favorite. I never get tired of wearing it."

Pedro, the valet, appeared out of nowhere with a tray full of Tex-Mex hors d'oeuvres and a huge, Texas-size margarita for me. My stomach was still in knots since this was the first time we had ever gone away where we would be spending the whole weekend together, and I still couldn't shake the whole 'kid' comment from earlier. I couldn't eat and had to restrain myself from downing my drink in one gulp.

So instead, I took in the surrounding scenery, which was pretty, but not really my cup of tea to be in so 'much' of it. Even though it was popular amongst the Texas elite to have a ranch (and the bigger, the better), I'd never been into this whole ranch scene. I preferred large cities with noise, bustle, and posh accommodations and frankly, things to do that *didn't* involve getting dirty. Out here in nature, I felt lost.

I'd lose my mind if I had to live here, I thought, but didn't say a word.

"Pedro makes one hell of a margarita, so watch out—you can't taste the tequila, but there's more in there than you think," Travis warned. "His family has been working for me for years."

"Thanks for the warning," I said as I took a small sip.

Suddenly, Pedro came running out of the house again. "Da plane, boss! Is'here," he said excitedly, pointing to the rose-colored sky.

I looked up and saw what appeared to be a small plane approaching at an extremely low altitude. In fact, it looked like it was ready to land on Travis's front lawn. I quickly realized that a huge, long lot at the edge of his property—what I thought was only cleared-out land—was actually an airstrip.

"Wait... what's going on?" I asked in semi-shock.

"Down here we ranch hop a lot via plane, and a few of my college buddies have ranches a couple of hours away, so I asked them to join us for dinner—I hope you don't mind? They're all couples and we'll have a good time yucking it up—it'll be fun. I was going to tell you over cocktails, but you took so long coming down I didn't have a chance."

Great, I thought. This was supposed to be our first romantic weekend away to get to know each other better, not a college reunion! But I held my tongue, for the comment about taking too long to get ready really stung. Now Travis had two strikes going against him so far today.

"Well then... I can't wait to meet them," I said, with a forced smile. What else could I say? It didn't really matter if I minded or not it seemed.

Suddenly I was having flashbacks to my marriage to Barc and then again whenever I was with Hunter and he pulled something like this... no, this isn't right... I decided right then and there I didn't want to ever be involved again with a man who didn't consider my feelings before he acted and I silently added a *third* strike. Travis was definitely out after this weekend. But with no other choice now but to accept my circumstances, I decided to give his friends a chance, still have fun, and go with the flow.

After all, the plane was already touching down, and I was stuck there anyway.

Chapter 21

❧

To my surprise, the first person off the plane was Jack—the fringe member of the Fearsome Foursome—"all growed up," as Oldie would say. Then came a few of Travis's fraternity brothers from college, who were all more Whitney's friends than mine, though I still recognized them even all these years later. They were just the vaguest of memories though.

But the biggest shock came when I saw who climbed out of the plane last—Emily—my old best-friend-turned-enemy, who I hadn't seen since the night she spurned me at my college graduation dinner. I couldn't believe she and Jack were still together after all these years! Seeing her brought back a flood of bad memories, and I could feel myself getting angry just at the mere sight of her.

Travis whispered in my ear, oblivious to my rage, "Jack refuses to get married, but he gave his girlfriend there Emily an engagement ring just to shut her up. These guys have been together since college, can you believe that?"

"Listen Travis, I know all about Emily," I told him. As I seethed about her, his words about the ring brought back painful memories of Hunter doing the same thing to me, but I let it all go as I continued, "She and I practically grew up together and I was there when Jack and her first hooked up... we were really close once, but she turned on me and now there's *major* bad blood between us. I really don't know if it's a good idea she's here."

"Whoa, really?" Travis said, clearly not knowing any of this. "That was such a long time ago; don't you think things have cooled off by now, babe?"

"I haven't seen her since college, since the night of our huge blow-out."

"Well... *humm*," he stammered as the whole gang made their way up the steps of the terrace to join us. "I guess we'll just see how things go, okay?"

We got up and greeted the group of guests. There was Brandon with his twenty-something, bimbo 'du jour' Samantha, who already appeared intoxicated, and Dean—or rather, "The Dean" as he was called—along with his wife, Bonnie, and of course, Jack and Emily.

"Do y'all remember Whitney St. John from college?" Travis said as he introduced me to everyone at once. They all nodded, and I could tell Emily was just as shocked to see me as I was to have seen her. "Well, believe it or not, this is her younger sister Melanie! She moved back to Houston after living in New York City for a bit."

"New York City?" the guys all said in unison, mimicking an old salsa commercial.

I laughed along uncomfortably as I felt all their eyes looking me up and down, especially Emily's, as they took in my ridiculous, expensive outfit and enormous necklace. I suddenly felt like an overdressed idiot. Everyone else was dressed in blue jeans and cowboy boots, including Travis.

My ignorance of appropriate ranch attire was embarrassing enough, but then 'The Dean' came up and asked me in a slurred, mocking Texan accent, "So, Melanie... what in the world is a girl from New York City doing with Travis on a ranch out in the middle of nowhere? And look 'atcha! Hell, looks like you're going to a cocktail party, darlin'—haven't you ever been on a ranch b'fore? What's up with this leather dress get-up?"

Travis came to my defense immediately. "Shut up!" he said to him sternly, then turned to me and whispered, "They've all had *way* too much to drink, as usual, already."

I was very grateful he stood up for me. No man ever had before besides Oldie.

Bonnie turned to the group and said, "Well I think she looks really cute, so everyone just leave Melanie alone!"

Emily finally came forward as she walked up and stood right in front of me, but not at all appearing very 'happy' to see me. She was already drunk. "She's right, you do look great, Melanie... it's been a *lonnng* time," she slurred.

I gave her a half-hearted hug and replied coldly, "It sure has, Emily."

"How's Victoria, huh?" she asked with only feigned interest.

"Modeling in New York, still on the hunt for Mr. Right, but otherwise, she's good," I said without meeting her eyes.

"Ha! No surprise there!" Emily said, almost gloating. "Poor little Victoria, never had any confidence with men, did she? So she never had good luck with them... but, I guess I shouldn't talk... I still haven't nailed down *this* one myself." She pulled Jack over to her side.

"Hey, NOW I remember YOU!" Jack said as he stared at me. He'd obviously been drinking as well. And then, never one to be very sensitive to social subtleties anyway, he added, "Man, we ain't seen you since we crashed that graduation party back in the day! Emily had a pretty sharp tongue at that party, *whew!*"

Leave it to Jack to bring everything out in the open, completely oblivious.

"She sure did," I said curtly, my arms folded. "But… she was also really drunk that night. Maybe even *so* drunk she doesn't remember what she said to me. Or maybe she didn't mean the things she said to me," I added pointedly, leaving the door wide open for an apology. So what if I was fishing? There was no way I could pretend I wasn't still pissed.

"Melanie," Emily laughed softly under her breath, her head cocked. "I *really* don't want to get into it here… but if you must know, I meant every word I said that night. Things I'd repeat to your face right here again tonight, if you'd like."

I nearly lunged at her. But instead, I shook the ice in my empty margarita glass. "How could you have been so cruel to me? I would have done anything for you!"

Emily just scoffed. "God, you're still so fake! All you ever do is try to make yourself look good, don't you see it? I mean, look at you now, in that 'outfit'—you always try so hard to be perfect, and it's not *real!*"

Jack chimed in, "Well, the only thing I remember about that night is you telling the *cops* that I couldn't drive… not cool, man! Took us to hell-n-back to get our keys back that night!"

"Yeah, that was messed up, Melanie!" Emily said, getting angry over it all over again. "You never rat out your friends to the COPS—"

I couldn't believe I was being so verbally assaulted by them—it was like college all over again.

Travis whistled to command both Emily and Jack's attention. "Hey, LISTEN UP! Leave my date alone, okay?" he told them both sternly. "The past is the past. Emily… Jack… just stay away from Melanie tonight if you have to. If you don't like her, or how she's dressed, or that she lived in New York, you can go piss up a rope for all I care! She's my date, and this is her first time to South Texas and I want to show her a good time, huh?"

Everyone whooped and hollered their approval.

Pedro must have been watching this whole unpleasant experience because suddenly he appeared in the doorway as he announced, "Dinner ready, senor and guests!"

Everyone started to relax as they followed Pedro into the house and towards the dining room. I let everyone go ahead of us and then pulled Travis aside as I threw my arms around him and kissed him passionately.

"Whoa!" he said, pleasantly surprised. "What was *that* for, kid?"

"For standing up for me…," I told him appreciatively. "Nobody I ever dated has *ever* stood up for me like that." I felt like we could suddenly work out our differences and all three strikes were now cleared from the slate. I wanted to give a man like this another chance and could feel myself falling for him even more than I had been before.

"Well, it's easy for me to choose you over them… I mean, you're a lot hotter than Jack!" Travis joked.

We laughed and kissed again, then went inside to join the others.

The main dining room was one of the most beautiful rooms I'd ever seen. The ceilings must have been at least twelve feet high and there was an enormous chandelier made out of deer antlers hanging above a very long, hand-carved, Baroque-styled dining table.

"Wow, it's gorgeous," I told Travis as we sat down at it along with the others. There was at least another ten feet of empty table space on either side of our group of eight now seated throughout the middle section. Emily sat as far away as she could from me, thankfully.

"I had this table made especially for this room," Travis boasted proudly. "It can easily seat up to twenty-four people, no problem."

I admired the incredible paintings hanging on the walls, some of which I recognized from my years at Sotheby's. In addition, there was an enormous, antique Aubusson rug underneath us. Travis had clearly done very well in the oil business.

After the way cocktail hour had gone, I was silently dreading dinner and was paranoid the group would start their interrogation of me all over again. But, to my relief, they only ignored me as they all reminisced about their 'good old college days,' exchanging the most ridiculous and immature stories I'd ever heard in the process.

Jack started it off by telling "butt stories," which basically recounted his sexual conquests with all of the prim and proper debutantes and sorority girls he'd bedded in college, including one poor girl who he later took to a country club event where he then blurted-out their 'private acts' to her whole family just to shock them.

Everyone at the table (except me) roared in laughter, and I looked at all of these near-middle-aged people and couldn't believe they were all still fixated on college. They talked and laughed about these events as if they happened yesterday. A shrink would have called it a case of 'arrested development.' On top of that, Emily would occasionally glare at me from across the table, clearly letting me know my presence was ruining her otherwise 'good time.'

I looked at my watch discreetly several times and hoped this boring evening would end.

"Okay, my turn!" The Dean said, smiling at Travis. "We all know one of good ol' Travis here's favorite indulgences in college was paying for a little something he called 'loveless copulation.'"

"Oooooo!" everyone said together teasingly.

My curiosity was finally piqued as well.

The Dean continued, now with a captive audience, "So, every now and again a group of us would stop by the world famous Chicken Ranch in Sealy. Well, Travis went off to one of the rooms with this girl whose tits were bigger than her head, I swear!" He paused to allow the group's hooting and laughing to die down. "And while we all finished with our 'needs' and then all met back up at the bar by nine like we always did—this time a damn extra hour goes by and Travis was *still* not there!"

Everyone *"Ooooooo'ed"* again like they were in Jr. High School. I was not enjoying hearing this story as much as I had thought I would either.

"What can I say?" Travis said proudly. "I was still getting my 'needs' met."

"Anyway," The Dean continued, "half a bottle of scotch later, we really wanted to go, so we decided to go take a peek at what the hell was going on. So we kicked in all the doors with 'keep out' signs, yelling 'Traaaaaavis! Where are yooooou?' into each one—the madam was so pissed she chased us all down the hall with a pistol, screaming, 'I'm going to shoot your little asses if you don't get out of my house... NOW!'"

The Dean paused again to let the laughter die down. "Travis finally ran out of the house wearing nothing but a cowboy hat and literally dove into the backseat of my brand new car butt-naked! He had to ride the entire way back to Austin wearing nothing but his *hat*—ha-ha!"

The entire table erupted with laughter. I was horrified.

"Needless to say, that was our *last* trip to the Chicken Ranch. After that, it was always Boy's Town," The Dean said, like it was something better than just another whorehouse.

Travis slammed his cup down and said in a very loud voice, "Road trip! Let's crank up the plane and hit Boy's Town... you know, for old time's sake!"

Everyone hooted and hollered instantly. I looked at Travis as if he'd gone mad, but everyone else seemed to be shouting their agreement like it was the greatest idea in the world.

I whispered to him, "Surely you must be joking! It's almost midnight! And I thought we had to get up early to go turkey hunting?"

Travis, who'd drank way too much tequila by now, said, "Come on Mel, it's been so long since any of us has been there. It's only forty minutes away by plane."

He summoned Pedro and instructed him, "We wanna go to Laredo for the after-party! Go wake up the pilots and tell them to be ready to take off in fifteen minutes."

Over-ruled and ignored I said, "Look, I've been a really good sport tonight Travis, but this is *really* over the top! I'm not going... period."

Travis was not used to being told no. "Melanie, be a trooper!" he pleaded. "All we want to do is fly across the border and yuk it up for an hour or two... we'll be back before you know it. And it's not that bad, really!"

I was too tired to argue and wasn't getting anywhere with him, so I followed the group to "da Plane" and we all climbed aboard. The sleepy pilots glared at us in annoyance, muttering something about "spoiled brats."

No kidding guys, I thought. *I'm with you!* I've had my 'being spoiled' moments, but this group could top the list of all-time spoiled brats!

Jack staggered around the plane swigging out of a bottle of tequila—the kind with the worm in it—and singing the old James Taylor song *Mexico*—apparently their 'theme song' for trips like this.

As promised, we took off and landed about forty minutes later in Laredo, Mexico. We were met by two cars and were driven straight to El Papagayo, 'Boy's Town'—the group's favorite old bar and whorehouse. We walked inside and every head in the room turned to look at 'the obvious Americans.' Everyone else besides us there were either young Mexican hookers or older Mexican men.

Brandon, The Dean, Samantha, and Bonnie all looked somewhat uneasy, even in their drunken states. Emily was so plastered by now I wasn't even sure she knew where she was.

"Let me take a look around," Jack said, and then went to talk to the bartender. Everyone perked up when he returned. "Guys, you're not going to believe this—there's a live lesbian show going on in the back right now! Let's go!"

All the other women—including Emily—wanted to go check it out, which I found disturbing.

This is the most surreal experience I've ever had, I thought. I held onto Travis's arm for dear life and said angrily, "There's no way in the world I'm going to watch a sleazy lesbian show! This place is beyond disgusting and quite frankly, I'm scared. Do you see the way everyone is glaring at us? I want to leave... and now!"

"Hey, calm down kid," Travis said. "Let's just get a drink at the bar and wait for the group there. Then we'll leave, I promise."

I was thankful he didn't put up a fight and became conflicted inside. For the second time that night Travis had put his attention on me instead of focusing on his buddies. No man I had ever dated had ever done that before. It felt good to be put first, and his constant reassurances that we were okay were adorable as we waited at the bar, but I was still mad at myself for being such a fool to have even come along with these drunken people in the first place.

Just as I was beginning to calm down, I heard a noise behind me that sounded like water pouring over a waterfall. I turned to see one of the

Mexican hookers calmly pouring a Negro Modelo—a dark Mexican beer—down the side of my brand new, $800 Gucci purse. Some of the liquid spilled inside it and I knew it was thoroughly drenched and ruined. I looked at the hooker in total disbelief as she laughed hysterically.

"Puta," she said harshly in broken English. "You go back where you come from... you're *not* wanted here." She pointed towards the front door.

"Okay, okay," Travis said, stepping in on my behalf yet again. "We're gone."

I was so upset and totally disgusted by the whole experience, I was shaking as Travis and I made our way back out the door. We quickly got into the backseat of one of the two cars waiting out front.

"Take us back to the airport," Travis told the driver. Then he turned to me. "I hate to say it, but you were right, Mel. Boy's Town is for trashy college kids.... not middle-aged oil men."

He was admitting I was *right?* Wow, another complete first! I kissed him.

"Wow, was that also for standing up for you?" he grinned.

"That was a thank you for getting me the hell out of there!" I said, and we continued to make out until we got to the airport, and it got even hotter once we were back on the plane. It would have escalated into even more too if not for the sudden appearance of the rest of the gang only a short time later. I was a little disappointed, for it would have been the first time I'd had sex since my marriage, and I knew I was ready to.

"There you guys are!" Jack said as he climbed aboard first. "Y'all were smart skipping *that* show... it was truly repulsive... and remember—this is ME talking here!"

The others all hurried to get settled in and we were airborne within minutes. Travis held me the whole way back to the ranch, but the romantic mood was definitely broken now.

It was 5:00 AM when I finally got to sleep, alone, since Travis and I were both too sleepy to do anything more once we arrived back at the ranch and said good-bye to the others. About an hour later, Maria knocked on my door loudly as she said, "Senora Melanie... the senor says it is time to go shoot the turkey!"

When I didn't answer, she let herself in. "Senora Melanie! Please, up now!"

I looked at her out of one squinted eye. She was in her crisp, little pink uniform, and I thought I must be hallucinating. I was so tired I could barely even lift my head off the pillow, much less respond to her.

Maria held out a bottle of ice cold Evian and two aspirin as she said, "This make you feel better."

"Thanks, Maria," I whispered with a hoarse voice. "But please tell 'el senor' I'm not going anywhere except back to *sleep.*" I pulled the covers over my head to prove my point.

"Please senora," Maria pleaded. "The senor will get muy anojado—very angry—if you do not shoot da turkey!"

"You can go tell su jeffe I don't care if he gets mad or not! Frankly, I don't give a damn what he thinks. I'm not going and that's final!"

Finally, Maria left.

A few minutes later, Travis showed up at my door and knocked on it as he entered. "Come on, kid," Travis ordered. "Up and at'em!"

I looked up and almost burst out laughing—he was dressed from head to toe in camouflage and even had black grease painted in strips across his cheeks, like jockeys wear in horse races, and he was holding a very large shotgun. He was such a sight! He looked like Daniel Boone about to go to battle. I covered my face with the sheet, laughing, as I said, "Travis, don't even try to talk me into this. I'm way too tired to do anything, much less hunt for a turkey."

Travis yanked the blankets off me and sat down on the bed as he tickled me playfully. I could tell he was trying to steal a peek at my breasts through my silk nightgown, but since it was black it allowed me to keep him in suspense.

"Stop it!" I said, grabbing his hand and holding it. We definitely had chemistry, that was for sure, as we stared into each other's eyes. He bent down and kissed me tenderly, then whispered in his deepest, sexiest voice, "Come on kid, it'll be fun... just you and me, out alone in nature..."

I would have rather we stayed right there in bed all day, but I didn't want our first time together to be when I was this tired—or when his face was covered in grease.

"Come on," Travis pleaded. "I don't want to go by myself."

"Oh, alright," I groaned. Once again, he was talking me into something I didn't want to do, and once again, I was letting him— but mostly because he was just so persuasively 'sexy' when he wanted to be. I didn't know how to say no to that.

Travis grinned and handed me a folded, complete camouflage outfit from L.L. Bean in just my size. "See? I've even got you covered, right?"

I grinned at his thoughtfulness... once again, another first for me with a man.

"Now go change and then let's haul ass—we're going to miss the best part of the day!" Travis said, and then left the room.

I changed quickly, shaking off my grogginess, and went downstairs and joined Travis. Pedro met us at the front door; then drove us out to the middle of scrub brush in a very big truck. Once the truck stopped, only Travis and I got out.

"Come on," Travis said, walking further into the brush.

"Where are we going?" I asked, not sure I *wanted* to go any further than where we currently stood.

"To the blind," he said.

"The what?"

"The turkey blind, where we'll find the *turkeys!*" he explained like I was Blakely's age.

We walked deeper into the brush and came to what I assumed must be the 'blind,' which turned out to be a sophisticated-looking version of a kid's tree house perched atop a large mesquite tree.

Travis smacked me on the butt, leaned over, and offered his interlaced hands as a 'step' as he said, "Ready to climb up?"

I gave Travis an icy look and felt like screaming—but who would hear me? I couldn't believe he had brought me all the way out here in the middle of nowhere and now expected me to climb up a tree too. I had to get away from him, so I walked off, having no idea where I was even going.

Travis screamed, "STOP RIGHT THERE MELANIE!"

I turned around and let him have it. "Do you think I'm some kind of adventure woman, or pioneer gal or something? Is this whole weekend some kind of joke or 'test' you put your dates through? Well forget it; I've had it with—"

"No—I mean, don't move! There are rattlesnakes everywhere out here!" Travis said frantically. "You can't go traipsing off without a guide! There are scorpions and poisonous cactus plants too—those you can't even *see!* And on top of that, Pedro has coyote traps all over the place. One false move and you'll lose an ankle. I'm serious. Please, come back over here."

I believed all those things were both possible and true, yet I could also tell Travis was trying to scare me. Still, no amount of L.L. Bean camouflage was going to protect me from all of *that,* so I quickly went back over to his side.

"Melanie, I was kidding about climbing the tree. There's wooden stairs on the other side." Travis pointed to them as he winked at me. "This blind is the most posh hunting blind you've ever been in—it has heat, electricity, *and* running water. I spent a Goddamn fortune on it, so I promise you, you'll be quite comfortable."

Again, I found myself conflicted as I saw both his softer side and how genuinely protective he was of me. So once again I found myself in a situation I wouldn't have been in if it weren't for this particular man... or rather, if I just weren't always giving in to his wishes, but I couldn't stop myself. It was like Travis had me hypnotized or something with his charm. *Still,* I thought, *who in their right mind would build a million-dollar ranch house way out here, much less call it a 'vacation?'*

I followed him like a smitten schoolgirl as we climbed up the stairs and entered the blind. Once inside, Travis pulled out two very cushioned chairs for us to take our positions in, in front of a large open window. I was dumbfounded at how incredibly comfortable it really was.

Travis whispered to me, "This is the time in the morning when the gobblers come to feed and look for a mate."

I had no idea what he was talking about. "What's a gobbler?"

"Oh, that's a male turkey. It's illegal to shoot a hen, but you can shoot the shit out of a gobbler! In fact, since you're here, I can shoot two. That's the limit."

I was horrified. "So you mean you just sit here and wait for the poor turkey to come around and then blow him away?"

"Yep. But you see, there's far too many turkeys out there. If I don't kill one or two of 'em, they'd probably starve to death or get eaten by another predator." Right after he finished his sentence a gobbler came up to the filled feeder on the ground below us and started pecking away at the food.

"Oh—*shshhh!*" Travis whispered at me, lifted his shotgun, and blew its head off.

I almost fainted on the spot. "That's sick... I'm going to be sick!"

Travis immediately climbed down the stairs of the blind to see what he had. "Oh baby, this thing is *huge!* It probably weighs at least fifteen pounds!" He shouted up at me, elated.

I couldn't care less how much it weighed. I didn't even want to look at it. He climbed back up into the blind and pulled out a small bottle of champagne from a tiny electric cooler to celebrate.

"Travis, it's like seven in the morning."

"So what? This has been a fabulous hunt!" He took out two plastic flutes and proceeded to pour us each a glass.

"How can you possibly call that a hunt? This wasn't a sport—it was a *slaughter*," I said as I sipped the champagne. "There was no skill involved—the bird came to *you!* My uncle hunts things all over the world and only uses a bow and arrow. Now *that's* truly a challenge!"

Travis said, "Kid, you may think it's too early in the morning for a celebratory alcoholic beverage, but I think it's too early for haughty editorials." He clicked my plastic champagne flute with his gleefully and then took a big swig.

I took another sip, but didn't feel like celebrating at all. Travis could sense it too. "Want to go, kid?" he asked.

I was glad he was being so sensitive to my feelings. "Yes, thank you."

We climbed back down to the ground and Travis called out for Pedro to bring the cooler, the truck, and the camera to come pick us up. He wanted a photo with his 'trophy gobbler.'

Once Pedro arrived, Travis picked up the dead bird by its legs and looked at me. "Mel, can you come over and stand by me on the *other* side? I promise, you don't have to touch the bird."

Is he able to read my mind now, or did he just defer a fight? I thought as I got into place; then smiled brightly for the camera as Pedro took our picture. We packed up and headed back to the ranch.

Travis was still wired from the kill once we reached it. "I want to get this sucker back to Houston and drop it off at JT's BBQ for them to smoke it on their mesquite grill before they close! We can have it for dinner tomorrow night."

I looked at him and said, "You must be kidding if you think I could possibly eat that thing after seeing you blow its head off. All that blood!"

"Jesus kid, it's not like it's going to look like that after it's been cooked! Go and pack your stuff and be ready to leave in about fifteen."

I felt like I'd been in boot camp all weekend, not on some multi-million dollar ranch. I was relieved to be leaving, but so exhausted I slept most of the long drive back. However, once I woke up I realized I shouldn't have.

"Where are we?" I asked, not recognizing the highway.

"Oh, I thought I'd try a different route home, but I guess it meant taking us a *bit* out of our way."

"Travis! We're going to be late now!"

"For what?" he said, not at all feeling any alarm.

"To have me back in time so I can pick up Blakely—from Barc," I reminded him.

Now he got it and looked concerned as he drove as fast as he could back to Houston, but it still wasn't fast enough as my scheduled pick-up time drew nearer and nearer. I finally called my mother. She agreed to go and get Blakely for me and wait back at my townhouse until I got home.

Great, I thought. This is just what Barc wants to have happen so he can keep saying I'm not a good mother. He'll probably call his lawyer about it immediately and have some ridiculous claim added to his custody suit.

Travis could sense my bad mood and truly felt bad. "I'm sorry Melanie. I forgot all about your strict schedule."

"I know," I said, realizing my first thoughts at the beginning of the weekend were now confirmed. Travis was not planning on ever having to worry about kids being in his life, and though he was the first man I'd been attracted to since my marriage, this definitely did not make us a match.

Travis dropped me off in front of my townhouse and I could see Blakely from the downstairs window looking out at me. She jumped up and down happily.

"Aw look... she's excited to see you!" Travis said, trying to ease my mood. "Just wait until she sees this turkey—she'll *really* be excited then!"

"There's no way you're meeting Blakely today *or* showing her that Travis—she's only a *child* for God's sake! I doubt she'd even know what a real turkey looks like, let alone a *dead* one! Jeez, you really have no idea how to be around children, do you?"

"No, I guess I don't."

"Listen," I said. "Thanks for the whole weekend, but I think we both know a lot of what happened was not really in sync with our 'different' lifestyles, wouldn't you say?"

Travis looked a bit surprised. "Well, we're still just getting to know each other."

I could see Blakely jumping up and down even more and knew I had to get inside. "I really have to go now, bye," I said curtly and jumped out with my bags.

Travis drove away and I truly did not expect to hear from him again. Sure, I hadn't dated in awhile and I knew we did have chemistry, but there was no way that weekend could be considered a success, by either one of us.

I dove right back into spending time with Blakely, running the business, and dealing with the stress of Barc still trying to gain sole custody of Blakely—even though he knew perfectly well she was better off with me. And he of course used the only time I ever sent my mother to pick her up from him as a 'big reason' why I was a completely unfit mother—Barc made it seem like I forgot all about my own kid and just abandoned her that day. I now felt my lawyer was right—he had filed this motion just so I would be forced to shell out forklifts of money in attorney's fees to fight this bogus lawsuit and hold onto legitimate parental rights that were already legally mine, and he was going to use every chance he could to keep making ridiculous claims until he took her away from me.

I knew Barc didn't really want sole custody of Blakely—he didn't want sole custody of a dog. I knew the constant care a small child requires would try his patience further than it could stretch; Barc was simply not a patient man. I had already begged and borrowed to get Blakely into a good preschool, attended every single one of her school activities, and spent time making sure she was learning extra things too by taking both swimming and gymnastics classes. Why in the world did Barc want to take her away from all that, and from me? He didn't want to be responsible for all those things. It just didn't make sense.

I was also sad about ending things with Travis, who I really liked, and the stress of everything made me want to go back to my daily shopping habit to help ease the anxiety, but I knew that wasn't the right way to handle things. So instead, I called Victoria. Luckily, she was fine with being my sounding board as I vented.

"Oh, that really sucks, Mel," Victoria said. "Is Barc still living with that nutcase Mimi?"

"Yes," I told her. "And they've already moved three times in the short time they've been together. She's so jealous of Barc's relationship with Blakely that she'll fly into a rage at a moment's notice too—he and Blakely have even had to leave the house in the middle of the night just to escape from her craziness!"

"Oh my!" Victoria sympathized.

"I know—he 'forgets' Blakely's old enough now to remember everything, and she told me Barc keeps a list of hotels as 'favorites' on his computer *and* a packed bag near the door in case they need to make a quick escape... so who is he kidding here? He thinks *he* has a more normal, stable environment for a child than *me?*"

"Can't you get all of this down as evidence for when you go back to court?"

"I'm keeping a journal about it all, but my lawyer says we're going to need a lot more proof."

"Oh Mel, I wish you could just enjoy being a mom without all this mess! How is everything else going?"

"It's *not,*" I told her truthfully. I hadn't heard from Travis all week, and still didn't expect to. "So please, tell me some happier news going on with you... dating anyone?"

"Not really," Victoria said sadly. "It seems I keep attracting nothing but losers or married men. And you won't believe what happened with my last date—or what was even *supposed* to be one."

"What?"

"A friend of mine wanted to fix me up with this great photographer she knew, so we made plans to have dinner last Saturday night—you know, as a blind date, but that afternoon while I was getting ready my friend called and said, 'I'm sorry, but Richard met a girl last night hon, and he's moving *in* with her.'"

"After only one *day?*" I said in disbelief.

"Yup. Apparently he said when they looked into each other's eyes it was like rubbing two wires together to hot-wire a car with nothing but sparks flying… Oh Mel, why does this always happen to me? Why can't I meet a *nice* guy?"

"I'm so sorry about this, really Vic, but obviously it's a blessing in disguise—there's something off about a guy who'd move in with a chick he's only known for twenty-four hours. I hate to say it but frankly, he did you a favor."

I could hear Victoria's voice choking up. "Yeah, well…"

My heart went out to her. "Look, you're a beautiful, accomplished woman," I told her, "and that intimidates a lot of men. But I know there's someone great out there just waiting for you."

"Thanks Mel. I sincerely hope that's true, for both of us still."

We hung up, but I doubted it was true for me anymore at all.

Then, to my surprise, Travis did call again later that week.

"Hi Mel, would you like to go bass fishing with me on Lake Livingston this weekend?" he asked. "I know its Barc's turn with Blakely again, and I *promise* you we'll be back in plenty of time for you to pick her up. No new routes!"

I was intrigued, but thought, *Who does this guy think he is? Doesn't he see we're COMPLETELY wrong for each other?* But still, I missed him a lot these past two weeks, and he was thinking of Blakely and about my strict schedule now. Maybe that meant he could handle having a child in his life. "Travis, I don't know anything about Lake Livingston," I said. "And the last time I went fishing was at camp twenty years ago."

"Great! I'll teach you everything you need to know. It'll be fun!"

"There won't be any spur-of-the-moment trips to Mexico this time, will there?"

"No, this time it's just you, me, and the fish! Well, and Robbie…"

"What?"

"Nothing! See you Saturday morning!"

I laughed. "I don't know how you rope me into these things, but okay, see you Saturday morning."

After the hunting experience I was nervous and tempted to bow out by the following afternoon. Being out in the middle of 'scrub brush land' was not my idea of a fun time; would being out on a lake be any better? But what could it hurt to at least try? So, I made the necessary preparations. This time I wanted to consider my wardrobe carefully—but I had no idea what I'd need to go 'bass fishing.' So once again I went back to the sporting goods store and asked a guy standing behind the fishing counter for some advice.

He returned a few minutes later with a shopping cart loaded with all kinds of fishing stuff. I stared at the cart full of the ugliest clothes I'd ever seen and decided not to argue—I just wanted to get out of there. I went to the check-out counter and paid a ridiculous amount of money for all of the fishing attire—close to $300. Just as I signed the credit card receipt, my cell phone rang.

I answered it. *"Hello?"*

"Hey kid, it's Travis. How are you doing?" he asked.

I was tempted to blast him and tell him I'd just spent $300 on hideous fishing clothes and that I was totally dreading this whole trip. But instead the sound of his voice made it suddenly all seem worth it, so I said, "Great, just having a relaxing afternoon shopping before going to pick up my daughter."

"Cool. I'm calling because I forgot to tell you something really important. You need to swing by a sporting goods store and buy a fishing license."

"A fishing license? I've never heard of such a thing. You really think I need a fishing license? I can almost guarantee you I won't catch one fish."

"It doesn't matter. To even drop a line in the water you need a license. It's the law. They usually sell them at the customer service desk at the front of the store—be sure and get a fresh water license, not salt water, okay?"

"Fine," I said and we hung up.

The guy behind the counter had overheard and was already getting out the necessary license for me. "That will be another twenty-two dollars," he said.

I took out my credit card again and sighed. *My new man is a complete pain in the ass,* I thought. But luckily, he was also very handsome, I reminded myself as I put my new fishing license in my Prada purse.

That evening I got a call from Barc five minutes *after* he was supposed to show up at the playground we had agreed to meet at so he could pick up Blakely for the weekend.

"I can't make it tonight," Barc slurred into the phone. He was obviously drunk, high, or possibly both. "Can you come back to the park in the morning, say ten and I'll get her then?"

"Sure, no problem," I said. "Sounds like you're in no state to watch her anyway—"

"BACK OFF BITCH!" Barc yelled; then hung up on me. I silently wished he had called my home phone instead, for I had begun to secretly tape-record all of his calls from there. I was also keeping a journal of everything he did that was questionable, uncooperative, abusive, or vulgar, and in only a few weeks I already had a lot of ammo to work with. Ms. Williams thought the tape recordings would be the best evidence overall to use in court though, for they clearly showed his tone of voice, abusiveness, and state of mind often. It just sucked that he called my cell phone more than my home line, and I couldn't put a 'bug' on it to record anything.

"Where's Dad?" Blakely asked as she ran up to me fresh from swinging across the monkey bars. I was amazed at her ability to tune into what
was going on whenever something like this happened to change our schedules—which was often lately.

"Oh, Daddy's not feeling well again, so it looks like you and I get to play
here all by ourselves tonight!"

"Yeah!" she said happily, and even with a bit of relief.

"Come on," I challenged her playfully. "I'll race you to the swings!"

The next morning, after I dropped off Blakely with Barc at the *second*
place he and Mimi requested that day by eleven o'clock, I then went back
home and called Travis to tell him I was finally all set to go. He seemed
very understanding and said it was no problem at all, for we weren't on any
particular timeline to get there anyway. I was glad, for with all the stress I
was under dealing with Barc, all I wanted to do for the next two days now
was relax and try not to think of Barc and Mimi doing anything neglectful or harmful to my precious Blakely. Getting away was actually a good
distraction.

Travis picked me up in his Cadillac and we drove to Lake Livingston,
which was only about a two hour drive from Houston. He pulled into the
driveway of a small, mom 'n pop-styled, rundown motel near the outskirts
of town and parked in a 'gues' (for the 't' was either faded or left out completely) parking spot.

"You *must* be kidding," I said. "We're staying *here?*" I thought he was
just messing with me, but no.

"Sorry Mel, it's this place or no place," Travis said, turning off the engine.
"It's the only motel in town. Besides, it's not that bad. I've stayed here dozens of times with my fishing buddies."

"So what happened to all of your 'fishing buddies' then, huh?" I asked,
thinking to myself that they probably got sick and tired of the accommodations. They were probably off fly-fishing in Colorado or salmon fishing
in Alaska, like most normal people of their means do. "Why do you want
me to join you on these expeditions anyway? It seems like you'd have much
more fun with the guys... people who like to hunt and fish and are used to
roughing it with you. I don't even know what I'm doing!"

"Mel, I want to share my interests with you. I've been hunting and fishing with the same guys since I was seven-years-old. Let's just go and check
in, okay?"

We did, and he then went and got both our bags and carried them into
our room. It was the most depressing place I'd ever seen—even worse than
the rat hole, which was saying *a lot.* It reeked of stale cigarette smoke which
had permeated the faded, nylon drapes and the worn, sickly, green-frayed

carpet. The chairs and dresser bore chips and scratches like war wounds. I immediately saw two cockroaches run across the floor. One of them drew up its wings and flew toward us. I screamed and ran out of the room. There was no way I was going to be dodging roaches all night.

"Travis, I'm sure you must be sick of hearing this, but you are out of your mind if you think I'm going to stay here. Forget it!"

"Jeez, calm down, Mel. It's just a fuckin' roach. They're everywhere this time of year. You're a Texan! Don't tell me you've never had any roaches in your house."

I barked at him, "No we have never had any roaches in our house! We have an *exterminator!*"

"All right then, let me call the front desk and see if we can't get a better room. Okay?"

"I don't even know why you're wasting our time. I can guarantee you this is as good as it gets in 'Livingston,' Texas."

He chose to ignore my snide comment and walked back to the front desk—after he discovered that the phone in our room was disconnected.

They immediately moved us to their best 'suite.' It was not much better than the first room, but at least it didn't stink and I didn't see any bugs. I unpacked and tried to calm down, dreading to even think of what might be living in the bed that we *couldn't* see. The bedspread matched the drapery in the same lame pattern of large purple, orange, and green flowers. It was brighter in some places than in others, indicating it was faded from sunlight. The faint smell of beer and the aroma of sour hops wafted upward. I winced, nauseous, and headed to the restroom. At least it was clean, thank God, and functional. I splashed some cold water on my face and picked up a small, shabby face towel, noticing it was mostly threadbare.

Travis knocked on the door. "Are you okay, Mel?"

Wow, he's really concerned about me, I thought as I looked in the bathroom mirror and smoothed my hair with my fingers. *I should give this more of a chance.*

"I think I'm allergic to this place," I said jokingly as I opened the door. I decided to make the best of it. After all, I was there with *him.*

Travis took my hand and led me to the bed like a true gentleman. I sat down and immediately sank into a deep hole in the lumpy, springy mattress while Travis laughed and went over to the portable cooler he had brought. He took out a good bottle of scotch—18-year-old Glenfiddich, extra smooth—poured some into a glass, then mixed it with a splash of water and some ice.

Good, I thought. *If anything could take the edge off of this day, Glenfiddich could.* "Make mine a double... no... on second thought, a triple, straight up."

Travis smiled and poured. He handed me my drink.

"Now, shall we go out onto the 'veranda' and enjoy the view?" he teased.

He dragged two disgusting-looking lawn chairs outside and we sat over-looking the highway as we enjoyed our cocktail hour. We each took a sip, then burst out laughing at the absurdity of our accommodations. It was extremely hot and very loud with all of the traffic going by. We only lasted about five minutes.

"I don't know about you, but I desperately need some AC," I said as I got up and slowly walked behind him, lightly stroking the base of his neck with my fingertips as I passed. He followed me back inside like a puppy dog.

I took another sip of my drink and the liquor burned as it glided down my throat; then numbed me as I took another, then another sip of the magic elixir. Travis watched with amusement, noticing respectfully that I could take my liquor 'neat.' Something clicked in my head and I finally realized that this was the way to his heart—through being outdoors with him and drinking like a man. We developed an easy-going camaraderie and close-ness sharing these otherwise vile experiences, one that was even stronger than the connection we had when we were out to dinner at the country clubs or some other fine restaurant. So now, instead of it being unbearable, it all became rather humorous to me.

It didn't take us long to each polish off our first drink. Travis poured us a second round. Then he put his arm around my waist and pulled me close to him.

What could be a better distraction from the drabness of our surroundings than this? I thought.

I noticed a tender, hot light in his eyes and no words between us were needed. I responded to the passionate desire of his lips eagerly. He had waited patiently for me to be ready for love, longer than most men would have put up with, that's for sure, and like before on the plane that time in Mexico, I was now sure I was ready for sex again.

I remembered Victoria complaining once back in New York that, "If you sleep with 'em they never call you back, and if you *don't* sleep with 'em they never call you back—so it's a no-win situation," but I always thought that that was a very depressing view on sex. If you felt the urge and the moment was right, why not just go for it and enjoy yourself?

I knew I was emotionally ready and willing to share myself with Travis for the first time since we had reconnected, which now seemed like ages ago. I kissed him with enough passion to make it clear that I was ready for intimacy too. My heart and emotions had been frozen for such a long time, but now they were alive and tingling inside me again. It felt great to be this close to a man—normal, even. And we made love like we had been doing it together all along... for hours...

Afterwards, things got comfortably quiet.

"So, what are we going to be doing for dinner?" I asked, somewhat afraid of the answer.

Travis laughed. "Well, I already know how you're going to react, but the only place to get a bite at this hour is the Dairy Queen down the road."

I laughed too, but not because I thought it was funny. "You're laughing, so I'm going to assume you're joking."

He said slowly and deliberately, "Melanie St. John, this is Lake Livingston, Texas, not New York City. Dairy Queens are like stop signs in Texas, where the hell have you been? C'mon, it's a rite of passage to eat there on a trip like this!"

I was becoming irritated, especially now I'd just slept with him, but I was stuck here and hungry, so I decided to make the best of it.

We went to the Dairy Queen and Travis ordered for us both. We drank our scotch out of Styrofoam cups and sat there talking for two hours. I refused to eat the food for fear of food poisoning, and he ate all of his cheeseburger and half of mine too. He noticed the time on his watch. "Oh man, it's almost ten. We'd better go. Our guide is picking us up at five."

"At *five?*" I said.

"Yes—five, A-M."

Here we go again, I thought. I just couldn't say no to this guy! I could tell I was facing another sleep-deprived weekend. What was it about him that made me put up with this kind of schedule and filth? He was completely the opposite of anyone I'd ever been attracted to before. Travis was such an outdoorsy Texan—a hunter and a fisherman—and roughing it seemed to be his middle name. There was something about this that actually intrigued me, but I couldn't put my finger on it.

We got our wake-up call at 5 AM, sharp. Once again, Travis pulled out the "correct" outfit for me to wear, and it fit perfectly.

What's up with this guy? I wondered. *And why does he have a closet full of women's hunting and fishing clothes—all mail-ordered from L.L. Bean?* He obviously had this down to a science.

I changed and met him and our guide, "Robbie," in the hotel lobby. Robbie was an authentic East Texan redneck complete with tattooed arms, a cut-off muscle T-shirt that said "Don't Mess With Texas," a toothpick hanging out of one side of his mouth, and a Marlboro red cigarette hanging out of the other. We hadn't had breakfast yet, and the smoke from Robbie's cigarette was making me queasy.

"Mel, I want to load all our gear into my car—so go ahead and ride with Robbie to the marina, will ya? I'll follow y'all in my Caddy. And don't worry, Robbie's a friend," Travis said when he saw my skeptical face.

I didn't have the energy to protest, so I climbed aboard the cab of Robbie's truck, which I could see he was using as a glorified garbage pit.

There were smashed beer cans all over the floor and an overstuffed, pullout ashtray filled with butts. A layer of bug carcasses and blue-gray smoke coated a windshield that hadn't been cleaned for years.

As we drove off, Robbie rode low and sparked up another Marlboro red. "Don't worry girlie, I used to be a truck driver," he assured me, and when he spoke I could see he was missing one of his front teeth. "Drove an eighteen-wheeler cross country for fifteen years, but lately I decided I needed something new, so now I race boats for a living. Got me a modified race boat for bass fishing that we're goin' out on today." He thought back about something he had said for a moment, then added, "The only good part of being a truck driver though were them road whores."

I'd only been half-listening, but suddenly the word 'whore' assaulted my consciousness.

"Yep, those gals were mighty 'fun,' know what I mean?" He chuckled, remembering fondly.

"How in the world could I know what you *mean?*" I scoffed.

Robbie laughed and said, "Listen girlie, you're *way* too uptight. I've known Travis a long-ass time, and you ain't gonna be around long if you keep this up. You just like all them other chicks he brings out here, and he's brought a *lot* of 'em, hear? They all stick-in-the-muds, whining about this thing or that thing... and then I never seen 'em again... Just sayin... All he wants is to find a nice girl he can have fun with. Is that so bad?"

"Did Travis put you up to saying all this to me?"

"No ma'am. I just like stickin' my nose where it don't belong," he said as he took a drag from his cigarette.

"I see. Well, thanks for telling me all this Robbie. I'm sure it's good to know. So uh.... how many girls are we talking?" I asked teasingly and Robbie grinned, knowing I was joking around.

Meanwhile I thought maybe this crazy redneck was right. Maybe I was being a little harsh on Travis. For whatever reason, he seemed to think all this outdoors stuff was a 'kick in the pants' kind of fun. As I was contemplating this, we finally reached the marina.

"Wait... this can't be right," I said to Robbie as I looked out of the truck window and saw lines of dilapidated trailers on cinder blocks. I'd never seen a trailer park in real life before and was completely stunned. "It looks like we're in the middle of a trailer park!"

Again, Robbie laughed out loud just as Travis pulled in beside us and we all climbed out.

"Just where the hell are we, Travis?" I asked him. "This place is appalling!"

Travis looked confused. "I told you, we're in some of the best fishing in the state! What's the problem?"

Irritated, I pointed to the depressing scene all around us. "This is a trailer park, not a State Park. We're in a friggin' slum, here! How can you ignore how horrible this place is? Why would you bring me here?"

"Uh, it never occurred to me *not* to? I guess I don't pay attention to the surroundings, considering it has nothing to do with the fishing. I dunno, maybe it's a guy thing?"

"What does being a *guy* have to do with anything?"

He snapped back, "This is the heart of East Texas, Mel. It is what it is."

"This isn't funny anymore, Travis. You're pushing me to my absolute limit here!"

Travis leaned forward and looked me straight in the eye as he said, "Well maybe that's the point, 'Princess,'" and walked away in a huff.

I, too, was upset, and we spent the next ten minutes pacing the dock on opposite ends while Robbie went and prepped the boat.

Travis finally came back over and put his arms around me. "I'm sorry this is upsetting to you, Mel, really. But I think you should stick this one out. We're gonna have fun out there, you know we will. Let's go and catch some fish and then I promise we'll get the hell out of dodge, okay?"

He leaned over and gave me a very sweet, sensitive kiss on my lips—as if to reassure me that everything really was going to be okay and that he really did care. I was instantly smitten again.

"Okay," I told him.

Robbie helped me climb aboard the modified, open-air, racing boat and Travis held onto me tightly as we sped out towards the deeper waters, together.

Chapter 22

"Hold on tight!" Robbie yelled as he floored the small boat out towards the middle of the lake. I was amazed at how fast he could make it go, but Travis had already explained to me that Robbie raced the boat during the week and took it out on fishing expeditions like this on weekends for extra cash. As we sped across the crest of the waves I thought of when Barc threw me overboard in Florida from the speed boat he had rented on our honeymoon, but knew Travis would never be the kind of man to do that to me, or anyone, ever. Though he still had his faults, deep down he had too much class for that and I felt safe being out here on the open water with him.

We finally reached the spot Robbie was looking for and he dropped the anchor. The sun was beginning to come up and all I could think about was how hot it was going to be soon.

"Oh my gosh, how fast were we going?" I gulped as the boat rocked back and forth, thinking for a moment I might be seasick. But luckily the moment passed.

Robbie said something about 'knots' which I didn't understand while he baited my hook and cast the line, then handed me the pole. Travis was too busy baiting his own hook and throwing out his own line to pay much attention to me anymore, so I settled into my seat and held onto the pole... wondering how long we were going to be out here doing this.

Within just a few minutes, I felt something tug at the end of my line.

"Hey—hey! There's something on my line! What do I do?" I yelled, panicking.

"Pull up on the rod and start reeling in the line!" Travis yelled back excitedly.

I flashed him a panicked and confused look. "This is no fish—this is like a baby whale! Can you please take over? My arms are killing me!" I pleaded.

Travis put down his pole and rushed over. I tried shoving the pole at him, but instead he got behind me and put his hands over mine. His arms felt safe, warm, and strong cuddled around me and I let him completely take over. After a small struggle, we reeled in a huge, white striped bass together. It must have weighed at least twenty pounds!

Robbie came running over and started snapping pictures with his disposable drugstore camera. Both boys looked thrilled.

Travis said, "Way to go, Mel! You're a natural. This one's definitely a keeper!" He playfully smacked my butt.

This started a run—I ended up catching twenty more fish that day, which was the limit, while Travis only caught one. His initial enthusiasm and excitement over my fishing success soon became embarrassment. "Jesus, you're kicking ass and taking names!"

"Beginners luck?" I offered.

"I don't know. You seem like a natural fisherman."

"Don't you mean 'fisherwoman?'" I joked.

We returned to the marina and gave all of the fish to Robbie to clean while Travis produced a celebratory bottle of champagne to honor my success.

"To you, kid," Travis said, truly impressed with me.

"And to you, for bringing me here," I offered back, feeling triumphant that I'd out-fished him. "You were right, I did have fun."

Travis looked at me with amusement; then recognized the 'challenge' I had in my eyes. "There's a huge and interesting world outside of Texas you know, Travis," I said. "And I want to show it to you... including places to hunt and fish that *aren't* in the backyard of a junkyard. I appreciate all these plebian experiences, really I do, but a girl can only take so much, got it? So if you ever want another date with me, *I'm* deciding where we go next time."

Travis laughed as he hugged me. "You're on, kid... after all, you can lead a horse to water, but you can't make him drink, *right?*"

Blakely's birthday was the following week, and I couldn't believe my baby girl was already turning five. I was planning a party at my mom's house for her with her whole class from preschool along with some family and friends of my own. I thought about inviting Travis, but decided against it since our relationship was still in the beginning stages and it was still my rule not to involve Blakely in my dating life. I was having fun with Travis and knew we were developing feelings for each other, but I still wasn't about to rush into any kind of permanent commitment to him like I did with Barc. I had learned from *that* mistake and was still paying for it dearly with his constant insults and accusations of me being a bad mother to our child.

"Oh Granny—the house is so pretty! Is it all for my party?" Blakely asked my mom when we arrived the day of the party and saw the bright, colorful pink, purple, and yellow tent and decorations covering a big part of the backyard and also inside the pool house. There were games set up like a carnival and a small petting zoo with an animal handler, ready to put on a show later.

Sondra was already there, filling the piñata with treats, and our family driver Ron was dressed as an old-fashioned soda jerk to serve ice cream floats and other treats at the soda fountain bar all afternoon long. It reminded me of the kinds of parties we had when Whitney and I were little, and I knew how much fun Blakely was going to have.

"Yes, birthday girl!" my mother told Blakely happily. "Now let's get ready to greet all your guests! Oh—here's one now!"

"Aunt Winnie!" Blakely yelled as my sister entered with a large present and put it on the gift table. There were already several packages there, some dropped off by guests who couldn't make it and the rest from me and my mom.

"Happy birthday baby!" Whitney said, hugging Blakely.

"I'm not a baby anymore, I'm *five* Aunt Winnie," Blakely corrected her.

"Oh, sorry, you're right. What college are you going to this fall?" Whitney teased.

"I'm going to all day *kindergarten!*" Blakely reminded her, and then ran off to greet one of her preschool friends and her mom as they arrived.

I smiled, silently praying she was right. I had already found the perfect private school to start her at in the fall which did have an all day kindergarten, but it was more than twice as much as the private preschool, and with so much of my money going towards the custody case I still wasn't sure how I was going to afford it all. But I had faith I'd find a way. After all, Blakely's education was important, and I'd take out a loan if I had to to pay for the best place I could find for her. I even planned to point this out during the trail as well as the fact that Barc had already missed several of his court-ordered, four hundred dollar a month 'minimum' child support payments this year. He claimed since he was "out of work" he couldn't come up with anything "sometimes," though I knew the drugs and partying he did on a daily basis weren't cheap and he certainly always found funds for that.

"So, sis," Whitney said, interrupting my thoughts just in time before they turned my mood sour. "How's it going with the 'leader' of the Fearsome Foursome? Still seeing him?"

"Yeah, and its fine," I said. I still felt a bit funny talking about Travis to Whitney since she knew so much about him that I still didn't know. But that was also a long time ago, so maybe he was a completely different person now too. He seemed to have grown up a lot, at least. "He treats me really well," I told her, "which is a nice change from all the other guys I've ever dated who didn't."

"Yeah, he's a charmer, that's for *sure,*" Whitney said in her typical 'dig-like' way. "And I hope he stays good to you Mel, really, but just remember, his nickname was 'Muy Malo' for a *reason.*"

I didn't respond, for I didn't know how to, but I knew she was right. That's why I was taking it slow and making sure he really was as good as he seemed to be so far. Only time would tell.

"Does he ever talk about any of the other 'Fearsome' members?" Whitney asked, somewhat timidly. I knew she meant Eva mainly, but we still never brought her up anymore. We had all just drifted apart our last couple of years in New York, and now that neither Whitney nor I even lived there it seemed pointless to keep in touch with her. Eva didn't take or want either of our advice or help when we offered it in regards to her drinking and drug problems, and now that she was an unhappy, regretful mom it was all just too much to watch her self-destruct even further. The only good thing I had heard about Eva's life since moving back to Texas was that her, Dawson, and the boys had finally moved out of that tiny, cramped apartment and into a big, beautiful mansion in an affluent part of Connecticut, just like Eva had always wanted. I was at least glad for her for *that.*

"Not really, but Austin calls him all the time, so sometimes he says to say 'hi' to you if I'm there."

"Oh, that's nice," Whitney said, and left it at that. "Did Mom tell you I'm going on a singles cruise to the Greek Isles?"

"No!" I said, glad to change the subject.

"Yup. I leave next week. I still can't believe I'm doing it, but, since I feel like I'm the *only* single woman around Houston these days, I figured why not try to go 'fishing' for a new man out at 'sea?'"

"Good for you," I told her warmly. "I hope you find a sexy Greek God this time!"

"Me too Squirt! Believe me—me *too!*"

Three days later, completely out of the blue, I received a call from Eva. It was just like when I saw both Hunter and Travis within days of each other after not seeing either of them for years. But it was as if Eva had 'felt' Whitney and me thinking about her at Blakely's birthday party, even when we had never spoken her name out loud. Fate sure was funny. Eva's call, however, was definitely not.

She phoned to tell me of her latest blowout with Dawson—and she didn't sound good at all. Eva was talking very slowly and slurring her words. "I'mm in Houstonn... for a feww days, Mell...," she said. "I'mm staying at myy parents' while they're innn... Argentina... it's an anniversary trip.

I'mm running out of Valiumm and alll of myy other meds and Dawson—
the bastard!—stopped writing mee scripts! So I'mm headed to Laredo—
wantt me to pick you up anythingg?"

After my last trip to Laredo across the border with Travis and his old college gang it was the last place I wanted to go back to, and I definitely felt
Eva shouldn't be going there at all. Besides being known for their whore-
houses it was also a well-known locale for picking up all kinds of drugs
with—or without—a prescription, and for her it would be like a kid being
in a candy store.

I sighed. "No I don't 'want' anything, Eva!" I told her firmly. "If a doctor hasn't prescribed you meds, you *shouldn't* be taking them! I'm worried
about you. I know you don't want to hear this again, but it's time you get
some help! You know, rehab or something..."

"Oh stooop being a *prude!* I'mm sooo tired of people getting onn my
case! I'm severely depressed Mell, I can't go off my meds! Believe me, I'll
gooo fucking nuuuts."

"You might be nuts ON them, Eva! I know we haven't talked in awhile,
but you're definitely *not* the same person I used to know and haven't been
the last few times I even saw or talked to you back in New York. I think
Dawson's right—you need to get clean. All that medication is really messing you up!"

"I'mm just sooo miserable I don't know what to dooo... can youu come
see mee while I'm in town?" she whimpered.

"Sure, Eva, I'll stop by tomorrow around one, okay? In the meantime,
just think about what I'm saying, and please, *don't* go down to Mexico. You
can never even be sure of what you're getting ther—"

She hung up before I could finish.

The next day, I went to visit her at her parents' house. But when I rang
the doorbell, no one answered. It was unlocked, so I let myself in.

"Eva!" I called out from the front hallway.

There was no answer.

"Eva! It's me, Melanie!" I called out as I walked around the whole downstairs. There was no one around, but evidence of someone having been in
both the kitchen and living room with dirty dishes, empty liquor bottles,
and lots of bottles of pills lying around. It reminded me of coming home
to my New York apartment and finding Barc's messes everywhere. I didn't
understand how anyone would want to live like this instead of trying to get
help and be sober.

"Eva! Are you home?" I yelled, now heading upstairs.

I went into two bedrooms that both looked unused. I then went into her
parents' master bedroom and saw the bed was disheveled and clothes were
scattered all over the floor, but there was no Eva. Then I finally discovered

her—she was in the master bathroom, and I couldn't believe how I found her. Eva was curled up in a ball in the dry, cold bathtub, completely naked and despondent. She was a pale, ghostly skeleton compared to the last time I saw her; she'd lost so much weight she looked anorexic. Dozens of half-empty prescription pill bottles laid all over the counter and floor. I picked some up and tried to read the names: Xanax, Valium, Chloral Hydrate, and others I didn't recognize. She'd clearly already come and gone from Laredo and had bought back a boatload of drugs.

"Oh Eva, what are you doing to yourself? You could kill a rhino with all this stuff!" I said, checking for a pulse on her thin wrist. She had one, but she could barely lift her head up to even look at me. She tried to talk, but I couldn't understand what she was saying. She mumbled something about going to the airport that night.

"Eva, you don't need to go to the airport, you need to go to the hospital. I'm calling nine-one-one."

She screamed, "NOOO! LEAVE MEE ALOOONE!" as she tried to sit up, but then slumped over against the wall, heavy with exhaustion.

Now that she faced me a bit more I could see part of a tattoo across the top of her pelvic bone that was not covered by thinning pubic hair. It was of "R.A.M."—the same tattooed initials Julie, the concubine Hunter had cheated on me with, had on her private area in all the photos Catherine had shown me. *Poor Eva,* I thought, thinking of what the Arab Sheik must have put her through that whole summer and fall. And here was a constant reminder.

Instead of 911, I decided to call her father, Dr. Helmut Mueller, figuring since he was a doctor he'd know what to do. I found the number to his cell phone on a desk in the bedroom and dialed it quickly. Luckily he answered right away.

"Dr. Mueller?" I said. "I'm sorry to disturb you, but this is Melanie St. John."

He sounded surprised to hear from me. "Well hello, Melanie! What can I do for you?"

"I know you're on vacation with your wife in Argentina, but I'm at your house right now with Eva—and she's in pretty bad shape. I found her lying naked in a bathtub, and it looks like she's taken quite a lot of prescription medication. She... she seems pretty messed up right now Dr. Mueller, and could really use some help."

There was a long, pregnant pause on the other end of the phone. He sighed. "I'm sorry you have to see that, Melanie."

"But what should I do? Should I call the hospital? She's totally incoherent, and it looks like she's taken a LOT of pills."

"Melanie... this is going to be hard for you to hear, but there's nothing you *can* do. We know all about her... 'problem.' Dawson's been prescribing all that medication to her for years, and we've begged him to stop, but he doesn't, for he says unless Eva *wants* to get help there's nothing any of us can do, and she really doesn't want our help. We sent her to rehab—several times now in fact—but it was pointless and all it did was end up costing me a small fortune. I was frankly tired of paying all those bills for something that didn't even work, so now I'm glad she refuses to even go back again. And we've tried planned interventions, but unless she accepts our offer of help *herself* at one of those, our hands are legally bound and the therapist just walks away without her that night, which they *always* seem to do— along with even more of my money... I thank you for the call, and my wife and I appreciate you looking after her, but the best thing you could do right now is to just go on your way."

I couldn't believe what I was hearing. By the sounds of it, her whole family and even her own husband had all written her off. "But Dr. Mueller... I'm serious. If someone doesn't do something, something *terrible* is going to happen to your daughter!"

All he could do was apologize... and agree.

I hung up the phone in disgust.

I looked over at Eva, so frail and incoherent, and started to cry. Why did everything suddenly feel so hopeless?

With disturbingly little effort, I picked her up and out of the bathtub and gently laid her across the bed. I could tell she hadn't bathed in several days, so I cleaned her up as best as I could with a warm washcloth and some lavender-scented soap. I felt like I was caring for an invalid—and yet, Eva was lying there, incapacitated from her own choices. I'd never seen someone so far gone, and I thought I had seen Barclay look pretty bad some days.

As I got out a small pail of soapy water and washed away some stale vomit that was crusted into her thinning hair, I spoke to her like we were really two old friends chatting away over coffee, even though Eva could only emit soft whines and whimpers back. I talked about Whitney's failed marriage and attempts at now starting a new love life, my recent trips with Travis, and about Blakely. I told her we should have Blakely and her twins play together one day when she was feeling better, and silently prayed that day would come.

After that I put a clean nightgown on her, tucked her into bed, and then sat in a chair opposite the bed and stared at her for awhile as she slept. I thought back to how full of life Eva had once been. She'd been the sultry, exotic 'hottie' of the Fearsome Foursome, a driven girl with heart, spunk, and street smarts. Here was a woman who'd clawed her way out of a self-hating middleclass family, connived her way into a loveless marriage, and done very ugly things in the name of self-preservation... she'd even managed to get herself across the border and back here in an intoxicated stupor—just to score her own drugs. How could someone so smart possess such jaw-dropping naiveté? Thinking she was out-smarting us all, Eva had made choices that were now directly responsible for her own suffering and self-destruction. She'd taken risks and fallen victim to ruthless predators like the Sheik, given up true love with Brian for 'security' with Dawson, and now, she was giving up being a wife and mother for these stupid pills.

By now her twin boys were around seven, and I could only hope that Dawson was caring for them—because Eva was clearly not. She couldn't even care for herself. To me, it looked like she'd given up entirely, even given up on living.

Finally, it was time to go, for I had to go pick up Blakely from preschool. I went down to the kitchen and found several bottles of water, a jar of peanut butter, and a bag of pretzels. I brought them back up to Eva's room and set them all on the nightstand next to the bed, imagining that when Eva awoke she'd want to eat and drink a little, just like Barc always did. I kissed her on the forehead and then let myself out.

On my drive to pick up Blakely, I found myself wondering if Eva would be healthier if Whitney or I had paid more attention to her in New York. I was still disgusted with how Eva's father had handled the situation too. Why didn't he DO something? I knew that if Oldie were here, he'd talk some sense into *both* him and her. But part of me also wondered if Helmut was right. Was Eva in too deep? What now? Would the love for her children be enough to pull her out of this situation? Deep down I knew that the decision to move forward was in Eva's hands... not mine, but, it was still hard not to worry about her as I sat in the carpool line at Blakely's preschool, waiting for my own precious, healthy, vigorous little girl to join me.

I planned on making sure the two of us would have nothing but fun and laughter in our home that night.

A week later Travis called to find out what I wanted to do on our next date, and I was glad to see he was thinking of my needs instead of solely his own. He had truly listened, which was another first for me with a man.

"I did some checking around," Travis said to me jokingly like he was James Bond again. "And word on the street is you like to be wined and dined, is that right, kid?"

"Yes," I laughed. I was truly ready to ditch the L.L. Bean wardrobe and have a real and intimate date with Travis—preferably involving satin and stilettos—and I had several places ready to suggest to him. But it turns out I didn't have to plan our next date after all.

"Well then, I think I found a nice, classy joint you'll just *love*—and it's a place you can dress to the 'nines' at, so wear only your best duds. Can I pick you up tomorrow night at seven?"

"Sounds great!" I said. I thought about telling him about Eva, but, like Whitney, Travis had lost touch with her and didn't really seem to care to bring her up anymore, so I decided not to. Whitney was busy packing for her "single's cruise" when I had called to tell her about my visit with Eva, and I didn't want to ruin her good mood right before her trip, so she didn't know anything either. It was as if I now had this big secret and wanted to tell someone, but there wasn't anyone to tell it to. I also secretly wondered if Eva had called Whitney while she was in town too, but if she had, Whitney never mentioned it to me.

"Good. See you then, doll," Travis said; then hung up.

I went to my closet to find the perfect, sexiest outfit to wear, truly looking forward to my romantic date ahead, for I really enjoyed being around Travis. If I excluded the "getting up at 4 AM" part and the "hiking through the mud" thing, there was definitely something very effortless about spending time with him. We were cut from the same cloth, same town, same schools, and we knew most of the same people. Conversations were always interesting but familiar, challenging but fun—even if I had to sit in a tree or on a hot lake to have them. But I was thrilled this next time together we would be back to our first few dates, when it was only in the finest of upscale surroundings with food I could actually eat.

The next day after I dropped Blakely off with Barc and Mimi, I went back home and got ready. Travis picked me up right on time and whisked me to one of the classiest French restaurants in all of Houston.

"You look *stunning* kid," he said as we finished a tin of Beluga caviar and our first glass of bubbly each.

"Thank you, so do you," I told him. And he truly did. In fact, I couldn't wait for our dinner to be over so we could go back to his place for 'dessert.'

Suddenly, my cell phone rang.

"I'm sorry Travis," I apologized. "But it might be Blak—"

"I know," he said understandably. "Go on, of course."

I looked down at my caller I.D. It was a number I didn't recognize. My heart skipped a beat—was everything okay with Blakely? Was Barc causing trouble somewhere?

I apologized to Travis again as I answered. "Hello?"

"Melanie? I don't know if you remember me, but it's Eva's sister, Angela," a shaky voice said on the other line. It was such a surprise to hear from her it took me several seconds to catch up to the words forming over the airwaves. "I'm sorry if this is a bad time, but I have some *terrible* news..."

Confusion and horror must have crept over my face as strange words were repeated by Angela, but they refused to make any sense in my head. The restaurant melted away as Travis's imploring eyes sought to find mine, but were ignored.

"NO! She wouldn't DO THAT!" I suddenly shouted into the phone, the very crowded and public restaurant I was in no longer a consideration. A concerned maître d' looked in the direction of our table. Travis looked at me, also very concerned, as he tried to decipher what was happening and leaned in towards the phone to eavesdrop.

On the other end of the line Angela was weeping and could barely talk. In between sobs, fragments of incomprehensible concepts pierced my consciousness: "...*both* boys... senseless tragedy....calling it murder-suicide... We all knew she was depressed you know, but how could she?... must have been *completely* out of her mind..."

"I'm so sorry, I'm so sorry," was all I could repeat, over and over.

"We're having people over to the house Sunday if you'd like to come, Mel... please do," Angela sniffled. "You were one of the few people she was close to, you know. There was... a note that said as much."

"Yes, absolutely—we'll be by in the afternoon Angela, okay? I'm just so sorry...."

She mumbled something and hung up, and I began to cry. "Oh God, Travis...! It was Eva's sister!"

Just from the bits and pieces of conversation he overheard along with now hearing her name, Travis put it all together. "Eva *Mueller?*" He shook his head in disbelief.

I nodded, still too in shock to speak.

"I can't believe she'd do that.... I've never heard of such a thing! It's just... just so *awful*," he said as he held me.

Travis told me he'd take me wherever I needed to go—and that he'd be there for me, no matter what. I exhaled, and held him back.

The next day I turned on CNN, and since Eva and Dawson now lived in such a prominent, affluent neighborhood, the story was being covered live by on-site reporters: "In the upstairs master bedroom of their Darien, Connecticut home, Eva Clarke—deceased wife of the renowned New York heart surgeon Dr. Dawson Clarke—in some sort of altered, inebriated state, took a twenty-two gauge rifle and shot her two twin sons in the head—then turned the gun on herself..."

The media was in an uproar as more details were then pronounced all over the news as I channel-surfed different stations: a next-door neighbor heard the shots and called 9-1-1... the paramedics arrived to find one of the bloodiest crime scenes that the normally quiet, upscale suburb had *ever* seen...

"Things just don't happen like this in our small town," the Chief of Police of Darien said in a short, punctuated interview.

The entire country was horrified, as was Eva's family in Houston. They made statements to the local press here: "We are just so shocked and so saddened," Dr. Mueller said. "Our grandchildren are gone and there's no fixing this..."

Dawson's family, understandably, were more publicly scathing: "Our daughter-in-law was a deeply troubled soul," Mr. Clarke said scornfully. "We will <u>never</u> forgive her for what she has done to our *family!*"

We all knew that Eva had threatened to kill herself before, but it had always been dismissed as the ravings of a dramatic, spoiled brat. No one could imagine she was serious—or that she was capable of something as barbaric as killing her own two sons, too.

By the next morning rumors of post-partum depression had began circulating, some thought by the Mueller family themselves—which helped 'explain away' Eva's evil act—she was a victim you see, not a 'murderer...'

"Hormones 'plummeting' after childbirth can cause severe depression in women like Eva," people and the media all said. "And, 'burdened' by the everyday concerns of modern motherhood, they can often go undiagnosed for years... leading to 'unfortunate' events like *this...*"

But I knew the truth, for I was the one who had left Eva in a puddle of her own misery that day; I was the one who walked away after I'd bought her father's story that she couldn't be helped anymore. I had felt it in my bones that something bad like this was going to happen. Eva's pain was just too great, and now something unimaginable had happened.

That afternoon, Travis held my hand as we stood on the front porch of the Mueller family home. I didn't have the courage to ring the bell, so he finally did. A stranger opened the door and we moved inside, heavy-footed. The act of putting one foot in front of the other took more concentration than it should have; my only hold on this grim reality was Travis's strong hand.

We entered the living room and were greeted by Eva's family members with soft hugs and whispers. There were not many other people besides family present. I was struck by how much both Dr. and Mrs. Mueller had aged since I'd last seen them, which was after Eva was brought home from being kidnapped. Shock and grief had transformed their faces practically beyond recognition. Besides that, there was also some disappointment mixed in, for I knew Eva's marriage into the Clarke family had been the pride and joy of their whole family's social aspirations, to redeem and liberate them all from the secret shame of immigration. But now Eva had shamed them even more, and their family's "failure" played out in their social circles, in public, and on every news outlet throughout the nation. Eva was gone forever, and with her, her father's hope for redemption was forever gone now too. Still, he was working the room like it was somewhat of a high society social event, and I didn't understand how he could put on such a brave face for the occasion. I guess all those years during World War II must have made him immune to death, even when it was his own daughter's.

Maybe he deserves this, I thought bitterly. Helmut was always too busy with his private practice or attending the next gala or charity event in Houston to ever stop and help his own daughter—or any of his children—growing up. And I knew I wasn't the only person who'd informed him of Eva's alcohol and drug problems. Plus, I also knew he had seen them firsthand. Why did he just blow it off? I kept looking at him and thinking, *He's a doctor... he could have done something!*

But as I perused the fireplace mantel, viewing the line of family photos which included Eva beaming with life as a happy child, standing next to a smiling Helmut and her proud mother—and then a lone, elegant photo of Eva on her wedding day, looking beautiful and still with a passion for life—resentment gave way to a deep, intense guilt. I wasn't excused, either. All Eva had really needed was a friend. Why couldn't *I* have listened more? Why couldn't *I* have visited her more when we both lived in New York?

I knew she was in trouble, mixing booze with hefty doses of prescription drugs, even back then. She just as easily could have overdosed at any time. If I had been a better friend to Eva, maybe she wouldn't have started down that treacherous slope—chasing the 'carrots' that Dawson dangled for her—and married the wrong man. But never in my wildest imagination did I think she would ever have murdered her own children—then again, how many times did Eva have to tell me she was miserable before I paid attention?

"Melanie..." a tearful Angela said, approaching me. "I'm glad you could come."

She looked at Travis questionably; there were no photos of the Fearsome Foursome from college, only photos of Eva with Whitney and occasionally me. I figured after the Sacred Greek Cross incident the whole family didn't want to ever remember Travis or Austin. I hadn't thought of that before now, but luckily it seemed no one was going to make an issue out of him being there with me. They just 'politely' ignored him.

Whitney was still in the Greek Isles, and though I left word for her on the ship, I still hadn't heard anything back. But then again, even if I had, there was no way she could leave the ship to be here now anyway. All I could think was she probably knew by now, but felt the same way she had that summer back in Monte Carlo when Eva went missing and she figured there was nothing she could do, so why spoil her own fun? I also knew she'd pay her respects as soon as she got back.

"I'm so sorry," I told Angela, sounding like a broken recorded still from before.

"Yeah," Travis added. I could tell he didn't know what else to say.

Angela told us that Eva had left a five page suicide note that she'd prepared days prior to the shooting. In it she said she couldn't stand being sober anymore and felt she was a slave to the addictions she couldn't control... she also explained she was a depressed housewife trapped in a loveless marriage, and the knowledge that she was being called a bad wife and mother all the time from her cheating husband was too much to bear. She said that in the end, Whitney and I were probably her only true friends ever, and that besides her family—whom she never saw—she felt like she had no one else left in the world. She ended it by saying she was lonelier than anyone could ever imagine, and she no longer wanted to live.

"But what about the children?" I asked. "Why them too?"

Angela shrugged. "From the looks of the note, it seemed Eva didn't plan on doing that, for she asked us all to help look after them... I guess she was so delusional or confused from the pills that day she either snapped, or simply didn't know what she was doing. The twins just happened to be at the house that day instead of off with the nanny as previously planned, so it was likely just very bad timing."

I couldn't help but cry. Angela was also a complete wreck and no longer able to socialize, so she excused herself.

Travis and I decided to cut our visit short, but as we made our way towards the front door a familiar face looking at the photos on the mantel caught my eye.

"Melanie!" Brian, Eva's ex-fiancée, said as he turned to hug me. "Nice to see you again."

"You too, Brian," I said, amazed at his appearance. He was at least forty pounds thinner and very muscular, his skin was all cleared up, and he had a slight tan. He was also dressed very 'prosperously' in a preppy, Ralph Lauren suit. As we chit-chatted I then found out that after Eva left him to pursue Dawson, he had gotten his engineering degree and then became the founder of a major energy conglomerate—which made millions—so he now divided his time between playing polo in Palm Beach and relaxing at his chateau in France.

What irony, I thought as Brian explained all this while I glanced over his shoulder at Eva's wedding photo. If Eva's motives had only been pure, she would have ended up with the love of her life *and* had the lifestyle she always dreamed of.

Brian's attractive wife came over to get him, and Travis used the opportunity to gently lead me out the front door, leaving the family and friends left behind to their own matters. Helmut never fully looked me in the eye as we waved our good-byes across the room.

On the drive home in a cold, air-conditioned car, we grieved in silence.

I wanted Travis to stay with me that night, but I had to go pick up Blakely from her weekend visitation with Barc, and I knew this was not the time to introduce her to him. It had to be when we were all at our best and happiest, not grieving like this. And besides that, I was still wondering if I should ever even introduce them at all. I only wanted it to be when I knew Travis and I were going to last, and I still didn't know that for sure.

As I sat alone at the fast food place Barc had asked me to wait for them at at five o'clock, I got irritated as the time ticked on. Being late for Barc was normal, but he was now almost a half hour late—and he wasn't picking up his cell when I repeatedly called it every five minutes.

Finally, at ten till six, the 'trio' all drove up in his sports car.

Blakely looked glad to see me as Barc let her out of the backseat near the curb up ahead of me and handed her her backpack, which had something pinned to it. I sat only ten feet away, but didn't want to get any closer to him as he told her good-bye. When she turned and ran up to me, I could see Mimi looking at me smugly from the passenger's seat, drinking out of an open beer bottle.

Classy, I thought, as Blakely now reached me and they sped off.

Blakely said, "Momma! Dad and Mimi went through the drive-thru, but instead of a Happy Meal, they got a 'married!'" She said it as if she couldn't believe it, and I couldn't either.

"What?" I asked her. "Blakely, what do you *mean,* honey?"

"Dad and Mimi are MARRIED!"

I then saw a round-trip plane ticket with Blakely's name and the destinations of "Las Vegas" and "Houston" flying in the breeze—it was what was pinned to her backpack. Underneath it was a pamphlet for the MGM Grand Hotel.

I wanted to scream, *That lunatic Mimi is now Blakely's step-mother?!* But I knew there wasn't anything I could do about it, so I kept calm as I put Blakely into the back of my car, gave her a book to look at, then stepped away from the curb as I called Barc immediately.

This time he answered on the first ring.

"Called to say congratulations *already?*" Barc said sarcastically. I could hear Mimi laughing hysterically in the background.

"So it's <u>true</u>?" I said. I guess a small, crazy part of me thought it might not be.

"YES! And believe me, it was *much* better than the friggin' circus YOU put me through—we went through a drive-thru wedding chapel, then got the 'wedding suite' at the Grand for the night... Blakely *loved* the lions!"

"Jesus Barc, are you out of friggin' mind? All this to get back at me? For what—leaving a loveless marriage? Because you're BORED? You're pathetic. The courts won't buy this!"

He just laughed. "Gotta go—we're still on our 'honeymoon' after *all*..." I heard Mimi making some loud, sloppy kissing sounds as he hung up.

I called Barc the next morning, praying he'd been incredibly drunk the weekend before and it was all a big joke. Plus, I wanted to get as much information about this as I could recorded for the trial. "Barc, *please* tell me you're just messing with me about all this," I pleaded over the phone.

"No joke—we're *married,* baby!" Barc said proudly. "I've finally found my 'soulmate' with Mimi—in fact, I've never been so 'in love' in my whole life!" he said sarcastically.

"Barc, everyone in Houston knows that woman is 'unstable.'" I chose my words carefully, knowing they were being recorded. "How could you do this? You *really* want her to be around Blakely *all* the time now?"

"You're just jealous, Mel. You had your chance. And now I can tell the judge that Blakely can have a 'two parent' home with *me.* No one's EVER going to want your fat, ugly ass again—so I've got you *beat!*"

I knew Barc wasn't going to talk seriously about this and also felt that the last comment alone could help prove that he was really doing this all just to win the case and get back at me, so I decided to end this whole nightmare of a conversation and make it clear what I wanted from him from now on. "God, I hate that I still have to talk to you, Barc. Please, DON'T call me anymore unless it's absolutely necessary and has to do with our child, got it Barclay?" I hung up on him.

I sat seething; Barc's antics made me delirious with rage, and I knew that's *really* why he did it. He finally found something he excelled at— making me crazy—and it was better than any chemical or herbal high he'd ever found. He seemed to become 'drunk' with the power of making my life chaotic and miserable, and I couldn't get away from him because he was the father of my child—and he reveled in that fact.

I was under so much stress now with Barc's latest stunt to try and win Blakely away from me in the custody battle that I wanted to go to a store and shop until I dropped, but I thought about Eva and realized giving in to any kind of an addiction wasn't a good thing to do, or a way to honor her memory. I wanted to show her at least someone learned from her mistake, so I stayed away from the stores and tried to deal with it on my own.

And for Travis, I was grateful. I emoted to him for days—consumed with anger and unruly bitterness towards Barc and Mimi, of course—but to him I made it seem like it was mostly about my feelings of true distain towards Dawson and Dr. Mueller for not doing more to help Eva. And at the same time, I was becoming more and more angry at Eva, too.

Travis could see how much I was hurting and tried to help me understand Eva's incomprehensible act. We both needed to discuss what happened with her and try to understand it all. We often talked and cried about
it until the wee hours of the morning, until we were physically and emotionally drained. I could see what a keenly perceptive and deeply emotional
person Travis really was now. Together, this raw, we were both real to each
other and felt vulnerable, safe, and freshly alive.

"I just don't understand it. Why didn't she just kill Dawson?" I asked
Travis as we sat in his kitchen, neither one of us touching the gourmet
lunch he had so wonderfully prepared that afternoon. "Why would she kill
her *babies?*"

Travis got up from the table and brought back a folder of research he
had found to support the idea that her actions fit a psychological profile
called the 'Medea Complex.' He explained to me that in clinical terms, the
Medea Complex describes a parent, usually the mother, who has a murderous hatred for her children in order to revenge their spouse or ex-spouse.

"See, there's a play based on Greek mythology about this daughter of a
king named 'Medea,'" he continued, pointing to more papers for the proof.
"She becomes the lover to a guy named Jason and they have a passionate
relationship, and she begs him to marry her and he does. They have two kids
together, but then later Jason is offered another king's daughter as a new
bride, and Jason abandons Medea for her. Medea becomes so enraged, her passion turns to intense hatred and she gets revenge on her husband's betrayal by
slaying their own two children... so see? As twisted as it sounds, it's possible
that in Eva's view, she was killing the boys in order to 'punish' Dawson...
she knew the only thing he cared about were those two little boys..." Travis
looked at me sadly. "Of course, we'll never know for sure though, kid." He
stroked the side of my arm with his hand, gently. "But the important thing
is not to blame yourself. This wasn't your fault, okay?" He made sure his eyes
met mine as he repeated, "This was *not* your fault, Melanie."

I studied the pages of research he had done on this for me and finally got
some clarity on it all. Medea was an enchantress, a high priestess with a hot
temper and a murderous rage inside her. She self-destructed and pushed
away everyone she ever loved, just like Eva did. I looked at Travis and realized I had to learn to let Eva's hard lessons and sad life be a warning that
no matter how uncomfortable I became, no matter how hard things got
between Barc and me, there were still always things in life worth fighting
for. Eva chose not to, but I chose to fight, and live.

I kissed Travis and told him how grateful I was to have him in my life. I
didn't want to ever let him think I was pushing him away, even if I was still
sometimes unsure of our future together. For now, we were close, like two
kindred spirits, and that was all that mattered.

Later that night I hugged Blakely tightly before tucking her into bed. I then watched her as she drifted off into a peaceful slumber. I just couldn't imagine a mother doing anything so horrible to her very own child.

For the next several weeks it seemed every time my cell phone rang, it was more bad news from my lawyer. There seemed to be no limit to the insidious things Barc would do to make me even crazier now that he and Mimi were "legally" a couple. In fact, I estimated the joy he sucked out of watching me hate him was even greater than any joy he got out of actually being a father, and that was perhaps the saddest part of all.

One night in late summer, I sat melancholy at one of my daughter's pee-wee softball games and looked around at all the other happy moms sitting around me with their 'families' intact: dad, baby, and the occasional older sibling. None of them seemed to have any care in the world except whether their daughter might hit the ball and run to a base. I was envious of them.

What happened to that for me? I thought. *How had I gotten here?*

I knew, of course, it was all by my own choices... but still, it made me upset to realize that I was not living the life I truly wanted. I wanted to be part of a family like I had grown up in, with a loving husband and father, and hopefully at least one happy, healthy, stable child. What was I waiting for? Was Travis the one who could give me all that? He seemed to be. Yet it was only six months since we had started dating. I didn't want to rush it in case things changed in time. Still, I knew I couldn't wait too long either or else Blakely would grow too used to it just being 'us' alone and not even welcome another person into our little secure, 'twosome' family. It had to be a delicate balancing act to decide if and when my relationship with Travis should last or end, just like it took all of these little peewee batter's instincts of exact timing, determination, and patience to finally connect at least once—hopefully—with the ball by the end of each game.

With part of a loan I took out, as well as some help from my mother, I was able to get Blakely into the private school that fall to start all day kindergarten. I also knew this was a place she could continue her education all through grade school as well. It was one of Houston's best, most elite schools by name alone—and I knew it would open many doors for her later on in life when she applied for prestigious high schools and colleges.

Though the stress of the financial responsibly was still all on me and not Barclay, I tried to keep it to myself and my lawyer and not burden my family or friends with the specifics of it anymore. They were probably just as tired as I was about hearing it all anyway.

Over the next month Travis and I took long walks and quiet fishing trips together where we talked and listened contemplatively to each other about our lives. I returned from each excursion a little more tolerant and confident of these outdoor adventures. And even though I knew I'd never truly share his passion for the rough and tumble treks he enjoyed so much, I was touched by his desire to keep including me in his world. I could feel myself broadening in ever-so-subtle ways, opening up like a blossom under Travis's strong and warm light. I basked in it and soon I wasn't dreading our expeditions; I was actually looking forward to them. I was also looking forward to creating a real future with him now.

As more time went by, life slowly normalized. My Saturday phone calls to Victoria were always a high point of my week and she helped me get through so many things; besides Travis, she was my other one true confidant.

One day Victoria called, sounding especially breezy as she said, "How's it going? How's the new guy?" She always had that sparkling enthusiasm that made me smile.

"Victoria! So good to hear from you! Better than ever, actually," I told her happily.

"Ooooh! Well then, tell him to find a friend, 'cause I'm coming to Houston for Thanksgiving!"

"No way! Oh Vic, it'll be so good to see you— we can really catch up."

"I know, I can't wait to see you too girl, I've missed you— that's why I'm coming! I haven't been to Texas in so long and you know, I just love that old TV show *Dallas*—it makes me want to come back and see those ranches and cowboys! The only men on horseback in New York are the snotty ones trotting past Ralph Lauren and Martha Stewart's estates in Bedford, or the polo players in Wellington. I'm hungry for a *real* man... Stetson hat, boots, twirlin' a rope... then later we'll see if he can twirl *me!*"

We laughed and made plans for when she arrived.

Upon hearing the news of Victoria's visit, Travis said, "So she wants a cowboy, huh? We'll get her a date with Austin! He's about as Texan as you can get, plus he's got a nice, tarnished, dubious past... prescription pills, booze, illicit drugs—just about anything you can do that's bad for ya."

"Uh... and just *how* does that make him a good date for my best friend?" I asked him with concern.

"You know, they might feel a 'kinship'—just kidding! I know Victoria's a prude and doesn't party like that. But now neither does he—Austin's cleaned-up after his divorce, I *promise*."

I punched him in the shoulder playfully. "Going back to the 'Fearsome Foursome,' huh? You sure that's *wise?*"

"It worked on you, didn't it?" he grinned.

Travis called Austin to see if he wanted to meet Victoria, and he was glad for the fix-up, for he said it had been a long time since he had had a date. Apparently after his divorce eight months ago, Austin went to rehab and got clean, and it was the first time since his parents died that he'd been fully sober for this long. And now his 'fix' was AA meetings, being a sponsor, and not much else. Travis claimed Austin had turned into a recluse and seldom went out at all anymore.

Yeah right, I thought. Who's fooling who? Still, Victoria was looking for a little 'country cowboy' action, and Austin certainly fit the bill. So the date was arranged.

Oddly, Austin insisted we go 'his' country club—which was very far and completely out of the way from where the other three of us were located. It was also, in my opinion, not as comfortable as Travis's club either. But when I protested, Travis explained that it was important to keep Austin in his "comfort zone." He said Austin was already nervous about meeting Victoria and didn't want any outside stresses or temptations around him that night—especially since it was a major holiday weekend and there was already a lot of 'pressure' about that just in general. I was happy to help Austin's sobriety cause, but a twinge of uncertainty crept into my mind. Was Austin ready to be seeing women? Was this a mistake?

Victoria showed up a week later and we had a wonderful reunion her first night. Blakely was thrilled to see her, for she now thought she had 'two' aunts.

The next night after Blakely went off with Barc and Mimi, I went back to my townhouse to get ready for our double date. Travis picked me up first; then we went and got Victoria at her hotel.

"You look beautiful," I told her as she got into Travis's backseat.

"Thanks Mel," she said, and I could tell she was a bit nervous.

When the three of us arrived at the country club, Austin was already seated and waiting, with one leg twitching like crazy.

"Hey, old sport. Great to see you, man," Travis said as we all approached him.

"Travis— way too long!" Austin said, sweating profusely. "Where have you been hiding?"

"With this great little gal," Travis said, pulling me close to his side playfully. "But first, please meet Victoria Lane, Mel's best friend from New York." He leaned in and pretended to whisper, "She's a 'model.'"

"I can see that," Austin said awkwardly, accidentally kissing Victoria's wrist instead of her hand as she held it out towards him. "Hi there, I'm Austin Brinkley. Let's all sit down."

An old, wrinkled waiter came by and knew just the right words to sooth Austin's anxious, nervous energy. He'd probably known him his whole life, I thought. "Hey Mr. B, how 'bout I fix you up with some crispy fried chicken, fresh corn on the cob, and mashed potatoes with extra gravy, just like you like it?"

Austin looked relieved. "Peyton, that would be perfect. Thanks for thinking of it!"

The comfort food worked as it arrived, and there was enough for all of us to enjoy.

As the evening went on Austin calmed down, and he and Victoria soon became very engrossed in conversation with each other. The connection was electric. Travis and I were beginning to feel invisible as we looked on like two doting parents instead of best friends.

"...Yep, if it weren't for Travis here, I probably would've snorted the last dime of my trust fund and ended up homeless... but I'm *completely* sober now," Austin said proudly.

"Wow!" Victoria said, eyes wide. "Well, it sounds like you've lived a very full, 'interesting' life."

"Yes ma'am... not proud of parts of it, but I'm doing much better now... especially since I've met *you* tonight."

They smiled shyly at each other as Victoria blushed. "Thank you."

Travis moved in a little closer to her. "How 'bout you?"

Victoria swooned. "*Me?* Well, I guess I feel the same way..."

"Then I think you should come back to see me in a couple of weeks. There's this big gala here at the club for the start of the Christmas holiday season. You wanna be my date?"

"Oh my gosh, I'd love to!"

Travis and I were delighted with ourselves. It seemed we had a love-match. I was glad something was finally going right again and had renewed hope for the future.

Chapter 23

*M*y temporary bubble of joy was brutally punctured the very next day though, after Victoria left and Blakely returned from her weekend with Barc and Mimi unkempt, withdrawn, and very needy. The sight of my beautiful baby girl in such a state made my heart break. She also insisted in speaking in a soft, 'baby's voice,' which she only used when she was really upset. She was quiet and didn't look at me as I strapped her into her car seat; instead, she stared listlessly out the window.

After we were safely on the road I asked, "So, how was the weekend with Dad and Mimi, baby?"

Silence. She seemed to have gone off into what I now called "Blakely's other world," a place where my daughter 'went' when she'd seen or done something bad—and I knew she'd experienced something worse than usual that weekend.

Finally, she spoke, "Dah and Mi-Mi went to look at new house while I was in car... he went away and left me alone. It was *hot*."

"He did *what?*" I nearly swerved off the road, for the red rage tearing at my eyeballs was blinding my eyesight.

Blakely repeated it, still in baby-talk, "He was gone for a long, *lonnng* time Mummy... and I was really, *really* hot the *whole* time."

"Were you scared, baby?"

She nodded as tears rolled down her face.

"Don't worry sweetheart, I'm *never* going to let that happen to you again, Mommy *promises*. Okay?"

She seemed relieved and I took her home, gave her a bubble bath, and cuddled her all night. I let her sleep in my bed next to me to make sure she felt safe and secure.

At 9:00 the next morning I called the best private detective agency in Houston and made an appointment to see its owner—who was also, coincidentally, its sole chief private investigator—Christopher Corey. After I explained my circumstances, he agreed to see me later that day.

Christopher was a big, burly, juiced up ex-cop and weight lifter who drove a Texan-style 4x4—not exactly my idea of a 'stealth' operation. But he only stared at me blandly when I questioned this and told me to look at his client roster if I had any doubts about his methods—he *always* got results—and deadbeat dads were his number one favorite targets.

I liked his no-nonsense attitude and enjoyed the fact that he thought Barc was a terrible excuse for a father too, though of course that information came only after my pronouncement of, "I don't care how long it takes or how much it costs—you have to get this asshole!" It was like pay dirt to his ears.

But despite the assurance and a hefty check made out to "Best P.I., Inc.," Barc busted Christopher on only day number *two* on the job. He came straight out of a burger joint and up to the mammoth 4x4 and asked Christopher, who was staring right at him, "Just what the *fuck* are you doing? Why are you following me?"

Christopher was ready with his short reply, "It's my job."

Barc got it instantly and shook his head in disbelief. "Melanie's hired you to find out what I'm up to now, *huh?*"

"To be frank, she doesn't give a flying fuck what you do, sir. Only what you do with her daughter on your 'borrowed' time, asshole."

"Fuck you! Get out of here!"

"Sorry to break it to you fella, but you're just gonna have to get used to me. I'm going to be on your ass like white on rice twenty-four-seven, whether you're out for a pack of smokes or a Roman Holiday. I'm paid to follow you to the end of the rainbow until the trial, you piece of shit, and it don't matter much whether you want me to or not. Better if things are just out in the open anyhow, don't ya think? Makes life a little easier..."

And it did. Barc soon got accustomed to Christopher being on his tail; so much so that after a while he forgot he was there at all. Barc became just as careless as he was before and as a result, Christopher was able to get incriminating videotape of Barc and Mimi during his very next weekend visitation; once again leaving Blakely alone in the car while they both purchased liquor—and also when they left her to play on the filthy floor of a restaurant underneath a table for three hours while they downed margaritas at the bar. But the worst was when Barc left Blakely in an unlocked car in the parking lot of a grocery store for nearly an hour. Any child rapist could have snatched her, the blazing, hot, Houston sun could have boiled her, or my curious little girl could have wandered off into the unknown all on her own.

Watching the tapes with Christopher later and now knowing for absolutely sure these offenses were taking place was excruciating—but in their discovery I became reaffirmed in my fight for full custody. I also wondered how many other times Barc had left our precious daughter unattended or neglected when Christopher wasn't filming him before this... the mere thought of it made me seethe.

Since Christopher had gathered and established a clear pattern of abuse and neglect on video for the courts, based on this proof, I countered with a new lawsuit in an attempt to wrestle sole custody of Blakely myself along with only minimal, four-hour, supervised visits every other weekend with Barc and Mimi.

Ms. Williams warned me that I might set Barc off by doing this, but I didn't care. I couldn't bear to watch my daughter be treated like a trophy. He showed off for effect and also to taunt me with, rather than to actually participate in Blakely's much-needed fraternal parenting. I knew "abuse" was a strong word to throw around in court, but poor judgment and bad parenting seemed like reasons enough for a showdown. I was also extremely worried about my daughter's fragile self-esteem, for Barc had once robbed me of all the self-esteem I once had and had convinced me I was fat, ugly, and stupid. Even when my heart told me it wasn't true, I still believed all the negativity because it was all I ever heard throughout our entire mar-riage—and Blakely heard it too. I now understood that Barc only put me down to make himself feel better, but it was a long and painful journey to understand this. I knew I couldn't change him, but I also knew that every time my defenseless daughter went to visit her father she could be at risk for his same verbal abuse. I tried to tell her how to protect herself from this negative energy—but it was difficult. I knew, for I was still dealing with it myself whenever I had to talk with him.

It took all my strength to put my case together with the evidence of videos, tape recordings, and journal entries, and I only hoped I could hold everything together until the trial date, which we still didn't have.

I told Christopher to continue to follow Barc up until our trial on the weekends he had my daughter only now and to try and gather even more evidence. I also gave him permission to intervene if ever necessary to keep her safe. Knowing he was following them the whole time they were together was the *only* thing that gave me some sense of peace about their mandatory visits now.

As the holidays approached, I tried to keep myself focused on only happy things, but it was difficult when so much stress and sadness over the whole custody battle as well as Eva's memory were always looming all around me. Then Travis showed up at my house one morning in a panic.

"Mel... you won't believe this... *I* don't believe this..." he stammered while pacing back and forth in my living room completely agitated. He had just received a devastating phone call from Austin's longtime house-keeper, Irene. She said she'd found Austin lying face down on the couch, not responding. She thought he was dead. Unsure what to do, she called the first number she could find on Austin's speed-dial, which was Travis's. Travis immediately called the paramedics, and then drove straight over to see me. "She *must* be mistaken, he *can't* be dead..." Travis said. "I have to go over there! Will you come?"

"Of course!" I said.

Travis drove so fast we got there before the ambulance arrived. Austin was still lying on the couch, deathly still. It looked like he'd passed out. Irene was pacing and crying.

Travis knelt beside Austin's body and tried to wake him up. He put his head on his chest and then wept softly. He could barely talk. "He was my best friend. He can't be gone..." Travis cried.

The paramedics arrived and confirmed what we knew, that Austin was gone. The coroner arrived half an hour later and they loaded his body onto a gurney. Travis helped cover Austin with a white sheet. As they wheeled him out of the house, Travis suddenly noticed Austin's cowboy boots in the corner of the living room. He ran out of the house shouting, "Wait! You can't take him away yet! He'd never want to go without his cowboy boots!"

Travis ran up to the ambulance with them. "He's been wearing these since college and we have to put them on him. I'm sure he'd want to be buried with them."

The paramedics looked at each other uncomfortably. One of them said, "With all due respect sir, the rigor mortis has set in, so they won't go on his feet right now. We can take the boots and give them to the mortician though."

Travis said, "Just let me handle the Goddamn boots!" and proceeded to try and shove Austin's uncooperative feet into them, but couldn't. Travis threw the boots down on the ambulance's floor and stormed away, while Austin and his boots drove off together.

Travis put his head between his hands, and wept. I went over and held him. He put his head on my shoulder as I silently vowed to be there for him like he had been there for me with Eva.

"Come on," he finally said. "Let's go help Irene clean up his things."

Travis and I walked back inside the house. We could hear Irene crying in the kitchen, so we decided to leave her to her grief momentarily as we picked up Austin's blazer from off the couch. We went upstairs to his master bedroom to put it away, but as we entered his walk-in closet my chin hit the floor.

Austin's closet was a mess and contained thousands of dollars worth of women's lingerie from Victoria's Secret to La Perla—all scattered in drawers, on hangers, even all over the floor. There was also a bevy of sex toys in plastic containers stacked up on one wall, along with a vast collection of X-rated magazines, triple-X-rated DVD's, and some unidentifiable objects whose functions only the most seasoned pervert could explain.

Travis was in complete shock as Irene came up behind us both. "Oh my God Irene!" Travis said to her. "What in the hell is all of *this?*"

"Austin's 'toys,'" Irene said. "And there's *a lot* more in here..." She pulled a key out of her apron pocket and we followed her back into the master bedroom, where she then opened a huge armoire crammed with all kinds of weird sexual paraphernalia. There were giant-sized dildos, vibrators, whips, chains, and blindfolds. A video camera had been installed and was pointed straight at the king-sized bed.

Travis smirked, speaking out loud like he was talking directly to Austin himself. "Goddamn, you old dog! I knew you were kinky, but this is fucking *epic!*" he said, eyeballing all the 'treasure.' "This is the damndest thing I've ever *seen!*"

Irene put her hands on her hips and said, "Well you're lucky—*I've* had to see it firsthand for over twenty *years!*"

"We have to get all of this shit out of here now—before the police or reporters or any of his relatives arrive," Travis said urgently. "This would completely sour his memory."

I agreed.

Travis turned to Irene in haste. "Go downstairs and get a box of those huge green garbage bags."

Irene ran down the stairs and returned a few moments later with the bags. We all furiously pulled all of the paraphernalia out of the armoire and walk-in closet and stuffed it into the big green leaf and lawn bags. By the time we were done we had filled six bags.

We all dragged the bags downstairs and threw them into the trunk of Irene's navy blue Buick.

"Irene," Travis instructed. "You need to haul ass and dump this stuff where no one will ever find it. Understand?"

She nodded and drove off.

Travis was still reeling from the exposure of Austin's subterranean life as we went back inside and sat down on the couch. I held him as he contemplated it all.

"I guess I didn't know him as well as I thought," Travis said, shaking his head. "And no wonder he seemed so nervous during his dinner date with Victoria now! Having a conversation with a *real* woman must have been hard for him—he obviously did most of his 'female entertaining' with whores in the dark, behind closed doors, and under the covers!"

"Oh my God, Victoria!" Things were happening so fast I had forgotten all about her. "I need to call and tell her... she's supposed to be coming down this week for him."

I stepped outside onto the patio and dialed her cell phone number.

"Hello?" Victoria answered cheerfully.

"Victoria honey..." I said. "It's me, Mel, and I have some *awful* news."

"Oh no—it's about Austin, right? Did he change his mind?"

"No... and I'm *so* sorry to have to tell you this, but, well... he just *died.*"

"What?"

"I know, I know—I'm so sorry, sweetie—it's all so surreal and Travis and I are still trying to wrap our heads around it too!"

Victoria choked up. "What happened?"

"We don't know—the ambulance just took his body away. Travis is a wreck."

"Oh God Mel, I'm just sick... I really liked him, you know? And I think he really liked me."

"He did. Travis could tell."

"God—it's like I'm a black widow or something!"

"Victoria ... you didn't cause this."

"I know Mel, but... sometimes it just feels like I'm not meant to be happy."

"Victoria—"

"Look, I don't want this to be about me right now... you need to go support Travis. I'll be okay."

"I hope so... call me later, okay?"

I didn't believe Austin could die so soon after Eva. It felt like Travis's and my whole world was crashing down. And he was right—it wasn't long before the police, reporters, relatives, and old 'acquaintances' were soon everywhere around Austin's estate, trying to decipher what happened to him. Theories abounded... Was it a relapsed overdose of something? A suicide? Anything to do with 'foul play'? It was all up for complete speculation as cell phones rang all over town. But none of it really made any sense.

Although Austin had had many notorious escapades in college and from his dubious past, it was now widely thought that his wild days were over. Lately Austin had only been seen socializing at one of his three elite country clubs, he attended an Episcopal Church service dutifully every weekend, and he generously supported many local charities, all the trappings of a true 'proper' Houston image. His death—and the timing of it—was clearly a mystery.

It also propelled Houston's communication and rumor networks into overdrive; no death had generated this much interest and attention in Texas since Howard Hughes's demise. Like Hughes, Austin had no children, so speculation of how many of his numerous relatives would be instantly catapulted into 'millionaire status' upon the reading of his will ran rampant.

The main headline in the Houston newspapers officially stated:

OILMAN FOUND DEAD IN POSH HOUSTON NEIGHBORHOOD

Austin Brinkley, 39, was found dead Saturday morning by his longtime housekeeper. He was discovered lying face down on the couch fully clothed. Paramedics say he died sometime during the night, cause of death unknown. Such a sudden and untimely death is hard for friends and family to accept...

And it was. But at least Travis and I had each other to lean on as we tried to get through this second shocking tragedy. And I tried not to feel guilty that despite all the bad things that were happening, I still felt good when Travis was around me. I knew I never wanted him not to be now, and hoped he felt the same.

When Eva died, I changed. And after Austin's death and the holidays finally passed, I noticed a change in Travis, too. It was as if he'd undergone a gentle metamorphosis. He was more conciliatory, more concerned with the feelings of others, and calmer overall in general. Our wounds seemed to understand each other. All along there had been a kinder, more considerate version of Travis tucked away in the corners of his mind, just waiting to get out. And in me, there was a stronger version of myself. It was just so sad that it took both of us losing someone we loved to finally have it happen in each of us.

I now felt secure enough about our relationship to introduce Travis to my other love—Blakely—and he was thrilled I finally arranged for it to happen. He knew my rule was only to do that once I felt there was a future with someone (and someone who would be a *positive* male role model for her, as well), so there was a subtle message underlining the whole afternoon as we all went to her favorite park to have a picnic and play.

It was also Valentine's Day, and Blakely told everyone at school the next day that she had a great time with her special 'Valentine's' date. She even showed them the beautiful pink rose and white teddy bear Travis had given her, which she adored. Travis thought she had made too big a deal about both of these seemingly small gifts to him, until I told him these were her first true gifts of affection from a father-like figure, for Barc always 'forgot' about doing things like that on holidays. Then he understood.

One cloudy spring evening a month later, Travis and I sat on the patio of our favorite Mexican cantina, Hasta La Vista.

The guitar player strummed, *Cuando Caliente el Sol Aqui en la Playa*— "When the Sun Sets on the Beach"—a common mariachi song about losing a loved one. The dour weather and melancholy music contributed to our somberness as we both tried not to think about what the final autopsy and police investigation from Austin's death both recently said—that the cause of death was still 'unknown'—but we clearly couldn't. How could a life just end unknowingly?

Suddenly Travis said, "That's it Melanie!"

"What?" I asked him.

"We need to quit all this 'gloom' we've had lately and take a *real* break from it all for awhile so we can just move on..."

"I agree, but to where?"

"Well, you once said you wanted to show me the world outside of Texas, so why don't you pick a place and I'll arrange it for next weekend while Blakely's with Barc. Someplace really special too, for it's almost our 'anniversary' of running into each other at the car wash, you know." He grinned.

I knew just where to take him—Palm Beach. He'd never been, and I had fond memories of being there with Blakely and Joy and always wanted to go back sometime with a man I truly loved for a romantic weekend. It would be the perfect place to celebrate our one-year anniversary of dating.

We stayed at the Breakers, or the 'grand dame hotel,' in a two-bedroom suite. The Duke and Duchess of Windsor had stayed there, as had the Rockefellers and the Vanderbilts. Travis enjoyed learning all about the history of it while I basked in the luxury. Our oceanfront suite was decorated in pale blue and cheerful yellow chintz, and it reminded me of the angelic clouds of a Fragonard painting. The bed was soft, warm linen with giant fluffy pillows. The deep blue of the Atlantic Ocean passed through the glass wall leading out to the balcony, and the salt air filled my lungs. The bathroom was cool marble with a whirlpool bathtub and a separate, glass-enclosed shower, both big enough for two. It was marvelous to be back.

Travis and I stepped out onto the terrace and let the fresh ocean breezes tickle our senses and stir our drinks. The heaviness of Houston lifted. I felt like being sexy and romantic for the first time in a long time. Though Travis had done his best to make me feel sexy and pretty overall again, I had to admit sometimes I still had my doubts that I could ever be. Barc's wounds had cut very deep. But now slowly, tenderly, Travis was finally healing them from deep inside me.

"It's great here," Travis said, hugging me from behind as we looked out at the vast ocean.

"Yeah, but mainly because I'm here with *you* now," I said, and kissed him lightly on the cheek. He held me tighter.

Standing there on the terrace, sipping Veuve Cliquot champagne, was wonderful. But as I looked around I also thought of some of the terrible memoires I had had there with Barc, and wondered if we should have gone someplace else. But since I felt comfortable with Travis I decided I should use the moment to finally reveal how destructive my first marriage had really been for me, in detail. I had only told Travis about it vaguely before, but now, I held nothing back. Then, feeling it was all still relevant, I also told him about how bad my relationship was with Hunter for so many long years. Travis listened to me for hours, intently.

"I had no idea either of them put you through so much hell!" he said, consoling me. He seemed to come alive with the news. He was sensitive, attentive, and sharply intelligent. I had never been with such a well-rounded man. Every aspect of him was attractive.

I was coming alive again too as I spoke about my past out loud. It was better than any therapy session I had ever had, and Travis even made me laugh about some of my heartache. He promised I'd never go back to being in a hellish relationship like that. His eyes were as blue as the ocean as he said it, and I believed him.

We wined, dined, and shopped on Worth Avenue, the famous shopping strip, for two straight days. Travis bought me a great cocktail dress at Chanel and a beautiful love bracelet from Cartier. When he bothered to change out of his Texan blue jeans and cowboy boots and into Armani slacks, a blazer, and Gucci loafers, he looked so handsome, like a true Palm Beacher—and I was proud to be on his arm.

The last night we were in town, Travis chartered a sailing yacht. We sailed down to Miami and had a fabulous dinner on the beach. He'd arranged for Joe's Stone Crab to cater it. They set up a small tent in the sand and had it decorated with palm trees, tiki torches, and lilac-scented votive candles placed everywhere. There were three waiters just for the two of us. We feasted on ice-cold stone crabs and champagne. Travis had obviously put a lot of thought into this dinner, and it was romantic and fun. We sailed back to Palm Beach with a full moon looking down on us.

We went back to our hotel suite, sat on the balcony, and talked until the sun peeked over the horizon. I had a hard time falling asleep, remembering the warmth of his lips, so I rested my head against his chest. I could feel that he wanted me, not only sexually, but totally. I felt respected, and for that, I was grateful.

"Would you like to join me in the shower?" Travis whispered seductively.

I was surprised, but unreservedly accepted his offer. It had been years, decades since I'd done such a thing, and I felt like a portentous teenager again. I let him lead me into the marble bathroom. My stomach was a bundle of nerves with excitement. Travis turned on the shower, turned around, and removed my shirt. I then returned the favor, and the next thing I knew, we were completely naked. He took my hand and we entered the shower, grins on our faces from ear-to-ear. We bathed each other head to toe, which caused obvious excitement on his part, and internally excited me. His soft lips then met mine, and our hands explored each other's bodies, causing a near eruption from both of us. He turned off the shower and we leapt straight back into bed without even drying off.

His gentle hands were all over me. Then he entered me, and all I could do was moan. We made love like I never had before, ever. Every thrust was incredible, every grunt genuine. When I came I was surprised by it, almost as if it had snuck up on me. And when he came I admired how hard he did, the strength and amount of energy he released, and I was proud. We looked into each other's eyes, and they danced together like Fred Astaire and Ginger Rogers. He held me tight, and together we rode waves of deep relaxation and a sense of satisfaction so complete, I dozed openly.

"We finally have our trial date all set!" Ms. Williams said excitedly upon my return. It was a month from Wednesday. I couldn't wait.

But during the final weeks of pretrial negotiations, Blakely became more and more withdrawn; it was as if she could feel the mounting tension between her father and me, and could sense that she was the center of it all. I tried spending extra time with her, showering her with love and affection, even more than usual, but she still kept going into "Blakely's other world" to escape. Between time spent planning my legal strategy, comforting Blakely, and keeping my business running—there was zero time left for Travis, let alone romance.

Yet Travis was completely understanding and supportive. He'd always thought Barc was a terrible father and a sack-of-shit husband, and now that he knew the full story he was even more convinced of that.

It wasn't long before I was losing sleep and losing weight. For the first time, a possibility loomed omnipresent, one I'd never fully considered before now; that—worst-case-scenario—I could actually lose custody of Blakely. From that moment on, that possibility, however unlikely, overtook everything in my life like a black, toxic cloud.

If I lose this case, what would I do? I thought to myself. I didn't even want to try and think up an answer, and I struggled to push hopeless thoughts like this out of my mind constantly. I used the adrenaline required to prepare for the pending legal battle to cut through these thoughts of despair as I repeated, "I have to win this! I'll beat Barc if it's the last thing I do!" like a broken record in my head. This and this alone propelled me through each day.

Two weeks before the trial, my phone rang right after I dropped Blakely off at school. I braced myself for the latest update from Ms. Williams, but it was Travis.

"Hey—are you okay, kid?" he asked, sounding truly concerned. "I haven't heard from you in a couple of days. You don't have to avoid me, you know. If there's a problem... I want to know about it."

I didn't want to overload Travis with any more of my problems. I had complained to him enough already I felt on our romantic weekend about my exes, I didn't want to burden him with all of this custody stuff too. Plus, it was hard to know where to begin. He didn't know what was *really* going on.

"Melanie, I meant what I said in Palm Beach... you've changed me."

"You've changed me too, Travis."

"I don't normally say this to women but... I think I'm falling in love with you. I just want you to know that."

My heart leapt out of my chest and caused me to fumble with the phone and I hit the horn of my BMW by accident. He loved me! I couldn't believe the timing—here was a moment I'd been waiting for, longed for—and yet, I'd almost been too upset by my problems to properly enjoy it.

"I love you too, Travis!" I said through half-laughter and half-tears.

"Well, I'm glad we finally got *that* out of the way," he said warmly. "Now spill it, kid. What's wrong? I know something's up."

I knew if I talked about what was really bothering me, I'd lose it. So I changed the subject and told him how much I'd enjoyed our trip to Palm Beach again. He wasn't having it.

"Meet me at the Petroleum club for lunch at one," he ordered, not asked.

I tried to protest, but Travis insisted. "No, no—we'll catch up then," he said, then hung up.

I kissed Travis hello brightly in the lobby once I arrived. It was so good to see him and he looked great. We were seated at a nice, quiet table, and despite trying to enjoy my lunch, the effort it took me to eat anything at all did not go by unnoticed.

"Kid, you've barely touched your food. Is everything okay?" Travis took my hand in his and looked at me with concerned eyes.

I didn't want to shut him out. After all, he now knew all my flaws and baggage, and for whatever reason, he still decided he wanted to be with me, no matter what, because he was here now. He kissed the inside of my wrist, and that was it—I lost it.

Tears rolled down my face and I could barely talk between sobs.

"Whatever it is Melanie, I'll fix it for you—I promise," Travis said with the same determination Oldie always spoke with.

I knew he meant it, but he didn't understand the situation really, and he didn't know what he was even promising. "No one can fix it," I gasped between sobs. "Barc is suing me for *sole* custody... and since he's 'married' the courts seem to think *that's* a better situation than being with a single mother, like me— no matter *what* I do to try and show he's not a good parent."

I then explained how Barc had used his family's money to hire the state's best attorneys and was coming after me with everything he had, forces I could never match, even with all my taped and recorded evidence of his neglect. And worse, he was also accusing me of being a bad mother and not providing a good home for our daughter.

Travis said dryly, "That's all a lot of B.S. Mel! I know what a good mother you are! And lately I've seen what a *great* mother you are because I've barely even seen you since you always put Blakely first. I'll even tell the courts that!"

Travis's unwavering support made me realize I was worthy of all that belonged to me, including my beloved daughter. I thanked him for helping me put things in perspective.

He squeezed my hand and the fierce focus in his eyes let me know his sincerity. "This has gone on long enough. He's trying to bulldog you—if he drags this thing out long enough you won't have enough to pay for a protracted legal battle, and he knows that. I swear I'll help you get through this. Let me have your lawyer's phone number."

I gave it to him and Travis left the room. He returned a few minutes later and sat down next to me confidently. "You don't have to worry about any of your legal fees anymore... and I'm adding *my* lawyer E.J. Gilbertson and his partner to your case, too."

"But I've met with him before. He was even more expensive than my current lawy—"

"I don't give a shit how much it COSTS!" Travis said. "I want that S.O.B. out of our lives!"

I could feel his strength transferring into my body like electricity. I'd never had a man so totally in my corner before, so willing to help me fight my battles. I felt like Oldie would be happy for me, and proud.

I didn't want to accept Travis's help financially and take on even more debt than I already had accumulated with my mother, but Travis assured me saving Blakely from Barc was worth the risk of *any* debt and not to worry about it. Besides, he knew I wasn't with him for his money anyway, for thanks to Oldie's solid investments of my trust fund, it was going to be worth millions once I could collect on it in a couple of years. So he knew money wouldn't be an issue for me anymore in the future, whether we were together or not. Besides that, he also said now it seemed we were creating a future together, he wanted to make sure we could go away for longer than just 'weekends' from time to time, and even that was worth paying a lawyer for, he joked.

Travis was such an enigma—a bad-boy college bachelor from hell, a bad-ass hunter from South Texas, a natural in the millionaire's playground of Palm Beach—and he could now add All-Around Hero to that list.

With Travis's support, I devised a strong counterattack against Barclay.

The next day, Lisa Williams, Travis, and I met with Travis' lawyer, E.J. Gilbertson and his partner, Bob Steele—a real piranha. E.J. only vaguely remembered me, so I explained the case to him and his partner thoroughly and also told them I knew Barc had only gotten married to project the illusion of a stable environment for Blakely. They could see that too after reviewing all the evidence I had accumulated. They assured me that Barc's lawsuit was frivolous and his accusations of me could not be proven. Nonetheless, we had to take the proceedings seriously—in part because Barc's lawyer, Robert 'Big Foot' Elliot and his entourage were E.J.'s accomplished, worthy adversaries. Big Foot won cases.

E.J. gave it to me straight: if no one was beating up or molesting Blakley, Barc's lack of common sense and questionable parenting skills would *not* win me sole custody *or* supervised visitations, at least not in the state of Texas.

But stubbornly, I refused to drop my claims. I knew that Barc really had no idea how to care for a child and worse, he still drank like a fish and partied constantly using cocaine and marijuana, and, I assumed, he was sleeping around on Mimi just like he did on me. I knew my ex-husband was not a good influence on my daughter and I prayed the court would agree with me.

E.J. and Bob said they would do their best to help, but I had to listen to them if we had any chance at all. They advised that Travis and I "cool things down" until after the trial so that Barc couldn't use our relationship against me in court. Barc was claiming 'inattentiveness,' saying I spent too much time working and with Travis—which was ludicrous considering I worked for a living and saw Travis only on weekends. Barc also complained that I 'traveled' too much—even more ridiculous of an accusation since lately, besides Palm Beach, I hadn't been anywhere since before the holidays. And when I did travel before that—which was mainly with Travis—it was always on weekends when Blakely was with Barc anyway.

"But still," E.J. said, "just the fact that you're not home and available is just more grist for Barc's mill—so until the trial date, stay in Houston."

I agreed as we went on to discuss the final item, which was that Barc was claiming I was 'irresponsible' with getting Blakely to her educational needs 'in a routine, consistent manner' by using 'another driver randomly'—which was also crazy since the 'other driver' he was referring to was always my mother. It was true that she drove Blakely to school a couple of times a week because of our hectic work schedules, and the days sometimes changed each week, but I was there every single day to pick Blakely up Monday through Friday without fail. Still, I wanted nothing to get in the way of my case, so I rearranged the schedule with my mother and took Blakely both to and from school for the next two weeks myself. Travis and I didn't see each other at all.

The day of the trial came, and I groaned as soon as I saw our judge. It turned out once you're assigned a particular judge in Texas Family Court, you're stuck with him forever; so we got the same hick judge who first awarded joint custody to Barc and me before. He would be presiding over our case again, and I dreaded his lumbering speeches and haughty attitude like last time.

We all met once again in a closed hearing, and as best I could I explained all my concerns for my child and her welfare. E.J. showed the video surveillance footage, which made Barc look like a fool, but the judge only scolded him briefly over it.

In fact, the judge looked incredibly weary as the morning went on and interrupted the whole proceedings by noon. "Look, this has gone on long enough," he said. "It's a waste of everyone's time, energy, and money. I established joint custody between you two long ago, and joint custody it will stay—just as I originally stated it—every other week for the father only, *period.*"

As he struck his gavel, I exhaled. I wouldn't have sole custody, but at least Barc wouldn't either. It was still a win!

As the judge retired to his chamber, E.J. made his move. He stood up, walked over to Barc and his lawyer Robert, and tore into them. "You two are a bunch of assholes! You've wasted MY time and a lot of Melanie's hard-earned money—are you satisfied now? This is a document I've drawn up that says if Barclay EVER files for sole custody again, he'll pay *all* the legal fees—his, hers, mine, and *all* the court costs."

E.J. shoved the thick stack of papers in front of Robert as he added, "I'm submitting this to the judge now too, and given his current state of mind I'm confident he'll sign it, so I suggest you do likewise."

Barc and Robert both fell silent. Then Robert slid the papers over in front of Barc. He looked down at them for a long moment, picked up a pen as if he were about to sign them; then threw the pen down in a fit of rage.

"You giant BITCH!" Barc screamed at me as he tossed the papers back at us. He knocked over his chair. "You think this is over just like that? No way in HELL I'm going to let this GO! You've got another thing coming BITCH... Just WAIT!"

Two hulking bailiffs ran over immediately and stood between us and the irate Barc; then led him and his lawyers away.

"Good day, gentlemen," E.J. said sarcastically to Robert, Barc, and the other members of their entourage as they were all escorted out of the court-room. I was relieved the moment they left.

"I doubt we'll be hearing from *them* anytime soon," E.J. said proudly. "They shouldn't screw with you again, not after I get the judge to sign this, too." He smiled triumphantly.

I hugged him, then Bob, and then Lisa. Lisa had tears in her eyes for me. Over the many months she helped me through this court battle, she'd become almost like a sister to me. I didn't have Oldie's vaunted legal advice, but Lisa had come in as a close second.

I returned home and was surprised to find a party being thrown at my town-house in my honor. A banner above my front door read "Congratulations!" and Travis was standing underneath it with a huge bouquet of red roses. As I approached him he handed the flowers to me and kissed me like I had just won a very big prize.

"Travis, what's all this?" I asked, happily surprised.

"It's a celebration of your victory, kid," he said.

"How'd you know I won? I hadn't even called you yet!"

"I never had any doubt!" Travis laughed. "You *did* win, right?"

"Well yeah, but—"

"But nothing! Come on in then..."

We went inside. The house was decorated beautifully for a victory cele-bration and my mom had prepared a wonderful feast. Whitney had Blakely in her arms, but Blakely scrambled down and ran to meet me when she saw me. She hugged me tightly and I held her for a long, long time.

"Did you beat Dad?" Blakely asked.

The way Whitney laughed I could tell she'd been coaching her to say that all morning.

"Yes, sweetie," I said. "I did beat Dad. You'll spend a few weekends with him and Mimi still, but otherwise you'll get to stay here with me like usual most of the time. Is that okay?"

"Yeah!" she cheered, jumping up and down in my arms.

I set her down and we both walked over to look at the cake my mother had prepared. The word "VICTORY" was written in bright red icing across the top. I found myself silently hoping that Blakely really didn't understand a lot of what was going on yet, and that when she got older, these would all be distant, faded memories. I didn't want her to remember how ugly the fight had gotten between her father and me, only that I had done all this to ensure her safety. In the meantime, I looked at Travis and my heart swelled. "Thank you so much, Travis. I couldn't have done this without you."

"Hey, all I did was pay. You fought the fight." He took me in his arms. "I love you, Mel," he whispered in my ear.

"I love you, too," I whispered back.

Whitney, Blakely, and my mother looked on approvingly. I could tell they all thought Travis fit in nicely with our family, and I could feel Oldie's approval too.

I couldn't believe the custody battle was finally over. Suddenly, the road ahead looked very rosy as I cut into our delicious-looking, red velvet victory cake.

Chapter 24

❦

*T*ravis proposed three months later in Monte Carlo, where long ago, in a past life, I had adventures, both severe and sublime. It was our first week-long trip together and we went to celebrate not only my legal victory, but also the fact that we could actually enjoy traveling together now without Barc's interference anytime we liked. My mother was happy to watch after Blakely, and I felt secure knowing everything was 'normal' again. I finally felt like an adult who could live her own life. And best of all, since Blakely was now six, she was old enough to call me on her cell phone whenever Barc or Mimi 'miss-behaved' on their visits, and I showed up right away to get her, without further protest from Barc. So I felt like she was going to be better from now on, too.

We stayed at the Hotel de Paris, and at first I worried that staying there, thick with memories, would be troubling. I remembered the long hallways, the white-gloved attendants, and being there with Oldie, still a massive, glowing ghost. I recalled his tantrums at the front desk and at the hotel bar when he was fretting and worrying about Whitney and Eva. I had worried too. I'd also taken a trip here with Barc once when Blakely was just a baby, a stab at rekindling our marriage. I remembered being heartbroken when instead of making love, Barc got drunk and started an argument with the valet, then passed out in the lobby. And also once upon a time, so very long ago now, I'd even vacationed here every summer with Hunter; when we were young, and I naively thought he was being faithful to me the whole time.

But this time, I was in Monte Carlo with Travis, and the ghostly echoes of memories were sepia and faded. This time, Monte Carlo felt just right.

He gave me a big, beautiful ring from Bulgari and said pointedly, "Melanie, you make me happy. You know I'm not the marrying type, but... now I want to make you happy. What do you say, kid... marry me?"

I looked deep into his eyes, searching for a crack in his armor, a glimmer of hesitation. I could find none. My soul said yes, but the words that came out were, "I love you, Travis. And the ring is beautiful. But isn't this awfully fast? We've only been dating a little over a year—and we both know how it worked out when I rushed things with my first husband."

"I don't know. Time means shit when you know you've got something good, right? Isn't that what married people say?"

"Still ... I'd like the opportunity to think about it."

I searched my soul along the salty beaches of the Mediterranean for the right answer. Travis was almost forty-years-old and had never been married. He was, quite literally, the last bachelor in town. I couldn't help but worry that I'd somehow hooked up with another, "I just want to be engaged, *to-be-engaged*" stags, who talked a big talk about marriage but deep down, wanted nothing to do with it. Another commitment-phobic faker, I feared.

On the other hand, Travis was the first person I'd ever dated who made me feel like I was part of a true partnership. He also seemed to have qualities that were lacking in all my past relationships: he was strong, consistent, and kind. He cared about me and never put me down. He challenged me to try new things and always called me out when I was being too petty, selfish, or spoiled. Most comforting of all, he was secure in who he was; with him, I felt strong, too. I could trust him to do his own thing, and never judged, bullied, or nagged him. I could be myself around him. And for the first time, I was starting to understand who 'myself' really was. He loved that person, whoever she was, and I, him.

We cruised the Mediterranean for the whole week and danced in all my favorite ports, sipped champagne, and cuddled under the stars. We fell in love deeper than I ever thought possible. If my life were built like a colossal, winding, whip-fast roller coaster of my emotions, I had now come full circle through it and was perched back at the top, wind-blown and exhilarated. I could look down at the valley of my life, on all my past relationships, and I realized that they all led up to this moment.

So on the last night of our trip, under a blue Mediterranean moon, I told Travis the answer to his question was most certainly, "Yes."

We landed back in Houston on a cloud. For days we made love and cooked each other meals and basked in a pre-honeymoon of bliss. Blakely could sense something had changed, but for the better—and we all instantly felt like the cozy little family I had always wanted.

I immediately started to make wedding plans, but Travis showed an 'enthusiasm' for changing the subject every time the conversation came up. For days he shoved off wedding talk like a bad cold. Panic clutched at my heart, but I went along with our engagement for awhile. I wore the ring proudly, but I knew I needed more now. I loved Travis, but there was no way I was going to settle for a long, drawn-out engagement—not after waiting for Hunter for all those years.

So one evening, after about a month of not talking about weddings or marriage at all, and after we'd finished a few margaritas at Hasta La Vista, I waited until we were both relaxed and in a good mood. Then I took a deep breath, pulled my daily planner out of my purse, pointed to the month of September on the calendar, and said, "Travis, I really, *truly* love you, but I'm not getting any younger and I have a small daughter to think about... So, if you're serious about getting married, there are five weekends next month in September. I want you to pick one, and let's get married. If you don't want to pick one, I'll have to end this relationship and move on. I know I want to be with you, but I have to think about Blakely and focus on our future."

He didn't say a word. Instead, Travis pulled out his cell phone and dialed. When the other end didn't pick up, he left a voice message. "Hey Shirley, it's your brother, Travis. Save the date for the third Sunday in September— I'm getting married! I'll get you details later." He hung up and grinned at me.

I jumped up out of my seat and hugged him tightly. He was already dialing his other sister.

Travis and I agreed we were too old for a grandiose wedding—something simple and tasteful would do just fine. He suggested a ten o'clock ceremony at his country club followed by a nice Sunday brunch reception at eleven-thirty.

With only a month to plan the whole wedding, I agreed. At this point I decided when, where, or how we got married didn't matter—Travis, the notorious bachelor, was onboard—time to sail! I thought back to Helen's words of wisdom with a shudder: "Marry 'em fast, honey!" But unlike Helen and countless other women, I knew I was in this thing for a lot more than simply safeguarding my family's future financial security. I couldn't deny I looked forward to finally not having to worry about Blakely's education, where we'd stay when my mother's generosity ran out on the townhouse, or even about paying for everyday household bills that could easily pile up. For even with my pending trust fund money coming to me soon, it was still nice to know I would now always have even *more* than enough—especially after learning what it was like to struggle all this time. And more importantly, I knew "marriage" wasn't exactly Travis's thing. So if he was serious about marrying me, as they said in Texas, it was time to 'fish or cut bait.'

We invited only close family and a few close friends—about seventy-five people in all. An old college buddy of Travis's named Barry Watkins, who was now a judge, was scheduled to perform the ceremony. He was known for marrying couples in their homes, country clubs, on the beach, or wherever their 'non-traditional' hearts desired... but Barry's real specialty was getting 'resistant' grooms down the aisle, and Travis and I both agreed he'd be perfect, 'just in case.'

Travis had given me no reason to think that he would be a resistant groom in reality though, of course. In fact, he went about being his usual, chipper self, going to work and chiming in on wedding arrangements whenever called upon, seemingly happy as a lark the whole time. But nonetheless I fretted, for I just didn't have very good feelings about marriage in general from my first experience with it. How could I *not* worry that this could be another mistake? That somehow, Travis would hurt me, too? But I tried to push those thoughts out of my mind.

If it weren't for my mother and Whitney, who staged a flurry of calls, menu-planning, and shopping trips to track down the perfect ivory cocktail dress, I never would have gotten it all done in such a short period of time. But, we all did.

And then, three days before our big day, I stood in line to pay for Blakely's flower girl dress at Nieman Marcus. It was all coming together just perfectly, and I finally felt relaxed and excited.

My cell phone rang. "Hello?" I answered cheerfully.

"Hey kid," Travis's sexy voice said. "Where are you? You free for lunch?"

"I can be," I replied, already anticipating seeing him.

"Great, cause I was going to see if you could meet up with E.J. at his office to sign a prenuptial agreement. He said it should only take a few minutes."

Muy Malo! I thought as ruby-red flags waved, my nostrils flared, and my wedged heels stomped the ground. *Oh my God—Whitney was right!* I tried not to shout as I said, "What friggin' prenuptial agreement, Travis? I've not heard one *word* about a prenup from you until NOW!"

"Whoa! Calm down Mel! I'm just trying to protect my assets. I've been working my ass off for almost twenty years—I'm sure you can appreciate that."

"Why am I just *now* just hearing about this? Why not last week or the week before that?"

He stammered, "I don't know, I guess I've been busy. And it's no big deal. Besides, it's not like I'm old hat at this or anything—how the hell do I know when we're supposed to go over all this stuff?"

I sighed. "Fine, let me see if I can get my attorney on the phone. When's the earliest we can *all* meet?"

"If not today, E.J. says he can only meet early Saturday morning."

I growled, "That's the day before our *wedding!* What happens if we can't get everything worked out?"

"Why wouldn't we get everything worked out? Mel, would you relax? It's just a standard, basic prenup—very simple, very routine."

"If you say so." I hung up with him and cursed the sky. This was it—the other ball had finally dropped. Travis was just like all the others. He was going to trap me and back me and my daughter into a corner, just like Barc did.

I yearned to talk to Oldie. I needed his guidance like never before… not only for legal advice, but for fatherly advice too. He'd see right through Travis's crap and give it to me straight.

As a distant second, I called Lisa Williams. She was in court, and by the time she called me back it was way past lunchtime.

Lisa listened to my situation and then replied, "I dunno, Mel… I smell a rat. But let's go to their 'meeting' Saturday morning and see what they have to say."

"I'm warning you, Lisa," I told her. "I'm not putting up with any bullshit this time!"

We met early Saturday morning at eight o'clock in E.J.'s office. It was not at all the same kind of friendly meeting we had all had together months before over my custody case with Barc. This time, the meeting immediately degenerated into cuss words and hot tempers between both Lisa and E.J., for it turned out that Travis was claiming the 'better part of the whole bottom half of Texas' as his sole, "separate property," for evidently he'd been slowly (and quietly) drilling oil wells in over twenty-seven counties for the past fifteen years. His assets were enormous; he had more property than I'd ever known about, and more wells than he'd ever admitted to me before.

I said to him angrily, "How is this all just coming out *now,* Travis? What *else* have you been hiding? I mean, you know about *my* trust fund coming to me in a couple of years—I disclosed it all to you long ago!"

"I know Mel, but I thought you'd be happy will all of this too—it's another good nest egg for us!" Travis said.

"Not if you're planning on keeping it all only yours, it's not. So what if you've been drilling halfway across the south—when, where, or how you're drilling is none of my business—I only know that I should have some claim on what's ours while we're together if this marriage ever ends, and that *is* my business!"

E.J. tried explaining it to me again in childlike tones, sugar-coating his sentences to convince me it all made perfect sense; Travis, simply put, was not 'pulling one over on me,' he was just trying to protect his oil wells. Nothing more.

The meeting was getting petty and underhanded, and I'd had enough. I wanted to tell E.J. off, but I kept my composure. Instead, I stood up and said to Lisa calmly, "Come on, let's go. I'm *not* signing anything so absurd." I looked Travis in the eye briefly and then glanced over at his fat lawyer friend. "You really must think I'm one stupid blond. This meeting is over... and unfortunately it looks like so is the wedding, too."

Lisa got up, put all of our papers into her briefcase, and we proceeded to head towards the door.

Travis jumped up and yelled, "Wait! Mel, you can't leave! We're getting married tomorrow!"

"No, we're not!" I told him. "I'm not a complete idiot. Come on, Lisa. I've heard enough for one day." I looked at E.J. "To pull this prenup thing on me less than twenty-four hours before the wedding is not only unprofessional, I think it's unethical. You both suck!"

I stormed out of the room. Lisa followed.

Travis chased after me. "Melanie, please come back! I know we can work out some kind of deal..."

"A *deal?*" I huffed. "A 'deal' means two parties negotiate. From where I sit, it looks like only one of us has all the cards... not to mention I'm hurt and disappointed that you'd ever even keep anything from me, Travis! I don't care what it is—I just didn't think we were ever going to have any secrets! Here I was thinking our marriage was going to be different, profound... <u>honest</u>! But *NO*—it looks like I've been deceived yet again!" I stifled a sob as I shoved my way past him in the hallway.

"I never thought you'd react like this!" Travis said, grabbing my shoulders to make sure I was looking right at him before he continued, "Melanie, I love you and I want to marry you. I wouldn't be here right now if that weren't true. Now please... come back into the room and let's try to work something out. I promise, I'll be more open-minded."

"It's just.... I'm *not* getting screwed again, Travis. Not this time. Not with Blakely to take care of," I said. Tears that had been gathering in my eyes now slid down my cheeks.

"I know. I know, kid. C'mere..." He wrapped his arms around me. For a moment, we warmed each other; then he said, "Will you please come back in?"

"Okay, just give me a moment with Lisa."

"Fine."

Travis went back into the room and Lisa and I went into a private conference room next door. I told her I originally had no intentions of calling off the wedding, but my emotions had gotten the best of me before. I had only wanted to call Travis's bluff, and now I intended to play the 'game,' but this time it was going to be by *my* rules. I knew it would be a tough challenge for our newly intense love, but if I didn't stand up and assert myself now in a true partnership, I knew I'd never survive this marriage. She completely understood.

"Listen Lisa, there's no way I'm signing what's on the table now," I said firmly. I could feel Oldie's presence in the room, and he was proud.

"What's your bottom line, then?" Lisa asked.

"He can keep his oil wells, but in return I want a substantial amount per month for alimony—a guaranteed amount per year—with a five year cap. If we make it past five years, then it's a fifty-fifty spilt on everything accumulated for the amount of time we were married. And under no circumstances do I ever lose the house we live in or not have enough to also get Blakely's college education paid for, got it? I also want a 'no cheating' clause—if he cheats, I get *everything*. If he doesn't agree to all of that, tell him that he can go have an overpriced brunch with his family and friends tomorrow for all I care."

"Ha! Alright, now we're talking!" Lisa chuckled. She was always game to play hardball. "Alright, then. I'll go back at 'em with a 'take it or leave it' attitude. You ready?"

I nodded firmly. We went back in, and Lisa laid out my demands.

Travis and E.J. listened patiently to our proposal and showed no reaction to anything, but then shear shock splashed across both their faces when it came to the 'no cheating clause.' When Lisa had finished explaining it, E.J. threw his hands up in the air and Travis said, "Are you two out of your friggin' minds? I don't know anyone's wife who gets <u>that</u> kind of money just for cheating!"

"Melanie wants what she wants—or the wedding's off, simple as that," Lisa said sternly.

"Mel, are you nuts?" Travis said, his eyes pleading with me to reconsider.

"First of all," I said as I stood up. "I'm not just 'anyone's wife'—I'm a woman who's been screwed around by men her entire life—and I made a promise to myself after my divorce to *never* let that happen again! Now, if someone had given me the chance, I would have explained all of this sooner than a mere twenty-four hours before our wedding... but as it is, I'm not going to be made vulnerable again—not for anyone, not even the man I love."

"I know Mel," Travis said. "But we just talked about all this in the hall, and it's not like I'm going to leave you high and dry. I'm gonna be real open-minded here... but you're asking too much."

"I know what I'm *worth*," I said firmly.

For eight long hours it then went, back and forth. At long last, with emotions raw and physical exhaustion setting in, we all scratched out an 'almost' equitable agreement. So far, I'd gotten everything I asked for but the no cheating clause and the house, but then again, Travis had helped build his house with his own two hands and I didn't know that before. I definitely didn't want to take that accomplishment away from him and was secretly glad he got it back. But I was standing firm on the no cheating clause.

"You should've been an attorney," E.J. said when it was all finally winding down. "You're one tough cookie."

I just blinked and said, "No, I'm just not going to let someone mess with me again. I have a daughter to provide for and, as you know, a deadbeat ex-husband who made my life hell. So now I know the drill... I may be older getting married this second time around, but at least I'm wiser."

Travis laughed. "Well, it really shows, kid." He came over and kissed me. "The 'wiser' part that is, for I think you're still just as gorgeous as the day I said good-bye to your sister in the airport—shit, I should've just married you back then!" He picked me up and spun me around, then put me back down as he turned to E.J. "Give her whatever she wants, E.J. I want her to know right now that there's no way some stupid prenup is going to stop me from marrying her, and all this is moot anyway because I'm *not* leaving her, I'm *never* cheating on her, and she needs to just stop worrying about all that crap starting right now."

I grinned.

"Hell, it would cost me too much if I ever even thought about doing any of that!" Travis joked, and I playfully punched him in the arm.

We took a collective breath in, and Travis and I both signed the final papers. We hugged and kissed while our lawyers shook hands. We were all exhausted, and Travis and I both went to our separate homes to get ready for our pending nuptials.

The next morning our family and friends gathered at Travis's country club. I was a bundle of nerves. Everyone was drinking Mimosas and laughing, but I was too shaky to drink anything—I hadn't seen Travis arrive yet, and it was making me uneasy as the clock now ticked a few minutes past ten. Did he have second thoughts about the final prenuptial agreement, or marrying me?

Guests, who knew we were running late, joked that perhaps Travis had gotten cold feet and was now a "runaway groom." After all, here was a man who'd managed to 'dodge the bullet' for almost twenty years, and no one would be particularly surprised if he didn't show up at all.

Fine, I silently fretted, resolving myself to this new reality as Victoria perfected my hair. *We'll just have fun and charge it to his account... then I'll move on with my life. I've done it before...*

"No worries," Whitney said as she entered my private dressing room. "Barry just heard from him—he's on his way... apparently he wasn't feeling well this morning and just overslept."

"See?" Victoria said to me cheerfully. "I knew he'd have a good reason!"

I paced my dressing room and directed scouts out to the parking lot to send word as soon as Travis arrived. Forty minutes later, he rushed into the club, indeed looking pale and sickly. It seemed he'd come down with some sort of stomach bug; whether related to the late, acid-inducing meal he had had the night before, or our stress-laced meeting all day yesterday, we'd never know, but he showed up anyway—sickly green, and very, very apologetic. I'd never been so relieved to see a man so in agony. He insisted it was the stomach flu, but part of me wondered if it was really the 'wedding flu,' for he seemed fine the day before. But still, no matter his state he showed up, "and that counts for something," I could hear both Oldie and Beau say, and they were right. That was *all* that mattered.

So on a verdant autumn morning, Melanie St. John and Travis Phillips exchanged vows under a blossoming grape vine on the country club patio, and all our loved ones clapped with delight. We had finally gone and done it—and Travis's boys whooped and hollered their approval from the back row as we exited the patio. Only time would tell whether Travis's 'wedding flu' would be a permanent, terminal condition and he'd have to cure it by becoming single again—but I hoped with my abundance of love and affection, we'd find the inner peace and contentment that had eluded both of us our whole lives.

The photographer told us he'd never seen a more miserable guy on his wedding day, and we all laughed as he clicked away on his camera. I knew our wedding photos would turn out terrible... a funny story for the grandkids, I mused.

At the reception, I tossed the bouquet and it flew towards Whitney, but with a sly sidestep she missed it. After a squalling skirmish with several other single gals, Victoria finally emerged, bouquet in hand. "Fantastic," she said sarcastically as she walked up to me. "Another one for my collection, huh Mel? I've got *two* of yours now! But a fat lot of good it's done me! Whitney should have caught this one, cheater!"

Whitney and the other women laughed.

"Ah Victoria," I told her. "Don't worry about it... the right guy will find you someday. Just don't look so hard."

"You've read my mind, Mel," Victoria said. "'Cause I've stopped looking, actually—what's the point? I probably just need to learn to be okay with me for now, you know? I make enough money modeling, I enjoy collecting art and traveling—what's the rush? I make a great aunt for now! Besides, Whitney's next." She winked.

"NO WAY!" shouted Whitney. "I'm through with all that junk."

I put my hands on my hips. "Really sis? Is that why you brought a nice, young, hot Indian hunk here as your 'date?'"

Whitney sighed with pleasure. "Yeah... Mohan's a *really* nice guy..."

"And that's my exit," Victoria said, sensing Whitney wanted some 'alone' time with me. "Congratulations again sweetie, I wish you the world," she said as she kissed my cheek and went off to dance with my friend Peter. It was already getting crowded on the dance floor and I was glad to see every-one having so much fun.

Whitney put her hand on my shoulder. "Mel, I have to tell you some-thing... you and Mom probably aren't going to be seeing me for awhile."

"Oh?"

"I'm going to India with Mohan tomorrow, and I plan on sticking around there for a bit."

My jaw dropped. "You're moving to *India?*"

"Not moving per se, but I'm going to spend some time there, see where my 'path' takes me. At least for six months, maybe even more. Mohan's shared a lot of interesting philosophies and experiences about living there with me and I want to experience some of those things first-hand. Remember when the Beatles made their famous visit to Rishikesh to visit the Maharishi Mahesh Yogi? It's something like that."

I looked at her suspiciously. "You're going there to party, aren't you?"

"Oh, most definitely that too!" She laughed. "Mohan's one of the ten richest men in India and he owns six fabulous estates in his homeland plus one in England! He has a private jet and we go to all these world-class, five-star hotels all over the world... Oh! And did you know that madras curry is the number one natural aphrodisiac in the *world?* Hey, why are you laughing?"

It took me a moment to catch my breath so I could explain. "I just can't believe you're going globe-trotting again like you're twenty-years-old, after all you've been through! And with an Indian man as your 'escort,' no less!"

"Oh Mel, don't be so provincial. Spending time with the family has been great, but the world is calling out to me right now. It's not even so much about Mohan... I just want to feel something different for awhile... get as far away as I can on the other side of the world. It might be just what I need to blur away my failed marriage, to clear my conscience. I'm not saying it's the right thing for everybody... it's just the right thing for *me* right now."

I sighed. "Well, you can't argue with that, sis." I hugged her, and then she spun away to socialize with Mohan and our mom over by the bar.

I watched Travis dancing with Blakely in the middle of the dance floor, hamming it up even in his sickly condition. They both looked so happy and I reveled at the memoires they were creating, good ones I hoped she especially would always cherish to help replace some of the bad. I knew I had married a first-class husband and father this time, and for all the right reasons.

I then looked at all our closest friends and family members who had attended and thanked them all silently for doing so. It was interesting to see where all our paths had led on such different roads up until here, right now... especially Whitney's, Victoria's, and my mom's—who was now doing just fine on her own without my dad and was proud to have such a busy, fulfilling life still. I thought about Oldie and knew he was smiling down at me, happy I stood up for myself with this one. I knew he was proud that I was once again his strong, confident, and very *bright* 'Lil' Bit.' I then thought about Eva and Austin and the crazy lives they'd each lived. I never expected either one of them to land where they now were, and yet, at certain points, it seemed I was only one step away from walking in each of their shoes myself at times, submitting to a similar fate, and I thanked God I didn't.

I thought about the choices I'd made, both good and bad. Some were definitely stupid, like staying with Hunter for all those years, blind to his games, weak for his excuses and gifts of leisure. Others didn't seem like 'choices' at all but rather tricked-coercions, like being talked into marrying Barclay when I could have listened to my own doubts, and also letting his abuses creep into my soul like abscesses and then letting them fester, unchecked, for five long years. In doing so, I had diseased us both. I knew what was right for me even then, but I didn't have the voice or the strength to stop the momentum of my life. I didn't even know who I was, then.

I looked pensively at the colorful petals of our bulging tulips on our floral centerpieces to try and take my mind off of all these disturbing thoughts of my past, but it didn't work. Maybe I couldn't have stopped any of it from happening, either. Because as I looked around at my sunny and blossomy wedding reception, I knew I'd never be where I was now if all of those other choices had not been made. I wouldn't have my beautiful daughter Blakely, for example; still twirling on the dance floor just a few feet away with her new, handsome step-dad, her quizzical nose and long blond hair bouncing to the music. And I wouldn't have a wonderful man in my life like Travis, who had surprised me and changed me and was growing with me, through new hardships and old wounds. Sure, he wasn't perfect… but who was? Certainly not me. I'd never even known the kind of love he offered before—and prenuptial agreement, financial security, or not—I was thankful he'd entered my life.

Gratitude was a new emotion for me; I explored it tenderly and with delicate hands. It felt good and pure. And a path with gratitude had to mean no regret.

Perhaps there's no such thing as a stupid choice. Maybe there's no such thing as a right or wrong choice either… there's only ever a single choice. Because if you listen hard enough to what's in your heart and honor it, you'll hear what you have to, and it will lead you to where you need to be. And if you don't listen, you might end up taking the long way around, like I did. Just as Whitney said, you have to make the choices that are right for you, no matter how little it makes sense. And you have to do it for yourself, not for anyone else.

The winds of fate might pull you to Bangladesh or blow you to the car-wash in your own hometown one otherwise very ordinary afternoon, but the only way to know your path for sure is to crouch low, listen hard, and be still enough to hear its internal whispers. And then, of course, be strong, brave, and smart enough to follow its lead.

With this knowledge, I knew I'd never be stupid by choice again.

About the Author

Leighton Summers is a sixth generation Texan who has traveled extensively throughout the U.S. and Europe her whole life. During her travels she was always surrounded by interesting, successful (and often eccentric) people who encouraged her to find her passion and live life to the fullest. Writing novels always intrigued her, and so one day while in New York City she took out her laptop in a café and decided to jot down some notes about how a female character created from her own world could "love smarter." Over the next four years the notes turned into both funny and sad adventures of a woman's quest for finding friendship, love, self, and family and she weaved them all together into this, her debut novel.

For more information or queries, please visit
www.StupidByChoice.net
or contact
author@StupidByChoice.net